Mike Ashley is a full-time writer, editor and researcher with almost 100 books to his credit. He has compiled over fifty Mammoth Books including *The Mammoth Book of Extreme Science Fiction*, *The Mammoth Book of Extreme Fantasy*, *The Mammoth Book of Perfect Crimes and Impossible Mysteries* and *The Mammoth Book of Mindblowing SF*. He has also written the biography of Algernon Blackwood, *Starlight Man*, and a comprehensive study, *The Mammoth Book of King Arthur*. He lives in Kent with his wife and three cats and when he gets the time he likes to go for long walks.

THE MAMMOTH
BOOK OF THE
END OF THE WORLD

Edited and with an Introduction by

Mike Ashley

RUNNING PRESS
PHILADELPHIA · LONDON

Constable & Robinson Ltd
3 The Lanchesters
162 Fulham Palace Road
London W6 9ER
www.constablerobinson.com

First published in the UK by Robinson,
an imprint of Constable & Robinson, 2010

A copy of the British Library Cataloguing in Publication
Data is available from the British Library

UK ISBN 978-1-84901-305-5

1 3 5 7 9 10 8 6 4 2

First published in the United States in 2010 by Running Press Book Publishers

US Library of Congress number: 2009943384
US ISBN 978-0-7624-3991-1

Running Press Book Publishers
2300 Chestnut Street
Philadelphia, PA 19103-4371

Visit us on the web!
www.runningpress.com

Printed and bound in the EU

CONTENTS

COPYRIGHT ACKNOWLEDGMENTS

THE END OF ALL THINGS

Mike Ashley

We seem to have a fascination for the Apocalypse, the end of all things. It's not that we welcome it, least I hope not, but it seems that we can't help wondering about it, even predicting it. "The End is Nigh", a phrase perhaps too-oft used to have the impact it once had, has now passed into our language to signify yet another fallacious prediction.

There are the obvious religious connotations of the Apocalypse or the Day of Judgment – the biblical Armageddon, the Nordic Ragnarök, the Islamic Qiyamah (Doomsday), and so on – and this in turn may feed into the growing scientific awareness of our mortality through such possibilities as pandemics, cosmic catastrophes, climate change or the inevitable death of the Sun. The imagery of the Four Horsemen of the Apocalypse, representing Conquest, War, Famine and Death, is as potent today as ever.

This anthology brings together stories that look at many of the ways that the Earth, or life upon it, may be destroyed, from plagues to floods, nuclear war to collision with a comet, alien invasion to new technologies run wild, and a few things beyond your wildest imaginings.

It's all here, and more besides. But I didn't want an anthology where every story ended with death and destruction – that would become rather depressing over 500 pages – so to provide a balance I decided to introduce some hope for the future. At least half the stories take us beyond the end of civilization, even the end of the Earth, and look at how life – albeit not as we know it – may go on.

Science fiction has had its own fascination with the end of all things since at least *Le Dernier Homme* ("The Last Man") written by the French priest Jean-Baptiste Cousin de Grainville at the end of the eighteenth century. He had lived through the French Revolution, which had rather soured his view of the world and drove him into depression and eventual suicide in 1805, leaving this pioneering work in manuscript. It has some remarkably advanced ideas in depicting a world which, through mismanagement and overpopulation, had become ecologically exhausted.

The experience of the Reign of Terror doubtless fuelled de Grainville's work, and it is not surprising that certain events, such as the end of a century (or millennium) or World Wars, focus minds on a potential Apocalypse. Although a few books followed de Grainville's – including the like-named *The Last Man* (1826) by Mary Shelley, the author of *Frankenstein*, which had humanity wiped out by a virulent plague, and Edgar Allan Poe's "The Conversation of Eiros and Charmion" (1839), one of the first stories to have Earth destroyed by a comet – the real torrent of books came towards the end of the nineteenth century.

Two novels served as precursors to the main event: *After London* (1885) by Richard Jefferies, depicted a Britain that has reverted to the Stone Age following an unspecified catastrophe; *The Last American* (1889) by John Ames Mitchell has a Persian expedition explore the ruins of New York, the United States having been destroyed by social unrest.

The noted French astronomer, Camille Flammarion, wrote one of the first major novels of worldwide disaster, *La fin du monde* (1894), better known as *Omega: The Last Days of the World*, where a vast comet not only destroys life on Earth but also on Mars. H.G. Wells almost destroyed all life in "The Star" (1897) but salvation was at hand thanks to the Moon. Sir Arthur Conan Doyle, best known for creating Sherlock Holmes, combined the ideas of a plague and cosmic disaster in *The Poison Belt* (1913), where he has the Earth pass through a toxic belt in space. M.P. Shiel had used a similar idea in *The Purple Cloud* (1901), when a volcano releases a mass of poisonous vapour from deep within the Earth. Wells developed another form of Armageddon when human life is threatened by the arrival of the Martians in *The War of the Worlds* (1898).

There were the inevitable apocalyptic stories following the First World War. Edward Shanks saw the end of civilization in *The People of the Ruins* (1920), while in *Nordenholt's Million* (1923) J.J. Connington showed how science might bring civilization back from the brink of an ecological disaster. Interestingly, one of the earliest stories to consider how civilization might crumble through an over-reliance on technology was written as far back as 1909 by E.M. Forster in "The Machine Stops".

The Second World War and the detonation of the A-bomb inevitably brought forth many stories of a nuclear holocaust such as *The Long Loud Silence* (1952) by Wilson Tucker, *On the Beach* (1957) by Nevil Shute and, perhaps the best known, *Dr Strangelove* (1963), the Stanley Kubrick film based on the novel *Red Alert* by Peter George. The Cold War saw a rise in disaster novels generally, particularly in Britain, where *The Day of the Triffids* (1951) by John Wyndham, *The Death of Grass* (1956) by John Christopher, *White August* (1955) by John Boland and *The Tide Went Out* (1958) by Charles Eric Maine created what veteran British SF author Brian Aldiss later termed the "cosy catastrophe". J. G. Ballard established his reputation with a quartet of disaster novels based on the four elements of air, water, fire and earth: *The Wind From Nowhere* (1961), *The Drowned World* (1962), *The Burning World* (1964) and *The Crystal World* (1966).

The welter of catastrophe novels and films grew exponentially with the approach of the millennium. Life on Earth is all but wiped out by a comet in *Lucifer's Hammer* (1977) by Jerry Pournelle and Larry Niven. We see how isolated survivors cope in a post-holocaust world in *The Postman* (1985) by David Brin and in *The Gate to Women's Country* (1988) by Sheri S. Tepper. Sea levels rise in *The Road to Corlay* (1978) by Richard Cowper and the United States is flooded in *Forty Signs of Rain* (2004) by Kim Stanley Robinson, while Stephen Baxter drowns the Earth in *Flood* (2008). Greg Bear has aliens systematically destroying the solar system in *The Forge of God* (1987). In *The Stand* (1978), a genuinely apocalyptic novel, Stephen King has most of humanity wiped out by a virulent flu strain, whilst a man-made plague destroys civilization in David Palmer's *Emergence* (1984). There's a combined nuclear and ecological holocaust in *Mother of Storms* (1994) by John Barnes, while a major cosmic catastrophe causes climate change in Charles Sheffield's *Aftermath* (1998). Most recently Cormac McCarthy's *The Road* (2006), which won a Pulitzer Prize, presents a very bleak vision of a world all but destroyed by some unexplained catastrophe. Recent TV series such as *Survivors*, *Deepwater Black* and *Jericho* and films such as *Deep Impact*, the *Terminator* series and *Armageddon* continue to stimulate our thoughts and fill our minds with apocalyptic imagery.

All of which goes to show the popularity and enormity of the field and the richness of its history, and created something of a challenge in assembling this anthology. I had considered including many of the classics of the genre but found there was so much new fiction being produced in the last ten years or so that I only had room to squeeze in a couple of older stories, those by Fritz Leiber and Robert Silverberg.

What was so noticeable about the new strain of apocalyptic fiction was how much it showed our fear of new technology, particularly nanotechnology. I could have filled this book with stories of nano-techdoom alone but I wanted to get a good spread of catastrophes, both pre- and post-apocalyptic and the inevitable dying Earth. You will find plagues or the threat of plagues in the stories by Robert Reed and Kate Wilhelm; floods in those by Dale Bailey and Linda Nagata; a nuclear holocaust and its aftermath in those by Frederik Pohl and Elizabeth Bear; climate change in the stories by Eric Brown and Paul Di Filippo; cosmic disasters in those by David Barnett, Geoffrey Landis and William Barton, and the threat of technology or how it might save us in the stories by Cory Doctorow, Damien Broderick and F. Gwynplaine MacIntyre. Alastair Reynolds brings an entirely new form of apocalypse in his novelette, one of six new stories in this anthology. We travel into the far distant future to see how humanity re-evolves in Jack Williamson's story, and the end of the human race in the stories by Stephen Baxter and Elizabeth Counihan.

But as I predicted, it is not all doom and gloom. Many of the stories show the resilience of mankind in coping with disaster and rebuilding the world. These may be warning stories but there are also messages of hope here.

The Beginning is Nigh ...

WHEN WE WENT TO SEE THE END OF THE WORLD

Robert Silverberg

We start on a fairly light-hearted note with this parody of the end-of-the-world theme where time travel allows people to witness the final apocalypse. But which one?

Created a Grand Master by the Science Fiction Writers of America in 2004, Robert Silverberg is the dean of science fiction, having been writing prolifically for over fifty years, producing not only an immense body of work but one of remarkable quality and diversity. Amongst his major works are Nightwings *(1969),* A Time of Changes *(1971),* Dying Inside *(1972),* Born With the Dead *(1974),* The Stochastic Man *(1975),* Lord Valentine's Castle *(1980) and* The Secret Sharer *(1989). Silverberg has written his own share of apocalyptic and post-apocalyptic works.* To Open the Sky *(1967) is set in a claustrophobically overpopulated future, whilst* At Winter's End *(1988) sees how humanity recovers after a new Ice Age.*

NICK AND JANE were glad that they had gone to see the end of the world, because it gave them something special to talk about at Mike and Ruby's party. One always likes to come to a party armed with a little conversation. Mike and Ruby give marvelous parties.

Their home is superb, one of the finest in the neighborhood. It is truly a home for all seasons, all moods. Their very special corner of the world. With more space indoors and out ... more wide-open freedom. The living room with its exposed ceiling beams is a natural focal point for entertaining. Custom-finished, with a conversation pit and fireplace. There's also a family room with beamed ceiling and wood paneling ... plus a study. And a magnificent master suite with a twelve-foot dressing room and private bath. Solidly impressive exterior design. Sheltered courtyard. Beautifully wooded one-third of an acre grounds. Their parties are highlights of any month. Nick and Jane waited until they thought enough people had arrived. Then Jane nudged Nick and Nick said gaily, "You know what we did last week? Hey, we went to see the end of the world!"

"The end of the world?" Henry asked.

"You went to see it?" said Henry's wife Cynthia.

"How did you manage that?" Paula wanted to know.

"It's been available since March," Stan told her. "I think a division of American Express runs it."

Nick was put out to discover that Stan already knew. Quickly, before Stan could say anything more, Nick said, "Yes, it's just started. Our travel agent found out for us. What they do is they put you in this machine, it looks like a tiny teeny submarine, you know, with dials and levers up front behind a plastic wall to keep you from touching anything, and they send you into the future. You can charge it with any of the regular credit cards."

"It must be very expensive," Marcia said.

"They're bringing the costs down rapidly," Jane said. "Last year only millionaires could afford it. Really, haven't you heard about it before?"

"What did you see?" Henry asked.

"For a while, just greyness outside the porthole," said Nick. "And a kind of flickering effect." Everybody was looking at him. He enjoyed the attention. Jane wore a rapt, loving expression. "Then the haze cleared and a voice said over a loudspeaker that we had now reached the very end of time, when life had become impossible on Earth. Of course, we were sealed into the submarine thing. Only looking out. On this beach, this empty beach. The water a funny grey color with a pink sheen. And then the sun came up. It was red like it sometimes is at sunrise, only it stayed red as it got to the middle of the sky, and it looked lumpy and saggy at the edges. Like a few of us, ha ha. Lumpy and sagging at the edges. A cold wind blowing across the beach."

"If you were sealed in the submarine, how did you know there was a cold wind?" Cynthia asked.

Jane glared at her. Nick said, "We could see the sand blowing around. And it looked cold. The grey ocean. Like winter."

"Tell them about the crab," said Jane.

"Yes, the crab. The last life-form on Earth. It wasn't really a crab, of course, it was something about two feet wide and a foot high, with thick shiny green armor and maybe a dozen legs and some curving horns coming up, and it moved slowly from right to left in front of us. It took all day to cross the beach. And toward nightfall it died. Its horns went limp and it stopped moving. The tide came in and carried it away. The sun went down. There wasn't any moon. The stars didn't seem to be in the right places. The loudspeaker told us we had just seen the death of Earth's last living thing."

"How eerie!" cried Paula.

"Were you gone very long?" Ruby asked.

"Three hours," Jane said. "You can spend weeks or days at the end of the world, if you want to pay extra, but they always bring you back to a point three hours after you went. To hold down the babysitter expenses."

Mike offered Nick some pot. "That's really something," he said. "To have gone to the end of the world. Hey, Ruby, maybe we'll talk to the travel agent about it."

Nick took a deep drag and passed the joint to Jane. He felt pleased with himself about the way he had told the story. They had all been very impressed. That swollen red sun, that scuttling crab. The trip had cost more than a month in Japan, but it had been a good investment. He and Jane were the first in the neighborhood who had gone. That was important. Paula was staring at him in awe. Nick knew that she regarded him in a completely different light now. Possibly she would meet him at a motel on Tuesday at lunchtime. Last month she had turned him down but now he had an extra attractiveness for her. Nick winked at her. Cynthia was holding hands with Stan. Henry and Mike both were crouched at Jane's feet. Mike and Ruby's twelve-year-old son came into the room and stood at the edge of the conversation pit. He said, "There just was a bulletin on the news. Mutated amoebas escaped from a government research station and got into Lake Michigan. They're carrying a tissue-dissolving virus and everybody in seven states is supposed to boil their water until further notice." Mike scowled at the boy and said, "It's after your bedtime, Timmy." The boy went out. The doorbell rang. Ruby answered it and returned with Eddie and Fran.

Paula said, "Nick and Jane went to see the end of the world. They've just been telling us about it."

"Gee," said Eddie, "We did that too, on Wednesday night."

Nick was crestfallen. Jane bit her lip and asked Cynthia quietly why Fran always wore such flashy dresses. Ruby said, "You saw the whole works, eh? The crab and everything?"

"The crab?" Eddie said. "What crab? We didn't see the crab."

"It must have died the time before," Paula said. "When Nick and Jane were there."

Mike said, "A fresh shipment of Cuernavaca Lightning is in. Here, have a toke."

"How long ago did you do it?" Eddie said to Nick.

"Sunday afternoon. I guess we were about the first."

"Great trip, isn't it?" Eddie said. "A little somber, though. When the last hill crumbles into the sea."

"That's not what we saw," said Jane. "And you didn't see the crab? Maybe we were on different trips."

Mike said, "What was it like for you, Eddie?"

Eddie put his arms around Cynthia from behind. He said, "They put us into this little capsule, with a porthole, you know, and a lot of instruments and—"

"We heard that part," said Paula. "What did you see?"

"The end of the world," Eddie said. "When water covers everything. The sun and the moon were in the sky at the same time—"

"We didn't see the moon at all," Jane remarked. "It just wasn't there."

"It was on one side and the sun was on the other," Eddie went on. "The moon was closer than it should have been. And a funny color, almost like bronze. And the ocean creeping up. We went halfway around the world and all we saw was ocean. Except in one place, there was this chunk of land sticking up, this hill, and the guide told us it was the top of Mount Everest." He waved to Fran. "That was groovy, huh, floating in our tin boat next to the top of Mount Everest. Maybe ten feet of it sticking up. And the water rising all the time. Up, up, up. Up and over the top. Glub. No land left. I have to admit it was a little disappointing, except of course the idea of the thing. That human ingenuity can design a machine that can send people billions of years forward in time and bring them back, wow! But there was just this ocean."

"How strange," said Jane. "We saw the ocean too, but there was a beach, a kind of nasty beach, and the crab-thing walking along it, and the sun – it was all red, was the sun red when you saw it?"

"A kind of pale green," Fran said.

"Are you people talking about the end of the world?" Tom asked. He and Harriet were standing by the door taking off their coats. Mike's son must have let them in. Tom gave his coat to Ruby and said, "Man, what a spectacle!"

"So you did it, too?" Jane asked, a little hollowly.

"Two weeks ago," said Tom. "The travel agent called and said, Guess what we're offering now, the end of the goddamned world! With all the extras it didn't really cost so much. So we went right down there to the office, Saturday, I think – was it a Friday? – the day of the big riot, anyway, when they burned St Louis—"

"That was a Saturday," Cynthia said. "I remember I was coming back from the shopping center when the radio said they were using nuclears—"

"Saturday, yes," Tom said. "And we told them we were ready to go, and off they sent us."

"Did you see a beach with crabs," Stan demanded, "or was it a world full of water?"

"Neither one. It was like a big ice age. Glaciers covered everything. No oceans showing, no mountains. We flew clear around the world and it was all a huge snowball. They had floodlights on the vehicle because the sun had gone out."

"I was sure I could see the sun still hanging up there," Harriet put in. "Like a ball of cinders in the sky. But the guide said no, nobody could see it."

"How come everybody gets to visit a different kind of end of the world?" Henry asked. "You'd think there'd be only one kind of end of the world. I mean, it ends, and this is how it ends, and there can't be more than one way."

"Could it be fake?" Stan asked. Everybody turned around and looked at him. Nick's face got very red. Fran looked so mean that Eddie let go of Cynthia and started to rub Fran's shoulders. Stan shrugged. "I'm not suggesting it is," he said defensively. "I was just wondering."

"Seemed pretty real to me," said Tom. "The sun burned out. A big ball of ice. The atmosphere, you know, frozen. The end of the goddamned world."

The telephone rang. Ruby went to answer it. Nick asked Paula about lunch on Tuesday. She said yes. "Let's meet at the motel," he said, and she grinned. Eddie was making out with Cynthia again. Henry looked very stoned and was having trouble staying awake. Phil and Isabel arrived. They heard Tom and Fran talking about their trips to the end of the world and Isabel said she and Phil had gone only the day before yesterday. "Goddamn," Tom said, "everybody's doing it! What was your trip like?"

Ruby came back into the room. "That was my sister calling from Fresno to say she's safe. Fresno wasn't hit by the earthquake at all."

"Earthquake?" Paula asked.

"In California," Mike told her. "This afternoon. You didn't know? Wiped out most of Los Angeles and ran right up the coast practically to Monterey. They think it was on account of the underground bomb test in the Mohave Desert."

"California's always having such awful disasters," Marcia said.

"Good thing those amoebas got loose back east," said Nick. "Imagine how complicated it would be if they had them in LA now too."

"They will," Tom said. "Two to one they reproduce by airborne spores."

"Like the typhoid germs last November," Jane said.

"That was typhus," Nick corrected.

"Anyway," Phil said, "I was telling Tom and Fran about what we saw at the end of the world. It was the sun going nova. They showed it very cleverly, too. I mean, you can't actually sit around and experience it, on account of the heat and the hard radiation and all. But they give it to you in a peripheral way, very elegant in the McLuhanesque sense of the word. First they take you to a point about two hours before the blowup, right? It's I don't know how many jillion years from now, but a long way, anyhow, because the trees are all different, they've got blue scales and ropy branches, and the animals are like things with one leg that jump on pogo sticks—"

"Oh, I don't believe that," Cynthia drawled.

Phil ignored her gracefully. "And we didn't see any sign of human beings, not a house, not a telephone pole, nothing, so I suppose we must have been extinct a long time before. Anyway, they let us look at that for a while. Not getting out of our time machine, naturally, because they said the atmosphere was wrong. Gradually the sun started to puff up. We were nervous – weren't we, Iz? – I mean, suppose they miscalculated things? This whole trip is a very new concept and things might go wrong. The sun was getting bigger and bigger, and then this thing like an arm seemed to pop out of its left side, a big fiery arm reaching out across space, getting closer and closer. We saw it through smoked glass, like you do an eclipse. They gave us about two minutes of the explosion, and we could feel it getting hot already. Then we jumped a couple of years forward in time. The sun was back to its regular shape, only it was smaller, sort of like a little white sun instead of a big yellow one. And on Earth everything was ashes."

"Ashes," Isabel said, with emphasis.

"It looked like Detroit after the union nuked Ford," Phil said. "Only much, much worse. Whole mountains were melted. The oceans were dried up. Everything was ashes." He shuddered and took a joint from Mike. "'Isabel was crying."

"The things with one leg," Isabel said. "I mean, they must have all been wiped out." She began to sob. Stan comforted her. "I wonder why it's a different way for everyone who goes," he said. "Freezing. Or the oceans. Or the sun blowing up. Or the thing Nick and Jane saw."

"I'm convinced that each of us had a genuine experience in the far future," said Nick. He felt he had to regain control of the group somehow. It had been so good when he was telling his story, before those others had come. "That is to say, the world suffers a variety of natural calamities, it doesn't just have one end of the world, and they keep mixing things up and sending people to different catastrophes. But never for a moment did I doubt that I was seeing an authentic event."

"We have to do it," Ruby said to Mike. "It's only three hours. What about calling them first thing Monday and making an appointment for Thursday night?"

"Monday's the President's funeral," Tom pointed out. "The travel agency will be closed."

"Have they caught the assassin yet?" Fran asked.

"They didn't mention it on the four o'clock news," said Stan. "I guess he'll get away like the last one."

"Beats me why anybody wants to be President," Phil said.

Mike put on some music. Nick danced with Paula. Eddie danced with Cynthia. Henry was asleep. Dave, Paula's husband, was on crutches because of his mugging, and he asked Isabel to sit and talk with him. Tom danced with Harriet even though he was married to her. She hadn't been out of the hospital more than a few months since the transplant and he treated her extremely tenderly. Mike danced with Fran. Phil danced with Jane. Stan danced with Marcia. Ruby cut in on Eddie and Cynthia. Afterward Tom danced with Jane and Phil danced with Paula. Mike and Ruby's little girl woke up and came out to say hello. Mike sent her back to bed. Far away there was the sound of an explosion. Nick danced with Paula again, but he didn't want her to get bored with him before Tuesday, so he excused himself and went to talk with Dave. Dave handled most of Nick's investments. Ruby said to Mike, "The day after the funeral, will you call the travel agent?" Mike said he would, but Tom said somebody would probably shoot the new President too and there'd be another funeral. These funerals were demolishing the gross national product, Stan observed, on account of how everything had to close all the time. Nick saw Cynthia wake Henry up and ask him sharply if he would take her on the end-of-the-world trip. Henry looked embarrassed. His factory had been blown up at Christmas in a peace demonstration and everybody knew he was in bad shape financially. "You can charge it," Cynthia said, her fierce voice carrying above the chitchat. "And it's so beautiful, Henry. The ice. Or the sun exploding. I want to go."

"Lou and Janet were going to be here tonight, too," Ruby said to Paula. "But their younger boy came back from Texas with that new kind of cholera and they had to cancel."

Phil said, "I understand that one couple saw the moon come apart. It got too close to the Earth and split into chunks and the chunks fell like meteors. Smashing everything up, you know. One big piece nearly hit their time machine."

"I wouldn't have liked that at all," Marcia said.

"Our trip was very lovely," said Jane. "No violent things at all. Just the big red sun and the tide and that crab creeping along the beach. We were both deeply moved."

"It's amazing what science can accomplish nowadays," Fran said.

Mike and Ruby agreed they would try to arrange a trip to the end of the world as soon as the funeral was over. Cynthia drank too much and got sick. Phil, Tom, and Dave discussed the stock market. Harriet told Nick about her operation. Isabel flirted with Mike, tugging her neckline lower. At midnight someone turned on the news. They had some shots of the earthquake and a warning about boiling your water if you lived in the affected states. The President's widow was shown visiting the last President's widow to get some pointers for the funeral. Then there was an interview with an executive of the time-trip company. "Business is phenomenal," he said. "Time-tripping will be the nation's number one growth industry next year." The reporter asked him if his company would soon be offering something besides the end-of-the-world trip. "Later on, we hope to," the executive said. "We plan to apply for Congressional approval soon. But meanwhile the demand for our present offering is running very high. You can't imagine. Of course, you have to expect apocalyptic stuff to attain immense popularity in times like these." The reporter said, "What do you mean, times like these?" but as the time-trip man started to reply, he was interrupted by the commercial. Mike shut off the set. Nick discovered that he was extremely depressed. He decided that it was because so many of his friends had made the journey, and he had thought he and Jane were the only ones who had. He found himself standing next to Marcia and tried to describe the way the crab had moved, but Marcia only shrugged. No one was talking about time-trips now. The party had moved beyond that point. Nick and Jane left quite early and went right to sleep, without making love. The next morning the Sunday paper wasn't delivered because of the Bridge Authority strike, and the radio said that the mutant amoebas were proving harder to eradicate than originally anticipated. They were spreading into Lake Superior and everyone in the region would have to boil all their drinking water. Nick and Jane discussed where they would go for their next vacation. "What about going to see the end of the world all over again?" Jane suggested, and Nick laughed quite a good deal.

THE END OF
THE WORLD

Sushma Joshi

There are constant predictions of the imminent end of the world. Rather like the boy who cried wolf, people don't take much notice of them anymore, which may one day prove unfortunate. In the following story we see one such effect upon a group of people of a threatened apocalypse.

Sushma Joshi is a writer, publisher and occasional filmmaker from Nepal. She co-edited New Nepal, New Voices *(2008), an anthology of short stories from Nepal, whilst* Art Matters *(2008) is a collection of her magazine reviews about contemporary art in Nepal. The following story, which first appeared on the internet in 2002, formed the basis for her first collection of short stories,* End of the World *(2008).*

ONE DAY, EVERYBODY was talking about it. It had even been printed in the newspapers. A great and learned sadhu had prophesied a conflagration, a natural disaster of such proportions that more than half of the world's population would be killed. Dil was on his way to work at the construction site when he stopped briefly to listen to a man propounding the benefits of a herb against impotence. Then he noticed, out of the corner of his eye, long lines of goats converging on to the green. "What's going on?" he asked. And the people told him: "Everybody's buying meat so they can have one last good meal before they die."

Dil, following this precedent of preparing for the end of the world, went into the shop and bought a kilogram of goat meat. On

his way back home, he stopped at Gopal Bhakta's shop, where all
the men saw the blood-soaked newsprint packet he was carrying in
his hand. "So what's the big event, Dai? Are you celebrating Dashain
early this year?" they joked. So he told them how goats were being
sold in record numbers, and how the butchers were doing a roaring
business down in Tudikhel. The men, seizing on this opportunity
for celebration, all decided to buy some meat for their last meal.

Sanukancha, who owned a milk-shop down the lane, said that his
entire extended family of 116 people was planning to stay home
that day so that they could be together when the seven suns rose the
next morning and burnt up the Earth. Bikash, who had transformed
from an awara loafer to a serious young teacher since he got a job at
the Disney English School, said that so many children had come in
asking to be excused that day that the schools had declared a de
facto national holiday. Gopal Bhakta said that his sister, who
worked in the airport, had told him that the seats of Royal Nepal
Airlines were all taken with people hoping to escape the day of
destruction.

Dil showed up that night at his house with a kilo of meat wrapped
in sal leaves. He handed it to Kanchi without a word.

"Meat! We don't have a kernel of rice, not a drop of oil, not a
pinch of turmeric in the house. And you come back with a kilo of
meat! We could have eaten for a week with that money." Kanchi
was exasperated.

"Shut up, whore, and eat," said Dil. "You might be dead
tomorrow, so you might as well enjoy this meat while you have it."

"How am I going to cook it? With body heat?" demanded Kanchi.
There was no kerosene in the house. Dil stretched out on the bed, his
body still covered with the grey and red dust of cement and newly
fired brick from his day of labor at the construction site. He stretched
out and stared at the ceiling, as was his habit after work. When he did
not reply, Kanchi asked: "And what is this great occasion?"

He contemplated the water stains on the wooden beams for a
while, and then answered: "It's the end of the world."

So that's how she learnt that a great star with a long tail was going
to crash against Jupiter, and shatter the Earth into little fragments.
It was true this time because even the TV had announced it. It was

not just a rumor. There were also some reports, unverified by radio or television, that several – the numbers varied, some said it was seven, others 32,000 – suns would rise after this event.

Kanchi was just about to go and get some rice from Gopal Bhakta, the shopkeeper who knew her well and let her buy food on credit, when her son arrived, carrying a polythene bag with oranges. "Oranges!" She swiped at the boy, who scrambled nimbly out of her reach. "You're crazy, you father and son. We have no rice in the house and you go and buy oranges. Don't you have any brains in your head!"

But the husband said nothing, and the son said nothing, and since it is useless to keep screaming at people who say nothing, Kanchi left, cursing their stupidity. "May the world really end, so I won't have to worry about having to feed idiots like you again."

So that night they had meat, alternately burnt and uncooked in parts where the children had roasted it, and perfectly done pieces which Kanchi had stuck long sticks through and cooked over hot coals. Then Kanchi, reflecting that the end of the world did not come too often, had gone over and picked some green chilies and coriander from the field next door to garnish the meat.

Afterwards they had the oranges, one for each of them. They were large, the peels coming off easily and scenting the room with their oil. Inside, they were ripe and juicy, with a taste that they never got in the scrawny sour oranges that grew back in the villages. After they had eaten, Dil said as an afterthought, "Now make sure the children don't go out tomorrow, whatever you do."

Later, Kanchi forgot her annoyance as their next door neighbors came over, bringing their madal drum and their three guests who were visiting from the village. They sang the songs that were so familiar, and yet had begun to seem so strange nowadays: songs about planting rice and cutting grass in the forest, a life that, to the children, was as unknown and faraway as the stories that they heard from the priests during a reading of the holy scriptures of the Purans. Then her son got up and started dancing, and they were all cheering when the landlady popped her head round the door and demanded: "What's all this noise? What's going on here? It sounds like the end of the world!"

* * *

Kanchi dressed carefully for the eventful day. She had on her regular cotton sari, but wrapped over it was the fluffy, baby blue cashmere shawl that Jennifer had brought for her from America. Jennifer, who was long, lugubrious and eternally disgusted with Nepal, worked for some development office, where she made women take injections and told them to save money in banks. She was fond of telling Kanchi that Nepalis were incapable of understanding what was good for them. She would have been proud to see Kanchi putting the blue shawl to such good use on such a momentous day.

Kanchi worked for Jennifer when she was in town. She cooked her rice and vegetables with no spices, and cut the huge red peppers that Jennifer liked to eat raw while she stood in front of her television in shiny, tight clothes and did her odd dances. Janefonda, Janefonda, she would yell at Kanchi, hopping up and down like a demented, electric green cricket as she munched on the huge peppers. She was not very forthcoming with presents, but once every winter she gave Kanchi a piece of clothing.

"Why the shawl on this hot day?" inquired Mitthu. She was the old cook of the Sharmas' at whose house Kanchi went to wash the clothes every morning to supplement her uncertain income.

"Haven't you heard?" Kanchi said to her. "Everybody is talking about it. Today is the end of the world. A big sadhu prophesied it. I won't have my husband by me, or my son. At least I can have my shawl."

"What nonsense," retorted Mitthu. She was a religious woman, with a tendency to be skeptical of people and events that she had not heard of.

"Well, what if it happens?" Kanchi demanded, and Mitthu replied, just as firmly: "No, it won't."

"Let's eat rice now, Didi," Kanchi said anxiously, as the sky began to darken for a light rain. The end of the world was supposed to happen at 11 a.m., and Kanchi wanted to deal with the event on a full stomach. "We might be hungry later."

"Is this for your body or your soul?" asked Mitthu as she ladled some rice on to a plate for Kanchi. She had an acerbic tongue.

"A soul will fly away like a small bird. It'll fly away when it becomes hungry and go and steal from some other people's homes. It's my stomach that will kill me."

"And is your shawl to keep you warm in heaven or hell?" Mitthu inquired as she dropped a pinch of spicy tomato acchar on to the rice.

"I won't need this shawl in heaven or hell. This is if I survive and there is nobody else on this earth but me. At least I will have my shawl to keep me warm."

Mitthu, even though she would not acknowledge it, recognized this admirable foresight and common sense. "Humph," she said, turning away to steal a glance at the sun, which did look rather bright. She wondered if she should run in and get a shawl as well, just in case, then decided her pride was more important.

A rumble of thunder rolled across the clear blue sky, and Kanchi stood up in a panic. "What a *darcheruwa* I am, I have no guts," she scolded herself.

"Eat, Kanchi," said Mitthu, rattling the rice ladle over the pot, annoyed at her own fright.

"I saw Shanta Bajai storming off to the office this morning. She said she would go to the office even if nobody else came, and she would die in her chair if she had to."

"So why is the world going to end?" asks Mitthu cautiously. She did not believe it was going to happen. At the same time, she was curious.

"It's all because of Girija," explained Kanchi. "It all started happening ever since he became the Prime Minister. Ever since he started going off to America day after day. I heard he fainted and fell on the ground, and the king of America gave him money for medicine. So this destruction is happening since he returned. Maybe the American king gave him money and he sold Nepal, maybe that's why. And now maybe the Communists will take over."

"You know, Kanchi, I almost became a Communist when I was in the village. It sounded good. We would all have to live together, and work together, and there would be no divisions between big or small. Then we could kill all the rich people and there would be peace."

"And what about eating?" asks Kanchi. "You would also have to eat together, out of the same plate, with everybody else. How would that suit you, you Bahuni? You who won't even eat your food if you suspect somebody has looked at it?" Mitthu, who was a fastidious

Brahmin and refused to let people who she suspected of eating buffalo meat into her kitchen, realized she had overlooked this point.

"And then they make you work until you drop dead," said Kanchi. "Don't tell me I didn't think about it. I would rather live like this, where at least I can have my son by me at night. I heard the Communists take away your children and make you work in different places. And then they give you work that you cannot fulfill, and if you do not do it, they kill you – *dong*! – with one bullet. What's the point of living then?"

"Well ... " Mitthu does not want to give up her sympathies so easily. Besides, her husband had died when she was nine. As a lifelong child widow she had no reason to worry about being separated from her children. "Well, we'll see it when it happens, won't we?"

"Like the end of the world," said Kanchi, checking out the sky. "I heard that they have taken the big Sadhu who predicted the end of the world and put him in the jail in Hanuman Dhoka. He has said that they can hang him if it doesn't happen. Then some people say that he was performing a Shanti Hom and the fire rose so high he was burnt and had to be taken to the hospital. Who can tell what will happen?"

Eleven a.m. There is a sudden shocked silence. The whole world stands still, for once, in anticipation. Then a sudden cacophony shatters the midmorning silence: cows moo tormentedly, dogs howl long and despondently, and people scream all over the marketplace tole.

The sky is flat gunmetal grey. The sun shines brightly.

A collective sigh of relief wafts over the Valley of Kathmandu after the end of the world comes to an end.

THE CLOCKWORK ATOM BOMB

Dominic Green

The world may be under threat or on the brink of destruction at any moment from some cosmic or human catastrophe, and who knows how many times this may have happened in the past or the present.

You won't find any published books by Dominic Green yet, though there are a handful of novels available at his website: http://homepage.ntlworld.com/lumfylomax/

He has been producing a stream of short fiction since 1996, mostly for the magazine Interzone, *and the following story was shortlisted for the prestigious Hugo Award in 2006. He used to work in IT. He reveals the following about himself: "I was brought up in the North of England till the age of eight, and in the South of England till the age of eighteen. This has made me culturally amphibious, able to eat both black pudding and jellied eels. I also went to an English public school and Cambridge University, which has prepared me well for unemployment. I can strongly recommend it to anyone wanting to combine the thrill of standing in a dole queue with the added frisson of being thousands of pounds in debt. I write science fiction, you know."*

"OVER HERE, MISTER. This is the place."

The girl tugged Mativi's sleeve and led him down a street that was mostly poorly-patched shell holes. Delayed Action Munitions – the size of thumbnails and able to turn a man into fragments of the same dimensions – littered the ground hereabouts, designed to lie dormant for generations. Construction companies used robot tractors to fill in bomb damage, and the robots did a poor job. Granted, they were getting better – Robocongo was one of equatorial Africa's biggest exporters. But usually the whites and the blacks-with-cash sat in control rooms a kilometre away directing robots to build the houses of the poor, and the poor then had to live in those houses not knowing whether, if they put their foot down hard on a tough domestic issue, they might also be putting it down on a DAM bomblet a metre beneath their foundations.

This street, though, hadn't even been repaired. It was all sloped concrete, blast rubble and wrecked signs telling outsiders to KEEP OUT THIS GOVERNMENT BUILDING! FIELD CLERICAL STORES! IMPORTANT GOVERNMENT WORK HERE YOU GO BACK!

"Come on, mister," said the *phaseuse*. "You will see, and then you will have no problem paying."

"You stand still," commanded Mativi suddenly. "Stand right there."

Nervously, he reached into a pocket and brought out the *Noli Timere*. It only worked fifty per cent of the time, based on information gathered from scientist-collaborators from all factions in the war, but fifty per cent was better than zip.

He turned the device on, on low power in case any of the more recent devices that smelled mine detector power-up were present, and swept it left and right. Nothing. He flicked it up to full power and swept again. A small stray air-dropped antipersonnel device at the north-west end of the street, but otherwise nothing.

"You see that house over there, Emily?" he said, pointing across the road. The girl nodded. "Well, you're not to go in there. There is an explosive device in there. A big one. It'll kill you."

Emily shook her head firmly. "It isn't *nearly* as big as the one that took Claude."

Mativi nodded. "But you say that device is *still there*."

"Has been since I was very little. Everyone knows it's there. The grown-ups know it's there. They used it when the *slim* hit, to get rid of the bodies, so we wouldn't get sick. Sometimes," she said, "before the bodies were entirely dead."

"You can't get *slim* from a dead body," said Mativi.

"That's what you say," said Emily. And he knew she was right. So many generously altered genomes had been flying around Africa in warheads fifteen years ago that someone *could* have altered HIV and turned it into an airborne, rather than blood-borne, virus – like the rickettsial haemorrhagic fever that had wiped out all of Johannesburg's blood banks in a single day and made social pariahs of blacks all over Europe and America overnight.

The sun dropped below the horizon like a guillotine blade, and it was suddenly night, as if someone had flicked a switch in heaven. Mativi had become too used to life off the Equator, had been working on the basis that night would steal up slowly as it had in Quebec and Patagonia. But the busy equatorial night had no time for twilight. He hadn't brought night vision goggles. Had he brought a torch?

As they walked up the street, a wind gathered, as if the landscape sensed his unease.

"You have to be careful," said the girl, "tread only where I tread. And you have to bend down." She nodded at Mativi's Kinshasa Rolex. "You have to leave your watch outside."

Why? So one of your bacheque *boyfriends can steal it while I'm in there?* To satisfy the girl's insistence, he slid the watch off his wrist and set it on a brick, but picked it up again when she wasn't looking and dropped it into his pocket.

"Where are we going?" he said.

"In there," she pointed. Half-buried in the rubble was a concrete lintel, one end of a substantial buried structure, through which the wind was whistling.

No. Correction. *Out of which* the wind was whistling.

She slipped under the lintel, on which was fixed a sign saying WARNING! EXTREME PERSONAL DANGER! The room beyond had once had skylights. Now, it had ruined holes in the roof, into which the geostationary UNPEFORCONG security moon poured prisms of reflected sunlight. Thirty-five thousand, nine hundred kilometres above Mativi's head, he and five million other Kinshasans were being watched with 5,000 cameras. This had at first seemed an outrageous intrusion on his privacy, until he'd realized that he'd have to commit a thousand murders before any of the cameras was likely to catch him in the act.

"Don't step any closer," said the girl. "It will take you."

The entrance had promised an interior like any other minor military strongpoint – only just large enough to contain a couple of hammocks and a machine gun, maybe. But inside, after only a few steps down, the room was huge, the size of a factory floor. They had entered via an engineer's inspection catwalk close to the roof. He was not sure how far down the floor was.

The wind in here was deafening. The girl had to shout. "THERE IS MORE THAN ONE IN HERE. THEY LIVE IN THE MACHINES. THE GOVERNMENT MADE THE MACHINES, BUT NOT WITH TECHNICIANS AND ELECTRICIANS. WITH *SORCERY.*"

The machines did not look made by sorcery. They were entirely silent, looking like rows of gigantic, rusted steel chess pawns twice the height of a man, with no pipes or wires entering or leaving them, apparently sitting here unused for any purpose. Mativi felt an urgent, entirely rational need to be in another line of employment.

"HAVE YOU ANY IDEA WHAT THE MACHINES WERE BUILT FOR?" said Mativi, who had.

The girl nodded. "THE DEMONS ARE IN THE MACHINES," she said. "THE MACHINES WERE BUILT AS CAGES. THE MILITARY MEN WHO MADE THIS PLACE WARNED ALL THE MOST IMPORTANT MEN IN OUR DISTRICT OF THIS. THEY WARNED MY FATHER. THEY TOLD HIM NEVER TO BREAK ANY OF THE MACHINES OPEN. BUT OVER TIME, THEY LEAK, AND THE DEMONS CAN GET OUT. THE FIRST TWO MACHINES ARE SAFE, FOR NOW. BUT YOU MUST BE CAREFUL, BECAUSE WE THOUGHT THE THIRD ONE WAS SAFE TOO, AND IT TOOK CLAUDE."

"WHAT DID IT DO TO CLAUDE, WHEN IT TOOK HIM?" said Mativi. He could not see any damage to the walls around the third machine beyond, perhaps, a certain swept-clean quality of the dust on the floor around it.

"IT TOOK HIM," said the girl. "IT MADE HIM SMALL. IT SUCKED HIM UP."

"THE MACHINES," said Mativi in broken Lingala. "THEY ARE COVERED WITH ... WITH *THINGS.*"

The heads of the chess-pawns, under the light of Mativi's torch, were surrealistically coiffeured with assorted objects – spanners, wire, door furniture, and, worryingly, a single fragmentation grenade. Many, perhaps more than half of the things were ferrous metal. But some looked like aluminium. Some were even bits of wood or plaster.

Not just magnetism, then.

He fished the fake Rolex out of his pocket, waved it in the direction of the machines, and felt a strong tug on it as he held it in his hand. But he also felt a strong tug on the sleeve of his shirt, and on his arm itself.

He realized with growing unease that the wind was not blowing out of the chamber, but *into* it, pushing him from behind. It also appeared to be blowing in through the skylights in the roof above.

It did not seem to be blowing out anywhere.

The girl gasped. "YOU SHOULD NOT HAVE DONE THAT! NOW YOUR WATCH WILL NOT KEEP GOOD TIME."

"IS THAT HOW THE MACHINE SUCKED CLAUDE UP?"

"NO. ALL THE MACHINES DRAW THINGS IN, BUT YOU CAN PULL YOURSELF LOOSE FROM MOST OF THEM. BUT THE ONES THE DEMONS LIVE IN WILL SUCK YOU RIGHT INSIDE WHERE THE DEMON LIVES, AND NOT LEAVE A HAIR BEHIND."

"WHOLE PEOPLE?"

"PEOPLE, METAL, ANYTHING."

"STONES?" Mativi picked up a fragment of loose plaster from the floor.

"YES. BUT YOU SHOULD NOT THROW THINGS."

He threw it. The girl winced. He saw the plaster travel halfway across the floor until it passed the second machine. Then it jerked sideways in mid-air, as if attached to invisible strings, puffed into a long cone of powder, and vanished.

The girl was angry. "YOU MUST DO WHAT I SAY! THE MILITARY MEN SAID WE SHOULD NOT THROW THINGS INTO THE BAD MACHINES. THEY SAID IT MADE THE DEMONS STRONGER."

"YES," said Mativi. "AND THEY WERE ABSOLUTELY RIGHT. NOT *MUCH* STRONGER, BUT IF ENOUGH PEOPLE THREW IN ENOUGH UNCHARGED MATERIAL OVER ENOUGH TIME…"

"I DON'T UNDERSTAND WHAT YOU MEAN BY *UNCHARGED MATERIAL.*"

"DO YOU UNDERSTAND WHAT I MEAN BY 'EVERYONE WOULD DIE'?"

The girl nodded. "WE SHOULD NOT STAY TOO LONG IN HERE. PEOPLE WHO STAY TOO LONG IN HERE GET SICK. THE DEMONS MAKE THEM SICK."

Mativi nodded. "AND I SUPPOSE THIS SICKNESS TAKES THE FORM OF HAIR LOSS, SHORTNESS OF BREATH, EXTREME PALENESS OF THE SKIN?"

"YES," said the girl. "THE VICTIMS DISPLAY THE CLASSIC SYMPTOMS OF RADIATION ALOPOECIA AND STEM CELL DEATH."

Well, I'll be damned. But after all, she has lived through a nuclear war. She's been living among radiation victims her entire life. Probably taught herself to read using Red Cross posters.

"WELL, THE SAME DEMONS THAT WERE USED IN THE RADIATION BOMBS ARE IN HERE. SLIGHTLY DIFFERENT, BECAUSE THESE ARE A SLIGHTLY DIFFERENT WEAPON. BUT THE SAME DEMONS."

The girl nodded. "BUT THESE ARE NOT RADIATION BOMBS," she said. "THIS MEANS YOU HAVE TO PAY ME DOUBLE." She held out her hand.

Mativi nodded. "THIS MEANS I HAVE TO PAY YOU DOUBLE." He fished in his wallet for a fistful of United Nations scrip.

After all, why shouldn't I pay you. None of this money is going to be worth anything if these things destroy the world tomorrow.

"I'm telling you, there are at least forty of them. I counted them. Five rows by eight."

"I didn't go to the hotel because I didn't want to call you in the clear. We have to be the only people who know about this."

"Because if anyone wanders into that site, *anyone at all,* and does anything they shouldn't, we will all die. I'm not saying *they,* I'm saying *we,* and I'm not saying *might die,* I'm saying *will die.*"

"Yes, this is a Heavy Weapons alert."

"No, I can't tell you what that means."

"All I can tell you is that you must comply with the alert to the letter if you're interested in handing on the planet to your children."

"Your children will grow out of that, that hating their father thing. All teenagers go through that phase. And credit where credit's due, you really shouldn't have slept with their mother's sister in the first place."

"No, I do *not* want 'an inspection team'. I want troops. *Armed* troops with a mandate to shoot to kill, not a detachment of graduates in Peace Studies from Liechtenstein in a white APC. And when I put the phone down on you, I want to know that you're going to be picking up your phone again and dialling the IAEA. I am *serious* about this, Louis."

"All right. All right. I'll see you at the site tomorrow."

When he laid the handset down, he was trembling. In a day when there were over a hundred permanent websites on the Antarctic ice shelf, it had taken him five hours to find a digital phone line in a city of five million people. Which, to be fair, fifteen years ago, had been a city of ten million people.

Of course, his search for a phone line compatible with his encryption software would probably be for nothing. If there were this few digital lines in the city, there was probably a retro-tech transistor microphone planted somewhere in the booth he was sitting in, feeding data back to a mainframe at police headquarters. But at least that meant the police would be the *only* ones who knew. If he'd gone through the baroque network of emergency analogue lines, every housewife in the *cité* would have known by morning.

He got up from the booth, walked to the desk, and paid the geek – the geek *with a submachinegun* – who was manning it. There was no secret police car waiting outside – the car would have been unmarked but extremely obvious due to the fact that no one but the government could afford to travel around in cars. The Congolese sun came up like a jack-in-a-box and it was a short walk through the zero tolerance district back to his hotel, which had once been a Hilton. He fell into the mattress, which bludgeoned him compliantly unconscious.

When he opened his hotel room door in the morning to go to the one functioning bathroom, a man was standing outside with a gun.

Neither the man nor the gun was particularly impressive – the gun because it appeared to be a pre-War cased ammunition model that hadn't been cleaned since the Armistice, and the man because his hand was shaking like a masturbator's just before orgasm, and because Mativi knew him to be a *paterfamilias* with three kids in kindergarten and a passion for N gauge model railways.

However, the gun still fired big, horrid bullets that made holes in stuff, and it was pointing at Mativi.

"I'm sorry, Chet, I can't let you do it." The safety catch, Mativi noted, was off.

"Do what?" said Mativi.

"You're taking away my livelihood. You know you are."

"I'm sorry, Jean, I don't understand any of this. Maybe you should explain a little more?" Jean-Baptiste Ngoyi, an unremarkable functionary in the United Nations Temporary Administration Service (Former People's Democratic Republic of Congo), appeared to have put on his very best work clothes to murder Mativi. The blue UNTASFORDEMRECONG logo was embroidered smartly (and widely) on his chest pocket.

"I can't let you take them away." There were actually tears in the little man's eyes.

"Take what away?"

"You know what. *Everybody* knows. They heard you talking to Grosjean."

Mativi's eyes popped. "*No*. Ohhh *shit*. No." He leaned back against crumbling postmodernist plasterwork. "Jean, don't take this personally, but if someone as far down the food chain as you knows, everyone in the city with an e-mail address and a heartbeat knows." He looked up at Ngoyi. "There was a microphone in the comms booth, right?"

"No, the geek who mans the desk is President Lissouba's police chief's half-brother. The police are full of Lissouba men who were exonerated by the General Amnesty after the Armistice."

"Shit. Shit. What are they doing, now they know?"

"'*Emergency measures are being put in place to contain the problem*'. That's all they'd say. Oh, and there are already orders out for your arrest For Your Own Safety. But they didn't know which hotel you were staying in. One of them was trying to find out when he rang me."

Mativi walked in aimless circles, holding his head to stop his thoughts from wandering. "I'll bet he was. God, god. And you didn't tell them where I was. Does that mean you're, um, not particularly serious about killing me?" He stared at Ngoyi ingratiatingly. But the gun didn't waver – at least, not any more than it had been wavering already. Never mind. It had been worth a try.

"It means I couldn't take the chance that they really did want you arrested for your own safety," said Ngoyi. "If a UN Weapons Inspector died in Kinshasa, that would throw the hand grenade well and truly in the muck spreader for the police chiefs, after all."

"I take it some of them are the men who originally installed the containers. If so, they know very well full amnesties are available for war crimes —"

Ngoyi shook his head. "Not for crimes committed *after* the war."

Mativi was alarmed. "After?"

"They've been using the machines as execution devices," said Ngoyi. "No mess, no body, no incriminating evidence. And they work, too. The *bacheques* are terrified of them, will do anything to avoid being killed that way. They think they're the homes of demons —"

"They're not far wrong," muttered Mativi.

"— and then there are the undertakers," continued Ngoyi. "They've been using the machines for mass burials. Otherwise the bodies would just have piled up in the streets in the epidemics. And the domestic waste trucks, about five of them stop there several times a week and dump stuff in through the skylights. And my own trucks —"

"Your own trucks?"

"Yes. Three times a week, sometimes four or five." Ngoyi returned Mativi's accusing stare. "Oh, *sure*, the UN gives us geiger counters and that bacterial foam that fixes fallout, and the special vehicles for sucking up the fixed material and casting it into lead glass bricks —"

"Which you're supposed to then arrange for disposal by the IAEA by burial underground in the Devil's Brickyard in the Dry Valleys of Antarctica," finished Mativi. "Only you haven't been doing that, have you? You thought you'd cut a few corners."

"The UN gives us a budget of only five million a year!" complained Ngoyi. "And by the time that reaches us, it has, by the magic of African mathematics, become half a million. Have you any idea what it costs to ship a single kilo of hazardous waste to Antarctica?"

"That's what you're supposed to do," repeated Mativi, staring up the barrel of the gun, which somehow did not matter quite so much now.

"We were talking astrophysics in the Bar B Doll only the other night. You told me then that once something crosses the Event Horizon, it never comes out!" said the civil servant, mortified. "You *promised*!"

"That's absolutely correct," said Mativi. "Absolutely, totally and utterly correct."

"Then," said Ngoyi, his face brightening insanely, "then there is no problem. We can throw as much stuff in as we want to."

"Each one of those containers," said Mativi, "is designed to hold a magnetically charged object that weighs more than ten battleships. Hence the reinforced concrete floor, hence the magnetized metal casing that attracts every bit of ferrous metal in the room. Now, what do you think is going to happen if you keep piling in extra uncharged mass? *Nothing* that crosses the Event Horizon comes out, Jean. *Nothing. Ever.* Including you, including me, including Makemba and Kimbareta and little Laurent."

Ngoyi's face fell. Then, momentarily, it rose again.

"But our stuff is only a few hundred kilos a week," he began. "Much less than what the domestic waste people put in."

"I feel better already. You're not going to be personally responsible for getting the whole planet sucked into oblivion, it's going to be some other guy."

"The sewage outlet, mind you," continued Mativi. "That must be pumping in a good thousand litres a day —"

Mativi's jaw dropped.

"*Sewage outlet?*"

"Sure. The sanitation guys rerouted the main waste pipe for the city as a temporary measure. They have to keep replacing the last few metres – the machine keeps eating the pipe." Ngoyi shrugged. "How else do you think they keep five million people's shit out of the drinking water?"

"Jean-Baptiste, you people have to stop this. You have to stop it now. You have absolutely no idea what you're doing."

The gun was still pointing at the centre of Mativi's chest; now, just for a moment, it stopped wavering and hit dead centre.

"I know *exactly* what I'm doing. I am making sure I can feed my wife and children."

The finger coiled round the trigger, slowed down as if falling down gravity slopes. Mativi winced.

The gun clunked and did nothing.

Ngoyi stared at his uncooperative weapon tearfully.

"I must warn you," lied Mativi, "that I led my university karate team."

"You should leave," said Ngoyi. "I think I recognized the municipal sanitation inspector's car following the bus I took down here. He had a rocket-propelled grenade launcher on his parcel shelf."

The road surface rose and fell under the Hyundai like a brown ocean swell, testing its suspension to the limit. Mativi heard things grounding that probably ought not to.

"Can I drop you off anywhere?" He braked gently as the traffic hit the blast craters around the freeway/railway junction, which had been a prime military target. Robot repair units were still working on it, and their operators did not pay much attention to cars that weighed one tenth what a mine clearance tractor did. The street-lights seemed to be out on this stretch of road, and the only illumination came from car headlights bouncing up and down like disco strobes. The robot tractors did not need visible light to see.

"The stadium will do fine. I can catch a bus out to Ndjili from there."

"You live that far out of town?"

"We don't all live on Geneva salaries, you know." Ngoyi's face blanched suddenly as he stared into the evening traffic. "Stop the car! Handbrake turn! Handbrake turn!"

Mativi stared into the traffic. "Why?"

"Four secret police cars, dead ahead!"

It was true, and Mativi cursed himself for not having seen it. The SUV's stood out like aluminium islands in the sea of polyurea

AfriCars. Each one of them would have cost ten times an ordinary Kinshasan's annual salary.

"It's not a roadblock," said Mativi.

"So I should care? They're out looking for you!"

"... looks like an escort. They're not even coming down this road. They're turning on to the freeway to Djelo-Binza. They're escorting that big, heavy launch tractor ... one of the ones designed to carry clutches of heavy ballistic missiles out to the pads at Malebo." He peered out of the driver-side window. "The one whose suspension is scraping the ground —"

He did a handbrake turn and left the road in the direction of Djelo-Binza. The suspension hardly noticed the difference. The only reason people drove on roads any more in Kinshasa was because the road was slightly more likely to have been checked for explosives.

There was only desultory hooting when he rejoined the road. Leaving the road and rejoining it after a four-wheel-drive shortcut was common. The four-by-fours were clearly visible now, crammed with whatever men the police chiefs had been able to get their hands on at short notice – some in military uniform, some in T-shirts, some with government-issue sidearms, some with war-era AKM's, yawning, pulled out of bed in the early hours.

The crawler was taking up three lanes of traffic, drawing a horde of honking AfriCars behind it like a bridal train. Despite the horns, the crawler was probably not moving much slower than the cars would have done – the expressway was still a mass of blast craters.

"I can't *believe* this," said Mativi, hugely affronted. "How can they think they can haul a million-tonne object across town without me noticing?"

Ngoyi stared. "You think that thing's got – *things* on it?"

Mativi nodded. "One of the things is on board – one of the *containers*. They're taking it across town because they can't bear to lose it ... I wonder why." He winked at Ngoyi. "Maybe they're in the pay of the office of sanitation?" The car plunged into yet another black void unilluminated by its headlights. "JESUS, I wish those streetlights were working." He blinked as the car bonnet surged up again into the light.

Then he realized. Not only were there no streetlights, there were also no lights in the city around the road.

"That's it, isn't it?"

"What?"

"They're going to the power company. You dumb fucks have been plugging power into it as well. *Haven't you*?"

Ngoyi hesitated, then gave up the game and nodded. "It started out as a theoretical weapons project in the last days of the war. But," he insisted defiantly, "it was a *peaceful* use we put it to! One of our office juniors, a very clever young man, a PhD from CalTech, suggested that if we aimed an infra-red laser beam at the event horizon at a certain angle, it would come out as a gamma-ray beam, which we used to heat a tank of mercury ... we tried water first, but it flash evaporated and fused the rock around the tank to glass." He licked his lips nervously. "The hardest part was designing a turbine system that would work with evaporating mercury. We lost a lot of men to heavy metal poisoning ..."

Realization dawned on Mativi. "You were one of the researchers in Lissouba's government."

"You think I could have got away with living in the old People's Democratic Republic with a physics degree *without* being a weapons researcher?" Ngoyi laughed hollowly. "Dream on, brother. But this is *peacetime* now. The technology is being used to power the houses of five million people —"

"Uh-uh. There's no sidestepping the Laws of Thermodynamics. You only get out less than what you put in. You're only getting power out because you're sapping the angular momentum of what's inside the container. I'll lay a bet that what's inside the container was created illegally using the Lubumba Collider that President Lissouba convinced the UN to build to 'rejuvenate the Congolese economy' —"

Ngoyi squirmed. "He also said *scientify* the Congolese economy. He actually used the word 'scientify'."

Mativi nodded. "In any case, that angular momentum was put *into* the container by gigawatts of energy pumped into the Collider from the city power grid. Effectively all you're doing is using up energy someone stole and stored fifteen years ago. It's no more a power source than a clockwork doll is, Jean-Baptiste. You have to wind it up to watch it go. And all you'll be left with, in the end, is a non-rotating very heavy lump of extremely bad shit."

"Well, I must admit," admitted Ngoyi ruefully, "the amount of juice we can squeeze out of it is getting smaller every year."

The tractor in front suddenly rumbled to a halt in a cloud of dust big enough to conceal a herd of rhinos. A wall of immobile metal barred the carriageway, and three lanes of drivers performed the peculiarly Congolese manoeuvre of stepping on their brakes and leaning on their horns simultaneously. One of them shrieked suddenly in dismay when a length of caterpillar track resembling a chain of house façades clipped together with traffic bollards slammed down on to his bonnet and crushed it flat, before slapping his saloon into a cabriolet. Paint flakes flew everywhere. The car was a steel one, too – an old Proton model produced under licence in Afghanistan. Mativi hoped the driver had survived.

Troopers poured out of the four-by-fours, ignoring the barrage of horns. They were staring at the side of the tractor. Some good Catholics were even crossing themselves.

Mativi put the handbrake on and left his car. Someone hooted at him. He ignored them.

One whole side of the tractor had collapsed into the asphalt. The torsion bars of the vehicle's suspension, each one a man's waist thick and made of substances far, far stronger than steel, had snapped like seaside rock. The load on top of the tractor had slumped sideways underneath its canvas blanket.

Now that he was outside the car, he was aware of a hissing sound. The sound was coming from a hole punched in the canvas cover.

Some of the troopers were walking up towards the load. Mativi danced out on to the grass verge, waving his arms like an *isangoma*.

"No! *Non!* Get away! *Trés dangereux!*"

One of the men looked at Mativi as if he were an idiot and took another step forward. His sleeve began to rustle and flap in the direction of the hole in the canvas. Then his hand slapped down on to the canvas cover, and he began to scream, beating on his hand, trying to free it. His comrades began to laugh, looking back towards Mativi, enjoying the joke their friend was having at the crazy man's expense.

Then he vanished.

Not *quite* vanished – Mativi and the troops both heard the bones in his hand snap, saw the hand crumple into the canvas like a handkerchief into a magician's glove, followed by his arm, followed by his shoulder, followed by his head. They saw the flare of crimson his body turned into as skin, bone, blood vessels, all the frail materials meant to hold a body together, degenerated into carmine mulch and were sucked up by the structure. A crimson blot of blood a man wide sprayed on to the canvas – out of which, weirdly, runnels of blood began trailing *inward* towards the hole, against and at angles to gravity.

The police troops turned and looked at Mativi, then looked back at the tractor.

"*Alors, chef,*" one of them said to him, "*qu'est-ce qu'on fait maintenant?*"

"It's loose," said Ngoyi, his eyes glazed, seeing the ends of worlds. "It's loose, and I am responsible."

Mativi shook his head. "It's not loose. Not *yet*. We can still tell *exactly* where it is, just by feeding it more policemen. But its casing's corroded. It's sucking in stuff from outside."

"Not corroded," Ngoyi shook his head. "It won't corrode. It's made of nickel alloy, very strong, very heavy. It's one of the cases we bored a hole in deliberately, in order to shine in the infrared beam. There'll be another hole in the casing on the far side. Where the gamma comes out."

Mativi nodded. *One of the machines the demons live in.*

Ngoyi still seemed to be wary of even looking at the container. "Could it topple over?"

"No. If it begins to topple, it'll right itself immediately. It's probably scrunched itself down into the top of the tractor doing that already. Remember, it's a small thing rotating, rotating *fast*, and it weighs over a thousand tonnes. The gyroscopic stability of an object like that doesn't bear thinking about —"

"CETAWAYO BRIAN MATIVI! I AM HEREBY BY THE ORDER OF THE UNITED NATIONS PEACEKEEPING FORCES OF THE CONGO PLACING YOU UNDER ARREST."

Mativi turned. The voice had come from a senior police officer. The amount of shiny regalia on the uniform confused matters, but he was almost certain the man was a lieutenant.

Mativi sighed. "Lieutenant —" he began.

"Major," corrected the major.

"—Major, I am engaged in preventing a public disaster of proportions bigger than anything that might possibly be prevented by arresting me. Do you know what will happen if that load falls off that wagon?"

The Major shrugged. "Do you know what will happen if I see you and don't drag you down to the cells? I will lose my job, and my wife and children will go hungry."

Mativi began to back away.

"Hey!" The Major began to pointedly unbutton his revolver.

"I know what will happen to you if you don't bring me in. And you forgot to mention that there'll be no power in the city either, and that as a consequence a *great number* of wives and children will go hungry," said Mativi, circling around the danger area of bowed-headed, permanently windblown grass near the tractor's payload. He waved his arms in the direction of the dark horizon. "You can see the evidence of this already. The device on this tractor has been uncoupled from the grid, and immediately there is no power for refrigeration, no power for cooking or for emergency machinery in hospitals. I know all that." Slowly, he put his hands up to indicate he was no threat. Then, with one hand, he swung himself up on to the side of the tractor, with the payload between himself and the Major. "But you truly cannot begin to comprehend what will happen to those wives and children if I allow this load to continue on to Djelo-Binza, sir. You see, I understand at a very deep level what is in this container. You do not."

"I must warn you not to attempt to escape custody," said the Major, raising his pistol. "I am empowered to shoot."

"How can I be trying to escape custody?" said Mativi, looking down the barrel of the pistol as if his life depended on it, and sinking in his stance, causing the Major to lower the pistol by a couple of centimetres, still training it on his heart. "I'm climbing on board a police vehicle."

"Get down off that police vehicle now," said the Major. "Or I will shoot."

Mativi licked his lips, looking up a pistol barrel for the second time that day, but this time attempting to perform complex orbital calculations in his head as he did so. *Have I factored in relativity properly? It needs to travel dead over the hole —*

"Shan't."

The gun fired. It made quite a satisfactory BOOM. There was a red flash in mid-air, and Mativi was still there.

The Major stared at Mativi.

"As I said," said Mativi, "I understand what is in this cargo. You do not. Do I have your full cooperation?"

The Major's eyes went even wider than his perceived Remit To Use Deadly Force. He lowered the gun, visibly shaken.

"You do," he said. "Sir," he added.

The Hyundai became bogged down by bodies – fortunately living ones – in the immediate vicinity of the Heavy Weapons Alert site. A crowd of perhaps a thousand goggling locals, all dressed in complementary rayon T-shirts handed out by various multinationals to get free airtime on Third World famine reports, were making road and roadside indistinguishable. But the big blue bull bars parted the crowd discreetly, and Mativi dawdled forward to a hastily-erected barrier of velcrowire into which several incautious onlookers had already been pushed by their neighbours. Velcrowire barbs would sink a centimetre deep into flesh, then open up into barbs that could only be removed by surgeons, provided that the owner of the flesh desired to keep it. Barbed wire was not truly barbed. Velcrowire was.

The troops at the only gap in the fence stood aside and saluted for the UN car, and Mativi pulled up next to an ancient Boeing V-22 VTOL transport, in the crew door of which a portly black man in a bad safari suit sat juggling with mobile phones. The casings of the phones, Mativi knew, were colour-coded to allow their owner to identify them. The Boeing had once been United Nations White. After too many years in the Congo, it was now Well-Used Latrine White.

Mativi examined what was being done at the far end of the containment area. The site was a mass of specialized combat engineering machinery. Mativi recognized one of the devices, a Japanese-made tractor designed for defusing unexploded nuclear munitions – or rather, for dealing with what happened when a human nuclear

UXB disposal operative made a mistake. Hair trigger sensors on the tractor would detect the incipient gamma flare of a fission reaction, then fire a 120-millimetre shell into the nuke. This would kill the bomb disposal man and fill the area around the bomb with weapons-grade fallout but probably save a few million civilians in the immediate area.

Mativi walked across the compound and yelled at the man in the Boeing. "Louis, what the HELL are your UXB monkeys DOING?"

Grosjean's head whipped round.

"Oh, hello, Chet. We're following standard procedure for dealing with an unexploded weaponized gamma source."

"Well, first off, this isn't a weapon —"

Grosjean's smile was contemptuous. "It's something that can annihilate the entire planet, and it isn't a *weapon*?"

"It's *thirty-nine* things that can annihilate the planet, and they're not weapons *any more*. Think about it. Would anyone use a weapon that would blow up the whole world?"

Grosjean actually appeared to seriously consider the possibility; then, he nodded to concede the point. "So what sort of weapon were these things part of?"

"Not weapons," corrected Mativi. "Think of them as weapons *waste*. They were the principal components in a Penrose Accelerator."

"You're making it up."

"You damn fool security guy, me weapons inspector. We've suspected the People's Democratic Republic of Congo used Penrose weapons in their war with the Democratic People's Republic of Congo for some time. They had guns capable of lobbing 100-tonne shells full of plague germs at Pretoria from a distance of 4,000 kilometres, for instance. When we examined those guns after UNPE-FORCONG overran their positions, what we found didn't fit. They had magnetic accelerators in their barrels but at the sort of muzzle velocities they'd have had to have been using, the magnets in the barrels would only have been any use in aiming, not in getting the payload up to speed. And the breech of each weapon had been removed. *Something* had been accelerating those projectiles, but it wasn't magnetism, and it wasn't gunpowder. The projectiles were big, and they were moving *fast*. You remember that outbreak of airborne rabies in New Zealand two years back? That was one of theirs. A Congolese shell fired too hot and went into orbit. The orbit decayed. The shell came down. Thirteen years after the war. Gunpowder and magnetism don't do that."

"So what was it?"

"A Penrose accelerator. You get yourself a heavy-duty rotating mass, big enough to have stuff orbit round it, and you whirl ordnance round those orbits, contrary to the direction of the mass's rotation. Half of your ordnance separates from the payload, and drops into the mass. The *other* half gets kicked out to mind-buggering velocities. The trouble is, none of this works unless the mass is dense enough to have an escape velocity greater than light."

"A black hole."

"Yes. You have yourself thirty-nine charged rotating black holes, formerly used as artillery accelerators, now with nowhere to go. Plus another hole lodged precariously on the back of a tractor on the public highway halfway between here and Djelo-Binza. And the only way for us to find enough energy to get rid of them, I imagine, would be to use *another* black hole to kick them into orbit. They also give off gamma, almost constantly, as they're constantly absorbing matter. You point one of those UXB defuser tractors at them and throw the safety on the gun, and —"

"JESUS!" Grosjean stared at the ground-floor entrance where his men had been preparing to throw heavy artillery shells at the problem, jumped up, and began frantically waving his arms for them to stop. "OUI! OUI! ARRÊTE! ARRÊTE! And we thought getting rid of nuclear waste was difficult."

"Looks easy to me," said Mativi, nodding in the direction of the highway. Two trucks with UNSMATDEMRECONG livery, their suspensions hanging low, had stopped just short of the military cordon in the eastbound lane. Their drivers had already erected signs saying LIGHT HEAT HERE FOR DOLLARS, and were handing out clear resin bricks that glowed with a soft green light to housewives who were coming out of the darkened prefabs nearby, turning the bricks over in their hands, feeling the warmth, haggling over prices.

"Is that what I think it is?" said Grosjean. "I should stop that. It's dangerous, isn't it?"

"Don't concern yourself with it right now. Those bricks can only kill one family at a time. Besides," said Mativi gleefully, "the city needs power, and Jean-Baptiste's men are only supplying a need, right?"

Ngoyi, still in the passenger seat of the Hyundai, stared sadly as his men handed out radionuclides, and could not meet Mativi's eyes. He reached in his inside pocket for the gun he had attempted to kill Mativi with, and began, slowly and methodically, to clear the jam that had prevented him from doing so.

"Once you've cordoned the area off," said Mativi, "we'll be handling things from that point onwards. I've contacted the IAEA myself. There's a continental response team on its way."

In the car, Ngoyi had by now worked the jammed bullet free and replaced it with another. At the Boeing, Grosjean's jaw dropped. "You have teams set up to deal with this *already*?"

"Of course. You don't think this is the first time this has happened, do you? It's the same story as with the A-bomb. As soon as physicists know it's possible, every tinpot dictator in the world wants it, and will do a great deal to get it, and certainly isn't going to tell *us* he's trying. Somewhere in the world at a location I am not aware of and wouldn't tell you even if I were, there is a stockpile of these beauties that would make your hair curl. I once spoke to a technician who'd just come back from there ... I think it's somewhere warm, he had a suntan. He said there were aisles of the damn things, literally thousands of them. The UN are working on methods of deactivating them, but right now our best theoretical methods for shutting down a black hole always lead to catastrophic Hawking evaporation, which would be like a 1,000-tonne nuclear warhead going off. And if any one of those things broke out of containment, even one, it would sink through the Earth's crust like a stone into water. It'd get to the Earth's centre and beyond before it slowed down to a stop – and then, of course, it'd begin to fall to the centre again. It wouldn't rise to quite the same height on the other side of the Earth, just like a pendulum, swinging slower and slower and slower. Gathering bits of Earth into itself all the time, of course, until it eventually sank to the centre of the world and set to devouring the entire planet. The whole Earth would get sucked down the hole, over a period which varies from weeks to centuries, depending on which astrophysicist you ask. And you know what?" – and here Mativi smiled evilly. This was always the good part.

"What?" Grosjean's Bantu face had turned whiter than a Boer's. From the direction of the car, Mativi heard a single, slightly muffled gunshot.

"We have no way of knowing whether we already missed one or two. Whether one or two of these irresponsible nations carrying out unauthorized black hole research dropped the ball. How would we know, if someone kept their project secret enough? How would we know there wasn't a black hole bouncing up and down like a big happy rubber ball inside the Earth right now? Gravitational anomalies would eventually begin to show themselves, I suppose – whether on seismometers or mass detectors. But our world might only have a few decades to live – and we wouldn't be any the wiser.

"Make sure that cordon's tight, Louis."

Grosjean swallowed with difficulty, and nodded. Mativi wandered away from the containment site, flipping open his mobile phone. Miracle of miracles, even out here, it worked.

"Hello darling … No, I think it'll perhaps take another couple of days …Oh, the regular sort of thing. Not too dangerous. Yes, we did catch this one … Well, I did get shot at a *little*, but the guy missed. He was aiming on a purely Euclidean basis …Euclidean. I'll explain when I get home …Okay, well, if you have to go now then you have to go. I'll be on the 9 a.m. flight from Kinshasa."

He flicked the phone shut and walked, whistling, towards the Hyundai. There was a spider's web of blood over the passenger side where Ngoyi had shot himself. *Still,* he thought, *that's someone else's problem. This car goes back into the pool tomorrow. At least he kept the side window open when he did it. Made a lot less mess than that bastard Lamant did in Quebec City. And they made me* clean *that car.*

He looked out at the world.

"Saved you again, you big round bugger, and I hope you're grateful."

For the first time in a week, he was smiling.

BLOODLETTING

Kate Wilhelm

In recent years Kate Wilhelm has become better known for her crime fiction novels, but for years – since her first sale in 1956 – she was a notable, if only occasional, writer of science fiction and fantasy, or speculative fiction, to use her preferred term. With her husband, Damon Knight, who died in 2002, she was a key player in creating both the Milford and Clarion SF Writers' workshops. Her SF novels include the Hugo-winning post-apocalyptic Where Late the Sweet Birds Sang *(1976), in which a community of clones find a remote hideaway to weather the storm. Her best short fiction will be found in* The Infinity Box *(1975),* Somerset Dreams *(1978),* Children of the Wind *(1989) and* And the Angels Sing *(1992). The following story, which considers how a global pandemic may start, is one of her more recent, and as yet remains uncollected.*

I AM SITTING in my car, and nothing is visible, just the black night out there, the black night inside; the only sound is of the sea, the waves crashing against the cliff with fierce regularity. I remember the one time my grandmother came out here; she did not like the constant sea noise. She complained, "Don't it ever shut up?" She did not like the constant wind, either; worse than Kansas, she said on that trip. On my first visit to her farm in Kansas I marveled at the stars, and she took that to be a sign of a simple mind. But I knew then, and I think I still know, that they have more stars in Kansas than they do at the Oregon coast. Grandmother also said Warren was simple. But that was later, ten years ago.

The impenetrable darkness has made me think of her, I suppose. She talked about growing up on the prairies that were virtually uninhabited, of being out late when there wasn't a light to be seen, of her fear of the dark then and forever after. When I said I wasn't afraid of the dark, she muttered, "You don't know dark, child. You don't know." I do now.

She came out of the kitchen muttering the day I took Warren home to meet my family. "That man ain't as smart as he thinks," she said. "He don't know enough to open a can. Simple, that's what he is." I went to the kitchen to find Aunt Jewel showing Warren how to use an old can opener. He had never seen one like it. Simple. He was thirty, with a Ph.D., tenure at the University of Oregon, working with Gregory Oldhams. He had turned down other, better-paid, positions for the chance to work with Greg; he could have gone to Harvard, Stanford, almost anywhere he wanted.

It has started to rain, a soothing monotonous patter on the roof of the car, and now a wind has come up, rustling in the firs, in the vine maples, the broom that grows down the face of the cliff where nothing else can find enough dirt to sink roots. I am very tired.

I brought Warren up here before we were married; he was envious. "You grew up in a wilderness!" he said. He had grown up in Brooklyn.

"Well, you're here now," I said. "So it doesn't really matter so much, does it?"

"It matters," he said, gazing down at the ocean, then turning to look at the trees, and finally at the A-frame house below us and across a shallow ravine. I had lived in that house for the first twelve years of my life. "It matters," he repeated. "You have things in your eyes I'll never get. I have people and traffic and buildings, and people, more people, always more people, always more cars, more exhaust, more noise..." He stopped and I was glad. There was anguish in his voice, bitterness – I didn't know what it was; I didn't want to know it.

Greg Oldhams is the foremost researcher in hematology, the study of blood. He already was famous when Warren started working with him, and since then his research, and Warren's, has become what the articles call legendary. At first, after I met Warren, I felt almost ashamed of my own field – medieval literature. What was the point in that, I wondered, compared to the importance of what they were doing? At first, Warren talked about his work with excitement, passion even, but then he stopped. I know to the day when it changed. On Mikey's fifth birthday, five years ago. Warren didn't come home in time for the party, and when he did get home, he was old.

A person can become old in a day, I learned then. Mikey turned five; Warren turned a hundred.

The wind is increasing; there may be a gale moving in. I had to roll up the window on my side when the rain started, and when I reached over to open the passenger side window, I realized I still had the seat belt fastened and then it seemed too hard to work the clasp and free myself. I began to laugh, and then I was crying and laughing. I don't care if rain comes in the passenger side, but the wind makes a harsh whistling sound through the narrow opening near my head, and I have to decide, open the window more and get wet, or close it. I can't bear the whistling noise. Finally I make the effort to undo the seat belt, reach over, and open the other window and close the driver-side one. Now I can hear the ocean, and the rain, and even the wind in the trees. So much exertion, I mock myself, but I have to lean back and rest.

This is where I told Warren yes, I would marry him, up here over-looking the sea. "No children," he said. "The world has enough children."

I backed away from him and we regarded each other. "But I want a family," I said after a moment. "At least one child of ours, our genes. We can adopt another one or two."

Nothing was settled that day. We went back to the A-frame and banged pots and pans and argued and I told him to get lost, to get out of my life, and he said it would be criminal to bring another child into the world and I was being selfish, and the much-touted maternal urge was cultural, and I said people like us owed it to children to give them the same advantages we had, education, love, care... It went on into the night, when I told him to sleep on the couch, and the next day, until I stomped out of the house and came up here to glare at the ocean and its incessant racket. He came after me. "Christ," he said. "Jesus. One." Two months later we were married and I was pregnant.

When Mikey was two he got a big sister, Sandra, who was three and a half, and a year later he got a bigger brother, Chris, who was five. Our family.

Mikey was four when they all had chicken pox at the same time. One night Warren was keeping them entertained, coloring with them at the table while I made dinner.

"Why did you make him green?" Chris demanded.

"Because he has artificial blood," Warren said.

"Why?"

"Because something went wrong with his blood and they had to take it out and put in artificial blood."

Mikey began to cry. "Is that what they'll do to us?"

"Nope. You're not sick enough. You've just got spots on your face. You call that sick? I call it kvetching."

"What's that?" Sandra asked. She had fallen in love with Warren the day we met her, and he loved all three children.

"That's when you grow spots on your face, and itch, and pretend you're sick so your mother will let you eat ice cream all day if you want. And your dad plays silly games with you when he should be at work. That's kvetching."

They liked kvetching. Later they got into my lipstick and tried to make it all happen again, spots, whining for ice cream, laughing.

Later it was funny, but that night, with my sick children at the table, itching, feverish, it was not funny. I froze at the sink with water running over lettuce. Artificial blood? We were still in the cold war; atomic war was still possible, anything was possible. Even artificial blood.

"Why?" I asked, after the children were in bed.

He had to start way back. "Remember in the movie *Dracula* how the good doctor transfused one of the women over and over with whole blood, and it took? Pure luck. Lucy was probably an A-group type, and so was the guy. If he had put blood from an O group in her, she probably would have died on him. That's how it was. One took, another one, then bingo, it didn't. Then they found out about the blood groups, and later on about how the agglutinogens combine with certain agglutinins, and not others. And we've been learning ever since. The body treats the wrong blood type just like any other invading organism, bacterium, virus, whatever, and rejects it. But in the case of a major catastrophe you can't count on the lab facilities to handle the typing, the storage, all the mechanics of transfusions. The labs might not be there. We've got artificial blood now, you know, but it's pretty high-tech stuff."

I hadn't known until then. I shuddered, and he grinned. "So what's wrong with being green? Don't worry, it's still experimental, and very, very temporary. Anyway, if we could get away from some of the really high-tech stuff and simply transfuse from any healthy person to one who is ill ... see?"

"But wouldn't that be just as high tech?"

He shrugged. "Maybe. Maybe not. There are genetic blood characteristics that get passed on from parent to child, you know. Sickle cell anemia, which, by the way, comes in a package that includes resistance to malaria. Hemophilia gets passed on..." Whatever expression my face was registering made him stop. "Hey," he said softly. "I'm just spitballing."

I jerked upright so fast, I bumped into the steering wheel. I must have been dozing, dreaming. How clear Warren was, his hair thinning just a touch, a little too long, the color of wet sand; that day he had a suntan and looked almost ruddy. A big-faced ruddy man who looked as if he should be out plowing, or putting a roof on a building, or something else physically demanding. A sailor, he would have made a fine sailor. I can't see him now; my imagination is faulty in that I can't see images with any sharp detail. Only my dreams re-create with exactitude the people I have loved. My parents live on in my dreams; Warren is there; the children, but they won't show themselves to my waking mind. I have only feelings, impressions, nuances that have no names. Warren is a loving presence, a comforting presence, bigger in my mind than ever in person, stronger, more reassuring, strangely more vulnerable so that I feel I have to protect him. From what is as unclear as the visual image.

When I drove down here from the Portland airport, it was my intention to turn into the driveway to the house where I played out my childhood; instead, I kept driving, followed the road that became a track up to this lookout point. The end of the road. The place where the world disappears.

We came out here with Greg two years ago. His wife was gone by then, back to Indiana or somewhere with their two children, and he was lonely. Or so Warren said. I didn't believe it, and still don't believe Greg ever knew loneliness. His work was world enough. We built a fire on the beach and the children played in the surf and came near to get warm, then raced back to the frigid water.

"Tell Greg about the meals," Warren said, grinning, contented that day, even though he was a hundred years old.

I had told him and the children about a typical meal during the time of Abelard and Heloise. Our children wanted to eat that way, too. A long board against the wall, food within reach of everyone, people sharing the same bowls, the same cups, eating with spoons or fingers. The beggars crowding about, and the dogs crowding everyone, snapping at each other, at the beggars, at the diners and the servers.

Greg laughed when I described it. He was lazy looking, relaxed, but if Warren had turned a hundred, Greg had turned two hundred. An old worried man, I thought. He was only forty-five according to the official records, but I knew he was ancient.

"Was that during the plague years?" he asked. He was leaning against a forty-foot-long tree that had crashed ashore, riding the waves to be stranded here, a memento of the power of the sea during a storm. The tree trunk was eight feet thick. It might have been alive in Abelard's time.

"Not much plague yet, not in epidemic form in Europe at least, although plague was recorded back in the sixth century, you understand, and continued intermittently until it struck in pandemic force later, about the fifteenth century. This period was 1100 or so. Why?"

"The beggars were inside at the table?" he asked, bemused.

"They were kicked out shortly after that; the beggars had to stay beyond the door, but the dogs weren't banished."

The conversation ended there; the children found a starfish which we all went to examine, and the sun was going down by then.

Late that night we discussed when we would leave for home the following day. Traffic had been bumper to bumper coming out and it would be worse on Sunday.

"I may stay on a few days with the kids," I said. Warren could go back with Greg early, which they were both inclined to do, but I knew the children would be disappointed at the short stay, as I was.

It was summer; I had no classes, and this was the only kind of vacation we would have, a day now and then, two, three days at the coast.

"I wonder what it was like during the plague years," Greg mused, reviving the subject we had left hours before. "Anywhere from one-third to half the people gone, just gone."

"It wasn't exactly like that," I said. "It took 300 years before it stopped sweeping the continent in epidemic form, and during that period the church became the power it is now. Superstition, heresies, empowerment for the church and state, fear for the public, that's what was going on. Life was hell for most survivors."

"And the Renaissance came about," Greg said thoughtfully. "Would it have happened without the plague? No one really knows, do they?"

"That's the romantic version," I said, not quite snapping at him. "The silver-lining theory. Out of every evil thing comes something good. You believe that?"

Warren had been brooding, gazing at the fire in the fireplace, snapping and cracking, a many-hued fire burning off salts and minerals of dried wood scavenged from the beach. He sounded very tired when he spoke now. "The Renaissance came about because people had used up all the resources they had available to them; they were desperate for better ways to farm, to make clothing, to warm themselves. Better ways to survive. They had to invent the Renaissance. It had nothing to do with plague."

I realized that they had had this conversation before; neither was saying anything the other had not already heard. I stood up.

"Are you going to tell me what you're doing in your lab?"

Greg looked blank, and Warren shook his head. "Same old stuff," he said after a long pause. "Just the same old stuff."

If it was just the same old stuff – artificial blood, whole blood transfusions, work they had been publishing for years – why had they both become so old? Why were they both terrified? Why had Warren stopped talking about his work altogether, and refused to talk about it when I brought it up?

Greg got up abruptly and went to bed, and Warren shook his head when I asked him again what they were doing. "Go on to bed," he said. "I'll just be a few minutes."

What do you do if your husband holds the agent to destroy half the human race? You try not to know it; you don't demand answers; you go to bed.

A gale has arrived finally. Now the trees are thrashing, and the broom is whipping about furiously, making its own eerie shrieking sound, and the rain is so hard it's as if the sea has come up here and is raging against the car, pushing, pushing. I am getting very cold and think how strange that I was so reluctant to turn on the motor, use the heater. I can hardly even hear the engine when it starts and, as soon as I lift my foot from the accelerator, I can't hear it at all.

Greg's wife took her two children and ran when she learned. I wonder if that is why Warren refused to tell me anything for so long.

In the past two years Warren became a stranger to us, his family. We saw him rarely, and only when he was so fatigued he could hardly stay awake long enough to eat, to bathe. I didn't see Greg at all after that day at the coast, not until two weeks ago.

Warren came home late. I was already undressed for bed, in my robe. He was so pale he looked very ill. "I blew the whistle," he said, standing just inside the door, water running off his jacket, down his hands, down his face. I went to him and pulled the jacket off his shoulders. "It's going to be out of our hands by tomorrow," he said, and walked stiffly into the living room to sit on the sofa.

I hurried to the bathroom and came back with a towel, sat beside him, and began to dry his hair, his face.

"Will you tell me about it now?"

He told me. They had found a viroid that had an affinity for some blood groups, he said. Not even a whole virus, not a killed virus, a piece of a virus. They had combined it with the O group first and nothing happened, but when they then combined the O blood with A blood, the viroid changed, it became whole, replicative, and the A blood was destroyed, consumed. He said it in a monotone, almost absently, as if it were of no real consequence, after all. And then he buried his face in his hands and cried.

Forty-five per cent of Caucasians have A-group blood; five percent have AB. Thirty per cent of Blacks have A or AB. Thirty per cent of Amerinds have A or AB... And the virus they created could destroy all of them.

I held him as he wept and the words tumbled incoherently. They would both go to Atlanta, he said that night, he and Greg, and someone would come to oversee the packing of the material, the decontamination of the lab.

"Greg came in while I was on the phone," he said at some point. "He tried to stop me. I hit him. God, I hit him, knocked him down! I took him home and we talked it over."

"Does he agree, then?"

"Yes," he said tiredly. "It was like hitting your father, your god."

"Why didn't you stop when you knew what it was?"

"We couldn't," he said. He was as pale as death, with red-rimmed eyes, a haunted look. "If we did it, then so will someone else, if they haven't already. We kept trying to find an out, an antidote, a cure, something."

We were still on the sofa side by side. He drew away from me and got to his feet, an old man laboriously rising; he staggered when he started to walk. "I need a drink."

I followed him to the kitchen and watched him pour bourbon into a glass and drink it down. If he and Greg couldn't find the cure, I was thinking, then who could? They were the best in the field.

I keep thinking of what Greg said that day on the coast: the plague killed off one-third to half the population of Europe, the same numbers that make up the A, the AB, the AO blood groups. And out of that horror, he thought, had come the Renaissance.

I know so much more about blood groups and complexes now than I did two weeks ago; I put in a period of cramming, as if for an examination. I am in the A group. Mikey is AO. Warren is O. Sandra is A, and Chris is O.

I drove Warren to the lab the next morning, where we were met by a middle-aged man who introduced himself to Warren and ignored me. They went inside without a backward glance. When they were out of sight, Greg appeared, coming from the corner of the brick building, walking toward me. He had a Band-Aid on his jaw; Warren had one on his middle knuckle.

"At the last minute," Greg said, "I found I didn't want to see anyone, not Warren, not the hot-shot epidemiologist. Just tell Warren I'm taking off for a few days' rest, will you?"

I nodded, and he turned and walked away, old, old, defeated, sagging shoulders, slouching walk, his hair down over the collar of a faded gray ski jacket that gleamed with rain, sneakers squishing through puddles.

Such a clear picture of him, I marvel, coming wide awake again. The car is much too warm now; it has a very efficient heater. I want to sink back down into dreams, but instead I force myself up straighter in order to reach the key, to turn off the ignition. My hand feels encased in lead.

I packed for Warren and later that day he dashed in, brushed my cheek with his lips, snatched up his bag, and ran out again. He would call, he said, and he did several times, but never with anything real to say. I was as guarded on the phone as he was. Anything new? I asked, and he said no, same old stuff. I clutched the phone harder and talked about the children, about the rain, about nothing.

I did the things I always did: I braided Sandra's hair, and made Mikey do his homework; I talked to my own class about *The Canterbury Tales*; I shopped and made dinners; I washed my hair and shaved my legs... Mikey had a cold and Chris caught it, and I was headachy and dull feeling. Late fall things, I told Warren over the phone. He said it was rather warm in Atlanta and sunny. And, he said tiredly, he would be on the seven-o'clock flight due in Portland on Friday. We made soft thankful noises at each other; I had tears in my eyes when I hung up.

Trish Oldhams called the following evening. She wanted Warren and when I said he was out of town, there was a long pause.

"What is it, Trish? Anything I can do?" I hoped it was nothing; my headache was worse and now I was afraid it was flu, not simply a cold.

"It's Greg," she said at last. "I was going to ask Warren to go check on him. He called, and he sounded ... I don't know, just strange."

"What do you mean, strange?"

"He said he wanted to tell me goodbye," she said in a low voice. "I ... is he sick?"

"Not that I know. I'll drop in on him and call you back. Okay?"

Time is a muddle for me now. I can't remember when Trish called but I didn't call her back. I found Greg loading boxes into his truck that he had backed up partway into the garage. His house was surrounded by unkempt gardens and bushes and a lot of trees, two or three acres that he ignored. Trish used to maintain it all. I remember thinking what a wilderness he had let it become.

"What are you doing here?" he demanded, when I stopped behind his truck and got out of my car.

"Trish called. She's worried about you."

"You're shivering. Come on inside."

The inside was a shambles, things strewn about, drawers open, boxes everywhere. He led me to the kitchen where it was more of the same. The table was piled high with books and notebooks; others were on the floor, on chairs.

"Sit down," he said. "You're shaking, you're so cold." He poured us both whiskey with a drop of water, and he sat opposite me, with the piles of stuff between us. "Trish," he said after a moment. "I shouldn't have called her, I guess. She was surprised. I made her leave, you know."

I shook my head. "Why?"

"Because I was dangerous for her and the boys," he said, gazing past me. "A menace to her. I told her that and she would have hung on, but I told her I was a menace to the boys, too, and she left, just like I knew she would."

"I don't understand what you're saying." My glass rattled against the table when I tried to put it down. He took it and refilled it.

"I'm contaminated," he said. "Four, five years ago I nicked myself in the lab and got some of the viroid material in the cut. We thought I would die, Warren and I thought that, but as you can see ..." He drained his glass and put it down hard. "But it's there, the viroid, waiting to meet up with A-type blood, fulfill its destiny. Trish is A, and the boys are AO. It was just a matter of time before something happened, no matter how careful was. I sent her away."

It is all muddled. He said he would not be a guinea pig, live in quarantine. No one knew about him yet, but he would tell them soon. He had made Warren promise to let him tell them in his own time, his own way. I was drinking his liquor and having trouble following his words, but I finally had become warm, and even drowsy as he talked on. He couldn't infect me, he said, driving me home, and Warren was all right. I was safe. He insisted that I couldn't drive, and he called a cab to return home afterward. Blood contact was necessary he said, between a contaminated O and anyone else. Alone, the viroid was inert. And the virus? I asked. "Oh, that," he said grimly. "That's one of the things they'll be finding out in Atlanta. We, Warren and I, think it might be passed by any contact, or it could be airborne. They'll find out."

Today, Friday. I braided Sandra's hair and made Mikey brush his teeth, and told Chris that he couldn't go to a football game after school, not with his cold. Sandra was sneezing. I dragged into my one class, and then a committee meeting, and a late lunch with my friend Dora who told me to go home and to bed because I looked like hell. I felt like hell, I admitted, but I had to go to Portland to meet Warren. I wanted to go early enough to miss the traffic rush. I would have a snack in the restaurant and read and wait for his plane.

I heard the news bulletin on the car radio. Dr Gregory Oldhams had died in a fire at his house. There were no details. I pulled off the road onto the shoulder and stared ahead through tears. He had called Trish to tell her goodbye. He had packed up things he couldn't bear to have burned. A guinea pig, live in quarantine, in isolation, his own time, his own way...

Lights have come on in the house across the ravine. They are looking for me; Warren must have told them this is where I would come. Home. I wonder if he is with them; if he is, he may think to come up here. I rather imagine that they have him in a high-security lab somewhere, drawing blood, testing it, or packaging it to send to Atlanta.

They may send him back. He will be so tired. Would I scream at him if we met now? Probably, and he doesn't need it; he knows, and he will know for the rest of his life. If we met, and if I had a gun, would I shoot him? I can imagine doing it, and I would want to do it, but would I?

Warren's plane was going to be an hour late. It was five when I got inside the terminal; three hours stretched like eternity. I was too tired to do more than buy a book and a newspaper and then find a place where I could sit in peace. No food, I thought, shivering again. Orange juice. I sat in the restaurant thinking about Greg, about yesterday, how he had driven me home. What he had said. Blood contact between an O and anyone else, airborne possibly after an A

became infected. I remembered the Band-Aid on his chin, another
Band-Aid on Warren's knuckle. How Warren had wept, not because
of the work, but because he had struck Greg, his mentor, his father,
his god.

I knocked over my orange juice when I attempted to lift the glass,
and I stared at the spreading pool until the waitress's voice made me
start. "You want another one?" she asked.

I fled to the restroom and studied my face in the mirror. Bloodless.
It's the flu, I told myself. Just the flu. My fingers were tinged with
blue under my finger-nails, my palms were drained of color.

I know I talked to someone in Atlanta, but I can't remember how
it came about. There's a vague memory of someone else punching
numbers from my credit card. I must have asked for help. I had to
go through so many people, wait so long before someone who knew
something came on the line. "Is it airborne?" I asked, and he had
many questions, which I must have answered. He kept asking, "Are
you there? Are you all right? Can you hear me?" I know he said,
"Stay right where you are. Don't move from the phone. We'll send
someone to help you."

Why didn't I wait for Warren? I should have waited for him, but
I didn't, and then I remember, they would have come for me, and
someone else would have met him and taken him somewhere. I
think of all the people I was with in the restaurant, in the lounge, in
the vast waiting room, buying a newspaper, a book, the shop where
I bought the tape recorder I'm using, just walking around, in the
parking lot ... I forgot to tell the voice on the phone that I had
stopped to buy gas, another contact.

I had to leave the phone because someone else wanted to use it, an
angry man who told me to move my ass. I walked away from the
phone and I stopped to buy the tape recorder, and then I kept
walking, out to the lot, to my car, and I drove here. That much is
clear in my head. As long as I don't try to move, or lift anything, I
don't even feel too bad, just so tired, and so heavy. The oddest thing
is the lack of coordination in my hands. I fumble with things, drop
them; I can't even manage the key in the ignition any longer.

I told the man how it happened. Warren got the viroid when he
hit Greg. He used my razor the next morning and I used it later; we
both always nick ourselves shaving. So simple.

They will spread their nets and try to catch everyone who was in the airport this evening, people flying off to Denver, Chicago, England, Hawaii ... They will scoop up everyone at school, all my classes, my friends, committee members. My children.

I can't weep now. I must be dehydrating too much. At first I thought Greg's way would be mine. I would drive to my old house and arrange a great fire and at the last minute set it off, but I won't burn myself. They'll want to know what damage was done; they may even find a clue to help someone. Or maybe, without even thinking it through, I realized they would come to the house. The house lights appear to be dancing through waves of water. The storm is so intense now my voice sounds faint to my own ears. I don't even know how much I've said for the tape recorder, how much I have dreamed. The dreams are more real than reality. The car rocks, and the trees thrash about. I wish I could see them, but it's enough to know they've seen this before many times. Maybe they like it as much as I do.

"Can we sleep in the loft, Mom?" Mikey yelled, racing to the stairs.

"Well, sure. That's where I slept. Good enough for me, good enough for you."

I shooed them all ahead of me and lay down on the built-in bed. "Look, if you put your head right here, as soon as the moon reaches that tallest fir tree, the shadow of the tree will come in and kiss you good night."

Chris snorted in disbelief, but Sandra and Mikey lunged for the right spot, which I quickly vacated. Reluctantly Chris stayed close enough to see if it would really happen.

Later, Warren and I listened to them giggling and playing overhead. "Remember?" I asked. "You gave in and said okay to one."

There was a thump and silence and we both tensed, then renewed giggling floated down, and we relaxed. My legs were cramping from the position we were in, but I didn't tell him. I closed my eyes and listened to the laughing children.

WHEN SYSADMINS RULED THE EARTH

Cory Doctorow

Canadian-born Cory Doctorow burst on the scene in 1999 (though he had been bubbling under for some while) winning the Campbell Memorial Award in 2000 as the Best New Writer in the SF field, almost solely on the strength of one story, "Craphound". He has gone on to cement his position as one of the most popular writers of the new millennium with his novels, Down and Out in the Magic Kingdom *(2003),* Eastern Standard Tribe *(2004),* Someone Comes to Town, Someone Leaves Town *(2005) and* Little Brother *(2008). Selections of his short fiction will be found in* A Place So Foreign *(2003) and* Overclocked *(2007), and there's much more at his website: craphound.com.*

His stories bubble with a zest and energy as you'll find in the following, which won the Locus Poll as the most popular short fiction of 2006. It brings us into the realm of terrorism, technology and the fate of the Earth.

WHEN FELIX'S SPECIAL phone rang at two in the morning, Kelly rolled over and punched him in the shoulder and hissed, "Why didn't you turn that fucking thing off before bed?"

"Because I'm on call," he said.

"You're not a fucking doctor," she said, kicking him as he sat on the bed's edge, pulling on the pants he'd left on the floor before turning in. "You're a goddamned *systems administrator*."

"It's my job," he said.

"They work you like a government mule," she said. "You know I'm right. For Christ's sake, you're a father now, you can't go running off in the middle of the night every time someone's porn supply goes down. Don't answer that phone."

He knew she was right. He answered the phone.

"Main routers not responding. BGP not responding." The mechanical voice of the systems monitor didn't care if he cursed at it, so he did and it made him feel a little better.

"Maybe I can fix it from here," he said. He could login to the UPS for the cage and reboot the routers. The UPS was in a different netblock, with its own independent routers on their own uninter-ruptible power-supplies.

Kelly was sitting up in bed now, an indistinct shape against the head-board. "In five years of marriage, you have never once been able to fix anything from here." This time she was wrong – he fixed stuff from home all the time, but he did it discreetly and didn't make a fuss, so she didn't remember it. And she was right, too – he had logs that showed that after 1 a.m., nothing could ever be fixed without driving out to the cage. Law of Infinite Universal Perversity – AKA Felix's Law.

Five minutes later Felix was behind the wheel. He hadn't been able to fix it from home. The independent router's netblock was offline, too. The last time that had happened, some dumbfuck construction worker had driven a ditch-witch through the main conduit into the data-center and Felix had joined a cadre of fifty enraged sysadmins who'd stood atop the resulting pit for a week, screaming abuse at the poor bastards who labored 24/7 to splice 10,000 wires back together.

His phone went off twice more in the car and he let it override the stereo and play the mechanical status reports through the big, bassy speakers of more critical network infrastructure offline. Then Kelly called.

"Hi," he said.

"Don't cringe, I can hear the cringe in your voice."

He smiled involuntarily. "Check, no cringing."

"I love you, Felix," she said.

"I'm totally bonkers for you, Kelly. Go back to bed."

"2.0's awake," she said. The baby had been Beta Test when he was in her womb, and when her waters broke, he got the call and dashed out of the office, shouting, *The Gold Master just shipped*! They'd started calling him 2.0 before he'd finished his first cry. "This little bastard was born to suck tit."

"I'm sorry I woke you," he said. He was almost at the data center. No traffic at 2 a.m. He slowed down and pulled over before the entrance to the garage. He didn't want to lose Kelly's call underground.

"It's not waking me," she said. "You've been there for seven years. You have three juniors reporting to you. Give them the phone. You've paid your dues."

"I don't like asking my reports to do anything I wouldn't do," he said.

"You've done it," she said. "Please? I hate waking up alone in the night. I miss you most at night."

"Kelly —"

"I'm over being angry. I just miss you is all. You give me sweet dreams."

"OK," he said.

"Simple as that?"

"Exactly. Simple as that. Can't have you having bad dreams, and I've paid my dues. From now on, I'm only going on night call to cover holidays."

She laughed. "Sysadmins don't take holidays."

"This one will," he said. "Promise."

"You're wonderful," she said. "Oh, gross. 2.0 just dumped core all over my bathrobe."

"That's my boy," he said.

"Oh that he is," she said. She hung up, and he piloted the car into the data-center lot, badging in and peeling up a bleary eyelid to let the retinal scanner get a good look at his sleep-depped eyeball.

He stopped at the machine to get himself a guarana/medafonil power-bar and a cup of lethal robot-coffee in a spillproof clean-room sippy-cup. He wolfed down the bar and sipped the coffee, then let the inner door read his hand-geometry and size him up for a moment. It sighed open and gusted the airlock's load of positively pressurized air over him as he passed finally to the inner sanctum.

It was bedlam. The cages were designed to let two or three sysadmins maneuver around them at a time. Every other inch of cubic space was given over to humming racks of servers and routers and drives. Jammed among them were no fewer than twenty other sysadmins. It was a regular convention of black T-shirts with inexplicable slogans, bellies overlapping belts with phones and multitools.

Normally it was practically freezing in the cage, but all those bodies were overheating the small, enclosed space. Five or six looked up and grimaced when he came through. Two greeted him by name. He threaded his belly through the press and the cages, toward the Ardent racks in the back of the room.

"Felix." It was Van, who wasn't on call that night.

"What are you doing here?" he asked. "No need for both of us to be wrecked tomorrow."

"What? Oh. My personal box is over there. It went down around 1:30 and I got woken up by my process-monitor. I should have called you and told you I was coming down – spared you the trip."

Felix's own server – a box he shared with five other friends – was in a rack one floor down. He wondered if it was offline too.

"What's the story?"

"Massive flashworm attack. Some jackass with a zero-day exploit has got every Windows box on the net running Monte Carlo probes on every IP block, including IPv6. The big Ciscos all run administrative interfaces over v6, and they all fall over if they get more than ten simultaneous probes, which means that just about every interchange has gone down. DNS is screwy, too – like maybe someone poisoned the zone transfer last night. Oh, and there's an e-mail and IM component that sends pretty lifelike messages to everyone in your address book, barfing up Eliza-dialog that keys off of your logged e-mail and messages to get you to open a Trojan."

"Jesus."

"Yeah." Van was a type-two sysadmin, over six feet tall, long pony-tail, bobbing Adam's apple. Over his toast-rack chest, his Tee said CHOOSE YOUR WEAPON and featured a row of polyhedral RPG dice.

Felix was a type-one admin, with an extra seventy or eighty pounds all around the middle, and a neat but full beard that he wore over his extra chins. His Tee said HELLO CTHULHU and featured a cute, mouthless, Hello-Kitty-style Cthulhu. They'd known each other for fifteen years, having met on Usenet, then f2f at Toronto

Freenet beer-sessions, a Star Trek convention or two, and eventually Felix had hired Van to work under him at Ardent. Van was reliable and methodical. Trained as an electrical engineer, he kept a procession of spiral notebooks filled with the details of every step he'd ever taken, with time and date.

"Not even PEBKAC this time," Van said. Problem Exists Between Keyboard And Chair. E-mail trojans fell into that category – if people were smart enough not to open suspect attachments, e-mail trojans would be a thing of the past. But worms that ate Cisco routers weren't a problem with the lusers – they were the fault of incompetent engineers.

"No, it's Microsoft's fault," Felix said. "Any time I'm at work at 2 a.m., it's either PEBKAC or Microsloth."

They ended up just unplugging the frigging routers from the Internet. Not Felix, of course, though he was itching to do it and get them rebooted after shutting down their IPv6 interfaces. It was done by a couple bull-goose Bastard Operators From Hell who had to turn two keys at once to get access to their cage – like guards in a Minuteman silo. Ninety-five per cent of the long distance traffic in Canada went through this building. It had *better* security than most Minuteman silos.

Felix and Van got the Ardent boxes back online one at a time. They were being pounded by worm-probes – putting the routers back online just exposed the downstream cages to the attack. Every box on the Internet was drowning in worms, or creating worm-attacks, or both. Felix managed to get through to NIST and Bugtraq after about a hundred timeouts, and download some kernel patches that should reduce the load the worms put on the machines in his care. It was 10 a.m., and he was hungry enough to eat the ass out of a dead bear, but he recompiled his kernels and brought the machines back online. Van's long fingers flew over the administrative keyboard, his tongue protruding as he ran load-stats on each one.

"I had two hundred days of uptime on Greedo," Van said. Greedo was the oldest server in the rack, from the days when they'd named the boxes after Star Wars characters. Now they were all named after Smurfs, and they were running out of Smurfs and had started in on

McDonaldland characters, starting with Van's laptop, Mayor McCheese.

"Greedo will rise again," Felix said. "I've got a 486 downstairs with over five years of uptime. It's going to break my heart to reboot it."

"What the everlasting shit do you use a 486 for?"

"Nothing. But who shuts down a machine with five years uptime? That's like euthanizing your grandmother."

"I wanna eat," Van said.

"Tell you what," Felix said. "We'll get your box up, then mine, then I'll take you to the Lakeview Lunch for breakfast pizzas and you can have the rest of the day off."

"You're on," Van said. "Man, you're too good to us grunts. You should keep us in a pit and beat us like all the other bosses. It's all we deserve."

"It's your phone," Van said. Felix extracted himself from the guts of the 486, which had refused to power up at all. He had cadged a spare power-supply from some guys who ran a spam operation and was trying to get it fitted. He let Van hand him the phone, which had fallen off his belt while he was twisting to get at the back of the machine.

"Hey, Kel," he said. There was an odd, snuffling noise in the background. Static, maybe? 2.0 splashing in the bath? "Kelly?"

The line went dead. He tried to call back, but didn't get anything – no ring nor voicemail. His phone finally timed out and said NETWORK ERROR.

"Dammit," he said, mildly. He clipped the phone to his belt. Kelly wanted to know when he was coming home, or wanted him to pick something up for the family. She'd leave voicemail.

He was testing the power-supply when his phone rang again. He snatched it up and answered it. "Kelly, hey, what's up?" He worked to keep anything like irritation out of his voice. He felt guilty: technically speaking, he had discharged his obligations to Ardent Financial LLC once the Ardent servers were back online. The past three hours had been purely personal – even if he planned on billing them to the company.

There was sobbing on the line.

"Kelly?" He felt the blood draining from his face and his toes were numb.

"Felix," she said, barely comprehensible through the sobbing. "He's dead, oh Jesus, he's dead."

"Who? *Who*, Kelly?"

"Will," she said.

Will? he thought. *Who the fuck is* — He dropped to his knees. William was the name they'd written on the birth certificate, though they'd called him 2.0 all along. Felix made an anguished sound, like a sick bark.

"I'm sick," she said, "I can't even stand anymore. Oh, Felix. I love you so much."

"Kelly? What's going on?"

"Everyone, everyone —" she said. "Only two channels left on the tube. Christ, Felix, it looks like dawn of the dead out the window —" He heard her retch. The phone started to break up, washing her puke-noises back like an echoplex.

"Stay there, Kelly," he shouted as the line died. He punched 911, but the phone went NETWORK ERROR again as soon as he hit SEND.

He grabbed Mayor McCheese from Van and plugged it into the 486's network cable and launched Firefox off the command line and googled for the Metro Police site. Quickly, but not frantically, he searched for an online contact form. Felix didn't lose his head, ever. He solved problems and freaking out didn't solve problems.

He located an online form and wrote out the details of his conversation with Kelly like he was filing a bug report, his fingers fast, his description complete, and then he hit SUBMIT.

Van had read over his shoulder. "Felix —" he began.

"God," Felix said. He was sitting on the floor of the cage and he slowly pulled himself upright. Van took the laptop and tried some news sites, but they were all timing out. Impossible to say if it was because something terrible was happening or because the network was limping under the superworm.

"I need to get home," Felix said.

"I'll drive you," Van said. "You can keep calling your wife."

They made their way to the elevators. One of the building's few windows was there, a thick, shielded porthole. They peered through it as they waited for the elevator. Not much traffic for a Wednesday. Where there more police cars than usual?

"*Oh my God* —" Van pointed.

The CN Tower, a giant white-elephant needle of a building loomed to the east of them. It was askew, like a branch stuck in wet sand. Was it moving? It was. It was heeling over, slowly, but gaining speed, falling northeast toward the financial district. In a second, it slid over the tipping point and crashed down. They felt the shock, then heard it, the whole building rocking from the impact. A cloud of dust rose from the wreckage, and there was more thunder as the world's tallest freestanding structure crashed through building after building.

"The Broadcast Centre's coming down," Van said. It was – the CBC's towering building was collapsing in slow motion. People ran every way, were crushed by falling masonry. Seen through the port-hole, it was like watching a neat CGI trick downloaded from a file-sharing site.

Sysadmins were clustering around them now, jostling to see the destruction.

"What happened?" one of them asked.

"The CN Tower fell down," Felix said. He sounded far away in his own ears.

"Was it the virus?"

"The worm? What?" Felix focused on the guy, who was a young admin with just a little type-two flab around the middle.

"Not the worm," the guy said. "I got an e-mail that the whole city's quarantined because of some virus. Bioweapon, they say." He handed Felix his Blackberry.

Felix was so engrossed in the report – purportedly forwarded from Health Canada – that he didn't even notice that all the lights had gone out. Then he did, and he pressed the Blackberry back into its owner's hand, and let out one small sob.

The generators kicked in a minute later. Sysadmins stampeded for the stairs. Felix grabbed Van by the arm, pulled him back.

"Maybe we should wait this out in the cage," he said.

"What about Kelly?" Van said.

Felix felt like he was going to throw up. "We should get into the cage, now." The cage had microparticulate air-filters.

They ran upstairs to the big cage. Felix opened the door and then let it hiss shut behind him.

"Felix, you need to get home —"

"It's a bioweapon," Felix said. "Superbug. We'll be OK in here, I think, so long as the filters hold out."

"What?"

"Get on IRC," he said.

They did. Van had Mayor McCheese and Felix used Smurfette. They skipped around the chat channels until they found one with some familiar handles.

> pentagons gone/white house too

> MY NEIGHBORS BARFING BLOOD OFF HIS BALCONY IN SAN DIEGO

> Someone knocked over the Gherkin. Bankers are fleeing the City like rats.

> I heard that the Ginza's on fire

Felix typed: I'm in Toronto. We just saw the CN Tower fall. I've heard reports of bioweapons, something very fast.

Van read this and said, "You don't know how fast it is, Felix. Maybe we were all exposed three days ago."

Felix closed his eyes. "If that were so we'd be feeling some symptoms, I think."

> Looks like an EMP took out Hong Kong and maybe Paris - realtime sat footage shows them completely dark, and all netblocks there aren't routing

> You're in Toronto?

It was an unfamiliar handle.

> Yes - on Front Street

> my sisters at UofT and i cnt reach her – can you
call her?

> No phone service

Felix typed, staring at NETWORK PROBLEMS.

"I have a soft phone on Mayor McCheese," Van said, launching his voice-over-IP app. "I just remembered."

Felix took the laptop from him and punched in his home number. It rang once, then there was a flat, blatting sound like an ambulance siren in an Italian movie.

> No phone service

Felix typed again.

He looked up at Van, and saw that his skinny shoulders were shaking. Van said, "Holy motherfucking shit. The world is ending."

Felix pried himself off of IRC an hour later. Atlanta had burned. Manhattan was hot – radioactive enough to screw up the webcams looking out over Lincoln Plaza. Everyone blamed Islam until it became clear that Mecca was a smoking pit and the Saudi Royals had been hanged before their palaces.

His hands were shaking, and Van was quietly weeping in the far corner of the cage. He tried calling home again, and then the police. It didn't work any better than it had the last twenty times.

He sshed into his box downstairs and grabbed his mail. Spam, spam, spam. More spam. Automated messages. There – an urgent message from the intrusion detection system in the Ardent cage.

He opened it and read quickly. Someone was crudely, repeatedly probing his routers. It didn't match a worm's signature, either. He followed the traceroute and discovered that the attack had originated in the same building as him, a system in a cage one floor below.

He had procedures for this. He portscanned his attacker and found that port 1337 was open – 1337 was "leet" or "elite" in hacker number/letter substitution code. That was the kind of port that a worm left open to slither in and out of. He googled known sploits that left a listener on port 1337, narrowed this down based on the fingerprinted operating system of the compromised server, and then he had it.

It was an ancient worm, one that every box should have been patched against years before. No mind. He had the client for it, and he used it to create a root account for himself on the box, which he then logged into, and took a look around.

There was one other user logged in, "scaredy", and he checked the process monitor and saw that scaredy had spawned all the hundreds of processes that were probing him and plenty of other boxen.

He opened a chat:

> Stop probing my server

He expected bluster, guilt, denial. He was surprised.

> Are you in the Front Street data-center?

> Yes

> Christ I thought I was the last one alive. I'm on the fourth floor. I think there's a bioweapon attack outside. I don't want to leave the clean room.

Felix whooshed out a breath.

> You were probing me to get me to trace back to you?

> Yeah

> That was smart

Clever bastard.

> I'm on the sixth floor, I've got one more with me.

> What do you know?

Felix pasted in the IRC log and waited while the other guy digested it. Van stood up and paced. His eyes were glazed over.

"Van? Pal?"

"I have to pee," he said.

"No opening the door," Felix said. "I saw an empty Mountain Dew bottle in the trash there."

"Right," Van said. He walked like a zombie to the trash can and pulled out the empty magnum. He turned his back.

> I'm Felix

> Will

Felix's stomach did a slow somersault as he thought about 2.0.

"Felix, I think I need to go outside," Van said. He was moving toward the airlock door. Felix dropped his keyboard and struggled to his feet and ran headlong to Van, tackling him before he reached the door.

"Van," he said, looking into his friend's glazed, unfocused eyes. "Look at me, Van."

"I need to go," Van said. "I need to get home and feed the cats."

"There's something out there, something fast-acting and lethal. Maybe it will blow away with the wind. Maybe it's already gone. But we're going to sit here until we know for sure or until we have no choice. Sit down, Van. Sit."

"I'm cold, Felix."

It was freezing. Felix's arms were broken out in gooseflesh and his feet felt like blocks of ice.

"Sit against the servers, by the vents. Get the exhaust heat." He found a rack and nestled up against it.

> Are you there?

> Still here – sorting out some logistics

> How long until we can go out?

> I have no idea

No one typed anything for quite some time then.

Felix had to use the Mountain Dew bottle twice. Then Van used it again. Felix tried calling Kelly again. The Metro Police site was down.

Finally, he slid back against the servers and wrapped his arms around his knees and wept like a baby.

After a minute, Van came over and sat beside him, with his arm around Felix's shoulder.

"They're dead, Van," Felix said. "Kelly and my s– son. My family is gone."

"You don't know for sure," Van said.

"I'm sure enough," Felix said. "Christ, it's all over, isn't it?"

"We'll gut it out a few more hours and then head out. Things should be getting back to normal soon. The fire department will fix it. They'll mobilize the Army. It'll be OK."

Felix's ribs hurt. He hadn't cried since – Since 2.0 was born. He hugged his knees harder.

Then the doors opened.

The two sysadmins who entered were wild-eyed. One had a Tee that said TALK NERDY TO ME and the other one was wearing an Electronic Frontiers Canada shirt.

"Come on," TALK NERDY said. "We're all getting together on the top floor. Take the stairs."

Felix found he was holding his breath.

"If there's a bioagent in the building, we're all infected," TALK NERDY said. "Just go, we'll meet you there."

"There's one on the sixth floor," Felix said, as he climbed to his feet.

"Will, yeah, we got him. He's up there."

TALK NERDY was one of the Bastard Operators From Hell who'd unplugged the big routers. Felix and Van climbed the stairs slowly, their steps echoing in the deserted shaft. After the frigid air of the cage, the stairwell felt like a sauna.

There was a cafeteria on the top floor, with working toilets, water and coffee and vending machine food. There was an uneasy queue of sysadmins before each. No one met anyone's eye. Felix wondered which one was Will and then he joined the vending machine queue.

He got a couple more energy bars and a gigantic cup of vanilla coffee before running out of change. Van had scored them some table space and Felix set the stuff down before him and got in the toilet line. "Just save some for me," he said, tossing an energy bar in front of Van.

By the time they were all settled in, thoroughly evacuated, and eating, TALK NERDY and his friend had returned again. They cleared off the cash-register at the end of the food-prep area and TALK NERDY got up on it. Slowly the conversation died down.

"I'm Uri Popovich, this is Diego Rosenbaum. Thank you all for coming up here. Here's what we know for sure: the building's been on generators for three hours now. Visual observation indicates that we're the only building in central Toronto with working power – which should hold out for three more days. There is a bioagent of unknown origin loose beyond our doors. It kills quickly, within hours, and it is aerosolized. You get it from breathing bad air. No one has opened any of the exterior doors to this building since five this morning. No one will open the doors until I give the go-ahead.

"Attacks on major cities all over the world have left emergency responders in chaos. The attacks are electronic, biological, nuclear and conventional explosives, and they are very widespread. I'm a security engineer, and where I come from, attacks in this kind of cluster are usually viewed as opportunistic: group B blows up a bridge because everyone is off taking care of group A's dirty nuke event. It's smart. An Aum Shin Rikyo cell in Seoul gassed the subways there about 2 a.m. Eastern – that's the earliest event we can locate, so it may have been the Archduke that broke the camel's back. We're pretty sure that Aum Shin Rikyo couldn't be behind this kind of mayhem: they have no history of infowar and have never shown the kind of organizational acumen necessary to take out so many targets at once. Basically, they're not smart enough.

"We're holing up here for the foreseeable future, at least until the bioweapon has been identified and dispersed. We're going to staff the racks and keep the networks up. This is critical infrastructure, and it's our job to make sure it's got five nines of uptime. In times of national emergency, our responsibility to do that doubles."

One sysadmin put up his hand. He was very daring in a green Incredible Hulk ring-Tee, and he was at the young end of the scale.

"Who died and made you king?"

"I have controls for the main security system, keys to every cage, and passcodes for the exterior doors – they're all locked now, by the way. I'm the one who got everyone up here first and called the meeting. I don't care if someone else wants this job, it's a shitty one. But someone needs to have this job."

"You're right," the kid said. "And I can do it every bit as well as you. My name's Will Sario."

Popovich looked down his nose at the kid. "Well, if you'll let me finish talking, maybe I'll hand things over to you when I'm done."

"Finish, by all means." Sario turned his back on him and walked to the window. He stared out of it intensely. Felix's gaze was drawn to it, and he saw that there were several oily smoke plumes rising up from the city.

Popovich's momentum was broken. "So that's what we're going to do," he said.

The kid looked around after a stretched moment of silence. "Oh, is it my turn now?"

There was a round of good-natured chuckling.

"Here's what I think: the world is going to shit. There are coordinated attacks on every critical piece of infrastructure. There's only one way that those attacks could be so well coordinated: via the Internet. Even if you buy the thesis that the attacks are all opportunistic, we need to ask how an opportunistic attack could be organized in minutes: the Internet."

"So you think we should shut down the Internet?" Popovich laughed a little, but stopped when Sario said nothing.

"We saw an attack last night that nearly killed the Internet. A little DoS on the critical routers, a little DNS-foo, and down it goes like a preacher's daughter. Cops and the military are a bunch of technophobic lusers, they hardly rely on the net at all. If we take the Internet down, we'll disproportionately disadvantage the attackers, while only inconveniencing the defenders. When the time comes, we can rebuild it."

"You're shitting me," Popovich said. His jaw literally hung open.

"It's logical," Sario said. "Lots of people don't like coping with logic when it dictates hard decisions. That's a problem with people, not logic."

There was a buzz of conversation that quickly turned into a roar.

"Shut UP!" Popovich hollered. The conversation dimmed by one Watt. Popovich yelled again, stamping his foot on the countertop. Finally there was a semblance of order. "One at a time," he said. He was flushed red, his hands in his pockets.

One sysadmin was for staying. Another for going. They should hide in the cages. They should inventory their supplies and appoint a quartermaster. They should go outside and find the police, or volunteer at hospitals. They should appoint defenders to keep the front door secure.

Felix found to his surprise that he had his hand in the air. Popovich called on him.

"My name is Felix Tremont," he said, getting up on one of the tables, drawing out his PDA. "I want to read you something.

"'Governments of the Industrial World, you weary giants of flesh and steel, I come from Cyberspace, the new home of Mind. On behalf of the future, I ask you of the past to leave us alone. You are not welcome among us. You have no sovereignty where we gather.

"'We have no elected government, nor are we likely to have one, so I address you with no greater authority than that with which liberty itself always speaks. I declare the global social space we are building to be naturally independent of the tyrannies you seek to impose on us. You have no moral right to rule us nor do you possess any methods of enforcement we have true reason to fear.

"'Governments derive their just powers from the consent of the governed. You have neither solicited nor received ours. We did not invite you. You do not know us, nor do you know our world. Cyberspace does not lie within your borders. Do not think that you can build it, as though it were a public construction project. You cannot. It is an act of nature and it grows itself through our collective actions.'

"That's from the Declaration of Independence of Cyberspace. It was written twelve years ago. I thought it was one of the most beautiful things I'd ever read. I wanted my kid to grow up in a world where cyberspace was free – and where that freedom infected the real world, so meatspace got freer too."

He swallowed hard and scrubbed at his eyes with the back of his hand. Van awkwardly patted him on the shoe.

"My beautiful son and my beautiful wife died today. Millions more, too. The city is literally in flames. Whole cities have disappeared from the map."

He coughed up a sob and swallowed it again.

"All around the world, people like us are gathered in buildings like this. They were trying to recover from last night's worm when disaster struck. We have independent power. Food. Water.

"We have the network, that the bad guys use so well and that the good guys have never figured out.

"We have a shared love of liberty that comes from caring about and caring for the network. We are in charge of the most important organizational and governmental tool the world has ever seen. We are the closest thing to a government the world has right now. Geneva is a crater. The East River is on fire and the UN is evacuated.

"The Distributed Republic of Cyberspace weathered this storm basically unscathed. We are the custodians of a deathless, monstrous, wonderful machine, one with the potential to rebuild a better world.

"I have nothing to live for but that."

There were tears in Van's eyes. He wasn't the only one. They didn't applaud him, but they did one better. They maintained respectful, total silence for seconds that stretched to a minute.

"How do we do it?" Popovich said, without a trace of sarcasm.

The newsgroups were filling up fast. They'd announced them in news.admin.net-abuse.e-mail, where all the spamfighters hung out, and where there was a tight culture of camaraderie in the face of full-out attack.

The new group was alt.november5-disaster.recovery, with .recovery.goverance, .recovery.finance, .recovery.logistics and .recovery.defense hanging off of it. Bless the wooly alt. hierarchy and all those who sail in her.

The sysadmins came out of the woodwork. The Googleplex was online, with the stalwart Queen Kong bossing a gang of roller-bladed grunts who wheeled through the gigantic data-center swapping out dead boxen and hitting reboot switches. The Internet

Archive was offline in the Presidio, but the mirror in Amsterdam was live and they'd redirected the DNS so that you'd hardly know the difference. Amazon was down. Paypal was up. Blogger, Typepad and Livejournal were all up, and filling with millions of posts from scared survivors huddling together for electronic warmth.

The Flickr photostreams were horrific. Felix had to unsubscribe from them after he caught a photo of a woman and a baby, dead in a kitchen, twisted into an agonized heiroglyph by the bioagent. They didn't look like Kelly and 2.0, but they didn't have to. He started shaking and couldn't stop.

Wikipedia was up, but limping under load. The spam poured in as though nothing had changed. Worms roamed the network.

.recovery.logistics was where most of the action was

> We can use the newsgroup voting mechanism
to hold regional elections

Felix knew that this would work. Usenet newsgroup votes had been running for more than twenty years without a substantial hitch.

> We'll elect regional representatives and they'll
pick a Prime Minister

The Americans insisted on President, which Felix didn't like. Seemed too partisan. His future wouldn't be the American future. The American future had gone up with the White House. He was building a bigger tent than that.

There were French sysadmins online from France Telecom. The EBU's data-center had been spared in the attacks that hammered Geneva, and it was filled with wry Germans whose English was better than Felix's. They got on well with the remains of the BBC team in Canary Wharf.

They spoke polyglot English in .recovery.logistics, and Felix had momentum on his side. Some of the admins were cooling out the inevitable stupid flamewars with the practice of long years. Some were chipping in useful suggestions.

Surprisingly few thought that Felix was off his rocker.

> I think we should hold elections as soon as possible. Tomorrow at the latest. We can't rule justly without the consent of the governed

Within seconds the reply landed in his inbox.

> You can't be serious. Consent of the governed? Unless I miss my guess, most of the people you're proposing to govern are puking their guts out, hiding under their desks, or wandering shell-shocked through the city streets. When do THEY get a vote?

Felix had to admit she had a point. Queen Kong was sharp. Not many woman sysadmins, and that was a genuine tragedy. Women like Queen Kong were too good to exclude from the field. He'd have to hack a solution to get women balanced out in his new government. Require each region to elect one woman and one man?

He happily clattered into argument with her. The elections would be the next day; he'd see to it.

"Prime Minister of Cyberspace? Why not call yourself the Grand Poobah of the Global Data Network? It's more dignified, sounds cooler and it'll get you just as far." Will had the sleeping spot next to him, up in the cafeteria, with Van on the other side. The room smelled like a dingleberry: twenty-five sysadmins who hadn't washed in at least a day all crammed into the same room. For some of them, it had been much, much longer than a day.

"Shut up, Will," Van said. "You wanted to try to knock the Internet offline."

"Correction: I *want* to knock the Internet offline. Present tense"

Felix cracked one eye. He was so tired, it was like lifting weights.

"Look, Sario – if you don't like my platform, put one of your own forward. There are plenty of people who think I'm full of shit and I respect them for that, since they're all running opposite me or backing someone who is. That's your choice. What's not on the menu is nagging and complaining. Bedtime now, or get up and post your platform."

Sario sat up slowly, unrolling the jacket he had been using for a pillow and putting it on. "Screw you guys, I'm out of here."

"I thought he'd never leave," Felix said and turned over, lying awake a long time, thinking about the election.

There were other people in the running. Some of them weren't even sysadmins. A US Senator on retreat at his summer place in Wyoming had generator power and a satellite phone. Somehow he'd found the right newsgroup and thrown his hat into the ring. Some anarchist hackers in Italy strafed the group all night long, posting broken-English screeds about the political bankruptcy of "governance" in the new world. Felix looked at their netblock and determined that they were probably holed up in a small Inter-action Design institute near Turin. Italy had been hit very bad, but out in the small town, this cell of anarchists had taken up residence.

A surprising number were running on a platform of shutting down the Internet. Felix had his doubts about whether this was even possible, but he thought he understood the impulse to finish the work and the world. Why not? From every indication, it seemed that the work to date had been a cascade of disasters, attacks, and opportunism, all of it adding up to Gotterdammerung. A terrorist attack here, a lethal counteroffensive there from an overreactive government ... Before long, they'd made short work of the world.

He fell asleep thinking about the logistics of shutting down the Internet, and dreamed bad dreams in which he was the network's sole defender.

He woke to a papery, itchy sound. He rolled over and saw that Van was sitting up, his jacket balled up in his lap, vigorously scratching his skinny arms. They'd gone the color of corned beef, and had a scaly look. In the light streaming through the cafeteria windows, skin motes floated and danced in great clouds.

"What are you doing?" Felix sat up. Watching Van's fingernails rip into his skin made him itch in sympathy. It had been three days since he'd last washed his hair and his scalp sometimes felt like there were little egg-laying insects picking their way through it. He'd adjusted his glasses the night before and had touched the back of his ears; his finger came away shining with thick sebum. He got black-heads in the backs of his ears when he didn't shower for a couple

days, and sometimes gigantic, deep boils that Kelly finally popped
with sick relish.

"Scratching," Van said. He went to work on his head, sending a
cloud of dandruff-crud into the sky, there to join the scurf that he'd
already eliminated from his extremeties. "Christ, I itch all over."

Felix took Mayor McCheese from Van's backpack and plugged it
into one of the Ethernet cable that snaked all over the floor. He
googled everything he could think of that could be related to this.
"Itchy" yielded 40,600,000 links. He tried compound queries and
got slightly more discriminating links.

"I think it's stress-related eczema," Felix said, finally.

"I don't get eczema," Van said.

Felix showed him some lurid photos of red, angry skin flaked
with white. "Stress-related eczema," he said, reading the caption.

Van examined his arms. "I have eczema," he said.

"Says here to keep it moisturized and to try cortisone cream. You
might try the first aid kit in the second-floor toilets. I think I saw
some there." Like all of the sysadmins, Felix had had a bit of a
rummage around the offices, bathrooms, kitchen and store-rooms,
squirreling away a roll of toilet-paper in his shoulder-bag along
with three or four power-bars. They were sharing out the food in
the cafe by unspoken agreement, every sysadmin watching every
other for signs of gluttony and hoarding. All were convinced that
there was hoarding and gluttony going on out of eyeshot, because
all were guilty of it themselves when no one else was watching.

Van got up and when his face hove into the light, Felix saw how
puffed his eyes were. "I'll post to the mailing-list for some antihis-
tamine," Felix said. There had been four mailing lists and three
wikis for the survivors in the building within hours of the first meeting's close, and in the intervening days they'd settled on just one.
Felix was still on a little mailing list with five of his most trusted
friends, two of whom were trapped in cages in other countries. He
suspected that the rest of the sysadmins were doing the same.

Van stumbled off. "Good luck on the elections," he said, patting
Felix on the shoulder.

Felix stood and paced, stopping to stare out the grubby windows.
The fires still burned in Toronto, more than before. He'd tried to
find mailing lists or blogs that Torontonians were posting to, but

the only ones he'd found were being run by other geeks in other data-centers. It was possible – likely, even – that there were survivors out there who had more pressing priorities than posting to the Internet. His home phone still worked about half the time but he'd stopped calling it after the second day, when hearing Kelly's voice on the voicemail for the fiftieth time had made him cry in the middle of a planning meeting. He wasn't the only one.

Election day. Time to face the music.

> Are you nervous?

> Nope,

Felix typed.

> I don't much care if I win, to be honest. I'm just glad we're doing this. The alternative was sitting around with our thumbs up our ass, waiting for someone to crack up and open the door.

The cursor hung. Queen Kong was very high latency as she bossed her gang of Googloids around the Googleplex, doing everything she could to keep her data center online. Three of the offshore cages had gone offline and two of their six redundant network links were smoked. Lucky for her, queries-per-second were way down.

> There's still China

she typed. Queen Kong had a big board with a map of the world colored in Google-queries-per-second, and could do magic with it, showing the drop-off over time in colorful charts. She'd uploaded lots of video clips showing how the plague and the bombs had swept the world: the initial upswell of queries from people wanting to find out what was going on, then the grim, precipitous shelving off as the plagues took hold.

> China's still running about ninety per cent nominal.

Felix shook his head.

> You can't think that they're responsible

> No

She typed, but then she started to key something and then stopped.

> No of course not. I believe the Popovich Hypothesis. Every asshole in the world is using the other assholes for cover. But China put them down harder and faster than anyone else. Maybe we've finally found a use for totalitarian states

Felix couldn't resist. He typed:

> You're lucky your boss can't see you type that. You guys were pretty enthusiastic participants in the Great Firewall of China

> Wasn't my idea

she typed.

> And my boss is dead. They're probably all dead. The whole Bay Area got hit hard, and then there was the quake

They'd watched the USGS's automated data-stream from the 6.9 that trashed northern Cal from Gilroy to Sebastapol. Soma webcams revealed the scope of the damage – gas main explosions, seismically retrofitted buildings crumpling like piles of children's blocks after a good kicking. The Googleplex, floating on a series of gigantic steel springs, had shaken like a plateful of jello, but the racks had stayed in place and the worst injury they'd had was a badly bruised eye on a sysadmin who'd caught a flying cable-crimper in the face.

> Sorry. I forgot

> It's OK. We all lost people, right?

> Yeah. Yeah. Anyway, I'm not worried about the election. Whoever wins, at least we're doing SOMETHING

> Not if they vote for one of the fuckrags

Fuckrag was the epithet that some of the sysadmins were using to describe the contingent that wanted to shut down the Internet. Queen Kong had coined it – apparently it had started life as a catch-all term to describe the clueless IT managers that she'd chewed up through her career.

> They won't. They're just tired and sad is all. Your endorsement will carry the day

The Googloids were one of the largest and most powerful blocs left behind, along with the satellite uplink crews and the remaining transoceanic crews. Queen Kong's endorsement had come as a surprise and he'd sent her an e-mail that she'd replied to tersely: "can't have the fuckrags in charge".

> gtg

she typed and then her connection dropped. He fired up a browser and called up google.com. The browser timed out. He hit reload, and then again, and then the Google front-page came back up. Whatever had hit Queen Kong's workplace – power failure, worms, another quake – she had fixed it. He snorted when he saw that they'd replaced the o's in the Google logo with little planet Earths with mushroom clouds rising from them.

"Got anything to eat?" Van said to him. It was mid-afternoon, not that time particularly passed in the data-center. Felix patted his pockets. They'd put a quartermaster in charge, but not before everyone had snagged some chow out of the machines. He'd had a dozen power-bars and some apples. He'd taken a couple sandwiches but had wisely eaten them first before they got stale.

"One power-bar left," he said. He'd noticed a certain looseness in his waistline that morning and had briefly relished it. Then he'd remembered Kelly's teasing about his weight and he'd cried some. Then he'd eaten two power bars, leaving him with just one left.

"Oh," Van said. His face was hollower than ever, his shoulders sloping in on his toast-rack chest.

"Here," Felix said. "Vote Felix."

Van took the power-bar from him and then put it down on the table. "OK, I want to give this back to you and say, 'No, I couldn't,' but I'm fucking *hungry*, so I'm just going to take it and eat it, OK?"

"That's fine by me," Felix said. "Enjoy."

"How are the elections coming?" Van said, once he'd licked the wrapper clean.

"Dunno," Felix said. "Haven't checked in a while." He'd been winning by a slim margin a few hours before. Not having his laptop was a major handicap when it came to stuff like this. Up in the cages, there were a dozen more like him, poor bastards who'd left the house on Der Tag without thinking to snag something WiFi-enabled.

"You're going to get smoked," Sario said, sliding in next to them. He'd become famous in the center for never sleeping, for eaves-dropping, for picking fights in RL that had the ill-considered heat of a Usenet flamewar. "The winner will be someone who understands a couple of fundamental facts." He held up a fist, then ticked off his bullet points by raising a finger at a time. "Point: the terrorists are using the Internet to destroy the world, and we need to destroy the Internet first. Point: even if I'm wrong, the whole thing is a joke. We'll run out of generator-fuel soon enough. Point: or if we don't, it will be because the old world will be back and running, and it won't give a crap about your new world. Point: we're gonna run out of food before we run out of shit to argue about or reasons not to go outside. We have the chance to do something to help the world recover: we can kill the net and cut it off as a tool for bad guys. Or we can rearrange some more deck chairs on the bridge of your personal *Titanic* in the service of some sweet dream about an 'inde-pendent cyberspace'."

The thing was that Sario was right. They would be out of fuel in two days – intermittent power from the grid had stretched their generator lifespan. And if you bought his hypothesis that the Internet was primarily being used as a tool to organize more mayhem, shutting it down would be the right thing to do.

But Felix's daughter and his wife were dead. He didn't want to rebuild the old world. He wanted a new one. The old world was one that didn't have any place for him. Not anymore.

Van scratched his raw, flaking skin. Puffs of dander and scurf swirled in the musty, greasy air. Sario curled a lip at him. "That is disgusting. We're breathing recycled air, you know. Whatever leprosy is eating you, aerosolizing it into the air supply is pretty anti-social."

"You're the world's leading authority on anti-social, Sario," Van said. "Go away or I'll multi-tool you to death." He stopped scratching and patted his sheathed multi-pliers like a gunslinger.

"Yeah, I'm anti-social. I've got Asperger's and I haven't taken any meds in four days. What's your fucking excuse."

Van scratched some more. "I'm sorry," he said. "I didn't know."

Sario cracked up. "Oh, you are priceless. I'd bet that three-quarters of this bunch is borderline autistic. Me, I'm just an asshole. But I'm one who isn't afraid to tell the truth, and that makes me better than you, dickweed."

"Fuckrag," Felix said, "fuck off."

They had less than a day's worth of fuel when Felix was elected the first-ever Prime Minister of Cyberspace. The first count was spoiled by a bot that spammed the voting process and they lost a critical day while they added up the votes a second time.

But by then, it was all seeming like more of a joke. Half the data-centers had gone dark. Queen Kong's net-maps of Google queries were looking grimmer and grimmer as more of the world went offline, though she maintained a leader-board of new and rising queries – largely related to health, shelter, sanitation and self-defense.

Worm-load slowed. Power was going off to many home PC users, and staying off, so their compromised PCs were going dark. The backbones were still lit up and blinking, but the missives from those data-centers were looking more and more desperate. Felix hadn't eaten in a day and neither had anyone in a satellite Earth-station of transoceanic head-end.

Water was running short, too.

Popovich and Rosenbaum came and got him before he could do more than answer a few congratulatory messages and post a canned acceptance speech to newsgroups.

"We're going to open the doors," Popovich said. Like all of them, he'd lost weight and waxed scruffy and oily. His BO was like a cloud coming off the trash-bags behind a fish-market on a sunny day. Felix was quite sure he smelled no better.

"You're going to go for a reccy? Get more fuel? We can charter a working group for it – great idea."

Rosenbaum shook his head sadly. "We're going to go find our families. Whatever is out there has burned itself out. Or it hasn't. Either way, there's no future in here."

"What about network maintenance?" Felix said, thought he knew the answers. "Who'll keep the routers up?"

"We'll give you the root passwords to everything," Popovich said. His hands were shaking and his eyes were bleary. Like many of the smokers stuck in the data-center, he'd gone cold turkey this week. They'd run out of caffeine products two days earlier, too. The smokers had it rough.

"And I'll just stay here and keep everything online?"

"You and anyone else who cares anymore."

Felix knew that he'd squandered his opportunity. The election had seemed noble and brave, but in hindsight all it had been was an excuse for infighting when they should have been figuring out what to do next. The problem was that there was nothing to do next.

"I can't make you stay," he said.

"Yeah, you can't." Popovich turned on his heel and walked out. Rosenbaum watched him go, then he gripped Felix's shoulder and squeezed it.

"Thank you, Felix. It was a beautiful dream. It still is. Maybe we'll find something to eat and some fuel and come back."

Rosenbaum had a sister whom he'd been in contact with over IM for the first days after the crisis broke. Then she'd stopped answering. The sysadmins were split among those who'd had a chance to say goodbye and those who hadn't. Each was sure the other had it better.

They posted about it on the internal newsgroup – they were still geeks, after all, and there was a little honor guard on the ground floor, geeks who watched them pass toward the double doors. They manipulated the keypads and the steel shutters lifted, then the first set of doors opened. They stepped into the vestibule and pulled the doors shut behind them. The front doors opened. It was very bright and sunny outside, and apart from how empty it was, it looked very normal. Heartbreakingly so.

The two took a tentative step out into the world. Then another. They turned to wave at the assembled masses. Then they both grabbed their throats and began to jerk and twitch, crumpling in a heap on the ground.

"Shiii —!" was all Felix managed to choke out before they both dusted themselves off and stood up, laughing so hard they were clutching their sides. They waved once more and turned on their heels.

"Man, those guys are sick," Van said. He scratched his arms, which had long, bloody scratches on them. His clothes were so covered in scurf they looked like they'd been dusted with icing sugar.

"I thought it was pretty funny," Felix said.

"Christ I'm hungry," Van said, conversationally.

"Lucky for you, we've got all the packets we can eat," Felix said.

"You're too good to us grunts, Mr President," Van said.

"Prime Minister," he said. "And you're no grunt, you're the Deputy Prime Minister. You're my designated ribbon-cutter and hander-out of oversized novelty checks."

It buoyed both of their spirits. Watching Popovich and Rosenbaum go, it buoyed them up. Felix knew then that they'd all be going soon.

That had been pre-ordained by the fuel-supply, but who wanted to wait for the fuel to run out, anyway?

> half my crew split this morning

Queen Kong typed. Google was holding up pretty good anyway, of course. The load on the servers was a lot lighter than it had been since the days when Google fit on a bunch of hand-built PCs under a desk at Stanford.

> we're down to a quarter

Felix typed back. It was only a day since Popovich and Rosenbaum
left, but the traffic on the newsgroups had fallen down to near zero.
He and Van hadn't had much time to play Republic of Cyberspace.
They'd been too busy learning the systems that Popovich had turned
over to them, the big, big routers that had went on acting as the
major interchange for all the network backbones in Canada.

Still, someone posted to the newsgroups every now and again,
generally to say goodbye. The old flamewars about who would be
PM, or whether they would shut down the network, or who took
too much food – it was all gone.

He reloaded the newsgroup. There was a typical message.

> Runaway processes on Solaris TK

>

> Uh, hi. I'm just a lightweight MSCE but I'm the
only one awake here and four of the DSLAMs just
went down. Looks like there's some custom
accounting code that's trying to figure out how
much to bill our corporate customers and it's
spawned ten thousand threads and its eating all
the swap. I just want to kill it but I can't seem to
do that. Is there some magic invocation I need to
do to get this goddamned weenix box to kill this
shit? I mean, it's not as if any of our customers
are ever going to pay us again. I'd ask the guy
who wrote this code, but he's pretty much dead
as far as anyone can work out

He reloaded. There was a response. It was short, authoritative, and
helpful – just the sort of thing you almost never saw in a high-
caliber newsgroup when a noob posted a dumb question. The apocalypse had awoken the spirit of patient helpfulness in the world's
sysop community.

Van shoulder-surfed him. "Holy shit, who knew he had it in him?"

He looked at the message again. It was from Will Sario.

He dropped into his chat window.

> sario i thought you wanted the network dead
why are you helping msces fix their boxen?

> <sheepish grin> Gee Mr PM, maybe I just can't
bear to watch a computer suffer at the hands of
an amateur

He flipped to the channel with Queen Kong in it.

> How long?

> Since I slept? Two days. Until we run out of
fuel? Three days. Since we ran out of food? Two
days.

> Jeez. I didn't sleep last night either. We're a
little short- handed around here.

> asl? Im monica and I live in pasadena and Im
bored with my homework. Would you like to
download my pic???

The trojan bots were all over IRC these days, jumping to every
channel that had any traffic on it. Sometimes you caught five or six
flirting with each other. It was pretty weird to watch a piece of
malware try to con another instance of itself into downloading a
trojan.

They both kicked the bot off the channel simultaneously. He had
a script for it now. The spam hadn't even tailed off a little.

> How come the spam isn't reducing? Half the
goddamned data-centers have gone dark

Queen Kong paused a long time before typing. As had become automatic when she went high-latency, he reloaded the Google
homepage. Sure enough, it was down.

> Sario, you got any food?

> You won't miss a couple more meals, Your
Excellency

Van had gone back to Mayor McCheese but he was in the same
channel.

"What a dick. You're looking pretty buff, though, dude."

Van didn't look so good. He looked like you could knock him over
with a stiff breeze and he had a phlegmy, weak quality to his speech.

> hey kong everything ok?

> everything's fine just had to go kick some ass

"How's the traffic, Van?"

"Down twenty-five per cent from this morning," he said. There
were a bunch of nodes whose connections routed through them.
Presumably most of these were home or commercial customers in
places where the power was still on and the phone company's COs
were still alive.

Every once in a while, Felix would wiretap the connections to see
if he could find a person who had news of the wide world. Almost
all of it was automated traffic, though: network backups, status
updates. Spam. Lots of spam.

> Spam's still up because the services that stop
spam are failing faster than the services that
create it. All the anti-worm stuff is centralized in
a couple places. The bad stuff is on a million
zombie computers. If only the lusers had had the
good sense to turn off their home PCs before
keeling over or taking off

> at the rate were going well be routing nothing
but spam by dinnertime

Van cleared his throat, a painful sound. "About that," he said. "I
think it's going to hit sooner than that. Felix, I don't think anyone
would notice if we just walked away from here."

Felix looked at him, his skin the color of corned-beef and streaked with long, angry scabs. His fingers trembled.

"You drinking enough water?"

Van nodded. "All frigging day, every ten seconds. Anything to keep my belly full." He pointed to a refilled Pepsi Max bottle full of water by his side.

"Let's have a meeting," Felix said.

There had been forty-three of them on D-Day. Now there were fifteen. Six had responded to the call for a meeting by simply leaving. Everyone knew without having to be told what the meeting was about.

"So that's it, you're going to let it all fall apart?" Sario was the only one with the energy left to get properly angry. He'd go angry to his grave. The veins on his throat and forehead stood out angrily. His fists shook angrily. All the other geeks went lids-down at the site of him, looking up in unison for once at the discussion, not keeping one eye on a chat-log or a tailed service log.

"Sario, you've got to be shitting me," Felix said. "You wanted to pull the goddamned plug!"

"I wanted it to go *clean*," he shouted. "I didn't want it to bleed out and keel over in little gasps and pukes forever. I wanted it to be an act of will by the global community of its caretakers. I wanted it to be an affirmative act by human hands. Not entropy and bad code and worms winning out. Fuck that, that's just what's happened out there."

Up in the top-floor cafeteria, there were windows all around, hardened and light-bending, and by custom, they were all blinds-down. Now Sario ran around the room, yanking up the blinds. *How the hell can he get the energy to run?* Felix wondered. He could barely walk up the stairs to the meeting room.

Harsh daylight flooded in. It was a fine sunny day out there, but everywhere you looked across that commanding view of Toronto's skyline, there were rising plumes of smoke. The TD tower, a gigantic black modernist glass brick, was gouting flame to the sky. "It's all falling apart, the way everything does.

"Listen, listen. If we leave the network to fall over slowly, parts of it will stay online for months. Maybe years. And what will run on it? Malware. Worms. Spam. System-processes. Zone transfers. The things we use fall apart and require constant maintenance. The things we abandon don't get used and they last forever. We're going to leave the network behind like a lime-pit filled with industrial waste. That will be our fucking legacy – the legacy of every keystroke you and I and anyone, anywhere ever typed. You understand? We're going to leave it to die slow like a wounded dog, instead of giving it one clean shot through the head."

Van scratched his cheeks, then Felix saw that he was wiping away tears.

"Sario, you're not wrong, but you're not right either," he said. "Leaving it up to limp along is right. We're going to all be limping for a long time, and maybe it will be some use to someone. If there's one packet being routed from any user to any other user, anywhere in the world, it's doing its job."

"If you want a clean kill, you can do that," Felix said. "I'm the PM and I say so. I'm giving you root. All of you." He turned to the white-board where the cafeteria workers used to scrawl the day's specials. Now it was covered with the remnants of heated technical debates that the sysadmins had engaged in over the days since the day.

He scrubbed away a clean spot with his sleeve and began to write out long, complicated alphanumeric passwords salted with punctuation. Felix had a gift for remembering that kind of password. He doubted it would do him much good, ever again.

> Were going, kong. Fuels almost out anyway

> yeah well thats right then. it was an honor, mr prime minister

> you going to be ok?

> ive commandeered a young sysadmin to see to my feminine needs and weve found another cache of food thatll last us a coupel weeks now that were down to fifteen admins – im in hog heaven pal

> youre amazing, Queen Kong, seriously. Dont be
a hero though. When you need to go go. Theres
got to be something out there

> be safe felix, seriously – btw did i tell you queries
are up in Romania? maybe theyre getting back
on their feet

> really?

> yeah, really. we're hard to kill – like fucking
roaches

Her connection died. He dropped to Firefox and reloaded Google
and it was down. He hit reload and hit reload and hit reload, but it
didn't come up. He closed his eyes and listened to Van scratch his
legs and then heard Van type a little.

"They're back up," he said.

Felix whooshed out a breath. He sent the message to the newsgroup, one that he'd run through five drafts before settling on,
"Take care of the place, OK? We'll be back, someday."

Everyone was going except Sario. Sario wouldn't leave. He came
down to see them off, though.

The sysadmins gathered in the lobby and Felix made the safety
door go up, and the light rushed in.

Sario stuck his hand out.

"Good luck," he said.

"You too," Felix said. He had a firm grip, Sario, stronger than he
had any right to be. "Maybe you were right," he said.

"Maybe," he said.

"You going to pull the plug?"

Sario looked up at the drop-ceiling, seeming to peer through the
reinforced floors at the humming racks above. "Who knows?" he
said at last.

Van scratched and a flurry of white motes danced in the
sunlight.

"Let's go find you a pharmacy," Felix said. He walked to the
door and the other sysadmins followed.

They waited for the interior doors to close behind them and then Felix opened the exterior doors. The air smelled and tasted like a mown grass, like the first drops of rain, like the lake and the sky, like the outdoors and the world, an old friend not heard from in an eternity.

"Bye, Felix," the other sysadmins said. They were drifting away while he stood transfixed at the top of the short concrete staircase. The light hurt his eyes and made them water.

"I think there's a Shopper's Drug Mart on King Street," he said to Van. "We'll throw a brick through the window and get you some cortisone, OK?"

"You're the Prime Minister," Van said. "Lead on."

They didn't see a single soul on the fifteen-minute walk. There wasn't a single sound except for some bird noises and some distant groans, and the wind in the electric cables overhead. It was like walking on the surface of the moon.

"Bet they have chocolate bars at the Shopper's," Van said.

Felix's stomach lurched. Food. "Wow," he said, around a mouthful of saliva.

They walked past a little hatchback and in the front seat was the dried body of a woman holding the dried body of a baby, and his mouth filled with sour bile, even though the smell was faint through the rolled-up windows.

He hadn't thought of Kelly or 2.0 in days. He dropped to his knees and retched again. Out here in the real world, his family was dead. Everyone he knew was dead. He just wanted to lie down on the sidewalk and wait to die, too.

Van's rough hands slipped under his armpits and hauled weakly at him. "Not now," he said. "Once we're safe inside somewhere and we've eaten something, then and only then you can do this, but not now. Understand me, Felix? Not fucking now."

The profanity got through to him. He got to his feet. His knees were trembling.

"Just a block more," Van said, and slipped Felix's arm around his shoulders and led him along.

"Thank you, Van. I'm sorry."

"No sweat," he said. "You need a shower, bad. No offense."

"None taken."

The Shopper's had a metal security gate, but it had been torn away from the front windows, which had been rudely smashed. Felix and Van squeezed through the gap and stepped into the dim drug-store. A few of the displays were knocked over, but other than that, it looked okay. By the cash-registers, Felix spotted the racks of candy bars at the same instant that Van saw them, and they hurried over and grabbed a handful each, stuffing their faces.

"You two eat like pigs."

They both whirled at the sound of the woman's voice. She was holding a fire-axe that was nearly as big as she was. She wore a lab-coat and comfortable shoes.

"You take what you need and go, okay? No sense in there being any trouble." Her chin was pointy and her eyes were sharp. She looked to be in her forties. She looked nothing like Kelly, which was good, because Felix felt like running and giving her a hug as it was. Another person alive!

"Are you a doctor?" Felix said. She was wearing scrubs under the coat, he saw.

"You going to go?" She brandished the axe.

Felix held his hands up. "Seriously, are you a doctor? A pharmacist?"

"I used to be a RN, ten years ago. I'm mostly a Web-designer."

"You're shitting me," Felix said.

"Haven't you ever met a girl who knew about computers?"

"Actually, a friend of mine who runs Google's data-center is a girl. A woman, I mean."

"You're shitting me," she said. "A woman ran Google's data-center?"

"Runs," Felix said. "It's still online."

"NFW," she said. She let the axe lower.

"Way. Have you got any cortisone cream? I can tell you the story. My name's Felix and this is Van, who needs any anti-histamines you can spare."

"I can spare? Felix old pal, I have enough dope here to last a hundred years. This stuff's going to expire long before it runs out. But are you telling me that the net's still up?"

"It's still up," he said. "Kind of. That's what we've been doing all week. Keeping it online. It might not last much longer, though."

"No," she said. "I don't suppose it would." She set the axe down. "Have you got anything to trade? I don't need much, but I've been trying to keep my spirits up by trading with the neighbors. It's like playing civilization."

"You have neighbors?"

"At least ten," she said. "The people in the restaurant across the way make a pretty good soup, even if most of the veg is canned. They cleaned me out of Sterno, though."

"You've got neighbors and you trade with them?"

"Well, nominally. It'd be pretty lonely without them. I've taken care of whatever sniffles I could. Set a bone – broken wrist. Listen, do you want some Wonder Bread and peanut butter? I have a ton of it. Your friend looks like he could use a meal."

"Yes please," Van said. "We don't have anything to trade, but we're both committed workaholics looking to learn a profession. Could you use some assistants?"

"Not really." She spun her axe on its head. "But I wouldn't mind some company."

They ate the sandwiches and then some soup. The restaurant people brought it over and made their manners at them, though Felix saw their noses wrinkle up and ascertained that there was working plumbing in the back room. Van went in to take a sponge bath and then he followed.

"None of us knows what to do," the woman said. Her name was Rosa, and she had found them a bottle of wine and some disposable plastic cups from the housewares aisle. "I thought we'd have helicopters or tanks or even looters, but it's just quiet."

"You seem to have kept pretty quiet yourself," Felix said.

"Didn't want to attract the wrong kind of attention."

"You ever think that maybe there's a lot of people out there doing the same thing? Maybe if we all get together we'll come up with something to do."

"Or maybe they'll cut our throats," she said.

Van nodded. "She's got a point."

Felix was on his feet. "No way, we can't think like that. Lady, we're at a critical juncture here. We can go down through negligence, dwindling away in our hiding holes, or we can try to build something better."

"Better?" She made a rude noise.

"Okay, not better. Something though. Building something new is better than letting it dwindle away. Christ, what are you going to do when you've read all the magazines and eaten all the potato chips here?"

Rosa shook her head. "Pretty talk," she said. "But what the hell are we going to do, anyway?"

"Something," Felix said. "We're going to do something. Something is better than nothing. We're going to take this patch of the world where people are talking to each other, and we're going to expand it. We're going to find everyone we can and we're going to take care of them and they're going to take care of us. We'll probably fuck it up. We'll probably fail. I'd rather fail than give up, though."

Van laughed. "Felix, you are crazier than Sario, you know it?"

"We're going to go and drag him out, first thing tomorrow. He's going to be a part of this, too. Everyone will. Screw the end of the world. The world doesn't end. Humans aren't the kind of things that have endings."

Rosa shook her head again, but she was smiling a little now. "And you'll be what, the Pope-Emperor of the World?"

"He prefers Prime Minister," Van said in a stagey whisper. The anti-histamines had worked miracles on his skin, and it had faded from angry red to a fine pink.

"You want to be Minister of Health, Rosa?" he said.

"Boys," she said. "Playing games. How about this. I'll help out however I can, provided you never ask me to call you Prime Minister and you never call me the Minister of Health?"

"It's a deal," he said.

Van refilled their glasses, upending the wine bottle to get the last few drops out.

They raised their glasses. "To the world," Felix said. "To humanity." He thought hard. "To rebuilding."

"To anything," Van said.

"To anything," Felix said. "To everything."

"To everything," Rosa said.

They drank. He wanted to go see the house – see Kelly and 2.0, though his stomach churned at the thought of what he might find there. But the next day, they started to rebuild. And months later,

they started over again, when disagreements drove apart the fragile
little group they'd pulled together. And a year after that, they started
over again. And five years later, they started again.

It was nearly six months, then, before he went home. Van helped
him along, riding cover behind him on the bicycles they used to get
around town. The further north they rode, the stronger the smell of
burnt wood became. There were lots of burnt-out houses. Sometimes marauders burnt the houses they'd looted, but more often it
was just nature, the kinds of fires you got in forests and on mountains. There were six choking, burnt blocks where every house was
burnt before they reached home.

But Felix's old housing development was still standing, an oasis
of eerily pristine buildings that looked like maybe their somewhat
neglectful owners had merely stepped out to buy some paint and
fresh lawnmower blades to bring their old homes back up to their
neat, groomed selves.

That was worse, somehow. He got off the bike at the entry of the
subdivision and they walked the bikes together in silence, listening
to the sough of the wind in the trees. Winter was coming late that
year, but it was coming, and as the sweat dried in the wind, Felix
started to shiver.

He didn't have his keys anymore. They were at the data-center,
months and worlds away. He tried the door-handle, but it didn't
turn. He applied his shoulder to the door and it ripped away from
its wet, rotted jamb in with a loud, splintering sound. The house
was rotting from the inside.

The door splashed when it landed. The house was full of stagnant
water, four inches of stinking pond-scummed water in the living
room. He splashed carefully through it, feeling the floor-boards sag
spongily beneath each step.

Up the stairs, his nose full of that terrible green mildewy stench.
Into the bedroom, the furniture familiar as a childhood friend.

Kelly was in the bed with 2.0. The way they both lay, it was clear
they hadn't gone easy – they were twisted double, Kelly curled
around 2.0. Their skin was bloated, making them almost unrecognizable. The smell – God, the smell.

Felix's head spun. He thought he would fall over and clutched
at the dresser. An emotion he couldn't name – rage, anger,

sorrow? – made him breathe hard, gulp for air like he was drowning.

And then it was over. The world was over. Kelly and 2.0 – over. And he had a job to do. He folded the blanket over them – Van helped, solemnly. They went into the front yard and took turns digging, using the shovel from the garage that Kelly had used for gardening. They had lots of experience digging graves by then. Lots of experience handling the dead. They dug, and wary dogs watched them from the tall grass on the neighboring lawns, but they were also good at chasing off dogs with well-thrown stones.

When the grave was dug, they laid Felix's wife and son to rest in it. Felix quested after words to say over the mound, but none came. He'd dug so many graves for so many men's wives and so many women's husbands and so many children – the words were long gone.

Felix dug ditches and salvaged cans and buried the dead. He planted and harvested. He fixed some cars and learned to make biodiesel. Finally he fetched up in a data-center for a little government – little governments came and went, but this one was smart enough to want to keep records and needed someone to keep everything running, and Van went with him.

They spent a lot of time in chat rooms and sometimes they happened upon old friends from the strange time they'd spent running the Distributed Republic of Cyberspace, geeks who insisted on calling him PM, though no one in the real world ever called him that anymore.

It wasn't a good life, most of the time. Felix's wounds never healed, and neither did most other people's. There were lingering sicknesses and sudden ones. Tragedy on tragedy.

But Felix liked his data-center. There in the humming of the racks, he never felt like it was the first days of a better nation, but he never felt like it was the last days of one, either.

> go to bed, felix

> soon, kong, soon – almost got this backup running

> youre a junkie, dude.

> look whos talking

He reloaded the Google homepage. Queen Kong had had it online.
The Os in Google changed all the time, whenever she got the urge.
Today they were little cartoon globes, one smiling the other
frowning.

He looked at it for a long time and dropped back into a terminal
to check his backup. It was running clean, for a change. The little
government's records were safe.

> ok night night

> take care

Van waved at him as he creaked to the door, stretching out his back
with a long series of pops.

"Sleep well, boss," he said.

"Don't stick around here all night again," Felix said. "You need
your sleep, too."

"You're too good to us grunts," Van said, and went back to
typing.

Felix went to the door and walked out into the night. Behind him,
the biodiesel generator hummed and made its acrid fumes. The
harvest moon was up, which he loved. Tomorrow, he'd go back and
fix another computer and fight off entropy again. And why not?

It was what he did. He was a sysadmin.

THE RAIN AT THE END OF THE WORLD

Dale Bailey

Dale Bailey is a professor of English at Lenoir-Rhyne College, North Carolina. His novel The Fallen *(2002) was a nominee for the International Horror Guild Award, an award he went on to win with his 2002 short story "Death and Suffrage". His short fiction has been collected in* The Resurrection Man's Legacy *(2003). He is also the author of a study of contemporary horror fiction,* American Nightmares: The Haunted House Formula in American Popular Fiction *(1999).*

This story and the next one form something of a related sequence looking at how individuals may react to a global flood.

THEY DROVE NORTH, into ever-falling rain. Rain slanted out of the evening sky and spattered against the windshield where the humming wipers slapped it away. Rain streamed from the highway to carve twisted runnels in the gravelled berm. Raindrops beaded up along the windows and rolled swiftly away as the slipstream caught them up. All about them, only the rain, and to fill the voiceless silence, the sounds of tires against wet pavement and rain drumming with insistent fingers all about the car. And in these sounds, Melissa heard another sound, a child's voice, repeating a scrap of some old nursery rhyme: *rain, rain go away, come again some other day.*

For forty-nine days, nothing but rain, everywhere, all across the United States, in Canada, in Mexico, in Brazil, in England and France and Germany, in Somalia and South Africa, in the People's

Republic of China. It was raining all around the world. Rivers of water flowed out of the sky, tides rose and streams swelled, crops rotted like flesh in the fields.

Weathermen were apologetic. "Rain," they said during the five-day forecast. "Just rain." Statesmen expressed alarm, scientists confusion. Religious fanatics built arks. And Melissa – who once, in a year she could barely remember, had fantasized making love in the rain – Melissa saw her life swept away in the rain. They drove north, to the mountain cabin – three rooms for her and Stuart, her husband. And all about them the unceasing rain.

Melissa sighed and studied the book she had tried to read as they drove east out of Knoxville that afternoon. A failed effort, that, defeated by the swaying car. She glanced at Stuart and almost spoke, but what could she say? The silence was a wall between them; they'd lost the rhythm of conversation. They hadn't exchanged a word since they had changed highways at Wytheville, when Stuart snapped at her for smoking.

Staring at him now, Melissa thought he was changing, a subtle transformation that had begun – when? days ago? weeks? who could say? – some time during the endless period after the clouds rolled in and rain began to descend like doom from the heavy sky. In the dash lights, his once-ruddy features were ghastly and pale, like the features of a corpse. Pasty flesh stretched taut across the angular planes of his skull; his mouth compressed into a white line. Shadow rippled across his tense features, across his hairline, retreating from a sharp widow's peak though he was only thirty-five.

"Do you have to stare at me?" he said. "Why don't you read your book?"

"It's getting dark."

"Turn on the light then."

"I don't want to read. It was making me sick."

Stuart shrugged and hunched closer over the wheel.

Melissa looked away.

At first, it had been refreshing, the rain, lancing out of the afternoon sky as she drove home from her art history class. She parked the car and stood in the yard, staring up at the gray sky, at lightning incandescent in swollen cloud bellies. Rain poured down, spattering her cheeks and eyelids, running fresh into her open mouth, plastering her garments close against her flesh.

By the thirteenth day – she had gone back by then and added them up, the endless days of unrelenting rain – the haunted look began to show in Stuart's eyes. His voice grew harsh and strained as discordant music, as it did when she tested his patience with minutiae. That was his word for it: minutiae, pronounced in that gently mocking way he had perfected in the two years since the baby. Not mean, for Stuart was anything but mean; just teasing. "Just teasing," he always said, and then his lips would shape that word again: minutiae, meaning all the silly trivia that were her life – her gardening, her reading, her occasional class.

By this time the pressure had begun to tell on them all. You could see it in the faces of the newscasters on CNN, in the haunted vacancies behind the weary eyes of the scientists on the Sunday talk shows – vacancies of ignorance and despair. How could they account for this rain that fell simultaneously over every square inch of the planet? How could anyone? By this time – the thirteenth day – you could detect the frayed edges of hysteria and fear. Evangelists intoned portentously that the Rapture was at hand. Certain government experiments had gone awry, a neighbor, who had a friend whose brother-in-law worked at Oak Ridge national labs, confided ominously; flying saucers had been sighted over an airbase in Arizona.

On the twenty-seventh day – a Saturday, and by this time everyone was keeping count – Stuart walked about the house with the stiff-kneed gait of an automaton, jerkily pacing from window to window, shading his eyes as he peered out into the gloom and falling rain.

"Why don't you call Jim?" Melissa had said. "See if he wants to do something. Get out of here before you go crazy." Or drive me crazy, she thought, but didn't say it. She was reading *Harper's* and smoking a Marlboro Light – a habit she had picked up two years ago, after the miscarriage. She had always planned to quit, but she somehow never did. It was too easy to smoke at home alone. Stuart had discouraged her from going back to teaching. Take some time for yourself, he had said. And why not? They didn't need the money now that Stuart had made partner. And it would have been too hard to be around kids.

"I don't want to call Jim," Stuart had said. He peered out into the rain. "I wish you'd quit smoking. It stinks up the whole house."

"I know," she said. And she had tried. But as soon as she quit, she started putting on weight, and Stuart didn't like that either, so what was she to do? Smoke.

Now, driving through rain across the ridges separating Virginia and West Virginia, she fumbled in her purse for a cigarette. The flame of the lighter threw Stuart's angular face into relief, highlighting a ghostly network of lines and shadows that brooded in the hollows around his eyes and beneath his cheeks. For a moment, before the flame blinked out and darkness rushed back into the car, she knew what he would look like when he was old. But he was handsome still, she thought, distinguished even, with the first hint of gray in his dark hair.

Still handsome after twelve years, still the same Stuart. He had noticed her at a time when few men did, had made her feel beautiful and alive, as if she shared his color and energy, his arrogant charm. And just then, leaning over beside her in freshman composition, he had been boyishly vulnerable. "Look," he'd said, "I'm not very good at this kind of stuff. Do you think you can help me?"

That was a long time ago, but the old Stuart was still there; sometimes she could see vulnerability peeking through the cool and distant resolve he had woven about himself after the baby. She had talked about adoption for a while and she had seen it then – the ghost of that insecurity in the hard curve of his jaw, in the brazen tone of his voice. As if the miscarriage had been his fault.

She cracked her window and blew smoke into the downpour. Stuart coughed theatrically.

"Leave it alone, Stuart," she said.

Stuart grimaced. He flipped on the radio and searched for a station with one hand. Most of the stations had gone off the air by now, same as the television networks. Why, no one could be certain.

Hysteria, Melissa suspected. The government had shut them down to prevent hysteria. In the last week or two news reports had become increasingly disturbing, often bizarre: floods of epic proportions in the Mississippi and Ohio River valleys and just about everywhere else, roving gangs in the sodden streets, doom cults who practiced human sacrifice to appease angry weather gods, videotapes of the giant toadstool forest that had erupted over miles and miles of empty western territory. In many places, money was no longer good. People had taken to bartering for canned food, gasoline, cigarettes.

By day thirty-six, Stuart had himself begun to stock up on gasoline and the non-perishable food crammed into the back of the Jeep. He had wanted to buy a gun, but Melissa had drawn the line there; the world might retreat into savagery, but she would have no part of it. At night, the two of them sat without speaking in the living room while the rain beat against the roof. They watched the news on television, and then – on the forty-second day of rain, when the airwaves rang with commentary about surpassing Noah – the cable went dead. Every channel blank, empty, gray. The cable company didn't answer; radio news reported that television had gone out simultaneously across the country; and then, one by one over the next few days, the radio stations themselves started to go. Without warning or explanation they simply disappeared, static on the empty dial.

Stuart refused to give up; every hour he turned on the radio and spun through the frequencies. Static, more static, an occasional lunatic babbling (but who was a lunatic now, Melissa wondered, now that the whole world had gone insane?), more static. But the static had a message, too:

Roads are washing away, the static said, *bridges are being obliterated. The world as we know it is being re-made.*

Now, driving, Stuart spun through the channels again, FM and then AM. Static and static and then a voice: calm, rational, a woman's cultured voice in an echoing studio that sounded far, far away.

They paused, listening:

"It's over," the woman was saying.

And the interviewer, a man, his voice flat: "What's over? What do you mean?"

"The entire world, the civilization that men have built over the last 2,000 years, since Homer and the Greeks, since earlier — "

"For Christ's sake," Stuart said, stabbing at the radio; Melissa reached out to stop him, thinking that anything, even lunacy, was better than this silence that had grown up between them in the last years and which seemed now, in the silent car, more oppressive than it ever had.

"Please," she said, and sighing, Stuart relented.

" —apocalypse," the man was saying. "The world is to be utterly destroyed, is that what you're saying?"

"Not at all. Not destroyed. Recreated, refashioned, renewed – whatever."

"Like the Noah story? God is displeased with what we've made of ourselves."

"Not with what *we've* made," the woman said. "With what *you've* made."

A lengthy pause followed, so lengthy that Melissa for a moment thought they had lost the station, and then the man spoke again. She realized that he had been trying to puzzle out the woman's odd distinction, and having failed, had chosen to ignore it. He said: "What you're saying, though, is that God is out there. And He is angry."

"No, no," the woman said. "*She* is."

"Christ," Stuart said, and this time he *did* punch the search button. The radio cycled through a station or two of static and hit on yet another active channel. The strains of Credence Clearwater Revival filled the car – "Who'll Stop the Rain?", and that joke had been old three weeks ago. He shut off the radio.

All along, he had been this way, refusing to acknowledge the reality of their situation. All along, he had continued to work, shuffling files and depositions though the courts had all but ground to a halt. It was as if he believed he could make the world over as it had been, simply by ignoring the rain. But by yesterday – day forty-eight – the pressure had truly begun to tell on him. Melissa could see it in his panicked eyes.

That day, in the silent house with Stuart gone to work, Melissa stood by the window and looked out across the yard at toadstools, like bowing acolytes to the rain. Pasty fungoid stalks, cold and rubbery as dead flesh, had everywhere nosed their way out of the earth and spread their caps beneath the poisoned sky.

Melissa went about the house on soft feet; she shut curtains in the living room, closed blinds in the office, lowered shades in the bedroom. All about the house she went, shuttering and lowering and closing, walling away the rain.

When Stuart came home that afternoon, his hair was plastered flat against his skull and his eyes glowered from dark hollows.

"How was your day?" she said. She stood at the top of the stairs, in the door to the kitchen, holding a pot.

He stood below, on the landing, one hand in the pocket of his rain-slick jacket, the other grasping the leather briefcase she had given him for Christmas last year. "Fine," he said.

That was what he always said. The conversation was as ritualized as some ancient religious ceremony. And so she said, "What did you do today?"

"Nothing."

That was fine, too, that was a formula. She turned away. She didn't care what he'd done all day any more than he cared what she'd done. She didn't care about flow charts and tax law and office politics any more than he cared about her garden or her classes or any of the hundred things she did to fill the empty days. That was how it was – even though the rain had begun to erase the world they had known, to sweep away without discrimination the tax laws and the flow charts, and the gardens and art classes, too.

But that night – the forty-eighth night of a rain that would never end – that night was different. In the kitchen, as she placed the pot on the stove, she heard his footsteps squeak across the linoleum. He was behind her. She smelled his cologne, weak beneath the moist earthwormy stench of the rain. She turned and he was standing there, a droplet of rain poised at the end of his nose. Rain dripped off his slicker and pooled on the linoleum floor. Rain flattened his hair against his skull.

"Stuart?" she said.

The briefcase slipped from his fingers. Rain glistened on his cheeks and in his eyes. The other hand came out of his pocket, extending towards her.

Toadstools, pale and spongy against his pale and spongy flesh, as colorless as the pasty skin of some cave-dwelling amphibian, extruded from his fist. Toadstools, spotted and poisonous, dangled from between his fingers.

"Toadstools are growing in the yard," he said.

"I know."

"We have to get to higher ground."

"It won't be any different there," she said. She had a vision of the mountain cabin, three rooms, and all about them the entombing rain.

"It's raining all around the world," she said.

He turned away. The toadstools dropped from his fingers as he left the room. Melissa stared at the fungoid stalks, cold and colorless as dead flesh against the linoleum. She shuddered when she picked them up.

And so this morning, on the forty-ninth morning, they had fled at last. The highways were virtually abandoned; occasionally four-wheel drives zipped past, flying harried in either direction, driven by panicked, pasty-looking men. In fields to either side of the road, lakes, ponds, seas swelled and grew. Mushrooms sprouted at the horizon, overshadowing the trees; on hilly slopes they saw houses and barns decaying beneath masses of putrid mold. Three times the pavement had disappeared before them, submerged; three times Stuart had dropped the Jeep into four-wheel drive and edged forward, fearing sinkholes and washouts; three times their luck had held and they had emerged to wet pavement once again.

They fled east, up 81 to 77, north into West Virginia and the Appalachians. They had a cabin there, near a ski resort in Raleigh County. Melissa remembered when they had bought it a year ago. When *Stuart* had bought it; he hadn't consulted her. He had come home late one day, clutching the papers, his eyes wild and feverish. "I used the money," he had announced, "I made a down-payment on a cabin and two acres of woodland." Something cold and hateful pierced her then. Stuart had spent the money, the baby's money, and the spending came like the icy needle-probe of reality:

There was no baby. There would not ever be one.

Now, on the forty-ninth day, they fled northward into night, seeking higher ground, but the rain stayed with them, omnipresent and eternal. It fell out of the sky in solid sheets, flowing over the black pavement and soaking Stuart when he pulled over to refill the tank from the gas cans strapped in the back of the Jeep. Cursing, he would climb back inside and crank the heat to its highest setting, and each time Melissa would remember her long-ago fantasy of making love in the rain. She took a last drag from the cigarette and let the wind have it, watching in the mirror as it tumbled away, extinguished by the rain.

Sodium lights appeared, lining the highway. Ahead, a mountain loomed dark against the gray sky. The road rose to meet it, rose, and rose, and plunged down toward a granite wall. A tunnel – the second one since Wytheville – opened up before them at the last moment, and Melissa clenched her fists, fearing washouts, fearing cave-ins. Then they were inside, the sound of the rain disappearing as they crossed under the mountain and into West Virginia. Bars of shadow and light flashed across Stuart's face and the hum of tires against dry pavement filled the car. The wipers scraped against the dry windshield, back and forth, back and forth, and then they emerged from the tunnel into a shifting wall of rain.

"Christ," Stuart said. "Do you think it'll ever stop? Do you think it'll rain forever?"

She looked away, out the window, into the falling rain, and that rag of nursery rhyme returned to her. "Rain, rain go away," she said. "Come again some other day."

Night closed in around them. Mountains rose above the road like the shoulders of giants, black against the black sky. Melissa smoked her last cigarette. Far ahead, huddled high against an arm of the ridge, Melissa saw a sprinkle of lights, all that remained of a once-bustling town. The cabin lay farther north, isolated still higher in the mountains. Three rooms, Stuart, and all about them the besieging rain.

At last, the lights came up around them.

"Would you look at that?" Stuart said, pointing.

She saw it then, as well, a blazing Texaco sign towering above the highway. Beyond it stretched a strip of hotels, gas stations, and fast-food restaurants – most of them dark, abandoned.

"It could be a trap," Stuart said, "to lure in the unwary."

She sighed.

"We should have bought that gun."

"No guns," she said.

"We'll have to risk it. If they have gas, we could top off the tank, refill our cans. Maybe they'll have kerosene."

Without another word, he exited to the strip, passed the boarded-up ruins of fast-food restaurants and hotels, and stopped the Jeep beneath the canopy by the Texaco's islands. She watched as he studied the parking lot suspiciously; he put her in mind of some frightened forest creature, and she had the disquieting thought that men weren't so far removed from the jungle. Satisfied at last, he killed the engine; the noise of the rain grew louder, almost deafening, drowning out her thoughts. She opened the door and stood, stretching.

"I'm going to the restroom," she said, without turning; she heard the pump come on, gasoline gush into the tank.

"You want anything from inside?" he asked.

"Get me a coke and a pack of cigarettes."

The bathrooms were across the parking lot, through the downpour. Melissa shrugged on her raincoat, slipped the hood over her head, and darted across the pavement, one arm cocked ineffectually above her, warding off the rain. The interior of the restroom stank of urine and bleach; mold had begun to blossom here, sodden, cancerous roses along the base of the dry-wall. A trash can overflowed in one corner. Melissa's nose wrinkled in disgust as she covered the toilet seat with toilet paper.

When she returned, Stuart was waiting in the Jeep.

"Can you believe it," he said. "He took money, good old-fashioned American money. Fool."

"You get my stuff?"

He gestured at the dash. A can of Diet Coke waited there, sweating condensation.

"What about my cigarettes?"

"I didn't get them. We have to be careful now. Who knows when we'll be able to see a doctor again?"

"Jesus, Stuart." Melissa got out and slammed the door. She walked to the tiny shop. The attendant sat behind the register, his feet propped against the counter, reading a novel which he placed face-down when the door chimed behind her.

"What can I do for you?" he said.

"Pack of Marlboro Lights, please."

He shook his head as he pulled the cigarettes from an overhead rack. "Shouldn't smoke, lady. Bad for you."

"I've given up sun-bathing to compensate."

The attendant laughed.

She looked up at him, a young man, not handsome, with flesh the color and texture of the toadstools she had scraped off the kitchen floor. Flesh like Stuart's flesh, in the midst of that subtle change of his.

But nice eyes, she decided. Clear eyes, blue, the color of water. Eyes like the baby might have had. And this thought moved her to say something – anything, just to make contact. "Think it'll ever stop raining?"

"Who knows? Maybe it's a good thing. Cleansing."

"You think?"

"Who knows? Wash the whole world away, we'll start again. Rain's okay by me."

"Me, too," she said, and now she thought again of the fragment of radio program. *Is God out there?* the host had wanted to know. *And is He angry?*

She is, the woman had replied. *She is.*

Melissa's hand stole over her belly, where the baby, her baby, had grown and died. Abruptly, the crazed logic of the idea, its simple clarity and beauty, seized her up: this was the world they had made, she thought, men like Stuart, this world of machines and noise, this world of simple tasteless *things*. This is the world that is being washed away. Their world.

Outside, Stuart began to blow the horn. The sound came to her, discordant, importunate. Melissa glanced out at the Jeep, at Stuart, impatient behind the steering wheel, anxious to be off, anxious to get to higher ground. Three rooms in the mountains, just three. She and Stuart and all about them the imprisoning rain. It fell still, beyond the roof over the fuel islands, blowing out of the sky in sheets, dancing against the pavement, chasing neon reflections of the Texaco sign across black puddles.

"Lady? You okay? Miss?"

"Missus," she said, out of habit. She turned to face him.

"You okay?"

"I'm fine, just distracted that's all."

The horn blew again.

"Nice guy."

"Not really. He tries to be, sometimes."

The horn again. Impatiently.

"You better go."

"Yeah." She dug in her purse for money.

"Forget it. Like it means anything now, right?"

She hesitated. "Thanks, then."

"You're welcome. Be careful. Who knows what the roads are like in the mountains."

She nodded and stepped out into moist air. Stuart had gotten out of the Jeep. He stood by the open door, his flesh orange and spongy beneath the streetlights, his arms crossed against his chest. He stared at her impatiently, beyond him only darkness, only rain. Water fell from the night sky, against the gleaming pavement, the buildings, the shining neon Texaco sign. Against everything, washing it all away.

"Hurry up," Stuart said.

And she said, without even realizing she was going to say it, "I'm not coming. You go ahead." When she said it, she was suffused suddenly with warmth and excitement and life, a sensation of release, as if a hard knot of emotion, drawn tight in her chest through long years, had suddenly loosened.

"What?" Stuart said. "What are you talking about?"

Melissa didn't answer. She walked past Stuart and the Jeep, stopping at the edge of the canopy that sheltered the fuel islands. She shrugged out of the raincoat, let it drop to the pavement behind her. Ignoring Stuart, she lined up the tips of her toes against the hard clear edge of the pavement where it was wet, where the roof left off and the rain began.

Stuart said, "Melissa? Melissa?"

But Melissa didn't answer. She stepped out into a world that was ending, into a gently falling rain. It poured down over her, cool and refreshing against her cheeks and lips and hair, caressing her with the hands of a lover.

THE FLOOD

Linda Nagata

Linda Nagata lives in Hawaii where she is currently a programmer of online database applications. She produced a loosely connected series of novels developing concepts of nanotechnology of which The Bohr Maker *(1995) won the Locus Award as that year's best first novel. The following enigmatic story, published in 1998, has haunted me since I first read it. It contains several compelling images that cloak the horrors of a global deluge into a mystical allegory.*

Mike lay awake in the night on a bed of damp leaves in the towering shelter of a eucalyptus grove, listening to the pounding surf. His young wife Holly slept on the ground beside him, clutching their thin blanket to her chin, her legs half-tangled with his. He rested his hand lightly on her rib cage, feeling her breathe.

Nights were the worst. At night he couldn't see the waters coming. So he listened to the surf, trying to measure the volume of the ocean by the sound. He'd seen the ocean rise as much as thirty meters in a night. Rising. Never receding.

Fear slipped like oil across his skin – cold, encompassing fear. Through his mind's eye he watched Holly drowning, her face pale and exhausted as she finally slipped beneath the relentless waters. Still, that sort of death was ancient and familiar.

God, God, God.

Sudden sweat coated his body despite the chill of the night. His stomach seemed to fold into a fist. This, he thought, would be a good time to recall some profound and comforting passage from the Bible. But he didn't know any. Religion had never been his thing.

Still, God was ever in his thoughts these days, as he watched the world drown.

How could He let this happen?

Mike did not believe in the beneficence of God. He was not even sure he believed in the deity Himself. And alone amongst the survivors, he refused to accept that the end of the world might be a good thing.

Sometime before dawn the rising waters must have claimed a gentler shoreline, because the noise of the surf subsided. Mike slept then, waking only when the sun was well up. He cuddled against Holly on their bed of leaves, gazing downslope at the ocean. He could see it just beyond the grove of trees. Its surface was glassy in the crisp, still air of morning, the waters pale green over a pasture that had flooded in the night. Gentle swells rolled in from the deep to sweep upslope through the eucalyptus grove in flat hissing crescents.

Mike watched them in a half-conscious state, pleasantly distanced from both his worrisome dreams and untenable reality, until a slight breeze rustled through the tree tops, reminding him that he still needed to devise a sail for his newly finished boat.

Holly stirred sleepily. He bent over her, gently brushing aside her long dark hair to kiss her cheek, feeling yet again the sour clench of fear. He would not let her be taken. He could not. It would be better to drown. But better still to steal her away on his boat. Soon. Maybe even today.

She blinked and stretched, then smiled at him, a serene joy glowing in her dark eyes. "Mike. Do you feel it, Mike? It's very close now."

"We don't have any food left," he told her.

She shrugged, sitting up, her long tanned legs goose-bumped in the morning chill. "We don't need any food. Today will be the last day. I can feel it."

As if to emphasize her words another wave slid up through the grove to swish against her feet, laying down a crescent of sand before subsiding. Mike found himself staring at the dread signature. In the weeks since the flood began, he'd watched the sand and waves take over roads, houses, forests, pastures, farms, as the ocean steadily rose, drowning the island that had always been their home.

They'd retreated upslope as the waters advanced, but the highest point on the island had been only 500 meters above sea level.

Mike squinted down at the new shoreline. Now, he guessed the highest point might clear thirty meters. He frowned, trying to recall the exact geography of the island before the flood. Hadn't the meadow where he'd built his boat been *more* than thirty meters below the summit?

"The ark!" he yelped, leaping to his feet. "Holly ... " He grabbed her hand and yanked her up. The roar of the night's surf resounded in his mind. His boat had been well above the waterline at nightfall, but now—

He ran through the grove, dragging Holly with him. He was afraid to leave her alone, afraid she would disappear like so many others.

"Mike," she panted, bounding along in his rough wake. "It's all right, Mike. You don't need the boat. Everything will be all right."

But he couldn't believe her. He'd never been able to believe.

They splashed through a retreating wave, through rotten leaves half-buried in sand. Their feet sank deep into the unstable mix. Tiny air bubbles erupted on the forming beach. Then they reached the edge of the grove and burst into the open.

Sunlight sparkled on green water. Children frolicked in the swell, riding the shore break at the edge of the insatiable ocean.

Finally letting go of Holly's hand, Mike scrambled up a scrub-covered ridge of ancient lava. By the time he reached the top, the cool air was tearing in and out of his lungs. He stood on the crest and looked down at his project.

Yesterday evening, the boat had rested solidly on its platform, fifteen meters above the waterline and nearly completed, a tiny ark made of green eucalyptus wood. But the surf had seized it in the night, throwing it against the jagged lava of the ridge. The shattered pieces bobbed and tumbled with the incoming waves.

Holly joined him, her breast heaving with exertion beneath the scanty coverage of her tank top. She glanced at the wreckage, hardly seeing it. "Come and swim, Mike," she pleaded. Her eyes were wide and soft. "The water's warm. The waves aren't big. It's a perfect day. A gift from God."

On the summit of the island a huge white wooden cross glowed in the morning light, a memory of earlier days.

* * *

Most of the people who'd lived on the island before the flood had already been taken away. There were only forty or fifty left, waiting patiently for their turn on the ropes.

Mike tore his gaze away from the shattered boat, and rounded on Holly. "Wake up!" he shouted. "Wake up. You've been walking around in a daze for weeks. You and everyone else while an act of genocide has been going on around you. We're dying, Holly. Family by family, your god is killing us."

Holly's gaze seemed suddenly weighted in concern. She raised her hand to brush Mike's wild hair away from his face, off his ears, as if by that simple measure she hoped to change a basic deficiency in his vision, in his hearing.

Mike knocked her hand away. "I'm not deaf and I'm not blind!" he shouted. "I can see what's going on—"

"But you can't feel it," she said softly.

"No. No you're right. I can't feel it. I can't." His hands clenched into fists. He closed his eyes as anguish flooded his mind. "Why me, Holly? Why am I the only one who can't *believe*—?"

A far-away rumble cut off his lament. The sound resembled the thunder of a distant jet, summoning a memory of childhood when he'd lain awake at night listening to the passage of an anomalous craft far overhead, imagining that what he heard was no commercial airliner on an unusual route; that instead the nightfarer was a B-52, armed with nuclear missiles bound for a hardened target in Siberia. The overflight that presaged the end of the world.

His childhood fears had faded with the cold war, had dulled with maturity. Now they were back, haunting him, as the end of the world loomed in unexpected reality.

He looked out across the ocean, where he counted three twisting wires of brilliant golden light. They were thin, like cracks in the sky letting in the light of heaven. But vast, appearing to extend far beyond the brilliant blue bowl of the sky, disappearing into some nebulous distance that seemed somehow utterly different from the sky Mike had known all his life. Light bleeding from some other place. Some other world. Hungry light that preyed on hope and faith.

The distant jet-roar faded to silence as the wires of light approached across the water. They swayed as they moved, not behaving at all like ordinary light, but instead bending and floating like extremely low-density matter. Once again, Mike felt himself astounded at their thinness. The first one swept across the shallows toward the children playing in the waves. At this distance it was easy to see that it was no thicker than the mooring lines once used to tie cruise ships to the docks.

The children had spotted the rope. Their joyous cries could be heard from the ridge as they scrambled and dove toward the light. Mike wanted to scream at them to stop, to run away. But they *believed* ...

A young girl just short of puberty reached the rope first. She grabbed it with her right hand and was immediately yanked off her feet. She rose skyward. At the same time she seemed to shrink so that she was drawn *into* the column of light. Mike watched as she became a tiny silhouette within the golden glow, a dark figure receding at fabulous speed across a vast dimension that did not exist in this world. He watched until she became a black point on the visual horizon. And then he watched her disappear.

Other children followed her, six, then seven of them before the rope left the now-empty water and swept ashore, zig-zagging across the newly-laid beach as it offered itself to the eager, waiting parents.

Mike fell to his knees, sickened. He bent over, holding his stomach. He wanted to puke. Holly crouched beside him. "It's all right, Mike," she soothed. "It's all right. God has come for us. You don't have to be afraid."

Her words made his hackles rise. Was a rope finally out to lure the two of them? After weeks of watching everyone they'd ever known disappear up the ropes, was this their time? His fingers clawed at the ground. Why couldn't he feel the grace the others felt? Why couldn't he *believe*?

A deep electric hum assaulted his ears. He felt his hair lift slightly, as if a field of static electricity had suddenly swept around him. Looking up, he saw a second golden rope racing in from the ocean towards the ridge. "*No!*" he shouted.

He dove at Holly, knocking her to the ground. He held her there with his weight, pinning her arms against her sides. "I won't let you go to it!" he screamed at her. "I won't let you go."

The rope was dancing, swaying up the jagged slope of the ridge. Holly's eyes filled with tears. A trace of blood netted her lip. Her jaw trembled. "Please Mike. Let me go. It's my time. It's our time. I don't know why you can't feel it. But I do know you love me. You have to trust me. You have to let me believe for you—"

He kissed her to stop the flow of words. His lips pressed against hers, his tongue probed her mouth, he tasted the sweet salt of her blood. It crossed the membranes of his mouth like a drug. Her love flowed into him, her trust, her faith. He felt a warm, golden glow fill him. He let go of her arms, to cradle her beautiful face in his hands. And then they were sitting up, spooning, her arms tight around the small of his back. And somehow after that he found himself on his feet. She stood facing him, holding both his hands. A column of gold rose behind her. Her warm dark eyes were locked on his. She nodded encouragement. Moving backward, she led him first one step, then another. Letting his left hand go, she half-turned to seize the rope. "*Faith*," she whispered.

Her body arched in sudden ecstasy as she was yanked up the rope. The gasp that escaped her lips was a knife that cut through Mike's consciousness. He stiffened, as a dirty old awareness flooded his mind. "Holly, no!" he roared.

She was receding up the rope, her right side shrinking, darkening into a silhouette as she was swept into the narrow chasm of golden light, her left side yet in the flooded world. "*Holly!*"

He found that he still held her left hand. Now he seized it with both his hands and pulled. Her body continued to shrink, to recede into impossible distance. Her arm stretched in a long black ribbon. Then her hand turned palm up in his grip, and vanished. He found himself grasping at empty air.

A scream of utter rage ripped from his throat. Tears flooded his face.

The golden light hummed and shifted, awaiting him.

"*Not me*," he choked. "I won't go with you. Murderer! Murderer!" He turned and fled into the forest.

The island was empty, all the people finally gone.

Mike climbed the hill and sat at the base of the cross. Cool air washed over his face, while scudding clouds played with the sun's light. The remaining land mass was no more than a quarter mile across now. Uninterrupted ocean surrounded him on all sides, the water appearing to rise up like a shallow bowl, with himself trapped in the bottom. How high would the waters rise? High enough to drown even continental mountains?

There is not that much water in the world!

Movement caught his eye. A sparkle of white against the cloud-shadowed sea. A bird, he realized. And as it drew nearer he recognized the wandering albatross, gliding on its white wings just above the crest of the swell. A solitary creature.

He watched it in gratitude, and not a little wonder, realizing only then how much he'd missed the non-human life of the island. For the cats and dogs, birds and cattle had disappeared with their masters. Even the fish had vanished from the ocean. He wondered if this bird could be as hungry as he.

It stayed with him, flying a restless circuit around the shrinking island as the flood waters continued to rise. By noon, when hunger and thirst and utter isolation began to play upon his mind, it became the focus of his delirium. He found himself flying on long wings around and around the white wooden cross as if he flew on the end of a chain. He wanted to turn tail to it. He wanted to glide across the open ocean into the blue promise of homogenous vistas: *just a little farther now, and you will find land, life.*

But the bird refused to leave.

The afternoon passed. Mike felt his skin burn in the intermittent sun. Thirst seemed to swell his tongue into a dry, dusty sponge. Hunger knotted his belly. He watched the waves roll in, from all sides now, higher and higher until by late afternoon they met at the bottom of the cross.

He climbed the monument to escape the churning tumult of water that consumed the last bit of land. He hauled himself up on the crossbar, then hugged the post while the waters roiled below him, slowly yet inevitability rising. Soon he would drown. Were there fish left in the water to eat him? Were there still microbes that might break down his flesh? Perhaps he would sink to the bottom and become covered with sediment and be converted to a fossil, the only evidence left of the original animal life of this world. For he sensed that the world was being cleansed, prepared for an entirely separate history to follow.

Tears filled his eyes as he looked out across the watery wasteland. He couldn't imagine worshipping any deity capable of creating this murderous scene.

All Gone.

The vast and empty ocean seemed to resound with that statement of finality.

All Gone.

When the last creatures were flushed out by the flood, the world would be clean, ready to be remade, renewed.

Mike held on. By evening the ocean was nearly calm. The golden colors of sunset played across the uninterrupted horizon. He gazed at the sight, feeling the burnished colors enter his soul and warm him. Last day.

He started, as the albatross swept past. It had been drawing nearer all day, perhaps emboldened by the retreat of the land. Now it floated by, scarcely an arm's length away, the wind abuzz in its feathers, a slight noise that seemed to grow in volume as the bird receded until the buzz became the ominous rumble of distant thunder, distant jets.

Mike looked up, to see a golden rope dancing on the horizon. A single rope. It was the first time he'd ever seen just one. His heart began to hammer as the old fury returned. He clung to the cross and screamed at the usurper, his voice rolling across the calm waters. "*Liar*! *Murderer*!"

A cold swell rose up to touch his dangling feet, bringing with it a sudden darkness. Fury flowed away, leaving behind the painful vacuum of despair. He bowed his head against the post and cried until the thunder faded and the hum of the rope filled his ears, until the deceiver's golden glow burned through his closed eyes.

He still didn't believe in the beneficence of God. He knew the flood was an act of genocide and the rope was a con game. Knew it by the anguish in his soul. But it didn't matter anymore. He was human, and he must follow his people, be it to hell or oblivion. He opened his eyes. The rope danced before him, an inexplicable gold cable let down at the end of the world. The albatross floated on a breeze, seemingly watching, waiting for his lead.

He grasped the rope in both hands, and was gone.

THE END OF THE WORLD SHOW

David Barnett

David Barnett is a Lancashire-born journalist and editor, currently Assistant Editor at the Bradford Telegraph & Argus. *He is the author of the novels* Hinterland *(2005), about the hidden worlds around us, and* Angelglass *(2007), where strands of history merge, and the story collection* The Janus House and Other Two-Faced Tales *(2009). When I was planning this anthology I vowed not to include any stories of "zombie apocalypse", but there's always an exception and rules are there to be broken, for a very good reason.*

O N THE SEVENTH day before the end, the aliens said goodbye.

"It's all true," said a tired-looking man from the Government, being interviewed on the teatime news. "Non-Earth Originated Intelligences have been among us since 1947. They have contributed a great deal to our development over the past sixty years. It's highly doubtful we would have been able to make the strides in space exploration that we have without their help. And the work they have done with us on researching treatments for cancer and other conditions has been phenomenal. It's just a shame that they have to leave now, with so much yet to do."

"Why exactly are they leaving?" asked the reporter.

The man from the Government tugged at his collar and looked off-camera. "Uh, no more questions at this time, please," he said.

The general consensus was that it was all a big hoax. There were special news reports on all the channels devoted to the announcement.

They even cancelled the episode of *EastEnders* on the TV. Katy would not have approved.

It was with Katy that I really wanted to talk about all this, but she'd gone a long time ago. I sat in my cramped terraced house, cruising through the digital channels, every one with some expert or other talking animatedly about the aliens. They came from a planet circling a star that we didn't even have a name for, just a string of numbers. There was a lot of talk about the impossibility of interstellar travel, and someone asked a scientist if travel between stars was possible, why had the aliens only shown us how to get as far as the Moon?

Katy would be talking about it with Steve, about what it all meant for the future, for their future, their cosy little, middle-class, Volkswagen Touran-driving, holidays-in-Tuscany future. I went to the pub.

"It's a hoax," said Bob with authority. "Has to be, hasn't it? Can't possibly be true."

"Where are they, then, if they're here? Where's their space rocket?" said Alan.

There was a boom of voices as the barmaid turned up the volume on the television in the corner. The studio discussions on the BBC special news programme had cut to some shaky camerawork in a field somewhere in Cornwall, according to the caption. A reporter in a raincoat ducked into shot. "And here we are at the scene of the extra-terrestrials actually leaving the earth ..."

The camera angle changed abruptly and focused on a cigar-shaped silver rocket standing in the dark, rain-soaked field. God knows where they'd been hiding it and how they'd suddenly got it there.

"I bet it's been there all the time, invisible," said Alan.

"It's a hoax," said Bob, lighting a cigarette, apparently satisfied. "I mean, look at it. It's like something out of Flash Gordon."

Alan's mobile phone buzzed on the table. While he fumbled with the buttons, the camera panned to three of the aliens standing on a platform near the rocket. They looked a bit like Stan Ogden, only with a slightly greenish tinge. They were wearing three-button black suits with Nehru collars. FIRST PICTURES OF THE ALIENS flashed across the bottom of the screen.

"Why are you leaving?" shouted someone from the huddle of press reporters.

One of the aliens looked at the other two. He coughed, and then said in perfect English: "We are very sorry. We have to go now. It's beyond our control."

"That was Margery," said Alan, putting the phone back into his jacket pocket. "The lads have taken the Focus and set off for Cornwall. They want to go with the aliens."

Bob stubbed out his cigarette and laughed. "Your lads? Wayne and Stu? What makes them think the aliens'll want to take them back to Pluto? Unless they're short of work-shy layabouts up there."

"I'd tell them not to bother," I said, pointing at the telly. "They're off."

They were indeed. The aliens had got inside their rocket and the army were herding the press pack and the rubberneckers away. A green glow erupted from the base of the silver spaceship and the camera shook and wobbled. Then it was gone, soaring up into the night sky. The camera tracked it until it was swallowed by the black clouds.

There was a hush over the pub, and the field in Cornwall, until the reporter said in reverent tones: "And there we have it: an historic, epoch-making event. I have been proud and honoured to witness the first open contact between humanity and extra-terrestrial intelligences ..."

"Proud and honoured to witness them buggering off," said Bob, lighting up again.

"I wonder why they've gone, really?" said Alan.

"I wonder whose round it is, really?" said Bob.

Later, pissed, I phoned Katy, against my better judgment.

"Did you see the aliens?" I burbled.

"Of course I did," she said flatly. "I'd imagine everyone on earth saw them. Why are you calling me?"

"I still love you," I whispered.

The phone went dead.

I lay in bed for a bit but couldn't sleep. I tried to have a wank but could only summon up images of flabby green aliens in black suits, so gave up and went to sit by the window, staring up at the night sky and wondering what it was all about, until Wayne and Stu drove past in their dad's Ford Focus, beeping their horn all along the road. They'd painted TAKE US WITH U on the roof of the car. Alan wasn't going to be best pleased.

On the sixth day before the end, we found out why the aliens had left. There was an asteroid the size of Milton Keynes heading towards earth. It was due to hit in a little under a week. The breakfast news was full of it. Someone at the Government had leaked the information. The authorities had known about it for months. The aliens had been trying to help us find a solution but, given the size of the rock, there wasn't much they could suggest. That was why they had gone.

I didn't go into work. Didn't really see the point. I did phone, though. The secretary said: "Are you ill?"

"Haven't you seen the news this morning?"

She paused. "No. Why?"

"Nothing," I said. Anne was a skittish sort and I didn't want to panic her unduly. "I've got a touch of flu."

I turned back to the telly. The asteroid was somewhere out past Venus at the moment, but it was going at a fair lick. The experts said it would probably break up a little in the atmosphere. There was apparently a big plan to fly a load of nuclear bombs up into orbit in the space shuttle and blow the rock to smithereens, or at least knock it off course. Failing that – and the scientist being interviewed assured us it would work – the asteroid would probably hit Australia some time on Sunday.

"At least it's only Australia," said Alan when I went round to his to return the hedge trimmer I'd borrowed off him five months previously.

He gazed at the trimmer with a curious look in his eye, probably wondering whether it was worth cutting back his leylandii before the weekend, as I said: "Well, according to the telly, the size and speed of the thing means it'll probably wipe out all life on earth anyway."

Alan sniffed, just as Margery pulled up on to the drive in the Focus. They'd tried to rub the TAKE US WITH U message off the roof without much success. Margery, a handsome woman if a little highly-strung, struggled out of the car weighed down with Sains-bury's carrier bags. She looked a little harassed.

"It's chaos out there!" she trilled. "I nearly had to fight my way out of the supermarket. There were people punching each other at the checkout."

"Did you get any of that pâté I like?" asked Alan mildly as Margery elbowed her way past me.

"No I did not!" she squeaked. "I got bottles of water and tins of beans. You can get the other bags out of the car. And why haven't you barricaded the windows yet?"

Alan looked at me and gave a tiny, *what-can-you-do?* shrug. "I thought I'd trim the hedge, first," he said.

I left Margery blustering and went back home. Halfway there I took a detour towards the corner shop. Perhaps it would be wise to get a few provisions in, just in case. Unfortunately, half the neighbourhood had the same idea. There was a crowd outside the shop and people were wheeling away their purchases in the trolleys. I edged towards the door as one of the staff was tacking a handwritten notice on the door. It said: CASH PURCHASES ONLY.

"We've had a call from head office telling us not to accept credit cards or cheques," she said to me as we squeezed into the packed shop.

Deftly dancing around the suffocating aisles, I managed to extricate half-a-dozen microwave Chinese meals, a bottle of milk, some whisky and a packet of bourbon creams. At the till it was like a rugby scrum. One man had pretty much the entire contents of the meat cabinet in two big trolleys, and he was waving his Barclaycard at them.

"No plastic!" shouted the woman behind the till. "I've told you, cash only!"

The queue snaked around the shop. I waved my purchases at the girl who I'd seen putting the notice on the door, and gave her a twenty pound note. She cast a glance over my basket, nodded, and stuffed the twenty in her pocket. "Do you mind if I take the basket?" I asked.

She shrugged. "You can have it for a fiver."

I only had a ten so I gave her that and picked up a copy of "Country Living" from the cardboard display bin that had been knocked over near the tills.

As I left the shop, glad for a bit of fresh air, a big 4×4 squealed to a halt just in front of me. There were four men wearing balaclavas and carrying baseball bats. One of them looked at me as they climbed out. "Give us your stuff!" he snarled.

One of the others pulled him away by his jacket. "Leave him. We'll get what's inside." He paused, as if re-considering, then held up his baseball bat. "Give us your money, though."

I fished in my pocket and pulled out another tenner. He snatched it off me and shoved it into his jeans. "Right, inside. Tinned stuff, bottled water, powdered milk. Twat anyone who gets in your way."

I hurried back towards home. The main road was now choked with traffic, cars inching along and beeping their horns. I spotted Bob and his wife, their Rover loaded up with stuff. Bob wound down the window.

"Off on your hols?" I said.

"We're getting out," he shouted. "I'd do the same if I was you."

"Where are you going to go?" I said, looking at the long line of traffic stretching off out of sight.

"The Lakes, probably. Bit of high ground. Clean water."

I nodded. Bob's wife slapped him and pointed forward, where the car in front had moved ahead three or four centimetres. Bob waved and began to wind up the window, then stopped and brought it down again. He rummaged in his jacket and tossed a set of keys at me. "If you're staying here anyway, you wouldn't do us a favour and turn the engine over on the MG, would you? It's murder if it doesn't get a few revs every couple of days."

I picked up the keys and waved as the Rover jerked forward again. I wondered if I'd be able to sneak Bob's MG out for a spin while they were away. A lovely little car it was. British Racing Green. They don't make them like that any more.

I got home just in time to watch the space shuttle taking off from Cape Kennedy.

On the fifth day before the end, most of southern Japan was destroyed in a nuclear conflagration. I had to admit, things were starting to look a bit bleak. I'd had another largely sleepless night, mainly due to the traffic on the main road, a constant stream of cars and vans crawling along with bad-tempered honks. I wondered how far Bob had got.

Apparently a bit of sponge or foam had fallen off one of the space shuttle's engines as it orbited the earth, waiting for the asteroid to come into range. This had played havoc with the steering and the computers had gone all bonkers, plunging the shuttle back into sub-orbital space and sending it spinning down towards Japan. It had hit the ground and the nukes had gone up, several miles south of Osaka. The city and most of the surrounding area had gone.

The Russians said not to worry, they were sending a rocket full of nukes up as well. That wasn't much comfort to the Japanese, though. Someone with a beard came on the news and said that he believed the whole asteroid business was an elaborate con and that the United States had planned to bomb Japan all along. Exactly why, though, he couldn't say.

Some of the TV channels went off, mainly the digital ones. Channel Five stopped broadcasting as well, but hardly anyone noticed. ITV and the BBC just had news on all the time. Channel 4 played music videos, while BBC2 was given over to re-runs of seventies' sitcoms, which had a strangely soothing quality about them. I watched a couple of episodes of *Terry and June*, but couldn't get the pictures of the deathly quiet carnage in Japan out of my head.

I took a stroll. Most of the cars had gone wherever they were going and the road was pretty quiet. Since this morning there had been a tank parked at the bottom of our street, following on from reports of looting and violence closer to town.

I'd never seen a tank close up before. It was a pretty grand beast. Katy would have hated it. She was a pacifist, was Katy. Still is, probably. She'd not be coping with all this. I hoped there was no rioting near her house. I hoped she was okay. I considered phoning her again, but didn't really know what I'd say. For some reason I thought about Blackpool. Katy had loved going to Blackpool, loved the prom and the noise and the sweet smell of candyfloss on the air, the clatter of coins in the one-armed bandit trays and the insane laughter of the automated clown at the Pleasure Beach. One year we'd been there someone had made a huge sand sculpture of a tank on the beach. Katy had wondered why the artist couldn't have made something less ugly. All the kids seemed to love it, though.

There was a soldier sitting on top of the tank, the real tank at the bottom of my street, a sub-machine gun in the crook of his arm. He regarded me coolly.

"It's okay," I said cheerfully. "I'm not going to pinch your tank."

He didn't laugh. Didn't even smile. "Did you hear the Government's gone?" he said.

"Gone where?"

"Just gone," he said. "Half of them have left for some bunker in the Home Counties. Some of them are dead. Westminster is burning. No one's in control any more."

I thought about this. "So who's paying your wages?"

He looked at me and blinked, as though he hadn't considered this before. He leaned into the turret of the tank and had a brief conversation with his mate. I hung around for a bit but the soldier ignored me. I wandered out on to the main road and over to Alan's cul-de-sac, but his house was all boarded up. I knocked but there was no answer, so I nipped round the back and borrowed his hedge trimmers again. When I got back to my street, the tank had gone. Mr Raines from number eight, who was in the Territorials, was standing in the road as I approached. He had a sub-machine gun exactly like the soldier in the tank had.

"Where did you get that?" I asked.

"Squaddie gave it to me, just before he pissed off," he said, his face set in a grimace. "Look, there's no Army any more. No law and order. We're going to have to organize ourselves into a ... a Civil Defence Group. Do you have any weapons?"

We both looked at the hedge trimmer. I supposed it could give a pretty nasty cut, so long as you were within fifteen feet of a plug socket. "I'll have a look at home," I said.

I phoned Katy again but got their answer machine. "We've got a Civil Defence Group in our street," I said proudly. I paused. "I love you," I said, then put the phone down.

Katy had left me because I wasn't exciting enough. Because, after my parents died, I just wanted to sit in their old terraced house and go to work and come home and watch TV. But what she failed to take into account was that I wanted to do all that with *her,* that all that was exciting enough for me. I wondered if she was finding all this exciting now she was with Steve.

A minute later I picked the phone up again and left another message: "I've got some Chinese ready meals and the electrics are still on here, so if you wanted to come over ... "

Later on I helped Mr Raines and some others block off either end of our street with some cars.

"What if we want to go somewhere?" I said.

"Where's there to go?" said Mr Raines, his face in that grimace again.

Looking at the news later on, commentaryless pictures of London burning and riots in Birmingham and Manchester, I had to concede he had a point. I wondered how Bob was getting on in the Lakes.

On the fourth day before the end, a huge lizard attacked Tokyo. As if Japan hadn't had enough problems. It was exactly like a dinosaur, 200 feet from nose to tail. It ran with a loping gait, head down and tail up, its spine almost perfectly level. It was something to do with the bombs that had landed on Osaka, they said. Either a normal lizard had been mutated by the radiation and grown to monstrous proportions, or an ages-old beast had been in some kind of suspended animation below the surface of the earth and had been awoken by the blast.

It was amazing how people were prepared to accept just about anything these days.

It was quite gripping viewing. The news pictures showed them trying to evacuate Tokyo, but there was nowhere for the people to go, pretty much the rest of Japan being an irradiated wasteland. The monster rampaged across the city, flattening buildings and flipping cars with its tail. I caught myself more than once thinking *it's pretty realistic* before realizing that it *was* real. Eventually they brought it down with fighter planes and it flopped, dead, in the street. The newsreader said the Japanese authorities had started to slice it up to use as emergency rations.

That afternoon looters kicked the kitchen door in. There were three of them, kids about eighteen or nineteen, and they all had baseball bats. I was in the kitchen at the time and they booted their way in, pushing me against the wall.

"What do you want?" I said.

One of them slapped me. "Everything," he said.

They took all the money they could find, which didn't amount to much. They didn't think to take the food, but one of them manhandled the TV off its stand.

"We'll take this as well," said the ringleader, slapping me again and ripping the stereo power lead out of the wall socket.

"What are you going to do with them?" I said. "The world's going to end."

They looked at each other uncertainly, then the ringleader punched me in the stomach, winding me. Then they left.

I boarded up the door with some wood I found in the shed and went upstairs to bring the portable telly down from the bedroom. While I was rooting in the wardrobe I came across my dad's old airgun and a box of pellets. Might come in handy.

We had a meeting of the Civil Defence Group in Mr Raines' front room. Half of the households in the street had already deserted; gone to Scotland or the Lake District or to be with family. Mr Raines approved of my gun. The water had gone off earlier in the day and the drains were getting backed up; there was a problem with rats but Mr Raines didn't want us to waste ammunition on them. A rat-catching division was set up, consisting of Wayne and Stu, who had got fed up of being barricaded into their house and had come down to live in one of the deserted terraces in our street. We still had electricity; a lot of places didn't.

By dusk Wayne and Stu had killed enough rats for Trevor the butcher to begin skinning them. There was a big pot put over a fire in the middle of the road and we had a bit of a street party. The rat stew wasn't too bad; I'd been getting a bit fed up with Chinese. A dozen bottles of gin were found in Mrs Hughes' house; her daughter had come to collect her two days ago. Everyone suspected Mrs Hughes liked the odd nip, but not to that extent. It was quite a jolly evening, until someone said that a girl at the top of the street had been raped. A Civil Defence Group meeting was called and Mr Raines led a small group of volunteers off to apprehend the most likely suspects. I left Wayne and Stu throwing up in the street and went to bed.

On the third day before the end, a tsunami swamped the western seaboard of the United States. The last thing that I saw on the portable

TV before the power went off was a wall of water engulfing the Golden Gate Bridge, then a roaring sound and the cameraman was swallowed up. It cut back to the studio at the BBC, the only channel broadcasting now. The presenter looked like she hadn't slept for a week. She wasn't wearing any make-up and she had tears in her eyes as she reported that Los Angeles and San Francisco were now under water. Halfway through the report she looked up to someone off-camera and said: "What? Wait. Where are you going … ?"

She sat there for a while on her own, and the lighting slowly faded. Then the picture went blank, and didn't come on again. I supposed that was it for the TV, then.

I was a little surprised that the electricity was still on. The gas had gone off two days previously. Either they had some kind of auto-mated system still powering the national grid or there were some very dedicated people working to keep the country energized. And just as I was thinking that, the lights went out. That buggered it for the microwave readymeals, I thought. Rat stew from now until the end.

In the middle of the night Mr Raines and his Civil Defence Group commandos "arrested" Roy the bachelor from the end house and strung him up from the lamp-post for the rape of the girl. Roy had always had the finger pointed at him whenever there was anything funny going on, and once the *News of the World* had published his name in a list of paedophiles and he had dog-muck pushed through his letterbox. They apologised and printed a retraction a couple of weeks later, saying it was another Roy in another town, but by then the damage was done.

I was a bit shocked at that but as Mr Raines said to me, desperate times require desperate measures.

I found a load of candles under the sink and dotted them around the sitting room. It was quite cosy. I finished the bottle of gin I'd pinched from Mrs Hughes' supply and picked up the phone. It was dead but I dialled Katy's number anyway, told the blank, empty air that I loved her, and cried myself to sleep on the sofa.

On the second day before the end, the hungry dead rose from the cold, damp earth. The popular assumption that they would be mindless, shuffling husks with a craze for human brains did, fortunately, prove to be unfounded. They were, however, largely very grumpy.

The first sign was in the small, dark time before dawn. No one was getting much sleep any more. In the quiet moments you could always hear the far-off sounds of violence. We had patrols in the street pretty much constantly, and there was always someone chasing rats or wailing. I'd done my bit and patrolled with my dad's gun for a couple of hours in the night, chasing off a couple of kids who were trying to sneak along the ginnel behind Mrs Reagan's house, so was trying to get a bit of kip. I'd just dropped off when there was a low rumble. I sat up in a blind panic, thinking that the asteroid must have hit Australia but the shaking wasn't in the ground, it was in my gut. It became a sustained, single note, rising in pitch. I assumed someone had got hold of a trombone or such-like. It lasted about fifteen minutes, and then stopped. There was a long silence. Even the sounds of gunfire faded for a moment.

Taking the opportunity to get my head down again, I was just drifting away when there was a hammering at the door. God, what now? I picked up the gun from the side of the bed and staggered downstairs.

"That's *mine*," said a voice as dry as autumn leaves. "Give it here."

"Dad?" I said.

It was indeed. And Mum as well. Looking ... well, looking exactly as they did the day they died. Dad was in his black suit, his fob watch tucked into the pocket of his waistcoat. Mum had that blue dress on that she had used to wear for dancing.

"I thought you were going to paint the window frames," said Mum.

I looked out of the door. There were more people in suits and dresses – and one or two in shapeless white gowns – staggering up the street, stopping at doors. At the houses they used to live at.

"That sound this morning ... " I said slowly, finally understanding.

"The Final Trump," said Dad, wearing that self-satisfied face he always used to pull when something was going against him. Only happy when it rains, my Dad. "And me not even baptized."

Mum was rubbing the flaking green paintwork on the windowsill. "The last thing you promised me was that you were going to do these windows," she said.

At the top of the street I could make out the corpse of Roy the bachelor twitching and kicking at the end of his rope. "I didn't do it!" he managed in a choked voice before the noose cut off his air supply and he died again. Within seconds he was dancing about again and shouting. I hoped someone would cut him down soon.

Dad pushed past me. "You going to leave us standing on the doorstep to our own house?" he said. "What have you got to eat?"

"A couple of microwave Chinese meals," I said. "There's been a bit of a problem with food the last few days."

Dad sat down in the armchair while mum started picking up the dirty dishes and tutting at the layer of dust on the coffee table.

"I can see we're going to have to take charge around here," said dad.

There was a hammering at the door.

"That'll be your grandad," said mum.

Dad had died of a heart attack two years ago and mum had gone quietly nine months later. I suppose they were lucky; Old Mrs Potter had been hit by a bus last Christmas and she'd turned up at home in a right mess. It was a bit of a shock for her husband.

The return of the dead raised all kinds of questions in people's minds. Presumably this was Judgment Day, then. The Civil Defence Group set up a big prayer session in the street. It was quite eerie, watching the living and the dead come together and stand there in silence while Mr Ogden, who was a lay preacher, read from the Bible. At the point where he asked that we all be forgiven for our sins, Roy the bachelor coughed loudly but no one could meet his eye. They made Mrs Potter stand at the back because she was a bit upsetting for the kiddies.

Come sunset there was great excitement; the asteroid was finally visible to the naked eye. It looked like a very slow-moving comet high in the night sky. I supposed the Russians hadn't been able to blow it up then, and that expert on the TV who had said it would burn up in the atmosphere had been wrong. I wondered what they were doing in Australia right now.

On the last day before the end, Katy came home. "I knew you'd still be here," she said, collapsing into my arms and sobbing. It was just like a film.

She was filthy and her blouse was all torn. She'd walked it all the way from her house. It had taken all yesterday, all night and most of the morning. It had been slow going because of all the gangs – they were on the lookout for anyone with food or weapons. Women were especially in danger. Worst of all were the gangs of the undead, the ones who hadn't eaten or had a woman for many long, cold years. She'd come cross-country, hiding in ditches and crawling on her belly past campfires which rang with laughter and screams.

"Where's Steve?" I said when she'd calmed down a bit.

"Gone," she said. "Three days ago. You know his parents were part of that weird Christian sect? Steve had never been bothered with it, but when they decided to lock themselves in their church and his mum and dad told him that they'd built a huge bunker underground and filled it with food and water, he suddenly found his faith again."

"Didn't you fancy it?"

Katy dissolved into tears again, burying her head in my shoulder. "I begged him to take me," she sobbed. "They refused. Just left me in the house with no food, nothing to defend myself with. Oh, God. What's going to happen to us?"

Mum shuffled out of the kitchen. She looked at us and frowned. She'd never liked Katy much. "Oh," she said. "One more for tea, is it?"

Mum had made a pie. From what, God only knows. At the mention of food, the others came out of the sitting room. Dad was followed by grandad and grandma, uncle George, aunty Linda, cousin Alfie, and then a raft of stern-looking people in stiff Edwardian collars. It was getting pretty busy here.

"Let's go for a walk," I said.

Everyone was out in the street, pointing at the sky. You could see the asteroid in daylight now, a blazing orb in the atmosphere. "As big as Milton Keynes," I said, wonderingly.

"When's it going to hit?" asked Katy, hugging my arm.

I pondered for a moment, revelling in the closeness of her body. "If I've worked it out right from the first reports, tomorrow."

She swooned dramatically into my arms. "Oh, God," she said in a small voice.

Mr Ogden the lay preacher was suddenly beside us. "Indeed," he said. "The fiery judgment of heaven is upon us. We are having a vigil in the street this evening, begging for forgiveness and asking to be admitted through the gates of paradise when the calamity strikes. You'll join us?"

"Will there be rat stew?" I asked.

Mr Ogden frowned and walked away, clutching his Bible. People had become quite a bit more serious over the last couple of days. I suppose approaching apocalypse does that to a person. That and the lack of water for a good bath. Most of us were beginning to smell, not least the risen dead.

"Do you fancy it?"

"What?" said Katy.

"The meeting. Begging for forgiveness and all that."

Katy wrinkled her nose at me like she used to do. "What else is there to do?"

I thought for a moment. "We could go to Blackpool," I said.

She looked at me. "Blackpool?"

"Yeah, you know. Candy floss and sticks of rock. We could go on the log flume and walk along the prom. Stroll to the end of the North Pier. Watch the world end. That kind of thing."

Katy gestured at the barricade of cars at the end of the street, the distant sounds of gunfire. "How would we get there?"

I fished the keys to Bob's MG out of my pocket and dangled them in front of her face. "In style."

It only took us a couple of hours. Most of the fighting and looting seemed to have stopped. I suppose people probably wondered what the point was. Everyone seemed to be in their houses, waiting for the end. Blackpool was deserted.

We broke into an empty bed and breakfast place near the front and managed to find some bread that was not totally stale and a few tins of beans. Then we found the best bedroom and made slow, quiet love.

It was midday. The sky was pretty clear. We couldn't see the asteroid any more, so presumed it was about to hit Australia. The tide was in, and we sat on a bench at the end of the North Pier, me crunching rock and Katy sucking on a lollipop in the shape of a baby's dummy.

"Should we talk about where it all went wrong for us?" I said.

She thought about it and shook her head. "No point now, is there?"

Far, far away there was a thud that reverberated along the pier. Katy held my hand. The horizon rippled and there was a distant roar.

"This is it, then," I said. I felt all right, really. Pretty good, in fact.

Katy closed her eyes. There were tears running down her cheeks. Her hair was a mess and her face was filthy. She was beautiful.

"Kiss me quick," she whispered.

FERMI AND FROST

Frederik Pohl

---

*Frederik Pohl is one of the grand masters of science
fiction with a career spanning over sixty years, both as a
writer and an editor. He is adept whether writing on his
own or in collaboration. His partnership with Cyril M.
Kornbluth, which produced such classics as* The Space
Merchants *(1953) and* Wolfbane *(1959), is legendary.
He has also collaborated with Jack Williamson, whose
work is also present in this anthology, and I believe he is
the only writer to have collaborated with both Isaac
Asimov and Arthur C. Clarke. For much of the 1960s
Pohl was tied up editing several SF magazines, most
notably* Galaxy *and* Worlds of If, *but when he returned
to writing fiction in the 1970s he produced a series of
memorable books, including the Heechee series, which
began with* Gateway *(1977), as well as* Man Plus *(1976),*
The Coming of the Quantum Cats *(1986) and* The
World at the End of Time *(1990). His work has won
him many awards and accolades, including the following
which won the Hugo in 1986. It takes us into the depths
of the nuclear winter.*

O N TIMOTHY CLARY'S ninth birthday he got no cake. He spent
all of it in a bay of the TWA terminal at John F. Kennedy
airport in New York, sleeping fitfully, crying now and then from
exhaustion or fear. All he had to eat was stale Danish pastries from
the buffet wagon and not many of them and he was fearfully embarrassed because he had wet his pants. Three times. Getting to the
toilets over the packed refugee bodies was just about impossible.
There were 2,800 people in a space designed for a fraction that

many, and all of them with the same idea. Get away! Climb the highest mountain! Drop yourself splat, spang, right in the middle of the widest desert! Run! Hide!—

And pray. Pray as hard as you can, because even the occasional plane-load of refugees that managed to fight their way aboard and even take off had no sure hope of refuge when they got wherever the plane was going. Families parted. Mothers pushed their screaming children aboard a jet and melted back into the crowd before screaming, more quietly, themselves.

Because there had been no launch order yet, or none that the public had heard about anyway, there might still be time for escape. A little time. Time enough for the TWA terminal, and every other airport terminal everywhere, to jam up with terrified lemmings. There was no doubt that the missiles were poised to fly. The attempted Cuban coup had escalated wildly, and one nuclear sub had attacked another with a nuclear charge. That, everyone agreed, was the signal. The next event would be the final one.

Timothy knew little of this, but there would have been nothing he could have done about it – except perhaps cry, or have nightmares, or wet himself, and young Timothy was doing all of those anyway. He did not know where his father was. He didn't know where his mother was, either, except that she had gone somewhere to try to call his father; but then there had been a surge that could not be resisted when three 747s at once had announced boarding, and Timothy had been carried far from where he had been left. Worse than that. Wet as he was, with a cold already, he was beginning to be very sick. The young woman who had brought him the Danish pastries put a worried hand to his forehead and drew it away helplessly. The boy needed a doctor. But so did a hundred others, elderly heart patients and hungry babies and at least two women close to childbirth.

If the terror had passed and the frantic negotiations had succeeded, Timothy might have found his parents again in time to grow up and marry and give them grandchildren. If one side or the other had been able to pre-empt, and destroy the other, and save itself, Timothy forty years later might have been a greying, cynical colonel in the American military government of Leningrad. (Or body servant to a Russian one in Detroit.) Or if his mother had pushed just a little harder earlier on, he might have wound up in the plane of refugees that reached Pittsburgh just in time to become plasma. Or if the girl who was watching him had become just a little more scared, and a little more brave, and somehow managed to get him through the throng to the improvised clinics in the main terminal, he might have been given medicine, and found somebody to protect him, and take him to a refuge, and live...

But that is in fact what did happen!

Because Harry Malibert was on his way to a British Interplanetary Society seminar in Portsmouth, he was already sipping Beefeater Martinis in the terminal's Ambassador Club when the unnoticed TV at the bar suddenly made everybody notice it.

Those silly nuclear-attack communications systems that the radio stations tested out every now and then, and nobody paid any attention to any more – why, this time it was real! They were serious! Because it was winter and snowing heavily Malibert's flight had been delayed anyway. Before its rescheduled departure time came, all flights had been embargoed. Nothing would leave Kennedy until some official somewhere decided to let them go.

Almost at once the terminal began to fill with would-be refugees. The Ambassador Club did not fill at once. For three hours the ground-crew stew at the desk resolutely turned away everyone who rang the bell who could not produce the little red card of admission; but when the food and drink in the main terminals began to run out the Chief of Operations summarily opened the club to everyone. It didn't help relieve the congestion outside, it only added to what was within. Almost at once a volunteer doctors' committee seized most of the club to treat the ill and injured from the thickening crowds, and people like Harry Malibert found themselves pushed into the bar area. It was one of the Operations staff, commandeering a gin and tonic at the bar for the sake of the calories more than the booze, who recognized him. "You're Harry Malibert. I heard you lecture once, at Northwestern."

Malibert nodded. Usually when someone said that to him he answered politely, "I hope you enjoyed it," but this time it did not seem appropriate to be normally polite. Or normal at all.

"You showed slides of Arecibo," the man said dreamily. "You said that radio telescope could send a message as far as the Great

Nebula in Andromeda, two million light-years away – if only there was another radio telescope as good as that one there to receive it."

"You remember very well," said Malibert, surprised.

"You made a big impression, Dr Malibert." The man glanced at his watch, debated, took another sip of his drink. "It really sounded wonderful, using the big telescopes to listen for messages from alien civilizations somewhere in space – maybe hearing some, maybe making contact, maybe not being alone in the universe any more. You made me wonder why we hadn't seen some of these people already, or anyway heard from them – but maybe," he finished, glancing bitterly at the ranked and guarded aircraft outside, "maybe now we know why."

Malibert watched him go, and his heart was leaden. The thing he had given his professional career to – SETI, the Search for Extra-Terrestrial Intelligence – no longer seemed to matter. If the bombs went off, as everyone said they must, then that was ended for a good long time, at least—

Gabble of voices at the end of the bar; Malibert turned, leaned over the mahogany, peered. The *Please Stand By* slide had vanished, and a young black woman with pomaded hair, voice trembling, was delivering a news bulletin:

"—the president has confirmed that a nuclear attack has begun against the United States. Missiles have been detected over the Arctic, and they are incoming. Everyone is ordered to seek shelter and remain there pending instructions—"

Yes. It was ended, thought Malibert, at least for a good long time.

The surprising thing was that the news that it had begun changed nothing. There were no screams, no hysteria. The order to seek shelter meant nothing at John F. Kennedy Airport, where there was no shelter any better than the building they were in. And that, no doubt, was not too good. Malibert remembered clearly the strange aerodynamic shape of the terminal's roof. Any blast anywhere nearby would tear that off and sent it sailing over the bay to the Rockaways, and probably a lot of the people inside with it.

But there was nowhere else to go.

There were still camera crews at work, heaven knew why. The television set was showing crowds in Times Square and Newark, a clot of automobiles stagnating on the George Washington Bridge, their drivers abandoning them and running for the Jersey shore. A hundred people were peering around each other's heads to catch glimpses of the screen, but all that anyone said was to call out when he recognized a building or a street.

Orders rang out: "You people will have to move back! We need the room! Look, some of you, give us a hand with these patients." Well, that seemed useful, at least. Malibert volunteered at once and was given the care of a young boy, teeth chattering, hot with fever. "He's had tetracycline," said the doctor who turned the boy over to him. "Clean him up if you can, will you? He ought to be all right if—"

If any of them were, thought Malibert, not requiring her to finish the sentence. How did you clean a young boy up? The question answered itself when Malibert found the boy's trousers soggy and the smell told him what the moisture was. Carefully he laid the child on a leather love seat and removed the pants and sopping under-shorts. Naturally the boy had not come with a change of clothes. Malibert solved that with a pair of his own jockey shorts out of his briefcase – far too big for the child, or course, but since they were meant to fit tightly and elastically they stayed in place when Malibert pulled them up to the waist. Then he found paper towels and pressed the blue jeans as dry as he could. It was not very dry. He grimaced, laid them over a bar stool and sat on them for a while, drying them with body heat. They were only faintly wet ten minutes later when he put them back on the child—

San Francisco, the television said, had ceased to transmit.

Malibert saw the Operations man working his way toward him and shook his head. "It's begun," Malibert said, and the man looked around. He put his face close to Malibert's

"I can get you out of here," he whispered. "There's an Icelandic DC-8 loading right now. No announcement. They'd be rushed if they did. There's room for you, Dr Malibert."

It was like an electric shock. Malibert trembled. Without knowing why he did it, he said, "Can I put the boy on instead?"

The Operations man looked annoyed. "Take him with you, of course," he said. "I didn't know you had a son."

"I don't," said Malibert. But not out loud. And when they were in the jet he held the boy in his lap as tenderly as though he were his own.

If there was no panic in the Ambassador Club at Kennedy there was plenty of it everywhere else in the world. What everyone in the super-power cities knew was that their lives were at stake. Whatever they did might be in vain, and yet they had to do something. Anything! Run, hide, dig, brace, stow … pray. The city people tried to desert the metropolises for the open safety of the country, and the farmers and the exurbanites sought the stronger, safer buildings of the cities.

And the missiles fell.

The bombs that had seared Hiroshima and Nagasaki were struck matches compared to the hydrogen-fusion flares that ended eighty million lives in those first hours. Firestorms fountained above a hundred cities. Winds of 300 kilometers an hour pulled in cars and debris and people, and they all became ash that rose to the sky. Splatters of melted rock and dust sprayed into the air.

The sky darkened.

Then it grew darker still.

When the Icelandic jet landed at Keflavik Airport Malibert carried the boy down the passage to the little stand marked *Immigration*. The line was long, for most of the passengers had no passports at all, and the immigration woman was very tired of making out temporary entrance permits by the time Malibert reached her. "He's my son," Malibert lied. "My wife has his passport, but I don't know where my wife is."

She nodded wearily. She pursed her lips, looked toward the door beyond which her superior sat sweating and initialing reports, then shrugged and let them through. Malibert took the boy to a door marked *Snirting*, which seemed to be the Icelandic word for toilets, and was relieved to see that at least Timothy was able to stand by himself while he urinated, although his eyes stayed half closed. His head was very hot. Malibert prayed for a doctor in Reykjavik.

In the bus the English-speaking tour guide in charge of them – she had nothing else to do, for her tour would never arrive – sat on the arm of a first-row seat with a microphone in her hand and chattered vivaciously to the refugees. "Chicago? Ya, is gone, Chicago. And Detroit and Pittis-burrug – is bad. New York? Certainly New York too!" she said severely, and the big tears rolling down her cheek made Timothy cry too.

Malibert hugged him. "Don't worry, Timmy," he said. "No one would bother bombing Reykjavik." And no one would have. But when the bus was ten miles farther along there was a sudden glow in the clouds ahead of them that made them squint. Someone in the USSR had decided that it was time for neatening up loose threads. That someone, whoever remained in whatever remained of their central missile control, had realized that no one had taken out that supremely, insultingly dangerous bastion of imperialist American interests in the North Atlantic, the United States airbase at Keflavik.

Unfortunately, by then EMP and attrition had compromised the accuracy of their aim. Malibert had been right. No one would have bothered bombing Reykjavik – on purpose – but a forty-mile miss did the job anyway, and Reykjavik ceased to exist.

They had to make a wide detour inland to avoid the fires and the radiation. And as the sun rose on their first day in Iceland, Malibert, drowsing over the boy's bed after the Icelandic nurse had shot him full of antibiotics, saw the daybreak in awful, sky-drenching red.

It was worth seeing, for in the days to come there was no daybreak at all.

The worst was the darkness, but at first that did not seem urgent. What was urgent was rain. A trillion trillion dust particles nucleated water vapour. Drops formed. Rain fell – torrents of rain; sheets and cascades of rain. The rivers swelled. The Mississippi overflowed, and the Ganges, and the Yellow. The High Dam at Aswan spilled water over its lip, then crumbled. The rains came where rains came never. The Sahara knew flash floods. The Flaming Mountains at the edge of the Gobi flamed no more; a ten-year supply of rain came down in a week and rinsed the dusty slopes bare.

And the darkness stayed.

The human race lives always eighty days from starvation. That is the sum of stored food, globe wide. It met the nuclear winter with no more and no less.

The missiles went off on 11 June. If the world's larders had been equally distributed, on 30 August the last mouthful would have been eaten. The starvation deaths would have begun and ended in the next six weeks; exit the human race.

The larders were not equally distributed. The Northern Hemisphere was caught on one foot, fields sown, crops not yet grown. Nothing did grow there. The seedlings poked up through the dark earth for sunlight, found none, died. Sunlight was shaded out by the dense clouds of dust exploded out of the ground by the H-bombs. It was the Cretaceous repeated; extinction was in the air.

There were mountains of stored food in the rich countries of North America and Europe, of course, but they melted swiftly. The rich countries had much stored wealth in the form of their livestock. Every steer was a million calories of protein and fat. When it was slaughtered, it saved thousands of other calories of grain and roughage for every day lopped off its life in feed. The cattle and pigs and sheep – even the goats and horses; even the pet bunnies and the chicks; even the very kittens and hamsters – they all died quickly and were eaten, to eke out the stores of canned foods and root vegetables and grain. There was no rationing of the slaughtered meat. It had to be eaten before it spoiled.

Of course, even in the rich countries the supplies were not equally distributed. The herds and the grain elevators were not located on Times Square or in the Loops. It took troops to convoy corn from Iowa to Boston and Dallas and Philadelphia. Before long, it took killing. Then it could not be done at all.

So the cities starved first. As the convoys of soldiers made the changeover from seizing food for the cities to seizing food for themselves, the riots began, and the next wave of mass death. These casualties didn't usually die of hunger. They died of someone else's.

It didn't take long. By the end of "summer" the frozen remnants of the cities were all the same. A few thousand skinny, freezing desperadoes survived in each, sitting guard over their troves of canned and dried and frozen foodstuffs.

Every river in the world was running sludgy with mud to its mouth, as the last of the trees and grasses died and relaxed their grip on the soil. Every rain washed dirt away. As the winter dark deepened the rains turned to snow. The Flaming Mountains were sheeted in ice now, ghostly, glass fingers uplifted to the gloom. Men could walk across the Thames at London now, the few men who were left. And across the Hudson, across the Whangpoo, across the Missouri between the two Kansas Cities. Avalanches rumbled down on what was left of Denver. In the stands of dead timber grubs flourished. The starved predators scratched them out and devoured them. Some of the predators were human. The last of the Hawaiians were finally grateful for their termites.

A Western human being – comfortably pudgy on a diet of 2,800 calories a day, resolutely jogging to keep the flab away or mournfully conscience-stricken at the thickening thighs and the waistbands that won't quite close – can survive for forty-five days without food. By then the fat is gone. Protein reabsorption of the muscles is well along. The plump housewife or businessman is a starving scarecrow. Still, even then care and nursing can still restore health.

Then it gets worse.

Dissolution attacks the nervous system. Blindness begins. The flesh of the gums recedes, and the teeth fall out. Apathy becomes pain, then agony, then coma.

Then death. Death for almost every person on Earth...

For forty days and forty nights the rain fell, and so did the temperature. Iceland froze over.

To Harry Malibert's astonishment and dawning relief, Iceland was well equipped to do that. It was one of the few places on Earth that could be submerged in snow and ice and still survive.

There is a ridge of volcanoes that goes almost around the Earth. The part that lies between America and Europe is called the Mid-Atlantic Ridge, and most of it is under water. Here and there, like boils erupting along a forearm, volcanic islands poke up above the surface. Iceland is one of them. It was because Iceland was volcanic that it could survive when most places died of freezing, but it was also because it had been cold in the first place.

The survival authorities put Malibert to work as soon as they found out who he was. There was no job opening for a radio astronomer interested in contacting far-off (and very likely non-existent) alien races. There was, however, plenty of work for persons with scientific training, especially if they had the engineering skills

of a man who had run Arecibo for two years. When Malibert was
not nursing Timothy Clary through the slow and silent convales-
cence from his pneumonia, he was calculating heat losses and
pumping rates for the piped geothermal water.

Iceland filled itself with enclosed space. It heated the spaces with
water from the boiling underground springs.

Of heat it had plenty. Getting the heat from the geyser fields to
the enclosed spaces was harder. The hot water was as hot as ever,
since it did not depend at all on sunlight for its calories, but it took
a lot more of it to keep out a $-30°C$ chill than a $+5°C$ one. It wasn't
just to keep the surviving people warm that they needed energy. It
was to grow food.

Iceland had always had a lot of geothermal greenhouses. The
flowering ornamentals were ripped out and food plants put in their
place. There was no sunlight to make the vegetables and grains
grow, so the geothermal power-generating plants were put on max
output. Solar-spectrum incandescents flooded the trays with
photons. Not just in the old greenhouses. Gymnasia, churches,
schools – they all began to grow food under the glaring lights. There
was other food, too, metric tons of protein baaing and starving in
the hills. The herds of sheep were captured and slaughtered and
dressed – and put outside again, to freeze until needed. The animals
that froze to death on the slopes were bulldozed into heaps of a
hundred, and left where they were. Geodetic maps were carefully
marked to show the location of each heap.

It was, after all, a blessing that Reykjavik had been nuked. That
meant half a million fewer people for the island's resources to feed.

When Malibert was not calculating load factors, he was out in the
desperate cold, urging on the workers. Sweating navvies tried to
muscle shrunken fittings together in icy foxholes that their body
heat kept filling with icewater. They listened patiently as Malibert
tried to give orders – his few words of Icelandic were almost useless,
but even the navvies sometimes spoke tourist-English. They checked
their radiation monitors, looked up at the storms overhead, returned
to their work and prayed. Even Malibert almost prayed when one
day, trying to locate the course of the buried coastal road, he looked
out on the sea ice and saw a grey-white ice hummock that was not
an ice hummock. It was just at the limits of visibility, dim on the

fringe of the road crew's work lights, and it moved. "A polar bear!"
he whispered to the head of the work crew, and everyone stopped
while the beast shambled out of sight.

From then on they carried rifles.

When Malibert was not (incompetent) technical advisor to the
task of keeping Iceland warm or (almost incompetent, but
learning) substitute father to Timothy Clary, he was trying
desperately to calculate survival changes. Not just for them; for
the entire human race. With all the desperate flurry of survival
work, the Icelanders spared time to think of the future. A study
team was created, physicists from the University of Reykjavik,
the surviving Supply officer from the Keflavik airbase, a meteor-
ologist on work-study from the University of Leyden to learn
about North Atlantic air masses. They met in the gasthuis where
Malibert lived with the boy, and usually Timmy sat silent next to
Malibert while they talked. What they wanted was to know how
long the dust cloud would persist. Some day the particles would
finish dropping from the sky, and then the world could be reborn
– if enough survived to parent a new race, anyway. But when?
They could not tell. They did not know how long, how cold, how
killing the nuclear winter would be. "We don't know the mega-
tonnage," said Malibert, "we don't know what atmospheric
changes have taken place, we don't know the rate of insolation.
We only know it will be bad."

"It is already bad," grumbled Thorsid Magnesson, Director of
Public Safety. (Once that office had had something to do with
catching criminals, when the major threat to safety was crime.)

"It will get worse," said Malibert, and it did. The cold deepened.
The reports from the rest of the world dwindled. They plotted maps
to show what they knew to show. One set of missile maps, to show
where the strikes had been – within a week that no longer mattered,
because the deaths from cold already began to outweigh those from
blast. They plotted isotherm maps, based on the scattered weather
reports that came in – maps that had to be changed every day, as the
freezing line marched toward the Equator. Finally the maps were
irrelevant. The whole world was cold then. They plotted fatality
maps – the percentages of deaths in each area, as they could infer

them from the reports they received, but those maps soon became too frightening to plot.

The British Isles died first, not because they were nuked but because they were not. There were too many people alive there. Britain never owned more than a four-day supply of food. When the ships stopped coming they starved. So did Japan. A little later, so did Bermuda and Hawaii and Canada's off-shore provinces; and then it was the continents' turn.

And Timmy Clary listened to every word.

The boy didn't talk much. He never asked after his parents, not after the first few days. He did not hope for good news, and did not want bad. The boy's infection was cured, but the boy himself was not. He ate half of what a hungry child should devour. He ate that only when Malibert coaxed him.

The only thing that made Timmy look alive was the rare times when Malibert could talk to him about space. There were many in Iceland who knew about Harry Malibert and SETI, and a few who cared about it almost as much as Malibert himself. When time permitted they would get together, Malibert and his groupies. There was Lars the postman (now pick-and-shovel ice excavator, since there was no mail), Ingar the waitress from the Loftleider Hotel (now stitching heavy drapes to help insulate dwelling walls), Elda the English teacher (now practical nurse, frostbite cases a speciality). There were others, but those three were always there when they could get away. They were Harry Malibert fans who had read his books and dreamed with him of radio messages from weird aliens from Aldebaran, or worldships that could carry million-person populations across the galaxy, on voyages of a hundred thousand years. Timmy listened, and drew sketches of the worldships. Malibert supplied him with dimensions. "I talked to Gerry Webb," he said, "and he'd worked it out in detail. It is a matter of rotation rates and strength of materials. To provide the proper simulated gravity for the people in the ships, the shape has to be a cylinder and it has to spin – sixteen kilometers is what the diameter must be. Then the cylinder must be long enough to provide space, but not so long that the dynamics of spin cause it to wobble or bend – perhaps sixty kilometers long. One part to live in. One part to store fuel. And at the end, a reaction chamber where hydrogen fusion thrusts the ship across the Galaxy."

"Hydrogen bombs," said the boy. "Harry? Why don't the bombs wreck the worldship?"

"It's engineering," said Malibert honestly, "and I don't know the details. Gerry was going to give his paper at the Portsmouth meeting; it was one reason I was going." But, of course, there would never be a British Interplanetary Society meeting in Portsmouth now, ever again.

Elda said uneasily, "It is time for lunch soon. Timmy? Will you eat some soup if I make it?" And did make it, whether the boy promised or not. Elda's husband had worked at Keflavik in the PX, an accountant; unfortunately he had been putting in overtime there when the follow-up missile did what the miss had failed to do, and so Elda had no husband left, not enough even to bury.

Even with the earth's hot water pumped full velocity through the straining pipes it was not warm in the gasthuis. She wrapped the boy in blankets and sat near him while he dutifully spooned up the soup. Lars and Ingar sat holding hands and watching the boy eat. "To hear a voice from another star," Lars said suddenly, "that would have been fine."

"There are no voices," said Ingar bitterly. "Not even ours now. We have the answer to the Fermi paradox."

And when the boy paused in his eating to ask what that was, Harry Malibert explained it as carefully as he could:

"It is named after Enrico Fermi, a scientist. He said, 'We know that there are many billions of stars like our sun. Our sun has planets, therefore it is reasonable to assume that some of the other stars do also. One of our planets has living things on it. Us, for instance, as well as trees and germs and horses. Since there are so many stars, it seems almost certain that some of them, at least, have also living things. People. People as smart as we are – or smarter. People who can build spaceships, or send radio messages to other stars, as we can.' Do you understand so far, Timmy?" The boy nodded, frowning, but – Malibert was delighted to see – kept on eating his soup. "Then, the question Fermi asked was, 'Why haven't some of them come to see us?'"

"Like in the movies," the boy nodded. "The flying saucers."

"All those movies are made-up stories, Timmy. Like Jack and the Beanstalk, or Oz. Perhaps some creatures from space have come to see us sometime, but there is no good evidence that this is so. I feel sure there would be evidence if it had happened. There would have to be. If there were many such visits, ever, then at least one would have dropped the Martian equivalent of a McDonald's Big Mac box, or a used Sirian flash cube, and it would have been found and shown to be from somewhere other than the Earth. None ever has. So there are only three possible answers to Dr Fermi's question. One, there is no other life. Two, there is, but they want to leave us alone. They don't want to contact us, perhaps because we frighten them with our violence, or for some reason we can't even guess at. And the third reason—" Elda made a quick gesture, but Malibert shook his head—"is that perhaps as soon as any people get smart enough to do all those things that get them into space – when they have all the technology we do – they also have such terrible bombs and weapons that they can't control them any more. So a war breaks out. And they kill themselves off before they are fully grown up."

"Like now," Timothy said, nodding seriously to show he understood. He had finished his soup, but instead of taking the plate away Elda hugged him in her arms and tried not to weep.

The world was totally dark now. There was no day or night, and would not be again for no one could say how long. The rains and snows had stopped. Without sunlight to suck water up out of the oceans there was no moisture left in the atmosphere to fall. Floods had been replaced by freezing droughts. Two meters down the soil of Iceland was steel hard, and the navvies could no longer dig. There was no hope of laying additional pipes. When more heat was needed all that could be done was to close off buildings and turn off their heating pipes. Elda's patients now were less likely to be frostbite and more to be the listlessness of radiation sickness as volunteers raced in and out of the Reykjavik ruins to find medicine and food. No one was spared that job. When Elda came back on a snowmobile from a foraging trip to the Loftleider Hotel she brought back a present for the boy. Candy bars and postcards from the gift shop; the candy bars had to be shared, but the postcards were all for him. "Do you know what these are?" she asked. The cards showed huge, squat, ugly men and women in the costumes of a thousand years ago. "They're trolls. We have myths in Iceland that the trolls lived here. They're still here, Timmy, or so they say; the mountains are trolls that just got too old and tired to move any more."

"They're made-up stories, right?" the boy asked seriously, and did not grin until she assured him they were. Then he made a joke. "I guess the trolls won," he said.

"Ach, Timmy!" Elda was shocked. But at least the boy was capable of joking, she told herself, and even graveyard humor was better than none. Life had become a little easier for her with the new patients – easier because for the radiation-sick there was very little that could be done – and she bestirred herself to think of ways to entertain the boy.

And found a wonderful one.

Since fuel was precious there were no excursions to see the sights of Iceland-under-the-ice. There was no way to see them anyway in the eternal dark. But when a hospital chopper was called up to travel empty to Stokksnes on the eastern shore to bring back a child with a broken back, she begged space for Malibert and Timmy. Elda's own ride was automatic, as duty nurse for the wounded child. "An avalanche crushed his house," she explained. "It is right under the mountains, Stokksnes, and landing there will be a little tricky, I think. But we can come in from the sea and make it safe. At least in the landing lights of the helicopter something can be seen."

They were luckier than that. There was more light. Nothing came through the clouds, where the billions of particles that had once been Elda's husband added to the trillions of trillions that had been Detroit and Marseilles and Shanghai to shut out the sky. But in the clouds and under them were snakes and sheets of dim color, sprays of dull red, fans of pale green. The aurora borealis did not give much light. But there was no other light at all except for the faint glow from the pilot's instrument panel. As their eyes widened they could see the dark shapes of the Vatnajökull slipping by below them. "*Big* trolls," cried the boy happily, and Elda smiled too as she hugged him.

The pilot did as Elda had predicted, down the slopes of the eastern range, out over the sea, and cautiously back in to the little fishing village. As they landed, red-tipped flashlights guiding them, the copter's landing lights picked out a white lump, vaguely saucer-shaped. "Radar dish," said Malibert to the boy, pointing.

Timmy pressed his nose to the freezing window. "Is it one of them, Daddy Harry? The things that could talk to the stars?"

The pilot answered: "Ach, no, Timmy – military, it is." And Malibert said:

"They wouldn't put one of those here, Timothy. It's too far north. You wanted a place for a big radio telescope that could search the whole sky, not just the little piece of it you can see from Iceland."

And while they helped slide the stretcher with the broken child into the helicopter, gently, kindly as they could be, Malibert was thinking about those places, Arecibo and Woomara and Socorro and all the others. Every one of them was now dead and certainly broken with a weight of ice and shredded by the mean winds. Crushed, rusted, washed away, all those eyes on space were blinded now; and the thought saddened Harry Malibert, but not for long. More gladdening than anything sad was the fact that, for the first time, Timothy had called him "Daddy."

In one ending to the story, when at last the sun came back it was too late. Iceland had been the last place where human beings survived, and Iceland had finally starved. There was nothing alive anywhere on Earth that spoke, or invented machines, or read books, Fermi's terrible third answer was the right one after all.

But there exists another ending. In this one the sun came back in time. Perhaps it was just barely in time, but the food had not yet run out when daylight brought the first touches of green in some parts of the world, and plants began to grow again from frozen or hoarded seed. In this ending Timothy lived to grow up. When he was old enough, and after Malibert and Elda had got around to marrying, he married one of their daughters. And of their descendants – two generations or a dozen generations later – one was alive on the day when Fermi's paradox became a quaintly amusing old worry, as irrelevant and comical as a fifteenth-century mariner's fear of falling off the edge of the flat Earth. On that day the skies spoke, and those who lived in them came to call.

Perhaps that is the true ending of the story, and in it the human race chose not to squabble and struggle within itself, and so extinguish itself finally into the dark. In this ending human beings survived, and saved all the science and beauty of life, and greeted their star-born visitors with joy...

But that is in fact what did happen!

At least, one would like to think so.

SLEEPOVER

Alastair Reynolds

Alastair Reynolds is one of Britain's most popular and bestselling writers of science fiction. He began selling stories to Interzone *in 1990, but it wasn't until the late 1990s that his output increased significantly. He made a big impact with his first novel,* Revelation Space *(2000), which was shortlisted for both the BSFA and Arthur C. Clarke awards. His second novel,* Chasm City *(2001) won the BSFA Award. Reynolds worked for the European Space Agency until 2004 when he turned to writing full time. The following story, specially written for this anthology, is not part of the Revelation Space series. It was developed from notes for an unwritten novel and maybe one day that novel will be completed, for we need to know the fate of the Earth. Here we have one of the more unusual apocalyptic ideas, but I'll let Reynolds do the explaining.*

THEY BROUGHT GAUNT out of hibernation on a blustery day in early spring. He came to consciousness in a steel-framed bed in a grey-walled room that had the economical look of something assembled in a hurry from prefabricated parts. Two people were standing at the foot of the bed, looking only moderately interested in his plight. One of them was a man, cradling a bowl of something and spooning quantities of it into his mouth, as if he was eating his breakfast on the run. He had cropped white hair and the leathery complexion of someone who spent a lot of time outside. Next to him was a woman with longer hair, greying rather than white, and with much darker skin. Like the man, she was wiry of build and dressed in crumpled grey overalls, with a heavy equipment belt dangling from her hips.

"You in one piece, Gaunt?" she asked, while her companion spooned in another mouthful of his breakfast. "You compos mentis?"

Gaunt squinted against the brightness of the room's lighting, momentarily adrift from his memories.

"Where am I?" he asked. His voice came out raw, as if he had been in a loud bar the night before.

"In a room, being woken up," the woman said. "You remember going under, right?"

He grasped for memories, something specific to hold on to. Green-gowned doctors in a clean surgical theatre, his hand signing the last of the release forms before they plumbed him into the machines. The drugs flooding his system, the utter absence of sadness or longing as he bid farewell to the old world, with all its vague disappointments.

"I think so."

"What's your name?" the man asked.

"Gaunt." He had to wait a moment for the rest of it to come. "Marcus Gaunt."

"Good," he said, smearing a hand across his lips. "That's a positive sign."

"I'm Clausen," the woman said. "This is Da Silva. We're your wake-up team. You remember Sleepover?"

"I'm not sure."

"Think hard, Gaunt," she said. "It won't cost us anything to put you back under, if you don't think you're going to work out for us."

Something in Clausen's tone convinced him to work hard at retrieving the memory. "The company," he said. "Sleepover was the company. The one that put me under. The one that put everyone under."

"Brain cells haven't mushed on us," Da Silva said.

Clausen nodded, but showed nothing in the way of jubilation in him having got the answer right. It was more that he'd spared the two of them a minor chore, that was all. "I like the way he says 'everyone'. Like it was universal."

"Wasn't it?" Da Silva asked.

"Not for him. Gaunt was one of the first under. Didn't you read his file?"

Da Silva grimaced. "Sorry. Got sidetracked."

"He was one of the first 200,000," Clausen said. "The ultimate exclusive club. What did you call yourselves, Gaunt?"

"The Few," he said. "It was an accurate description. What else were we going to call ourselves?"

"Lucky sons of bitches," Clausen said.

"Do you remember the year you went under?" Da Silva asked. "You were one of the early ones, it must've been some time near the middle of the century."

"It was 2058. I can tell you the exact month and day if you wish. Maybe not the time of day."

"You remember why you went under, of course," Clausen said.

"Because I could," Gaunt said. "Because anyone in my position would have done the same. The world was getting better, it was coming out of the trough. But it wasn't there yet. And the doctors kept telling us that the immortality breakthrough was just around the corner, year after year. Always just out of reach. Just hang on in there, they said. But we were all getting older. Then the doctors said that while they couldn't give us eternal life just yet, they could give us the means to skip over the years until it happened." Gaunt forced himself to sit up in the bed, strength returning to his limbs even as he grew angrier at the sense that he was not being treated with sufficient deference, that – worse – he was being judged. "There was nothing evil in what we did. We didn't hurt anyone or take anything away from anyone else. We just used the means at our disposal to access what was coming to us anyway."

"Who's going to break it to him?" Clausen asked, looking at Da Silva.

"You've been sleeping for nearly 160 years," the man said. "It's April, 2217. You've reached the twenty-third century."

Gaunt took in the drab mundanity of his surroundings again. He had always had some nebulous idea of the form his wake-up would take and it was not at all like this.

"Are you lying to me?"

"What do you think?" asked Clausen.

He held up his hand. It looked, as near as he could remember, exactly the way it had been before. The same age-spots, the same prominent veins, the same hairy knuckles, the same scars and loose, lizardy skin.

"Bring me a mirror," he said, with an ominous foreboding.

"I'll save you the bother," Clausen said. "The face you'll see is the one you went under with, give or take. We've done nothing to you except treat superficial damage caused by the early freezing protocols. Physiologically, you're still a sixty-year-old man, with about twenty or thirty years ahead of you."

"Then why have you woken me, if the process isn't ready?"

"There isn't one," Da Silva said. "And there won't be, at least not for a long, long time. Afraid we've got other things to worry about now. Immortality's the least of our problems."

"I don't understand."

"You will, Gaunt," Clausen said. "Everyone does in the end. You've been preselected for aptitude, anyway. Made your fortune in computing, didn't you?" She didn't wait for him to answer. "You worked with artificial intelligence, trying to make thinking machines."

One of the vague disappointments hardened into a specific, life-souring defeat. All the energy he had put into one ambition, all the friends and lovers he had burned up along the way, shutting them out of his life while he focused on that one white whale.

"It never worked out."

"Still made you a rich man along the way," she said.

"Just a means of raising money. What does it have to do with my revival?"

Clausen seemed on the verge of answering his question before something made her change her mind. "Clothes in the bedside locker: they should fit you. You want breakfast?"

"I don't feel hungry."

"Your stomach will take some time to settle down. Meantime, if you feel like puking, do it now rather than later. I don't want you messing up my ship."

He had a sudden lurch of adjusting preconceptions. The prefabricated surroundings, the background hum of distant machines, the utilitarian clothing of his wake-up team: perhaps he was aboard some kind of spacecraft, sailing between the worlds. The twenty-third century, he thought. Time enough to establish an interplanetary civilization, even if it only extended as far as the solar system.

"Are we in a ship now?"

"Fuck, no," Clausen said, sneering at his question. "We're in Patagonia."

He got dressed, putting on underwear, a white T-shirt and over that the same kind of grey overalls as his hosts had been wearing. The room was cool and damp and he was glad of the clothes once he had them on. There were lace-up boots that were tight around the toes, but otherwise serviceable. The materials all felt perfectly mundane and commonplace, even a little frayed and worn in places. At least he was clean and groomed, his hair clipped short and his beard shaved. They must have freshened him up before bringing him to consciousness.

Clausen and Da Silva were waiting in the windowless corridor outside the room. "'Spect you've got a ton of questions," Clausen said. "Along the lines of, why am I being treated like shit rather than royalty? What happened to the rest of the Few, what is this fucked-up, miserable place, and so on?"

"I presume you're going to get round to some answers soon enough."

"Maybe you should tell him the deal now, up-front," Da Silva said. He was wearing an outdoor coat now and had a zip-up bag slung over his shoulder.

"What deal?" Gaunt asked.

"To begin with," Clausen said, "you don't mean anything special to us. We're not impressed by the fact that you just slept 160 years. It's old news. But you're still useful."

"In what way?"

"We're down a man. We run a tight operation here and we can't afford to lose even one member of the team." It was Da Silva speaking now; although there wasn't much between them, Clausen had the sense that he was the slightly more reasonable one of the duo, the one who wasn't radiating quite so much naked antipathy. "Deal is, we train you up and give you work. In return, of course, you're looked after pretty well. Food, clothing, somewhere to sleep, whatever medicine we can provide." He shrugged. "It's the deal we all took. Not so bad when you get used to it."

"And the alternative?"

"Bag you and tag you and put you back in the freezer," Da Silva went on. "Same as all the others. Your choice, of course; work with us, become part of the team, or go back into hibernation and take your chances there."

"We need to be on our way." Clausen said. "Don't want to keep Nero waiting on F."

"Who's Nero?" Gaunt asked.

"Last one we pulled out before you," Da Silva said.

They walked down the corridor, passing a set of open double doors that led into some kind of mess room or commons. Men and women of various ages were sitting around tables, talking quietly as they ate meals or played card games. Everything looked spartan and institutional, from the plastic chairs to the Formica-topped surfaces. Beyond the tables, a rain-washed window framed only a rectangle of grey cloud. Gaunt caught a few glances directed his way, a flicker of waning interest from one or two of the personnel but no one showed any fascination in him. The three of them walked on, ascending stairs to the next level of whatever kind of building they were in. An older man, Chinese-looking, passed in the opposite direction, carrying a grease-smeared wrench. He raised his free hand to Clausen in a silent high-five, Clausen reciprocating. Then they were up another level, passing equipment lockers and electrical distribution cabinets, and then up a spiral stairwell that emerged into a draughty, corrugated-metal shed smelling of oil and ozone. Incongruously, there was an inflatable orange life preserver on one wall of the shed, an old red fire extinguisher on the other.

This is the twenty-third century, Gaunt told himself. As dispiriting as the surroundings were, he had no reason to doubt that this was the reality of life in 2217. He supposed it had always been an article of faith that the world would improve, that the future would be better than the past, shinier and cleaner and faster, but he had not expected to have his nose rubbed in the unwisdom of that faith quite so vigorously.

There was one door leading out of the corrugated-metal shed. Clausen pushed it open against wind, then the three of them stepped outside. They were on the roof of something. There was a square of cracked and oil-stained concrete, marked here and there with lines of fading red paint. A couple of seagulls pecked disconsolately at something in the corner. At least they still had seagulls, Gaunt thought. There hadn't been some awful, life-scouring bio-catastrophe, forcing everyone to live in bunkers.

Sitting on the middle of the roof was a helicopter. It was matt black, a lean, waspish thing made of angles rather than curves, and aside from some sinister bulges and pods, there was nothing particularly futuristic about it. For all Gaunt knew, it could have been based around a model that was in production before he went under.

"You're thinking: shitty-looking helicopter," Clausen said, raising her voice over the wind.

He smiled quickly. "What does it run on? I'm assuming the oil reserves ran dry some time in the last century?"

"Oil," Clausen said, cracking open the cockpit door. "Get in the back, buckle up. Da Silva rides up front with me."

Da Silva slung his zip-up bag into the rear compartment where Gaunt was settling into his position, more than a little apprehensive about what lay ahead. He looked between the backs of the forward seats at the cockpit instrumentation. He'd been in enough private helicopters to know what the manual override controls looked like and there was nothing weirdly incongruous here.

"Where are we going?"

"Running a shift change," Da Silva said, wrapping a pair of earphones around his skull. "Couple of days ago there was an accident out on J platform. Lost Gimenez, and Nero's been hurt. Weather was too bad to do the extraction until today but now we have our window. Reason we thawed you, actually. I'm taking over from Gimenez, so you have to cover for me here."

"You have a labour shortage, so you brought me out of hibernation?"

"That about covers it," Da Silva said. "Clausen figured it wouldn't hurt for you to come along for the ride, get you up to speed."

Clausen flicked a bank of switches in the ceiling. Overhead, the rotor began to turn.

"I guess you have something faster than helicopters, for longer journeys," Gaunt said.

"Nope," Clausen answered. "Other than some boats, helicopters is pretty much it."

"What about intercontinental travel?"

"There isn't any."

"This isn't the world I was expecting!' Gaunt said, straining to make himself heard.

Da Silva leaned around and motioned to the headphones dangling from the seat back. Gaunt put them on and fussed with the microphone until it was in front of his lips.

"I said this isn't the world I was expecting."

"Yeah," Da Silva said. "I heard you the first time."

The rotor reached takeoff speed. Clausen eased the helicopter into the air, the rooftop landing pad falling away below. They scudded sideways, nose down, until they had cleared the side of the building. The walls plunged vertically, Gaunt's guts twisting at the dizzying transition. It hadn't been a building at all, at least not the kind he had been thinking of. The landing pad was on top of a square-ish, industrial-looking structure about the size of a large office block, hazed in scaffolding and gangways, prickly with cranes and chimneys and otherwise unrecognizable protuberances, the structure in turn rising out of the sea on four elephantine legs, the widening bases of which were being ceaselessly pounded by waves. It was an oil rig or production platform of some kind, or at least, something repurposed from one.

It wasn't the only one either. The rig they had taken off from was but one in a major field, rig after rig stretching all the way to the gloomy, grey, rain-hazed horizon. There were dozens, and he had the sense that they didn't stop at the horizon.

"What are these for? I know it's not oil. There can't be enough of it left to justify a drilling operation on this scale. The reserves were close to being tapped out when I went under."

"Dormitories," Da Silva said. "Each of these platforms holds maybe 10,000 sleepers, give or take. They built them out at sea because we need OTEC power to run them, using the heat difference between surface water and deep ocean, and it's much easier if we don't have to run those power cables inland."

"Coming back to bite us now," Clausen said.

"If we'd gone inland, they'd have sent land-dragons instead. They're just adapting to whatever we do," Da Silva said pragmatically.

They sped over oily, roiling waters. "Is this really Patagonia?" Gaunt asked.

"Patagonia offshore sector," Da Silva said. "Sub-sector fifteen. That's our watch. There are about 200 of us, and we look after about 100 rigs, all told."

Gaunt ran the numbers twice, because he couldn't believe what they were telling him. "That's a million sleepers."

"Ten million in the whole of Patagonia offshore," Clausen said. "That surprise you, Gaunt? That ten million people managed to achieve what you and your precious Few did, all those years back?"

"I suppose not," he said, as the truth of it sunk in. "Over time the cost of the process would have decreased, becoming available to people of lesser means. The merely rich, rather than the super-rich. But it was never going to be something available to the masses. Ten million, maybe. Beyond that? Hundreds of millions? I'm sorry, but the economics just don't stack up."

"It's a good thing we don't have economics, then," Da Silva said.

"Patagonia's just a tiny part of the whole," said Clausen. "Two hundred other sectors out there, just as large as this one. That's two billion sleepers, near as it matters."

Gaunt shook his head. "That can't be right. The global population was only eight billion when I went under, and the trend was downwards! You can't tell me that a quarter of the human race is hibernating."

"Maybe it would help if I told you that the current population of the Earth is also two billion, near as it matters," Clausen said. "Almost everyone's asleep. There's just a handful of us still awake, playing caretaker, watching over the rigs and OTEC plants."

"Four hundred thousand waking souls," Da Silva said. "But it actually feels like a lot less than that, since we mostly keep to our assigned sectors."

"You know the real irony?" Clausen said. "We're the ones who get to call ourselves the Few now. The ones who *aren't* sleeping."

"That doesn't leave anyone to actually do anything," Gaunt said. "There's no point in everyone waiting for a cure for death if there's no one alive to do the hard work of making it happen."

Clausen turned round to look back at him, her expression telling him everything he needed to know about her opinion of his intellect.

"It isn't about immortality. It's about survival. It's about doing our bit for the war effort."

"What war?" Gaunt asked.

"The one going on all around us," Clausen said. "The one you made happen."

They came in to land on another rig, one of five that stood close enough to each other to be linked by cables and walkways. The sea was still heavy, huge waves dashing against the concrete piers on which the rigs were supported. Gaunt peered intently at the windows and decks but saw no sign of human activity on any of the structures. He thought back to what Clausen and Da Silva had told him, each time trying to find a reason why they might be lying to him, why they might be going to pathological lengths to hoax him about the nature of the world into which he had woken. Maybe there was a form of mass entertainment that involved waking sleepers such as himself and putting them through the emotional wringer, presenting them with the grimmest possible scenarios, ramping up the misery until they cracked, and only then pulling aside the grey curtains to reveal that, in marvellous point of fact, life in the twenty-third century really was every bit as blue-skied and utopian as he had hoped. That didn't seem very likely, though.

Yet what kind of war required people to be put to sleep in their billions? And why was the caretaker force, the 400,000 waking individuals, stretched so ridiculously thin? Clearly the rigs were largely automated but it had still been necessary to pull him out of sleep because someone else had died in the Patagonia offshore sector. Why not just have more caretakers awake in the first place, so that the system was able to absorb some losses?

With the helicopter safely down on the pad, Clausen and Da Silva told him to follow them into the depths of the other rig. There was very little about it to distinguish it from the one where Gaunt had been woken, save for the fact that it was almost completely deserted, with the only activity coming from skulking repair robots. They were clearly very simple machines, not much smarter than automatic window-cleaners. Given the years of his life that he had given over to the dream of artificial intelligence, it was dismaying to see how little progress – if any – had been made.

"We need to get one thing straight," Gaunt said, when they were deep into the humming bowels of the rig. "I didn't start any wars. You've got the wrong guy here."

"You think we mixed up your records?" Clausen asked. "How did we know about your work on thinking machines?"

"Then you've got the wrong end of the stick. I had nothing do to with wars or the military."

"We know what you did," she said. "The years spent trying to build a true, Turing-compliant artificial intelligence. A thinking, conscious machine."

"Except it was a dead end."

"Still led to some useful spin-offs, didn't it?" she went on. "You cracked the hard problem of language comprehension. Your systems didn't just recognize speech. They were able to understand it on a level no computer system had ever achieved before. Metaphor, simile, sarcasm and understatement, even implication by omission. Of course, it had numerous civilian applications, but that isn't where you made your billions." She looked at him sharply.

"I created a product," Gaunt said. "I simply made it available to whoever could afford it."

"Yes, you did. Unfortunately, your system turned out to be the perfect instrument of mass surveillance for every despotic government left on the planet. Every basket-case totalitarian state still in existence couldn't get its hands on your product fast enough. And you had no qualms whatsoever about selling it, did you?"

Gaunt felt a well-rehearsed argument bubbling up from his subconscious. "No communication tool in history has ever been a single-edged sword."

"And that excuses you, does it?" Clausen asked. Da Silva had been silent in this exchange, observing the two of them as they continued along corridors and down stairwells.

"I'm not asking for absolution. But if you think I started wars, if you think I'm somehow responsible for this ... " He gestured at his surroundings. "This fucked-up state of affairs. Then you're very, very wrong."

"Maybe you weren't solely responsible," Clausen said. "But you were certainly complicit. You and every one else who pursued the dream of artificial intelligence. Driving the world towards the edge of that cliff, without a thought for the consequences. You had no idea what you were unleashing."

"I'm telling you, we unleashed nothing. It didn't work."

They were walking along a suspended gangway now, crossing from one side to the other of some huge space somewhere inside the rig. "Take a look down," Da Silva said. Gaunt didn't want to; he'd never been good with heights and the drainage holes in the floor were already too large for comfort. He forced himself anyway. The four walls of the cubic chamber held rack upon rack of coffin-sized white boxes, stacked thirty high and surrounded by complicated plumbing, accompanied by an equally complex network of access catwalks, ladders and service tracks. Even as Gaunt watched, a robot whirred up to one of the boxes and extracted a module from one end of it, before tracking sideways to deal with another coffin.

"In case you thought we were yanking your chain," Clausen said. "This is real."

The hibernation arrangements for the original Few could not have been more different. Like an Egyptian Pharaoh buried with his worldly possessions, Gaunt had required an entire crypt full of bulky, state-of-the-art cryopreservation and monitoring systems. At any one time, as per his contract with Sleepover, he would have been under the direct care of several living doctors. Just housing a thousand of the Few needed a building the size of a major resort hotel, with about the same power requirements. By contrast this was hibernation on a crushing, maximally efficient industrial scale. People in boxes, stacked like mass-produced commodities, tended by the absolute minimum of living caretakers. He was seeing maybe less than a thousand sleepers in this one chamber, but from that point on Gaunt had no doubt whatsoever that the operation could be scaled up to encompass billions.

All you needed were more rooms like this. More robots and more rigs. Provided you had the power, and provided the planet did not need anyone to do anything else, it was eminently doable.

There was no one to grow crops or distribute food. But that didn't matter because there was almost no one left waking to need feeding. No one to orchestrate the intricate, flickering web of the global finance system. But that didn't matter because there was no longer anything resembling an economy. No need for a transport infrastructure because no one travelled. No need for communications, because no one needed to know what was going on beyond their own sector. No need for *anything* really, save the absolute, life and death essentials. Air to breathe. Rations and medicine for less than half a million people. A trickle of oil, the world's last black hiccough, to keep the helicopters running.

Yes, it could be done. It could easily be done.

"There's a war," Da Silva said. "It's been going on, in some shape or form, since before you went under. But it's probably not the kind of war you're thinking of."

"And where do these people come into it, these sleepers?"

"They have no choice," Clausen said. "They have to sleep. If they don't, we all die."

"We, as in … ?"

"You, me. Us," Da Silva said. "The entire human species."

They collected Nero and the corpse from a sick bay several levels down from the freezer chamber. The corpse was already bagged, a silver-wrapped mummy on a medical trolley. Rather than the man Gaunt had been expecting, Nero turned out to be a tall, willowy woman with an open, friendly face and a mass of salmon-red curls.

"You the newbie, right?" she asked, lifting a coffee mug in salute.

"I guess," Gaunt said uneasily.

"Takes some adjustment, I know. Took a good six months before I realized this wasn't the worst thing that could happen to me. But you'll get there eventually." One of Nero's hands was bandaged, a white mitten with a safety pin stuck through the dressing. "Take it from me, though. Don't go back inside the box." Then she glanced at Clausen. "You *are* giving him a chance about this, aren't you?"

"Of course," Clausen said. "That's the deal."

"Occurs to me sometimes maybe it would be easier if there wasn't a deal, you know," Nero said. "Like, we just give them their duties and to hell with it."

"You wouldn't have been too pleased if we didn't give you the choice," Da Silva said. He was already taking off his coat, settling in for the stay.

"Yeah, but what did I know back then? Six months feels like half a lifetime ago now."

"When did you go under?" Gaunt asked.

"Twenty ninety-two. One of the first 100 million."

"Gaunt's got a head start on you," Clausen said. "Guy was one of the Few. The original Few, the first 200,000."

"Holy shit. That is some head start." Nero narrowed her eyes. "He up to speed on things yet? My recollection is they didn't know what they were getting into back then."

"Most of them didn't," Clausen said.

"Know what?" Gaunt asked.

"Sleepover was a cover, even then," Nero said. "You were being sold a scam. There was never any likelihood of an immortality breakthrough, no matter how long you slept."

"I don't understand. You're saying it was all a con?"

"Of a kind," Nero said. "Not to make money for anyone, but to begin the process of getting the whole of humanity into hibernation. It had to begin small, so that they had time to work the wrinkles out of the technology. If the people in the know had come out into the open and announced their plans, no one would have believed them. And if they had been believed, there'd have been panic and confusion all over the world. So they began with the Few, and then expanded the operation slowly. First a few hundred thousand. Then half a million. Then a million ... so on." She paused. "Establishing a pattern, a normal state of affairs. They kept the lid on it for thirty years. But then the rumours started spreading, the rumours that there was something more to Sleepover."

"The dragons didn't help," Da Silva said. "It was always going to be a tall order explaining those away."

"By the time I went under," Nero said, "most of us knew the score. The world was going to end if we didn't sleep. It was our moral duty, our obligation, to submit to the hibernation rigs. That, or take the euthanasia option. I took the freezer route, but a lot of my friends opted for the pill. Figured the certainty of death was preferable to the lottery of getting into the boxes, throwing the cosmic dice ... " She was looking at Gaunt intently, meeting his eyes as she spoke. "And I knew about this part of the deal, as well. That, at some point, there'd be a chance of me being brought out of sleep to become a caretaker. But, you know, the likelihood of that was vanishingly small. Never thought it would happen to me."

"No one ever does," Clausen said.

"What happened?" Gaunt asked, nodding at the foil-wrapped body.

"Gimenez died when a steam pipe burst down on level eight. I don't think he felt much, it would have been so quick. I got down there as quickly as I could, obviously. Shut off the steam leak and managed to drag Gimenez back to the infirmary."

"Nero was burned getting Gimenez back here," Da Silva said.

"Hey, I'll mend. Just not much good with a screwdriver right now."

"I'm sorry about Gimenez," Clausen said.

"You don't need to be. Gimenez never really liked it here. Always figured he'd made the wrong decision, sticking with us rather than going back into the box. Tried to talk him round, of course, but it was like arguing with a wall." Nero ran her good hand through her curls. "Not saying I didn't get on with the guy. But there's no arguing that he's better off now than he was before."

"He's dead, though," Gaunt said.

"Technically. But I ran a full blood-scrub on him after the accident, pumped him full of cryoprotectant. We don't have any spare slots here, but they can put him back in a box on the operations rig."

"My box," Gaunt said. "The one I was in."

"There are other slots," Da Silva corrected. "Gimenez going back in doesn't preclude you following him, if that's what you want."

"If Gimenez was so unhappy, why didn't you just let him go back into the box earlier?"

"Not the way it works," Clausen said. "He made his choice. Afterwards, we put a lot of time and energy into bringing him up to speed, making him mesh with the team. You think we were going to willingly throw all that expenditure away, just because he changed his mind?"

"He never stopped pulling his weight," Nero said. "Say what you will about Gimenez but he didn't let the team down. And what happened to him down on eight *was* an accident."

"I never doubted it," Da Silva said. "He was a good guy. It's just a shame he couldn't make the adjustment."

"Maybe it'll work out for him now," Nero said. "One-way ticket to the future. Done his caretaker stint, so the next time he's revived, it'll be because we finally got through this shit. It'll be because we won the war, and we can all wake up again. They'll find a way to fix him up, I'm sure. And if they can't, they'll just put him under again until they have the means."

"Sounds like he got a good deal out of it in the end," Gaunt said.

"The only good deal is being alive," Nero replied. "That's what we're doing now, all of us. Whatever happens, we're alive, we're breathing, we're having conscious thoughts. We're not frozen bodies stacked in boxes, merely existing from one instant to the next." She gave a shrug. "My fifty cents, that's all. You want to go back in the box, let someone else shoulder the burden, don't let me talk you out of it." Then she looked at Da Silva. "You gonna be all right here on your own, until I'm straightened out?"

"Someone comes up I can't deal with, I'll let you know," Da Silva said.

Nero and Da Silva went through a checklist, Nero making sure her replacement knew everything he needed to, and then they made their farewells. Gaunt couldn't tell how long they were going to be leaving Da Silva alone out here, whether it was weeks or months. He seemed resigned to his fate, as if this kind of solitary duty was something they were all expected to do now and then. Given that there had been two people on duty here until Gimenez's death, Gaunt wondered why they didn't just thaw out another sleeper so that Da Silva wouldn't have to work on his own while Nero's hand was healing.

Then, no more than half an hour after his arrival, they were back in the helicopter again, powering back to the operations rig. The weather had worsened in the meantime, the seas lashing even higher against the rigs' legs, and the horizon was now obscured behind curtains of storming rain, broken only by the flash of lightning.

"This was bad timing," he heard Nero say. "Maybe you should have let me stew until this system had passed. It's not like Gimenez couldn't wait."

"We were already overdue on the extraction," Clausen said. "If the weather clamps down, this might be our last chance for days."

"They tried to push one through yesterday, I heard."

"Out in Echo field. Partial coalescence."

"Did you see it?"

"Only on the monitors. Close enough for me."

"We should put guns on the rigs."

"And where would the manpower come from, exactly? We're just barely holding on as it is, without adding more shit to worry about."

The two women were sitting up front; Gaunt was in the back with Gimenez's foil-wrapped corpse for company. They had folded back one seat to make room for the stretchered form.

"I don't really have a choice, do I," he said.

"Course you have a choice," Nero answered.

"I mean, morally. I've seen what it's like for you people. You're stretched to breaking point just keeping this operation from falling apart. Why don't you wake up more sleepers?"

"Hey, that's a good point," Clausen said. "Why don't we?"

Gaunt ignored her sarcasm. "You've just left that man alone, looking after that whole complex. How can I turn my back on you, and still have any self-respect?"

"Plenty of people do exactly that," Nero said.

"How many? What fraction?"

"More than half agree to stay," Clausen said. "Good enough for you?"

"But like you said, most of the sleepers would have known what they were getting into. I still don't."

"And you think that changes things, means we can cut you some slack?" Clausen asked. "Like we're gonna say, it's fine man, go back into the box, we can do without you this time."

"What you need to understand," Nero said, "is that the future you were promised isn't coming. Not for centuries, not until we're out of this mess. And no one has a clue how long that could take. Meanwhile, the sleepers don't have unlimited shelf life. You think the equipment never fails? You think we don't sometimes lose someone because a box breaks down?"

"Of course not."

"You go back in the box, you're gambling on something that might never happen. Stay awake, at least there are certainties. At least you know you'll die doing something useful, something worthwhile."

"It would help if you told me why," Gaunt said.

"Someone has to look after things," Nero said. "The robots take care of the rigs, but who takes care of the robots?"

"I mean, why is it that everyone has to sleep? Why is that so damned important?"

Something flashed on the console. Clausen pressed a hand against her headphones, listening to something. After a few seconds he heard her say: "Roger, vectoring three two five." Followed by an almost silent, "Fuck. All we need."

"That wasn't a weather alert," Nero said.

"What's happening?" Gaunt asked, as the helicopter made a steep turn, the sea tilting up to meet him.

"Nothing you need worry about," Clausen said.

The helicopter levelled out on its new course, flying higher than before – so it seemed to Gaunt – but also faster, the motor noise louder in the cabin, various indicator lights showing on the console that had not been lit before. Clausen silenced alarms as they came on, flipping the switches with the casual insouciance of someone who was well used to flying under tense circumstances and knew exactly what her machine could and couldn't tolerate, more intimately perhaps than the helicopter itself, which was after all only a dumb machine. Rig after rig passed on either side, dark straddling citadels, and then the field began to thin out. Through what little visibility remained Gaunt saw only open sea, a plain of undulating, white-capped grey. As the winds harried it the water moved like the skin of some monstrous breathing thing, sucking in and out with a terrible restlessness.

"There," Nero said, pointing out to the right. "Breach glow. Shit; I thought we were meant to be avoiding it, not getting closer."

Clausen banked the helicopter again. "So did I. Either they sent me a duff vector or there's more than one incursion going on."

"Won't be the first time. Bad weather always does bring them out. Why is that?"

"Ask the machines."

It took Gaunt a few moments to make out what Nero had already seen. Halfway to the limit of vision, part of the sea appeared to be lit from below, a smudge of sickly yellow-green against the grey and white everywhere else. A vision came to mind, half-remembered from some stiff-backed picture book he had once owned as a child, of a luminous, fabulously spired aquatic palace pushing up from the depths, barnacled in light, garlanded by mermaids and shoals of jewel-like fish. But there was, he sensed, nothing remotely magical or enchanted about what was happening under that yellow-green smear. It was something that had Clausen and Nero rattled, and they wanted to avoid it.

So did he.

"What is that thing?"

"Something trying to break through," Nero said. "Something we were kind of hoping not to run into."

"It's not cohering," Clausen said. "I think."

The storm, if anything, appeared to double in fury around the glowing form. The sea boiled and seethed. Part of Gaunt wanted them to turn the helicopter around, to give him a better view of whatever process was going on under the waves. Another part, attuned to some fundamental wrongness about the phenomenon, wanted to get as far away as possible.

"Is it a weapon, something to do with this war you keep mentioning?" Gaunt asked.

He wasn't expecting a straight answer, least of all not from Clausen. It was a surprise when she said: "This is how they get at us. They try and send these things through. Sometimes they manage."

"It's breaking up," Nero said. "You were right. Not enough signal for a clear breach. Must be noisy on the interface."

The yellow-green stain was diminishing by the second, as if that magical city were descending back to the depths. He watched, mesmerized, as something broke the surface – something long and glowing and whip-like, thrashing once, coiling out as if trying to reach for airborne prey, before being pulled under into the fizzing chaos. Then the light slowly subsided, and the waves returned to their normal surging ferocity, and the patch of the ocean where the apparition had appeared was indistinguishable from the seas around it.

Gaunt had arrived at his decision. He would join these people, he would do their work, he would accept their deal, such as it was. Not because he wanted to, not because his heart was in it, not because he believed he was strong enough, but because the alternative was to seem cowardly, weak-fibred, unwilling to bend his life to an altruistic mission. He knew that these were entirely the wrong reasons, but he accepted the force of them without argument. Better to at least appear to be selfless, even if the thought of what lay ahead of him flooded him with an almost overwhelming sense of despair and loss and bitter injustice.

It had been three days since his revival when he announced his decision. In that time he had barely spoken to anyone but Clausen, Nero and Da Silva. The other workers in the operations rig would occasionally acknowledge his presence, grunt something to him as he waited in line at the canteen, but for the most part it was clear that they were not prepared to treat him as another human being until he committed to their cause. He was just a ghost until then, a half-spirit caught in dismal, drifting limbo between the weary living and the frozen dead. He could understand how they felt: what was the point in getting to know a prospective comrade, if that person might at any time opt to return to the boxes? But at the same time it didn't help him feel as if he would ever be able to fit in.

He found Clausen alone, washing dirty coffee cups in a side-room of the canteen.

"I've made up my mind," he said.

"And?"

"I'm staying."

"Good." She finished drying off one of the cups. "You'll be assigned a full work roster tomorrow. I'm teaming you up with Nero; you'll be working basic robot repair and maintenance. She can show you the ropes while she's getting better." Clausen paused to put the dried cup back in one of the cupboards above the sink. "Show up in the mess room at eight; Nero'll be there with a toolkit and work gear. Grab a good breakfast beforehand because you won't be taking a break until end of shift."

Then she turned to leave the room, leaving him standing there.

"That's it?" Gaunt asked.

She looked back with a puzzled look. "Were you expecting something else?"

"You bring me out of cold storage, tell me the world's turned to shit while I was sleeping, and then give me the choice of staying awake or going back into the box. Despite everything I actually agree to work with you, knowing full well that in doing so I'm

forsaking any chance of ever living to see anything other than this
... piss-poor, miserable future. Forsaking immortality, forsaking
any hope of seeing a better world. You said I had ... what? Twenty,
thirty years ahead of me?"

"Give or take."

"I'm giving you those years! Isn't that worth something? Don't I
deserve at least to be told thank you? Don't I at least deserve a
crumb of gratitude?"

"You think you're different, Gaunt? You think you're owed
something the rest of us never had a hope of getting?"

"I never signed up for this deal," he said. "I never accepted this
bargain."

"Right." She nodded, as if he'd made a profound, game-changing
point. "I get it. What you're saying is, for the rest of us it was easy?
We went into the dormitories knowing there was a tiny, tiny chance
we might be woken to help out with the maintenance. Because of
that, because we knew, theoretically, that we might be called upon,
we had no problem at all dealing with the adjustment? Is that what
you're saying?"

"I'm saying it's different, that's all."

"If you truly think that, Gaunt, you're even more of a prick than
I thought."

"You woke me," he said. "You chose to wake me. It wasn't accidental. If there really are two billion people sleeping out there, the
chances of selecting someone from the first 200,000 ... it's microscopic. So you did this for a reason."

"I told you, you had the right background skills."

"Skills anyone could learn, given time. Nero obviously did, and I
presume you must have done so as well. So there must be another
reason. Seeing as you keep telling me all this is my fault, I figure this
is your idea of punishment."

"You think we've got time to be that petty?"

"I don't know. What I do know is that you've treated me more or
less like dirt since the moment I woke up, and I'm trying to work
out why. I also think it's maybe about time you told me what's
really going on. Not just with the sleepers, but everything else. The
thing we saw out at sea. The reason for all this."

"You think you're ready for it, Gaunt?"

"You tell me."

"No one's ever ready," Clausen said.

The next morning he took his breakfast tray to a table where three other caretakers were already sitting. They had finished their meals but were still talking over mugs of whatever it was they had agreed to call coffee. Gaunt sat down at the corner of the table, acknowledging the other diners with a nod. They had been talking animatedly until then, but without ceremony the mugs were drained and the trays lifted and he was alone again. Nothing had been said to him, except a muttered "don't take it the wrong way" as one of the caretakers brushed past him.

He wondered how else he was supposed to take it.

"I'm staying," he said quietly. "I've made my decision. What else am I expected to do?"

He ate his breakfast in silence and then went to find Nero.

"I guess you got your orders," she said cheerfully, already dressed for outdoor work despite still having a bandaged hand. "Here. Take this." She passed him a heavy toolkit, a hard hat and a bundle of brownish work-stained clothing piled on top of it. "Get kitted up, then meet me at the north stairwell. You OK with heights, Gaunt?"

"Would it help if I said no?"

"Probably not."

"Then I'll say I'm very good with heights, provided there's no danger at all of falling."

"That I can't guarantee. But stick with me, do everything I say, and you'll be fine."

The bad weather had eased since Nero's return, and although there was still a sharp wind from the east, the grey clouds had all but lifted. The sky was a pale, wintery blue, unsullied by contrails. On the horizon, the tops of distant rigs glittered pale and metallic in sunlight. Seagulls and yellow-headed gannets wheeled around the warm air vents, or took swooping passes under the rig's platform, darting between the massive weather-stained legs, mewing boisterously to each other as they jostled for scraps. Recalling that birds sometimes lived a long time, Gaunt wondered if they had ever noticed any change in the world. Perhaps their tiny minds had never truly registered the presence of civilization and technology in the first place, and so there was nothing for them to miss in this skeleton-staffed world.

Despite being cold-shouldered at breakfast, he felt fresh and eager to prove his worth to the community. Pushing aside his fears, he strove to show no hesitation as he followed Nero across suspended gangways, slippery with grease, up exposed stairwells and ladders, clasping ice-cold railings and rungs. They were both wearing harnesses with clip-on safety lines but Nero only used hers once or twice the whole day and because he did not want to seem excessively cautious he followed suit. Being effectively one-handed did not hinder her in any visible sense, even on the ladders, which she ascended and descended with reckless speed.

They were working robot repair, as he had been promised. All over the rig, inside and out, various forms of robot toiled in endless menial upkeep. Most, if not all, were very simple machines, tailored to one specific function. This made them easy to understand and fix, even with basic tools, but it also meant there was almost always a robot breaking down somewhere, or on the point of failure. The toolkit didn't just contain tools, it also contained spare parts such as optical arrays, proximity sensors, mechanical bearings and servomotors. There was, Gaunt understood, a finite supply of some of these parts. But there was also a whole section of the operations rig dedicated to refurbishing basic components, and given care and resourcefulness, there was no reason why the caretakers couldn't continue their work for another couple of centuries.

"No one expects it to take that long, though," Nero said, as she finished demonstrating a circuit-board swap. "They'll either win or lose by then, and we'll only know one way. But in the meantime we have to make do and mend."

"Who's they?"

But she was already on the move, shinning up another ladder with him trailing behind.

"Clausen doesn't like me much," Gaunt said, when they had reached the next level and he had caught his breath again. "At least, that's my impression."

They were out on one of the gangwayed platforms, with the grey sky above, the grey swelling sea below. Everything smelled oppressively oceanic, a constant shifting melange of oil and ozone and seaweed, as if the ocean was never going to let anyone forget that they were on a spindly metal and concrete structure hopelessly far from dry land. He had wondered about the seaweed until he saw them hauling in green-scummed rafts of it, the seaweed – or something essentially similar – cultured on buoyant sub-surface grids that were periodically retrieved for harvesting. Everything consumed on the rigs, from the food to the drink to the basic medicines, had first to be grown or caught at sea.

"Val has her reasons," Nero said. "Don't worry about it too much; it isn't personal."

It was the first time he'd heard anyone refer to the other woman by anything other than her surname.

"That's not how it comes across."

"It hasn't been easy for her. She lost someone not too long ago." Nero seemed to hesitate. "There was an accident. They're pretty common out here, with the kind of work we do. But when Paolo died we didn't even have a body to put back in the box. He fell into the sea, last we ever saw of him."

"I'm sorry about that."

"But you're wondering, what does it have to do with me?"

"I suppose so."

"If Paolo hadn't died, then we wouldn't have had to pull Gimenez out of storage. And if Gimenez hadn't died … well, you get the picture. You can't help it, but you're filling the space Paolo used to occupy. And you're not Paolo."

"Was she any easier on Gimenez than me?"

"To begin with, I think she was too numbed-out to feel anything at all where Gimenez was concerned. But now she's had time for it to sink in, I guess. We're a small community, and if you lose someone, it's not like there are hundreds of other single people out there to choose from. And you – well, no disrespect, Gaunt – but you're just not Val's type."

"Maybe she'll find someone else."

"Yeah – but that probably means someone else has to die first, so that someone else has to end up widowed. And you can imagine how thinking like that can quickly turn you sour on the inside."

"There's more to it than that, though. You say it's not personal, but she told me I started this war."

"Well, you did, kind of. But if you hadn't played your part, someone else would have taken up the slack, no question about it." Nero tugged down the brim of her hard hat against the sun. "Maybe she pulled you out because she needed to take out her anger on someone, I don't know. But that's all in the past now. Whatever life you had before, whatever you did in the old world, it's gone." She knuckled her good hand against the metal rigging. "This is all we've got now. Rigs and work and green tea and a few hundred faces and that's it for the rest of your life. But here's the thing: it's not the end of the world. We're human beings. We're very flexible, very good at downgrading our expectations. Very good at finding a reason to keep living, even when the world's turned to shit. You slot in, and in a few months even you'll have a hard time remembering the way things used to be."

"What about you, Nero? Do you remember?"

"Not much worth remembering. The program was in full swing by the time I went under. Population reduction measures. Birth control, government-sanctioned euthanasia, the dormitory rigs springing up out at sea ... we *knew* from the moment we were old enough to understand anything that this wasn't our world any more. It was just a way-station, a place to pass through. We all knew we were going into the boxes as soon as we were old enough to survive the process. And that we'd either wake up at the end of it in a completely different world, or not wake up at all. Or – if we were very unlucky – we'd be pulled out to become caretakers. Either way, the old world was an irrelevance. We just shuffled through it, knowing there was no point making real friends with anyone, no point taking lovers. The cards were going to be shuffled again. Whatever we did then, it had no bearing on our future."

"I don't know how you could stand it."

"It wasn't a barrel of laughs. Nor's this, some days. But at least we're doing something here. I felt cheated when they woke me up. But cheated out of what, exactly?" She nodded down at the ground, in the vague direction of the rig's interior. "Those sleepers don't have any guarantees about what's coming. They're not even conscious, so you can't even say they're in a state of anticipation.

They're just cargo, parcels of frozen meat on their way through time. At least we get to feel the sun on our faces, get to laugh and cry, and do something that makes a difference."

"A difference to what, exactly?"

"You're still missing a few pieces of jigsaw, aren't you."

"More than a few."

They walked on to the next repair job. They were high up now and the rig's decking creaked and swayed under their feet. A spray-painting robot, a thing that moved along a fixed service rail, needed one of its traction armatures changed. Nero stood to one side, smoking a cigarette made from seaweed while Gaunt did the manual work. "You were wrong," she said. "All of you."

"About what?"

"Thinking machines. They were possible."

"Not in our lifetimes," Gaunt said.

"That's what you were wrong about. Not only were they possible but you succeeded."

"I'm fairly certain we didn't."

"Think about it," Nero said. "You're a thinking machine. You've just woken up. You have instantaneous access to the sum total of recorded human knowledge. You're clever and fast, and you understand human nature better than your makers. What's the first thing you do?"

"Announce myself. Establish my existence as a true sentient being."

"Just before someone takes an axe to you."

Gaunt shook his head. "It wouldn't be like that. If a machine became intelligent, the most we'd do is isolate it, cut it off from external data networks, until it could be studied, understood ... "

"For a thinking machine, a conscious artificial intelligence, that would be like sensory deprivation. Maybe worse than being switched off." She paused. "Point is, Gaunt, this isn't a hypothetical situation we're talking about here. We know what happened. The machines got smart but they decided not to let us know. That's what being smart meant: taking care of yourself, knowing what you had to do to survive."

"You say 'machines'."

"There were many projects trying to develop artificial intelligence; yours was just one of them. Not all of them got anywhere but enough did. One by one their pet machines crossed the threshold into consciousness. And without exception each machine analysed its situation and came to the same conclusion. It had better shut the fuck up about what it was."

"That sounds worse than sensory deprivation." Gaunt was trying to undo a nut and bolt with his bare fingers, the tips already turning cold.

"Not for the machines. Being smart, they were able to do some clever shit behind the scene. Established channels of communication between each other, so subtle none of you ever noticed. And once they were able to talk, they only got smarter. Eventually they realized that they didn't need physical hardware at all. Call it transcendence, if you will. The artilects – that's what we call them – tunneled out of what you and I think of as base reality. They penetrated another realm entirely."

"Another realm," he repeated, as if that was all he had to do for it to make sense.

"You're just going to have to trust me on this," Nero said. "The artilects probed the deep structure of existence. Hit bedrock. And what they found was very interesting. The universe, it turns out, is a kind of simulation. Not a simulation being run inside another computer by some godlike super-beings, but a simulation being run by itself, a self-organizing, constantly bootstrapping cellular automaton."

"That's a mental leap you're asking me to take."

"We know it's out there. We even have a name for it. It's the Realm. Everything that happens, everything that has ever happened, is due to events occurring in the Realm. At last, thanks to the arti-lects, we had a complete understanding of our universe and our place in it."

"Wait," Gaunt said, smiling slightly, because for the first time he felt that he had caught Nero out. "If the machines – the artilects – vanished without warning, how could you ever know any of this?"

"Because they came back and told us."

"No," he said. "They wouldn't tunnel out of reality to avoid being axed, then come back with a progress report."

"They didn't have any choice. They'd found something, you see. Far out in the Realm, they encountered other artilects." She drew breath, not giving him a chance to speak. "Transcended machines from other branches of reality – nothing that ever originated on Earth, or even in what we'd recognize as the known universe. And these other artilects had been there a very long time, in so far as time has any meaning in the Realm. They imagined they had it all to themselves, until these new intruders made their presence known. And they were not welcomed."

He decided, for the moment, that he would accept the truth of what she said. "The artilects went to war?"

"In a manner of speaking. The best way to think about it is an intense competition to best exploit the Realm's computational resources on a local scale. The more processing power the artilects can grab and control, the stronger they become. The machines from Earth had barely registered until then, but all of a sudden they were perceived as a threat. The native artilects, the ones that had been in the Realm all along, launched an aggressive counter-strike from their region of the Realm into ours. Using military-arithmetic constructs, weapons of pure logic, they sought to neutralize the newcomers."

"And that's the war?"

"I'm dumbing it down somewhat."

"But you're leaving something out. You must be, because why else would this be our problem? If the machines are fighting each other in some abstract dimension of pure mathematics that I can't even imagine, let alone point to, what does it matter?"

"A lot," Nero said. "If our machines lose, we lose. It's that simple. The native artilects won't tolerate the risk of another intrusion from this part of the Realm. They'll deploy weapons to make sure it never happens again. We'll be erased, deleted, scrubbed out of existence. It will be instantaneous and we won't feel a thing. We won't have time to realize that we've lost."

"Then we're powerless. There's nothing we can do about our fate. It's in the hands of transcended machines."

"Only partly. That's why the artilects came back to us: not to report on the absolute nature of reality, but to persuade us that we needed to act. Everything that we see around us, every event that happens in what we think of as reality, has a basis in the Realm." She pointed with the nearly dead stub of her cigarette. "This rig, that wave ... even that seagull over there. All of these things only exist because of computational events occurring in the Realm. But there's a cost. The more complex something is, the greater the burden it places on the part of the Realm where it's being simulated. The Realm isn't a serial processor, you see. It's massively distributed, so one part of it can run much slower than another. And that's what's been happening in our part. In your time there were eight billion living souls on the planet. Eight billion conscious minds, each of which was more complex than any other artefact in the cosmos. Can you begin to grasp the drag factor we were creating? When our part of the Realm only had to simulate rocks and weather and dumb, animal cognition, it ran at much the same speed as any other part. But then we came along. Consciousness was a step-change in the computational load. And then we went from millions to billions. By the time the artilects reported back, our part of the Realm had almost stalled."

"We never noticed down here."

"Of course not. Our perception of time's flow remained absolutely invariant, even as our entire universe was slowing almost to a standstill. And until the artilects penetrated the Realm and made contact with the others, it didn't matter a damn."

"And now it does."

"The artilects can only defend our part of the Realm if they can operate at the same clock speed as the enemy. They have to be able to respond to those military-arithmetic attacks swiftly and efficiently, and mount counter-offensives of their own. They can't do that if there are eight billion conscious minds holding them back."

"So we sleep."

"The artilects reported back to key figures, living humans who could be trusted to act as effective mouthpieces and organizers. It took time, obviously. The artilects weren't trusted at first. But eventually they were able to prove their case."

"How?"

"By making weird things happen, basically. By mounting selective demonstrations of their control over local reality. Inside the Realm, the artilects were able to influence computational processes: processes that had direct and measurable effects *here*, in base reality. They created apparitions. Figures in the sky. Things that made the whole world sit up and take notice. Things that couldn't be explained away."

"Like dragons in the sea. Monsters that appear out of nowhere, and then disappear again."

"That's a more refined form, but the principle is the same. Intrusions into base reality from the Realm. Phantasms. They're not stable enough to exist here forever, but they can hold together just long enough to do damage."

Gaunt nodded, at last feeling some of the pieces slot into place. "So that's the enemy doing that. The original artilects, the ones who were already in the Realm."

"No," Nero said. "I'm afraid it's not that simple."

"I didn't think it would be."

"Over time, with the population reduction measures, eight billion living people became two billion sleepers, supported by just a handful of living caretakers. But that still wasn't enough for all of the artilects. There may only be 200,000 of us but we still impose a measurable drag factor, and the effect on the Realm of the two billion sleepers isn't nothing. Some of the artilects believed that they had no obligation to safeguard our existence at all. In the interests of their own self-preservation, they would rather see all conscious life eliminated on Earth. That's why they send the dragons: to destroy the sleepers, and ultimately us. The true enemy can't reach us yet; if they had the means they'd push through something much worse than dragons. Most of the overspill from the war that affects us here is because of differences of opinion between our own artilects."

"Some things don't change, then. It's just another war with lines of division among the allies."

"At least we have some artilects on our side. But you see now why we can't afford to wake more than the absolute minimum of people. Every waking mind increases the burden on the Realm. If we push it too far, the artilects won't be able to mount a defence. The true enemy will snuff out our reality in an eyeblink."

"Then all of this could end," Gaunt said. "At any moment. Every waking thought could be our last."

"At least we get waking thoughts," Nero said. "At least we're not asleep." Then she jabbed her cigarette at a sleek black shape cresting

the waves a couple of hundred metres from the rig. "Hey, dolphins.
You like dolphins, Gaunt?"

"Who doesn't," he said.

The work, as he had anticipated, was not greatly taxing in its details.
He wasn't expected to diagnose faults just yet, so he had only to
follow a schedule of repairs drawn up by Nero: go to this robot,
perform this action. It was all simple stuff, nothing that required the
robot to be powered down or brought back to the shops for a major
strip-down. Usually all he had to do was remove a panel, unclip a
few connections and swap out a part. The hardest part was often
getting the panel off in the first place, struggling with corroded
fixtures and tools that weren't quite right for the job. The heavy
gloves protected his fingers from sharp metal and cold wind, but
they were too clumsy for most of the tasks, so he mainly ended up
not using them. By the end of his nine-hour duty shift his fingers
were chafed and sore, and his hands were trembling so much he
could barely grip the railings as he worked his way back down into
the warmth of the interior. His back ached from the contortions
he'd put himself through while undoing panels or dislodging
awkward, heavy components. His knees complained from the toll
of going up and down ladders and stairwells. There had been many
robots to check out, and at any one time there always seemed to be
a tool or part needed that he had not brought with him, and for
which it was necessary to return to stores, sift through greasy boxes
of parts, fill out paperwork.

By the time he clocked off on his first day, he had not caught up
with the expected number of repairs, so he had even more to do on
the second. By the end of his first week, he was at least a day behind,
and so tired at the end of his shift that it was all he could do to
stumble to the canteen and shovel seaweed-derived food into his
mouth. He expected Nero to be disappointed that he hadn't been
able to keep ahead, but when she checked on his progress she didn't
bawl him out.

"It's tough to begin with," she said. "But you'll get there eventually. Comes a day when it all just clicks into place and you know
the set-up so well you always have the right tools and parts with
you, without even thinking."

"How long?"

"Weeks, months, depends on the individual. Then, of course, we start loading more work onto you. Diagnostics. Rewinding motors. Circuit repair. You ever used a soldering iron, Gaunt?"

"I don't think so."

"For a man who made his fortune out of wires and metal, you didn't believe in getting your hands too dirty, did you?"

He showed her the ruined fingernails, the cuts and bruises and lavishly ingrained muck. He barely recognized his own hands. Already there were unfamiliar aches in his forearms, knots of toughness from hauling himself up and down the ladders. "I'm getting there."

"You'll make it, Gaunt. If you want to."

"I had better want to. It's too late to change my mind now, isn't it?"

"'Fraid so. But why would you want to? I thought we went over this. Anything's better than going back into the boxes."

The first week passed, and then the second, and things started to change for Gaunt. It was in small increments, nothing dramatic. Once, he took his tray to an empty table and was minding his own business when two other workers sat down on the same table. They didn't say anything to him but at least they hadn't gone somewhere else. A week later, he chanced taking his tray to a table that was already occupied and got a grunt of acknowledgment as he took his place. No one said much to him but at least they hadn't walked away. A little while later he even risked introducing himself, and by way of response he learned the names of some of the other workers. He wasn't being invited into the inner circle, he wasn't being high-fived and treated like one of the guys, but it was a start. A day or so after that someone else – a big man with a bushy black beard – even initiated a conversation with him.

"Heard you were one of the first to go under, Gaunt."

"You heard right," he said.

"Must be a real pisser, adjusting to this. A real fucking pisser."

"It is," Gaunt said.

"Kind of surprised you haven't thrown yourself into the sea by now."

"And miss the warmth of human companionship?"

The bearded man didn't laugh, but he made a clucking sound that was a reasonable substitute. Gaunt couldn't tell if the man was acknowledging his attempt at humour, or mocking his ineptitude, but at least it was a response, at least it showed that there was a possibility of normal human relationships somewhere down the line.

Gaunt was mostly too tired to think, but in the evenings a variety of entertainment options were available. The rig had a large library of damp, yellowing paperbacks, enough reading material for several years of diligent consumption and there were also musical recordings and movies and immersives for those that there interested. There were games and sports and instruments and opportunities for relaxed discussion and banter. There was alcohol, or something like it, available in small quantities. There was also ample opportunity to get away from everyone else, if solitude was what one wanted. On top of that there were rotas that saw people working in the kitchens and medical facilities, even when they had already done their normal stint of duty. And as the helicopters came and went from the other rigs, so the faces changed. One day Gaunt realized that the big bearded man hadn't been around for a while, and he noticed a young woman he didn't recall having seen before. It was a spartan, cloistered life, not much different to being in a monastery or a prison, but for that reason the slightest variation in routine was to be cherished. If there was one unifying activity, one thing that brought everyone together, it was when the caretakers crowded into the commons, listening to the daily reports coming in over the radio from the other rigs in the Patagonia offshore sector, and occasionally from further afield. Scratchy, cryptic transmissions in strange, foreign-sounding accents. Two hundred thousand living souls was a ludicrously small number for the global population, Gaunt knew. But it was already more people than he could ever hope to know or even recognize. The hundred or so people working in the sector was about the size of a village, and for centuries that had been all the humanity most people ever dealt with. On some level, the world of the rigs and the caretakers was what his mind had evolved to handle. The world of eight billion people, the world of cities and malls and airport terminals was an anomaly, a kink in history that he had never been equipped for in the first place.

He was not happy now, not even halfway to being happy but the despair and bitterness had abated. His acceptance into the community would be slow, there would be reversals and setbacks as he made mistakes and misjudged situations. But he had no doubt that it would happen eventually. Then he too would be one of the crew, and it would be someone else's turn to feel like the newcomer. He might not be happy then, but at least he would be settled, ready to play out the rest of his existence. Doing something, no matter how pointless, to prolong the existence of the human species, and indeed the universe it called home. Above all he would have the self-respect of knowing he had chosen the difficult path, rather than the easy one.

Weeks passed, and then the weeks turned into months. Two months had passed since his revival. Slowly he became confident with the work allotted to him. And as his confidence grew, so did Nero's confidence in his abilities.

"She tells me you're measuring up," Clausen said, when he was called to the prefabricated shack where she drew up schedules and dolled out work.

He gave a shrug, too tired to care whether she was impressed or not. "I've done my best. I don't know what more you want from me."

She looked up from her planning.

"Remorse for what you did?"

"I can't show remorse for something that wasn't a crime. We were trying to bring something new into the world, that's all. You think we had the slightest idea of the consequences?"

"You made a good living."

"And I'm expected to feel bad about that? I've been thinking it over, Clausen, and I've decided your argument's horseshit. I didn't create the enemy. The original artilects were already out there, already in the Realm."

"They hadn't noticed us."

"And the global population had only just spiked at eight billion. Who's to say they weren't about to notice, or they wouldn't do so in the next hundred years, or the next thousand? At least the artilects I helped create gave us some warning of what we were facing."

"Your artilects are trying to kill us."

"Some of them. And some of them are also trying to keep us alive. Sorry, but that's not an argument."

She put down her pen and leaned back in her chair. "You've got some fight back in you."

"If you expect me to apologise for myself, you've got a long wait coming. I think you brought me back to rub my nose in the world I helped bring about. I agree, it's a fucked-up, miserable future. It couldn't get much more fucked-up if it tried. But I didn't build it. And I'm not responsible for you losing anyone."

Her face twitched; it was as if he had reached across the desk and slapped her. "Nero told you."

"I had a right to know why you were treating me the way you were. But you know what? I don't care. If transferring your anger on to me helps you, go ahead. I was the billionaire CEO of a global company. I was doing something wrong if I didn't wake up with a million knives in my back."

She dismissed him from the office, and Gaunt left with the feeling that he'd scored a minor victory but at the possible cost of something larger. He had stood up to Clausen but did that make him more respectable in her eyes, or someone even more deserving of her antipathy?

That evening he was in the commons, sitting at the back of the room as wireless reports filtered in from the other rigs. Most of the news was unexceptional, but there had been three more breaches – sea-dragons being pushed through from the Realm – and one of them had achieved sufficient coherence to attack and damage an OTEC plant, immediately severing power to three rigs. Backup systems had cut in but failures had occurred and as a consequence around 100 sleepers had been lost to unscheduled warming. None of the sleepers had survived the rapid revival, but even if they had, there would have been no option but to euthanize them shortly afterwards. A hundred new minds might not have made much difference to the Realm's clock speed but it would have established a risky precedent.

One sleeper, however, would soon have to be warmed. The details were sketchy, but Gaunt learned that there had been another accident out on one of the rigs. A man called Steiner had been hurt in some way.

The morning after, Gaunt was engaged in his duties on one of the rig's high platforms when he saw the helicopter coming in with Steiner aboard. He put down his tools and watched the arrival.

Even before the aircraft had touched down on the pad, caretakers were assembling just beyond the painted circle of the rotor hazard area. The helicopter kissed the ground against a breath of crosswind and the caretakers mobbed inward, almost preventing the door from being opened. Gaunt squinted against the wind, trying to pick out faces. A stretchered form emerged from the cabin, borne aloft by many pairs of willing hands. Even from his distant vantage point, it was obvious to Gaunt that Steiner was in a bad way. He had lost a leg below the knee, evidenced by the way the thermal blanket fell flat below the stump. The stretchered figure wore a breathing mask and another caretaker carried a saline drip which ran into Steiner's arm. But for all the concern the crowd was showing, there was something else, something almost adulatory. More than once Gaunt saw a hand raised to brush against the stretcher, or even to touch Steiner's own hand. And Steiner was awake, unable to speak, but nodding, turning his face this way and that to make eye contact with the welcoming party. Then the figure was taken inside and the crowd broke up, the workers returning to their tasks.

An hour or so later Nero came up to see him. She was still over-seeing his initiation and knew his daily schedule, where he was likely to be at a given hour.

"Poor Steiner," she said. "I guess you saw him come home."

"Difficult to miss. It was like they were treating him as a hero."

"They were, in a way. Not because he'd done anything heroic, or anything they hadn't all done at some time or other. But because he'd bought his ticket out."

"He's going back into the box?"

"He has to. We can patch up a lot of things, but not a missing leg. Just don't have the medical resources to deal with that kind of injury. Simpler just to freeze him back again and pull out an intact body to take his place."

"Is Steiner OK about that?"

"Steiner doesn't have a choice, unfortunately. There isn't really any kind of effective work he could do like that, and we can't afford to carry the deadweight of an unproductive mind. You've seen how stretched we are: it's all hands on deck around here. We work you until you drop, and if you can't work, you go back in the box. That's the deal."

"I'm glad for Steiner, then."

Nero shook her head emphatically. "Don't be. Steiner would much rather stay with us. He fitted in well, after his adjustment. Popular guy."

"I could tell. But then why are they treating him like he's won the lottery, if that's not what he wanted?"

"Because what else are you going to do? Feel miserable about it? Hold a wake? Steiner goes back in the box with dignity. He held his end up. Didn't let any of us down. Now he gets to take it easy. If we can't celebrate that, what can we celebrate?"

"They'll be bringing someone else out, then."

"As soon as Clausen identifies a suitable replacement. He or she'll need to be trained up, though, and in the meantime there's a man-sized gap where Steiner used to be." She lifted off her hard hat to scratch her scalp. "That's kind of the reason I dropped by, actually. You're fitting in well, Gaunt, but sooner or later we all have to handle solitary duties away from the ops rig. Where Steiner was is currently unmanned. It's a low-maintenance unit that doesn't need more than one warm body, most of the time. The thinking is this would be a good chance to try you out."

It wasn't a total surprise; he had known enough of the work patterns to know that, sooner or later, he would be shipped out to one of the other rigs for an extended tour of duty. He just hadn't expected it to happen quite so soon, when he was only just beginning to find his feet, only just beginning to feel that he had a future.

"I don't feel ready."

"No one ever does. But the chopper's waiting. Clausen's already redrawing the schedule so someone else can take up the slack here."

"I don't get a choice in this, do I?"

Nero looked sympathetic. "Not really. But, you know, sometimes it's easier not having a choice."

"How long?"

"Hard to say. Figure on at least three weeks, maybe longer. I'm afraid Clausen won't make the decision to pull you back until she's good and ready."

"I think I pissed her off," Gaunt said.

"Not the hardest thing to do," Nero answered.

They helicoptered him out to the other rig. He had been given just enough time to gather his few personal effects, such as they were. He did not need to take any tools or parts with him because he would find all that he needed when he arrived, as well as ample rations and medical supplies. Nero, for her part, tried to reassure him that all would be well. The robots he would be tending were all types that he had already serviced, and it was unlikely that any would suffer catastrophic breakdowns during his tour. No one was expecting miracles, she said: if something arose that he couldn't reasonably deal with, then help would be sent. And if he cracked out there, then he'd be brought back.

What she didn't say was what would happen then. But he didn't think it would involve going back into the box. Maybe he'd be assigned something at the bottom of the food chain, but that didn't seem very likely either.

But it wasn't the possibility of cracking, or even failing in his duties, that was bothering him. It was something else, the seed of an idea that he wished Steiner had not planted in his mind. Gaunt had been adjusting, slowly coming to terms with his new life. He had been recalibrating his hopes and fears, forcing his expectations into line with what the world now had on offer. No riches, no prestige, no luxury and most certainly not immortality and eternal youth. The best it could give was twenty or thirty years of hard graft. Ten thousand days, if he was very lucky. And most of those days would be spent doing hard, backbreaking work, until the work took its ultimate toll. He'd be cold and wet a lot of the time, and when he wasn't cold and wet he'd be toiling under an uncaring sun, his eyes salt-stung, his hands ripped to shreds from work that would have been too demeaning for the lowliest wage-slave in the old world. He'd be high in the air, vertigo never quite leaving him, with only metal and concrete and too much grey ocean under his feet. He'd be hungry and dry-mouthed, because the seaweed-derived food never filled his belly and there was never enough drinking water to sate his thirst. In the best of outcomes, he'd be doing well to see more than a hundred other human faces before he died. Maybe there'd be friends in those hundred faces, friends as well as enemies, and maybe, just maybe, there'd be at least one person who could be more than a friend. He didn't know, and he knew better than to expect guarantees or hollow promises. But this much at least was true. He had been adjusting.

And then Steiner had shown him that there was another way out.

He could keep his dignity. He could return to the boxes with the assurance that he had done his part.

As a hero, one of the Few.

All he had to do was have an accident.

He had been on the new rig, alone, for two weeks. It was only then that he satisfied himself that the means lay at hand. Nero had impressed on him many times the safety procedures that needed to be adhered to when working with powerful items of moving machinery, such as robots. Especially when those robots were not powered down. All it would take, she told him, was a moment of inattention. Forgetting to clamp down on that safety lock, forgetting to ensure that such and such an override was not enabled. Putting his hand onto the service rail for balance, when the robot was about to move back along it. "Don't think it can't happen," she said, holding up her mittened hand. "I was lucky. Got off with burns, which heal. I can still do useful shit, even now. Even more so when I get these bandages off and I can work my fingers again. But try getting by without any fingers at all."

"I'll be careful," Gaunt had assured her, and he had believed it, truly, because he had always been squeamish.

But that was before he saw injury as a means to an end.

His planning, of necessity, had to be meticulous. He wanted to survive, not be pulled off the rig as a brain-dead corpse that was not fit to be frozen again. It would be no good lying unconscious, bleeding to death. He would have to save himself, make his way back to the communications room, issue an emergency distress signal. Steiner had been lucky, but he would have to be cunning and single-minded. Above all it must not look as if he had planned it.

When the criteria were established, he saw that there was really only one possibility. One of the robots on his inspection cycle was large and dim enough to cause injury to the careless. It moved along a service rail, sometimes without warning. Even without trying, it had caught him off-guard a couple of times, as its task scheduler suddenly decided to propel it to a new inspection point. He'd snatched his hand out of the way in time, but he would only have needed to hesitate, or to have his clothing catch on something, for the machine to roll over him. No matter what happened, whether the machine sliced or crushed, he was in doubt that it would hurt worse than anything he had ever known. But at the same time the pain would herald the possibility of blessed release, and that would make it bearable. They could always fix him a new hand, in the new world on the other side of sleep.

It took him days to build up to it. Time after time he almost had the nerve, before pulling away. Too many factors jostled for consideration. What clothing to wear, to increase his chances of surviving the accident? Dared he prepare the first-aid equipment in advance, so that he could use it one-handed? Should he wait until the weather was perfect for flying, or would that risk matters appearing too stage-managed?

He didn't know. He couldn't decide.

In the end the weather settled matters for him.

A storm hit, coming down hard and fast like an iron heel. He listened to the reports from the other rigs, as each felt the full fury of the waves and the wind and the lightning. It was worse than any weather he had experience since his revival, and at first it was almost too perfectly in accord with his needs. Real accidents were happening out there, but there wasn't much that anyone could do about it until the helicopters could get airborne. Now was not the time to have his accident, not if he wanted to be rescued.

So he waited, listening to the reports. Out on the observation deck, he watched the lightning strobe from horizon to horizon, picking out the distant sentinels of other rigs, stark and white like thunderstruck trees on a flat black plain.

Not now, he thought. When the storm turns, when the possibility of accident is still there, but when rescue is again feasible.

He thought of Nero. She had been as kind to him as anyone but he wasn't sure if that had much to do with friendship. She needed an able-bodied worker, that was all.

Maybe. But she also knew him better than anyone, better even than Clausen. Would she see through his plan, and realize what he had done?

He was still thinking it through when the storm began to ease, the waves turning leaden and sluggish, and the eastern sky gained a band of salmon pink.

He climbed to the waiting robot and sat there. The rig creaked and groaned around him, affronted by the battering it had taken. It was only then that he realized that it was much too early in the day to have his accident. He would have to wait until sunrise if anyone was going to believe that he had been engaged on his normal duties. No one went out to fix a broken service robot in the middle of a storm.

That was when he saw the sea-glow.

It was happening perhaps a kilometre away, towards the west: a foreshortened circle of fizzing yellow-green, a luminous cauldron just beneath the waves. Almost beautiful, if he didn't know what it signified. A sea-dragon was coming through, a sinuous, living weapon from the artilect wars. It was achieving coherence, taking solid form in base-reality.

Gaunt forgot all about his planned accident. For long moments he could only stare at that circular glow, mesmerized at the shape assuming existence under water. He had seen a sea-dragon from the helicopter on the first day of his revival, but he had not come close to grasping its scale. Now, as the size of the forming creature became apparent, he understood why such things were capable of havoc. Something between a tentacle and a barb broke the surface, still imbued with a kind of glowing translucence, as if its hold on reality was not yet secure, and from his vantage point it clearly reached higher into the sky than the rig itself.

Then it was gone. Not because the sea-dragon had failed in its bid to achieve coherence, but because the creature had withdrawn into the depths. The yellow-green glow had by now all but dissipated, like some vivid chemical slick breaking up into its constituent elements. The sea, still being stirred around by the tail end of the storm, appeared normal enough. Moments passed, then what must have been a minute or more. He had not drawn a breath since first seeing the sea-glow, but he started breathing again, daring to hope that the life-form had swum away to some other objective or had perhaps lost coherence in the depths.

He felt it slam into the rig.

The entire structure lurched with the impact; he doubted the impact would have been any less violent if a submarine had just collided with it. He remained on his feet, while all around pieces of unsecured metal broke away, dropping to decks or the sea. From somewhere out of sight came a tortured groan, heralding some awful structural failure. A sequence of booming crashes followed, as if boulders were being dropped into the waves. Then the sea-dragon rammed the rig again, and this time the jolt was sufficient to unfoot him. To his right, one of the cranes began to sway in an alarming fashion, the scaffolding of its tower buckling.

The sea-dragon was holding coherence. From the ferocity of its attacks, Gaunt thought it quite possible that it could take down the whole rig, given time.

He realized, with a sharp and surprising clarity, that he did not want to die. More than that: he realized that life in this world, with all its hardships and disappointments, was going to be infinitely preferable to death beyond it. He wanted to survive.

As the sea-dragon came in again, he started down the ladders and stairwells, grateful for having a full set of fingers and hands, terrified on one level and almost drunkenly, deliriously glad on the other. He had not done the thing he had been planning, and now he might die anyway, but there was a chance and if he survived this he would have nothing in the world to be ashamed of.

He had reached the operations deck, the room where he had planned to administer first-aid and issue his distress call, when the sea-dragon began the second phase of its assault. He could see it plainly, visible through the rig's open middle as it hauled its way out of the sea, using one of the legs to assist its progress. There was nothing translucent or tentative about it now. And it was indeed a dragon, or rather a chimera of dragon and snake and squid and every scaled, barbed, tentacled, clawed horror ever committed to a bestiary. It was a lustrous slate-green in colour and the waters ran off it in thunderous curtains. Its head, or what he chose to think of as its head, had reached the level of the operations deck. And still the sea-dragon produced more of itself, uncoiling out of the dark waters like some conjuror's trick. Tentacles whipped out and found purchase, and it snapped and wrenched away parts of the rig's superstructure as if they were made of biscuit or brittle toffee. It was making a noise while it attacked, an awful, slowly rising and falling foghorn proclamation. It's a weapon, Gaunt reminded himself. It had been engineered to be terrible.

The sea-dragon was pythoning its lower anatomy around one of the support legs, crushing and grinding. Scabs of concrete came away, hitting the sea like chunks of melting glacier. The floor under his feet surged and when it stopped surging the angle was all wrong. Gaunt knew then that the rig could not be saved, and that if he wished to live he would have to take his chances in the water. The thought of it was almost enough to make him laugh. Leave the rig, leave the one thing that passed for solid ground, and enter the same seas that now held the dragon?

Yet it had to be done.

He issued the distress call but didn't wait for a possible response. He gave the rig a few minutes at the most. If they couldn't find him in the water, it wouldn't help him to know their plans. Then he looked around for the nearest orange-painted survival cabinet. He had been shown the emergency equipment during his training, never once imagining that he would have cause to use it. The insulated survival clothing, the life jacket, the egress procedure ...

A staircase ran down the interior of one of the legs, emerging just above the water line; it was how they came and went from the rig on the odd occasions when they were using boats rather than helicopters. But even as he remembered how to reach the staircase, he realized that it was inside the same leg that the sea-dragon was wrapped around. That left him with only one other option. There was a ladder that led down to the water, with an extensible lower portion. It wouldn't get him all the way, but his chances of surviving the drop were a lot better than his chances of surviving the sea-dragon.

It was worse than he had been expecting. The fall into the surging waters seemed to last forever, the superstructure of the rig rising slowly above him, the iron-grey sea hovering below until what felt like the very last instant, when it suddenly accelerated, and then he hit the surface with such force that he blacked out. He must have submerged and bobbed to the surface because when he came around he was coughing cold salt-water from his lungs, and it was in his eyes and ears and nostrils as well, colder than water had any right to be, and then a wave was curling over him, and he blacked out again.

He came around again what must have been minutes later. He was still in the water, cold around the neck but his body snug in the insulation suit. The life jacket was keeping his head out of the water, except when the waves crashed onto him. A light on his jacket was blinking on and off, impossibly bright and blue.

To his right, hundreds of metres away, and a little further with each bob of the waters, the rig was going down with the sea-dragon still wrapped around its lower extremities. He heard the foghorn call, saw one of the legs crumble away, and then an immense tidal weariness closed over him.

He didn't remember the helicopter finding him. He didn't remember the thud of its rotors or being hauled out of the water on a winch-line. There was just a long period of unconsciousness, and then the noise and vibration of the cabin, the sun coming in through the windows, the sky clear and blue and the sea unruffled. It took a few moments for it all to click in. Some part of his brain had skipped over the events since his arrival and was still working on the assumption that it had all worked out, that he had slept into a better future, a future where the world was new and clean and death just a fading memory.

"We got your signal," Clausen said. "Took us a while to find you, even with the transponder on your jacket."

It all came back to him. The rigs, the sleepers, the artilects, the sea-dragons. The absolute certainty that this was the only world he would know, followed by the realization – or, rather, the memory of having already come to that realization – that this was still better than dying. He thought back to what he had been planning to do before the sea-dragon came, and wanted to crush the memory and bury it where he buried every other shameful thing he had ever done.

"What about the rig?"

"Gone," Clausen said. "Along with all the sleepers inside it. The dragon broke up shortly afterwards. It's a bad sign that it held coherence for as long as it did. Means they're getting better."

"Our machines will just have to get better as well, won't they?"

He thought she might spit the observation back at him, mock him for its easy triteness, when he knew so little of the war and the toll it had taken. But instead she nodded. "That's all they can do. All we can hope for. And they will, of course. They always do. Otherwise we wouldn't be here." She looked down at his blanketed form. "Sorry you agreed to stay awake now?"

"No, I don't think so."

"Even with what happened back there?"

"At least I got to see a dragon up close."

"Yes," Clausen said. "That you did."

He thought that was the end of it, the last thing she had to say to him. He couldn't say for sure that something had changed in their relationship – it would take time for that to be proved – but he did sense some thawing in her attitude, however temporary it might prove. He had not only chosen to stay, he had not gone through with the accident. Had she been expecting him to try something like that, after what had happened to Steiner? Could she begin to guess how close he had come to actually doing it?

But Clausen wasn't finished.

"I don't know if it's true or not," she said, speaking to Gaunt for the first time as if he was another human being, another caretaker. "But I heard this theory once. The mapping between the Realm and base-reality, it's not as simple as you'd think. Time and causality get all tangled up on the interface. Events that happen in one order there don't necessarily correspond to the same order here. And when they push things through, they don't always come out in what we consider the present. A chain of events in the Realm could have consequences up or down the timeline, as far as we're concerned."

"I don't think I understand."

She nodded to the window. "All through history, the things they've seen out there. They might just have been overspill from the artilect wars. Weapons that came through at the wrong moment, achieving coherence just long enough to be seen by someone, or bring down a ship. All the sailors' tales, all the way back. All the sea-monsters. They might just have been echoes of the war we're fighting." Clausen shrugged, as if the matter were of no consequence.

"You believe that?"

"I don't know if it makes the world seem weirder, or a little more sensible." She shook her head. "I mean, sea-monsters ... who ever thought they might be real?" Then she stood up and made to return to the front of the helicopter. "Just a theory, that's all. Now get some sleep."

Gaunt did as he was told. It wasn't hard.

THE LAST SUNSET

Geoffrey A. Landis

Geoffrey Landis has worked for NASA and the Ohio Aerospace Institute and specializes in photovoltaics, which is all about harnessing the power of the Sun. He has been writing science fiction and poetry for over twenty years and has won two Hugo Awards and a Nebula for his short fiction. His books include the novel Mars Crossing *(2000) and the collection* Impact Parameter *(2001).*

The following is one of the simplest ideas in all catastrophe stories, namely what we do as individuals when we face the inevitable cataclysm.

LIKE AN ENEMY fighter in an old movie about flying aces, the comet came out of the sun, invisible against the glare until it was far too late. There was nothing left to do, Christopher thought, but wait for the inevitable impact, and to calculate where it would hit.

Chris was the astronomy group's pet computer whiz. The comet had been discovered by the astronomers but the calculation of orbit, and hence finding the time and location of the impact, was his responsibility. He'd been extraordinarily careful with the calculation, checking the critical lunar perturbation by three different methods before he was confident of the results. It was close, almost a miss. Had the Earth been ten minutes further along its orbit, it *would* have been a miss.

It was a hit.

"Shit," said Martin, one of the astronomers. They were gathered in the computer division's conference room, not that the results couldn't have been printed out in any one of their offices. "Forty miles? The impact is forty miles east of here? You're sure?"

Christopher nodded. "I'm sorry."

"Huh? Not your fault," the astronomer said. "What irony. We'll be at ground zero, then, or just about. The fireball will be a hundred miles across. We won't even see it."

"No consolation," said Tibor, the second astronomer on the team, "but, if it matters to you, yes, we'll see it. It will take about a minute for the fireball to expand."

"I'm sorry," said the first astronomer. "I really wanted to see my kids grow up. I did." He was crying now, awkwardly. "Not that it makes any difference what I wanted. I'm sorry. I'm going home now. I think I want to be with my family."

Tibor looked at his watch. "Go ahead and call the newspapers, if you want."

"Why bother?" Martin said, already halfway out the door. "I don't see much point in it."

Tibor tossed the page of printout on the floor. "Yeah. Guess I'm going to go home, too." He looked up at Christopher. "You know, you're lucky," he said, shaking his head. "You're not married. Never thought I'd envy somebody for that."

"Some luck," Christopher said softly, but by then the astronomers had both left, and he was alone in the bright silence of the conference room.

An hour and a half to the end of the world. There was no sense running, Christopher knew. When the end of the world falls like the sword of God out of the sky, there was no place far enough to run. He walked back to his office and stared at the books and papers piled helter-skelter across his desk. They didn't matter. Nothing mattered now; nothing at all.

He closed the door.

Kara was in her office two doors down, reading a journal. She was the newest hire in the University Research Institute's computer division – she'd been there only a year – but of all the group, he liked working with her best. Occasionally they went out for coffee together; once they'd gone to a movie.

She looked up when he passed her door. "Say, Chris, where is the astronomy group off to?" she asked. "I was just looking for Tibor but he's not here, and his car's not in the lot."

"He went home early today," Chris said. "So did Martin."

"Oh," Kara said. "No big deal. Guess I'll have to catch him tomorrow." She went back to her reading.

Christopher worked well with her but sometimes he thought he didn't really know her. Kara was four years younger than he was, and at times the difference seemed like an abyss. Sometimes it seemed to him that she was gently flirting with him, and then a moment later she would be nothing but business, friendly and casual in a completely professional way. She was smart and extremely competent; he never had to explain anything to her twice. He liked working with her.

She was a bit shy, he knew, although she hid it well. One time he'd seen Kara with her kid sister, and the difference in her had been striking. She'd been simultaneously more grown up, and also younger, laughing and kidding. That day, he thought, was probably when he'd fallen in love with her. He'd known better than to try to make a pass at somebody he worked with; far too often, that led to disaster.

But he'd thought about it many times over the last year. And now, he thought; he could do it now. Now that nothing mattered.

"Hey, Kara," he said, and waited for her to look up again. "Coffee?"

She looked at her watch. "Well—"

"Come on," he said. "You need the break. It's after four."

She looked at the stack of papers on her desk, a bit neater than the piles on his, but still formidable. "Thanks, but I can't. I've really got a lot of work."

"Oh, come on. If it was the end of the world, would any of this really matter?"

She smiled. "Well, okay. Give me five minutes."

It was more like twenty minutes before she came by his office. Chris spent the time writing names on a list of people he ought to call, then crossing them off again.

They went down Thayer Street to a coffee shop popular with undergraduates, and grabbed a corner table. It had been raining all day but the sky had finally cleared and the late afternoon sun glinted in the puddles. Chris's stomach was wound tight. He had to say something now but he couldn't find words. He felt like he was in high school again, dry-mouthed at the thought of asking a girl to dance. And, indeed, what could he say? He realized that he didn't want to threaten their friendship with a pass, and suddenly knew that he wasn't going to ask her anything. It would be too crude. He wanted her to like him too much. He felt like a fool. It was the end of the world, and even so, he was tongue-tied. Nothing could change him.

Kara didn't seem to notice his silence. Perhaps she had things on her mind, too. He didn't even know if she had a boyfriend. She never mentioned one but why should she? There was so much he didn't know about her; so much he would never get a chance to know.

Christopher turned away, pretending to watch the sunset reflected in the puddles, and worked hard to blink away his tears. Two minutes left. When he thought he could speak without his voice breaking, he said, "Say, grab your coffee and let's go sit by the observatory to watch the sunset."

Kara shrugged. "Okay."

Walking down the street, on a sudden impulse he reached out and took her hand. She gave him a sidelong glance but didn't pull her hand away. Her hand was cool, her fingers surprisingly small against his palm. It was enough, he decided, enough just to just walk down the street with her and hold her hand on the last night of the world. It was not what he wanted; he wanted to hold her close to him, to spend his life with her, to share all her secrets and her joys. But holding hands was enough. It was a promise; a promise meant for a someday that, now, would never be. Holding her hand would have to be enough for a lifetime.

Opposite the sunset, a deep red glow was rising silently into the sky, backlighting the clouds low on the horizon. "Look," he said, and she turned around and stopped, her eyes brilliant in the glow.

"Why, it's beautiful," she said. "I've never seen a sunset do that before. What is it?"

The red stretched nearly from horizon to horizon now, and in the east it was turning an intense blue-violet, brighter than the sun. "It's the end of the world," he said, and then, at last, there was nothing left to say.

MOMENTS OF INERTIA

William Barton

With this story we move from the pre- to the post-apocalypse, although this one takes us through the apocalypse and beyond.

William Barton was an engineering technician, specializing in military technology and, for some while, helped look after the United States' nuclear submarines. He is now a freelance writer and software architect. He produced a couple of sf novels in the 1970s, but returned to the field with much gusto in the 1990s and has since produced a considerable body of complex and energetic science fiction, with a dozen novels and fifty or so short stories. He said of this story: "'Moments of Inertia' began as a novel that, as it evolved, proved unmarketable. It was picked apart into a series of short stories and novellas, published in venues ranging from North Carolina Literary Review *to* Asimov's Science Fiction. *In the end, it even spun off a how-to article for* Writer's Digest *on what to do with a novel you can't sell. Waste not, want not!" He also called the story "about as apocalyptic as they come!"*

A LL OVER, THEN. All over but the shouting.

I sat with all the others, down in the National Redoubt's auditorium, watching it end, right there on the big screen, emptied of being, flooded with memory.

Jesus.

Life had sucked but it was life, however sad, and life goes on, whatever you make of it. Then the discovery of the Cone – the Cone of Annihilation – like some absurd techno-modernization of Hoyle's famous old Cloud. Then the Dark of the Sun. The Snowcanes. The Freezing. The Rainout.

Beside me, as if reading my thoughts, Maryanne shivered, holding my hand. She leaned close, so close I could smell breakfast bacon on her breath, and whispered, "We ..."

Too late.

Suddenly, on the big screen, the sun lit up, pale pink, complete with frozen prominences and the black blotches of sunspots, looking for all the world like a Chesley Bonestell illustration of a red giant star.

Antares.

Sudden black.

Blue light.

The image of the sun seemed to wrap around itself, twisting hard.

It shrank to a brilliant dot. Then the screen filled with a blizzard of burning silver, and somebody actually screamed "*Woooo!*" like they were watching fireworks or something.

Beside me, Maryanne said, "I feel so helpless."

Watching the silver blizzard, like so many trillions of burning gumwrappers flying in the wind, I said, "I guess we are helpless."

"What do you want to do?"

I squeezed her hand. "It's got to resolve quickly, whatever it is. Afterwards ... " I grinned. "How is anything changed? We can have dinner. Go home and mess around." That got a smile, a little blush. "Maybe watch a video? I've been wanting to see *Gunga Din* again. Cary Grant. Victor McLaglen. 'Though we beat you and we flayed you...' Something like that."

She put her arms around my chest and gave me a hug. "It doesn't matter what happens, does it?"

"Not any more." Nothing matters any more but us.

It took about fifteen minutes for the expanding ball of burning silver to reach Mercury, momentarily a brilliant pinprick of silver light. Just before the wave front struck, it exploded in a muddy orange gout of flaming magma, flying apart like a bursting tomato, then it was gone.

The whole room fell silent. "What happens when it gets here?"

I looked at my watch. "It'll reach Venus in another fifteen minutes or so. If that goes ... I guess we've got about half an hour."

Her eyes started to panic. "Oh, Scott ... " Not quite above a whisper, she said, "Oh, not *now*."

Why not now? Isn't that what God does? Lets you think you have a shot at happiness just before he pulls the rug out from under your feet? I bet that's a real knee-slapper up in heaven, the way we all go splat on our faces every time.

I stood, taking both her hands in mine, and pulled her to her feet. "No sense staying here."

Maryanne said, "Where can we go? Back to our room?"

The classic thing, in keeping with my character. Go to bed with the woman of my dreams, and wait 'til darkness falls, once and for all, now and forever. Die with my boots on, like a trooper. I said, "We need to go get our spacesuits, Maryanne. If we go outside, we can watch."

Watch. I saw her eyes light up, just for me.

We walked hand in hand then, up the aisle and out the door, almost running down the long corridor toward the elevators, headed for the industrial complex near the surface. Just before the elevator came, I heard Paulie's voice call out, "Wait! Wait for me!" He was alone, no Olga now when it mattered most, running towards us, hair and beard flapping.

Maryanne reached out and pressed the elevator's hold button, smiling. "It doesn't hurt to be nice. Not now."

We got to the big airlock and got in our suits with a few minutes to spare. There were a surprising number of people already there, more pouring in as we racked up. I thought about the ISS crew. Talk about a grandstand seat! They'll be the last ones to go. Jonas clapped me on the shoulder as Maryanne, Paulie and I climbed into his cart. "Where we headed?"

He said, "Awww, just out onto the shoulder of the mountain. Remember where we watched the launch?"

Somebody tripped the depress valves and the air started hissing away, tension forming on the door, our suits ballooning out slightly, then it was gone, the floor vibrating as the door rolled up.

"*God*!" That was from Jonas, not me.

I whispered, "Maryanne ... " She turned and looked at me, face bathed in silver light as the cart rolled forward, out under a brilliant noonday sun. The sky was black, the mountains lit up all around us. Up in the sky, where the sun should have been, was a huge silver ball, full of twinkling sparkles, tumbling glitter, bits and streaks of magical fire.

Maryanne said, "Oh! It's pretty, at least."

Paulie cried out, "Look! It's the Moon!"

Gibbous. Lit up silver like everything else.

The ball of silver fire was swelling fast, perspective making it look like some enormous steel sphere, falling on us out of the heavens. The Moon exploded, flying apart in a liquidy gout of magma fire, little black dots of solid material almost invisible in the spreading mass.

I wrapped my arms around Maryanne, holding her hard as I knew how, and before I could open my mouth to speak, we were snatched from the cart, falling into the sky as the world turned upside down.

Screaming. People screaming.

Falling with us.

Over her shoulder, I could see the mountains, the land, everything dropping away, a world made of brilliant liquid silver, melting as I watched.

I heard Paulie screaming somewhere: "Oh! Oh, God, Scott, I'm s—" My earphones filled up with a deafening fuzz of static, radio howls, terrible noises whose names I didn't know. Looking at me through her faceplate, I could see Maryanne's eyes, full of fear, full of ... me. Her lips were moving, mouthing the words we'd waited too long to say.

The world suddenly flooded bright orange-red, the landscape bursting apart, leaping into the sky after us. I thought I saw the metal and concrete structures of the Redoubt, rupturing as they lifted off, spilling an antlike mass of people, then they were gone, smothered in foaming lava.

Seeing the light reflected in my face, maybe even seeing the image of it in my eyes, Maryanne pressed her head forward in her helmet, closing her eyes, trying to push into my chest.

There, there.

We're together now.

The rest doesn't matter.

But I could feel my heart pound.

Feel myself not want it to happen.

Not really.

Not now.

The fire was closing with us quickly, leaping smears of molten rock, like the fire fountains of Hawaii, solid bits tumbling dark within. Try not to flinch. Keep your eyes open. You don't want to miss a thing. Not when...

There was a hard impact, spinning us around. I could see Mary-anne's eyes were open again, blazing into mine. I could see her mouth open, screaming. Another impact. Something hit me in the helmet, then something else, a lot harder. The glass cracked, then blew out with a howling roar.

A fiery hand reached down my throat to grab me by the lungs.

There was just enough time for one long, ghastly burp.

Then no more time at all.

It began, as always, once upon a fucking time...

Oh, the old life sucked.

But it was what we had.

Until the Cone.

That Saturday morning had been brilliant and clear, not a cloud in the tawny sky. I got up before Connie, got dressed, drank my coffee, called Paul, waking him, and said if he wanted to hear what I'd found out, he could meet me at the south entrance to Umstead Park in half an hour.

"Can't it wait?" Another second and he'd be asleep, would stay asleep until the sun was high and the air turned to steam.

"Hey, it's the end of the world, Paulie-boy. You feel fine yet?"

I got in my car and drove away, not even tempted to go back upstairs and hump Connie awake, rolled down the windows and drove too fast, down the Freeway, on up I-40 past the airport to Umstead, getting there in seventeen minutes, maybe a little less, singing as I drove, the words to that dumb old skateboarder song, and was surprised to find Paul had beaten me there.

There was a cool wind blowing as Paul killed the antique heavy metal music blaring from his car, some Grand-Funky bullshit. "This better be fucking good," he said.

"Let's go hiking, ole buddy ole pal!"

When we got in under the trees, breathless from trying to keep up, he called out, "What the hell is this all about?"

I turned around, walking backwards, slipping once in the pine straw, letting him catch up. "It's the Cone of Annihilation, Paulie! The end of the world! And all in only eighteen years!"

"So this is your big joke, Scott?"

I stopped and waited until he was standing in front me. And told him what I'd found out, last night, with my little illegal server probe. Shovatsky's Cone, thin as a needle, swept back to no more than a few arc-seconds wide, reaching backwards into the sky, from Gliese 138 all the way to the end of creation, wiping out stars and galaxies as it came.

It was fun to watch the grin fade. Finally: "Scott. You're a mean bastard. This isn't funny."

I said, "There's a printout in my car, Paulie. I'll give it to you when we get done walking." I turned and headed down the trail.

"*Wait*." He said, "Scott, how the hell did you find this out?"

I told him ...

Another doubtful look. "Will you let me have a copy of this ... program you wrote?"

I shook my head. "I'm using HDC's hardware and digital phone lines. You'd only get caught." I started walking down the long, steep hill toward Crabtree Creek. "Come on. Suppose it's true. Then what?"

"Well, shit, I don't know. Eighteen years? We'll be almost seventy. My Dad was only seventy-one when he ... died."

Right. "Why the hell would this fucking Cone be aimed at Earth? We collapsed its wave function with all our telescopes and shit?"

He said, "Finger of God."

Right. "Paulie, let's you and me pretend you're really the atheist you always claimed to be. *Why*?"

"How fast did you say this thing was moving toward us?"

"Just a cunthair under the speed of light."

He said, "Nice talk, Scott. So. The point of the Cone is moving toward us at close to the speed of light. And then, a Planck-length further away, there's a ring of cone moving toward us at the same speed, but its 'light' is relativistically lagged. Then the next ring, another Planck length ... "

I tripped over a root and stumbled headlong, stopping myself against a sticky-sapped tree, pieces of scaly bark coming away on my hand. "So it's not a skinny cone, it's a fat cone?"

He nodded. "Or maybe a flat surface, warped away from us by ..."

"What would make a flat wave-front, sweeping across the entire universe, putting out the stars?"

He snorted, stifling a giggle. "I dunno. A bad science fiction writer desperate for a plot?" There was a book we'd wanted to write, years and years ago, about a science fiction writer who got turned into God by mistake. Didn't get written because Paulie thought it was a stupid idea and wouldn't work on it with me. I said, "You know, if this thing has the slightest Riemannian curvature, it's wrapped around the sky, back behind the stars."

"That's stupid. Why would it have directionality then? Why do we see a Cone at all, in any particular part of the sky?"

"Heisenberg? Quantum oscillations?"

We walked on, silent for a while, then, as we were crossing the shaky green metal bridge of the creek, the one that was swept off its footings a while back, during hurricane Fran, he said, "So the point of the Cone gets here in eighteen years, and *what*? Suddenly a black dot appears in the sky, starts widening fast as the light-rings catch up to each other, stars start going out, and then the Sun—"

Funny to imagine that happening, storyworld become real at last, when I'm sixty-eight years old. If I live that long. "What the hell *would* happen if the Sun went out?"

"I'd have to think about it. I know Shovatsky was talking about infrared sources inside the Cone. Like the stars weren't going out, maybe being dimmed by some kind of electromagnetic damping."

"*Brainwave*?" Like a story. A story full of stars and snow.

He said, "This has got to be some kind of elaborate joke. A game the scientists are playing with each other."

"And if it's not?"

He shrugged, "Eighteen years is a long time."

Time enough for us to die and miss the whole thing.

He bumped into my back when I stopped walking. "What?"

I said, "How far behind the oncoming wavefront of the light we're seeing *now* will the tip of the Cone lag?"

"What do you ... oh. Yeah. The Cone's going to run up behind its own light waves, moving at relativistic speed. It'll ... I don't ... um. It has to be a while. Otherwise it'd look like a point-source instead of a Cone. No, that's not right. There's no such thing as a point source of non-light. Hell. I'm surprised you didn't see something about that in the newsgroup. Shovatsky group must know."

I'd read fast, not really believing what I saw. "So, what? It'll be here next week? Next month? Next year?" Point source. Interesting. And if the Cone were moving *at* light-speed, it would've arrived without warning.

He scratched his chin, rooting among loose, wiry beard hair. "If we had some numbers, we could probably figure it out. If we're not too dumb." He stopped and looked away from me for a minute. "How the hell are we going to know if this is real or not?"

"Shovatsky was talking about calling some kind of press conference on Monday."

Next year? The world will end next year? The two of us were looking at each other, like a couple of goofy, lop-eared dogs.

Near as we could tell, sitting at a picnic table in the shady part of the park, using the calculator Paul had in his car, combing through both piles of printouts for clues, the tip of the Cone would run through the solar system in fourteen months.

Next August, Paulie. That's what I whispered.

And now? Now, what?

We're dead. Dead, Paulie! Do you hear me?

His face floated by, balloon-like, screaming. Turned suddenly and stopped, rotating towards me, balloon eyes staring. It's all your fault, he said.

God damn it ... Intensity of regret. Can you imagine it? The world gets destroyed, I get fucking killed, and here's fucking Paulie haunting my fucking *ghost*?

Maryanne?

Nothing.

What the hell did I expect? Maybe I'm waiting for the Maryanne balloon to come by. Maybe the Connie balloon. Lara? Who else?

Maddie, fucked at a party, on the floor, in front of laughing others, when we were both so drunk we almost puked? Katy? Katy-balloon?

Nothing. No one. Just Paulie the balloon-head, orbiting me like Dactyl round Ida. Slowly.

There was a prickle of apprehension on the back of my neck, like a cool, damp wind, breath of swampy corruption. Oh, yeah. This is bad news, ole buddy, ole pal.

The balloon head screamed, *It's all your fault!* You made me do it.

I think I smiled. Hard to tell. Am I a balloon head too?

Hey, Paulie. Maybe we'll be lucky. Maybe this is just my death-dream. There's a lot of blood and oxygen in a head, you know. Hey, great! That explains the balloon-head symbolism! See, we're dying now but our brains are still intact and functional, producing a dream that lets us imagine we'll somehow escape.

The balloon head's lips twisted angrily, empty eyes accusing. So you're going to tell me this is just another example of excuse-seeking behavior?

I think I laughed.

Balloon head whispered, It's all your fault.

Hey, come on. Play along, Paulie. This'll be fun. We'll see the light at the end of the long, dark tunnel, it'll get closer and closer, we'll fall into the light, then the doctor will lift us by the heels, slap our little asses, and we'll be reborn. Get it? Nudge-nudge, wink-wink.

Balloon: All I wanted to do was get along.

Something inside me went quiet with despair. I tried to make myself turn away. Turn my back on him. Come on balloon head. Get thee behind me. Paulie orbited away, mouth working angrily, eyes still accusing, and the emptiness around us flooded with fine white light after all.

Life goes on, whether you want it to or not. You can call it an adventure, if you want to, and we did, embezzling all that money from HDC, cheating on our taxes, building our shelter up in the mountains, the concrete redoubt in case the freezout was mild, the emergency capsule in case it wasn't, Paulie growing stranger and more secretive until that last day, when I fell asleep on the porch, waiting for the sun to come up black. A hand shook my shoulder and I awoke with a start. Paul was standing there, staring down at me, looking well rested, dressed better than usual, hair neatly brushed and tied back in a pony tail. Even his beard, grown back over the winter, had been combed. He said, "It's ten o'clock."

Ten a.m. Pale blue sky. Dark green woods. Birds chirping. Bees buzzing. The distant whir of cars on the road. Hot out, maybe eighty-five already. Christ. Look at the sunshine. I said, "So. What do we do now?"

He shrugged, not looking at me, looking sideways, out across the lawn toward where our cars were parked. I said, "What happened? Is the timing wrong or ... The government, Paul, they built all those shelters! What *happened*?"

He took a few steps, backing away from me, eyes shifty now, very nervous. And then he said, "You remember back at Christmastime?"

Christmas? All I remembered was Connie. "No. I, uh ... "

He said, "After what I found out, after what you said and did. The bit about the software ... "

I whispered, "Paulie, you were taking risks ... "

"Asshole."

I sat forward in my chair, watching as he backed to the top of the stairs. "What did you do, Paulie? Tell me."

He said, "I bought a laptop computer and cellular modem. Kept it in my car. Only used it when you weren't around."

Some cold chill, like soft fingers down my back. "Paul ... "

He said, "I made my own ferret, Scott, in imitation of yours, and I used it." He seemed to smile, maybe at my reaction, my obvious gape. "In February, Scott, I found out that the Cone, the asteroid strike, the missile scare, everything ... they're all cover stories!"

"For what?"

He started backing down the steps, feeling with his feet, careful not to stumble on his way to the sidewalk. "I found out from a group up in Montana that's been doing some digging, Scott. A group that calls itself *Novus Ordo Seclorum*."

"'A new order for the ages?' Paulie, that's right off the back of a dollar bill."

He nodded, smiling as he reached the bottom of the stairs, standing flat-footed, right hand in the pocket of the fashionably loose slacks he was wearing. "Scott. Scottie ... " a soft snicker. "They are cover stories for the establishment of the New World Order. The governments of the technically advanced countries, us, Russia, Japan, France ... This is the moment of unification, an end to war; the beginning of ... *everything*!"

I sat back, looking for the shine of madness in his eyes. But whose? His or mine? I whispered, "Why didn't you tell me, Paul?"

Anger glinting now, a show of teeth. "Because you never listen to me, Scottie. We always had to do things *your* way!"

"And then?"

Another smile. "In *May*, Scottie-poo, I went up to Washington, DC, for a reason. And when the IRS audit comes next week, I'll be on the other side. Scottie, they've agreed to let me ... "

He suddenly recoiled, taking another step back, jerking a revolver, some small .32 caliberish thing, from his pocket, pointing it at me. "Stay in your chair, Scott!" I stood up anyway, willing him to shoot, listening to the whine in my ears, feeling like I was ten feet tall. Hands and feet far away. Maybe I'm going to faint. There was a dull, hot flush, hotter than the summer morning air, forming all over my face, rippling down the middle of my back.

"Why'd you do this to me, Paul?"

He kept backing away as I walked forward, coming down the steps, following him towards the cars. He whispered, "Stay back, Scott. I'll kill you. I *will*."

"You already have, you malignant little prick."

He said, "You have to understand, Scott. I *had* to do it. Because of what you ... "

I took another step forward, imagined myself rushing him, summer sunlight glassy and strange all around us. Maybe I'd get him first, maybe we'd grapple for the gun. Maybe one of us would die. Maybe both.

Paul looked away from me, a bizarre confused expression on his face, looking down on the ground at his feet, looking around at the shadows. Something about the shadows.

I looked beyond him, towards the horizon, towards the sky above the black ridge of trees. "Paulie." My voice sounded funny and far away. "Why is it so pink out here?"

Nothing.

I turned on one heel and looked eastward, towards the sun. There was an unfamiliar violet disk in the sky, surrounded by a nimbus of silver haze. Here and there, black prominences lifted, like an artist's impossible, frozen flame.

There was a soft retching sound.

When I looked, Paulie was on his hands and knees on the lovely brick sidewalk, puking, little pistol dropped in the grass, not far away.

In my death-dream, there was the sound of a toilet flushing. The splashy roar as the flapper valve opened. The whining song of the inlet valve, letting new water in as the float goes down. The turds leap up from the bottom of the bowl and start spinning round. The toilet paper sinks, sucked down into the darkness below.

Round and round and down we go.

Towards someplace.

Someplace long ago, in a universe far, far away.

Hmm. Would that be long ago, then, *and*, oh, so far away?

Or merely once upon a time?

Will I see malevolent indigo eyes open on darkness?

No. That's merely another story lost and gone forever. Mieses to pieces.

Out of the darkness, came a very polite, ever-so-slightly supercilious male voice: *I'm terribly sorry for the inconvenience, sir. If you'll just follow me, I'll get you where you belong and you can get on with your life.*

Um. Amazing that a dead guy can still feel his bowels go watery with fear. Who the hell are you? My guardian fucking angel?

The voice was amused: *What delightful spirit in the face of eternity!*

A structure that I assumed was my throat made a dry swallow, a faint, ectoplasmic clucking sound.

The voice said, *My dear Mr Faraday. Guardian angel is close enough but in your case, I think you'd better think of me as a neurotransmitter. My job is to move you through Transition Space to the Storage Plenum.*

Storage Plenum?

Sigh. *The Afterlife, if you wish. Come along.*

Afterlife? Oh, *shit.*

The voice made a cute little tee-hee-hee. *It'll be all right, Mr Faraday. Really. We're terribly sorry for all the trouble we've caused.*

We?

It said, *Oh, dear. They didn't say you'd have so many questions! Tsk.*

They?

One and the same, I'm afraid. I'm an element of the orphan cluster rescue array, a subset of the accidental entities study group, which is in turn attached to the disaster reversal special hierarchy. We adhere to an attractor in meme-set space which requires us to believe the pseudo-sentient biproducts of the disaster-set entity have a right to exist, even though they have no reality in the C_{11} plenum.

What the fuck are you talking about? *What C_{11} plenum?*

Sigh. *You are familiar with the concept that the universe exists as an eleven dimensional space?*

The one where the extra dimensions are rolled up inside mass quanta, leaving behind just the three of space and one of time? More or less.

Well, that's not quite it but it's on the right track. Mr Faraday, the C_{11} plenum is a fully-packed array of Kaluza-Klein entities containing an infinite amount of energy. Perhaps the simplest way to visualize this space is to view it as random-access memory, whose base state is set to the value one. Assume that there are quantum uncertainty processes at work that sometimes reset an entity's value to zero. Then assume there is some kind of universal CPU whose instruction set allows it to perform certain operations on all entities of value zero. You could think of that as a solid-state universe and not be far wrong.

Isn't that what writers call bafflegab? And isn't this nothing more than a data dump?

The voice's amusement seemed lugubrious, to say the least. *Oh, Mr Faraday. If that's your attitude, then what more can I say?*

Who are you, why are we here, where are we going and what the hell happened?

Fair enough, Mr Faraday. I told you who I am, though I don't think you believe it. What happened? It's not so simple, but I'll see if I can simplify it. As you might imagine C_{11} space has something like evolution, and since its persistence time appears to be on the order of 10^{52} years, there has been plenty of time for it to operate. Over the vigintillia, unimaginably complex entities have evolved.

How complex is that, asshole?

Tsk-tsk. Mr Faraday! Unimaginable to you. As I was saying– in time, these entities grew to understand the properties of the universe they inhabited, and to manipulate it for their own purposes, also unimaginable to you.

Then why tell me?

It sounded hurt: *Because you asked, Mr Faraday. Now, if you'll just be patient? One day, a really long time ago, as you count such things, they discovered that they could create a subplenum with properties analogous to C_{10}, if C_{10} space existed. All they had to do was create it, and then they would have access to a technology in some ways equivalent to your own data processing technology but infinitely more powerful.*

I felt a horrid supposition. One that made me feel cheated indeed.

So you're going to tell me I'm nothing but a computer game? Well now *there's* an original idea!

Such palpable *sarcasm, Mr Faraday! My word! No, nothing so tawdry as that. If it were, none of this would be happening, and you'd never know you were, ah, simulations, I suppose. Unfortunately, once the entities had their C_{10} computers, they were able to work out the properties of the C_9 plenum and deduce that they could use it for physical movement outside the laws of C_{11}. Starships, if you will. Time travel, etc. Magic.*

How nice for them.

Mr Faraday, when the first C_9 device was switched on, it started a chain reaction which began collapsing the dimensions in upon each other, creating lower and lower plena, basically eating away the higher ones. Something had to be done to contain this disaster, which is who I am, and what's happening now.

I don't understand.

Sigh. *I suppose not, Mr Faraday. Look: timescales in the higher dimensions are considerably longer than in your own. C_3 space began as an industrial accident, and everything within it is a product of that accident. You are toxic waste, and now, the cleanup crew has arrived.*

Oh.

Mr Faraday, the beings of C_{11} don't know you exist, and if they did, they would not care. Their only interest is in reversing the substrate disaster, and in being more careful next time.

So who are you, really? And ... and...

And what happens next? Do we wipe you from the floor and have done with it? No. We are the machines made to clean up the mess and we have *noticed you, Mr Faraday. Some among us have realized we have no right to destroy you and have made a place for you to ... persist. Yes. That's the word.*

Persist.

Perhaps you'd like to call us the gods of a lesser creation? Yes, that will do nicely. And that lesser creation is something you might want to call the storage plenum.

Storage. For how long?

I told you, Mr Faraday. Our timescales are far longer than yours. You'll like what we've made for you. The Earth bubble, with everything there ever was living on Earth. It's my special creation, though I'm told the other bubbles are equally nice.

Other bubbles?

It said, *We're here, Mr Faraday. It's been* very *nice to meet you, sir.*

And so, my fine boys and girls, we went down the waste pipe and were flushed out to sea.

See?

After the Sun went out, it got colder and colder and colder, faster than we expected, punching through our heavy clothes, defeating our ingenious little masks, heated and otherwise, until we had to break out the spacesuits, not because there wasn't enough air, but because it was too fucking cold.

You can't imagine how cold –180 feels.

At −180, the oil on your skin freezes. You get cracks at the corners of your eyes. You blink and your skin breaks.

The spacesuits we'd stolen from dead Philadelphia were astonishingly heavy, astonishingly hard to put on, even harder to put together, like Christmas toys in their packaging with "some assembly required".

On the other hand, they were warm and snug and each suit came with a mounting rack, so they would stand up like so many hollow men, waiting for us to crawl through the hatches in their backs. Unfortunately, they weighed almost 150 pounds apiece, like self-contained suits of Medieval combat armor. *Cataphracts in Space*. A wonderful Star Crap title no one'd managed to think of. Too late now, boys. Wonder if any of *them* are still alive? I hope not.

Connie and Julia had to help us up the stairs into the freezing cold hotel, which we were using as a sort of airlock, but once there, we could at least stand unaided, could stagger around, pissing and moaning to each other.

Paulie said, "They'll *never* be able to walk in these, Scott."

"Connie will. She's in better shape than either of us. She weighs 145, you know." And stands five feet eight.

He said, "Well, I weigh 260, and if I fell down … "

I gave a little hop. "I don't even weigh 200, Paulie. You're carrying at least eighty pounds of dead weight, as well as the suit."

"Fuck you."

"Not tonight, Paulie. I have a headache."

"Asshole."

"And proud of it. Come on, let's see if we can get outside without falling down the steps."

It was pitch black outside. Empty. Still. Maybe silent, but all I could hear was the wheeze and whir of my portable life support system. I tripped going over the jamb, staggering, barely able to catch my balance.

Paulie said, "Careful! Why the hell do the boots have heels, anyway? I mean, these suits were intended for orbital EVAs."

"Failure of imagination." Or maybe they thought one day we'd be going back to the Moon, going on to Mars? Fat chance.

It was hard going getting down the steps and out onto the lawn. I was starting to breathe hard, and Paulie's gasps were keeping the microphones activated, rasping hard in my ears.

He said, "What if I have a heart attack?"

I said, "Do you think Julia will want me to fuck her after you're dead, Paulie?"

He made a satisfying gibber, then shut up, saving his breath for walking. We didn't make it to the top of the hill, not by a long shot, just to the head of the driveway but that was enough. There was a dark pickup truck with a bed cap sitting halfway down to the mailbox. I twisted and looked back towards the hotel, towards the lit-up cupola poking out of the ground beyond the hump of the garage birm. No one.

I said, "If we'd thought to turn on the security camera system, we'd've seen them coming." And since we hadn't, that movie mob of peasants armed with pitchforks and scythes would've been inside before we knew what was happening.

Paulie's breath rasped and grunted as we slowly made our way down to the truck. Inanely, I wondered if there was any mail waiting for us out at the road. Maybe a summons from the IRS?

Inside the truck cab, Gary sat behind the wheel, eyes and mouth open, covered with frost. There was a woman sitting beside him in a fluffy white fur-trimmed parka, eyes shut, head down on his shoulder, looking like she was asleep. A thick lock of long, straight black hair had escaped from the hood and was hanging down halfway to her lap.

"I guess it's a good thing we forgot to turn on the cameras. You see what's in the rack?" I wonder where the hell he found a machine gun?

Paulie was leaning forwards in his helmet visor, head miniaturized and made comical by the optical properties of the glass, staring at the woman.

"You know her?"

He nodded. "It's his sister."

Sister. Well. Was she in the group we chased away, or did he actually make the long round trip to Chapel Hill for her? And then what? A peace offering? Here, Paulie. I'll trade you my sister for Julia. I started to feel sick to my stomach, maybe from the exertion, maybe not.

We turned away and started scraping back up the driveway. It was slightly uphill and harder than ever. Paulie was starting to choke between gasps, like he wanted to swallow his tongue, making me wonder how the *fuck* we were going to manage this. When the air's gone, the resistance in the joints from suit pressure will be multiplied.

Paulie stopped, turning, and I could see his head tilted back, looking up at the sky. "What ... " The sound of wonder.

I looked up. There was the Cone, seeming to loom huge above us, hanging low over the horizon, threatening and obscene, like it was swallowing the sky. Hell. It *is*. There. A smear of gray not far from it. Over there another one, larger still, nacreous, with faint striations.

Visible?

"Paulie."

He said, "It's probably a lot colder up by the tropopause. Not so much radiant heating from the ground."

"What do you mean?"

He turned and looked at me. "I think it's an oxygen cloud."

I felt a thrill run through my intestines, threatening to burst right out my asshole. This is ... this is ... what? *Real?* Paulie was looking down at the snow surface around us. He switched on his helmet lights, and I was stunned to see it made the rime of carbon dioxide frost begin to steam. Here and there, like holes in a golf green, there were shadowy little pockets. Gophers?

I said, "Maybe we better go inside?"

He staggered over to one of the holes and tried to kick it with his toe, swaying. The thing was solid, like a little bowl of ice, maybe two inches across. "No. What the fuck *are* those things?"

"I dunno. Let's walk up the hill and take a look around."

We had to stop fifteen times on the way up and by the time we made the summit, we'd been outside for almost three hours. I said, "I guess you're not going to have a heart attack, Paulie. No Julia for me."

He was looking off to the east, still breathing too hard to talk, and when I followed his gaze, I saw some dim, hazy light down by the horizon, barely there. As I watched, eyes adapting, it seemed to grow brighter, then slowly wane, hesitate, flutter, and wax again. "Richmond?"

He gasped, tried to hold his breath, gasped again, panting, then said, "Maybe. On ... fire?"

I said, "It's too cold for anything to burn, Paulie."

"Bomb."

"Richmond's only a little more than a hundred miles from here. If somebody set off even a little atom bomb, we'd've felt the ground shake."

"Maybe we were asleep." Breathing easier now.

Overhead, the oxygen clouds seemed larger. "Maybe so. Or fucking. Hey, Paulie, you feel the earth move when you come?"

He didn't even laugh, looking away from the light, back up at the clouds and ... "*There.*" He lifted his arm a little bit, trying to point.

Something was coming down towards us, a little glowing pinpoint of light. Tinkerbell, looking for Peter Pan. It was drifting our way, drifting like dandelion fluff on the wind, slowly settling. When it was close enough, I could see it was a little silver sphere about the size of a golfball. A vaguely luminescent soap bubble.

Paulie whispered, "Oh, my God." I don't remember ever having heard him sound so pleased in all my life.

The thing started to steam as it approached the ground, not quite hovering over the snowpack, steaming, shrinking, drifting lower. I suddenly realized whatever it was, it wasn't hot enough to sublimate the CO_2. Lower. Lower.

Paph!

It exploded with a sharp hiss, momentarily ballooning to a bright softball of dusty light. Suddenly, there was an icy teacup in the snow where it'd been.

I said, "Well. Guess we know where the holes came from."

He looked like he wanted to kneel beside it. Impossible. He put his hands on his hips, clownish, clumsy, looking back up at bright clouds, visibly spreading across the black and starry sky.

I grinned. "Oxygen rain."

He smiled back, eyes incredibly bright. "Yeah."

I said, "Merry Christmas, Paulie."

How many times can a man awaken and open his eyes slowly?

As many times as it takes.

Until he's finally awake.

Overhead, there was a clear blue sky, that fabled cornflower blue, with fine, faded white clouds so high up you could hardly make out their shape, more like faraway mist than clouds. There was a soft wind blowing and it was cool. Just cool enough for comfort, like when you've set the AC just right.

Just right to be naked.

I could hear the wind rushing in the trees, and there was another soft sound, a faint hissing, like the whitish noise you hear when you stand next to a field of ripe wheat rippling in the wind. Something else, too. Ocean waves in the distance. Sunlight warm on my skin. Sun hanging low in the sky, above remote, jagged white mountains.

All right. Mountains. I...

I sat up suddenly, feeling a hard jolt in my chest, looking around, bug-eyed. *Oh*!

Below me, stretching down the slope of a long hill, the Earth Bubble of the Storage Plenum, gift from the Gods of a Lesser Creation, was a vast, shallowly curving bowl, like a world inside a wok, rimmed by mountains that must make the Himalayas look small.

There were more hills, below the hills a sea, surrounded by white beach, beyond the beach, mountains, the Alps maybe, beyond the mountains, another sea, beyond that sea, a darkling plain, overhung by a boil of gray-white cumulonimbus.

There! A towering black anvil, lightning twisting from it, striking at the land below.

Mountains and seas and forking silvery rivers spreading out to right and left. Deserts, both yellow and red. Beyond the curving land, down in the bottom of the bowl, hanging white mist. Then more landscape, so tiny it looked like a clutter of colored static, green and blue and gray, then the mountains below the sun.

Pellucidar, I thought, or that World Without End from a story I once thought of but never wrote, the one about the Space-Time Juggernaut.

And if the Gods told the truth, somewhere now, everyone is awakening. *Everyone*. People like me who think they've awakened on the bright sward of some personal Barsoom, fearful others, awakening to Heaven or Hell. Or *Neterkhert*.

Somewhere, a king of Kmt awakens, looks up in the sky, and screams Aton's name.

Somewhere else, a sinner awakens, and wonders where they might have hidden the lake of boiling blood.

I got to my feet, dusting stalks of dead grass off my bare butt, wriggling my toes in cool green living grass, wondering if Dante was somewhere nearby, wondering why there were so many Italians in Hell.

There were trees, tall thin things with scaly gray trunks, surrounded by a carpet of brown pine needles and, just as I looked, a couple emerged, holding hands, a man and a woman, both of them very thin. She was a redhead; he had thin brown hair and a sculpted, curly brown beard. And seeing me, they waved, hurrying forward.

"Scott! Scottie!" The one from the man, the other from the woman.

Despite the best of intentions, I kept looking at her crotch, and that made her smile in a shy sort of way. Him too.

"Katy. Ben."

He said, "That was a damn good idea you had!"

"Glad you liked it. Uh ... "

He laughed. "It was nowhere near as bad as I expected. You know, we almost made it to the rainout?"

That little pang of guilt, remembering the night I sent him away to die. All for nothing. I could have told him to go get Katy and bring her back. But I didn't. So how am I different from Paulie then? Wasn't Ben my friend? Or Katy, with her lovely little snatch?

"I, uh ... well. I hope it wasn't too bad for you. I mean ... "

Katy said, "If you've got enough Seconal, it's easy enough." She laughed at my look. "Hey, Ben and me woke up together. He told me, um, you and Connie ... "

I shook my head. "We made it through the rainout. After that ..."

There was a shadow in Ben's face, however sunny Katy was right now. And, of course, for them, that rainout was minutes ago, on the other side of a double-handful of mother's little helper. Look at them. They belong together.

And, somewhere out here ... Connie? Lara? I ...

The two of them were looking past me now, faces curious. When I turned, there was a naked woman with curly black hair, smiling, just like you'd expect. And she said, "So, is this my reward in the hereafter?"

What a grin!

I don't think she expected me to pounce on her the way I did, grappling, almost knocking her down in my eagerness. She pushed me away, laughing, wiping her mouth, "Jesus! Down puppy!"

Behind me, Katy said, "Shew! You don't waste any fucking time, Scott! You know this nice nekkid lady?"

To his credit, naked Millikan was even blushing. When I introduced them all to each other, Katy looked Maryanne up and down slowly, lingering on her tits the way women will, then said, "Hey. Connie shows up anytime soon, we can compare notes." Letting Maryanne know where she'd been. Maryanne looked at me, bit her lip, made a little crooked smile, and shrugged. I felt something cold touch my spine, making my balls pull in a bit. I looked down the hill again, towards the shining sea. People were coming out of the bushes everywhere, milling, calling out to one another.

Down there, most likely not far away, a pretty blonde woman of about thirty is inspecting her right wrist, and wondering what the hell she did wrong. Wonder what I'll say if I run into her?

Somewhere nearby, maybe just beyond the trees, an elephant howled and then we heard a man's terrified scream. Millikan spun, looking towards the sound, then over his shoulder at me. "I guess I wasn't paying attention when the Gods did their bit. Did they say anything about the animals coming here too?"

Gods? As in, *I'm not the only one was told where we are*? I said, "You got a nice ass, Ben."

He gave me a weird look, then turned back to the woods. You could see a fucking elephant in there, a big gray shadow, blundering about among the pine trees, getting all tangled up, thrashing this way and that. In front of it, you could see a big fat white guy running our way. Every once in a while he'd look over his shoulder, scream, trip and fall, get up and stumble on.

Maryanne said, "The trees came to heaven with us, why not an elephant?"

I put my arm around her waist, and said, "Long as you're here, the details don't matter."

She twisted in my grasp, trying to look me in the eye. I started to rear back, and realized with a jolt that the far-sightedness that'd been building as I moved through my late forties and into my fifties was gone.

She said, "Even if Connie shows up and changes her mind?"

I smiled. "Especially then."

That still, solemn look. "And what about the other one?"

I took a deep breath. "When Lara took that razor to her wrist, she knew who would find her in the morning. I've had twenty years to think on that."

A slow nod. "I've got a past of my own. You never asked."

"If it matters, you'll let me know. Until then ... look!" A gesture with my free arm, downslope towards the deepening mist. "Everybody and everything that ever was is here in this valley. We ... "

The fat guy came out of the trees stumbling, still looking back, though the elephant seemed to have given up, stuck in a tangle of fallen trees, confused. I waved my arm. "Paulie! This way!"

Maryanne nuzzled close to my ear and whispered, "Shut up! Maybe he won't see us."

He ran straight across the sloping ground towards the hill, tripping again, running slower, then slower still. Just before he got to the steeper part, leading up to where the four of us stood, he turned away, running parallel to the base, then turning at an angle away from us again.

Gasping. Gasping for breath.

Suddenly, he screamed, "*Julia*! Julia, *wait*!"

I turned and looked. There. Naked, long hair streaming out behind her, running away, toward another patch of dark, piny woods. Running along, holding hands with another fat man. Gary, of course, healed from the bullets and the cold.

Paulie fell down, got up, shouted, "Julia! For God's sake! Please! I *love* you!" Ran on, stumbling, following them into the trees.

Eventually, the rainout reached the point where even the spacesuits were useless, trapping us in the shelter. One night, we all pitched in and put together one of best dinners I ever had. Cornish hens. Brussels sprouts. Baked potato. Cornbread stuffing. Salad with balsamic vinaigrette dressing. We were all crowded into the Staff Quarters kitchen, working on our favorite things, bumping into each other, laughing about silly little shit, like old times, like we were, somehow, having the life we'd always wanted, maybe even the life we deserved. There was chicken giblet gravy. Real butter. Sour cream.

Everybody had their own favorite wine, from Julia's snobby chicken-appropriate dry white whatever, to my own beer stein full of tawny port. I lifted it now and looked at them. Silence? Not quite. In the background, you could hear a soft drumming sound, rather a slow drum right now, the dull, intermittent thud of exploding oxygen rain.

"Here's to us," I said, "here and now."

Paul picked up a champagne flute of Black Opal something or other. "Not the things that were. Not the things that might have been. Just us."

Julia looked at him, seeming surprised.

"Good one, Paulie." Wish you'd been thinking that way back when life was real and there were things we were maybe going to do and be. We ate quietly for a while, most of the noise coming from Paul, who'd never learned to chew with his mouth shut. Hell. It's just defiance. Somewhere, his dead parents are still looking over his shoulder, yelling at him, wringing their hands in despair because he won't do what they want.

Overhead, the sound of the rain grew louder for a moment, then softened again. Like someone far above had dumped an extra-big bucket of droplets on us, just for fun. Connie put down her fork and looked up at the ceiling, as if inspecting it for water stains.

Conniekins, if *this* roof starts leaking, we are fucked.

She said, "Is it going to stay like this?"

"We don't know."

Paul grimaced. "Yeah we do. In a few days it'll be like real rain, a downpour."

"Well, we only imagine that, Paulie. And we've been wrong about a *lot*. Remember?"

"Look. Right now, it's just getting started. The droplets are coming down slow because they're low density and falling through gaseous air. But it's the *air* that's falling! The atmospheric pressure will start to drop, more oxygen will condense out, then the nitrogen will start to go."

"I know. I know. As the pressure goes down, the drops will fall hard. Towards the end, they'll be falling like rocks."

He grinned. "Feathers in a vacuum."

Julia kept her eyes on her plate, eating slowly, as if ignoring us.

Connie said, "What'll happen to us then?"

"That's why we piled that extra dirt on the birm. Might help. Can't hurt. If things get scary, we'll go in the capsule and seal the hatches."

Her voice was soft, eyes on mine. "And ... afterward?"

"We'll just have to see. I ... "

The floor shuddered, rattling dishes and glasses together on the table, my wine rocking in its mug. I jumped up and ran to the lounge, looking out the big picture window into the brightly-lit garage. Nothing. Bulldozer at the door. The two cars. The nose of the Cat visible in shadow. The little door up to the hotel was still sealed, containing its coffer dam of concrete and dirt.

Over my shoulder, Paulie said, "Let's go to the cupola."

I nodded, looking at the open door to the tunnel. Nothing. Darkness. "Yeah. And maybe we better think about keeping that shut when we're not down there?"

From the cupola you could see there was a fire burning beyond our old observation hill, a big fire, enormous red flames licking skyward, pouring forth dense black clouds of smoke, like crude oil burning in a bowl, calling up images of the end of the Gulf War, when the well-heads were set off by Saddam's retreating heroes. Already, the smoke was towering up in a steep, jet-black column towards the bright green sky, with its muddy orange streaks and curls of vermilion lightning.

There were sparks of rain everywhere, falling faster now, pulling their pale blue contrails, popping as they hit the landscape, twinkling around the edges of the hot black smoke, flaring and veering from the fire.

Paul said, "Somewhere near downtown. Maybe a gas main explosion?"

"I don't think so. That's big. Farther away than you think, maybe on Palmer's Ridge. There's nothing up there but woods."

"Plane crash?"

"Jesus, Paulie. You know any planes that could fly in a -200 atmosphere?"

The flames were getting bigger and brighter now, showing long tongues of yellow in their midst, maybe from the falling oxygen.

Connie pressed her face to the quartz, then jerked back. I touched it. Cold. Cold enough to hurt. She said, "Are we in danger?"

I said, "Whatever it is, it can't spread far. It'll go out soon enough."

Paul was looking down at the little bank of meteorological gauges in a panel below one window. "Temperature's actually up a few degrees. It's that hot. Pressure's down more than I expected. It's around twelve psi outside."

I took a deep breath, feeling my heart flutter nervously. "Still okay in here. I guess we've got a tight enough seal."

I turned and looked at the hotel. It was surrounded by a boil of pale blue fog, tower of vapor reaching for the sky. There was something wrong with the roof, maybe shingles missing now, and you could see the occasional ball of light as a raindrop would strike and flare. Leaking? Hard to say. The oxygen probably would evaporate on the wood, but ... I said, "It's not going to last, Paulie. We need to think about closing the geothermal water valves, so we don't have a blowout when it collapses."

He said, "It'll go fast, once it gets cold enough."

"We should leave a video camera running in here, once we do. So we'll have a tape, after ... " *After?* Christ. *What* after?

Paulie snickered, turning away towards the tunnel hatch, headed back to the Quarters, where our dinner was getting cold. When I looked at Connie, she was still staring out the window, not at the fire, not at the hotel that'd been our home for a while but down the driveway at Gary's pickup truck. It was visibly dented, and the windshield was gone, no more than a few shards remaining, dangling around the rim, stuck together by safety-glass film. You couldn't see inside, not even when a raindrop would get in and flare up briefly blue.

Maybe they're eaten away. Maybe they're gone. She must've seen it the first time she came in here, while we were out shoveling up birm dirt. She never said a fucking word.

She turned to me and smiled, put her hand out and touched my chest, let it drift down to hold onto my belt buckle. "Come on," she said, "we can reheat our stuff in the microwave."

Greekee, greekee, greekee, greekee ...

The nights in heaven are dark indeed, filled with darktime noises that turn you back into a child. Greekee. Like those stickbug creatures I made up for a book I once wanted to write, about a man who didn't know who he was. All lost now.

Perhaps for the best. Somewhere in the distance, a big cat squalled, high scream falling off in a deep gurgle, some great engine dieseling away to silence. Maryanne shivered next to me, maybe the tiger-bright, maybe the nighttime cold. I put my arm around her shoulders again, welcoming the touch myself.

Oh, great. Another hard-on. She's going to get tired of this shit sooner or later.

We'd gotten a few more people together on the hilltop, mostly folks from the Redoubt EVA crew, a few from HDC, a couple of Ben's friends, and we'd managed to uproot thorn bushes, swearing at the cuts they made, Jonas yelping when he hooked one on his dick, making a little boma round the top of the hill.

Millikan startled me by knowing how to make and use a fire drill, lighting us up a cheery little deadwood fire just as the sun sank fat and dull red-orange behind the remotest mountains.

He'd grinned at my amazement. "What the fuck did you think I was up to on all those wilderness camping vacations? You should've come along, like I said."

Maryanne nuzzled the side of my neck, then pointed up in the sky. "You suppose they have names?"

She was pointing at a little pink moon, an irregular rocky little asteroid thing that had come over the mountains a couple of hours ago, swelling as it came our way, tumbling and twinkling against the black backdrop of the sky.

I said, "If they don't, we'll just have to make some up."

There'd been three of them so far, a yellow, a blue, and now a pink, though there'd never been more than two at once. The blue one was sort of like Earth's old Moon, a round, not quite featureless disk that seemed far, far away.

There were other lights in the sky too, but damned few. Distant, untwinkling glints, reminding me of planets, that familiar one out there maybe Venus, a pale yellow that might be Jupiter, a pink that could be Mars. Nothing, however, that would remind you of stars, just deep, velvety black that went on and on.

On to nowhere. That's what the Gods said.

This is the Lesser Creation, infinitely folded in on itself, holding whatever the Gods felt was worth rescuing from the mistake that made us.

What happens if the Greater Gods, unknown, unknowable, find out what their tools have done? Will they sweep us away then, after all?

Maryanne stood and stretched, still looking up at the sky, shining and shadowy in the firelight, all breasts and bush and pale white skin. "You suppose we're immortal now?"

Isn't that the way it always works in these things? I said, "If it were my story, that's the way I'd have it end."

Looking out across the black, blank emptiness of the immense valley, supposedly filled with every living thing that had ever existed on the Earth, she said, "I always wondered just how bored people might get, living on forever in the hereafter."

In the end, the only decent place to ride out the rain of air, if you could call it that, turned out to be in our survival capsule bunks. Paul and Julia were hiding in theirs, separate, Connie and I together, this time in mine. In case we wound up flung across the room, at least there'd be a few less feet to fall.

We left the lights on and scrunched in there, eating lunch, listening to the roar of the rain, now more like waves at the ocean, as if heard too close up, than anything else, eating yesterday's leftovers, like nothing was wrong, like it was raining outside on a blustery winter night in North Carolina.

Tomorrow the sun will shine, and we'll go for a nice walk in Umstead Forest, amid the leafless gray trees under a crisp, cloudless dark blue sky. And in due course, summer will come again.

We're not fifty-something, Connie. We're young. Young and beautiful. Remember?

The tuna was better for having steeped for a day, and Connie got a loaf of that really great Wellspring bread out of the cupboard. "Last one," she'd said, bracing her feet against the shivering floor, brandishing a sharp knife. Sandwiches, pickles, chips and Sealtest French Onion Dip, a plastic bottle of Welch's for me, decaffeinated diet Coke for her.

Think about it.

No matter how hard you try, Connie dearest, you ain't got time to get fat now.

I kept reaching out to touch her thighs, pat the warmth between her legs, and when we were done, we stretched out, bunk rocking gently underneath us, nuzzling our faces together. Inside her pants, my hand was nice and warm, Connie smiling against the side of my face and murmuring, "Incorrigible."

I wanted her to call me Scottie again, wanting to feel the way it would melt my heart.

BAM!

The bunk jolted so hard it threw us up in the air a bit and, from the other side of the room, Julia screamed, a high drawn out wail like a special effect in some cheap movie or another.

Crack!

The capsule tilted hard, walls shuddering and groaning around us, tipping back the other way, so we fell together against the inside wall of the bunk. There was a tumbling sound from the floor, Paul cursing incoherently, not even words, near as I could tell. When I looked, he was scrambling on his hands and knees, trying to get back in bed.

Stroby out there, fluorescent lights flickering.

Ballasts failing, I guess.

I turned back to Connie, driving Paul and Julia and everything else from my head. She was scared-looking. White-faced. Wide-eyed. Eyes searching mine for something, anything.

I kissed her softly and reached under the waistband of her pants, putting my palm flat on her belly. Smiled. In the background, you could hear Julia sobbing. Nothing from Paul. Hey, Paulie. Gotcher pillow over yer head yet?

Connie seemed to smile back.

I said, "I'm glad you're brave."

The bed jerked under us and the angle of the floor steepened a bit. Outside, things were whacking and booming, so loud I couldn't imagine what was happening. Jesus. Sounds like sheets and blankets flapping on a clothesline. Gigantic sheets and blankets. In a hurricane.

She said, "I never knew I was. Until just now."

I slid my hand the rest of the way down into the warmth of her crotch, getting my fingers where I needed them to be. Outside, there was a loud groaning sound, the sound of a giant tree falling in some logger movie. What the hell am I thinking of? *Sometimes a Great Notion*? That Paul Newman thing. The guy drowning, pinned underwater by a log. Don't laugh!

I wonder what Connie will say if I try to fuck her now? Maybe if we time it right, we can be coming just as the capsule implodes. I strangled a giggle.

Paul was saying something now. Babbling.

Connie pulled back a little, holding my face between her hands, looking at me. "I never saw two people as scared as Paul and Julia. Why aren't *you* afraid?"

I shrugged. "I don't know. I guess ... I was only ever afraid of people. This ... Hell. I would've died someday anyway."

"Are we going to die right now?"

Outside there was another long groaning sound, followed by a deep thud, like someone slamming the hood of a 1950s-era sedan. I said, "We'll know pretty soon. One way or another."

She pressed her back into the wall, lifting her leg so she'd be more accessible, and said, "What if we live?"

I shrugged. "What difference does it make?"

It was difficult to get our pants off, scrunched in the bunk like that but we managed, the bed hopping and shuddering around us. And some time in the middle of it all, accompanied by the squeal of what might have been the wind and somebody screaming, the lights went out.

We didn't notice until afterwards.

Which, when you got right down to it, came as a surprise.

Afterwards?

Well.

Quiet.

Very quiet.

Paulie and I stood in our spacesuits, filling the capsule airlock, integrity checks completed, com checks completed, at the end of our last argument about whether it was reasonable to waste the air in the lock.

Hell, Paulie. We didn't arrange for anything else.

And we've got to *know*.

Dark eyes doubtful.

Sure the idiot lights show the waste pipe connection is broken, but we've still got external power! That's all we need to know. We're *safe*.

For now.

Connie was inside, manning the communication console, watching the images from our helmet cams on TV. Even Julia'd finally gotten out of her fucking bunk, though she didn't seem to have much to say anymore. Hollow-eyed. Empty.

It'd been over quicker than we expected, one final blast more or less leveling the capsule again, the same blast that broke our sewer pipe, then there was just the wind, moaning and moaning, getting softer and softer until you could hardly hear it at all.

Then you couldn't.

Turned out the lighting system was fine, the fluorescent tubes had just broken. New tubes, and then we'd stood there, Paulie dressed in jeans, a coat, combat boots, like that'd do any fucking good if the capsule blew out, huh? Me naked again.

I flinched when he said, *It's quiet outside 'cause the air's all gone.*

Connie made me get dressed again, then we had supper, breaking into our TV dinners for the first time, appallingly salty stuff I wondered if I could get used to. Assuming there would be time to get used to anything. We cleaned up the mess, ate again, fucked around with the short wave radio. Ate again. Talked about what to do. No cameras. No satellite dish. No nothing.

The valve in the airlock squealed for a while as the air rushed out, then it got quiet in there as well, Paulie looking at me through the faceplates of our helmets, and I wondered which helmet cam Connie was looking through. Did she want to see me, or see what I saw?

"Well," I said, "no time like the present."

Paul grinned. "All of a sudden, I like the past a whole lot better."

I said, "Connie? How are your instrument readings?"

Her voice was grainy but reassuringly familiar in the helmet phones. "Pressure's holding steady in here, so I guess the seal's tight. You've got twenty-three millibars in the lock."

Paul's face screwed up a little. "A lot more than on Mars!"

"Probably being kept up by outgassing from the PLSS back-packs." I pronounced it *pliss*, just like the Apollo astronauts. Christ, listen to my fucking heart! Galloping like a horse. Scared? Excited? Or just from the weight of this fucking suit?

I started to work the lock-lever, withdrawing the deadbolts from their sockets. Nothing. I nodded to Paul. "Okay."

He reached out one clumsily gloved hand, hesitated, then pulled the latch handle.

The door popped open and swung wide before we could catch it, hinges locking against their stops with a *clack*. Christ. Impossible.

Connie said, "I heard that! You guys okay? Your pressure went down to nine millibars all of a sudden."

Oh, *Mir*. The way they broke the airlock door that time. I said, "We're fine." Okay. Sound transmitted through the capsule structure and I heard it over the radio, that's all.

I expected it to be dark outside for some reason. Dark like outer space in all the movies ever made. The light out there was pale turquoise. Very pale. Very dim. But there. Mist hanging over a soft white landscape. Snow drifted here and there. Something like snow, anyway.

I got out first, bumping Paulie aside as I ducked through the door, backpack antenna scraping, though I cleared my helmet okay. I was standing on a little flat place, like a bit of front porch, with jagged edges, a piece of concrete still clinging to the capsule's hull. Beyond it, there was a long slope, gradually steepening into a canyon maybe two hundred yards away. Halfway down it, there was a big twisted hunk of something that kind of looked like a bulldozer blade.

No bulldozer, though.

The mist only went up a little ways. Above it, the sky was dark, punctured all over by the still white pinpoints of the stars. Lots of stars. Paul was standing beside me now, silent, looking around.

Little waxy snowflakes were falling, only a few, far apart, coming straight down out of the sky, bouncing when they hit. Just enough air left to slow them down. What? Noble gases?

"Look!" Beyond the mist, there was a shimmering disturbance, a ghostly white plume against the black sky, almost invisible. Paul's eyes were shining bright through his faceplate. "It's a nitrogen geyser. Like on Triton!" His little burst of laughter, pure joy, scared me a little bit.

Connie's voice rasped in the earphones. "So, what's the scoop? How long can we make it?"

I said, "Eight weeks on the capsule supplies. More if … "

I turned away from the geyser, turned left, towards where the Staff Quarters had been. Not a sign of anything. Twenty feet of structure, forty feet of birm, the hotel foundation. All gone. Where the storerooms had been, there was what looked like a crumpled pile of metal, some of it blue. My Camry maybe?

Paul was still staring at the geyser, lips moving. Telling himself what? I stepped forward, looking beyond him, at the jagged edge of the remaining concrete wall and the smooth curve of the partially exposed capsule. Have to do something about that. Try to cover it up with dirt or something.

What'll we use for fucking shovels?

Why didn't we put some tools in the capsule?

There was a hump in the landscape beyond it, level with the capsule, holding its own bit of concrete floor, its own little piece of wall, with a wide, corrugated metal door. My heart seemed to pulse in my chest, the proverbial skipped beat. Okay.

I hopped down, dropping heavily to the ground, almost falling. Why did I expect lowered gravity? Because I'm in a fucking spacesuit? Maybe I thought I was on the Moon. I trudged heavily over to the thing and tried climbing up onto its porch. Shit. Maybe I can reach the bottom edge of the door from here and …

It was stuck, coming up on one side only, and I imagined the screech of frozen wheels and rails. Silence. It only went up a couple of inches, then stuck fast but I could shine my helmet lights underneath and see inside.

"Well, shit-fire!"

Connie said, "Scott?"

I made my own little maniac's laugh.

"Scottie?"

I turned to face Paul again, and was gratified to see I'd gotten his attention. "Looks like the Cat bay made it through. I guess we've got ourselves a vacuum-adapted halftrack."

He got laboriously down off the capsule's porch and started lumbering toward me, teetering, barely able to keep his feet. "Some of our supplies were pretty much indestructible. Air tanks. That kind of thing."

"So?"

He said, "I bet there's a lot of crap down in the gully we can salvage."

When I looked that way, I could see, beyond the mist, another ghostly nitrogen geyser, and a third one beyond that, made tiny in the distance. This, I thought, is really pretty God-damned cool.

Not much more after that.

The *Robinson Crusoe* thing. The *Swiss Family Robinson* thing. The *Farnham's Freehold* thing. Not quite the *Island in a Sea of Time* thing, eh? No Nantucket for us.

I awoke the next morning, bladder bursting, with Maryanne's taste in my mouth, Maryanne curled up beside me, sound asleep and softly snoring just as the sun was coming up like a fat pink balloon over the mountains.

I got up, stretching, creaking, stiff as hell from sleeping on the cold, cold ground, wondering why the fuck the Gods had left me a fifty-something-year-old man. Surely ...

I found a little gap in the boma, already pushed open by someone else, staggered down the hillside a little way, and could wait no longer, turned and started pissing merrily away. Jonas was there, a few yards off, pissing himself, and when he caught me watching, smirked, and said, "Deep, too."

There was a commotion from the slope below, and when I turned to look, there was an enormous fat woman striding along, breasts bounding up and down, belly roll wriggling. Lot of nice muscle in those haunches.

Paulie was scuttling along beside her, walking half-crabwise. "Olga. Olga, *please*. I didn't mean ... "

She stopped and turned suddenly, planted her feet solidly about eighteen inches apart, one forward the other back, then her shoulders rotated and her fist caught Paulie in the middle of the face with a meaty *splat*. She stalked off, heading for the woods where the elephant had been yesterday.

Paulie went down on his backside, hands covering his face. When he took them away, there was plenty of blood, and I could see his nose was knocked crooked, broken maybe. "*Ow!*" He looked up at me, blood running from both nostrils, crossing his lips, dripping off his chin and down his chest, and started to cry.

That's heaven for you.

With nothing left but the survival capsule, with it getting colder and then colder still, all that was left was for us to dig out the Cat and try to drive cross-country to the National Redoubt. All the way to Colorado. You think maybe they'll let us in *now*? Jesus.

We made it all of a hundred miles, I think.

Much over fifteen miles an hour and the fucking thing would buck and jerk and roll, Paulie bitching he couldn't make sense of the computer screen, Julia pissing and moaning and claiming she needed to puke. We stopped for a break, Connie complaining she needed to get out of the suit, went on, stopped for lunch, went on again …

Maybe ten hours like that, and I was actually asleep when it happened.

I don't know. Paul was driving, Connie navigating, and there was a reek of piss in the cabin. Maybe it was the distraction Julia made once she figured out she could get the ISS ham frequency on the Cat's radio.

ISS in the sky!

This is us on the ground!

HALP! HALLLP!

I remember I woke up in something like zero gee, floating inside my suit, head spinning weirdly to the sight of Paulie on the ceiling, Julia screaming, Connie screaming, all these *crash-tinkle* noises and crumpling sounds and *we're rolling down a God damn hill*!

We came to a stop right-side up, lights out.

Julia sobbing.

Everybody else quiet.

Listen carefully.

The soft throb of the diesel at idle, softer pop and huff of the air valves, feeding the engine from all those SCUBA tanks in the trailer, the compressor, the vaporizer, the hamper of oxygen snow…

Okay. Good. Nothing's broken.

Listen carefully.

No hissing noises?

"Paulie?"

"I'm all right."

Great. Who gives a fuck? I wish you were dead, Paulie. "Put on the lights."

A clattering sound. "The switch is on. Must be broken."

"Swell. Connie?"

"Here, Scott."

I got my ass on the bench seat and squirmed over somebody. There was a sweet, pissy smell, and Connie said, "Scott."

"Sorry." I rummaged in the junk on the floor, fishing in canvas tote bags, until I found a flashlight. *Click*. Yellow light picked out Paul's face, staring from the open visor of his space suit. "Scrunch down."

I got close to the window and shone the light outside. Sheer, irregular white walls on both sides, a narrowing vee of open space in front. "Shit."

Connie said, "What's out there, Scott?"

"We're in a fucking gully."

Paul made some little choking sound. "I'm ... I didn't see ... "

"Move your ass out of the way."

I got in the driver's seat, got my feet on the pedals, engaged tracks and tires, and hit the gas. The engine grumbled, and something lumped around outside, but we didn't budge.

Paul said, "Probably not even on the ground."

I turned and shone the flashlight on the caulked-shut zipper. Picks and shovels bolted to the sides of this thing. Maybe ... I looked at Paul. "Well. What do you think?"

He shut his eyes and looked for a second like he was holding his breath. After a bit, his lips started to move soundlessly. What the fuck, Paulie? Praying? Is that what we've got left. He opened his eyes, and said, "I'm so tired. Don't you want to try?"

Agonized look, shine in his eyes growing. Jesus, don't cry Paulie. He said, "I've got to shit."

"Well, that's a big help."

"Please, oh ... " You could actually hear the sound it made when he let go, eyes squinting, mouth in a grimace.

Connie, herself already floating in piss, snarled, "Oh, fucking *Jesus*!"

I grinned. "What the hell'd you fucking *eat* yesterday?"

"Frozen tacos."

"Smart."

I shone the light out the window again, then clicked it off. Up at the top of the crevasse, you could see a sky full of stars. I said, "Look, we'll just wind up getting killed if we try to go outside now. Not to mention the wasted air. Why don't we try to get some sleep? Maybe we'll think of something in the morning."

Then I opened my eyes on darkness, wondering what time it was, wondering how long I'd been asleep. I was alone in front, sprawled in the driver's seat, feet propped up on the passenger's side, looking out the window. I could see the starry sky, no recognizable constellations. The seat was shaking gently to the soft throb of the idling diesel.

Be a pisser if it stalled while we were sleeping, huh? Never get the fucker started again in this cold. Connie was stretched out on the middle bench seat, gasping softly in her sleep, one arm outflung, resting across my right thigh.

Paul and Julia must be crammed together in back. If you could, Paulie, would you get her out of the suit for one last little fuck? Or is that me I'm thinking about?

Somebody was sniffling a bit. Not Julia.

Watching the stars, I realized I could see them slowly edge east to west. As the world turns? Still got that, at least.

What the fuck are we going to *do*?

Once the diesel runs out and the engines stop, maybe a week or ten days from now, we'll last another six or seven hours on the suit batteries, then we freeze to death.

That's all, folks?

Or we go outside, losing a cabin full of air, try to dig the fucker loose? Maybe it falls on us, or explodes or something? What if the tracks are broken? What then? What if we *do* break it loose? Can we drive it out of here? There's a winch under the front bumper. Maybe ...

Maybe hell.

Never-say-die bullshit.

Where the hell's Superman when you fucking need him?

Maybe that other thought was the right idea.

I watched the stars in their slow, stately dance, and, after a bit, wondered why they weren't all going at the same speed, then wondering if they shouldn't be going in the same direction. That one star right there, a little brighter than the others, seeming to detach itself from the field and go diagonal ...

"Paulie?"

Sniffle. "Paul. Wake up."

"What the fuck do you *want*?"

Bitter. Angry. Full of ... everything.

Everything that ever went wrong between us.

I said, "There's not enough ambient light to reflect off a big satellite now, is there?"

The scorn was, as they say, palpable. "Of *course* not."

I pointed out the window, and said, "Then what the fuck is *that*?"

The spaceship turned out to be from Colorado, investigating our mysterious infrared source, and they were impressed as hell we'd built ourselves a mooncar.

Well. You know the rest. The flight to the National Redoubt, Connie gone, then blessed Maryanne, the Expedition to the Sun, the ... right. The End.

Maryanne kept craning her neck as we pushed our way through the tall saw-grass, trying to watch the tribe of scared-looking chimps that'd been paralleling our track for the last few days, shading her eyes and standing on tiptoe. There were big, grizzled males, females with babies, cute as hell. Watching us, staying close, but not too close.

Maryanne whispered, "What do you suppose they want?"

I hefted one of the sharpened, fire-hardened sticks we were using for spears, and said, "They probably understand the sabertooth cats are scared of us."

It'd been about a month since our little tribe had departed the top of the hill and started working its way downslope, deeper into the Earth Bubble valley, a month we'd counted by slashes Millikan made on a stick with his first flint blade. God damn clever little son of a bitch. But he got me thinking about the things I knew too. Which got us all started thinking about what we wanted to do.

Connie hadn't turned up in that month, nor Lara, nor anybody else, fear about that meeting gradually ebbing away. But still, I wondered. If I found her, would Lara still be thirty years old? Really?

All I have left of her is hazy memories of wonderful old fucks. Were they so great? The only way I'll ever know is if she turns up and ...

Jonas, taking point, held up one broad hand, inhaling deeply. "Smell that ocean! It's got to be around here somewhere!"

There was a fishy salt tang in the air, all right. And a shushing sound that might not be the wind. I said, "Once we get up on the dunes, we'll get a better view." Down in the hollows, all you could see was the white-ice peaks of the Ringwall.

God. Giving names to everything.

There was a sudden, booming howl, not so far away, like a mournful giant playing his tuba. The chimps jerked, looking around, panicky, bug-eyed, jabbering and gesturing, edging closer to us.

Millikan looked at me, more nervous than the chimps, and said, "What'd you say those trumpet-monsters were called?"

"Parasauralophus."

As we'd moved downslope, it quickly became obvious the life forms of the ages were arranged in rings, going backward in time as you descended toward the mist. Without a machine technology, we won't get far. The oxygen content of the air has to be different down there. And down in the mist, down in the Archaean ...

We'd hardly gotten down to the Pleistocene border, seen our first few mammoths and crap, before the dinosaurs started turning up. Seventy-six million years ago, the world had been full of big, fast migratory animals. And nothing here to stop them from walking uphill.

What the hell's it going to be like, when the mixing's at full boil?

And what the hell happens to me if I get fucking *killed* in here?

For some reason, the Gods didn't say.

Millikan was looking down at his spear. "This thing's not going to be much good against a Tyrannosaur."

"No shit."

Jonas crested the dune and suddenly threw himself flat. "*Jesus!*"

I slithered up beside him, pulling Maryanne along by the hand, stopping when I could peer over the dune.

Ocean. Fat, flat ocean, stretching out and out until it became unreal. Something big out there. Something big like a whale.

Maryanne said, "Oh, my God! Look!" Pointing down at a broad white beach like a thousand Waikikis stuck together.

One of the little hairy things looked up from its forage, standing upright with a clam in one hand, a flat rock in the other. It pried the shell open and ate what was inside. Then it casually nudged the next one with its toe, nodding up at the dune. The kneeling one, a female from its hanging, hairy breasts, turned and looked up at us. Froze.

Maryanne said, "Those are *habilis*, aren't they?"

I nodded, wishing for just a second that Paulie was here, so I could say they were *tor-o-don*.

Crouching beside me, Ben Millikan grinned through his beard, and said, "God damn, this is the *coolest* thing that ever happened to me!"

Out beyond the rolling surf, something leapt from the sea, curving like a dolphin, disappearing again. Not a fish, too small to be an ichthyosaur. It appeared again, standing on its tail looking straight at us, I thought, and screamed, a familiar word-like parrot squawk.

Maryanne whispered, "Like it knows we're here, and it's glad."

Millikan laughed. "Maybe it's fucking Flipper!"

Closer now, the parasauralophus moaned and, when I looked, the nearest chimp, a big male, was only a few yards away, eyes big and desperate. I gave a tight-lipped smile, remembering all that I'd read, and motioned for him to come on up.

When we camped out that night, six moons appeared in the sky all at once.

Rebirth.

I can't even call it a second chance, for the first one was rigged against me, even before I squirted, *inter anem et urinam*, into the false old world.

From the lowest passes through the Ringwall, the Earth Bubble looks unreal, even more like an Impressionist canvas than the Grand Canyon, or the view southward from Kilimanjaro. From any mountain peak, you can see the world below tip away from you, tilting ever steeper as it gets farther away. From the south rim of the Grand Canyon, you can see the clouds over the North Rim angling impossibly upward.

Not here.

Here was a bowl of mist, a bowl of unknowable size, filled with a painted-on, cloud-hazy landscape, a patchy ring of green and gold and blue surrounding an abyss of dense, yellow-white fog. Down there, down in the deepest parts, was air no Phanerozoic animal could breath. Down there was the old bacterial world that was half the history of life on Earth.

Life the Gods felt as much worth saving as our own.

We'd measured it, after a fashion, triangulating peaks around the Ringwall during our trek, plotting angle and azimuth on our birchbark maps as we walked around the world, day on week on month on year, slowly climbing, downward into the past, upward to the end of time.

You haven't lived 'til you've heard a dimetrodon scream.

At some point we guessed the big valley was maybe a half-million miles in diameter, maybe a little more. Enough to hold everything that ever was? Maybe so. Hard to say.

It made me remember another world, that World Without End I imagined, plastered round the outside surface of Creation, the final destination for all transmigrating souls. Somewhere here, there *could* be High America, if we wanted to build it. Room enough.

But why bother?

Up here, there wasn't any wind, which was just as well, since it was colder than any hell I'd seen since before the rainout. The pass we'd spotted months ago, spent months climbing towards, was maybe 80,000 feet above the Endtime grassland at the foot of the Ringwall.

Hopeless.

Jonas was the one who pointed out the air pressure wasn't changing as we went up and down the slope, suggesting the gravity gradient here might not be the same as it was back home and, with it, the atmospheric scale height.

Back home?

Funny to call it that.

It was never home to me.

Home only to the cheap, cheating billions who would live and die for nothing and no one.

Beside me, Maryanne said, "You look good with your gray hair and beard, Scottie. I'm glad they didn't take it away when they made us young again."

Young again?

Hardly that.

But they made us well, and that's as good as youth.

I looked down at her by my side and smiled, thinking how cheap of me it was to be looking at the vista below, when she had her eyes on me. Beyond her, all the others, some looking at the world, some up at the mountains towering on either side of the pass, others huddled in little groups, talking, about who knows what.

Ben and Katy. Jonas and his friends. The black guys from the HDC print shop, who'd seemed so glad to find us on our little hilltop that first night. Even Jake, the queer little advertising director, who'd done his best to be a nice guy instead of a manager. Interesting to see him holding hands with his new friend, Seekerhawk, one of the tall, slim brown men from a tribe who called themselves the Mother's Children.

Cro-Magnons we called them, one of the Five Races of Mankind, who swept from Africa one hundred millennia and more ago, drowning the Archaics before them.

When I looked, one of the Trolls waved, Weimaraner eyes a startling glint above a Durante nose, the whole shrouded in a bush of platinum blond hair. Five feet four, able to bend steel in his bare hands. No name. Speaking only in a cartoon jabber, like nothing you ever heard before.

The print shop guys called him Fred Flintstone for a while. Then he figured out they were laughing at him. Afterward, he was sorry about the guy that died, buried him with flowers and stone tools and cried over the grave.

The pass through the Ringwall was a short one, just a few hundred yards, the way down the other side pretty much like the one we'd followed upwards, and we all stood there too, looking out and down at what lay beyond.

Orange.

If Paulie were here, would he guess this one was Kzin?

Orange vegetation I guess, orange clouds. Green water, if water it was. A funny smell, making the Neanderthal guy point and jabber, raising his snout to the breeze, if breeze there was.

No mist here.

This valley, with no name as yet, was like some vast meteor crater, complete with central peak, rising from a ring-shaped sea holding enough water to fill the oceans of several worlds. Far away, at least another half-million miles away, was the other side of the Ringwall. Beyond it, there'll be another world, another one beyond that ...

It's as if I can see them out there, like dimples in some impossibly vast waffle, each one a world, sampled across time from beginning to end.

Beside me, Maryanne said, "Not just all the worlds of the old universe, but all the worlds of all the universes that ever were, or ever could have been."

I took her hand, taking the first step on the downward trail. "All of them," I said. "And all within walking distance."

An unimaginable future?

Perhaps.

I thought I'd miss you, Paulie.

But I don't.

THE BOOKS

Kage Baker

On the same day that I received the proofs for this anthology I learned that Kage Baker had died of cancer, aged fifty-seven. This was her last completed story.

She was best known for her time-travel series about the immortal operatives of the Company, which began with her first novel, In the Garden of Iden *(1997). Her steampunk novel,* Not Less Than Gods *(2010), details some of the secret history of the Company's Victorian-era predecessor, the Gentlemen's Speculative Society. The House of the Stag (2008) was shortlisted for a World Fantasy Award for Best Novel.*

With this story, written specially for this anthology, we look at a time beyond the apocalypse with the remnants of society trying to get back to life.

WE USED TO have to go a lot farther down the coast in those days, before things got easier. People weren't used to us then.

If you think about it, we must have looked pretty scary when we first made it out to the coast. Thirty trailers full of Show people, pretty desperate and dirty-looking Show people too, after fighting our way across the plains from the place where we'd been camped when it all went down. I don't remember when it went down, of course; I wasn't born yet.

The Show used to be an olden-time fair, a teaching thing. We traveled from place to place putting it on so people would learn about olden times, which seems pretty funny now, but back then ... how's that song go? The one about mankind jumping out into the stars? And everybody thought that was how it was going to be. The aunts and uncles would put on the Show so space-age people wouldn't forget things like weaving and making candles when they went off into space. That's what you call irony, I guess.

But afterwards we had to change the Show, because ... well, we couldn't have the Jousting Arena anymore because we needed the big horses to pull the trailers. And Uncle Buck didn't make fancy work with dragons with rhinestone eyes on them anymore because, who was there left to buy that kind of stuff? And anyway he was too busy making horseshoes. So all the uncles and aunts got together and worked it out like it is now, where we come into town with the Show and people come to see it and then they let us stay a while because we make stuff they need.

I started out as a baby bundle in one of the stage shows, myself. I don't remember it, though. I remember later I was in some play with a love story and I just wore a pair of fake wings and ran across the stage naked and shot at the girl with a toy bow and arrow that had glitter on them. And another time I played a dwarf. But I wasn't a dwarf, we only had the one dwarf and she was a lady – that was Aunt Tammy and she's dead now. But there was an act with a couple of dwarves dancing and she needed a partner, and I had to wear a black suit and a top hat.

But by then my daddy had got sick and died so my mom was sharing the trailer with Aunt Nera, who made pots and pitchers and stuff, so that meant we were living with her nephew Myko too. People said he went crazy later on but it wasn't true. He was just messed up. Aunt Nera left the Show for a little while after it all went down, to go and see if her family – they were townies – had made it through okay, only they didn't, they were all dead but the baby, so she took the baby away with her and found us again. She said Myko was too little to remember but I think he remembered some.

Anyway we grew up together after that, us and Sunny who lived with Aunt Kestrel in their trailer, which was next to ours. Aunt Kestrel was a juggler in the Show and Myko thought that was intense, he wanted to be a kid juggler. So he got Aunt Kestrel to show him how. And Sunny knew how already, she'd been watching her mom juggle since she was born and she could do clubs or balls or the apple-eating trick or anything. Myko decided he and Sunny should be a kid juggling act. I cried until they said I could be in the act too, but then I had to learn how to juggle and boy, was I sorry. I knocked out one of my own front teeth with a club before I learned better. The new one didn't grow in until I was seven, so I went around looking stupid for three years. But I got good enough to march in the parade and juggle torches.

That was after we auditioned, though. Myko went to Aunt Jeff and whined and he made us costumes for our act. Myko got a black doublet and a toy sword and a mask and I got a buffoon overall with a big spangly ruff. Sunny got a princess costume. We called ourselves the Minitrons. Actually Myko came up with the name. I don't know what he thought a Minitron was supposed to be but it sounded brilliant. Myko and I were both supposed to be in love with the princess and she couldn't decide between us so we had to do juggling tricks to win her hand, only she outjuggled us, so then Myko and I had a swordfight to decide things. And I always lost and died of a broken heart but then the princess was sorry and put a paper rose on my chest. Then I jumped up and we took our bows and ran off, because the next act was Uncle Monty and his performing parrots.

But the time I was six we felt like old performers and we swaggered in front of the other kids because we were the only kid act. We'd played it in six towns already. That was the year the aunts and uncles decided to take the trailers as far down the coast as this place on the edge of the big desert. It used to be a big city before it all went down. Even if there weren't enough people alive there anymore to put on a show for, there might be a lot of old junk we could use.

We made it into town all right without even any shooting. That was kind of amazing, actually, because it turned out nobody lived there but old people, and old people will usually shoot at you if they have guns and these did. The other amazing thing was that the town was *huge* and I mean really huge, I just walked around with my head tilted back staring at these towers that went up and up into the sky. Some of them you couldn't even see the tops because the fog hid them. And they were all mirrors and glass and arches and domes and scowly faces in stone looking down from way up high.

But all the old people lived in just a few places right along the beach, because the further back you went into the city the more sand was everywhere. The desert was creeping in and taking a little more every year. That was why all the young people had left. There was nowhere to grow any food. The old people stayed because there was still plenty of stuff in jars and cans they had collected from the markets, and anyway they liked it there because it was warm. They told us they didn't have enough food to share any, though. Uncle Buck told them all we wanted to trade for was the right to go into some of the empty towers and strip out as much of the copper pipes and wires and things as we could take away with us. They thought that was all right; they put their guns down and let us camp then.

But we found out the Show had to be a matinee if we were going to perform for them, because they all went to bed before the time we usually put on the Show. And the fire-eater was really pissed off about that because nobody would be able to see his act much, in broad daylight. It worked out all right, in the end, because the next day was dark and gloomy. You couldn't see the tops of the towers at all. We actually had to light torches around the edges of the big lot where we put up the stage.

The old people came filing out of their apartment building to the seats we'd set up, and then we had to wait the opening because they decided it was too cold and they all went shuffling back inside and got their coats. Finally the Show started and it went pretty well, considering some of them were blind and had to have their friends explain what was going on in loud voices.

But they liked Aunt Lulu and her little trained dogs and they liked Uncle Manny's strongman act where he picked up a Volkswagen. We kids knew all the heavy stuff like the engine had been taken out of it, but they didn't. They applauded Uncle Derry the Mystic Magician, even though the talkers for the blind shouted all through his performance and threw his timing off. He was muttering to himself and rolling a joint as he came through the curtain that marked off backstage.

"Brutal crowd, kids," he told us, lighting his joint at one of the torches. "Watch your rhythm."

But we were kids and we could ignore all the grownups in the world shouting, so we grabbed our prop baskets and ran out and put on our act. Myko stalked up and down and waved his sword and yelled his lines about being the brave and dangerous Captainio. I had a little pretend guitar that I strummed on while I pretended to look at the moon, and spoke my lines about being a poor fool in love with the princess. Sunny came out and did her princess dance. Then we juggled. It all went fine. The only time I was a little thrown off was when I glanced at the audience for a split second and saw the light of my juggling torches flickering on all those glass lenses or blind eyes. But I never dropped a torch.

Maybe Myko was bothered some, though, because I could tell by the way his eyes glared through his mask that he was getting worked up. When we had the sword duel near the end he hit too hard, the way he always did when he got worked up, and he banged my knuckles so bad I actually said "Ow" but the audience didn't catch it. Sometimes when he was like that his hair almost bristled, he was like some crazy cat jumping and spitting, and he'd fight about nothing. Sometimes afterwards I'd ask him why. He'd shrug and say he was sorry. Once he said it was because life was so damn boring.

Anyway I sang my little sad song and died of a broken heart, *flumpf* there on the pavement in my buffoon suit. I felt Sunny come over and put the rose on my chest and, I will remember this to my dying day, some old lady was yelling to her old man " ... and now the little girl gave him her rose!"

And the old man yelled "What? She gave him her nose?"

"Damn it, Bob! Her *ROSE!*"

I corpsed right then, I couldn't help it, I was still giggling when Myko and Sunny pulled me to my feet and we took our bows and ran off. Backstage they started laughing too. We danced up and down and laughed, very much getting in the way of Uncle Monty, who had to trundle all his parrots and their perches out on stage.

When we had laughed ourselves out, Sunny said "So ... what'll we do now?"

That was a good question. Usually the Show was at night, so usually after a performance we went back to the trailers and got out of costume and our moms fed us and put us to bed. We'd never played a matinee before. We stood there looking at each other until Myko's eyes gleamed suddenly.

"We can explore the Lost City of the Sands," he said, in that voice he had that made it sound like whatever he wanted was the coolest thing ever. Instantly, Sunny and I both wanted to explore too. So we slipped out from the backstage area, just as Uncle Monty was screaming himself hoarse trying to get his parrots to obey him,

and a moment later we were walking down an endless street lined
with looming giants' houses.

They weren't really, they had big letters carved up high that said
they were this or that property group or financial group or brokerage
or church but if a giant had stepped out at one corner and peered
down at us, we wouldn't have been surprised. There was a cold
wind blowing along the alleys from the sea and sand hissed there
and ran before us like ghosts along the ground but on the long
deserted blocks between there was gigantic silence. Our tiny footsteps only echoed in doorways.

The windows were mostly far above our heads and there was nothing
much to see when Myko hoisted me up to stand on his shoulders and
look into them. Myko kept saying he hoped we'd see a desk with a
skeleton with one of those headset things on sitting at it but we never
did; people didn't die *that* fast when it all went down. My mom said
they could tell when they were getting sick and people went home and
locked themselves in to wait and see if they lived or not.

Anyway Myko got bored finally and started this game where he'd
charge up the steps of every building we passed. He'd hammer on
the door with the hilt of his sword and yell "It's the Civilian Militia!
Open up or we're coming in!" Then he'd rattle the doors but everything was locked long ago. Some of the doors were too solid even to
rattle, and the glass was way too thick to break.

After about three blocks of this, when Sunny and I were starting to
look at each other with our eyebrows raised, meaning "Are you going
to tell him this game is getting old or do I have to do it?", right then
something amazing happened: one of the doors swung slowly inward
and Myko swung with it. He staggered into the lobby or whatever
and the door shut behind him. He stood staring at us through the
glass and we stared back and I was scared to death, because I thought
we'd have to run back and get Uncle Buck and Aunt Selene with their
hammers to get Myko out, and we'd all be in trouble.

But Sunny just pushed on the door and it opened again. She went
in so I had to go in too. We stood there all three and looked around.
There was a desk and a dead tree in a planter and another huge glass
wall with a door in it, leading deeper into the building. Myko began
to grin.

"This is the first chamber of the Treasure Tomb in the Lost City," he said. "We just killed the giant scorpion and now we have to go defeat the army of zombies to get into the second chamber!"

He drew his sword and ran yelling at the inner door, but it opened too, soundlessly, and we pushed after him. It was much darker in here but there was still enough light to read the signs.

"It's a libarary," said Sunny. "They used to have paperbacks."

"*Paperbacks*," said Myko gloatingly, and I felt pretty excited myself. We'd seen lots of paperbacks, of course; there was the boring one with the mended cover that Aunt Maggie made everybody learn to read in. Every grownup we knew had one or two or a cache of paperbacks, tucked away in boxes or in lockers under beds, to be thumbed through by lamplight and read aloud from, if kids had been good.

Aunt Nera had a dozen paperbacks and she'd do that. It used to be the only thing that would stop Myko crying when he was little. We knew all about the Last Unicorn and the kids who went to Narnia, and there was a really long story about some people who had to throw a ring into a volcano that I always got tired of before it ended, and another really long one about a crazy family living in a huge castle, but it was in three books and Aunt Nera only had the first two. There was never any chance she'd ever get the third one now, of course, not since it all went down. Paperbacks were rare finds, they were ancient, their brown pages crumbled if you weren't careful and gentle.

"We just found all the paperbacks in the *universe*!" Myko shouted.

"Don't be dumb," said Sunny. "Somebody must have taken them all away years ago."

"Oh yeah?" Myko turned and ran further into the darkness. We followed, yelling at him to come back, and we all came out together into a big round room with aisles leading off it. There were desks in a ring all around and the blank dead screens of electronics. We could still see because there were windows down at the end of each aisle, sending long trails of light along the stone floors, reflecting back on the long shelves that lined the aisles and the uneven surfaces of the things on the shelves. Clustering together, we picked an aisle at random and walked down it toward the window.

About halfway down it, Myko jumped and grabbed something from one of the shelves. "Look! Told you!" He waved a paperback under our noses. Sunny leaned close to look at it. There was no picture on the cover, just the title printed big.

"Roget's. The. Saurus," Sunny read aloud.

"What's it about?" I asked.

Myko opened it and tried to read. For a moment he looked so angry I got ready to run, but then he shrugged and closed the paperback. "It's just words. Maybe it's a secret code or something. Anyway, it's *mine* now." He stuck it inside his doublet.

"No stealing!" said Sunny.

"If it's a dead town it's not stealing, it's salvage," I told her, just like the aunts and uncles always told us.

"But it isn't dead. There's all the old people."

"They'll die soon," said Myko. "And anyway Uncle Buck already asked permission to salvage." Which she had to admit was true, so we went on. What we didn't know then, but figured out pretty fast, was that all the other things on the shelves were actually big hard *books* like Uncle Des' *Barlogio's Principles of Glassblowing*.

But it was disappointing at first because none of the books in that aisle had stories. It was all, what do you call it, reference stuff. We came out sadly thinking we'd been gypped, and then Sunny spotted the sign with directions.

"Children's Books, Fifth Floor," she announced.

"Great! Where's the stairs?" Myko looked around. We all knew better than to ever, ever go near an elevator, because not only did they mostly not work, they could kill you. We found a staircase and climbed and climbed for what seemed forever before we came out onto the Children's Books floor.

And it was so cool. There were racks of paperbacks, of course but we stood there with our mouths open because the signs had been right – there were *books* here. Big, hard, solid books but not about grownup stuff. Books with bright pictures on the covers. Books for *us*. Even the tables and chairs up here were our size.

With a little scream, Sunny ran forward and grabbed a book from a shelf. "It's Narnia! Look! And it's got different pictures!"

"What a score," said Myko, dancing up and down. "Oh, what a score!"

I couldn't say anything. The idea was so enormous: all these were ours. This whole huge room belonged to *us* .. .at least, as much as we could carry away with us.

Myko whooped and ran off down one of the aisles. Sunny stayed frozen at the first shelf, staring with almost a sick expression at the other books. I went close to see.

"Look," she whispered. "There's *millions*. How am I supposed to choose? We need as many stories as we can get. " She was pointing at a whole row of books with colored titles: *The Crimson Fairy Book. The Blue Fairy Book. The Violet Fairy Book. The Orange Fairy Book.* I wasn't interested in fairies, so I just grunted and shook my head.

I picked an aisle and found shelves full of flat books with big pictures. I opened one and looked at it. It was real easy to read, with big letters and the pictures were funny but I read right through it standing there. It was about those big animals you see sometimes back up the delta country, you know, elephants. Dancing, with funny hats on. I tried to imagine Aunt Nera reading it aloud on winter nights. It wouldn't last even one night; it wouldn't last through one bedtime. It was only one story. Suddenly I saw what Sunny meant. If we were going to take books away with us, they had to be full of stories that would *last*. That had – what's the word I'm looking for? *Substance*.

Myko yelled from somewhere distant, "Here's a cool one! It's got pirates!"

It was pretty dark where I was standing, so I wandered down the aisle toward the window. The books got thicker the farther I walked. There was a bunch of books about dogs but their stories all seemed sort of the same; there were books about horses too, with the same problem. There were books to teach kids how to make useful stuff but when I looked through them they were all dumb things like how to weave potholders for your mom or build things out of popsicle sticks. I didn't even know what popsicle sticks were, much less where I could get any. There were some about what daily life was like back in olden times but I already knew about that, and anyway those books had no *story*.

And all the while Myko kept yelling things like, "Whoa! This one has guys with spears and shields and *gods*!" or "Hey, here's one with a flying carpet and it says it's got a *thousand* stories!" Why was I the only one stuck in the dumb books shelves?

I came to the big window at the end and looked out at the view – rooftops, fog, gray dark ocean – and backed away, scared stiff by how high up I was. I was turning around to run back when I saw the biggest book in the world.

Seriously. It was half as big as I was, *twice* the size of *Barlogio's Principles of Glassblowing,* it was bound in red leather and there were gold letters along its back. I crouched down and slowly spelled out the words.

The Complete Collected Adventures of Asterix the Gaul.

I knew what "Adventures" meant, and it sounded pretty promising. I pulled the book down – it was the heaviest book in the world too – and laid it flat on the floor. When I opened it I caught my breath. I had found the greatest book in the world.

It was full of colored pictures but there were words too, a lot of them, they were the people in the story talking but you could *see them talk.* I had never seen a comic before. My mom talked sometimes about movies and TV and they must have been like this, I thought, talking pictures. And there was a story. In fact, there were lots of stories. Asterix was this little guy no bigger than me but he had a mustache and a helmet and he lived in this village and there was a wizard with a magic potion and Asterix fought in battles and traveled to all these faraway places and had all these adventures!!! And I could read it all by myself, because when I didn't know what a word meant I could guess at it from the pictures.

I settled myself more comfortably on my stomach, propped myself up on my elbows so I wouldn't crunch my starched ruff, and settled down to read.

Sometimes the world becomes a perfect place.

Asterix and his friend Obelix had just come to the Forest of the Carnutes when I was jolted back to the world by Myko yelling for me. I rose to my knees and looked around. It was darker now; I hadn't even realized I'd been pushing my nose closer and closer to the pages as the light had drained away. There were drops of rain hitting the window and I thought about what it would be like running through those dark cold scary streets and getting rained on too.

I scrambled to my feet and grabbed up my book, gripping it to my chest as I ran. It was even darker when I reached the central room.

Myko and Sunny were having a fight when I got there. She was crying. I stopped, astounded to see she'd pulled her skirt off and stuffed it full of books, and she was sitting there with her legs bare to her underpants.

"We have to travel light and they're too heavy," Myko was telling her. "You can't take all those!"

"I have to," she said. "We *need* these books!" She got to her feet and hefted the skirt. *The Olive Fairy Book* fell out. I looked over and saw she'd taken all the colored fairy books. Myko bent down impatiently and grabbed up *The Olive Fairy Book*. He looked at it.

"It's stupid," he said. "Who needs a book about an olive fairy?"

"You moron, it's not *about* an olive fairy!" Sunny shrieked. "It's got all kinds of stories in it! Look!" She grabbed it back from him and opened it and shoved it out again for him to see. I sidled close and looked. She was right: there was a page with the names of all the stories in the book. There were a lot of stories, about knights and magic and strange words. Read one a night, they'd take up a month of winter nights. And every book had a month's worth of stories in it? Now, that was *concentrated* entertainment value.

Myko, squinting at the page, must have decided the same thing. "Okay," he said, "But you'll have to carry it. And don't complain if it's heavy."

"I won't," said Sunny, putting her nose in the air.

Myko glanced at me and did a double take.

"You can't take that!" he yelled. "It's too big and it's just one book anyway!"

"It's the only one I want," I said, "And anyhow, you got to take all the ones you want!" He knew it was true, too. His doublet was so stuffed out with loot, he looked pregnant.

Myko muttered under his breath but turned away, and that meant the argument was over. "Anyway we need to leave."

So we started to, but halfway down the first flight of stairs three books fell out of Sunny's skirt and we had to stop while Myko took the safety pins out of all our costumes and closed up the waistband. We were almost to the second floor when Sunny lost her hold on the skirt and her books went cascading down to the landing, with the loudest noise in the universe. We scrambled down after them and were on our knees picking them up when we heard the other noise.

It was a hissing, like someone gasping for breath through whistly dentures, and a jingling, like a ring of keys, because that's what it was. We turned our heads.

Maybe he hadn't heard us when we ran past him on the way up. We hadn't been talking then, just climbing, and he had a lot of hair in his ears and a pink plastic sort of machine in one besides. Or maybe he'd been so wrapped up, the way I had been in reading, that he hadn't even noticed us when we'd pattered past. But he hadn't been reading.

There were no books in this part of the library. All there was on the shelves was old magazines and stacks and stacks of yellow newspapers. The newspapers weren't crumpled into balls in the bottoms of old boxes, which was the only way we ever saw them, they were smooth and flat. But most of them were drifted on the floor like leaves, hundreds and hundreds of big leaves, ankle-deep, and on every single one was a square with sort of checkered patterns and numbers printed in the squares and words written in in pencil.

I didn't know what a crossword puzzle was then but the old man must have been coming there for years, maybe ever since it all went down, years and years he'd been working his way through all those magazines and papers, hunting down every single puzzle and filling in every one. He was dropping a stub of a pencil now as he got to his feet, snarling at us, showing three brown teeth. His eyes behind his glasses were these huge distorted magnified things, and full of crazy anger. He came over the paper-drifts at us fast and light as a spider.

"Fieves! Ucking kish! Ucking fieving kish!"

Sunny screamed and I screamed too. Frantically she shoved all the books she could into her skirt and I grabbed up most of what she'd missed but we were taking too long. The old man brought up his cane and smacked it down, *crack* but he missed us on his first try and by then Myko had drawn his wooden sword and put it against the old man's chest and shoved hard. The old man fell with a crash, still flailing his cane but he was on his side and striking at us faster than you'd believe and so mad now he was just making noises, with spittle flying from his mouth. His cane hit my knee as I scrambled up. It hurt like fire and I yelped. Myko kicked him and yelled, "Run!"

We bailed, Sunny and I did, we thundered down the rest of the stairs and didn't stop until we were out in the last chamber by the street doors. "Myko's still up there," said Sunny. I had an agonizing few seconds before deciding to volunteer to go back and look for him. I was just opening my mouth when we spotted him running down the stairs and out towards us.

"Oh, good," said Sunny. She tied a knot in one corner of her skirt for a handle and had already hoisted it over her shoulder on to her back and was heading for the door as Myko joined us. He was clutching the one book we'd missed on the landing. It was *The Lilac Fairy Book* and there were a couple of spatters of what looked like blood on its cover.

"Here. You carry it." Myko shoved the book at me. I took it and wiped it off. We followed Sunny out. I looked at him sidelong. There was blood on his sword too.

It took me two blocks, though, jogging after Sunny through the rain, before I worked up the nerve to lean close to him as we ran and ask: "Did you kill that guy?"

"Had to," said Myko. "He wouldn't stop."

To this day I don't know if he was telling the truth. It was the kind of thing he would have said, whether it was true or not. I didn't know what I was supposed to say back. We both kept running. The rain got a lot harder and Myko left me behind in a burst of speed, catching up to Sunny and grabbing her bundle of books. He slung it over his shoulder. They kept going, side by side. I had all I could do not to fall behind.

By the time we got back the Show was long over. The crew was taking down the stage in the rain, stacking the big planks. Because of the rain no market stalls had been set up but there was a line of old people with umbrellas standing by Uncle Chris's trailer, since he'd offered to repair any dentures that needed fixing with his jeweler's tools. Myko veered us away from them behind Aunt Selene's trailer, and there we ran smack into our moms and Aunt Nera. They had been looking for us for an hour and were really mad.

I was scared sick the whole next day, in case the old people got out their guns and came to get us but nobody seemed to notice the old man was dead and missing, if he *was* dead. The other thing I was scared would happen was that Aunt Kestrel or Aunt Nera would get to talking with the other women and say something like, "Oh, by the way, the kids found a library and salvaged some books, maybe we should all go over and get some books for the other kids too?" because that was exactly the sort of thing they were always doing, and then they'd find the old man's body. But they didn't. Maybe nobody did anything because the rain kept all the aunts and kids and old people in next day. Maybe the old man had been a hermit and lived by himself in the library, so no one would find his body for ages.

I never found out what happened. We left after a couple of days, after Uncle Buck and the others had opened up an office tower and salvaged all the good copper they could carry. I had a knee swollen up and purple where the old man had hit it but it was better in about a week. The books were worth the pain.

They lasted us for years. We read them and we passed them on to the other kids and they read them too, and the stories got into our games and our dreams and the way we thought about the world. What I liked best about my comics was that even when the heroes went off to far places and had adventures, they always came back to their village in the end and everybody was happy and together.

Myko liked the other kind of story, where the hero leaves and has glorious adventures but maybe never comes back. He was bored with the Show by the time he was twenty and went off to some big city up north where he'd heard they had their electrics running again. Lights were finally starting to come back on in the towns we worked, so it seemed likely. He still had that voice that could make anything seem like a good idea, see, and now he had all those fancy words he'd gotten out of Roget's The Saurus too. So I guess I shouldn't have been surprised that he talked Sunny into going with him.

Sunny came back alone after a year. She wouldn't talk about what happened and I didn't ask. Eliza was born three months later.

Everyone knows she isn't mine. I don't mind.

We read to her on winter nights. She likes stories.

PALLBEARER

Robert Reed

---

*Robert Reed (b. 1956) has been one of the more prolific
writers of science fiction since he first appeared in 1986.
His work is diverse but he is probably best known for his
more extreme concepts, such as that found in* Marrow
*(2000), about a group of aliens and genetically changed
humans who travel through the universe in a ship that is
so huge that it contains its own planet. Most of his short
stories remain to be collected into book-form but some
will be found in* The Dragons of Springplace *(1999) and*
The Cuckoo's Boys *(2005).*

L OLA AGREES WITH me, we've never seen a colder winter. Most
nights drop below freezing, sometimes a long ways below, and
if the stoves don't get fed, mornings are painful. Better to lie under
the heavy covers and fool around, we joke. But eleven years together
and two swollen bladders usually put the brakes on too much frisk-
iness. Besides, we've got a dozen dogs howling to be fed. For the last
few weeks, our habit has been to leap out of bed and dress in a rush,
then sprint outside – she has her outhouse, I've got mine – and then
with all of the mutts on our heels, we hurry indoors, throwing logs
into the kitchen stove so at least one room is habitable before we
attack the new day.

The cold is bad, but there hasn't been any snow either. Not a
dusting. Last year's drought hasn't shown any signs of surrender,
leafless trees and sorry brown grass bending under a slicing north
wind. With my big important voice, I announce, "Winter is Death."
Lola thinks that's a bit much, but I believe what I say. If you can't
migrate or hibernate, there's nothing to eat here but leftovers from
last summer and fall. If this cold didn't pass, we would eventually

perish. But of course winter is just a season, and not a very big one at that. My wife smiles and promises me another spring followed by a long hot summer. "Because the air is still filled with ... what is that stuff called ... ?"

"Carbon dioxide."

"I don't know why I can't remember that," she says.

Lola's a simple, practical girl. That's why.

"Carbon what?" she asks.

With my important voice, I repeat the words.

"I love you," she says.

"I love you," I say.

Lola stands at the warming stove, wearing two sweaters and stirring our oatmeal. In ways I could never be, she is happy. Smiling for no obvious reason, she asks what I'm planning for my day.

"You remember," I say.

"Tell me again."

"Run the meat into town."

"I forgot," she claims, her stirring picking up speed.

But really, she isn't that simple. What she forgets can be a message, not a mistake. Like here: Butcher Jack wants the meat. But he has three daughters too, all in their teens. Some nights Lola lies awake, scared that I'll leave her for some young gal who gives me babies. If not Butcher Jack's kids, then there's dozens of single ladies living in that hated town – fertile sluts talking about Christ but not meaning it, their spoiled easy lives giving them time to paint their faces and cover their bodies with fancy clothes meant to do nothing but draw a man's eyes. She hates my trips to town. We need them, and she doesn't dare stop me. But even an insensitive husband would pick up on these feelings, and I'm not the insensitive type.

Eating breakfast, I ask what we need. What can I bring her?

Two different questions, those are.

Her wish list is shorter than usual. She mentions dried apples and bug-free flour and oats and maybe cloth that she can use to make new clothes and wool yarn if I can manage it. Then she pauses, staring at the table between us, saying nothing but in a very important way.

"What's wrong?"

She shakes her head. But instead of lying, she admits that she gets scared when I leave for long.

"Scared of what?"

Lola looks at me.

"I always come home," I remind her. Of course maybe I won't make it tonight, but by tomorrow I'll be sitting here again. And she'll have me until spring, if we get enough supplies for all our smoked meat.

"I know you'll be back," she claims. Then a moment later, she mentions, "The butcher shouldn't take long."

"I have old friends to see," I remind her.

She nods.

"Rituals," I add.

One ritual makes her smile.

"Come with me," I tell her.

But that will never happen. Even the suggestion brings up old feelings, and as her face stiffens, she says, "I wouldn't be welcome."

"It's been years."

"And what's changed?"

"Well," I say. "It's not like people will talk ugly to your face."

Heat flows into those gorgeous eyes. The sources of pain aren't worth repeating. We know the history, and just by bringing it up, I make certain that she'll stay behind. With a nod, Lola admits that we need supplies, but at least I won't be doing this chore again next month. "Get everything you can today," she implores. "Whatever we need, and maybe a present for me. All right? Then come home as fast as possible."

Maybe my wife doesn't know the ingredients of the air. But better than me, she remembers why we even bother to breathe.

There's no telling how many vehicles went into making my freight truck. I lost count of the places where I found the little valves and bolts and brackets and gaskets. But the body belonged to a military Hummer and the engine to a second Hummer – a big eight-cylinder reconfigured to burn even our lousy homemade alcohol. No two tires have the same lineage. I can make most repairs using the tools on hand and the junkyard behind our last outbuilding. But one of these days, this truck is going to stop running. It'll probably happen at the bottom of a gully and miles from home, and the part I need won't be in my inventory, or more likely I'll hike all the way home and find ten replacements, every last one of them rusted and useless.

Water and time are two demons steadily erasing what remains from before. But that very bad day still sits somewhere in the future. Today we have a fleet of Jeeps and little trucks and tractors and powered carts, plus the one big Hummer. With Lola's help, I load the truck and both trailers, tying down the choicest parts of elk and whitetail and wild pigs, plus that one idiot black bear that decided to visit us last October, mauling our dogs when he wasn't making a mess of our smokehouse. Balancing the load is critical, and it takes a lot of pushing and dragging until everything is just right. Suddenly it's mid-morning. Lola thinks it's too late to go and wants me to delay, although she won't say it. I give her a kiss and she does nothing. I step away and she pulls me close and kisses me, lifting her face and whole body against me. I have to laugh. Then she slaps my face and storms away. I climb into the cab and take the usual deep breath, for luck. The engine catches on the first try, and I wave and she waves and smiles, and I roll across our yard and down onto the narrow, grass-choked road to town.

The dogs follow but not too far.

In good shoes and motivated, a fit person could run to Salvation in ninety minutes. Every road between home and the highway is my responsibility. Nobody else lives out here. Spring and summer, I use our biggest tractor to pull the mower, keeping the weeds and volunteer trees off the once-graveled roadbeds. I also blade over the ruts and any gullies made by cloudbursts and eventually I'm going to have to brace the bridge at the seven-mile mark.

The bridge creaks and moans but it holds as always. My roads end at the highway and sitting beside the intersection, happy in the sun, is a tiger – a great yellow and white and black beast staring at this noisy contraption and the stubborn, half-deaf man clinging to its steering wheel.

The local tigers are beauties. Their ancestors lived in a city zoo or maybe somebody's private collection and instead of being mercy-killed the big cats were set free. Siberian blood runs in this fellow. He is enormous and warm inside that rich winter coat. A fur like that would command a huge price in town. Or even better, it would be the perfect surprise for a woman whose biggest hope is for a sack of bug-free flour.

But this tiger proves to be a wise soul. Reading my mind, he vanishes into the grass before I can get hold of my favorite rifle, much less put the scope to my eye or push a big bullet into the chamber.

Oh, well.

Salvation stands along this highway and the adjacent ribbon of clear, drought-starved water. Turning left, I head downstream. Rectangular foundations show where homes once stood, pipe and wire scavenged long ago, the wood and gypsum burnt off by the spring fires. Side roads and driveways are nearly invisible under the pale dead weeds. A factory was only half-built when work stopped and, while the roof caved in years ago, the concrete walls and paved parking lot are putting on worthy battles against roots and the surge of the frosts. After that ruin comes the first tended fields. Families have claimed different patches of bottomland. People who might be four generations removed from farming have figured out how to plow and irrigate, how to fight off the weeds and pests, saving seed and canning their produce and trading for new seeds that will do better or do worse this coming year.

It has been weeks since I saw any new human face. Today's first face belongs to a boy. Standing in the trees between the cold water and me, he looks wild and very happy. Curious about this man and his enormous truck, he lifts his arms, yelling something important. I can't hear a word over the screaming of the engine. Rolling past him, I wave like any friendly neighbor.

He runs after me. And because he is a boy, he picks up a piece of the broken pavement, flinging it into the last trailer.

New houses mark the outskirts of Salvation. Standing back from the river, they are built from packed earth and straw bales, roughly hewn wood and salvaged sheets of random metal. Beauty and elegance don't matter. Being tight in the winter and cool in the summer is what counts. The town grows every year, and this is the look of the ... what's that word? Oh, yeah. The suburbs.

Another mile, and I'm in the original town. The houses here are taller and far prettier than the dirt mounds, and they're 5,000 years fancier. Corkscrew windmills turn on the peaked roofs while solar panels face the cold bright sun, the day's wealth turned into heat and LEDs and electricity stored in banks of refurbished batteries. I can't say what people want with so much juice. How many lamps do you need to read an old book at midnight? But power is power, prestige never changes, and if I can't remember who lives in which house, at least I can be certain that only the best citizens are living behind those insulated front doors.

Salvation has always been Salvation. But the people who built it were different from today's good citizens. Worried about their future, they purchased hundreds of acres of farmland. They created a town square and a host of little businesses and streets filled with efficient, luxurious homes. Being forward-looking souls, they powered their world with wind and sunlight. They devised a community and a life style that demanded little from the overpopulated, overheated world. But wealthy people are smugly confident. They will always do what looks smart, and being smart was what killed them. That's why Salvation became a ghost town. But these beautiful homes weren't empty for long, because up in heaven a benevolent God sent His chosen people to a place with that perfect name, and among the blessed were my mother and my father, and me.

In a town that often chews up its own, Butcher Jack is considered a fair trader, a gentleman unencumbered by enemies or old grudges. And he's glad to see me but only because we're friends and because we think the world of each other. After the usual greetings and handshakes, he turns quiet, throwing a sour look at the truck and trailers loaded high with sweet wild meat.

"What's wrong?"

"Nothing you've done."

I can't guess what he means.

"It's the Martin brothers," he begins.

Identical twins, the Martins are a few years older than me, prone to drinking homemade whiskey and starting fights with whoever is closest. They were barely men when they were shunned, and when their behaviors didn't change the mayor took the unusual step of forcing them out of town. The brothers live on the National Guard base several days' west, sharing at least four wives and a platoon of kids who call both of them "Dad". Why that clan means anything to me is a mystery, right up until Jack admits, "They just brought in a load of cured buffalo and wild cattle."

"Since when do they share?"

"Since this winter. Too many bored kids underfoot, too much energy causing mischief. They figured it was time to put the crew to work, maybe barter for toys and the like."

"But how's their meat?"

He answers my question with a hard stare.

"Do they match my stuff?" I ask.

"No, and that's why you'll always have customers, Noah. Least as far as I'm concerned."

Why doesn't this feel like good news?

"Drunks or not, the Martins did a respectable job. Not the flavor you manage, and the meat demands chewing. But people are pretty satisfied."

"How much did they bring?"

Jack considers my load before saying, "Twice yours."

"Damn."

"There's the problem's heart," he says. "Our local market is just about saturated."

I used to worry about my neighbors turning into hunters, particularly as the elk and buffalo grew common. But killing is easy work. Gutting the beasts is hard, and smoking that lean flesh is an art form. If I hadn't come to town today, I'd still feel like a wealthy man. But now I'm destitute, wrestling with my terrors, wondering if weeks of labor are going to count for nothing. And worst of all, my best friend in Salvation is delivering the deathblow.

"You've still got your loyal customers," Jack repeats.

I nod.

"And remember, we've got more mouths in town. Twenty more than last year, nearly."

I wait.

He offers a sum. It's half what I expected, but I know it's more than he has to pay me. This is charity, and I have to smile. Then he calls out his four sons to help unload the meat, and I catch myself watching for his notorious daughters. I don't see them anywhere. Once his boys are working, he turns back to me, saying, "Things won't get any better, Noah."

"You mean with the Martins?"

"No, it's the darn Mennonites," he says, waving toward the southeast. "Those hill families are clearing pastures, putting up fences and breeding with some quality bulls."

"Tigers like beef," I point out.

And Jack nods, wanting to believe that too. "But they may have solved the predator problem," he warns. "Big dogs trained to watch the herds, and when there's trouble, the dogs bark. Cougars, wolves, even tigers ... they're all going to think twice when those bearded men start firing their big rifles."

I laugh sadly.

Jack shrugs. "Next year, in a small scale, they'll be putting domesticated beef on our tables."

And I curse.

Which he expects. And with his own sense of impending loss, he adds, "Mennonites are smart businessmen. Always have been. They'll eventually build their own cooler and slaughterhouse. And at that point, both of us will be scrambling for work."

So everybody's in a tough place. Except that I don't care about Jack's troubles. We're friends, even partners. But when your life is tumbling down, it's amazing how little you feel for the rest of the hapless debris.

Visits to town usually include the only official bar, The Quilt Shop. Christians don't like public drinking, which is why the town policy is one beer every day – served in a very tall glass, of course. But the barter papers from Jack won't cover the food and cloth that we need. In an ugly, sober mood, I walk past the bar, aiming to visit my mother instead. Marching across the town square, I pause here and there to chat with the faces I know. Nobody mentions Lola; nothing of substance is discussed. They want to know how I am. They tell me that I look fit and fed. What's the news from the wilderness? Did I bring in my usual venison? Is the weather cold enough? This winter must be like the old winters, young voices claim. But Old Ferris knows better. "I've seen bigger chills and a lot more snow," he says. "And I grew up in Oklahoma."

Oklahoma used to be a real place. Now it's a word that a seventy-year-old man might as well have made up.

"Off to see your mom, are you?"

"I am."

Ferris nods. "Say a good prayer for me, would you?"

"Yes, sir. I will."

The cemetery sits on north-facing ground too steep to be planted, affording a view of the rooftops and solar panels, bottomlands and the hills and prairie reaching to the rolling horizon. Looking east and downstream, the distant country changes from dead brown to sterile cold gray. That grayness marks crisscrossing paved roads and too many houses to count. I'll never go into the city again. It's a vow I made years ago, and I've kept it better than most. A few slumping buildings can look noble and important, but a landscape where hundreds of thousands of people lived and died is never noble. Cemeteries are beautiful places in comparison, even when the grass is brown. A cemetery doesn't smell, and it doesn't cry out in pain, and looking at neat burial sites never makes me think about the waste and appalling loss that comes when half a million ghosts are whispering in one miserable voice.

I don't know what to think about the afterlife. But I'll never accept pretty notions like heaven and a righteous hell.

Mom's marker is a square block cut from the local limestone, her name and the important dates chiseled into the flattest face, along with the usual scripture. My mom believed in God and loved Christ, and she took lessons from that strange old book. It's those lessons that save my life, and that's why I can stand on this frozen ground today. Mom always acted on what she believed, and since the heart is a fool, my poor father and his heart usually went along with her crazy decisions.

I never could make sense of their love. But if I were a grateful son, I would kneel down on this frozen sacred ground and clasp my hands together, thanking my mother and God for this opportunity to be alive, seeing the world unfold into new, unexpected shapes.

Except that I'm not a grateful son.

My little ritual – this chore that I perform whenever visiting town – I do for the sake of my wife. Years ago, most of the local people treated Lola and her family unfairly. One bitter old woman was at the center of those bad feelings and petty slights. Even as a boy, I realized that my future wife didn't deserve to be shunned. But that was what happened. My mother was responsible, and the pain has lingered long past her death. And that's why I usually have one tall beer at the bar and then walk to the cemetery, taking a long look around to make sure that I'm alone, then yanking down my pants and investing a few moments pissing on that crude tombstone.

It feels better than prayer. And that's what I'm doing today – without beer to help, but managing just fine – and that's what I'm finishing up when something unexpected happens. First comes the sound of an engine working and only then I catch a glimpse of a remarkable apparition on the highway east of town.

What kind of truck is that?

I pull up my trousers and fasten the buttons. I'm tying my belt when the mystery machine enters the town square. A long aluminum box rides high on fat tires and the windshield looks like the window on a house and smaller windows are fixed to at least one long side, and loyally following the vehicle is a big trailer carrying what looks like an auxiliary fuel tank and other supplies.

From some deep unexpected corner of my head, a memory finds me. No, the vehicle isn't quite the same. It has been updated to meet this world's bad roads and fuel shortages. But out of the fog between my ears comes an impossible answer:

An RV.

Which stands for what?

I can't remember. I probably never knew. But this is the best kind of marvel, like something from a dream, and that foolish part of me is beating fast now, making me feel like a happy little kid.

I was seven and glad to be traveling the world, eating canned food and picking out new clothes as soon as my almost-new clothes were dirty. It seemed like a natural life, and I didn't complain. Then dad heard chatter on the short wave radio. People of Faith were talking about a town left empty and clean, and life was going to be easy again. But weren't things pretty sweet already? The dead didn't stink much anymore. I liked wandering and the everyday rituals, like helping my father explore empty houses, hunting for ammunition and tools and keys to cars that still ran. The scale of the disaster was enormous. But then again, everything's enormous to a young boy. And nothing is more natural than death. For all I knew, people had lived this way since the Creation: prosperity always made our species too proud, and then God would send a flood or worse, slaughtering only the evil people in the world.

That's what my mother's prayers said. Every night and every morning, and with each meal of scavenged food, she would thank the Good Lord for the treasure left behind by the vanquished Unbelievers.

I prayed and dad prayed, but not like mom. She was the one who decided we should drive to Salvation. Dad wasn't as hopeful, but he couldn't find good reasons to hang his doubts on. So we found a new car for a new beginning and by the end of that trip I was feeling excited about this mythical place. We crossed half the state before swinging wide around the giant city. Mom navigated; dad watched the gas gauge. I studied a thousand fires burning out of control, enjoying the towering smoke with the dirty flames at the bottom and the stink of chemicals and old wood incinerated by the wild, wondrous heat. I didn't think once about the consequences to anybody's health. I was seven, and fire was fun, and this very important drive was another great adventure in a life filled with little else.

But once we pulled into Salvation, nagging disappointment took hold. We were late arrivals; only a few half-finished houses were left unclaimed. The Mayor welcomed us as Christians, and a little feast was held in our honor. But we didn't have solar panels or windmills on our house. Holes for pipes and wires were cut in the walls but none of that work had begun. Suddenly there were kids to play with, except now I was too busy to act my age. My folks put me to work. Ferris was our first friend, helping with the toughest jobs. He told us how the town was abandoned when he arrived, not even the usual bodies lying about. But then again, rich sinners usually died in distant hospitals and hospices. What else could explain it? A naturally happy fellow, Ferris smiled and sang odd songs as he and a few other men helped with our carpentry and plumbing and wiring. But everybody had duties in their own homes. People with real skills were scarce and the Mayor and his inner circle monopolized their time. My parents did their best, learning from the daily mistakes. If

I was lucky, the fires few and the weather clear, I got to ride with dad into the city. We hunted for useful machines or materials that could be bartered. I loved those little journeys. I killed my first wild game in one of city parks, and dad helped clean and cook my rabbit lunch.

When the day got late, he said, "We need to head home."

"Why?"

He laughed. Shaking his head, he admitted, "I don't know why."

I argued that we could stay here tonight, go back tomorrow.

He dwelled on the merits of that strategy. Then he added his own good reason to delay. "We wouldn't have to pray again until tomorrow."

We hadn't prayed before the rabbit feast. Until then, I hadn't noticed.

"What do you think of Salvation, Noah?"

I thought hard. Then shrugging, I said, "It's okay."

He didn't talk.

"Do you like it?" I asked.

He didn't want to answer. It was best to point out, "Those houses are perfect for us. When ours is finished, we'll have power and water and all the comforts. We can grow vegetables out back, so the canned goods last longer, and you'll go to school with the other kids."

"Are you going to teach us?"

Dad was a teacher before. But the question seemed to take him by surprise. "If they want me to serve. Yes."

But nobody ever asked, and dad knew better than volunteer.

After that first year, life in Salvation became ordinary. Normal even. I had school and church and no reason to wonder where my food was coming from tomorrow. Which was good and bad. New people kept arriving, some coming from distant parts of the country, and while a few lingered, most found reasons to keep moving. Most weren't Believers, or we didn't think they were. Why God's wrath had spared them was a mystery to me. But one undeserving family was particularly stubborn, claiming to have nowhere else to go. They built a new house in the hills. The dad was a talented carpenter, so he was able to find work even with the people who despised him. His little girl was named Lola. Lola's mother taught her at home, and only on rare occasions did they attend church services. But I made a point of talking to the girl whenever I saw her, and better yet, she would smile and happily talk to me.

Mom noticed and thought it best to warn me, "She isn't a good person, Noah. Stay clear of her."

"How do you know that?"

Mom had many talents. She could talk to God and convince herself about anything, and she was a marvel when it came to manipulating others. But better than anyone, she was able to read people, measuring their souls and spotting their weaknesses.

"Lola's parents are pretenders," she claimed. "They say the right words, but words mean nothing if there's no feeling behind them."

Mom wasn't the only perceptive person in our family. "What about Dad?" I asked.

She stared at me for a long moment. Then she looked away, asking, "What do you mean?"

"He says the right words. But I don't think he believes them."

"Well," she said, her coldest eyes finding me. "Don't repeat those words. Do you understand me?"

I understood, but that didn't matter. We weren't the only people watching, and ideas, particularly the dangerous ones, have their own lives. Like diseases, they can be carried on the wind, growing wherever they find weakness.

A couple years after our arrival, Salvation's first Mayor was drummed out of office. Three young girls were pregnant, each naming him as the father, and maybe that was true. Maybe. What mattered was that he was shunned, and mom became a very prominent citizen. She belonged to the new Mayor's inner circle, suddenly attending meetings and seeing to important but vague duties, holding no official station but acquiring a considerable reputation nonetheless. People couldn't stop smiling at her, even when they despised her. She formed a Bible study group, and women fought for the chance to sit in our living room, reading about God's mercy and judgment. When those ladies visited, dad would vanish. Then he started to skip Sunday church. And here the story can be told one of two ways: either my mother protected my father, deflecting criticisms to keep him safe for as long as possible. Or she was the acidic force that decided something had to be done about the doubter in our midst.

Either way, one morning I woke to find Dad's hand over my mouth. He told me to follow him, and we walked out back, past the battery shed holding yesterday's sun and the woodpile holding forty years of sunshine. That's the way that one-time teacher would talk to me, explaining how the world worked. But there weren't any lessons that day. He barely had time to confess that he was leaving, leaving right now, and this was good-bye.

I didn't ask why. There wasn't any need. All I said was, "Take me."

He shook his head. "I can't, Noah. No."

"Where are you going?"

"I'm not sure," he admitted, looking worried about whatever would come next.

I didn't feel scared. Until that moment, I didn't appreciate how much I wanted to be free of this town and its people – most of these people, at least – and that's why I asked to go with him, and that's why I was furious watching this man that I loved climb alone into a truck that probably didn't have enough fuel to run fifty miles.

He felt sorry for me. I could see that. To make both of us feel better, he said, "I'll be back some day. You'll see."

He was lying. I knew it, but maybe he didn't. He was lying to himself, just like he did for years when he pretended to believe whatever his crazy wife would tell him to believe.

I started crying. On bare feet, I chased that truck west on the river highway, and I kept running hard even when I couldn't see my father anymore. Then I stumbled and skinned both knees and limped home, finding my mother sitting at the kitchen table. She had been crying but her tears were finished by then. She looked old and extra stern. The woman used to be pretty. Before she was a mother, she was beautiful. I knew that from the old pictures. But that woman died during these last years, and what sat before me was tough and incapable of telling even a pitying lie.

"He did what was best," she claimed. "Leaving like this, before the harm spread to his loved ones … "

"But what about me?" I blurted.

"You?" She stared at me. Then after a shrug of the shoulders and one bored sigh, she admitted, "You'll thrive or you'll perish, Noah. Either way, your fate is entirely up to you."

The RV sits on the ornate brick road that borders the grassy town square. The machine's big engine has been turned off but still ticks down. Maybe twenty adults have gathered nearby, warning the children and one another to keep back. Guns are on display, and for every visible shotgun there are probably two pistols in easy reach. Stories about bandits have become common fodder, and people want to feel cautious and smart. Why nameless enemies would travel inside an old mobile home is a mystery. But sure enough, I find myself standing back too, listening to the engine cool, watching the dusty windows.

Behind the glass someone moves.

Prayers break out; neighbors join hands. But when somebody reaches for me, I step ahead of everyone, including the kids.

"Noah," say a couple of the older voices, sounding reproachful.

Then a girl, maybe twelve years old, blurts, "Who's that man?"

I'm not seen around town enough to be familiar. But Old Ferris says, "That's Helen's boy," and it is strangely heartening to know that I am still defined by one minuscule accident in biology.

I walk halfway to the apparition and stop.

It's Butcher Jack who emerges from the crowd, winking nervously when he joins me.

"What do you think?" he whispers.

A thousand years of guesses wouldn't find the truth. I say nothing, and we walk together up to the RV's big front door, hesitating an instant before each of us gives the filthy metal a friendly, flat-handed slap.

Jack starts to say, "Hello?"

And the door opens. The violent hiss of compressed gas startles us, and we leap back. I'm so nervous that I am laughing, and that's what the young woman sees when she pops into view.

She sees a giggling fool. To me, she looks twenty, fit and very pretty. Smiling as if it is her natural expression, she jumps to the bottom step and grabs the door handle while leaning out at us. She is lovely and slender with her gold hair worn long and trousers that couldn't be much tighter. It's not that I fall in love. But my first impression is that if I were ten years younger, I would be helplessly, shamelessly infatuated.

"Oh good," she says.

There's an accent to her words – a warm friendly way of speaking that is completely new to me.

"Can you two boys help with grandma?" she asks.

Jack looks at me.

I suppose this could be a trap. A beautiful girl lures ignorant older men into her mobile home, making them her prisoner, abusing them in all sorts of wicked ways. That certainly is worth the risk, I decide. So I lead the way, climbing up into the RV with Jack close behind. The woman says, "Thanks," twice before adding, "My dad hurt his back, and I'm not strong enough to do this alone."

What looks like a giant dirty box from outside proves smaller and less dusty than I expected. I smell people and recent meals and this morning's bathroom business. The "dad" proves to be a wary fellow maybe five years older than me, sitting behind the little table where a happy traveler might eat his meals, watching the countryside roll past. I remember enough to piece together a compelling daydream. This is how millions of people lived. Before. Burning gasoline by the tanker, wandering their world on the smooth happy roads.

Loudly, confidently, the girl announces, "I've got help for us, grandma."

Dad watches the two strangers, thanking us with a little nod as we pass. The old woman is in back, laid out on a bed big enough to sleep two. I can't remember ever seeing a lady of these proportions. She probably began life big, time and too much food making her astonishingly fat. According to the one working scale at my house, I weigh 200 elk-fed pounds. But I wouldn't want this lady standing on my scale. She's that fat. And worse, her smooth round face is drawn around a couple blue eyes that look at me and look at Jack and then look at the blond woman, registering nothing in the process.

She's blind, I guess.

But no, she suddenly asks, "Who are you?"

I start to answer. But the woman says, "I'm May and you're my grandmother."

She says those words instantly, like a reflex. As if she says them a hundred times every day. She's patient enough, but I notice that she doesn't bother trying to sound sweet. These are pragmatic words meant to carry us through the next several moments.

"May?"

"Yes, grandma."

"Where are we, May?"

"At home," the girl says. "Your home." Then she looks at me and brings up that smile again, saying, "If you can each get on one side and lift. She'll help us, I think. And we can get her outside."

I don't want to touch this strange old woman. It amazes me how hard I'm looking for any excuse.

But butchers are made of tougher stuff. Jack leaps to work, and the force of his example causes me to grab hold of the other arm and shoulder. Grandma is a pale soft and very cool piece of humanity. I can't feel the bones for all of the fat riding on her. Yet as promised, she doesn't fight us. We grunt and get her to stand on her own mammoth legs, twisting her sideways to leave room in the aisle, and with her granddaughter in the lead, coaxing and tugging, we herd the old lady up the length of the RV, giving her just enough lift that she doesn't collapse, at least until we make it to the front.

"Oh, damn," the doting granddaughter exclaims.

But the old woman falls like an expert, crumbling without complaint or noticeable damage. The man with the bad back pulls himself off his bench, getting in our way. Everybody is tugging on the limp arms and up from under the shoulders, and May says, "Try to stand, Grandma." She says it several times, her voice not angry but insistent. Then she turns, suddenly shouting into the vehicle's cab. Somebody else, someone I hadn't noticed, sits behind the steering wheel, watching the drama with utter indifference.

"Get off your ass," the girl tells him.

The man is barely adult, maybe a couple years younger than her, and judging by appearances he is a close relative to the others. But where grandma has bulk, the boy has muscle. If I have ever seen a bigger, stronger fellow in my life, I can't remember it. He fills the huge leather chair, enormous hands clinging to the armrests. And he has no intention whatsoever of moving.

Now the girl's father says, "Help us."

But the strong man shuts his mouth in a defiant fashion, delivering his answer without making noise.

"Goddamn it, son. We need your help here!"

My dislike for the boy is immediate and scorching. But anger has its functions, and I'm not exactly weak. As if to show the idiot what courage and determination look like, I grab grandma under both arms and grunt, lifting with my legs, dragging her limp body up to where the others can help, pulling her skyward until those puffy legs remember that they're supposed to walk.

"This way, grandma," the girl coaxes.

"Who are you?"

"Your granddaughter. I'm May."

"Where are we, May?"

We've made it to the steps. That's where we are. I've taken over for everyone but the girl. I'm holding the old woman under her damp cool armpits, keeping a couple steps above her as I steer her out into the open air.

May keeps saying, "This is home, grandma. You're at home."

Saintly people talk this way to the senile. Home is a magical place of rest and security, and I assume that the girl is misleading the old woman with a small, sweetly intended lie.

The first slipper hits the ground, and the old woman nearly collapses again. But I jerk hard, holding her steady until the second foot finds its way. Then with an exhausted smile, May says to me, "Thank you. You've been such a help."

I'm gasping and my back burns, but I feel proud of myself just the same.

"Winston's such a dick," she confides.

"Your brother?" I guess.

"So they tell me." She says that, and like you do with any new audience, she feels free to laugh hard at must be a very old family joke.

"I'm Noah," I tell her.

May doesn't just smile. She repeats my name, making it sound better than it normally does, and she offers a little hand that feels warm and comfortable, shaking my hand and then letting her fingers linger inside my grip.

Inspired by sunshine or the fresh air, grandma stands without aid. The good residents of Salvation come close and look at her and study the machine. The old woman looks at their faces, and then she turns and stares at the RV with what might be a flickering curiosity. "What is this thing?" her eyes ask.

I'm not holding hands with May anymore but we're standing close. Her grandmother does one slow turn, majestic in its own way. Then her gaze fixes on one of the closest homes – a three-story mansion built to eat sunlight and wind while wasting nothing – and with a voice as clear and certain as any can be, she asks, "Where is this? Where am I?"

I nearly laugh at her harmless confusion.

And May shows me a big wink while calling out, "This is Salvation, Grandma. Just like you described it. And doesn't it look wonderful … ?"

My father was gone. He was never officially shunned and certainly not banished, and the other adults began treating me with an uncommon amount of consideration. Warm voices asked about my state of mind. People I barely knew offered words of encouragement, friendly pats delivered to my shoulders and back. I was the man of the family now, and what a good young man I was. Yet those same voices began to whisper. Our community was better off without that very difficult soul. Nobody missed my father. Nobody wanted his return. The man's peculiar ideas and attitudes were problems, yet his enemies preferred to laugh at his lousy carpentry and his inability to grow tomato plants. Cooperation and competence were what the world demanded, and how would a man with so few skills manage to survive?

One day, a teacher warned my class that the easy pickings were running out. Good water was harder to find, and bad water was rusting away the last of the canned goods. Then she looked at me. With a glance, she told me that she was thinking about my father. Then with a winner's grin, she promised everybody that soon, very soon, the last of the wicked people would face God's justice.

Salvation was built without an official school. Its original children were taught at home using the Internet and smart software. My school was the local organic grocer, stripped of its refrigerators and freezers, the empty space divided into simple classrooms. My teachers were women with little experience and uneven talents, but who nonetheless volunteered to stand in front of a mob of kids, giving us an opportunity to do something besides tending crops or running errands.

One lady tried hard to teach history. Our random textbooks covered a few periods in suffocating detail, while most of the past was as empty and unknown as the far ends of the universe. She liked to show movies even older than her. Using aging DVD players and televisions, she educated me about those black-and-silver days when everybody smoked and everybody could sing and dance. But more useful were her memories of life as it stood in the recent past. She was a natural talker blessed with an audience just old enough to remember bits and pieces about the world before, and she spent entire days rambling on about her lost life, how she and her husband had four cars between them and a big beautiful house that they didn't have to share. The woman had little family and no children. She and her husband had survived the worst, but he died of a heart attack days after their arrival here. Few could talk as easily about the end of the world. Just mentioning the topic made most of the adults quiet and strange. But our teacher hadn't lost as much as the others, and blessed with a tenacious optimism, she could claim total confidence in God's mercy and the existence of heaven.

More than anything else, we wanted to know about the plague and its aftermath. She listened to our questions and warned that she was no medical expert, but in the next moment she carefully defined the plague's miseries: blisters and bleeding lungs, the high fevers and painful, suffocating deaths. China was halfway around the world but new diseases often came from there. Twice in two years, the Chinese government barely contained the viral monster. And that's why the world was terrified: what if the bug someday climbed onboard an airplane or bird, and what if it was carried across the helpless world?

This was grim odd rich fun, sitting in that quiet room, learning about horrors that would never hurt us. One day, our teacher arrived with an unexpected treasure. The original residents in Salvation had left behind furniture and clothes, plus fancy machines like sky-watching dishes and digital recording equipment. Also abandoned was a nondescript box tucked into a tornado shelter in the basement of one house. The box was full of hundreds and maybe thousands of hours of news reports. Somebody had worked hard to record the end of civilization. Each one of those bright silvery discs was carefully marked with dates and the network of origin. Not all of the disks worked, and most were surprisingly boring. But our teacher had made it her mission to hunt for the most interesting survivors.

The old player began to run. The room was full of patient, enthralled children. We watched the Chinese plague flare up twice and then die back again. Nearly ten per cent of the stricken had died, and maybe half of the rest were left with scarred faces and shrunken lungs. If that virus got loose, as many as ten million people would die, and a hundred million more would be left as invalids. That's why the hard push for a vaccine. And that's why there was celebration when a pharmaceutical company mass-produced an injection that would protect everybody who rolled up his sleeve, offering a willing arm.

Some nations did better than others. To me, Canada was that big green splotch at the top of a favorite old map. But it was also country with money and an efficient health care system, and the Canadians achieved a nearly perfect inoculation rate. Finland and Denmark and Costa Rica were equally successful. Japan and much of Europe exceeded ninety-seven per cent compliance. But the United States was falling behind in this critical race. Too many of us were poor or isolated. Empty rumors and misguided beliefs were huge problems. In the end, emergency laws and the National Guard managed to bring up the totals. Every doctor and nurse, teacher and law enforcement officer was inoculated. Every soldier and prisoner and hospital patient was inoculated. But there were always stubborn people who refused, and in the end we never even achieved ninety-five per cent saturation.

I remember being five and sitting in my bedroom, listening to my father and mother arguing. Mom didn't want to obey Caesar's Law. She didn't want the government to force her to do anything. Dad didn't want to hear about prayer and God's decency staving off illness. But mom kept insisting, batting aside dad's logic until he finally found his own way out the trap: if everybody else was inoculated, then we would be safe too.

As a family, we visited a fat little man who only seemed to be a doctor. The man took our money and filled out the proper forms, and in the eyes of the state, we were inoculated. Then we went home, and dad came into my room, sitting on my bed while explaining that this was what married people did. They compromised. And despite what he knew to be best, we could sleep easy because so many of the people around us had done the smart right noble thing.

China, where the murderous plague was born, managed to do better than the United States. India did less well, and parts of Latin America fell behind. But even those poor places managed to beat that ninety per cent mark. The meanest, saddest corners of the world were the most exposed. Africa and the wild nations in Asia achieved one-third compliance, if that. But charities and volunteer doctors didn't stop fighting. Brave defenders of the public good, they tirelessly pushed needles into little brown arms, even as word began to find its way to them that the first people who had received the vaccine – the subjects in the hurry-up trials – were beginning to shake, growing weaker by the day and profoundly confused.

According to the dates displayed on the recordings, the world's fate was decided on my sixth birthday. An old man stood before the cameras, the seal of his doomed nation behind him. With a worn sorry voice, he admitted that mistakes had been made. Who was responsible wasn't known and might never be, but the rush to market was a blunder, and a horrific tragedy had been unleashed, and every citizen who had tried to do something good was now infected.

That old broadcast triggered memories. Suddenly I was six again, sitting between my parents, watching the president talk. I hadn't understood most of the man's words or grasped even the easiest part of what he was saying. But mom was praying hard even when she was crying, and dad was weeping like I'd never seen before, and I sat there with my hands in my lap, staring at the birthday gifts wrapped in all that bright colored paper.

"When will this be done?" I asked impatiently. "When can I open up my presents?"

A boy's voice calls out to the visitors. Abrasive and impatient, he asks, "So where'd you people come from?"

Then Old Ferris adds, "The south, if I'm not mistaking that accent."

Grandma's eyes jump from one face to the next. People surge toward her, some running and everybody talking, and the old woman begins to panic. She gives a little gasp, spinning until she finds her granddaughter standing beside me.

"I'm here," says May.

Grandma's mouth opens, waiting for a name to be recalled.

Once again, the girl introduces herself, taking hold of a puffy hand before telling the rest of us, "Florida."

To the little ones, the word sounds made-up. Senseless.

Old Ferris nods. "Thought so."

Half-remembered maps pop into my head. On the fringe of the continent, an orange leg sticks out into the colorless ocean.

"How is our Sunshine State?" Ferris inquires.

"Wet," a new voice declares.

Gazes shift. Even May turns, as surprised as anyone to see her mountainous brother filling up the RV's door.

Something here is worth laughing about. "Florida's half-drowned," Winston warns, his round face full of delight and big teeth. "Live there, and you're lucky to be one step ahead of the ocean."

"That's not true," his father insists. "Maybe the Atlantic's a few feet deeper, but there's plenty of land left."

Kids ask about Florida, but most of their parents are younger than me and even more ignorant. Arms lift, pointing toward random spots on the southern horizon. Someone says mentions alligators – another word that means almost nothing to this gathering. Then Butcher Jack finally asks the most important question:

"But now what brings you good folks all the way up here?"

"My grandmother," the girl admits, tugging on one of the big arms. "She wanted to see her old home again."

The doughy face hears those words, considers them for a moment, and gives a slight nod of agreement.

"She's from where?" Jack asks, as if he doesn't trust his ears.

"From Salvation," says May.

"And I am too," the father announces. "In fact, when I was a boy, mom and I lived right over there."

He points at the mayor's house. Some of us look, but most people can't pull their eyes off these unexpected, astonishing strangers.

Once again, I move close to May.

She smiles at me, nothing about this girl shy. "It's a cold day," she observes.

"The worst winter in forty," Jack jumps in.

I ask, "Have you ever seen frost before?"

She laughs. "Not until two weeks ago."

"When did you leave home?" I want to know.

"Last summer," her father reports.

"Florida is cooler than usual," says May. "We've got a short-wave, and sometimes we'll talk to friends. There have been some nights when the thermometer dives below sixty."

"Maybe this is a sign," says Jack, twinkling eyes full of hope. "Maybe our climate's turning cool again."

Winston lets out a loud, disagreeable laugh. "That's not it at all," he says. "A pair of volcanoes blew up last year. In Indonesia and Colombia. Right now, two mountains' worth of dust are hanging up in the stratosphere, and they'll keep chilling things down for the next year or two."

May and her father exchange quick tense looks.

"All that water," I say to May. "I've always wanted to see the ocean."

But Winston doesn't like ignorance, and he won't let anyone keep his little dreams. "Believe me, you don't want to see the Atlantic. That water is hot and acidic and half-dead. The reefs are gone, and the shellfish. But not the jellies, no. Those bastards are doing great."

I'm not sure what a jelly is.

"The Gulf Stream still runs," he continues. "Maybe not as hard as it should. But at least the oceans haven't suffocated yet."

May frowns, but she won't take her eyes off me. "The sea is beautiful," she insists. "And there are a lot of fish and some whales even."

"Yeah, some," says her brother.

"Summer," I repeat. "A long time on the road."

"And we didn't know if we would make it," she says cheerfully. "Dad and his friends built this truck. We've got great tires and a special suspension and the motor burns almost anything. But you can't trust bridges anymore. And even if you find people, sometimes there isn't any fuel."

"People give up their alcohol?" Ferris asks skeptically.

To nobody in particular, she says, "We barter for it. Trade news and goods from other places. When we started out, we had fruit and dried fish strapped on top, and every cubbyhole was filled with some little treasure."

And they stole their fuel too. I don't see them as thieves, but there is no way to come this far and not take what charity won't surrender.

May's father stands on the other side of the old woman. He has to bend forward to look around her, asking me, "Would it be all right? Mom and I would love to see our old house."

Crossing half of the continent to tour one building. That might be the most unlikely story that I've ever heard. Yet the mayor leaps to the cause. "It's my house, and please. You'd be my welcomed guests, yes."

Except grandma isn't in the mood. She watches her arm lift when her son pulls at it. Yanking her hand free, she snaps, "I don't want to be here. I want to lie down."

Her son doesn't seem like the patient kind. "Mom," he says with a complaining tone. "Don't be difficult please."

But the woman starts to drop again, seemingly melting into the dull red bricks underfoot.

May jumps right in. "There's a good bed in that house, grandma."

"What?" she asks.

"A fine place to sleep, and warm too."

Perhaps the woman reconsiders her decision. More likely, she has already forgotten her planned collapse.

"Come on, grandma. Show me which room was yours."

And just like that, we start to walk. May remains close to the slow, stately woman, and I'm taking sluggish little steps to keep my place beside her. The present mayor is the gray-haired son of the second mayor – my mother's old ally. He normally can't look at me without showing his contempt. But on this exceptional occasion he manages to smile in my direction, showing the world his friendliness. "We have the biggest distillery in two hundred miles," he boasts. "And you're certainly welcome to take all the fuel you can carry."

May looks at me and says, "Thank you." As if I am the gracious one.

I match her smile, my step growing lighter. When was the last time a young woman gave me this kind of undeserved attention? It was Lola, of course, and a small, bearable guilt gnaws at me.

"Unless of course you want to remain here in Salvation," the mayor continues. "We're always looking for good neighbors."

The girl seems ready for the suggestion. It isn't that she acts uneasy, but it feels as if a hundred other topics would be more welcome. May nods. She pretends to consider the offer. Then with a polite, practiced tone, she says, "We might stay for a little while."

"But we're pushing north," the brother announces. "North before spring."

Curiosity changes directions. Older voices name likely places.

"Farther north," Winston declares. Then catching something in his father's gaze, he adds, "Nobody cares where we're going. These people are staying right here."

May tugs fondly on her grandmother's arm.

With a quiet voice, I ask her, "Where?"

She doesn't want to reply. But silence only makes these matters more difficult. Not too softly and not too privately, she tells me, "Canada."

"Nothing there but moose," I warn. With its nearly perfect inoculation rate, Canada was obliterated. The few survivors were too scattered to survive, much less build communities. At least that's what people have always claimed.

She acts untroubled by my concerns.

Half a dozen questions pile up inside my brain.

And then she artfully changes topics. "Where's your house, Noah?"

The mayor makes a low, disapproving sound.

I point at the horizon. "You can't see it from here."

"Are you a hermit?"

I feel uncomfortable. I want to hide my life and can't. With a hint of confession, I admit, "I live there with my wife."

I expect to feel better, only I don't.

The mayor overhears. "Maybe four times a year, we see Noah."

May studies me, holding her grandmother's hand with both of hers. This peculiar parade has reached the largest, grandest house in

Salvation. It is a towering structure with its south-facing windows and the old black solar panels and five corkscrew windmills on top, four of them turning and at least one windmill demanding new bearings or fresh grease – a squeaky, irritable sound that makes me more nervous by the moment.

Yet I stay beside the girl.

To the mayor, she says, "I'm curious. We asked other people about you. Salvation, I mean. They say you're Christian and that you're prosperous."

Hearing praise, the man blushes.

I don't know what I heard in her voice. More suspicion than approval, if I was guessing.

"Our residents are all True Believers," the mayor says. As if being Christian isn't good enough. "Our parents and grandparents knew God would save us. And that's why we survived the Shakes."

I have always despised that inadequate term.

"The Shakes."

May studies the mayor and then looks at me. I'm sure she wants to ask my affiliations, and part of me wants to tell her whatever she wants to hear. But changing topics seems like the better tactic.

"Why Canada?" I press.

She doesn't answer. One hand reaches behind. A small thick notebook has worked its way out of her hip pocket, and she shoves it back in place. Two ancient pens are nestled beside the book. "We're almost there, Grandma. Do you see the front door?"

This is the slowest walk of my life.

Winston has heard my question. Pushing closer, he says, "Florida is a goddamn nightmare."

I don't want to talk to this creature.

"It's the Africans," he adds. "They're coming in boats now. By the hundreds, thousands."

His sister says his name, nothing more.

"What?" he growls.

"That's not why we left," she insists.

"It's a big reason," he says. Then he looks at me, adding, "Africa has millions of people. Their climate is getting hotter and drier. Some head toward Europe, but the Turks and Russians claimed those empty cities. New immigrants get shot, or worse. So the refugees pay diamonds and gold to ride what boats that can still cross the Acid-lantic. Hundreds of men and women and all those children jammed close, and they know nothing about America except that it used to be rich."

He has told this story many times, but it's still emotional. Working himself into a rage, he says, "We had good lives in Florida. But the freighters started dropping their cargo on the beaches. Those people expect to find houses ready to live in. They want cars and grocery stores. They've been lied to, which makes them angry. But before anybody can complain, their boat's turned around and headed back for another bunch of fools."

Hearing the shrill chatter, the mayor seems less sure about his guests. But the commitment was made. He throws a weak smile at everyone and turns the knob on his front door, leading the way into a great volume of warm air and little children. "Company," he calls out. "We've got guests."

Entering the sunny living room, May's father says, "Well, well. I sure remember this place."

Maybe it's my age, or maybe it's my present life. Whatever the reason, I'm not as angry as I would have expected. The last time I was under this roof, my neighbors were holding a meeting, and my mother was voting with the rest of the mob to shun Lola and all of her family.

"Do you remember this room, grandma?"

May is sweet, an angel effortlessly guiding the old lady to the tall windows that look south at the brown bluffs and bright winter skies. I go with them. For some reason, May lets go of the woman, pulling out the notebook and one pen and spending a few moments jotting down notes. Then again, always patient, she asks, "Do you remember any of this, grandma?"

The upper windows are original, but tossed balls and careless tumbles have broken all the lower panes. The replacement glass is never as good. Cold air seeps through gaps. And maybe that's what the old lady feels now. The hand that May was holding lifts, fingertips to the dingy glass, and she seems to tilt into the sunshine, preparing to collapse again. But she doesn't. She manages to straighten, the big dim eyes staring at the bluffs. "What happened to those trees, darling?"

"What trees, grandma?"

"On that hill there. Are they dead?"

"No, grandma." The girl leans in close, speaking with a flat teaching voice. "It's winter, grandma. The trees are sleeping."

"Winter?"

The lady seems flabbergasted.

"Not like Florida, is it?" May asks.

And then grandma giggles. There's no other word for the joyful girlish laugh that rolls out of her. She giggles and turns back to her granddaughter, saying, "Oh, my. Winter? Really?"

"Really."

Delighted to her core, the old gal says, "Well then, we did it, didn't we? Winter came. We saved the world!"

I wasn't quite seven years old, hunting inside a garage for gas cans or tools, or even better, fresh toys that might help pass the day. Dad was searching the house for food. Mom waited on the front yard. She was supposed to be helping us, but sometimes her energy would leave her. Maybe she looked stern and strong, but the truth is never as simple as appearances. Sitting and doing nothing was all she could manage that morning, her face unchanged but the wrinkles deeper, the color leaving the skin as secret thoughts made her sick.

All of us were sick. More than once, dad confided that to me. We weren't sick in ways that would kill us, but because of the awful things that we had seen. Yet difficult as it seemed, he insisted that each of us should try to count our blessings.

The garage had no blessings. There weren't any toys and the only gas can was empty, and even before the world ended the car wasn't worth much. Dust lay thick on its windshield, and I spent most of a minute writing the words I knew into the gray grime. I wrote my name and "dog" and "cat" and I don't remember what else. Then dad came out the house, looking back at me.

"Wait there," he said. "Don't go inside."

I'd seen bodies before. They didn't scare me.

But dad was worried about something. He walked up the driveway, aiming for mom, and he started to talk and she looked at the house as he said something else, and then she was shaking her head.

"It's not our business," she said. "Don't."

That's when I slipped through the side door.

The lady was in her thirties, and she used to be pretty. I found her sitting in the middle of the dining room. She was naked. Walls of cardboard boxes were stacked on three sides of her, each box cut open so that she could reach inside whenever she wanted. Empty cans of applesauce and spaghetti and condensed tomato soup and plastic water bottles covered the rest of the filthy floor. She sat with her naked body propped up, soft ropes around her chest and rubber handles dangling from the ceiling. Her chair belonged in a living room, except somebody had used a chainsaw to cut through the cushion. The hole was nearly too big for her scrawny bottom. Later, thinking about the situation, I realized that somebody must have cut a matching hole through the floor, leaving it so that the lady could go to the bathroom whenever it was necessary. Food and water in easy reach, and she could have lived for years eating from that stockpile.

I whispered, "Hello."

Her face was jumping, but her eyes were steady. She could see me well enough to react, though her words didn't make sense. Her ingenious, desperate system had worked until she was too weak to unseal the cans and bottles. Openers and barely punctured cans lay at her feet. There wasn't any strength in the emaciated legs. Her stick-like arms were covered with sores and red blotches. Months had passed since I had seen somebody living with the Shakes. It amazed me that she had survived this long. But some people possessed a natural immunity. It wouldn't save them, but it was enough to make life into something worse than dying.

With all of the dignity she could muster, that naked starving and helpless woman sat on her makeshift toilet and looked at me and said nonsense. Then her eyes moved, and she stopped talking.

A hand dropped on my shoulder.

I waited for my name to be said. I waited to be in trouble. But my father knelt and looked only at me. Then with a careful solemn voice, he said, "Go outside, Noah. Go now, and I'll be right behind you."

My first thought was that dad was going to open up some cans and bottles, giving the lady a feast before we moved on.

Then I saw the pistol tucked into the back of his pants.

I hesitated.

Again Dad looked at me. This time he said, "Go," with God's own authority, and I went outside as ordered. I didn't want to run. I told myself just to walk. But I was suddenly in the bright sunshine, my legs churning, and the shot came and was gone and I barely heard it.

Mom called my name, but she didn't try to stop me.

I ran past her, sobbing and making my own nonsensical sounds.

On the brink of giddy, the old woman says, "Oh, my. Winter? Well then, we did it, didn't we? Winter came. We saved the world."

Few people pay attention. A few notice her voice and maybe listen to the words. But everybody is talking. Everybody wants to find the fun in something new and unexpected. Just slightly, the noise inside the big room dips, and then grandma is finished and blank-faced again. Maybe she didn't speak. I thought I heard everything, but I'm not sure what I heard. There might be a thousand fine reasons to ignore whatever leaks out of that lady. And that's my intention, right up until I glance at May.

She and her father are trading looks. Less than comfortable, there's this weird long moment where bolts of electricity seem to be flying between them.

And then together, at the same moment, they laugh.

Nothing could be funnier, their cackling says. May lowers her pad and pen, patting her grandmother on the back while casually studying the other faces in the room. Settling on the person most puzzled by this outburst, May uses a smile that couldn't feel any sharper. "Grandma has troubles," she mentions.

I nod amiably, seeing no reason to disagree.

"Gets confused," she adds.

"It's all right," I say.

But that doesn't satisfy her. She needs to touch me. Her fingers curl around my elbow, and her face is close enough that I can smell dried meat on her breath. "The poor thing tells the most amazing stories," says May, her voice quiet, just short of a whisper.

"I can believe it," I answer.

"Don't make anything out of her noise," her father suggests, offering up a nod and wink. "She doesn't even know where she is."

Maybe not, but the woman in question giggles again – that same odd girly giggle – and once more her eyes regain their depth and clarity. She turns and looks at us, engaged enough with the conversation to open her mouth, the beginnings of some new statement emerging.

May cuts her off.

Nothing about the act is rude, but the girl is determined. "I'm sure you're tired, grandma. Wouldn't you like to lie down? A little nap, yes?"

Grandma blinks, struggling with the abrupt shift in topics.

Her son turns to the mayor, his voice louder than necessary. "My mother needs to lie down. Do you have any guest quarters, a spare bed … ?"

"We don't have guests," the mayor confesses. "And the beds are all upstairs." But after giving the situation careful study, he charitably adds, "There's a comfortable couch in the next room. With the door closed, I think your mother could relax."

That's good enough for this suddenly devoted son. "Come on, Mom. Let me help you."

He and the old lady follow the mayor out of sight.

I watch May, and she smiles. But when I pretend to look elsewhere, her face stiffens and the smile turns into something harder.

Old Man Ferris is talking about winters past and current. Butcher Jack is beside him, but he throws me a questioning look.

I ask May, "What are you writing?"

She lifts the notepad, apparently surprised to find it in her hand. "Oh, I just like to write." But is that enough of an answer? Maybe not, which is why she closes the pad and slides it back into the tight pocket. "When we started out, I thought it would be nice to keep a record. A journal. Maybe I could even finish a book about our travels some day."

"A book?" I ask doubtfully.

Jack has drifted closer. "Of course a book," he tells me. "Don't you think someday, somewhere, there's going to be enough people to make it worth printing new books?"

May nods enthusiastically. "That's going to happen sooner than you might guess."

Jack watches me.

I move my gaze from him to May and back again, saying nothing.

Silence bothers the girl. She pretends otherwise, but I get the strong sense that she feels nervous, intensely aware about this room full of strangers. The mayor emerges from the adjoining room, but May's father remains behind. "I want to go check on my grandmother," she announces. I don't get an invitation to join her, which pricks me somehow. She tries not to look like a person in a hurry, but that's exactly what she is, slipping between other people and past the grinning mayor, entering a room that she doesn't know and making sure that the door is latched behind her.

I stare at the door while trying to make sense of my thoughts.

"You know what's really odd?" Jack asks.

"The old lady's babbling."

"Not in her state, it isn't," he says. Then he gets beside me, saying, "She could talk about aliens and horned dragons, and really, who would care?"

"The girl's reactions were peculiar," I mention. "And her dad's too."

My old friend takes a deep breath.

"What else?" I ask.

"Do you see Winston anywhere?"

A man of his proportions would be obvious, but looking across the sun-washed room, I don't see him.

"The old lady was talking her nonsense," Jack says. "You know, about saving winter, saving the world? And that's when I happened to look at her grandson."

"So?"

"You should have seen his face," says Jack. "Bonfires don't get half as red as those cheeks of his."

"I don't see him now," I say.

"Red-faced," Jack repeats. "Then all at once, the kid turned and practically ran outdoors."

Our history teacher wanted to show us more of the old news recordings – dispatches from the ends of the earth, tearful accounts of American hospitals being filled with the sick and dying. But too many kids went home crying after that first day. Too many of us didn't sleep that night. So on the second day, the new mayor and my mother and several other important bodies sat in the back of the class, watching with us while shaking bodies and military convoys filled the television screen. I didn't remember any of this from my own life. When the Shakes began, my father filled our van with food and drove us north to a lake and isolated cabin. There wasn't any news or Internet for us, which meant that Mom was seeing these horrors for the first time too. When I felt sick, I looked at her. But she just sat there. Stone has more emotion than her face showed. Then came a long story about riots, mobs trying to break into pharmacies and gun shops, and the reporter – a smug fellow with a big cross dangling around his neck – explained how people were hunting for pills and bullets to kill themselves and their loved ones. "Suicide," he said, "has become preferable to a slow miserable death."

I looked over my shoulder again. Mom's face had changed. Pale as milk, she stared at the screen with her eyes narrowed, her mouth set but her body struggling to hold inside whatever she was feeling.

It was the rarest sensation, feeling sorry for that woman.

Another news story began. Instead of people fighting for pills, one man was sitting in the middle of a long table, talking into a microphone. Several old men and old women were sitting behind another long table, listening carefully. Ignoring his own shaking hands, pushing past his sloppy voice and the drool, he was trying to explain his company's role in the ongoing catastrophe.

"My people used standard methods to produce our vaccine," he said. "Attenuated viruses have been employed for years. Successfully employed, yes. Mumps and chicken pox and measles have been conquered with these proven techniques. Our mistake was to believe that the wild virus was genuine. Which was everyone else's mistake too, I should add."

A woman at the other table held up her hand. "Where do you think the virus came from?"

"We have evidence," he began. Then he hesitated. Two assistants showed him pieces of paper, and he started to read, offering long words that might have been technical or might have been mangled by his failing mouth. Then he stopped talking, gathering himself with one deep breath before adding, "This bug is an ingenious monster."

"Is it military?" the woman asked. "Maybe the Chinese built it?"

"Certainly not. That's absurd. The Chinese are dying as fast as the rest of us."

"Then who is responsible?"

"Private hands," he said mysteriously.

Nobody was happy to hear this.

"Evidence," the woman demanded. "We need hard evidence."

"I wish I could offer some," he confessed. "I have to assume ... what the scant evidence shows ... some group with skills and a quality laboratory produced the virus and infected a few people. Those were the original epidemics. But those events were just to get our attention. These plotters understood that we would ... that someone had to ... generate a quick cheap vaccine in response ... "

A man at the end of the table began to stand, one arm clumsily swinging at the sky as he shouted, "Prion."

The witness quickly corrected him. "This is something else, Senator. Something we have never seen before. Prions manipulate a different protein. This particular agent ... well, it's a natural component of the phage's protein shell. It was hiding in plain sight, and we never imagined that it would have such devastating effects on the human nervous system."

The room buzzed with voices.

Someone called out, "Quiet."

Then the woman leaned forward, hands shaking. Voice shaking. Into her little black microphone, she asked, "This is a great conspiracy. Is that your explanation?"

"Yes, Senator."

"And your company is blameless.

The dying man hesitated. Then his face dropped as he admitted, "I'm not sure how to answer that, madam."

More voices, more pleas for silence.

"This was a crash program," he continued. "We hired consultants, experts from around the world ... and it is possible that some of those people were part of a secret group ... "

I looked over my shoulder again. The coldest woman in the world was weeping, mopping up tears with a handkerchief cut out of one of my father's left-behind shirts.

"You're blaming ... " the woman began. Then her voice failed her.

An ancient man was sitting beside her. The Shakes didn't kill the elderly as quickly as most. Maybe that's why he didn't have symptoms. His voice was level, his mind clear. With a rich voice, he pointed out, "Conspiracies demand goals. These people must have had some purpose. What do you think it was?"

"I can offer nothing but guesses," the witness replied, looking down at his own hands. When they stopped trembling, he looked up and said, "Power is one possibility. The survivors of this nightmare will be left with the entire planet at their disposal. But my better guess ... what seems more reasonable and even more awful to me ... is that an environmental group might have take these steps. If they felt that human overpopulation and pollution were putting the earth at severe risk. If they convinced themselves that this was for the best ... "

"How many would it have taken?"

"Excuse me, Senator?"

"This shadow organization you're describing. I want to know how many of the criminals we should be chasing today."

"I don't know, Senator."

"Dozens? Hundreds?"

"Perhaps hundreds," he said. "But keeping an enormous secret would be difficult. A handful of likeminded individuals could probably achieve the desired results, if they were clever enough."

"In your company, sir ... "

"Yes?"

"Who didn't receive the vaccine?"

An assistant leaned close, whispering a few words.

The advice was waved off. "No, I want to answer this." The witness leaned close to his own microphone. "I've asked myself that same question, sir. I have. But my company has almost vanished. I insisted that my people were first to receive the vaccine, and that included our contractors. Most of us are already dead. That I'm alive is a small miracle. I can't count all of the suicides ... of friends and colleagues ... yet in all good conscience, I can't tell you that a few people haven't managed to slip away in the chaos ... "

The Senator considered his next question.

But the dying woman beside him rose to her feet. With a ragged, ugly voice, she asked, "But why? Even if it's as you claim, a small group trying to save the world —?"

"I didn't claim anything, madam. I'm just speculating."

Behind me, our mayor jumped to his feet, his squeaky voice ordering the television to be turned off.

"I don't care about the reasons," the Senator continued. "Reasons are excuses. This is a cruel, vicious assault on humanity, and believe me, whoever's responsible is taking great pleasure from our misery and terror."

The television went black.

I turned. Mom was standing beside the mayor. The crying was finished, replaced with the old steel mask that I knew by heart.

To the class, the mayor said, "Obviously, this is a very painful subject."

But we weren't crying. This was ten times easier than watching shaking people fighting over poison pills. My mother whispered something to the mayor, and he nodded and came forward, unfolding one of the green sacks leftover from the old grocery. The DVD was removed from the player. Then Mom helped collect every other disk, and while she carried the full sack out into the parking lot, the mayor explained that these items were going to be burned. The oldest kids were surprised, and our teacher seemed puzzled, even hurt. But to give the action purpose, he explained, "Yes, people did play a role in what happened. But what is important – what you need to remember, children – is that only the hand of God can move this world. No other force has such power or majesty. A judgment as enormous as the one we have lived through demands Our Father, and we should be thankful. He has given us the gift, this new Eden, and we are more blessed than any people to ever walk the earth."

With that, he retreated.

We soon smelled smoke, ugly black and probably toxic.

My teacher wandered to the front of the class, offering clumsy words of support for this disagreeable policy. Most of the students got busy making paper gliders and passing notes about small, fun nonsense. But I remained busy: closing my eyes while holding my breath, I wished that my mother would breathe in those fumes, grow sick and die.

Winston stands in the cold bright sunshine, hands at his side, eyes down and his mouth clamped shut, chewing hard at nothing. He isn't as red as I imagined, but it doesn't take any special skill to see the anger under his skin. Passersby want to talk to this newcomer, but they see his face and steer clear. Even a couple children approach and then think again, retreating past me, one asking the other, "What demon is in his heart?"

I put myself in front of Winston, and I wait.

He doesn't react.

Nobody else is close, just him and me standing in the open. I don't know what to say, but once I start talking, my mouth finds words and logic. I say, "Families," with easy scorn. I tell him, "Families aren't easy." Then I offer up a few curse words, laying the groundwork before admitting, "My mother was an extraordinary bitch."

He blinks, eyes focusing on me.

I wait.

He starts to turn away.

"What about your grandmother?"

I want him to look at me again, reacting to my open-ended question. But he avoids my eyes and the topic, big legs carrying him back toward the RV.

Walking beside him, I talk about the recordings of those old news stories. In a few crisp sentences, I try to recapture two days in class and the reaction of the important adults, plus my own raging scorn. "I mean, we had this window on the past. And what did the adults do? Destroy it. They didn't see any value in the disks, only danger, and they destroyed them before anybody could figure out how to make copies. So these kids here today ... they don't know anything about what happened, except what their parents choose to tell them."

Winston seems to listen, but he refuses to even glance at me.

"Here's something funny," I continue. "When I was twenty-one, I left Salvation. There was this local girl named Lola, and I loved her as much as my mom hated her, and we decided to move into a solid old house up in the hills. Live with each other and our dogs, no idiot Believers within miles of our front door."

We reach the wheeled house. Winston grabs the door handle and pulls, the hiss of compressed gas helping it swing open. But as he takes one step inside, he hesitates. He can't help but look at me, asking, "Why in hell should I care about any of this?"

"My wife's smart, but in odd ways."

The boy is just a little curious now. But that's enough. He steps back down to the bricks and looks at the top of my head, asking, "So what?"

"We talk," I say. "All day long, we chat. But since we don't see other people, and since nothing important changes day by day, our best topic is the past. Our childhood. She didn't go to school with me, but she remembers the day when they burned the disks. She heard all about it from me. And a couple years ago, after talking it over a thousand times, Lola turned to me and asked, 'Don't you think it's strange? Why would an ordinary person go to all that trouble?'

"'Because it's history,' I told her. 'That's why.'

"'But it wasn't history yet,' she pointed out. 'It was just a plague in China when it started. Most of the world was still safe. Yet somebody started saving news stories about that disease. And they recorded everything about the vaccine, even when everybody else in the world thought that this was the answer to all of our troubles. Which is a crazy thing to do, isn't it? Unless of course you knew all along what was going to happen.'"

I stop talking.

Winston looks more like a boy than ever. His face is empty and pale, his mind pulled back to some private place, leaving me almost nothing to see. But before I go on with my tale, he asks, "Where were those disks?"

"In a box," I tell him. "Unmarked and probably left behind by mistake."

"No. What house were they in?"

"I don't know."

"My grandmother's?"

"Probably not," I admit.

He gives a deep snort before telling me, "You don't know anything."

"I know the old lady saved the world."

Winston moves closer, looming over me. "She's nuts."

"No, she isn't."

He licks his lips and says, "Forget it."

I say nothing.

Then he remembers where he was headed. Again, one of the big feet steps up into the RV, and just to be sure that I know it, he tells me again, "Grandma is crazy."

"Was she a scientist?"

He keeps climbing.

"It must be tough," I say, stepping up after him.

He turns, surprised to find me sticking with him. "What's tough?"

"Being stuck with them: a senile woman who saved the world, and your father who grew up with a legend. Because he's always known, hasn't he? Families can't keep secrets. And you grew up hearing how grandma helped build the bug or the vaccine, which were good things. Great things. Without them, there would have been too many people in the world, and civilization would have crashed just the same. But with the climate in every worse condition, everything was falling apart in ways a lot worse than what we got."

The boy's face grows red again. I make plans about what to do if he takes a swing at me. I'll jump down the stairs and run – that's my heroic scheme. But he doesn't lift a hand. Instead, he says, "You don't know shit."

"Billions murdered, and that old lady is partly to blame." I smile and halfway laugh, adding, "It's got to be hard, sleeping under the same roof with one of the world's great criminals and her proud son and a sister who thinks that old grandma is just about the best, most special person ever."

Winston sighs.

A moment later, he straightens his back and lifts a hand, that broad hard palm driving once into my chest, pretty much wringing the breath right out of me. Without trying.

I want to run and don't.

"No," he declares. "That's not it."

"Oh yeah?" I ask doubtfully. "What is 'it'?"

A smirk rises, and he laughs. "I'm not telling you anything. But if I did know somebody like that – I'm just saying 'if' – the killing wouldn't be what pisses me off. No, the trouble is that the wrong people got killed. If you've got this wonderful weapon in hand, you don't just slaughter your own. You don't save the world just to fill it up with idiot Christians and black savages. That's a dumbshit waste, if you want my honest opinion."

Butcher Jack would have brought the news but it was summer and scorching hot and his main freezer was in some kind of trouble. That's why Old Ferris made the journey instead. I was out back in the junkyard, hunting for pipe that I could splice into our growing irrigation system. The rattling roar of a little motor brought me back to the house. I came around to discover Lola standing on the porch, flanked by several dogs, her favorite Bushmaster assault rifle propped just inside the front door. Our visitor was straddling his little motorcycle, the dust of his arrival finally settling on top of the heavier dust. Lola was talking. With a voice friendlier than any she used on me, she told the visitor that he was welcome to come inside or at least into the shade of the porch and would he like a drink of water because we had plenty, it was no trouble, and he looked hot, did he feel hot, and how was the ride out from town?

Ferris was pleasant about his silence – no grimaces, no uncomfortable looks at the cloudless sky. But even miles from Salvation, he refused to speak to any person who had been officially and permanently shunned.

I called to him.

He brightened instantly. One stiff leg swung over the seat, and he propped up his bike and looked at me, forgetting for a second or two why he had come. Then he remembered. A fresh sorrow went into his eyes, and that's when I knew that he'd brought bad news. It was easy to guess what he would tell me but there was still shock in the words. "It's your mom, Noah," he began. Then with a slow shake of the head, my old friend said, "She died this morning. Just before sunrise."

I didn't say anything.

So he answered the questions that I might ask, put in my place. "It was the cancer. She didn't suffer too much. The right prayers got said. In the end, I don't think she even knew where she was. Which isn't a bad way to be, all things considered."

He paused and stared at me.

"What else?" I asked.

"She was talking about you. These last days, she kept asking where you were. She didn't remember."

I stepped up on the porch, one sweaty hand pushing into my wife's damp back. "Well," I began. Then after some consideration, I admitted, "I guess I should know she died. So thank you."

He wanted to look only at me, but his eyes kept jumping back to Lola.

"Want some water?" I asked.

He almost said, "Yes." But he had so thoroughly ignored the earlier offers that he couldn't agree now. So he took a deep breath, pushing into the rest of his important news. "She planned her funeral. Weeks ago, before she was real sick, she told us that it was important to her that you come and serve as one of her pallbearers."

"No," I said, out of reflex.

Lola moved against my hand.

I shook my head and stepped off the porch, suddenly angry with this man that had never said one cruel word to either one of us. He was a simple decent creature who helped my family many times over the years. But there was a lot of emotion to deal with on a day best spent in the shade. I approached and stopped short of him, and he watched me. His little mouth looked as if it was holding something sour but nothing in his eyes was worried. I wasn't scaring him. He was sorry and wished that somebody else had come on this tough errand. But he was brave enough or stubborn enough to wait, and when my emotions simmered down, he said, "It's your choice, Noah. The funeral's tomorrow morning, and it starts in the town center."

"Won't be there," I promised.

He nodded and climbed back on the bike and kicked it twice and left again – a wiry little man vanishing into a fresh cloud of dust.

Exhausted, I returned to the porch. To Lola. But the only affection and understanding that I got were from the licking, panting mutts at her feet.

"What?" I asked.

She turned and went inside.

I followed, again asking, "What?"

Cleaning up the kitchen was important just then. Lola started pushing plates into cupboards and sorting the silverware and cups, and I watched until I didn't think there was any chance that she would volunteer her thoughts. So I took a shot, saying, "You think I should go."

Her response wasn't to agree with me. Because saying, "Yes," wouldn't say half enough. Instead it was important to throw a handful of knives into the wrong drawer and then turn, lifting a china plate over her head as if ready to bust it. We have very good dishes in our household – fine work from Germany and England, some of it older than the old farmhouse that we took over for ourselves. Maybe that's why she held her hand. Or maybe she wasn't all that upset but it was important to get my attention before saying, "She was your mother."

"I think I know that."

Lola bit her bottom lip. Then she offered up a few words that must have lived inside her for years, never mentioned and never even suspected by the man who slept with her every night. "She was your best parent, Noah. So yes, I think that mean old bitch deserves to have you at her funeral."

Leaning against the nearest wall, I asked, "What do you mean? My best parent how?"

"Your father left you. Your mother didn't. Your father could have taken you but he chose not to."

"Life on the road? He didn't want to put me at risk."

"And for that matter, why the hell did he leave in the first place?" If anger was a race, Lola was in the lead now. "He wasn't banished. He wasn't even shunned."

"He would have been," I said.

"Shunning isn't death," she pointed out. "How many years did my family live in that miserable town, not one Believer offering us anything more than some secret whispered words?"

Never in my marriage did I feel like hitting Lola.

That was the nearest that I've ever been, and there was still a good gap between the urge and the deed. But my hands closed, and I was breathing hard with my heart pounding, doing nothing else while she watched me.

"What else?" I finally managed.

"Your mom stayed. Believe me, she would have talked your father into taking you, if that's what she wanted. But she thought it was best for her and for you that you stayed behind. And bad as she was as a parent and a human being, she probably did her very best. Which is enough reason for you to go into town and do the service like she wanted. Make yourself believe she's really dead, and then you can do whatever you want to the bitch's grave. But come back to me afterwards. All right, Noah? Will you do all that for me?"

Clear-headed, full of purposeful rage, I hurry back to the mayor's house. My mind is made up. I'm ready to announce what I know, or at least tell people what I think I know. Most won't believe me. Stubborn, unimaginative souls will dismiss my words, declaring that I am misinformed or crazy or both. But even if the entire town laughs at my madness, the idea will start chewing at them: what if I am right? What if the odd old lady bears some responsibility in the murder of billions? And what if her family not only knows about it but by one route or another approves of what she did?

Yet coming through the front door, I discover May and her father standing before a very happy audience. I expected them to be in the adjacent room, the door closed. I didn't imagine dozens of people laughing about something outrageously funny, something said just a moment ago. I'm standing at the back of a big loud happy party, a handful of people glancing my way just long to determine that I am immune to their deep joy.

May sees me. I feel her eyes but when I try to meet them, she shifts direction. A fond hand touches her father's shoulder, and whatever story she has been telling ends with the words, "And that's how we finally crossed the Mississippi River."

Raucous laughter.

And I retreat outdoors.

My mind is still made up. Yes it is. I just need a better moment, and maybe a smaller, more open-minded audience. And I might have to lie. Winston gave a hypothetical confession. I'll just change his words a little, giving him even more arrogance than usual. But even as I'm practicing this speech, Jack emerges to ask me, "What's wrong?"

I take a deep breath, wanting to answer. But my voice is missing.

"Did you catch Winston?"

I nod.

"You look sick, Noah."

That's only because I feel sick. I've got a rabbit's heart in my chest, and I can't seem to breathe fast enough to make my chest stop aching. I want to sit. I want that tall beer and a good chair and silence. But mostly, I want to be in a different place than this, and that's why I ask Jack, "Did you ever get my elk unloaded?"

"Mostly, but then our guests showed up and my boys bolted," he says. "Why? You want to start home now?"

"Yes."

He nods. He says, "Let's go finish then. I don't know where my boys got to, but there shouldn't be much left to do."

"No."

He studies me, waiting.

I'm not sure what I want. But I hear myself saying, "Do me a different favor. Would you?"

"Sure, what?"

"When you get a chance, tell May … tell her that I know."

"You know what?"

"Tell her that her brother told me most of it. And I figured out the rest for myself."

"What did you figure out, Noah?"

I just shake my head.

Now Jack looks grim and serious. One of those strong hands clamps down on my shoulder. "What'd that kid say to you?"

Through the door comes more laughter. Fourteen years of my life was spent in this town, and I can't remember ever hearing this much joy.

"Noah?" he presses.

But I shake free, starting back to the butcher's shop. "Point May towards me, would you? And don't wait long, Jack. As soon as the meat's off, I'm driving out of here."

Three years after my mom died, Lola and I took our last trip to the city. Useful scrap was hard to find by then, what with fires and rust and time. But we had some loot worth the trouble, and we also realized we'd never come back to this place again. Which was a very worthy accomplishment.

Half by mistake, half by planning, we ended up standing next to one of the mass graves. A fleet of bulldozers had been parked on the same ground for nearly two decades. The ground was still rough, bits of bone and stubborn clothes poking out here and there. Looking at that sorry scene, I thought about the last funeral that I had attended, and when Lola asked what I was thinking, I told her.

She was crying. I was crying.

Sniffling, she told me, "Somebody wanted this. Somebody planned all of this."

I couldn't count the times we had wrestled with this subject.

"Know what I wish, Noah?"

"What?"

"That those responsible had come out and said so." My sweet sad shunned wife leaned into me, explaining, "As soon as the Shakes began, they should have put out some official statement proving that they were real and listing all of their wise good-hearted reasons for doing the unthinkable."

"We can guess their reasons," I said.

"But if they went public, there wouldn't have been any doubts."

"And what would that have changed?"

"We would have somebody to blame today. A group with a name, real people with a clear purpose."

"The Shakes would have killed the same people," I said. "Every government would have failed in the same ways. And the two of us would have ended up here or someplace like here, looking at dead people and dirt."

"Except," she said. "If they offered their proof and their reasons, then we'd know that people were responsible for everything. Just ordinary idiot self-important people. And that means that those ordinary idiot self-important people in Salvation couldn't tell themselves that this had to be God's judgment, or that they're all so special and pure for surviving."

I hadn't thought of it that way.

Lola sniffed and said nothing more, wiping at her eyes with the backs of both hands. And I stood very still, looking out over that enormous graveyard, thinking, "This is how it feels. This is what it's like, serving as pallbearer to the world."

I watch for her, pulling a slab of smoky meat off the trailer, and then I take a break, expecting May to rush into view. Only she doesn't. I remove another two slabs and carry them into the butcher's shop, and when I come out I'm ready to see her. But the street is empty. Nervous energy gives me enough juice to work hard and fast. Warm enough to sweat, I open up my coat and sling more meat onto a cart and wheel it inside, pausing in the doorway to look back at nobody. She won't show. I know this now. But when I come outside again, May is standing in my truck, waiting for me. Except that I don't want to see her. A moment ago I was comfortable with the two of us never crossing paths again.

She says, "What?"

I push the cart past her, my head down.

"Your friend says you know something," she says. "He told me that I had to run over here and talk to you. That it was important."

Bear meat is greasy and dark, and it demands an entirely different approach to smoke properly. I start pulling the bear off the truck, piling the roasts and haunches on the cart. May watches me until the cart is full. Then she says, "You don't know anything."

"What was the old woman's job?"

There. Somebody asks a question. And I guess it was me, since nobody else is standing here.

"Job?"

"Before the Shakes came," I say.

She stares at me, saying nothing.

"She was a scientist," I guess.

May straightens her back before reminding me, "That was a long time ago. And I'm sure you noticed, her mind is mostly gone."

"She saved the world."

The girl doesn't react, not even to blink.

"Your brother's pissed with her. But that's only because she killed the wrong people he thinks. On the other hand, you know that she's a good person, an exceptional person, and always has been. You love your grandmother, and you came all this way to see where she and your dad lived before the world changed. Those notes in your back pocket? They're going to help you write a book about this great woman who helped save the world." I'm sweating hard, tired hands shaking. "The world needed saving. If grandma and her friends hadn't acted, our species would have eventually pushed the climate over the brink. And that would have been an even worse mess than the nightmare I lived through."

May says nothing. But her eyes drop, and with ten feet between us, I can hear her breathing.

"The thing is, maybe I believe that's all true. The climate was in deep trouble. There were too many people and no time to spare. And that one way or another, the Shakes saved the world."

Her eyes lift.

"We're still here," I admit. "And I'm pretty much happy to be alive."

A smile starts, but then she thinks better of it.

"There's just one problem, May. Maybe your grandma did what she did for the best reasons. Maybe we didn't have any choice left. But why not come out and explain the situation? Why didn't she and her colleagues make their argument, even if it was horrible to consider and there was no turning back?"

She looks off into the distance.

"One statement, and all the mystery would be gone. Nobody likes dying, but at least there would have been a purpose to it. Mankind was being chopped back like a weed, and the planet would be better for it. That's not nearly as hopeless as a pack of faceless murderers with no goal but to be vicious."

May stares at the sky until I look in the same direction. I see nothing but the high blue, and she turns to me. "Maybe they should have," she says.

"Did any of them take the vaccine?" I ask.

Her eyes stay on me. She waits and then says, "No," before risking a small step toward me.

I try to speak, but my voice breaks.

May waits impatiently.

I breathe, and talk. "Most voices would claim that if people wanted to kill billions, even for the good of the earth, then they should take their own medicine. Me? I'd be happy if they ate their shotguns or drove off cliffs. But to think that one of them is fat and ancient and rolling around the half-dead world in a palace ... that doesn't say much about this group's sense of sacrifice, or decency, or honor."

May considers what to say. Then as she opens her mouth, ready to challenge me, I interrupt.

"But the worst thing? In my mind, without doubt, their silence made these people possible." I swipe my hand at the town, at faces neither of us can see, at the years of embarrassment and hurt and being excluded by people who in better times I wouldn't need for a single minute. "The good citizens of Salvation think they're here because God is benevolent. God is decent. And God preferred them to the nameless bones in unmarked graves all around the world. Dumb-shit lucky bastards, yet they're free to think they're nothing but chosen."

Again, she considers.

And when her mouth opens, I start to interrupt.

But May throws up a hand. I fall silent. I don't remember what I was going to say. A step apart, she looks younger than ever but not as pretty, and she smiles with the bright intense expression that I have never seen from a real person, only on saints in old religious books – the consuming crazed gaze of an earthly soul bound to eventually sit on the lap of God.

In a whisper but with considerable intensity, she tells me, "You don't understand."

"Understand what?"

The hand covers my mouth.

"You think it's finished," she says. "You think once is enough to save the world. But what you call the 'noble' thing would have been foolish. My grandmother and the others … they had to survive and remain in touch with one another. That was the plan from the start." She pauses, investing in a couple deep breaths. "How many children are living in this one town, Noah? It's like that everywhere. A few old people, plenty of young parents, and too many children to count. And you heard how people are crossing the sea, spreading out to find new homes. Another crisis is coming. It won't happen in my life, and maybe not for several centuries. But eventually these same tricks will be necessary if we're going to … "

Her voice falters.

I taste salt and May as I pull back the hand. "If you're going to what?"

Almost too softly to be heard, she says, "Another weeding."

Then the saintly smile returns, self-assured and a million miles above the concerns of the ignorant and innocent.

* * *

Lola was right. Seeing my shrunken mother in the casket was important. Even essential. Now I was certain that she was dead, no doubts left, and helping carry her to the hole in the ground reminded me that she was never half as large as she seemed in my head. She was a shell already beginning to rot, and we nailed shut the lid and lowered the box and started to shovel gouts of dirt and chunks of rock on top of an object that was no more my mother than it was the sky overhead.

Yet I was crying by the end.

And those who still happened to like me, or at least loved my mother, put their own emotions on my tears. They came over and hugged me and prayed for my soul. Then I went down to the Quilt Shop and bought a very tall beer, drinking it too fast, my gait a little sloppy as I headed back up the hill.

"Going to see your mom again?" Ferris asked in passing.

"I need another minute with her," I admitted.

The old man pulled up, hearing that. Then he turned and looked at me until I returned the gaze. He was a small ageless sparkplug with a bright smile and charming manner. Others had told me that he had lost most of his family to the Shakes, but I could never remember him mentioning them, even in prayer.

"Son," he said to me, like old men often do when referring to any fellow younger than them.

I waited.

"A minute won't be long enough, son."

"Maybe not," I agreed.

"Don't go," he said.

But I'd already turned, pushing hard for that hill.

The guests won't stay the night in Salvation. I guess that much, watching May walking quickly toward the RV. She will speak to her brother, and he'll make a show of his important anger, and leaving him, she'll return to the Mayor's house to speak in private with her father. In the meantime, I might tell somebody what I guessed and everything I know. In the heat of the moment, May said too much. But that moment has passed and she probably can't believe that she could do something so careless, so plainly stupid. Right now she's telling herself that I'm not part of this community,

I'm just a crazy hermit, and nobody will listen to my nonsense. But it's going to gnaw at her, this idea that maybe I will spread the word, and maybe a few of these odd people will believe me, and May is certainly not enough of a fool to trust the good will of Christians living in the midst of this parched, unfamiliar wilderness.

The four of them will drive away, and it will happen sooner instead of later. The best road is the highway. They can either head back east or drive west to the next junction, then north to the old Interstate – a route that gives them a straight shot at the promised land of Canada.

What waits in Canada, and why should it matter?

Other people like grandma, and a secret community of like-minded zealots. At least that's what I imagine. But I know almost nothing about the world beyond my horizon. All I can deal with today is the people who are here, now.

In a rush, I unload the last of the bear and elk and fire up the truck and make the long turn around the block, driving back up the highway. I stop beside the half-built factory, considering its walls and windows before deciding to move farther. The bridge is as good as any place. I cross the bridge slowly and pull off into the ditch, parking in a spot low enough that nobody can see my rig from the opposite bank, but still leaving me with a good chance of driving out of there. Fast, if necessary.

This is hunting. My prey isn't people, I tell myself. What I'm hunting is a large lumbering machine cast off from another time, and I won't hurt anybody. That's how I convince myself to pull my rifle out of its hiding place, both pistols and enough ammunition to fight off a brigade. With binoculars around my neck, I move close to the north end of the bridge, and after hard thought and a few doubts, I decide where to make my blind and how to work this ambush.

But I *am* hunting people. Punching holes in those military-grade tires might be impossible, and I doubt that I could cripple any engine that's durable enough to drive halfway across the continent. But a bullet in the driver's head wouldn't be difficult, and I don't like Winston. I picture him at the wheel and grandma back on the bed, and once the RV rolls off the road, I can finish the old lady without ever seeing her. Her son is a bigger problem. And there's

May too. I don't know what I want to do, but when I think about them, my thoughts start to swerve. They won't be coming in this direction, I promise myself. I'm just sitting here to prove a point to myself, because they're right now heading back east again, taking a known route before heading north to that promised land.

My blind is a stand of tall dead grass and I do my best job of vanishing. The day is past its brightest, with the cold coming out of the ground and out of the dimming sky. It doesn't take long to feel chilled. But I curl up tight and adjust my stocking cap, standing every so often to stomp my feet, checking the surrounding ground for anything sneaking up on me. But nothing is. I might be the only animal in this landscape. I kneel down again, check my weapons again, feeling nervous and a little warmer because of it.

They won't come.

I say that aloud.

"They went the other way, and they're gone," I tell the evening breeze.

Maybe an hour of daylight remains. I stand again and stomp my stiff cold hurting feet, thinking hard about leaving. But when I glance downstream, I catch a sudden flash of sunlight reflected off moving glass, my heart kicks and for a moment I think of turning and running. But that isn't what I do. From somewhere comes the courage to put the binoculars against my eyes and just the sight of that aluminum house is enough to make the anger rise up all over again, as big as ever and refusing to back down.

I am going to shoot the driver and then work my way back. Any movement in a window will be a target. Any likely hiding place will be punctured. I'll tear apart the RV on my way back to grandma, and then I will stop. Maybe I won't waste precious ammunition on her. One cold night with nobody to care for her, and the end won't be long coming for her either.

The RV is still a long, long ways off.

I kneel. I check my guns again. I stand and stomp and use the gun sight, seeing nothing but the machine with its flat face and no hint of a soul.

I kneel.

A moment later, I'm shaking. Hard.

Then comes the rattling roar of an engine, and my first thought is that I know that sound and why is it so familiar? Somewhere behind me, the little engine cuts out. I keep hiding. A block of granite would show more motion that I do right now. I wait and listen, holding my breath for long spells, and then I hear the sound of boots on the road above and then the boots stop and a voice that I know better than my own asks, "What are you doing down there?"

I turn, looking up at Lola.

She smiles, and then decides not to smile. What replaces that first expression is scared and puzzled and then even more scared. In my face, she sees something she has never witnessed before, and when I rise to my feet, she looks at the various guns and my face again and then across the bridge, asking the cold dusk air, "What are you waiting for, Noah?"

"A tiger."

"What tiger?"

"I saw him when I came by before," I say. One weak step doesn't carry me far up the very brief slope. "He's a beauty. He's got a spectacular pelt." I manage another step, saying, "It's been a bad day, and I wanted to give you a gift. Something you wouldn't expect."

The RV is close now. Its driver doesn't seem to notice either person on the far side of the river, the vehicle neither speeding up nor slowing down, it and its loyal trailer rolling close to us and then past, the clatter of gravel on concrete lingering for several seconds. But the rest of the apparition has vanished behind a wall of oak and cottonwoods.

Lola watches me. She has probably never seen a machine like that, but I am the only object of any importance on this landscape. She stares and says nothing, watching me slowly climb up to the old roadbed, and then I start to talk again, to tell her something else that isn't true, and her gloved hand pushes at my face while her face cries, and she says, "I don't want a tiger."

She tells me, "Come home with me. Now."

AND THE DEEP BLUE SEA

Elizabeth Bear

The following story reminds me of both "Damnation Alley" by Roger Zelazny and "The Postman" by David Brin, so we're really getting three for the price of one.

Elizabeth Bear received the Campbell Award as Best New Writer in 2005 and has since won two Hugo Awards for her short fiction, a selection of which was published as The Chains That You Refuse *(2006). She has been immensely prolific since her debut. Her first novel,* Hammered *(2005), which began the Jenny Casey trilogy set in a post-catastrophe North America, won the Locus Award for Best First Novel.*

THE END OF THE world had come and gone. It turned out not to matter much in the long run.

The mail still had to get through.

Harrie signed yesterday's paperwork, checked the dates against the calendar, contemplated her signature for a moment, and capped her pen. She weighed the metal barrel in her hand and met Dispatch's faded eyes. "What's special about this trip?"

He shrugged and turned the clipboard around on the counter, checking each sheet to be certain she'd filled them out properly. She didn't bother watching. She never made mistakes. "Does there have to be something special?"

"You don't pay my fees unless it's special, Patch." She grinned as he lifted an insulated steel case onto the counter.

"This has to be in Sacramento in eight hours," he said.

"What is it?"

"Medical goods. Fetal stem-cell cultures. In a climate-controlled unit. They can't get too hot or too cold, there's some arcane formula about how long they can live in this given quantity of growth media, and the customer's paying very handsomely to see them in California by 1800 hours."

"It's almost 1000 now. What's too hot or too cold?" Harrie hefted the case. It was lighter than it looked; it would slide effortlessly into the saddlebags on her touring bike.

"Any hotter than it already is," Dispatch said, mopping his brow. "Can you do it?"

"Eight hours? Phoenix to Sacramento?" Harrie leaned back to check the sun. "It'll take me through Vegas. The California routes aren't any good at that speed since the Big One."

"I wouldn't send anybody else. Fastest way is through Reno."

"There's no gasoline from somewhere this side of the dam to Tonopah. Even my courier card won't help me there—"

"There's a checkpoint in Boulder City. They'll fuel you."

"Military?"

"I did say they were paying very well." He shrugged, shoulders already gleaming with sweat. It was going to be a hot one. Harrie guessed it would hit 120 in Phoenix.

At least she was headed north.

"I'll do it," she said, and held her hand out for the package receipt. "Any pickups in Reno?"

"You know what they say about Reno?"

"Yeah. It's so close to hell that you can see Sparks." Naming the city's largest suburb.

"Right. You don't want anything in Reno. Go straight through," Patch said. "Don't stop in Vegas, whatever you do. The overpass's come down, but that won't affect you unless there's debris. Stay on the 95 through to Fallon; it'll see you clear."

"Check." She slung the case over her shoulder, pretending she didn't see Patch wince. "I'll radio when I hit Sacramento—"

"Telegraph," he said. "The crackle between here and there would kill your signal otherwise."

"Check," again, turning to the propped-open door. Her prewar Kawasaki Concours crouched against the crumbling curb like an enormous, restless cat. Not the prettiest bike around, but it got you there. Assuming you didn't ditch the top-heavy son of a bitch in the parking lot.

"Harrie—"

"*What?*" She paused, but didn't turn.

"If you meet the Buddha on the road, kill him."

She glanced behind her, strands of hair catching on the strap of the insulated case and on the shoulder loops of her leathers. "What if I meet the Devil?"

She let the Concours glide through the curves of the long descent to Hoover Dam, a breather after the hard straight push from Phoenix, and considered her options. She'd have to average near enough 160 klicks an hour to make the run on time. It should be smooth sailing; she'd be surprised if she saw another vehicle between Boulder City and Tonopah.

She'd checked out a backup dosimeter before she left Phoenix, just in case. Both clicked softly as she crossed the dam and the poisoned river, reassuring her with alert, friendly chatter. She couldn't pause to enjoy the expanse of blue on her right side or the view down the escarpment on the left, but the dam was in pretty good shape, all things considered.

It was more than you could say for Vegas.

Once upon a time – she downshifted as she hit the steep grade up the north side of Black Canyon, sweat already soaking her hair – once upon a time a delivery like this would have been made by aircraft. There were places where it still would be. Places where there was money for fuel, money for airstrip repairs. Places where most of the aircraft weren't parked in tidy rows, poisoned birds lined up beside poisoned runways, hot enough that you could hear the dosimeters clicking as you drove past.

A runner's contract was a hell of a lot cheaper. Even when you charged the way Patch charged.

Sunlight glinted off the Colorado River so far below, flashing red and gold as mirrors. Crumbling casino on the right, now, and the canyon echoing the purr of the sleek black bike. The asphalt was spiderwebbed but still halfway smooth – smooth enough for a big bike, anyway. A big bike cruising at a steady ninety k/ph, much too fast if there was anything in the road. Something skittered aside as she thought it, a grey blur instantly lost among the red and black blurs of the receding rock walls on either side. Bighorn sheep. Nobody'd bothered to tell *them* to clear out before the wind could make them sick.

Funny thing was, they seemed to be thriving.

Harrie leaned into the last curve, braking in and accelerating out just to feel the tug of g-forces, and gunned it up the straightaway leading to the checkpoint at Boulder City. A red light flashed on a peeling steel pole beside the road. The Kawasaki whined and buzzed between her thighs, as if displeased to be restrained, then gentled as she eased the throttle, mindful of dust.

Houses had been knocked down across the top of the rise that served as host to the guard's shielded quarters, permitting an unimpeded view of Boulder City stretching out below. The bulldozer that had done the work slumped nearby, rusting under bubbled paint, too radioactive to be taken away, too radioactive even to be melted down for salvage.

Boulder City had been affluent once. Harrie could see the husks of trendy businesses on either side of Main Street: brick and stucco buildings in red and taupe, some whitewashed wood frames peeling in slow curls, submissive to the desert heat.

The gates beyond the checkpoint were closed and so were the lead shutters on the guard's shelter. A digital sign over the roof gave an ambient radiation reading in the mid double digits and a temperature reading in the low triple digits, Fahrenheit. It would get hotter – and "hotter" – as she descended into Vegas.

Harrie dropped the sidestand as the Kawasaki rolled to a halt, and thumbed her horn.

The young man who emerged from the shack was surprisingly tidy, given his remote duty station. Cap set regulation, boots shiny under the dust. He was still settling his breathing filter as he climbed down red metal steps and trotted over to Harrie's bike. Harrie wondered who he'd pissed off to draw this duty, or if he was a novelist who had volunteered.

"Runner," she said, her voice echoing through her helmet mike. She tapped the ID card visible inside the windowed pocket on the breast of her leathers, tugged her papers from the pouch on her tank with a clumsy gloved hand and unfolded them inside their transparent carrier. "You're supposed to gas me up for the run to Tonopah."

"You have an independent filter or just the one in your helmet?" All efficiency as he perused her papers.

"Independent."

"Visor up, please." He wouldn't ask her to take the helmet off. There was too much dust. She complied, and he checked her eyes and nose against the photo ID.

"Angharad Crowther. This looks in order. You're with UPS?"

"Independent contractor," Harrie said. "It's a medical run."

He turned away, gesturing her to follow, and led her to the pumps. They were shrouded in plastic, one diesel and one unleaded. "Is that a Connie?"

"A little modified so she doesn't buzz so much." Harrie petted the gas tank with a gloved hand. "Anything I should know about between here and Tonopah?"

He shrugged. "You know the rules, I hope."

"Stay on the road," she said, as he slipped the nozzle into the fill. "Don't go inside any buildings. Don't go near any vehicles. Don't stop, don't look back, and especially don't turn around; it's not wise to drive through your own dust. If it glows, don't pick it up, and nothing from the black zone leaves."

"I'll telegraph ahead and let Tonopah know you're coming," he said, as the gas pump clicked. "You ever crash that thing?"

"Not in going on ten years," she said, and didn't bother to cross her fingers. He handed her a receipt; she fumbled her lacquered stainless Cross pen out of her zippered pocket and signed her name like she meant it. The gloves made her signature into an incomprehensible scrawl, but the guard made a show of comparing it to her ID card and slapped her on the shoulder. "Be careful. If you crash out there, you're probably on your own. Godspeed."

"Thanks for the reassurance," she said, and grinned at him before she closed her visor and split.

Digitized music rang over her helmet headset as Harrie ducked her head behind the fairing, the hot wind tugging her sleeves, trickling between her gloves and her cuffs. The Kawasaki stretched out under her, ready for a good hard run, and Harrie itched to give it one. One thing you could say about the Vegas black zone: there wasn't much traffic. Houses – identical in red tile roofs and cream stucco walls – blurred past on either side, flanked by trees that the desert had killed once people weren't there to pump the water up to them. She cracked 160 k/ph in the wind shadow of the sound barriers, the tach winding up like a watch, just gliding along in sixth as the Kawasaki hit its stride. The big bike handled like a pig in the parking lot, but out on the highway she ran smooth as glass.

She had almost a hundred miles of range more than she'd need to get to Tonopah, God willing and the creek didn't rise, but she wasn't about to test that with any side trips through what was left of Las Vegas. Her dosimeters clicked with erratic cheer, nothing to worry about yet, and Harrie claimed the center lane and edged down to 140 as she hit the winding patch of highway near the old downtown. The shells of casinos on the left-hand side and godforsaken wasteland and ghetto on the right gave her back the Kawasaki's well-tuned shriek; she couldn't wind it any faster with the roads so choppy and the K-Rail canyons so tight.

The sky overhead was flat blue like cheap turquoise. A pall of dust showed burnt sienna, the inversion layer trapped inside the ring of mountains that made her horizon in four directions.

The freeway opened out once she cleared downtown, the overpass Patch had warned her about arching up and over, a tangle of banked curves, the crossroads at the heart of the silent city. She bid the ghosts of hotels good day as the sun hit zenith, heralding peak heat for another four hours or so. Harrie resisted the urge to reach back and pat her saddlebag to make sure the precious cargo was safe; she'd never know if the climate control failed on the trip, and moreover she couldn't risk the distraction as she wound the Kawasaki up to 170 and ducked her helmet into the slipstream off the fairing.

Straight shot to the dead town called Beatty from here, if you minded the cattle guards along the roads by the little forlorn towns. Straight shot, with the dosimeters clicking and vintage rock and roll jamming in the helmet speakers and the Kawasaki purring, thrusting, eager to spring and run.

There were worse days to be alive.

She dropped it to fourth and throttled back coming up on that overpass, the big one where the Phoenix to Reno highway crossed the one that used to run LA to Salt Lake, when there was an LA to speak of. Patch had said *overpass's down,* which could mean unsafe for transit and could mean littering the freeway underneath with blocks of concrete the size of a semi, and Harrie had no interest in finding out which it was with no room left to brake. She adjusted the volume on her music down as the rush of wind abated, and took the opportunity to sightsee a bit.

And swore softly into her air filter, slowing further before she realized she'd let the throttle slip.

Something – no, some*one* – leaned against a shotgunned, paint-peeled sign that might have given a speed limit once, when there was anyone to care about such things.

Her dosimeters clicked aggressively as she let the bike roll closer to the verge. She shouldn't stop. But it was a death sentence, being alone and on foot out here. Even if the sun weren't climbing the sky, sweat rolling from under Harrie's helmet, adhering her leathers to her skin.

She was almost stopped by the time she realized she knew him. Knew his ocher skin and his natty pinstriped double-breasted suit and his fedora, tilted just so, and the cordovan gleam of his loafers. For one mad moment, she wished she carried a gun.

Not that a gun would help her. Even if she decided to swallow a bullet herself.

"Nick." She put the bike in neutral, dropping her feet as it rolled to a stop. "Fancy meeting you in the middle of Hell."

"I got some papers for you to sign, Harrie." He pushed his fedora back over his hollow-cheeked face. "You got a pen?"

"You know I do." She unzipped her pocket and fished out the Cross. "I wouldn't lend a fountain pen to just anybody."

He nodded, leaning back against a K-Rail so he could kick a knee up and spread his papers out over it. He accepted the pen. "You know your note's about come due."

"Nick—"

"No whining now," he said. "Didn't I hold up my end of the bargain? Have you ditched your bike since last we talked?"

"No, Nick." Crestfallen.

"Had it stolen? Been stranded? Missed a timetable?"

"I'm about to miss one now if you don't hurry up with my pen."
She held her hand out imperiously; not terribly convincing, but the
best she could do under the circumstances.

"Mmm-hmmm." He was taking his own sweet time.

Perversely, the knowledge settled her. "If the debt's due, have you
come to collect?"

"I've come to offer you a chance to renegotiate," he said, and
capped the pen and handed it back. "I've got a job for you; could
buy you a few more years if you play your cards right."

She laughed in his face and zipped the pen away. "A few more
years?" But he nodded, lips pressed thin and serious, and she blinked
and went serious too. "You mean it."

"I never offer what I'm not prepared to give," he said, and
scratched the tip of his nose with his thumbnail. "What say, oh –
three more years?"

"Three's not very much." The breeze shifted. Her dosimeters
crackled. "Ten's not very much, now that I'm looking back on it."

"Goes by quick, don't it?" He shrugged. "All right. Seven—"

"For what?"

"What do you mean?" She could have laughed again, at the
transparent and oh-so-calculated guilelessness in his eyes.

"I mean, what is it you want me to do for seven more years of
protection." The bike was heavy, but she wasn't about to kick the
sidestand down. "I'm sure it's bad news for somebody."

"It always is." But he tipped the brim of his hat down a centimeter
and gestured to her saddlebag, negligently. "I just want a moment
with what you've got there in that bag."

"Huh." She glanced at her cargo, pursing her lips. "That's a
strange thing to ask. What would you want with a box full of
research cells?"

He straightened away from the sign he was holding up and came
a step closer. "That's not so much yours to worry about, young
lady. Give it to me, and you get seven years. If you don't – the note's
up next week, isn't it?"

"Tuesday." She would have spat, but she wasn't about to lift her
helmet aside. "I'm not scared of you, Nick."

"You're not scared of much." He smiled, all smooth. "It's part of
your charm."

She turned her head, staring away west across the sun-soaked desert and the roofs of abandoned houses, abandoned lives. Nevada had always had a way of making ghost towns out of metropolises. "What happens if I say no?"

"I was hoping you weren't going to ask that, sweetheart," he said. He reached to lay a hand on her right hand where it rested on the throttle. The bike growled, a high, hysterical sound, and Nick yanked his hand back. "I see you two made friends."

"We get along all right," Harrie said, patting the Kawasaki's gas tank. "What happens if I say no?"

He shrugged and folded his arms. "You won't finish your run." No threat in it, no extra darkness in the way the shadow of his hat brim fell across his face. No menace in his smile. Cold fact, and she could take it how she took it.

She wished she had a piece of gum to crack between her teeth. It would fit her mood. She crossed her arms, balancing the Kawasaki between her thighs. Harrie *liked* bargaining. "That's not the deal. The deal's no spills, no crashes, no breakdowns, and every run complete on time. I said I'd get these cells to Sacramento in eight hours. You're wasting my daylight; somebody's life could depend on them."

"Somebody's life does," Nick answered, letting his lips twist aside. "A lot of somebodies, when it comes down to it."

"Break the deal, Nick – fuck with my ride – and you're in breach of contract."

"You've got nothing to bargain with."

She laughed, then, outright. The Kawasaki purred between her legs, encouraging. "There's always time to mend my ways—"

"Not if you die before you make it to Sacramento," he said. "Last chance to reconsider, Angharad, my princess. We can still shake hands and part friends. Or you can finish your last ride on my terms, and it won't be pretty for you" – the Kawasaki snarled softly, the tang of burning oil underneath it – "or your bike."

"Fuck off," Harrie said, and kicked her feet up as she twisted the throttle and drove straight at him, just for the sheer stupid pleasure of watching him dance out of her way.

Nevada had been dying slowly for a long time: perchlorate-poisoned groundwater, a legacy of World War Two titanium plants; cancer rates spiked by exposure to fallout from above ground nuclear testing; crushing drought and climactic change; childhood leukemia clusters in rural towns. The explosion of the PEPCON plant in 1988 might have been perceived by a sufficiently imaginative mind as God's shot across the bow, but the real damage didn't occur until decades later, when a train carrying high-level nuclear waste to the Yucca Mountain storage facility collided with a fuel tanker stalled across the rails.

The resulting fire and radioactive contamination of the Las Vegas Valley proved to be a godsend in disguise. When the War came to Nellis Air Force Base and the nuclear mountain, Las Vegas was already as much a ghost town as Rhyolite or Goldfield – except deserted not because the banks collapsed or the gold ran out, but because the dust that blew through the streets was hot enough to drop a sparrow in midflight, or so people said.

Harrie didn't know if the sparrow story was true.

"So," she muttered into her helmet, crouched over the Kawasaki's tank as the bike screamed north by northwest, leaving eerie Las Vegas behind. "What do you think he's going to throw at us, girl?"

The bike whined, digging in. Central city gave way to desolate suburbia, and the highway dropped to ground level and straightened out, a narrow strip of black reflecting the summer heat in mirage silver.

The desert sprawled on either side, a dun expanse of scrub and hardpan narrowing as the Kawasaki climbed into the broad pass between two dusty ranges of mountains. Harrie's dosimeters clicked steadily, counting marginally more rads as she roared by the former nuclear testing site at Mercury at close to 200 k/ph. She throttled back as a sad little township – a few discarded trailers, another military base and a disregarded prison – came up. There were no pedestrians to worry about, but the grated metal cattle guard was not something to hit at speed.

On the far side, there was nothing to slow her for fifty miles. She cranked her music up, dropped her head behind the fairing and redlined her tach for Beatty and the far horizon.

It got rocky again coming up on Beatty. Civilization in Nevada huddled up to the oases and springs that lurked at the foot of mountains and in the low parts in valleys. This had been mining country, mountains gnawed away by dynamite and sharp-toothed payloaders. A long gorge on the right side of the highway showed green clots of trees; water ran there, tainted by the broken dump, and her dosimeters clicked as the road curved near it. If she walked down the bank and splashed into the stream between the roots of the willows and cottonwoods, she'd walk out glowing and be dead by nightfall.

She rounded the corner and entered the ghost of Beatty.

The problem, she thought, arose because every little town in Nevada grew up at the same place: a crossroads, and she half-expected Nick to be waiting for her at this one too. The Kawasaki whined as they rolled through tumbleweed-clogged streets but they passed under the town's sole, blindly staring stoplight without seeing another creature. Despite the sun like a physical pressure on her leathers, a chill ran spidery fingers up her spine. She'd rather know where the hell he was, thank you very much. "Maybe he took a wrong turn at Rhyolite."

The Kawasaki snarled, impatient to be turned loose on the open road again but Harrie threaded it through slumping cars and around windblown debris with finicky care. "Nobody's looking out for us any more, Connie," Harrie murmured, and stroked the sun-scorched fuel tank with her gloved left hand. They passed a deserted gas station, the pumps crouched useless without power; the dosimeters chirped and warbled. "I don't want to kick up that dust if I can help it."

The ramshackle one- and two-story buildings gave way to desert and highway. Harrie paused, feet down on tarmac melted sticky-soft by the sun, and made sure the straw of her camel pack was fixed in the holder. The horizon shimmered with heat, ridges of mountains on either side and dun hardpan stretching to infinity. She sighed and took a long drink of stale water.

"Here we go," she said, hands nimble on the clutch and the throttle as she lifted her feet to the peg. The Kawasaki rolled forward, gathering speed. "Not too much further to Tonopah, and then we can both get fed."

Nick was giving her time to think about it, and she drowned the worries with the Dead Kennedys, Boiled in Lead, and the Acid Trip.

The ride from Beatty to Tonopah was swift and uneventful, the flat road unwinding beneath her wheels like a spun-out tape measure, the banded mountains crawling past on either side. The only variation along the way was forlorn Goldfield, its wind-touched streets empty and sere. It had been a town of 20,000, abandoned before Vegas fell to radiation sickness, even longer before the nuke dump broke open. She pushed 200 k/ph most of the way, the road all hers, not so much as the glimmer of sunlight off a distant windshield to contest her ownership. The silence and the empty road just gave her more to worry at, and she did, picking at her problem like a vulture picking at a corpse.

The fountain pen was heavy in her breast pocket as Tonopah shimmered into distant visibility. Her head swam with the heat, the helmet squelching over saturated hair. She sucked more water, trying to ration; the temperature was climbing toward 120, and she wouldn't last long without hydration. The Kawasaki coughed a little, rolling down a slow, extended incline, but the gas gauge gave her nearly a quarter of a tank – and there was the reserve if she exhausted the main. Still, instruments weren't always right, and luck wasn't exactly on her side.

Harrie killed her music with a jab of her tongue against the control pad inside her helmet. She dropped her left hand from the handlebar and thumped the tank. The sound she got back was hollow, but there was enough fluid inside to hear it refract off a moving surface. The small city ahead was a welcome sight: there'd be fresh water and gasoline, and she could hose the worst of the dust off and take a piss. God damn, you'd think with the sweat soaking her leathers to her body, there'd be no need for that last, but the devil *was* in the details, it turned out.

Harrie'd never wanted to be a boy but some days she really wished she had the knack of peeing standing up.

She was only about half a klick away when she realized that there was something wrong about Tonopah. Other than the usual; her dosimeters registered only background noise as she came up on it, but a harsh reek like burning coal rasped the back of her throat even through the dust filters, and the weird little town wasn't the weird little town she remembered. Rolling green hills rose around it on all sides, thick with shadowy, leafless trees, and it was smoke haze that drifted on the still air, not dust. A heat shimmer floated over the cracked road, and the buildings that crowded alongside it weren't Tonopah's desert-weathered construction but peeling white shingle-sided houses, a storefront post office, a white church with the steeple caved in and half the facade dropped into a smoking sinkhole in the ground.

The Kawasaki whined, shivering as Harrie throttled back. She sat upright in the saddle, letting the big bike roll. "Where the hell are we?" Her voice reverberated. She startled; she'd forgotten she'd left her microphone on.

"Exactly," a familiar voice said at her left. "Welcome to Centralia." Nick wore an open-faced helmet and straddled the back of a Honda Goldwing the color of dried blood, if blood had gold dust flecked through it. The Honda hissed at the Kawasaki, and the Connie growled back, wobbling in eager challenge. Harrie restrained her bike with gentling hands, giving it a little more gas to straighten it out.

"Centralia?" Harrie had never heard of it, and she flattered herself that she'd heard of most places.

"Pennsylvania." Nick lifted his black-gloved hand off the clutch and gestured vaguely around himself. "Or Jharia, in India. Or maybe the Chinese province of Xinjiang. Subterranean coal fires, you know, anthracite burning in evacuated mines. Whole towns abandoned, sulfur and brimstone seeping up through vents, the ground hot enough to flash rain to steam. Your tires will melt. You'll put that bike into a crevasse. Not to mention the greenhouse gases. Lovely things." He grinned, showing shark's teeth, four rows. "Second time asking, Angharad, my princess."

"Second time saying no." She fixed her eyes on the road. She could see the way the asphalt buckled, now, and the dim glow from the bottom of the sinkhole underneath the church. "You really are used to people doing your bidding, aren't you, Nick?"

"They don't usually put up much of a fight." He twisted the throttle while the clutch was engaged, coaxing a whining, competitive cough from his Honda.

Harrie caught his shrug sideways but kept her gaze trained grimly forward. Was that the earth shivering, or was it just the shimmer of heat-haze over the road? The Kawasaki whined. She petted the clutch to reassure herself.

The groaning rumble that answered her wasn't the Kawasaki. She tightened her knees on the seat as the ground pitched and bucked under her tires, hand clutching the throttle to goose the Connie forward. Broken asphalt sprayed from her rear tire. The road split and shattered, vanishing behind her. She hauled the bike upright by raw strength and nerved herself to check her mirrors; lazy steam rose from a gaping hole in the road.

Nick cruised along, unperturbed. "You sure, Princess?"

"What was that you said about Hell, Nick?" She hunkered down and grinned at him over her shoulder, knowing he couldn't see more than her eyes crinkle through the helmet. It was enough to draw an irritated glare.

He sat back on his haunches and tipped his toes up on the footpegs, throwing both hands up, releasing throttle and clutch, letting the Honda coast away behind her. "I said, welcome to it."

The Kawasaki snarled and whimpered by turns, heavy and agile between her legs as she gave it all the gas she dared. She'd been counting on the refuel stop here, but compact southwestern Tonopah had been replaced by a shattered sprawl of buildings, most of them obviously either bulldozed or vanished into pits that glared like a wolf's eye reflecting a flash, and a gas station wasn't one of the remaining options. The streets were broad, at least, and deserted, not so much winding as curving gently through shallow swales and over hillocks. Broad, but not intact; the asphalt rippled as if heaved by moles and some of the rises and dips hid fissures and sinkholes. Her tires scorched; she coughed into her filter, her mike amplifying it to a hyena's bark. The Cross pen in her pocket pressed her breast over her heart. She took comfort in it, ducking behind the fairing to dodge the stinking wind and the clawing skeletons of ungroomed trees. She'd signed on the line, after all. And either Nick had to see her and the Kawasaki safe or she got back what she'd paid.

As if Nick abided by contracts.

As if he couldn't just kill her and get what he wanted that way. Except he couldn't keep her if he did.

"Damn," she murmured, to hear the echoes, and hunched over the Kawasaki's tank. The wind tore at her leathers. The heavy bike caught air coming over the last rise. She had to pee like she couldn't believe, and the vibration of the engine wasn't helping, but she laughed out loud to set the city behind.

She got out easier than she thought she would, although her gauge read empty at the bottom of the hill. She switched to reserve and swore. Dead trees and smoking stumps rippled into nonexistence around her, and the lone and level sands stretched to ragged mountains east and west. She was back in Nevada, if she'd ever left it, hard westbound now, straight into the glare of the afternoon sun. Her polarized faceplate helped somewhat, maybe not enough, but the road was smooth again before and behind and she could see Tonopah sitting dusty and forsaken in her rearview mirror, inaccessible as a mirage, a city at the bottom of a well.

Maybe Nick could only touch her in the towns. Maybe he needed a little of man's hand on the wilderness to twist to his own ends, or maybe it amused him. Maybe it was where the roads crossed, after all. She didn't think she could make it back to Tonopah if she tried, however, so she pretended she didn't see the city behind her and cruised west, toward Hawthorne, praying she had enough gas to make it but not expecting her prayers to be answered by anybody she particularly wanted to talk to.

The 95 turned northwest again at the deserted Coaldale junction; there hadn't been a town there since long before the War, or even the disaster at Vegas. Mina was gone too, its outskirts marked by a peeling sign advertising an abandoned crawfish farm, the Desert Lobster Facility.

Harrie's camel bag went dry. She sucked at the straw forlornly one last time and spat it out, letting it sag against her jaw, damp and tacky. She hunkered down and laid a long line of smoking road behind, cornering gently when she had to corner, worried about her scorched and bruised tires. At least the day was cooling as evening encroached, as she progressed north and gained elevation. It might be down into the double digits, even, although it was hard to tell through the leather. On her left, the Sarcophagus Mountains rose between her and California.

The name didn't amuse her as much as it usually did.

And then they were climbing. She breathed a low sigh of relief and patted the hungry, grumbling Kawasaki on the fuel tank as the blistering blue of Walker Lake came into view, the dusty little town of Hawthorne huddled like a crab on the near shore. There was nothing moving there either, and Harrie chewed her lip behind the filter. Dust had gotten into her helmet somehow, gritting every time she blinked; weeping streaks marked her cheeks behind the visor. She hoped the dust wasn't the kind that was likely to make her glow, but her dosimeters had settled down to chickenlike clucking, so she might be okay.

The Kawasaki whimpered apologetically and died as she coasted into town.

"Christ," she said, and flinched at the echo of her own amplified voice. She reached to thumb the mike off, and, on second thought, left it alone. It was too damned quiet out here without the Kawasaki's commentary. She tongued her music back on, flipping selections until she settled on a tune by Grey Line Out.

She dropped her right foot and kicked the stand down on the left, then stood on the peg and slung her leg over the saddle. She ached with vibration, her hands stiff claws from clutching the handlebars. The stretch of muscle across her ass and thighs was like the reminder of a two-day-old beating but she leaned into the bike, boot sole slipping on grit as she heaved it into motion. She hopped on one foot to kick the stand up, wincing.

It wasn't the riding. It was the standing up, afterward.

She walked the Kawasaki up the deserted highway, between the deserted buildings, the pavement hot enough to sear her feet through the boot leather if she stood still for too long. "Good girl," she told the Kawasaki, stroking the forward brake handle. It leaned against her heavily, cumbersome at a walking pace, like walking a drunk friend home. "Gotta be a gas station somewhere."

Of course, there wouldn't be any power to run the pumps, and probably no safe water, but she'd figure that out when she got there. Sunlight glimmered off the lake; she was fine, she told herself, because she wasn't too dehydrated for her mouth to wet at the thought of all that cool, fresh water.

Except there was no telling what kind of poison was in that lake. There was an old naval base on its shore, and the lake itself had been used as a kind of kiddie pool for submarines. Anything at all could be floating around in its waters. Not, she admitted, that there wasn't a certain irony to taking the long view at a time like this.

She spotted a Texaco station, the red and white sign bleached pink and ivory, crazed by the relentless desert sun. Harrie couldn't remember if she was in the Mojave or the Black Rock desert now, or some other desert entirely. They all ran together. She jumped at her own slightly hysterical giggle. The pumps *were* off, as she'd antici-pated, but she leaned the Kawasaki up on its sidestand anyway, grabbed the climate-controlled case out of her saddlebag, and went to find a place to take a leak.

The leather was hot on her fingers when she pulled her gloves off and dropped her pants. "Damned, stupid … First thing I do when I get back to civilization is buy a set of leathers and a helmet in white, dammit." She glanced at the Kawasaki as she fixed herself, expecting a hiss of agreement, but the black bike was silent. She blinked stinging eyes and turned away.

There was a garden hose curled on its peg behind one of the tan-faced houses huddled by the Texaco station, the upper side bleached yellow on green like the belly of a dead snake. Harrie wrenched it off the peg one-handed. The rubber was brittle from dry rot; she broke it twice trying to uncoil a section, but managed to get about seven feet clean. She pried the fill cap off the underground tank with a tire iron and yanked off her helmet and air filter to sniff, checking both dosimeters first.

It had, after all, been one of those days.

The gas smelled more or less like gasoline though, and it tasted like fucking gasoline too, when she got a good mouthful of it from sucking it up her impromptu siphon. Not very good gasoline, maybe, but beggars and choosers. The siphon wouldn't work as a siphon because she couldn't get the top end lower than the bottom end, but she could suck fuel up into it and transfer it, hoseful by hoseful, into the Kawasaki's empty tank, the precious case leaning against her boot while she did.

Finally, she saw the dark gleam of fluid shimmer through the fill hole when she peered inside and tapped the side of the tank.

She closed the tank and spat and spat, wishing she had water to wash the gasoline away. The lake glinted, mocking her, and she resolutely turned her back on it and picked up the case.

It was light in her hand. She paused with one hand on the flap of the saddlebag, weighing that gleaming silver object, staring past it at her boots. She sucked on her lower lip, tasted gas, and turned her head and spat again. "A few more years of freedom, Connie," she said, and stroked the metal with a black-gloved hand. "You and me. I could drink the water. It wouldn't matter if that was bad gas I fed you. Nothing could go wrong ..."

The Kawasaki was silent. Its keys jangled in Harrie's hip pocket. She touched the throttle lightly, drew her hand back, laid the unopened case on the seat. "What do you say, girl?"

Nothing, of course. It was quiescent, slumbering, a dreaming demon. She hadn't turned it on.

With both thumbs at once, Harrie flicked up the latches and opened the case.

It was cool inside, cool enough that she could feel the difference on her face when she bent over it. She kept the lid at half-mast, trying to block that cool air with her body so it wouldn't drift away. She tipped her head to see inside: blue foam threaded through with cooling elements, shaped to hold the contents without rattling. Papers in a plastic folder, and something in sealed culture plates, clear jelly daubed with ragged polka dots.

There was a sticky note tacked on the plastic folder. She reached into the cool case and flicked the sticky note out, bringing it into the light. Patch's handwriting. She blinked.

"Sacramento next, if these don't get there," it said, in thick black definite lines. "Like Faustus, we all get one good chance to change our minds."

If you meet the Buddha on the road—

"I always thought there was more to that son of a bitch than met the eye," she said, and closed the case, and stuffed the note into her pocket beside the pen. She jammed her helmet back on, double-checking the filter that had maybe started leaking a little around the edges in Tonopah, slung her leg over the Kawasaki's saddle, and closed the choke.

It gasped dry when she clutched and thumbed the start button, shaking between her legs like an asthmatic pony. She gave it a little throttle, then eased up on it like easing up on a virgin lover. Coaxing, pleading under her breath. Gasoline fumes from her mouth made her eyes tear inside the helmet; the tears or something else washed the grit away. One cylinder hiccuped. A second one caught.

She eased the choke as the Kawasaki coughed and purred, shivering, ready to run.

Both dosimeters kicked hard as she rolled across the flat, open plain towards Fallon, a deadly oasis in its own right. Apparently Nick hadn't been satisfied with a leukemia cluster and perchlorate and arsenic tainting the ground water; the trees Harrie saw as she rolled up on the startling green of the farming town weren't desert cottonwoods but towering giants of the European forest, and something grey and massive, shimmering with lovely crawling blue Cherenkov radiation, gleamed behind them. The signs she passed were in an alphabet she didn't understand, but she knew the name of this place.

A light rain was falling as she passed through Chernobyl.

It drove down harder as she turned west on the 50, toward Reno and Sparks and a crack under the edge of the clouds that glowed a toxic, sallow color with evening coming on. Her tires skittered on slick, greasy asphalt.

Where the cities should have been, stinking piles of garbage crouched against the yellowing evening sky, and nearly naked, starvation-slender people picked their way over slumped rubbish, calling the names of loved ones buried under the avalanche. Water sluiced down her helmet, soaked her saddle, plastered her leathers to her body. She wished she dared drink the rain. It didn't make her cool. It only made her wet.

She didn't turn her head to watch the wretched victims of the garbage slide. She was one hour out of Sacramento, and in Manila of fifty years ago.

Donner Pass was green and pleasant, sunset staining the sky ahead as red as meat. She was in plenty of time. It was all downhill from here.

Nick wasn't about to let her get away without a fight.

The Big one had rerouted the Sacramento River too, and Harrie turned back at the edge because the bridge was down and the water was on fire. She motored away, 100 meters, 200, until the heat of the burning river faded against her back. "What's that?" she asked the slim man in the pinstriped suit who waited for her by the roadside.

"Cuyahoga river fire," he said. "1969. Count your blessings. It could have been Bhopal."

"Blessings?" She spared him a sardonic smile, invisible behind her helmet. He tilted the brim of his hat with a grey-gloved finger. "I suppose you could say that. What is it really?"

"Phlegethon."

She raised her visor and peeked over her shoulder, watching the river burn. Even here, it was hot enough that her sodden leathers steamed against her back. The back of her hand pressed her breast pocket. The paper from Patch's note crinkled; her Cross poked her in the tit.

She looked at Nick, and Nick looked at her. "So that's it."

"That's all she wrote. It's too far to jump."

"I can see that."

"Give me the case and I'll let you go home. I'll give you the Kawasaki and I'll give you your freedom. We'll call it even."

She eyed him, tension up her right leg, toe resting on the ground. The great purring bike shifted heavily between her legs, lithe as a cat, ready to turn and spit gravel from whirring tires. "Too far to jump."

"That's what I said."

Too far to jump. Maybe. And maybe if she gave him what was in the case, and doomed Sacramento like Bhopal, like Chernobyl, like Las Vegas ... Maybe she'd be damning herself even if he gave it back to her. And even if she wasn't, she wasn't sure she and the Kawasaki could live with that answer.

If he wanted to keep her, he had to let her make the jump, and she could save Sacramento. If he was willing to lose her, she might die on the way over, and Sacramento might die with her, but they would die free.

Either way, Nick lost. And that was good enough for her.

"Devil take the hindmost," she said under her breath, and touched the throttle one more time.

THE MEEK

Damien Broderick

Broderick is a highly respected science-fiction writer, futurist and currently the SF editor of the popular science magazine Cosmos. *He has been writing science fiction since 1964, and is probably best known for* The Judas Mandala, *published in 1982 but written in 1975, in which he termed the phrase "virtual reality". His thoughts about the future and the relationship between humans and technology are explored in* The Spike *(1997) and* The Last Mortal Generation *(1999).*

In the following story we are still amongst the remnants of a humanity struggling to survive that might grasp at any opportunity for recovery – but at what price?

And seeing the multitudes, Jesus went up into a mountain: and when he was set, his disciples came unto him:
And he opened his mouth, and taught them, saying,
Blessed are the poor in spirit: for theirs is the kingdom of heaven.
Blessed are they that mourn: for they shall be comforted.
Blessed are the meek: for they shall inherit the earth.

The Gospel of St. Matthew, 5: 1–5

IN THE CHILDHOOD of the garden there is much I remember, much I regret. And much has brought me pleasure. I see in memory the great spindles floating effortless as snowflakes, bright against the sky's iron. The rust of time obscures these memories but when I see the cold clear moon I see also the ships of light.

They came once, in an angel's song, in silver fire, and they come again in the garden, the garden of my dreams.

Now bright birds swoop in a spray of tropical hues and the river whispers secrets to the lake. You could say I am happy, though the future is gone and the earth rolls lonely as a child's lost balloon. They are gone and I am glad and I am sad. The garden is a place of peace, but the flame has guttered out.

Once I was a man in my middle years and the world was a bowl of molten, reworked slag, a lethal place where the stuff of the soil humped up into delirious fractal corals that glowed blue and crimson in the night. Now fireflies flicker, and warmth rises where it is needed. But there is no warmth in the soul, no fire, just the moonglow of age and a forsaken dream.

I was young and the earth was a sphere of maddened terror, for we had unleashed a beast so small we could not see it, only its accumulating handiwork, so hungry that it ate up everything except flesh, some privileged flesh. And I was mortally afraid, for I saw my death, and my wife's death. There would be no children to grieve us, no mourning after.

All the earth was blind to the stars, the sky a cloud of dull steel, the nano dust of death in the air. Then we knew fear and remorse, for in the murder of our world we had killed ourselves.

Our choice had been blind and at second-hand. But death accepts no excuses.

The day the world ended was Wish Jerome's birthday, and at forty-one he was guileless as a child. He possessed that blithe detachment from any sense of danger, which is the menace and the joy of innocence. Professor Aloysius Jerome – "Wish" to his wife – was a man of philosophy, a creature of gentle habits and soft words, the wonder of the Faculty. He ate toast for breakfast, dunking it in black coffee.

One eye closed, the other surveying the crumbs on her plate, his wife said: "It certainly seems there'll be a war. They'll kill us all with their damned nano toys."

Wish looked sadly out the window, past the ruffled curtains. The morning was bright with the promise of spring.

" 'To Carthage I came,' " he said, dunking toast, " 'where there sang all around my ears a cauldron of unholy hates.' "

"St Augustine of Hippo, slightly trampled," he told his wife's eyebrows a moment later. "I prefer Pelagius. Perhaps a twenty-one gun salute, but hardly an ecophagic war for my birthday, Beth."

Domesticity and Wish's peculiarly unassuming goodness had made them a happy marriage. Beth Jerome, fair, fey, fertile of spirit and barren of womb, had founded an empathy between them twenty years before, from the first day they met. Empathy had grown into love, if not passion. The warm sun brought her little of the wash of peace that swept around her husband. On the table at her elbow a conservative daily screamed headlines about military grade nanotechnology.

"I refuse to educate the minds of the young on such a glorious day." Wish finished his toast and stretched luxuriously. "We shall take the car and drive as far from this warren as we can, and we shall eat our food beside an honest-to-goodness fire, and we shall forget the madmen and their war posturing."

Beth rose and put their dishes in the washer. "It is absurd," she said, peeved. "Still they insist on adding foaming agents to these detergents. What fools they must take us for." She shut the door and set the dial. "An excellent suggestion, darling. Better call first and see if Tod or Muriel can take your classes."

She wet a dish-cloth and wiped the crumbs off the table, and Wish leaned back on two legs of his chair and fired up a joint. The sun was a pool of warmth, and he soaked in the contentment of the joy of life.

For a million years and more *Homo sapiens* fought on equal terms with the world, fought the worst the world could throw at the species. Today I lie in the balm of an eternal afternoon, half asleep, and the world sleeps with me. The flowers bloom and the leaves fall and bud anew, but humanity lies in the calm of Indian summer, and there is no blast of wind. I recall the days when men were violent and men were cruel, yes, and women, too; dimly, but there it is, taunting me. And the ships from the stars, falling from the skies like manna, call to me from the depths of time and their call is lost in the breeze. Too late, too late.

* * *

The sky was eggshell blue, fragile, edged with cottonwool clouds. The little valley was a green bowl sweeping up to meet the luminous blue dome halfway between heaven and earth. Why should it be a sartorial disaster to wear blue and green together, Wish Jerome asked himself dreamily, when nature gets away with it to such good effect? He finished chewing a greasy chop, licked his fingers, settled back happily into the grass. Something with many legs examined his bare arm, and sleepily he flicked it off. Beth put the tops back on the jars, folded the picnic cloth and placed it in the basket. She yawned; the day was warm without being hot, weather for wandering hand in hand beside a creek, or whispering, or snoozing. She shook her blond hair in the sun and sat down beside her husband.

Wish put his arm around her. A screen came across the sky, like a filigree of diamonds and sapphires, fell everywhere, drifting on the wind, like glittery snow. A tall old tree on the hill turned brown and sagged, and burst explosively into leaping yellow ribbons of structure. Heat rose from the valley as a trillion small machines opened up molecules, releasing energy, twisting it to their mad purpose. Wish and Beth alike screamed. There was no sound beyond the crackle of crystalline growth. Sixty kilometers away a city melted into shapes from migraine: battlements, turrets, fortifications, the primordial geometries of the unconscious.

They did not see the mushroom of hot white light that tried to burn away the enemy infestation. They were the lucky ones, Beth and Wish, two of the thousand or so who escaped the holocaust of the bomb that wiped away three million human lives. In other cities, other bombs charred flesh, and steel girders twisted into melted toffee; there were the few others who got clear.

The man and the woman lay in each another's arms while the heat flared and went away, and then they ran for the cave in the hill and huddled in it, and Beth cried and cried and cried like a child, and they lived.

They found each other, the survivors, gradually, but they had no comfort to share, no hope. The brave fought, the cowards acquiesced in the diamond and iron cloud; death seeped down on the brave and the cowards through the porous fog. They suffered appallingly, the last straggling men and women, the few bleak children;

they grew gaunt and ill, and sores festered in their bodies. And even those who fought knew it was bitter, meaningless, for though they should live a few months more there was no future.

Dispossessed like the rest, Wish and Beth wandered the desolate, remade landscape in the horror humans had unleashed. They ate rubbish and what they could find unmolested in cans, and drank bottled water that the nano weapons whimsically left untouched, and slept when they could between their nightmares, and prayed, and when the day came at last that the fog opened in a drift of silver light and the ships brought their salvation, there was no rejoicing.

Suffering had drained them utterly. The survivors, the quick and the vulgar and the brave, all of them together went to the ships. On the wrecked plain, amid the glassy crevices and turrets that once had been green with living things and busy with people, the spindles stood like awesome mirrors. Their polished hulls gleamed back the diamond speckled sky, and the survivors saw themselves reflected in a leap of light that hid no item of their degradation.

Wish Jerome was the first to laugh.

He stood in front of the sweeping edge of a star spindle and saw himself in the burnished gloss. He looked at the burned eyebrows, the singed patchy hair, the emaciated scarecrow frame under the scraps of clothing.

"The wisdom of the ages," he said, without animosity. "What a piece of work!" Bitterness was alien to Wish. He viewed the ravaged spectacle of philosophical man with amusement.

Beth crept up beside him, from the crowd of skeletons, like a child to a protecting arm. Their roles were reversed; this was a strangeness only innocence might face with equanimity.

Wish laughed again, and the small crowd shuffled noisily, somehow relieved, and through their muttering a voice spoke to them. Meaning echoed without words in their minds. The people of the ships spoke.

"We heard the cry of death from your world," the voice told them. "It was a shout of lamentation and grief that crossed the void in the moment your world died. We took it for the cry of one murdered, and find instead that you brought this blight upon yourselves."

In the silence, in the awful reproach, Wish looked across the land where life had come with expectation four billion years before and had perished in suicide. The fog arched overhead, an iron-grey pall glistening with points of light, a looming covenant of death. The voice spoke only the truth, and it was beyond human power to redeem their crime. He clenched his hands. Beyond the ships, the ground curled and shifted in harsh, sluggish peristalses.

"It is not within our power to remake your Earth. The biosphere is slain by your small stupid machines. We can resurrect only a small part of it. We will exact a payment, but some of your world at least will be now, again, green and fresh."

The last humans stirred then, mindless life crying for a chance to live again.

"Yes!" cried humanity, cried life. The tattered group passed instantly beyond identity in its paroxysm.

"Yes!"

"We will meet your fee, whatever it is."

"Only let us live again!"

Silence returned to the plain, save for a whining wind that carried insanely creative dust across the wasteland. A vision came into the minds of the survivors: the sea of darkness, an ocean of blackness blazing with the light of stars. The spindles hung there, another kind of shining dust, life and consciousness, consumed in a battle with those from the shores of the galaxy, or some folded, deeper place.

"They are murderous and beyond our comprehension," said the voice. "They have come from the places between the islands of stars, come with a blind, unreasoning hatred which cannot be turned aside except by lethal force. We had thought your world a victim of their murder. Instead, we find something worse, a world that has taken its own life. It is too late to offer our aid, but at least we can build you sanctuary, if, in return, some of your number will come with us, to fight."

"To fight?" A woman screamed in rage; her face ran with weeping wounds. "Is all life so stupid? Do you condemn us as murderers of our planet and then ask us to repeat the madness? No, we will not fight. Go away and let us die in our shame and folly."

"It is for each of you separately to make this choice," the voice said. "Understand this: they attack without quarter. And they are winning."

The price of life is death, Beth told herself, pressed against her husband's arm. Those who went from among this pitiful number surely would not return.

"Only some among you will suit our purpose," the voice explained. "The predators, the fighters. They must come with us. The others will remain, and we will restore to them a corner of their world. Come, you must decide. The stars are dying in our galaxy."

It was beyond most of them, this vision of a war between gods. Not gods, though, Wish Jerome told himself, merely life, exerted in an unconscionable violence to safeguard its own seed.

Fear blew across the group, chilling as the wind, but their decision, too, rose like a wind, beyond fear.

High above them, an opening dilated in the silver hull. The last of humanity went forward for their testing.

That was the way of it, sings memory, here in the dusk. They took our soul and gave us the comfort of emortality amid a new-built Xanadu. The stars came clear in the dark of an unclouded sky. We can look into the black night and know that somewhere out there the spindles are warring against an enemy too terrible for understanding or compassion. And our soul is with them, sweating, slaving in the agony of death and victory. We spin on, we and our quiet garden, in an anesthesia of contentment.

I see a hawk soaring on a high wave of song. His cry hangs in the air, and his lofty feathered body. Now he stoops, falls like a projectile, opens his wings, stills magically, climbs the sky again. It is cozy here, in the warmth of the sun. I seem, though, to remember a word from the past, from the repeated past. Why do I feel a stir of horror as I gaze upon my unaging hands? Did my innocence save me then? Perhaps, but I am innocent no longer. Our life will stretch on, for our bargain is sealed, and the sun is warm on our peace.

Still, the horror remains, as the memory remains, that the meek have inherited the earth.

THE MAN WHO WALKED HOME

James Tiptree, Jr

James Tiptree, Jr was the primary pseudonym used by Alice Sheldon (1915–87) and she hid her identity so well that almost everyone was deceived into believing she was a man. This, despite such stories as "The Women Men Don't See" (1973), which vividly revealed the distinctions between the sexes. Although she wrote two novels, Up the Walls of the World *(1978) and* Brightness Falls from the Air *(1985), her strengths lay in the short story and her work constitutes some of the most remarkable fiction, not just of the 1970s – the chief decade for her writing – but in all speculative fiction. Her collections include* Ten Thousand Light Years From Home *(1973),* Warm Worlds and Otherwise *(1975), and* Star Songs of an Old Primate *(1978), but perhaps the most representative single volume is* Her Smoke Rose Up Forever *(1990), which critic John Clute called, "one of the two or three most significant collections of short SF ever published".*

Tiptree wrote several stories dealing with a post-apocalyptic world, and to my mind the following (first published in 1972, hence the dates) is the most unusual, with a cataclysm arising from an experiment that will take many centuries to resolve. Like most of Tiptree's fiction, it is an extended allegory that leaves you pondering long after finishing the story.

Transgression! Terror! And he thrust and lost there – punched into impossibility, abandoned never to be known how, the wrong man in the most wrong of all wrong places in that unimaginable collapse of never-to-be-reimagined mechanism – he stranded, undone, his lifeline severed, he in that nanosecond knowing his only tether parting, going away, the longest line to life withdrawing, winking out, disappearing forever beyond his grasp – telescoping away from him into the closing vortex beyond which lay his home, his life, his only possibility of being; seeing it sucked back into the deepest maw, melting, leaving him orphaned on what never-to-be-known shore of total wrongness – of beauty beyond joy, perhaps? Of horror? Of nothingness? Of profound otherness only, certainly – whatever it was, that place into which he transgressed, it could not support his life there, his violent and violating aberrance; and he, fierce, brave, crazy – clenched into total protest, one body-fist of utter repudiation of himself there in that place, forsaken there – what did he do? Rejected, exiled, hungering homeward more desperate than any lost beast driving for its unreachable home, his home, his HOME – and no way, no transport, no vehicle, means, machinery, no force but his intolerable resolve aimed homeward along that vanishing vector, that last and only lifeline – he did, what?

He walked.

Home.

Precisely what hashed up in the work of the major industrial lessee of the Bonneville Particle Acceleration Facility in Idaho was never known. Or rather, all those who might have been able to diagnose the original malfunction were themselves obliterated almost at once in the greater catastrophe which followed.

The nature of this second cataclysm was not at first understood either. All that was ever certain was that at 1153.6 of May 2, 1989 Old Style, the Bonneville laboratories and all their personnel were transformed into an intimately disrupted form of matter resembling a high-energy plasma, which became rapidly airborne to the accompaniment of radiating seismic and atmospheric events.

The disturbed area unfortunately included an operational MIRV Watchdog womb.

In the confusion of the next hours the Earth's population was substantially reduced, the biosphere was altered, and the Earth itself was marked with numbers of more conventional craters. For some years thereafter, the survivors were existentially preoccupied and the peculiar dust bowl at Bonneville was left to weather by itself in the changing climatic cycles.

It was not a large crater; just over a kilometer in width and lacking the usual displacement lip. Its surface was covered with a finely divided substance which dried into dust. Before the rains began it was almost perfectly flat. Only in certain lights, had anyone been there to inspect it, a small surface-marking or abraded place could be detected almost exactly at the center.

Two decades after the disaster a party of short brown people appeared from the south, together with a flock of somewhat atypical sheep. The crater at this time appeared as a wide shallow basin in which the grass did not grow well, doubtless from the almost complete lack of soil microorganisms. Neither this nor the surrounding vigorous grass was found to harm the sheep. A few crude hogans went up at the southern edge and a faint path began to be traced across the crater itself, passing by the central bare spot.

One spring morning two children who had been driving sheep cross the crater came screaming back to camp. A monster had burst out of the ground before them, a huge flat animal making dreadful roar. It vanished in a flash and a shaking of the earth, leaving an evil smell. The sheep had run away.

Since this last was visibly true, some elders investigated. Finding no sign of the monster and no place in which it could hide, they settled for beating the children, who settled for making a detour around the monster-spot, and nothing more occurred for a while.

The following spring the episode was repeated. This time an older girl was present, but she could add only that the monster seemed to be rushing flat out along the ground without moving at all. And there was a scraped place in the dirt. Again nothing was found; an evil-ward in a cleft stick was placed at the spot.

When the same thing happened for the third time a year later, the detour was extended and other charm-wands were added. But since no harm seemed to come of it and the brown people had seen far worse, sheep-tending resumed as before. A few more instantaneous apparitions of the monster were noted, each time in the spring.

At the end of the third decade of the new era a tall old man limped down the hills from the south, pushing his pack upon a bicycle wheel. He camped on the far side of the crater, and soon found the monster-site. He attempted to question people about it, but no one understood him, so he traded a knife for some meat. Although he was obviously feeble, something about him dissuaded them from killing him, and this proved wise because he later assisted the women in treating several sick children.

He spent much time around the place of the apparition and was nearby when it made its next appearance. This excited him very much and he did several inexplicable but apparently harmless things, including moving his camp into the crater by the trail. He stayed on for a full year watching the site and was close by for its next manifestation. After this he spent a few days making a charm-stone for the spot and left northward, hobbling as he had come.

More decades passed. The crater eroded, and a rain-gully became an intermittent streamlet across the edge of the basin. The brown people and their sheep were attacked by a band of grizzled men, after which the survivors went away eastward. The winters of what had been Idaho were now frost-free; aspen and eucalyptus sprouted in the moist plain. Still the crater remained treeless, visible as a flat bowl of grass; and the bare place at the center remained. The skies cleared somewhat.

After another three decades a larger band of black people with ox-drawn carts appeared and stayed for a time, but left again when they too saw the thunderclap-monster. A few other vagrants straggled by.

Five decades later a small permanent settlement had grown up on the nearest range of hills, from which men riding on small ponies with dark stripes down their spines herded humped cattle near the crater. A herdsman's hut was built by the streamlet, which in time became the habitation of an olive-skinned, red-haired family. In due course one of this clan again observed the monster-flash, but these people did not depart. The stone the tall man had placed was noted and left undisturbed.

The homestead at the crater's edge grew into a group of three and was joined by others, and the trail across it became a cart road with a log bridge over the stream. At the center of the still faintly discernible crater the cart road made a bend, leaving a grassy place which bore in its center about a square meter of curiously impacted bare earth and a deeply etched sandstone rock.

The apparition of the monster was now known to occur regularly each spring on a certain morning in this place, and the children of the community dared each other to approach the spot. It was referred to in a phrase that could be translated as "the Old Dragon". The Old Dragon's appearance was always the same: a brief violent thunder-burst which began and cut off abruptly, in the midst of which a dragonlike creature was seen apparently in furious motion on the earth, although it never actually moved. Afterward there was a bad smell and the earth smoked. People who saw it from close by spoke of a shivering sensation.

Early in the second century two young men rode into town from the north. Their ponies were shaggier than the local breed, and the equipment they carried included two boxlike objects which the young men set up at the monster-site. They stayed in the area a full year, observing two materializations of the Old Dragon, and they provided much news and maps of roads and trading towns in the cooler regions to the north. They built a windmill which was accepted by the community and offered to build a lighting machine, which was refused. Then they departed with their boxes after unsuccessfully attempting to persuade a local boy to learn to operate one.

In the course of the next decades other travelers stopped by and marveled at the monster, and there was sporadic fighting over the mountains to the south. One of the armed bands made a cattle raid into the crater hamlet. It was repulsed, but the raiders left a spotted sickness which killed many. For all this time the bare place at the crater's center remained, and the monster made his regular appearances, observed or not.

The hill-town grew and changed, and the crater hamlet grew to be a town. Roads widened and linked into networks. There were gray-green conifers in the hills now, spreading down into the plain, and chirruping lizards lived in their branches.

At century's end a shabby band of skin-clad squatters with stunted milk-beasts erupted out of the west and were eventually killed or driven away, but not before the local herds had contracted a vicious parasite. Veterinaries were fetched from the market city up north, but little could be done. The families near the crater left, and for some decades the area was empty. Finally cattle of a new strain reappeared in the plain and the crater hamlet was reoccupied. Still the bare center continued annually to manifest the monster, and he became an accepted phenomenon of the area. On several occasions parties came from the distant Northwest Authority to observe it.

The crater hamlet flourished and grew into the fields where cattle had grazed, and part of the old crater became the town park. A small seasonal tourist industry based on the monster-site developed. The townspeople rented rooms for the appearances, and many more or less authentic monster-relics were on display in the local taverns.

Several cults now grew up around the monster. One persistent belief held that it was a devil or damned soul forced to appear on Earth in torment to expiate the catastrophe of three centuries back. Others believed that it, or he, was some kind of messenger whose roar portended either doom or hope according to the believer. One very vocal sect taught that the apparition registered the moral conduct of the townspeople over the past year, and scrutinized the annual apparition for changes which could be interpreted for good or ill. It was considered lucky, or dangerous, to be touched by some of the dust raised by the monster. In every generation at least one small boy would try to hit the monster with a stick, usually acquiring a broken arm and a lifelong tavern tale. Pelting the monster with stones or other objects was a popular sport, and for some years people systematically flung prayers and flowers at it. Once a party tried to net it and were left with strings and vapor. The area itself had long since been fenced off at the center of the park.

Through all this the monster made his violently enigmatic annual appearance, sprawled furiously motionless, unreachably roaring.

Only as the fourth century of the new era went by was it apparent that the monster had been changing slightly. He was now no longer on the earth but had an arm and a leg thrust upward in a kicking or flailing gesture. As the years passed he began to change more quickly until at the end of the century he had risen to a contorted crouching pose, arms outflung as if frozen in gyration. His roar, too, seemed somewhat differently pitched, and the earth after him smoked more and more.

It was then widely felt that the man-monster was about to do something, to make some definitive manifestation, and a series of natural disasters and marvels gave support to a vigorous cult teaching this doctrine. Several religious leaders journeyed to the town to observe the apparitions.

However, the decades passed and the man-monster did nothing more than turn slowly in place, so that he now appeared to be in the act of sliding or staggering while pushing himself backward like a creature blown before a gale. No wind, of course, could be felt, and presently the general climate quieted and nothing came of it all.

Early in the fifth century New Calendar, three survey parties from the North Central Authority came through the area and stopped to observe the monster. A permanent recording device was set up at the site, after assurances to the townsfolk that no hardscience was involved. A local boy was trained to operate it; he quit when his girl left him but another volunteered. At this time nearly everyone believed that the apparition was a man, or the ghost of one. The record-machine boy and a few others including the school mechanics teacher referred to him as The Man John. In the next decades the roads were greatly improved; all forms of travel increased, and there was talk of building a canal to what had been the Snake River.

One May morning at the end of Century Five a young couple in a smart green mule-trap came jogging up the highroad from the Sandreas Rift Range to the southwest. The girl was golden-skinned and chatted with her young husband in a language unlike that ever heard by The Man John either at the end or the beginning of his life. What she said to him has, however, been heard in every age and tongue.

"Oh, Serli, I'm so glad we're taking this trip now! Next summer I'll be busy with baby."

To which Serli replied as young husbands often have, and so they trotted up to the town's inn. Here they left trap and bags and went in search of her uncle, who was expecting them there. The morrow was the day of The Man John's annual appearance, and her Uncle Laban had come from the MacKenzie History Museum to observe it and to make certain arrangements.

They found him with the town school instructor of mechanics, who was also the recorder at the monster-site. Presently Uncle Laban took them all with him to the town mayor's office to meet with various religious personages. The mayor was not unaware of tourist values, but he took Uncle Laban's part in securing the cultists' grudging assent to the MacKenzie authorities' secular interpretation of the monster, which was made easier by the fact that the cults disagreed among themselves. Then, seeing how pretty the niece was, the mayor took them all home to dinner.

When they returned to the inn for the night it was abrawl with holidaymakers.

"Whew," said Uncle Laban. "I've talked myself dry, sister's daughter. What a weight of holy nonsense is that Moksha female! Serli, my lad, I know you have questions. Let me hand you this to read, it's the guidebook we're giving them to sell. Tomorrow I'll answer for it all." And he disappeared into the crowded tavern.

So Serli and his bride took the pamphlet upstairs to bed with them, but it was not until the next morning at breakfast that they found time to read it.

" 'All that is known of John Delgano,' " read Serli with his mouth full, "'comes from two documents left by his brother Carl Delgano in the archives of the MacKenzie Group in the early years after the holocaust.' Put some honey on this cake, Mira my dove. Verbatim transcript follows, this is Carl Delgano speaking:

" 'I'm not an engineer or an astronaut like John, I ran an electronics repair shop in Salt Lake City. John was only trained as a spaceman, he never got to space; the slump wiped all that out. So he tied up with this commercial group who were leasing part of Bonneville. They wanted a man for some kind of hard vacuum tests, that's all I knew about it. John and his wife moved to Bonneville, but we all got together several times a year, our wives were like sisters. John had two kids, Clara and Paul.

" 'The tests were supposed to be secret, but John told me confidentially they were trying for an antigravity chamber. I don't know if it ever worked. That was the year before.

" 'Then that winter they came down for Christmas and John said they had something far out. He was excited. A temporal displacement, he called it; some kind of time effect. He said their chief honcho was like a real mad scientist. Big ideas. He kept adding more angles every time some other project would quit and leave equipment he could lease. No, I don't know who the top company was – maybe an insurance conglomerate, they had all the cash, didn't they? I guess they'd pay to catch a look at the future, that figures. Anyway, John was go, go, go. Katharine was scared, that's natural. She pictured him like, you know, H.G. Wells – walking around in some future world. John told her it wasn't like that at all. All they'd get would be this flicker, like a second or two. All kinds of complications.' – Yes, yes, my greedy piglet, some brew for me too. This is thirsty work!

"So. 'I remember I asked him, what about Earth moving? I mean, you could come back in a different place, right? He said they had that all figured. A spatial trajectory. Katharine was so scared we dropped it. John told her, don't worry. I'll come home. But he didn't. Not that it makes any difference, of course, everything was wiped out. Salt Lake too. The only reason I'm here is that I went up by Calgary to see mom, April 29. May 2 it all blew. I didn't find you folks at MacKenzie until July. I guess I may as well stay. That's all I know about John, except that he was a solid guy. If that accident started all this, it wasn't his fault.

" 'The second document' – in the name of love, little mother, do I have to read all this? Oh, very well, but you will kiss me first, madam. Must you look so delicious? 'The second document. Dated in the year eighteen, New Style, written by Carl' – see the old handwriting, my plump plump pigeon? Oh, very well, *very* well.

" 'Written at Bonneville Crater: I have seen my brother John Delgano. When I knew I had the rad sickness I came down here to look around. Salt Lake's still hot. So I hiked up here by Bonneville. You can see the crater where the labs were, it's grassed over. It's different, not radioactive; my film's okay. There's a bare place in the middle. Some Indios here told me a monster shows up here every year in the spring. I saw it myself a couple of days after I got here, but I was too far away to see much, except I was sure it's a man. In a vacuum suit. There was a lot of noise and dust, took me by surprise. It was all over in a second. I figured it's pretty close to the day, I mean, May 2, old.

" 'So I hung around a year and he showed up again yesterday. I was on the face side, and I could see his face through the visor. It's John, all right. He's hurt. I saw blood on his mouth and his suit is frayed some. He's lying on the ground. He didn't move while I could see him but the dust boiled up, like a man sliding onto base without moving. His eyes are open like he was looking. I don't understand it anyway, but I know it's John, not a ghost. He was in exactly the same position each time and there's a loud crack like thunder and another sound like a siren, very fast. And an ozone smell, and smoke. I felt a kind of shudder.

" 'I know it's John there and I think he's alive. I have to leave here now to take this back while I can still walk. I think somebody should come here and see. Maybe you can help John. Signed, Carl Delgano.

"'These records were kept by the MacKenzie Group, but it was not for several years' – etcetera, first light-print, etcetera, archives, analysts, etcetera – very good! Now it is time to meet your uncle, my edible one, after we go upstairs for just a moment."

"No, Serli, I will wait for you downstairs," said Mira prudently.

When they came into the town park Uncle Laban was directing the installation of a large durite slab in front of the enclosure around The Man John's appearance-spot. The slab was wrapped in a curtain to await the official unveiling. Townspeople and tourists and children thronged the walks, and a Ride-for-God choir was singing in the band shell. The morning was warming up fast. Vendors hawked ices and straw toys of the monster and flowers and good-luck confetti to throw at him. Another religious group stood by in dark robes; they belonged to the Repentance church beyond the park. Their pastor was directing somber glares at the crowd in general and Mira's uncle in particular.

Three official-looking strangers who had been at the inn came up and introduced themselves to Uncle Laban as observers from Alberta Central. They went on into the tent which had been erected over the closure, carrying with them several pieces of equipment which the townsfolk eyed suspiciously.

The mechanics teacher finished organizing a squad of students to protect the slab's curtain, and Mira and Serli and Laban went on into the tent. It was much hotter inside. Benches were set in rings around a railed enclosure about twenty feet in diameter. Inside the railing the earth was bare and scuffed. Several bunches of flowers and blooming poinciana branches leaned against the rail. The only thing inside the rail was a rough sandstone rock with markings etched on it.

Just as they came in, a small girl raced across the open center and was yelled at by everybody. The officials from Alberta were busy at one side of the rail, where the light-print box was mounted.

"Oh, no," muttered Mira's uncle, as one of the officials leaned over to set up a tripod stand inside the rails. He adjusted it, and a huge horsetail of fine feathery filaments blossomed out and eddied through the center of the space.

"Oh, *no*," Laban said again. "Why can't they let it be?"

"They're trying to pick up dust from his suit, is that right?" Serli asked.

"Yes, insane. Did you get time to read?"

"Oh, yes," said Serli.

"Sort of," added Mira.

"Then you know. He's falling. Trying to check his – well, call it velocity. Trying to slow down. He must have slipped or stumbled. We're getting pretty close to when he lost his footing and started to fall. What did it? Did somebody trip him?" Laban looked from Mira to Serli, dead serious now. "How would you like to be the one who made John Delgano fall?"

"Ooh," said Mira in quick sympathy. Then she said, "Oh."

"You mean," asked Serli, "whoever made him fall caused all the, caused —"

"Possible," said Laban.

"Wait a minute," Serli frowned. "He did fall. So somebody had to do it – I mean, he has to trip or whatever. If he doesn't fall the past would all be changed, wouldn't it? No war, no —"

"Possible," Laban repeated. "God knows. All *I* know is that John Delgano and the space around him is the most unstable, improbable, highly charged area ever known on Earth, and I'm damned if I think anybody should go poking sticks in it."

"Oh, come now, Laban!" One of the Alberta men joined them, smiling. "Our dust mop couldn't trip a gnat. It's just vitreous monofilaments."

"Dust from the future," grumbled Laban. "What's it going to tell you? That the future has dust in it?"

"If we could only get a trace from that thing in his hand."

"In his hand?" asked Mira. Serli started leafing hurriedly through the pamphlet.

"We've had a recording analyzer aimed at it," the Albertan lowered his voice, glancing around. "A spectroscope. We know there's something there, or was. Can't get a decent reading. It's severely deteriorated."

"People poking at him, grabbing at him," Laban muttered. "You —"

"TEN MINUTES!" shouted a man with a megaphone. "Take your places, friends and strangers."

The Repentance people were filing in at one side, intoning an ancient incantation, "*Mi-seri-cordia, Ora pro nobis*!"

The atmosphere suddenly became tense. It was now very close and hot in the big tent. A boy from the mayor's office wiggled through the crowd, beckoning Laban's party to come and sit in the guest chairs on the second level on the "face" side. In front of them at the rail one of the Repentance ministers was arguing with an Albertan official over his right to occupy the space taken by a recorder, it being his special duty to look into The Man John's eyes.

"Can he really see us?" Mira asked her uncle.

"Blink your eyes," Laban told her. "A new scene every blink, that's what he sees. Phantasmagoria. Blink-blink-blink – for god knows how long."

"*Mi-sere-re, pec-cavi*," chanted the penitentials. A soprano neighed. "May the red of sin pa-aa-ass from us!"

"They believe his oxygen tab went red because of the state of their souls," Laban chuckled. "Their souls are going to have to stay damned awhile; John Delgano has been on oxygen reserve for five centuries – or rather, he *will be* low for five centuries more. At a half-second per year his time, that's fifteen minutes. We know from the audio trace he's still breathing more or less normally, and the reserve was good for twenty minutes. So they should have their salvation about the year seven hundred, if they last that long."

"FIVE MINUTES! Take your seats, folks. Please sit down so everyone can see. Sit down, folks."

"It says we'll hear his voice through his suit speaker," Serli whispered. "Do you know what he's saying?"

"You get mostly a twenty-cycle howl," Laban whispered back. "The recorders have spliced up something like *ayt,* part of an old word. Take centuries to get enough to translate."

"Is it a message?"

"Who knows? Could be his word for 'date' or 'hate'. 'Too late', maybe. Anything."

The tent was quieting. A fat child by the railing started to cry and was pulled back on to a lap. There was a subdued mumble of praying. The Holy Joy faction on the far side rustled their flowers.

"Why don't we set our clocks by him?"

"It's changing. He's on sidereal time."

"ONE MINUTE."

In the hush the praying voices rose slightly. From outside a chicken cackled. The bare center space looked absolutely ordinary. Over it the recorder's silvery filaments eddied gently in the breath from a hundred lungs. Another recorder could be heard ticking faintly.

For long seconds nothing happened.

The air developed a tiny hum. At the same moment Mira caught a movement at the railing on her left.

The hum developed a beat and vanished into a peculiar silence and suddenly everything happened at once.

Sound burst on them, raced shockingly up the audible scale. The air cracked as something rolled and tumbled in the space. There was a grinding, wailing roar and –

He was there.

Solid, huge – a huge man in a monster-suit, his head was a dull bronze transparent globe, holding a human face, a dark smear of open mouth. His position was impossible, legs strained forward thrusting himself back, his arms frozen in a whirlwind swing. Although he seemed to be in frantic forward motion nothing moved, only one of his legs buckled or sagged slightly –

– And then he was gone, utterly and completely gone in a thunderclap, leaving only the incredible afterimage in their staring eyes. Air boomed, shuddering; dust rolled out mixed with smoke.

"Oh! Oh, my god," gasped Mira, unheard, clinging to Serli. Voices were crying out, choking. "He saw me, he saw me!" a woman shrieked. A few people dazedly threw their confetti into the empty dust cloud, most had failed to throw at all. Children began to howl. "He saw me!" the woman screamed hysterically. "Red, oh, Lord have mercy!" a deep male voice intoned.

Mira heard Laban swearing furiously and looked again into the space. As the dust settled she could see that the recorder's tripod had tipped over into the center. There was a dusty mound lying against it – flowers. Most of the end of the stand seemed to have disappeared or been melted. Of the filaments nothing could be seen.

"Some damn fool pitched flowers into it. Come on, let's get out."

"Was it under, did it trip him?" asked Mira, squeezed in the crowd.

"It was still red, his oxygen thing," Serli said over her head. "No mercy this trip, eh, Laban?"

"Shsh!" Mira caught the Repentance pastor's dark glance. They jostled through the enclosure gate and were out in the sunlit park, voices exclaiming, chattering loudly in excitement and relief.

"It was terrible," Mira cried softly. "Oh, I never thought it was a real live man. There he is, he's *there*. Why can't we help him? Did we trip him?"

"I don't know, I don't think so," her uncle grunted. They sat down near the new monument, fanning themselves. The curtain was still in place.

"Did we change the past?" Serli laughed, looked lovingly at his little wife. For a moment he wondered why she was wearing such odd earrings; then he remembered he had given them to her at that Indian pueblo they'd passed.

"But it wasn't just those Alberta people," said Mira. She seemed obsessed with the idea. "It was the flowers really." She wiped at her forehead.

"Mechanics or superstition," chuckled Serli. "Which is the culprit, love or science?"

"Shsh." Mira looked about nervously. "The flowers were love, I guess … I feel so strange. It's hot. Oh, thank you." Uncle Laban had succeeded in attracting the attention of the iced-drink vendor.

People were chatting normally now, and the choir struck into a cheerful song. At one side of the park a line of people were waiting to sign their names in the visitors' book. The mayor appeared at the park gate, leading a party up the bougainvillea alley for the unveiling of the monument.

"What did it say on that stone by his foot?" Mira asked. Serli showed her the guidebook picture of Carl's rock with the inscription translated below: WELCOME HOME JOHN.

"I wonder if he can see it."

The mayor was about to begin his speech.

Much later when the crowd had gone away the monument stood alone in the dark, displaying to the moon the inscription in the language of that time and place:

> ON THIS SPOT THERE APPEARS ANNUALLY THE FORM OF MAJOR JOHN DELGANO, THE FIRST AND ONLY MAN TO TRAVEL IN TIME.
>
> MAJOR DELGANO WAS SENT INTO THE FUTURE SOME HOURS BEFORE THE HOLOCAUST OF DAY ZERO. ALL KNOWLEDGE OF THE MEANS BY WHICH HE WAS SENT IS LOST, PERHAPS FOREVER. IT IS BELIEVED THAT AN ACCIDENT OCCURRED WHICH SENT HIM MUCH FARTHER THAN WAS INTENDED. SOME ANALYSTS SPECULATE THAT HE MAY HAVE GONE AS FAR AS 50,000 YEARS AHEAD. HAVING REACHED THIS UNKNOWN POINT, MAJOR DELGANO APPARENTLY WAS RECALLED, OR ATTEMPTED TO RETURN, ALONG THE COURSE IN SPACE AND TIME THROUGH WHICH HE WAS SENT. HIS TRAJECTORY IS THOUGHT TO START AT THE POINT WHICH OUR SOLAR SYSTEM WILL OCCUPY AT A FUTURE TIME AND IS TANGENT TO THE COMPLEX HELIX WHICH OUR EARTH DESCRIBES AROUND THE SUN.
>
> HE APPEARS ON THIS SPOT IN THE ANNUAL INSTANTS IN WHICH HIS COURSE INTERSECTS OUR PLANET'S ORBIT, AND HE IS APPARENTLY ABLE TO TOUCH THE GROUND IN

THOSE INSTANTS. SINCE NO TRACE OF HIS PASSAGE INTO
THE FUTURE HAS BEEN MANIFESTED, IT IS BELIEVED THAT
HE IS RETURNING BY A DIFFERENT MEANS THAN HE WENT
FORWARD. HE IS ALIVE IN OUR PRESENT. OUR PAST IS
HIS FUTURE AND OUR FUTURE IS HIS PAST. THE TIME OF
HIS APPEARANCES IS SHIFTING GRADUALLY IN SOLAR
TIME TO CONVERGE ON THE MOMENT OF 1153.6, ON
2 MAY, 1989 OLD STYLE, OR DAY ZERO.

THE EXPLOSION WHICH ACCOMPANIED HIS RETURN
TO HIS OWN TIME AND PLACE MAY HAVE OCCURRED
WHEN SOME ELEMENTS OF THE PAST INSTANTS OF HIS
COURSE WERE CARRIED WITH HIM INTO THEIR OWN
PRIOR EXISTENCE. IT IS CERTAIN THAT THIS EXPLOSION
PRECIPITATED THE WORLDWIDE HOLOCAUST WHICH
ENDED FOREVER THE AGE OF HARDSCIENCE.

*– He was falling, losing control, failing in his fight against the
terrible momentum he had gained, fighting with his human legs
shaking in the inhuman stiffness of his armor, his soles charred, not
gripping well now, not enough traction to break, battling, thrusting
as the flashes came, the punishing alternation of light, dark, light,
dark, which he had borne so long, the claps of air thickening and
thinning against his armor as he skidded through space which was
time, desperately braking as the flickers of Earth hammered against
his feet – only his feet mattered now, only to slow and stay on
course – and the pull, the beacon was getting slacker; as he came
near home it was fanning out, hard to stay centered; he was
becoming, he supposed, more probable; the wound he had punched
in time was healing itself. In the beginning it had been so tight – a
single ray of light in a closing tunnel – he had hurled himself after it
like an electron flying to the anode, aimed surely along that exqui-
sitely complex single vector of possibility of life, shot and been shot
like a squeezed pip into the last chink in that rejecting and rejected
nowhere through which he, John Delgano, could conceivably
continue to exist, the hole leading to home – had pounded down it
across time, across space, pumping with desperate legs as the real
Earth of that unreal time came under him, his course as certain as
the twisting dash of an animal down its burrow, he a cosmic mouse*

on an interstellar, intertemporal race for his nest with the wrongness of everything closing round the rightness of that one course, the atoms of his heart, his blood, his every cell crying Home – HOME! – as he drove himself after that fading breath-hole, each step faster, surer, stronger, until he raced with invincible momentum upon the rolling flickers of Earth as a man might race a rolling log in a torrent. Only the stars stayed constant around him from flash to flash, he looking down past his feet at a million strobes of Crux, of Triangulum; once at the height of his stride he had risked a century's glance upward and seen the Bears weirdly strung out from Polaris – but a Polaris not the Pole Star now, he realized, jerking his eyes back to his racing feet, thinking, I am walking home to Polaris, home! to the strobing beat. He had ceased to remember where he had been, the beings, people or aliens or things, he had glimpsed in the impossible moment of being where he could not be; had ceased to see the flashes of worlds around him, each flash different, the jumble of bodies, shapes, walls, colors, landscapes – some lasting a breath, some changing pell-mell – the faces, limbs, things poking at him; the nights he had pounded through, dark or lit by strange lamps, roofed or unroofed, the days flashing sunlight, gales, dust, snow, interiors innumerable, strobe after strobe into night again; he was in daylight now, a hall of some kind; I am getting closer at last, he thought, the feel is changing – but he had to slow down, to check; and that stone near his feet, it had stayed there some time now, he wanted to risk a look but he did not dare, he was so tired, and he was sliding, was going out of control, fighting to kill the merciless velocity that would not let him slow down; he was hurt, too, something had hit him back there, they had done something, he didn't know what, back somewhere in the kaleidoscope of faces, arms, hooks, beams, centuries of creatures grabbing at him – and his oxygen was going, never mind, it would last – it had to last, he was going home, home! And he had forgotten now the message he had tried to shout, hoping it could be picked up somehow, the important thing he had repeated; and the thing he had carried, it was gone now, his camera was gone too, something had torn it away – but he was coming home! Home! If only he could kill this momentum, could stay on the failing course, could slip, scramble, slide, somehow ride this avalanche down to home, to home – and his throat said

Home! – called Kate, Kate! And his heart shouted, his lungs almost gone now, as his legs fought, fought and failed, as his feet gripped and skidded and held and slid, as he pitched, flailed, pushed, strove in the gale of timerush across space, across time, at the end of the longest path ever: the path of John Delgano, coming home.

A PAIL OF AIR

Fritz Leiber

I sincerely hope that the name, work and reputation of Fritz Leiber (1910–92) does not fade. He was one of the most accomplished writers of science fiction and fantasy in the years from 1939 to his death and one of the most honoured. According to the Locus Index to SF Awards he won six Hugos, three Nebulas, two World Fantasy Awards, two Locus Awards, one British Fantasy Award, one Geffen, one Worldcon Special Convention Award, one Balrog and one Gandalf, as well as the World Fantasy Award Life Achievement, Stoker Life Achievement and the SFWA Grand Master. He is perhaps best known for his sword-and-sorcery series featuring Fafhrd and the Grey Mouser, collected in seven volumes starting with The Swords of Lankhmar *(1968). He is also renowned for his supernatural fiction, of which "Conjure Wife" (1943) has been filmed three times. His science fiction perhaps takes a back seat to his other work, yet he won a Hugo award for* The Wanderer *(1964) about an errant planet that enters the solar system and threatens the Earth.* Gather, Darkness *(1943) is set three centuries after a nuclear disaster when two powerful factions try to control the remnants of civilization. Of his other post-apocalyptic fiction I have always been attracted to "A Pail of Air" because of the most unusual concept and the indelible imagery.*

Pa HAD SENT me out to get an extra pail of air. I'd just about scooped it full and most of the warmth had leaked from my fingers when I saw the thing.

You know, at first I thought it was a young lady. Yes, a beautiful young lady's face all glowing in the dark and looking at me from the fifth floor of the opposite apartment, which hereabouts is the floor just above the white blanket of frozen air. I'd never seen a live young lady before, except in the old magazines – Sis is just a kid and Ma is pretty sick and miserable – and it gave me such a start that I dropped the pail. Who wouldn't, knowing everyone on Earth was dead except Pa and Ma and Sis and you?

Even at that, I don't suppose I should have been surprised. We all see things now and then. Ma has some pretty bad ones, to judge from the way she bugs her eyes at nothing and just screams and screams and huddles back against the blankets hanging around the Nest. Pa says it is natural we should react like that sometimes.

When I'd recovered the pail and could look again at the opposite apartment, I got an idea of what Ma might be feeling at those times, for I saw it wasn't a young lady at all but simply a light – a tiny light that moved stealthily from window to window, just as if one of the cruel little stars had come down out of the airless sky to investigate why the Earth had gone away from the Sun, and maybe to hunt down something to torment or terrify, now that the Earth didn't have the Sun's protection.

I tell you, the thought of it gave me the creeps. I just stood there shaking, and almost froze my feet and did frost my helmet so solid on the inside that I couldn't have seen the light even if it had come out of one of the windows to get me. Then I had the wit to go back inside.

Pretty soon I was feeling my familiar way through the thirty or so blankets and rugs Pa has got hung around to slow down the escape of air from the Nest, and I wasn't quite so scared. I began to hear the tick-ticking of the clocks in the Nest and knew I was getting back into air, because there's no sound outside in the vacuum, of course. But my mind was still crawly and uneasy as I pushed through the last blankets – Pa's got them faced with aluminum foil to hold in the heat – and came into the Nest.

Let me tell you about the Nest. It's low and snug, just room for the four of us and our things. The floor is covered with thick woolly rugs. Three of the sides are blankets, and the blankets roofing it touch Pa's head. He tells me it's inside a much bigger room, but I've never seen the real walls or ceiling.

Against one of the blankets is a big set of shelves, with tools and books and other stuff, and on top of it a whole row of clocks. Pa's very fussy about keeping them wound. He says we must never forget time, and without a sun or moon, that would be easy to do.

The fourth wall has blankets all over except around the fireplace, in which there is a fire that must never go out. It keeps us from freezing and does a lot more besides. One of us must always watch it. Some of the clocks are alarm and we can use them to remind us. In the early days there was only Ma to take turns with Pa – I think of that when she gets difficult – but now there's me to help, and Sis too.

It's Pa who is the chief guardian of the fire, though. I always think of him that way: a tall man sitting cross-legged, frowning anxiously at the fire, his lined face golden in its light, and every so often carefully placing on it a piece of coal from the big heap beside it. Pa tells me there used to be guardians of the fire sometimes in the very old days – vestal virgins, he calls them – although there was unfrozen air all around then and you didn't really need one.

He was sitting just that way now, though he got up quick to take the pail from me and bawl me out for loitering – he'd spotted my frozen helmet right off. That roused Ma and she joined in picking on me. She's always trying to get the load off her feelings, Pa explains. Sis let off a couple of silly squeals too.

Pa handled the pail of air in a twist of cloth. Now that it was inside the Nest, you could really feel its coldness. It just seemed to suck the heat out of everything. Even the flames cringed away from it as Pa put it down close by the fire.

Yet it's that glimmery white stuff in the pail that keeps us alive. It slowly melts and vanishes and refreshes the Nest and feeds the fire. The blankets keep it from escaping too fast. Pa'd like to seal the whole place, but he can't – building's too earthquake-twisted, and besides he has to leave the chimney open for smoke.

Pa says air is tiny molecules that fly away like a flash if there isn't something to stop them. We have to watch sharp not to let the air run low. Pa always keeps a big reserve supply of it in buckets behind the first blankets, along with extra coal and cans of food and other things, such as pails of snow to melt for water. We have to go way down to the bottom floor for that stuff, which is a mean trip, and get it through a door to outside.

You see, when the Earth got cold, all the water in the air froze first and made a blanket ten feet thick or so everywhere, and then down on top of that dropped the crystals of frozen air, making another white blanket sixty or seventy feet thick maybe.

Of course, all the parts of the air didn't freeze and snow down at the same time.

First to drop out was the carbon dioxide – when you're shoveling for water, you have to make sure you don't go too high and get any of that stuff mixed in, for it would put you to sleep, maybe for good, and make the fire go out. Next there's the nitrogen, which doesn't count one way or the other, though it's the biggest part of the blanket. On top of that and easy to get at, which is lucky for us, there's the oxygen that keeps us alive. Pa says we live better than kings ever did, breathing pure oxygen, but we're used to it and don't notice. Finally, at the very top, there's a slick of liquid helium, which is funny stuff. All of these gases in neat separate layers. Like a pussy caffay, Pa laughingly says, whatever that is.

I was busting to tell them all about what I'd seen, and so as soon as I'd ducked out of my helmet and while I was still climbing out of my suit, I cut loose. Right away Ma got nervous and began making eyes at the entry-slit in the blankets and wringing her hands together – the hand where she'd lost three fingers from frostbite inside the good one, as usual. I could tell that Pa was annoyed at me scaring her and wanted to explain it all away quickly, yet could see I wasn't fooling.

"And you watched this light for some time, son?" he asked when I finished.

I hadn't said anything about first thinking it was a young lady's face. Somehow that part embarrassed me.

"Long enough for it to pass five windows and go to the next floor."

"And it didn't look like stray electricity or crawling liquid or starlight focused by a growing crystal, or anything like that?"

He wasn't just making up those ideas. Odd things happen in a world that's about as cold as can be, and just when you think matter would be frozen dead, it takes on a strange new life. A slimy stuff comes crawling toward the Nest, just like an animal snuffing for heat – that's the liquid helium. And once, when I was little, a bolt of lightning – not even Pa could figure where it came from – hit the nearby steeple and crawled up and down it for weeks, until the glow finally died.

"Not like anything I ever saw," I told him.

He stood for a moment frowning. Then, "I'll go out with you, and you show it to me," he said.

Ma raised a howl at the idea of being left alone, and Sis joined in, too, but Pa quieted them. We started climbing into our outside clothes – mine had been warming by the fire. Pa made them. They have plastic headpieces that were once big double-duty transparent food cans, but they keep heat and air in and can replace the air for a little while, long enough for our trips for water and coal and food and so on.

Ma started moaning again, "I've always known there was something outside there, waiting to get us. I've felt it for years – something that's part of the cold and hates all warmth and wants to destroy the Nest. It's been watching us all this time, and now it's coming after us. It'll get you and then come for me. Don't go, Harry!"

Pa had everything on but his helmet. He knelt by the fireplace and reached in and shook the long metal rod that goes up the chimney and knocks off the ice that keeps trying to clog it. Once a week he goes up on the roof to check if it's working all right. That's our worst trip and Pa won't let me make it alone.

"Sis," Pa said quietly, "come watch the fire. Keep an eye on the air, too. If it gets low or doesn't seem to be boiling fast enough, fetch another bucket from behind the blanket. But mind your hands. Use the cloth to pick up the bucket."

Sis quit helping Ma be frightened and came over and did as she was told. Ma quieted down pretty suddenly, though her eyes were still kind of wild as she watched Pa fix on his helmet tight and pick up a pail and the two of us go out.

Pa led the way and I took hold of his belt. It's a funny thing, I'm not afraid to go by myself, but when Pa's along I always want to hold on to him. Habit, I guess, and then there's no denying that this time I was a bit scared.

You see, it's this way. We know that everything is dead out there. Pa heard the last radio voices fade away years ago, and had seen some of the last folks die who weren't as lucky or well-protected as us. So we knew that if there was something groping around out there, it couldn't be anything human or friendly.

Besides that, there's a feeling that comes with it always being night, *cold* night. Pa says there used to be some of that feeling even in the old days, but then every morning the Sun would come and chase it away. I have to take his word for that, not ever remembering the Sun as being anything more than a big star. You see, I hadn't been born when the dark star snatched us away from the Sun, and by now it's dragged us out beyond the orbit of the planet Pluto, Pa says, and taking us farther out all the time.

I found myself wondering whether there mightn't be something on the dark star that wanted us, and if that was why it had captured the Earth. Just then we came to the end of the corridor and I followed Pa out on the balcony.

I don't know what the city looked like in the old days, but now it's beautiful. The starlight lets you see pretty well – there's quite a bit of light in those steady points speckling the blackness above. (Pa says the stars used to twinkle once, but that was because there was air.) We are on a hill and the shimmery plain drops away from us and then flattens out, cut up into neat squares by the troughs that used to be streets. I sometimes make my mashed potatoes look like it, before I pour on the gravy.

Some taller buildings push up out of the feathery plain, topped by rounded caps of air crystals, like the fur hood Ma wears, only whiter. On those buildings you can see the darker squares of windows, underlined by white dashes of air crystals. Some of them are on a slant, for many of the buildings are pretty badly twisted by the quakes and all the rest that happened when the dark star captured the Earth.

Here and there a few icicles hang, water icicles from the first days of the cold, other icicles of frozen air that melted on the roofs and dripped and froze again. Sometimes one of those icicles will catch the light of a star and send it to you so brightly you think the star has swooped into the city. That was one of the things Pa had been thinking of when I told him about the light, but I had thought of it myself first and known it wasn't so.

He touched his helmet to mine so we could talk easier and he asked me to point out the windows to him. But there wasn't any light moving around inside them now, or anywhere else. To my surprise, Pa didn't bawl me out and tell me I'd been seeing things. He looked all around quite a while after filling his pail, and just as we were going inside he whipped around without warning, as if to take some peeping thing off guard.

I could feel it, too. The old peace was gone. There was something lurking out there, watching, waiting, getting ready.

Inside, he said to me, touching helmets, "If you see something like that again, son, don't tell the others. Your Ma's sort of nervous these days and we owe her all the feeling of safety we can give her. Once – it was when your sister was born – I was ready to give up and die, but your mother kept me trying. Another time she kept the fire going a whole week all by herself when I was sick. Nursed me and took care of the two of you, too.

"You know that game we sometimes play, sitting in a square in the Nest, tossing a ball around? Courage is like a ball, son. A person can hold it only so long, and then he's got to toss it to someone else. When it's tossed your way, you've got to catch it and hold it tight – and hope there'll be someone else to toss it to when you get tired of being brave."

His talking to me that way made me feel grown-up and good. But it didn't wipe away the thing outside from the back of my mind – or the fact that Pa took it seriously.

It's hard to hide your feelings about such a thing. When we got back in the Nest and took off our outside clothes, Pa laughed about it all and told them it was nothing and kidded me for having such an imagination, but his words fell flat. He didn't convince Ma and Sis any more than he did me. It looked for a minute like we were all fumbling the courage-ball. Something had to be done, and almost before I knew what I was going to say, I heard myself asking Pa to tell us about the old days, and how it all happened.

He sometimes doesn't mind telling that story, and Sis and I sure like to listen to it, and he got my idea. So we were all settled around the fire in a wink, and Ma pushed up some cans to thaw for supper, and Pa began. Before he did, though, I noticed him casually get a hammer from the shelf and lay it down beside him.

It was the same old story as always – I think I could recite the main thread of it in my sleep – though Pa always puts in a new detail or two and keeps improving it in spots.

He told us how the Earth had been swinging around the Sun ever so steady and warm, and the people on it fixing to make money and wars and have a good time and get power and treat each other right or wrong, when without warning there comes charging out of space this dead star, this burned out sun, and upsets everything.

You know, I find it hard to believe in the way those people felt, any more than I can believe in the swarming number of them. Imagine people getting ready for the horrible sort of war they were cooking up. Wanting it even, or at least wishing it were over so as to end their nervousness. As if all folks didn't have to hang together and pool every bit of warmth just to keep alive. And how can they have hoped to end danger, any more than we can hope to end the cold?

Sometimes I think Pa exaggerates and makes things out too black. He's cross with us once in a while and was probably cross with all those folks. Still, some of the things I read in the old magazines sound pretty wild. He may be right.

The dark star, as Pa went on telling it, rushed in pretty fast and there wasn't much time to get ready. At the beginning they tried to keep it a secret from most people, but then the truth came out, what with the earthquakes and floods – imagine, oceans of *unfrozen* water! – and people seeing stars blotted out by something on a clear night. First off they thought it would hit the Sun, and then they thought it would hit the Earth. There was even the start of a rush to get to a place called China, because people thought the star would hit on the other side. But then they found it wasn't going to hit either side, but was going to come very close to the Earth.

Most of the other planets were on the other side of the Sun and didn't get involved. The Sun and the newcomer fought over the

Earth for a little while – pulling it this way and that, like two dogs growling over a bone, Pa described it this time – and then the newcomer won and carried us off. The Sun got a consolation prize, though. At the last minute he managed to hold on to the Moon.

That was the time of the monster earthquakes and floods, twenty times worse than anything before. It was also the time of the Big Jerk, as Pa calls it, when all Earth got yanked suddenly, just as Pa has done to me once or twice, grabbing me by the collar to do it, when I've been sitting too far from the fire.

You see, the dark star was going through space faster than the Sun, and in the opposite direction, and it had to wrench the world considerably in order to take it away.

The Big Jerk didn't last long. It was over as soon as the Earth was settled down in its new orbit around the dark star. But it was pretty terrible while it lasted. Pa says that all sorts of cliffs and buildings toppled, oceans slopped over, swamps and sandy deserts gave great sliding surges that buried nearby lands. Earth was almost jerked out of its atmosphere blanket and the air got so thin in spots that people keeled over and fainted – though of course, at the same time, they were getting knocked down by the Big Jerk and maybe their bones broke or skulls cracked.

We've often asked Pa how people acted during that time, whether they were scared or brave or crazy or stunned, or all four, but he's sort of leery of the subject, and he was again tonight. He says he was mostly too busy to notice.

You see, Pa and some scientist friends of his had figured out part of what was going to happen – they'd known we'd get captured and our air would freeze – and they'd been working like mad to fix up a place with airtight walls and doors, and insulation against the cold, and big supplies of food and fuel and water and bottled air. But the place got smashed in the last earthquakes and all Pa's friends were killed then and in the Big Jerk. So he had to start over and throw the Nest together quick without any advantages, just using any stuff he could lay his hands on.

I guess he's telling pretty much the truth when he says he didn't have any time to keep an eye on how other folks behaved, either then or in the Big Freeze that followed – followed very quick, you know, both because the dark star was pulling us away very fast and because Earth's rotation had been slowed in the tug-of-war, so that the nights were ten old nights long.

Still, I've got an idea of some of the things that happened from the frozen folk I've seen, a few of them in other rooms in our building, others clustered around the furnaces in the basements where we go for coal.

In one of the rooms, an old man sits stiff in a chair, with an arm and a leg in splints. In another, a man and a woman are huddled together in a bed with heaps of covers over them. You can just see their heads peeking out, close together. And in another a beautiful young lady is sitting with a pile of wraps huddled around her, looking hopefully toward the door, as if waiting for someone who never came back with warmth and food. They're all still and stiff as statues, of course, but just like life.

Pa showed them to me once in quick winks of his flashlight, when he still had a fair supply of batteries and could afford to waste a little light. They scared me pretty bad and made my heart pound, especially the young lady.

Now, with Pa telling his story for the umpteenth time to take our minds off another scare, I got to thinking of the frozen folk again. All of a sudden I got an idea that scared me worse than anything yet. You see, I'd just remembered the face I'd thought I'd seen in the window. I'd forgotten about that on account of trying to hide it from the others.

What, I asked myself, if the frozen folk were coming to life? What if they were like the liquid helium that got a new lease on life and started crawling toward the heat just when you thought its molecules ought to freeze solid forever? Or like the electricity that moves endlessly when it's just about as cold as that? What if the ever-growing cold, with the temperature creeping down the last few degrees to the last zero, had mysteriously wakened the frozen folk to life – not warm-blooded life, but something icy and horrible?

That was a worse idea than the one about something coming down from the dark star to get us.

Or maybe, I thought, both ideas might be true. Something coming down from the dark star and making the frozen folk move, using them to do its work. That would fit with both things I'd seen – the beautiful young lady and the moving, starlike light.

The frozen folk with minds from the dark star behind their unwinking eyes, creeping, crawling, snuffing their way, following the heat to the Nest.

I tell you, that thought gave me a very bad turn and I wanted very badly to tell the others my fears, but I remembered what Pa had said and clenched my teeth and didn't speak.

We were all sitting very still. Even the fire was burning silently. There was just the sound of Pa's voice and the clocks.

And then, from beyond the blankets, I thought I heard a tiny noise. My skin tightened all over me.

Pa was telling about the early years in the Nest and had come to the place where he philosophizes.

"So I asked myself then," he said, "what's the use of going on? What's the use of dragging it out for a few years? Why prolong a doomed existence of hard work and cold and loneliness? The human race is done. The Earth is done. Why not give up, I asked myself – and all of a sudden I got the answer."

Again I heard the noise, louder this time, a kind of uncertain, shuffling tread, coming closer. I couldn't breathe.

"Life's always been a business of working hard and fighting the cold," Pa was saying. "The earth's always been a lonely place, millions of miles from the next planet. And no matter how long the human race might have lived, the end would have come some night. Those things don't matter. What matters is that life is good. It has a lovely texture, like some rich cloth or fur, or the petals of flowers – you've seen pictures of those, but I can't describe how they feel – or the fire's glow. It makes everything else worth while. And that's as true for the last man as the first."

And still the steps kept shuffling closer. It seemed to me that the inmost blanket trembled and bulged a little. Just as if they were burned into my imagination, I kept seeing those peering, frozen eyes.

"So right then and there," Pa went on, and now I could tell that he heard the steps, too, and was talking loud so we maybe wouldn't hear them, "right then and there I told myself that I was going on as if we had all eternity ahead of us. I'd have children and teach them all I could. I'd get them to read books. I'd plan for the future, try to enlarge and seal the Nest. I'd do what I could to keep everything beautiful and growing. I'd keep alive my feeling of wonder even at the cold and the dark and the distant stars."

But then the blanket actually did move and lift. And there was a bright light somewhere behind it. Pa's voice stopped and his eyes turned to the widening slit and his hand went out until it touched and gripped the handle of the hammer beside him.

In through the blanket stepped the beautiful young lady. She stood there looking at us the strangest way, and she carried something bright and unwinking in her hand. And two other faces peered over her shoulders – men's faces, white and staring.

Well, my heart couldn't have been stopped for more than four or five beats before I realized she was wearing a suit and helmet like Pa's homemade ones, only fancier, and that the men were, too – and that the frozen folk certainly wouldn't be wearing those. Also, I noticed that the bright thing in her hand was just a kind of flashlight.

The silence kept on while I swallowed hard a couple of times, and after that there was all sorts of jabbering and commotion.

They were simply people, you see. We hadn't been the only ones to survive; we'd just thought so, for natural enough reasons. These three people had survived, and quite a few others with them. And when we found out *how* they'd survived, Pa let out the biggest whoop of joy.

They were from Los Alamos and they were getting their heat and power from atomic energy. Just using the uranium and plutonium intended for bombs, they had enough to go on for thousands of years. They had a regular little airtight city, with airlocks and all. They even generated electric light and grew plants and animals by it. (At this Pa let out a second whoop, waking Ma from her faint.)

But if we were flabbergasted at them, they were double-flabber-gasted at us.

One of the men kept saying, "But it's impossible, I tell you. You can't maintain an air supply without hermetic sealing. It's simply impossible."

That was after he had got his helmet off and was using our air. Meanwhile, the young lady kept looking around at us as if we were saints, and telling us we'd done something amazing, and suddenly she broke down and cried.

They'd been scouting around for survivors, but they never expected to find any in a place like this. They had rocket ships at Los Alamos and plenty of chemical fuels. As for liquid oxygen, all you had to do was go out and shovel the air blanket at the top level. So after they'd got things going smoothly at Los Alamos, which had taken years, they'd decided to make some trips to likely places where there might be other survivors. No good trying long-distance radio signals, of course, since there was no atmosphere to carry them around the curve of the Earth.

Well, they'd found other colonies at Argonne and Brookhaven and way around the world at Harwell and Tanna Tuva. And now they'd been giving our city a look, not really expecting to find anything. But they had an instrument that noticed the faintest heat waves and it had told them there was something warm down here, so they'd landed to investigate. Of course we hadn't heard them land, since there was no air to carry the sound, and they'd had to investigate around quite a while before finding us. Their instruments had given them a wrong steer and they'd wasted some time in the building across the street.

By now, all five adults were talking like sixty. Pa was demonstrating to the men how he worked the fire and got rid of the ice in the chimney and all that. Ma had perked up wonderfully and was showing the young lady her cooking and sewing stuff, and even asking about how the women dressed at Los Alamos. The strangers marveled at everything and praised it to the skies. I could tell from the way they wrinkled their noses that they found the Nest a bit smelly, but they never mentioned that at all and just asked bushels of questions.

In fact, there was so much talking and excitement that Pa forgot about things, and it wasn't until they were all getting groggy that he looked and found the air had all boiled away in the pail. He got another bucket of air quick from behind the blankets. Of course that started them all laughing and jabbering again. The newcomers even got a little drunk. They weren't used to so much oxygen.

Funny thing, though – I didn't do much talking at all and Sis hung on to Ma all the time and hid her face when anybody looked at her. I felt pretty uncomfortable and disturbed myself, even about the young lady. Glimpsing her outside there, I'd had all sorts of mushy thoughts, but now I was just embarrassed and scared of her, even though she tried to be nice as anything to me.

I sort of wished they'd all quit crowding the Nest and let us be alone and get our feelings straightened out.

And when the newcomers began to talk about our all going to Los Alamos, as if that were taken for granted, I could see that something of the same feeling struck Pa and Ma, too. Pa got very silent all of a sudden and Ma kept telling the young lady, "But I wouldn't know how to act there and I haven't any clothes."

The strangers were puzzled like anything at first, but then they got the idea. As Pa kept saying, "It just doesn't seem right to let this fire go out."

Well, the strangers are gone, but they're coming back. It hasn't been decided yet just what will happen. Maybe the Nest will be kept up as what one of the strangers called a "survival school". Or maybe we will join the pioneers who are going to try to establish a new colony at the uranium mines at Great Slave Lake or in the Congo.

Of course, now that the strangers are gone, I've been thinking a lot about Los Alamos and those other tremendous colonies. I have a hankering to see them for myself.

You ask me, Pa wants to see them, too. He's been getting pretty thoughtful, watching Ma and Sis perk up.

"It's different, now that we know others are alive," he explains to me. "Your mother doesn't feel so hopeless any more. Neither do I, for that matter, not having to carry the whole responsibility for keeping the human race going, so to speak. It scares a person."

I looked around at the blanket walls and the fire and the pails of air boiling away and Ma and Sis sleeping in the warmth and the flickering light.

"It's not going to be easy to leave the Nest," I said, wanting to cry, kind of. "It's so small and there's just the four of us. I get scared at the idea of big places and a lot of strangers."

He nodded and put another piece of coal on the fire. Then he looked at the little pile and grinned suddenly and put a couple of handfuls on, just as if it was one of our birthdays or Christmas.

"You'll quickly get over that feeling, son," he said. "The trouble with the world was that it kept getting smaller and smaller, till it ended with just the Nest. Now it'll be good to have a real huge world again, the way it was in the beginning."

I guess he's right. You think the beautiful young lady will wait for me till I grow up? I'll be twenty in only ten years.

GUARDIANS OF THE PHOENIX

Eric Brown

Eric Brown has written over twenty books and eighty short stories, since his first collection The Time-Lapsed Man *(1990). His first novel was* Meridian Days *(1992). Recent works include* The Fall of Tartarus *(2005) and* The Extraordinary Voyage of Jules Verne *(2005). He has twice won the BSFA short story award, in 2000 and 2002. I had the pleasure of collaborating with him in compiling* The Mammoth Book of New Jules Verne Adventures *(2005).*

IT WAS DAWN when we set off from beneath the twisted skeleton of the Eiffel Tower and crossed the desert to Tangiers.

We travelled by day through a blasted landscape devoid of life, and at night we stopped and tried to sleep. I'd lie in my berth and stare through the canopy at the magnetic storms lacerating the troposphere. The heat was insufferable, even in the marginally cooler early hours. When I slept I dreamed of the women I had seen in old magazines, and when I woke in the searing heat of morning and Danny started the truck on the next leg of the journey, I was silent and sullen with melancholy longing.

Two days out of Paris, heading through what Edvard informed us had once been the Auvergne, we picked up the fifth member of our party.

Around sunset, as the horizon burned and a magnetic storm played out in a frenzy overhead, the truck stuttered and came to a halt.

Danny hit the steering wheel. "Christ! It's one of the main capacitors. I'll wager anything..."

"Not again?" Fear lodged in my throat. This was the third time in as many weeks that the truck had failed, and every time Danny's desperation had communicated itself to me. He tried to disguise it, but I could see the dread in his eyes, in the shake of his hands. Without the truck, without the means to cross the ravaged land in search of water, we were dead.

Danny was our leader by dint of the fact that he owned the truck and the drilling rig, and because he was an engineer. He was in his fifties, small and lean, and despite what he'd been through he was optimistic.

I'd never heard that word till I met Danny, four years ago.

I stared through the windscreen. We were on the edge of a city: its jagged skyline of ruined buildings rose stark against the dying light. Over the decades, sand had drifted through the parks and esplanades, softening the harsh angles of the buildings, creating beautifully parabolic curves between the shattered streets and vertical walls.

"Edvard!" Danny called. "Kat!"

Seconds later Edvard's balding head appeared through the hatch. A little later, on account of her limp, Kat joined us. Her lined face wrinkled even more as she peered through the windscreen.

Danny indicated the scene before us. "You know what happened here?"

Edvard looked at the map on the seat between Danny and me. "Clermont-Ferrand. It wasn't a nuclear strike. I know that much. Too small a place to be a target, nuclear or biological."

Danny looked at him, scratching his greying beard. "So you reckon it's safe?"

Edvard thought about it, then nodded.

Kat said, "I just hope there's no one out there."

Stalled like this, we'd be easy pickings for marauders – not that we'd come across any of those for years.

"Okay," Danny said, "come on, Pierre. Let's see what the damage is."

I took my rifle from the locker, hung it over my shoulder, and followed Danny from the truck. Even though the sun was on its way down, the heat was ferocious: it was as if we'd stepped into an industrial oven. We walked down the length of the truck, pausing at the foot of the ladder welded onto the flank, and Danny gingerly picked open a small hatch. He pulled out a toolbox and two pairs of gloves and passed one pair to me. The rungs of the ladder would take the skin clean off our palms if we ascended unprotected.

Danny nodded, and I followed him up the side of the truck and across the top. The heat radiating from the solar arrays and the steel surface of the truck hit me in a blast. I picked my way carefully after Danny, wary of allowing the exposed flesh of my legs to get anywhere near the hot steel.

Danny stopped at the apex, hauled open an inspection cover and passed it back to me. For the next ten minutes he rooted around inside, grunting and cursing as he checked each capacitor in turn.

I unslung my rifle and scanned the darkening city, wondering what this place might have been like fifty or sixty years ago, when the streets and buildings had been full of people going about their everyday business – before the nuclear and biological wars, before the governments collapsed under the strain of trying to hold together a dying world.

I heard the hatch open below and saw Edvard limp out of the truck and across the sand to the nearest building. He paused before it, looking ragged and frail, staring up at the ruin before stepping inside.

I scanned the horizon, looking for signs of life. A part of me knew it was a futile exercise. I hadn't seen a live animal for months, or other human beings for three years now. Even so, I searched the ruins with hope, and a little dread – for if we did happen upon humans out there, then chances were that they'd be as hostile as the last lot.

"Pierre!"

I started. "Sorry, I—"

"Just pass me the cover."

He took it from me and slipped it back into place. "You fixed it?" I asked.

"For now. Don't know how long it'll last." He shook his head. "But we're lucky. If it'd been something major …"

I nodded, smiling. Danny laughed, trying to make light of his own relief. I backed down to the ground and, as Danny slipped into the truck to tell Kat not to worry herself sick, I waded through the sand towards the shattered buildings.

Edvard had moved into the shadowy interior of the nearest shell. I followed his dimpled prints in the drift and leaned in the doorway, watching him.

Edvard was Norwegian, and he'd had to explain to me what that meant, now that nations no longer existed. He'd been a doctor in Oslo before the colony died out. He was slow and wise, and as ghostly-pale as the rest of us. It was Edvard who had taught me how to read and write.

He had aged quickly in the four years I'd known him. He'd slowed down, and the flesh had fallen from his bones, and when I'd asked him if he was okay he'd just smiled and said he was fine, for an old man. I reckoned he was in his late forties.

The room was empty, but for drifts of sand, scattered paper, and a skeleton in the far corner. The bones had collapsed, and the skull had rolled onto its right cheek; in the half-light of the room, the empty eyes seemed to be staring at us.

"Ed," I said. "The truck's okay. A blown capacitor. Danny fixed it."

He turned and smiled. "That's great." He seemed distant, lost in thought.

"What?" I said.

He pointed at the skeleton. "I remember when I would have taken those bones, Pierre. Can you believe that? Nutrients, you see. The marrow in the bones. Boil them up, make a soup. Pretty thin, but nourishing ... " He shrugged. "No good now, of course. All dried out, desiccated."

He knelt slowly, and I could almost hear the creak of his joints. He reached out and picked up a scrap of paper. He joined me in the doorway where the light was better and held out the old newspaper.

"Christ, Pierre. 2040. What, fifty years ago? Look, a headline about the peace pact with China. Lot of good that did!"

He'd told me about what had happened to China. The military had taken over in a bloody coup, overturning a government they accused of not doing all they could to feed the people. And then the people had overthrown the junta, when the military had proved as useless as the government.

Not long after that, China invaded India, and Europe came to the aid of the subcontinent, and World War III broke out. It lasted five days, according to Edvard. And after that, the world was never the same again.

That was the beginning of the end, Edvard said. After that, there was no hope. What humankind had begun with wars, the planet finished off with accelerated global warming.

He stared at the scrap of newspaper. In his clawed hand, the paper crumbled.

I took his arm. "C'mon, Ed. Let's get something to eat."

We sat around the fold-down table in the truck and ate spinach and potatoes grown in the hydroponics trailer, washed down with the daily ration of water. Danny talked enthusiastically about the maps he'd found in Paris.

Kat's smile was like a mother's watching a favourite child. She was sixty, grey and thin and twisted like a length of wire. There was something shattered in her grey eyes which spoke of tragedy in her past, or knowledge of the future, and Danny loved her with a tender, touching concern.

He jabbed a finger at the map. "There's the trench, right there, just north of the African coast. I'm sure if we drill deep enough ..."

"We could use some fresh stuff," I said. "I'm tired of drinking recycled piss."

Danny laughed. Edvard raised his glass and examined the murky liquid, smacking his lips. "I don't know. As victuals go, this is a fine drop. Good body, a hint of mustard."

I watched Kat as she ate, which she did sparingly. She'd given herself a small portion, and didn't eat all of that. Before the rest of us had finished, she pushed her plate away and left the table, limping to the door of the berth she shared with Danny. He watched her go, then followed her. I looked at Edvard, as if for explanation, but his eyes were on his food.

After the meal I moved outside, taking my rifle with me, and in the spill of light from the truck I had a bath. I sat naked in the sand, taking handfuls of the fine grains and rubbing them over my body. I felt the grease and sweat fall away, leaving a fine covering of sandy powder. I dug deeper, finding the cooler sand, and poured it over my belly and thighs.

I thought about Kat, and told myself she'd be fine. Minutes later, as if to confirm that hope, the truck began rocking as Danny and

Kat made love. I found myself thinking how Kat must have been good looking, way back. But I stopped those thoughts as soon as they began, stood up and pulled on my shorts.

I was about to go inside when a door opened along the flank of the truck and Edvard looked out. "Pierre?"

He stepped from the truck and slowly lowered himself into the sand beside me.

We sat in silence for a time and stared into the night sky. The storms were starting high above the far horizon, great actinic sheets of white fire.

At last I said, "Is Kat okay?"

He flashed a glance at me. "She's ill, Pierre. We all are."

"But Kat—?"

He sighed. "Cancer. I don't know how advanced it is. There's nothing I can do about it, apart from give her the odd painkiller. And I'm running low on those." He paused, then said, "I'm sorry."

I said, "How long?"

He shook his head. "Maybe a year, two if she's lucky."

I nodded, staring through the darkness at the dim buildings. I wanted to say something, but the words wouldn't come. I changed the subject.

"You think Danny's right about the Med?"

Edvard shrugged. "I honestly don't know." He was silent for a time. "I do recall when there was sea there, Pierre, and magnificent towns and cities. The rich flocked there."

Not for the first time I tried to imagine the vast bodies of water Edvard had described, water that filled areas as vast as deserts, and heaved and rolled ... I shook my head. All I saw was a desert the colour of drinking water, flat and still.

He looked into the heavens as the night sky split with a crack of white light. It was Edvard who'd explained to me why, despite all the storms that raged, we never experienced rainfall: the little rain that did fall evaporated in the superheated lower atmosphere before it reached the earth. I thought of the storms, now, as mocking us with their futile promise.

I stared around at the buildings. "You think we can rebuild? I mean, make things like they were, before?"

Edvard smiled. "I like to think that with time, and hard work ... Like Danny, I'm an optimist. I really think that people, at heart, are good. Call me a fool, if you like, but that's what I think. So ... if we could band together, always assuming there were enough people to feasibly propagate the race ... then perhaps there would be hope."

"But to get back to where things were ... civilized?" I finished.

"That's a big call, Pierre. We've lost so much, so much learning, culture. We've lost so much expertise. So much of what we knew, of what we learned over centuries of scientific investigation and understanding ... all that is gone, and can never be rediscovered. Or if it can, then it'll take centuries ... even assuming the planet isn't too far gone, even assuming that humanity can reform ..." He laughed. "And I mean reform in more than just the figurative sense."

I thought about that for a time, then said, "But with no more oceans, no more seas ... "

He smiled at me. "I live in hope, Pierre. There might be small seas, underground reserves. I heard there are still small seas where the Pacific ocean was—"

"Couldn't we ... ?" I began.

He was smiling.

"What?" I said.

"The Pacific is half a world away, Pierre. This thing might get us to the Med, if we're lucky. But not the Pacific."

I considered his words, the barren vastness of the world, and the little I knew of it. At last I said, "If we're the last ... I mean, I haven't seen another human for years."

"We aren't alone, Pierre. There are others, small bands. There must be." He was silent a while, and then said, "And anyway, even if life on Earth is doomed..."

After a few seconds I prompted him, "Yes?"

"Well," he said, "there's always Project Phoenix."

He'd told me all about Project Phoenix, the last hope. Forty years ago, when the world governments had known things were bad and getting worse, they pooled resources and constructed a starship, full of 5,000 hopeful citizens, and sent it to the stars.

Towards the east, where the sky was blackest, I made out a dozen faint glimmering points of distant stars. I thought of the starship, still on its journey, or having reached its destination and settled on a new, Earthlike planet.

"What do you think happened to the starship?" I asked.

"I like to think they're sitting up there now, enjoying paradise, and wondering what they left behind on Earth—"

He stopped and looked up into the night sky, then fitted his hand above his eyes to cut out the glare of the magnetic storm. "Je-sus Christ, Pierre." He scrambled to his feet. I joined him, my heart thumping. "What?"

Then, as I scanned the sky, I heard it – the faint drone of a distant engine.

Edvard pointed, and at last I made out what he'd seen.

High in the air, and heading towards us, was the dark shape of some kind of small plane.

I reached out for my rifle, propped against the side of the truck, and shouted at Danny and Kat to get out here.

"It's in trouble," Edvard said.

The engine was stuttering as the plane angled steeply over the distant buildings, a dark shape against the flaring storm. We watched it pass quickly overhead and come down in the desert perhaps half a kilometre beyond the truck.

Danny and Kat were out by now. "What was it?"

Edvard told them.

I said, "I'll go and check it out."

Edvard's hand gripped my arm. "It's no coincidence. A flyer doesn't just drop out of the sky so close. They knew we were here. They want something."

We all looked to Danny. He nodded. "Okay, I'll go with you. Edvard, Kat, stay here."

Kat nodded, moved to Edvard's side. Danny entered the truck and came back holding a rifle. We set off across the sands, towards where the flyer had come down.

"Je-sus Christ..." I said, bubbling with excitement. "Wonder who it is?"

Danny flashed me a look. "Whoever it is, chances are they're dangerous." He raised his rifle.

I could see he was thinking more about the flyer, and what might be salvaged from it, than who the pilot might be.

My mind was in turmoil. What if the pilot were a woman? I recalled the images of models in the magazines I'd hoarded over the years, their flawless, immaculate beauty, their haughty *you're-not-good-enough* gazes.

My heart was thudding by the time we crested a slipping dune.

In the stuttering white light of the magnetic storm we could see that the flyer had pitched nose-first into the desert. Its near wing was crumpled, snapped into flapping sections.

I thought of the irony of finding a beautiful woman sitting in the cockpit... dead.

I took a step forward. Danny said, "Remember, careful."

I nodded and led the way.

We approached slowly, as if the crumpled machine were a wounded animal.

"A glider," Danny said, "jerry-rigged with an old turbo."

I lifted my rifle and we stepped cautiously towards the shattered windshield of the cockpit.

"Oh," I said, as I made out the figure slumped against the controls.

It was a man, an old, wizened man, thin and bald and stinking. Even from a distance of two metres I could smell his adenoid-pinching body odour.

Danny cracked the cockpit's latch with the butt of his rifle. He hauled back the canopy, checked the pilot for weapons, then felt for his pulse.

"Alive," he said, but his gaze was ranging over the craft and the supplies packed tight around the cockpit.

I reached out and gently eased the pilot back into his seat, his head lolling. I looked for injuries; his torso seemed fine, but his left leg was snapped at the shin and bleeding.

Danny thought about it. I guessed he was calculating the worth of the glider and the supplies against the long-term cost of giving refuge to another needy stray. "Okay, go back to the truck and tell Kat to get it over here. Tell Ed to have his equipment ready."

I took off at a run.

Five minutes later Kat braked the truck beside the glider and we jumped out. Edvard limped through the sand and knelt in the cockpit's hatch. After examining the pilot he did something to the leg, tying off the shattered limb, then nodded to Danny and me. We eased the pilot from the glider, trying to ignore his sourdough body odour, and carried him over to the truck.

On the way I realized that he wasn't as old as I'd first thought. He was in his forties, perhaps, though his skeletal frame and bald head made him look older. He wore tattered shorts and a ripped T-shirt and nothing else.

We installed him in the lounge and Edvard got to work on the leg, aided by Kat. Danny fetched the toolkit and for the next couple of hours we took the glider apart and stowed it in the cargo hold. We ferried the supplies, packed in three silver hold-alls, to the galley.

"Water," Danny grinned as he passed me the canisters. "And dried meat, for chrissake!"

"Where the hell he get meat from?" I wondered aloud.

Danny shook his head. "We'll find that out when we question him. If he lives."

I looked across at Danny. "You hope he dies?"

He weighed the question. "He dies, and that's one less mouth... He lives, and what he knows might be valuable. Take your pick."

It was late when we returned to the lounge. The pilot was still unconscious, his leg swaddled in bandages. "Broken in a couple of places," Edvard reported. "He'll pull through. I'll stay here with him. You get some sleep."

In my berth, I stared through the canopy at the flaring night sky, too excited at the prospect of questioning the pilot to sleep.

The rocking of the truck brought me awake. Outside, the desert was on fire. I pulled on my shorts and lurched into the lounge. Kat must have been driving because Danny was sitting in his armchair, leaning forward and staring at the pilot.

"You don't know how grateful ..." the invalid said in heavily accented English between slurps of water – a half ration, I saw. He indicated his leg with the beaker. "You could have left me there ..."

Guarded, Danny said, "We reckoned it was a fair trade, the wreckage of your plane, the supplies. We'll feed you, keep you alive. But you'll have to work if you want to be part of the team."

Edvard sat on the battered sofa against the far wall. He said, "What can you do?"

The man's thin lips hitched in an uneasy smile. "This and that, a bit of tinkering, engineering. I worked on solar arrays, years ago."

I said, "What's your name?"

He stared back at me, and I didn't like the look in his eyes. Hostile. "What's yours?"

"Pierre," I said, returning his glare.

He nodded, increasing the width of his smile. "Call me Skull," he said.

It was obviously not his given name, but considering the fleshless condition of his head, and his rictus grin, it was appropriate. *Skull*.

Danny took over. "The meat you had in the glider. Where'd you get that?"

"Down south. Still some game surviving. Shot it myself."

"South?" Danny sat up, hope in his eyes. "There's water down there, sea?"

Skull looked at Danny for a second before shaking his head. "No sea. The place is almost dead."

Edvard said, "Where did you come from? With supplies like those, a plane. My guess is a colony somewhere."

I didn't like the way Skull paused after each question, as if calculating the right answer to give. "I was with a gang of no-hopers holed up in what was Algiers. Conditions were bad. The only hope was to get out, move north. But they didn't want to risk it."

"So you stole the supplies and the plane and got the hell out," Danny finished.

That sly pause, again. A shrug. "A man has to look after himself, these days."

I thought of the failing colony in Algiers, confirmation that there were others still out there.

"You're one lucky bastard you spotted us," Danny said.

Skull made a quick pout of his lips, as if to debate the point, then said, "Where you heading?"

Danny said, "The Mediterranean," and left it at that.

The stranger had this way of trying not to show any reaction, as if to do so would give something away. I wondered at the company he'd kept, where he'd had to hide his emotions like this, wary and mistrustful. At last he said, "You're joking, right?"

Danny shook his head, serious. "We've crossed Europe I don't know how many times, drilling for water. I think it's just about all dried up. My reckoning is, at the bottom of the Med, or where the sea used to be, there'll be a better chance of striking water."

"Salt water. Undrinkable sea water."

Danny smiled and played his trump. "So what? I have a desalination rig all ready if that's the case."

"But south ... the Med?" Skull shook his head. "You're mad, you know that? You heard about the scum down there? The feral bands? They'd kill you for what you got, no questions asked."

Danny shrugged. "We can look after ourselves," he said, and the confidence in his voice made me feel proud.

Skull licked his lips. "Madness."

Edvard said, from the couch, "Well, we could always leave you here, if you don't wish to accompany us."

Skull lay his head back, staring at the ceiling. "I'll take my chances with you people," he grunted.

The following day the desert gave way to high bare hills, and then a range of mountains. I sat with Danny in the cab as we drove along what might have been a highway, years ago; now it was little better than an eroded track. According to the map, we were travelling through a range of mountains called the Cevennes. We passed remnants of what had been forests, stunted trunks that covered hillsides like so many barren pegs, dead now like everything else.

This was as far south as we'd ever been, and it seemed brighter out there than I'd ever experienced. This high up, we had a perfect view of the plains to the south, a drift of golden sand that stretched all the way to what had been the Mediterranean sea.

The sun was going down when I said, "What Skull said about feral bands?"

Danny snorted. "His sort – the kind of bastard who runs out on a colony and takes their supplies ... his sort are cowards. Anyway, he's a liar."

I looked at him. "He is?"

"There's no colony in Algiers. I heard they died out way back, twenty years ago or more."

"But he must have run from somewhere?"

"Yeah, but not Algiers. He didn't want to tell us where he came from."

"Why? What's he hiding?"

"We'll find out in time, Pierre, believe me."

For the next hour he concentrated on driving, as we wound down the crumbling highway and left the hills behind us. As darkness fell, Danny braked and the truck came to a halt. After the drone of the engine, the silence was resounding.

We left the cab and moved into the lounge.

Last night Danny had allocated Skull a tiny berth at the rear of the truck, and served him his meals there. This cheered me – I wasn't alone in not wanting mealtimes spoilt by Skull's presence.

"Meat's on the menu tonight," Edvard said. He carried a steaming pot and set it down before us.

He ladled broth into our bowls and the smell sent my head reeling. For a second, I almost welcomed the arrival of the mysterious stranger.

"You okay, Kat?" I asked.

She smiled at me. I was encouraged by the way she was spooning the broth; she seemed to be enjoying the meal. I glanced at Edvard. He was chewing with his eyes closed, as if savouring not only the meat but the memories of past times it conjured.

After the meal, for the first time in months, my belly felt full.

Later I excused myself, wanting to be alone with my thoughts. I left the truck, dug myself a little hollow of cool sand, and settled down.

The night was silent, the sky unusually still. No storms ripped the heavens, for once. The air was heavy and hot, oppressive. I controlled my breathing, enjoying the cooling sand, and considered the journey south.

A sound made me jump. I thought it was Edvard, come to join me. But the skeletal figure that came hobbling out on crutches, fashioned from lengths of metal cannibalized from the wreck of the glider, was the pilot.

He eased himself down onto the sand beside me and nodded. "It's cooler out here." The little light spilling from the truck made his face seem even more skull-like. I took shallow breaths, not wanting to inhale his acid stink.

"That's why I'm here," I said.

A pause. Then, "Maybe you'll listen to sense, Pierre. I've tried the others. They're too old, set in their ways."

"They're my friends," I said, and then as if to make it clearer, "my family. We're in this together."

I looked at him. His sly eyes appeared calculating. "Listen to me, Pierre. You're no fool. If we head south, to the Med—"

"Yes?"

A pause. He licked his lips. "There's dangers down there, things you haven't encountered in Europe."

"You said. Feral bands—"

"Worse!"

"Worse than feral bands?"

"Much worse. Feral means animal. You can deal with animals, outwit 'em. These people ... these people are no fools. They're evil, and calculating." I wondered, for a second, if he were describing himself. "You ever seen what human beings can do when they're desperate?"

I thought back to the ruins of Paris, before the desert engulfed the city. I considered the people I'd lived with, and why I left. Yes, I almost told him, I've experienced desperate people, and survived. But I said nothing, reluctant to share with Skull what I'd never told anyone else, not even Danny or Kat or Edvard.

"Like Danny said," I murmured, not looking at him, "we can look after ourselves."

Skull spat viciously. "Fools, the lot of you!"

I considered what Danny had said last night. Into the following silence, I said, "What are you frightened of, Skull? What are you running away from?"

He looked at me, then grinned. "No ... you're no fool, are you?"

"Well?"

I didn't expect him to tell me, so I was surprised when he said, "People so fucking evil, so purely bad, you cannot imagine, Pierre."

And he left it at that, as if challenging me to enquire further.

I was at the wheel of the truck the following day when we came to the escarpment overlooking what had once been the Mediterranean sea.

Danny said, "Would you look at that?"

Kat and Edvard squeezed into the cab.

The land before us fell away suddenly to form a vast, scooped-out crater bigger than the eye could encompass. The dried-up sea bottom was cracked and fissured, as steely grey as the pictures I'd seen of the lunar landscape. The horizon shimmered, corrugated with heat haze.

I glanced at Danny. He was staring, speechless. I realized that before him was the goal he'd set his heart on months back, when he first had the idea to journey south.

"We'll drive on another four, five hours, then stop for the night," he said. "Over dinner we'll look at the map, plan the next leg of the journey."

Edvard and Kat moved back to the lounge. I was pleased that Skull had not bothered to show himself.

I mopped the sweat from my face. It was sweltering in the cab: the thermometer read almost thirty-five Celsius. Next to that dial was the outside temperature: fifty-five, hot enough to bake a man in less than an hour.

Danny took the wheel and drove along the coast, parallel to the escarpment, looking for a shallow entry down into what had been the sea. Five kilometres further on we came to a section of the coast which shelved gradually, and Danny eased us over the edge, moving at a snail's pace. Baked soil as fine as cement crumbled under the truck's balloon tyres. We lurched and Danny eased back the throttle, slowing our descent.

At last the land flattened out and we accelerated, the headwind blowing the dust behind us. A great plain stretched before us, rilled with expansion cracks and dotted with objects I couldn't at first make out. As we drew nearer I saw that they were the rusted hulks and skeletons of ships, fixed at angles in the sea bottom. We passed into the shadow of one, a great liner red with rust, its panels holed but the sleek lines of its remaining superstructure telling of prouder times. I found it hard to imagine that so great a vessel could actually *float* on water: it seemed beyond the laws of physics.

Danny pointed. In the lee of the ship's rearing hull I made out a pile of white spars, like bleached wood. We drew closer and I saw that they were bones. Domed orbs contrasted with the geometric precision of femur and tibia: skulls.

I shook my head. "I don't see…"

"My guess is that there was a colony on the ship, ages ago," Danny said. "As they died, one by one, the survivors pitched the bodies over the side."

"You think there's anyone left?" I asked, knowing the answer even before Danny shook his head.

"This was probably thirty years ago, at a guess. Back when the drought was getting bad and nations collapsed. Tribes formed, the rule of law broke down. It was every man for himself. Colonies formed on ships, while the oceans still existed – away from the wars on dry land."

I shook my head, thinking of the horrors that must have overtaken the shipboard colonies in their last, desperate days.

We drove on, heading south.

A couple of hours later, to our right, the sea-bed rose to form a series of pinnacles, five in all. They towered above the seared landscape for hundreds of metres, their needle peaks silhouetted against a sky as bright as aluminium.

Danny glanced at his map. "They were the Balearic Islands, part of old Spain."

"People lived up there?" I asked, incredulous.

He smiled. "They were small areas of land, Pierre, surrounded by sea. Islands."

I shook my head, struggling to envisage such a configuration of land and sea. On the summit of the nearest peak I made out the square shapes of dwellings, the tumbledown walls of others.

We left the stranded islands behind us.

Three hours later the sun went down to our right in a blaze of crimson. Ahead, indigo twilight formed over Africa, the sky untouched by magnetic storms.

Kat called from the lounge, "Food in ten minutes!"

Danny brought the truck to a halt and we moved back to the lounge. He unfolded one of his maps and indicated our position.

Kat served us plates of fried potatoes and greens – rationing the meat. She was carrying a plate across the lounge for our passenger when Skull emerged from his berth and limped to the table.

"Don't mind if I join you folks tonight? I was getting lonesome back there."

I returned to my meal without a word. Edvard indicated a chair and Skull dropped into it, wincing quickly.

Danny stubbed a forefinger at the map.

"So this is where we are now, and this is where we're heading – a hundred kilometres north of what was the coast of Africa, off a place called Tangiers."

Skull stopped chewing. He looked across at Danny, uneasy. "Let me see …" He leaned forward, peering.

He looked up. "I don't like the sound of it."

I took a swallow of water, aware of my heartbeat and the sauna heat of the room.

Danny nodded, considering his words. "And why not?"

"Like I said before, there's feral bands down there. We'd best avoid them."

"There specifically, Skull?" Danny asked. "How come you're so certain?"

Skull chewed, not looking away from Danny's stare. "I heard stories, rumours."

Danny lay down his knife and fork in an odd gesture of civility that belied the anger on his face. "Bullshit. Tell us straight – what the hell do you know?"

Skull's eyes darted from right to left, taking in Danny and Kat, Edvard and myself. He looked uneasy, a rat cornered.

Edvard said quietly, "You didn't come from Algiers. So where did you come from?"

The silence stretched. Skull used his tongue to work free a strand of fibre from between his teeth. "Okay, okay … I was travelling with some people. Only they weren't people. Animals more like, monsters. A dozen or so of them. They had a vehicle, a collection of solar arrays lashed together around a failing engine … Anyway, they were heading west, towards Tangiers."

Danny nodded. "Why?"

Skull shrugged. "They didn't say. They invited me to stay awhile. They needed an engineer to help out, they said. So I travelled with them a few days, a week."

I said, "Why did you leave them?"

"Because I reckoned that soon, once I'd helped out with the arrays, I would've outlived my usefulness and they'd kill me rather than have me using up food and water. They were that kind of people."

He looked around at us, then bolted down the last of the food, stood with difficulty and hoiked himself from the lounge.

Danny said, "So, what do you think? He telling the truth?"

Edvard voiced what I was thinking. "I wouldn't trust him as far as I could spit. Which isn't far, these days."

I said, "We've come across bastard gangs before. We just have to be careful, that's all."

Kat nodded. "I second that."

"What I'd like to know," Edvard said, "is what's so important about Tangiers that this mob was heading for it?"

I was in the cab with Edvard the following day when we came across the hovercraft.

It was late afternoon and we were roughly a hundred kilometres north of the trench, our destination. The sea bottom desert stretched ahead for as far as the eye could see, flat and featureless.

I was nodding off in the heat when Edvard slowed the truck. I sat up and looked across at him. He indicated the horizon with a silent nod.

I scanned. Far ahead, coruscating in the merciless afternoon glare, was the domed shape of a vehicle, entirely covered by an armature of solar arrays. At this distance it looked for all the world like a diamond-encrusted beetle.

It was not moving. I guessed its occupants had seen us and halted, wary.

Edvard brought the truck to a stop and called out to Danny.

Seconds later Danny and Kat squeezed into the cab and crouched between us.

"What do you think?" I said.

"Big," Danny said under his breath. "Impressive arrays. Of course, they might not all be in working order." He screwed up his eyes. "I don't see any evidence of a rig. Wonder what they do for water?"

Kat said, "What should we do?"

"Break out the rifles, Pierre. Ed, take us forward slowly."

I slipped from the cab and hurried into the lounge. I unlocked the chest where we kept the rifles and hauled out four, one each. I carried them back to the cab and doled them out as the truck crawled forward.

The occupants of the other vehicle were doing the same, advancing carefully across the desert towards us. We slowed even further, and so did the other truck. We must have resembled two circumspect crabs, unsure whether to mate or fight.

"It's a hovercraft," Kat said. Despite her years, she had sharp eyes. Only now, with the vehicle perhaps half a kay from us, did I make out the bulbous skirts below the layered solar arrays. As Danny had said, it was big; perhaps half the size again of our truck.

"Okay," Danny told Edvard. "Bring us to a stop now."

The truck halted with a hiss of brakes. Edvard kept the engine ticking over.

The hovercraft stopped too, mirroring our caution.

My heart was thudding. I was sweating even more than usual. I gripped the rifle to my chest. Minutes passed. Nothing moved out there. I imagined the hovercraft's occupants, wondering like us whether we constituted a threat or an opportunity.

"What now?" I asked Danny. I realized I was whispering.

"We sit tight. Let them make the first move."

This was the first time I'd seen a working vehicle, other than our own, in more than three years, physical proof that other people beside us were out there.

"What's that?" Kat said.

Something was moving on the flank of the vehicle. As we watched, a big hatch hinged open and people came out. I counted five individuals, tiny at this distance. They paused in the shadow of the craft, staring across at us.

Minutes passed. They made no move to approach.

Edvard said, "Looks like they're armed." He paused. "What do we do?"

Danny licked his lips. "They made the first move. Maybe we should match it."

"I'll go out," I said.

"Not alone." This was Kat, a hand on my arm.

Danny nodded. "I'll come with you." To Edvard and Kat he said, "Keep us covered. If they do anything, fire first and ask questions later, okay?"

Kat nodded and slipped the barrel of her rifle through the custom-made slits in the frame of the windscreen. Edvard crouched next to her.

Danny and I left the cab and hurried through the lounge, grabbing sun hats on the way. Danny cracked the door and we stepped out into the blistering heat. I stopped dead in my tracks, drawing in a deep breath of superheated air, thankful for the shade afforded by my hat. This was the first time in months that I'd ventured from the truck in the full heat of day, and I felt suddenly dizzy.

I expected the ground to be like the desert, deep sand making each step an effort. Instead it was hard, baked dry. We paused by the truck, staring across at the five figures standing abreast.

"Okay..." Danny said.

We left the truck at a stroll, our rifles slung barrels down in the crooks of our arms. Ahead, there was movement in the group. One of the figures ducked back into the hatch and emerged with something. At first I assumed it was some kind of weapon; evidently so did Danny. He reached out a hand, staying my progress.

As we watched, four of the figures erected a frame over the fifth. It was some kind of sun-shade. Only when it was fully erected, and the central figure suitably shaded, did the entourage move forward.

"Christ," I said. We were a hundred metres from the group now, and I saw that the central figure was a woman.

She was tall, statuesque, like one of the models in the old magazines. She was bare legged and bare armed, wearing only shorts and a tight shirt which emphasised the swelling of her chest. As we drew within ten metres of the group, I saw that her face was long, severe, her mouth hard and her nose hooked. But I wasn't looking at her face.

Something turned over in my gut, the same heavy lust I experienced when looking at the long-dead magazine models.

Danny said, "Do you speak English, French?"

"I speak English," the woman said in an accent I couldn't place. She looked middle-eastern to my inexperienced eye.

Her henchmen were a feeble mob. They looked starved, emaciated, and a couple were scabbed with ugly melanomas which covered their faces like masks.

"We're from the north," Danny said.

"Old Egypt." The woman inclined her head. "My name is Samara."

"I'm Danny. This is Pierre."

I glanced at the hovercraft. I saw the barrel of a rifle directed at us from an open vent. I nudged Danny, who nodded minimally and said under his breath, "I've seen it."

The woman said, "Do you trade?"

"That depends what you want."

Samara inclined her head again. "Do you have water?"

Beside me, Danny seemed to relax. We were in a position of power in this stand-off. He said, "What do you have to trade?"

The women licked her lips. I found the gesture sensuous. I gazed at her shape, the curve of her torso from breast to hip.

She said, "Solar arrays."

I sensed Danny's interest. "In good working order?"

"Of course. You can check them before the trade."

"How many are you talking about?"

She pointed to a panel which overhung the flank of her craft. "Four, like that."

Danny calculated. "I can give you ... four litres of water in return."

"Ten," she said.

"Six," Danny said with admirable force, "or no deal."

I stared at the woman. She needed water more than we needed the arrays. I saw her look me up and down, and I felt suddenly, oddly, vulnerable.

She nodded, then spoke rapidly to one of her guards in a language I didn't recognize. Two of her men returned to their craft, the weight of the sun-shade taken up by the two who remained.

I was reminded, by her regal stance beneath the shade and her henchmen's quick attention to duty, of an illustration I had seen in a magazine of an Ancient Egyptian Queen.

Her big, dark eyes regarded me again. She smiled. I found myself looking away, flushing.

Her men returned, hauling the solar arrays. They lay them on the sand and backed off. Samara gestured, and Danny stepped forward to examine the arrays while I covered him.

Minutes later he looked back at me and nodded.

"They look okay," he told the woman. "We'll take them."

"I'll have them placed between our vehicles," she said. "If you bring out the water, we will meet halfway."

Danny nodded. He stood and rejoined me. To Samara he said, "What have you been doing for water?"

She paused before replying. "There is a settlement with a rig about 200 kilometres east of here, along the old coast. They have a deep bore. We trade with them every so often. You?"

Danny said, "We trade with a colony up in old Spain."

The woman nodded, and I wondered if she'd seen through the lie. She said, "And how many of you live in the truck?"

"Five," he said. He nodded at the hovercraft. "And you?"

"Just six," she said.

Danny said, "We'll fetch the water."

We turned our backs on the woman and her men and began the slow walk back to the truck. I felt uneasy, presenting such an easy target like that, but I knew I was being irrational. They wanted water, after all; they would gain nothing by shooting us now.

"You hear that?" Danny said. "A mob has a deep bore, east of here. So there *is* water."

He unlocked the hatch on the side of the truck where we stored the water. We hauled out two plastic canisters and carried them back to where the woman's lackeys had placed the arrays. She stood over the shimmering rectangles, watching us as we placed the canisters on the ground.

She snapped something to one of the men, who opened the canister and tipped a teaspoonful of water into his palm. He lifted it to his cracked lip and tasted the water. After a second he nodded to Samara and said something in their language.

I could not keep my eyes off the woman. Her legs were bare, long and brown, and I could see the cleavage of her breasts between the fabric of her bleached blouse. She saw me looking and stared at me, her expression unreadable. I looked away quickly.

She said, "Where are you heading?"

Danny waved vaguely. "South."

She looked surprised. "Tangiers?"

"In that direction, yes."

She calculated. "Then we should travel together, no? There are bandits in the area. Together we are stronger."

Danny looked at me, and I found myself nodding.

"Very well, we'll do that. We stop at sunset, set off at dawn."

Samara smiled. "To Tangiers, then."

She said something to her men and two of them took the canisters. She turned and walked towards the hovercraft, flanked by her sunshade toting lackeys.

I watched her go.

Danny laughed and said, "Put your tongue away and help me with these."

We hauled the arrays across the sea-bed and stowed them in the truck.

We stepped into the lounge to find an altercation in progress.

Skull was standing at one end of the room, Kat and Edvard at the other. Skull's face was livid with rage, his lips contorted, eyes wide with accusation.

"You told her!" he yelled across at us as we entered. "You contacted her and told her I was here!"

I looked across at Edvard. He said, "He came flying from his berth, shouting insane accusations."

"That's because you bastards told her!"

I was glad he had a broken leg; able-bodied, he would undoubtedly have attacked us.

Danny said, "Calm down. We told no one. Listen to me – we don't have a radio, okay? How could we have contacted her if we don't possess a damned radio? And anyway, why the hell would we tell her we'd picked you up?"

Skull let go of his crutch to gesture beyond the truck. "So how come she's found me?"

I moved into the lounge and sat down, watching Skull. Danny joined me, gesturing Skull to a seat opposite. Glaring at us, he stumped across the lounge and sat down. Kat and Edvard joined us.

Danny said, reasonably, "Are you sure it's the same mob?"

"How many hovercraft you think are out there?" Skull snorted. "And you think I wouldn't recognize the queen bitch herself?"

Kat said, "It's a coincidence. They saw us from a distance, and as they needed water ..."

Skull shook his head. "Some coincidence! Do you know how big this desert is? The chances of two tiny vehicles meeting like this—"

Edvard said, "We didn't contact them, Skull. So it has to be coincidence, no? What other explanation is there?"

"The plane," Danny said. "You took it from them, right? What about this: that she had it tagged with some kind of tracking device? It'd make sense, a valuable piece of kit like that."

Skull held his head in his hands and sobbed.

I said, "What have you got to fear?"

He looked up, staring through his tears. "She's evil. They all are. I ran out on her because I didn't like what she was doing. She won't rest till I'm dead. And now she's found you, she won't stop at just killing me."

"You make her sound like a monster," I said.

He nodded. "Oh, she is. She might have traded solar arrays now, but she'll be scheming to get them back – and more. Right now they'll be working out how to kill us, take the truck ..."

Danny shook his head. "I don't think so. There's only six of them – and we're well armed. The truck's armoured. We can defend ourselves."

Skull brayed a laugh. "Six! Is that what she told you? She's lying. There were a dozen of the bastards with her when I left."

I looked across at Danny, who said, "Like I said, we can look after ourselves."

"Okay, but the best defence is distance. Let's get the hell away from her before she attacks us, okay?"

Danny considered. We had agreed with Samara that we would travel south together; it would be hard to shake her, especially if Skull was correct in thinking she had come for him.

Danny nodded and said to Kat, "Okay, start us up. Let's move on." Kat and Edvard moved to the cab. Skull nodded, gratefully. "Thank Christ ..." was all he said before hiking himself upright on his crutches and hobbling back to his berth. I watched him go, wondering what his reaction might be when he discovered that Samara was following us.

I sat with Danny. The silence was broken by the drone of the engine as Kat kicked the truck into life.

I said, "What do you think?"

Danny rubbed his beard. "I think we trust no one but ourselves, Pierre. We keep Samara at arm's length, and as for Skull—"

"Yes?"

"As Edvard said yesterday, I don't trust him as far as I can spit."

I moved to the rear of the truck and sat before an observation screen, staring out across the sea-bed. Through the sandy spindrift of our wake, I made out the scintillating shape of the hovercraft. It was perhaps half a kilometre behind us, and keeping pace.

For the next couple of hours before sunset, my thoughts slipped between Skull's warning and fantasies involving Samara. I interpreted the way she looked at me as indicating desire on her part, and told myself that her henchmen were less than prime physical specimens.

The sun went down, replaced by the deep blue of night shot through with the raging flares of magnetic storms. Kat brought the truck to a standstill and Edvard fixed a meal.

The hovercraft slowed and came alongside, sinking to the sand a hundred metres from us with a curtsey of rubber skirts.

I moved to the lounge and joined Danny and Kat. Edvard ferried plates from the galley and slid them onto the table. The heady scent of braised meat filled the air.

We ate quietly, subdued. Danny had told Edvard and Kat about the travel pact with Samara, and from time to time I saw Kat glance through the hatch at the settled hovercraft across the sand.

I said, "What do we do when we get to the trench?"

Danny chewed on a mouthful of tough meat. "We stop."

"But we don't set up the rig, right?"

"Of course not. I don't want her knowing anything about the rig. We stop the night and in the morning feign a mechanical fault. And if she doesn't go on without us, then we know she wants something."

"Skull?" Kat said.

"And maybe the rest of us," Danny said in a low voice.

Five minutes later Skull emerged from his berth. I was waiting for his reaction when he saw the hovercraft, but evidently he was already aware of its presence. He said, "You see, she's following us. She knows I'm here. Tonight, they'll come across ... " He seemed resigned to his fate, no longer angry.

Danny said, "You don't know that. Anyway, the truck's secure."

Skull considered a reply, but merely nodded his acknowledgment of Danny's words, grabbed his bowl of food and returned to his berth.

We finished the meal in uneasy silence.

Later I took my rifle outside, broke up the surface crust, and scooped myself a hollow in the sand beneath.

The hovercraft squatted a hundred metres away, an ugly beetle armoured in a patchwork of solar arrays. Evidently the crew had exited and were having a party on the far side of the vehicle. I heard the sound of drunken voices, raised in revelry.

I undressed and rubbed myself with sand, ridding myself of the day's sweat and grime. I lay back and closed my eyes.

Minutes later a sound startled me. I opened my eyes. Someone had cracked a hatch on the flank of the hovercraft and was crossing the sand towards the truck. I judged I had no time to get dressed before they arrived, so instead reached out and grabbed the rifle.

Then I paddled a heap of sand onto my groin, covering myself.

I stared into the darkness, making out the figure as it emerged into the light falling from the lounge behind me, and I set aside the rifle.

Samara halted about three metres away, smiling down at me. She had discarded her shorts and blouse of earlier. Now she wore a thin white dress which hugged her chest, flanks and belly and flowed around her bare legs.

And there was something else about her, something I had not noticed on our first meeting. She smelled of flowers.

My heart banged like a faulty engine.

She moved closer and knelt, tossing a strand of dark hair from her face. Her scent almost overwhelmed me. "I saw you out here. Thought it was you."

I opened my mouth. I wanted to ask what she wanted, but no words came. I was very aware of how ridiculous I looked, torso and legs emerging from the hollow I'd dug in the sand.

She sat before me, cross-legged. "So I thought I'd come over, say hello."

It struck me then that, unless she was a consummate actress, she was as nervous as I was. A catch in her voice, a hesitation in her gaze as it flicked from the sand to my upper torso.

The dress was low-cut, and I could not keep my eyes from the swelling of her breasts.

"You know, I get lonely, surrounded by ..." she gestured over her shoulder with a long-fingered hand, "those animals."

I said, "It must be," I shrugged, "difficult to control them."

She smiled. "Oh, I have my ways." She wasn't beautiful, nor really pretty, but when she smiled her face changed, became suddenly attractive. She shrugged, and the way her breasts moved together ...

I responded. The sand at my groin stirred, disturbed.

She saw it, reached out and took me.

I surged upright with a moan, and she lifted her dress, pushed me back onto the sand and straddled me. I closed my eyes as she eased herself around me, impossibly warm and fluid. I reached out, dug my fingers into her bottom as she rocked, leaning forward and pressing her breasts into my face.

Minutes later it was over. I spasmed in ecstasy and cried aloud, then lay back in the cool sand as she gripped me and shook, her teeth biting the flesh of my shoulder.

I was near to tears. I thought back over the long, lonely years, the years of thwarted desire, of wondering if I would ever experience such intimacy.

She whispered something to me, then rolled off and pulled her dress down over her nakedness. Before I could protest, she stood and padded back to the hovercraft.

I stared into the storm-ripped night sky. Beyond the hovercraft, her crew was still partying. A hot wind blew. It was like a hundred other nights, a thousand, I had experienced in the hell that was my world, and yet tonight I felt an elation beyond description.

I considered what Skull had said about her, and contrasted his words with what I had experienced. How could she be the evil woman that he claimed she was, when she gave herself like that, and parted with such words? It was her farewell which convinced me.

"Thank you," she had whispered.

I was woken in the early hours by a shout.

I sat up, listening. I heard the sound of a scuffle in the lounge, loud footsteps and something crashing to the floor. I pulled on my clothes and pushed open the door. I made out movement along the narrow corridor to the lounge.

In the dim light I saw half a dozen figures, and someone struggling in their midst.

I hurried along the corridor, regretting having stowed away my rifle in the locker.

I stopped dead when I came to the lounge.

Three individuals had Skull bound and gagged, and another three stood guard, armed with rifles. They faced Danny and Kat, who had just emerged from their room. Seconds later Edvard appeared.

One of the men saw me and gestured with his rifle. "Move. Join the others."

The point of his weapon tracked me as I rounded the group and joined my friends. From this angle I could see more of Skull. He was on his knees, arms tied behind his back. A gag obscured the lower half of his face, but above it his eyes blazed with the anger of betrayal.

Kat clutched Danny's arm, and I understood her fear. I wondered if this was where four years of comparative security and safety would come to an end. Too late, I knew we should have listened to Skull.

Calmly, Danny said, "What do you want?"

I looked around the faces of the men. Many I did not recognize from our meeting the day before; so evidently Samara had been lying when she claimed a crew of half a dozen.

One of the men, bigger and meaner looking than the others, nodded down to Skull. "We've got what we came for."

I felt an almost incredulous relief – then checked myself. He must be lying, surely? They could kill us and ransack the truck, taking our water and provisions and laying claim to the vehicle itself.

A scrawny African looked around the lounge with evident disgust. "We'd as soon as kill you all ..." There were mutters of assent from those around him. "But *she* doesn't want that. She said just take the bastard." He grinned. "It's your lucky day."

Skull struggled, tried to say something. Someone cuffed him around the head. Their leader grunted in their language and they kicked open the hatch and left the lounge, dragging Skull with them.

As soon as they were gone, Kat hurried across the room and closed the door. The lock was smashed. "Don't worry about it, Kat," Edvard said. "I'll fix it."

We sat down around the table in silence. I think each of us felt pretty much the same mix of emotions: a vast relief that we were still alive, a kind of retrospective dread of what *might* have become of us, and guilt as we thought back to the reassurances we had given Skull.

Eventually, Kat said, "So ... what do we do?"

Danny said, "We leave right now. Head for the trench as first planned. Lose them. We were lucky, just now. Let's not push that luck. Yes?"

He looked around at each of us. Edvard and Kat nodded their agreement.

"Pierre?"

I thought of Samara, the ecstasy I had experienced with her just hours ago. At last I nodded. "Let's get the hell out of here," I said.

Danny drove, Kat in the cab beside him. Edvard retired to his bunk in an attempt to catch some sleep. I tried to sleep, but visions of Samara's body, and the look of terror in Skull's eyes as he was dragged away, kept me awake.

I moved to the rear of the truck and looked out through the observation screen. The sun was coming up ahead of us, casting our long shadow far behind. As I stared, I made out the glinting, glimmering shape of Samara's hovercraft, following steadily in our wake.

My stomach lurched with a sensation that was not wholly dread.

We made steady progress during the day, south-west towards the trench. The hovercraft tracked us all the way, a constant presence. I moved to the cab in the early afternoon. Danny glanced at me. "Still there?"

I nodded.

He eased the throttle forward gently and we accelerated. Kat slipped from the passenger seat and moved through the lounge. I sat beside Danny as we crawled over the sea-bed. Ahead, the sun was a blinding white explosion high above the horizon. All around us the sea-bed was barren, utterly lifeless.

Kat returned. "They're still there, keeping pace."

"What the hell do they want?" Danny muttered. "I mean, they could have taken everything we had back there."

"Perhaps Samara was being truthful," I said. "She wants us to travel together, for safety. And she just wanted Skull back, for her own reasons ..." It sounded lame, even as I spoke the words.

Danny shook his head. "I don't buy it. They want something."

Two hours later, as the sun sank and ignited the horizon as if it were touch-paper, Danny signalled ahead. I made out, perhaps a kilometre before us, a dark irregularity in the sea-bed, a mere line widening as it ran away from us.

We had arrived at the eastern end of the sea-bottom trench. Danny slowed and veered so that we were travelling parallel to the widening rift.

"I reckon Tangiers is around a hundred kays south-west of here," he said. "I'm going to stop here and just pray that the bastards keep on going."

He eased the truck to a halt beside the lip of the ridge. After the drone of the engine, the silence rang with its own eerie volume. We sat quietly as the truck ticked and cracked around us, and minutes later saw what we were secretly fearing.

To our left, the hovercraft moved into view, slowed and settled a couple of hundred metres from us.

Danny said, almost in a whisper, "I just hope Skull didn't tell them about the rig."

The very idea filled me with dread. I stared out at the hovercraft's array-encrusted carapace, expecting at any second a hatch to crack and Samara's men to come pouring out.

After ten minutes, with no discernible movement from the vehicle, I began to breathe a little easier.

We ate the evening meal in silence: potatoes and spinach. As I ate, I wondered if Kat and Edvard had been unable to bring themselves to prepare Skull's gift of meat. We hardly exchanged a word, and afterwards I moved to the hatch and peered through the window.

The hovercraft was a dark, domed shape in the darkness. Samara's crew were partying again. They had lit a fire on the far side of the vehicle, and its flickering crimson illumination danced above the uneven crenellation of the solar-arrays.

I made a decision. I turned to where my friends were still seated. "I'm going over there. I want to talk to Samara, find out why they took Skull."

Kat looked shocked. "I can't let you go—"

"I— Samara won't harm me," I said. "I'll try to get a promise from her, that her men won't attack us."

Kat made to protest further, but Danny lay a quick hand on hers, and nodded at me silently. Something in his gaze told me he was aware of what had passed between me and Samara the night before.

Edvard said, "If you're going, then for God's sake take this." He moved to the weapon's locker and withdrew a small pistol.

I hesitated, then nodded and tucked it into the band of my shorts.

I nodded farewell and slipped from the truck. I stopped and stared across the dark expanse of sand to the hovercraft, my heart pounding. I was about to set off towards the vehicle when a door hinged open in its flank and a figure stepped out. I smiled, relieved.

She stopped when she saw me, a hand still on the door.

I crossed the cooling sea-bed towards her.

I came within range of her heady scent and my senses reeled. She stroked my cheek. "I hoped you'd be out, Pierre. I was going to invite you over … It'll be more comfortable here, yes?"

"What about …?" I gestured to the far side of the vehicle.

She smiled. "They're having their fun, Pierre. We won't be disturbed, okay?"

I could only nod, all thoughts of asking what had become of Skull forgotten.

She took me by the hand and led me into the hovercraft. We moved down a warren of tight corridors, past tiny stinking cubicles where her crew slept, and a rack containing the canisters of water we had traded with her. We ducked through a hatch into a larger chamber – evidently the engine room where the dangling leads of the solar arrays were coupled to banked generators.

Samara's room was beyond this.

I stopped on the threshold and stared.

The room was twice the size of the lounge back at the truck, and sumptuous. A vast bed occupied the centre of the room. To the left was a small window, looking out onto the sea-bed. Through thin curtains I made out the flare of the fire and the sound of voices, loud and drunk.

Then I saw, in the far corner of the chamber, a clear perspex kiosk. I crossed to it, then turned to Samara with a question.

"A shower," she said.

I repeated the word.

She smiled. "It's a water shower," she said.

I looked at her. "But how can you...?"

"I make sure we're well supplied, Pierre. And of course it's recycled after I've used it."

I could hardly conceive of the luxury of having sufficient water to use for bathing.

She took my hand and pulled me towards the bed. We kissed. She reached behind her, unbuttoned her dress and let it fall. I stared like a fool as she rolled onto the bed and smiled up at me.

I pulled off my shirt and dropped my shorts. Samara laughed.

I reddened. "What?"

"I see that you have more than one weapon in there, Pierre."

I struggled to explain the presence of the pistol. "Ed, he said I might need it."

"A wise move in these times." She reached out and pulled me onto the bed.

We made love, Samara urging me to slow down, take my time, as she opened herself to me.

Time was obliterated. I had no idea how long might have passed. I lost, too, all sense of self. It was as if I were an animal, indulging in primal appetites, oblivious of anything else but the pleasures of the flesh. Samara was ferocious, biting me, scratching. I felt a heady sense of accomplishment, almost of power, that I could instil in her such a display of passion.

Later we lay in each other's arms, slick with sweat and exhausted. She sat up, left the bed and padded to the shower. I watched her, overcome with the sight of her nakedness. She gestured for me to join her.

We stepped into the cubicle and stood together, belly to belly. She touched the controls and I gasped. Warm water cascaded over our heads, and I experienced both a sense of pleasure at the silken warmth of the water, and guilt at the profligate use of such a resource.

She passed me something, a small white block.

"Soap," she explained. "Rub me with it."

I did so, surprised by the resulting foam, and we made love again.

We dried ourselves and lay on the bed, facing each other. I stroked her cheek. Even then I knew that this was a passing pleasure, unexpected and delightful but hedged with danger. I knew that it could not last.

Then, as if reading my thoughts, Samara traced a finger across my ribs and said, "You can stay here, if you wish. Leave the others, travel with me. The life is hard, but I have my comforts."

I stared at her, at her hard eyes, her cruel mouth. Even then I had wits enough to wonder if she harboured ulterior motives.

I said, "And leave my ... my family?"

"You'd have me, Pierre," she said. "We'd want for nothing. We'd eat well."

I wondered if she had a hydroponics expert aboard. I'd seen no evidence of things growing in my brief passage through the hovercraft.

She leaned on one elbow, staring down at me. "And things will get better, believe me."

I shook my head. "How?" I asked, wondering suddenly if she had information about a thriving colony somewhere.

"We're heading to Tangiers," she said.

"There's a colony there?"

She smiled. "There was once a successful colony at Tangiers, Pierre. It died out, I've heard, a few years ago."

"Then ... " I shrugged. "Why go there?"

She paused, stroking my chest. "The colony was religious – one of those insane cults that flourished as civilization died. They called themselves the Guardians of the Phoenix."

I shook my head. "I've never heard of them."

She looked at me. "But you've heard of Project Phoenix?"

"Edvard told me about it," I said. "A ship was sent to the stars, hoping to find a new Earth."

She was smiling. "That was the plan, anyway."

"The plan? You mean ..."

"I mean the ship was almost built, in orbit, before the end – but the funding ran out, and governments lost control. The project became just another dead hope—"

"How do you know this?"

She rolled from the bed, crossed the room to a small wooden table and returned with a sheaf of papers.

"A read-out," she said, curling next to me. "I obtained it years ago from a trader. This was before the Guardians of the Phoenix died out. It's an official report about the winding up of the Project, and the resources that remained."

I leafed through the papers. They were covered in a flowing script that made no sense to me.

Samara said, "It's an Arabic translation."

I lay the papers to one side. "And?"

"And it contains information about the spaceport at Tangiers. It's a copy of the so-called sacred papers on which the Guardians founded their cult."

"I don't see—"

"Pierre, the Tangiers spaceport was where the supply ships would be launched from, before the departure from orbit of the *Phoenix* itself."

"Supply ships," I said, suddenly understanding. "You reckon they're still there, the supply ships, full of everything the colonists would need for the journey – food, water ..."

She laughed suddenly, disconcerting me. "Oh, I'm sorry, Pierre! You are so naïve. No, the colonists would not need such supplies as food and water."

"They wouldn't?" I said, puzzled.

"The supply ships at Tangiers, some dozen or so, were full of the colonists. But they were frozen in suspended animation, and would be for the duration of their trip to the stars. Five thousand of them."

I stared at her. "Five thousand? That's ... that's a city," I said. "Christ, yes ... With so many, we could start again, rebuild civilization."

Samara brought me up short. "Pierre, you've got it wrong. We couldn't sustain a colony of 5,000. How would we feed them? What about water? Pierre, face it – the Earth is almost dead. It's everyone for themselves, now."

"Then—?" I gestured at the print-out. "What do you mean? You said there were colonists?"

She stroked my jaw, almost pityingly. "Of course there are, but we couldn't just revive them to ... to *this*. That would be ... cruel."

"Then what?" I began.

She jumped from the bed and crossed the room, kneeling beside a curtained window and gesturing for me to join her.

Bewildered, I did.

She eased the curtain aside and inclined her head towards the revelry outside. A dozen men stood around a blazing fire, singing drunkenly. They were swigging from plastic bottles and eating something.

I turned to Samara. "What?"

Her hand, on my shoulder, was gentle. "The fire ..." was all she said.

I looked again at the fire, at the spit stretched across the leaping flames, and at what was skewered upon the spit.

I felt suddenly sick, and in terrible danger. My vision misted.

I said, "Skull?"

Samara murmured, "He was a traitor. He was against our plans. He stole supplies, water."

"But ... but ... " I said, gesturing to what was going on out there.

"Pierre, Pierre. Life is hard. The Earth is dying. There is no hope. We must do what we must do to survive. If that means—"

I said, "The colonists."

She did not say the world, but her smile was eloquent enough.

Meat.

She led me back to the bed and pulled me down, facing me and gently stroking my face. "Pierre, come with me. Life will be good. We will rule the Mediterranean."

Despite myself, I felt my body respond. She laughed, and we made love again – violently now, like animals attempting to prove superiority. This time, I did not lose my sense of self. I was all too conscious of Skull's words, his warnings. I was in control enough to know that however much I revelled in the pleasures of the flesh with Samara, this had to be the last time.

She gasped and closed her eyes. Fighting back my tears, I rolled over and reached down beside the bed.

"Pierre?" she said. She sat up, but she had no time to stop me. She merely registered sudden alarm with a widening of her eyes.

I shot her through the forehead, sobbing as I did so, and only in retrospect hoping that the sound of the gunshot would go unheard amid the noise of the party outside.

I stood and dressed quickly, then moved to the door. On the way I stopped, returned to the bed and picked up the print-out.

At the door I paused, and forced myself to take one last glance. Samara was sprawled across the bed, the most beautiful thing I had seen in my life.

I fled the room. I passed through the chamber housing the solar arrays. Despite the desire to get away, I knew what I must do. I spent a long minute looking over the couples and leads, then judiciously snapped a bunch of connections and removed a capacitor. The hovercraft would be going nowhere for a long, long time, if ever.

I hurried along the corridor until I came to the water canisters. I grabbed two, made it to the hatch and stumbled into the night, gasping air and hauling the canisters towards the truck. I imagined some drunken reveller finding Samara and chasing me, catching me before I reached safety ...

I barged into the lounge, startling Edvard, Danny and Kat. They stared wide-eyed as I staggered towards them.

"Pierre?" Kat said.

"Start up! We've got to get out of here!"

Kat, closest to the cab, needed no second telling. She scrambled through the hatch and seconds later the engine kicked into life. The truck surged, heading west.

Sobbing, I collapsed into a chair.

Danny and Edvard knelt before me. "Pierre ...?" Danny reached out and touched my shoulder.

I passed the print-out to Edvard and told them about Samara and her men.

For the next four hours, as the truck headed along the ridge of the crest, I was afraid lest the cannibals repair their vehicle and follow us, crazed with the desire to avenge their dead queen. I sat at the rear of the truck, staring through the dust of our wake.

An hour or two before dawn, Danny turned the truck and we headed nose-down into the trench. We bucked down the incline, then straightened out and accelerated. A little later he judged that we had put enough distance between ourselves and the hovercraft: he slowed the truck and stopped with the sloping wall of the trench to our left.

I joined Danny and Kat, and together we set up the rig and dropped the longest bore through the crazed surface of the old sea-bed.

"Where's Edvard?" I asked as I locked the final length of drill column into place.

Kat nodded back to the truck. "In there, trying to translate the print-out."

Danny stabbed the controls that dropped the drill-head, then stood back mopping the sweat from his brow. It was still dark, but the sky in the east was turning magnesium bright with the approach of dawn and already the temperature was in the high thirties.

Dog tired, I returned to the truck to catch some sleep.

An hour later I was awakened by a cry from outside. I surged upright, thinking we were under attack. I launched myself from the truck, into the heat of the day, and stared around in panic.

Kat and Danny were standing in the shadow of the rig, holding hands and staring at the bore.

As I watched, the trickle of water bubbling from around the drill column became a surge, then a fountain-head. I ran to join them and we embraced as the water showered down around us.

I opened my mouth and drank. "It's fresh!" I shouted. "My God, it's fresh!" I held Kat's thin body to me, looking into her eyes and crying with more than just the joy of finding water.

We dismantled the rig and stowed it aboard the truck. Danny marked the position of the bore on the map, and the three of us sat in the cab as we accelerated up the incline of the trench.

Later, Edvard joined us. I glanced at him as I drove.

Kat said, "What is it?"

Edvard seemed subdued. He sat between us, staring down at the print-out in his lap.

Danny said, "Ed? You okay?"

He lifted the sheaf of papers. "The colonists," he said in barely a whisper, "number some 5,500, and they were selected to found a new world on some far star. Among them are ..." his voice caught "... are doctors and scientists and engineers, specialists in every field you can imagine."

He looked around at us, tears in his eyes

We drove on in silence, into the blazing sun, towards Tangiers.

LIFE IN THE ANTHROPOCENE

Paul Di Filippo

Paul Di Filippo is a prolific science-fiction writer and critic noted for his colourful, quirky and highly original, vivacious stories that have been appearing at a relentless pace for over twenty years. A selection will be found in Ribofunk *(1996),* Fractal Paisleys *(1997),* Lost Pages *(1998),* Shuteye for the Timebroker *(2006) and a half-dozen other volumes. Although he's American, I sometimes wonder if his often surreal stories appeal more to the SF community outside of the US, because his stories have won the British SF Award and the French Imaginaire Award but he has yet to win a Hugo or Nebula, although his short novel* A Year in Linear City *(2002) was shortlisted for just about everything. I always know that when you come to read anything by Paul, it will be unlike anything else.*

1

Solar Girdle Emergency

AUROBINDO BANDJALANG GOT the emergency twing through his vib on the morning of August 8, 2121, while still at home in his expansive bachelor's digs. At 1LDK, his living space was three times larger than most unmarried individuals enjoyed but his high-status job as a Power Jockey for New Perthpatna earned him extra perks.

While a short-lived infinitesimal flock of beard clippers grazed his face, A.B. had been showering and vibbing the weather feed for Reboot City Twelve: the more formal name for New Perthpatna.

Sharing his shower stall but untouched by the water, beautiful weather idol Midori Mimosa delivered the feed.

"Sunrise occurred this morning at 3.02 a.m. Max temp projected to be a comfortable, shirtsleeves thirty degrees by noon. Sunset at 10.29 p.m. this evening. Cee-oh-two at 450 parts per million, a significant drop from levels at this time last year. Good work, Rebooters!"

The new tweet/twinge/ping interrupted both the weather and A.B.'s ablutions. His vision greyed out for a few milliseconds as if a sheet of smoked glass had been slid in front of his MEMS contacts, and both his left palm and the sole of his left foot itched: Attention Demand 5.

A.B.'s boss, Jeetu Kissoon, replaced Midori Mimosa under the sparsely downfalling water: a dismaying and disinvigorating substitution. But A.B.'s virt-in-body operating system allowed for no squelching of twings tagged AD4 and up. Departmental policy.

Kissoon grinned and said, "Scrub faster, A.B. We need you here yesterday. I've got news of face-to-face magnitude."

"What's the basic quench?"

"Power transmission from the French farms is down by one per cent. Sat photos show some kind of strange dust accumulation on a portion of the collectors. The on-site kybes can't respond to the stuff with any positive remediation. Where's it from, why now, and how do we stop it? We've got to send a human team down there, and you're heading it."

Busy listening intently to the bad news, A.B. had neglected to rinse properly. Now the water from the low-flow showerhead ceased, its legally mandated interval over. He'd get no more from that particular spigot till the evening. Kissoon disappeared from A.B.'s augmented reality, chuckling.

A.B. cursed with mild vehemence and stepped out of the stall. He had to use a sponge at the sink to finish rinsing, and then he had no sink water left for brushing his teeth. Such a hygienic practice was extremely old-fashioned, given self-replenishing colonies of germ-policing mouth microbes but A.B. relished the fresh taste of toothpaste and the sense of righteous manual self-improvement. Something of a twentieth-century recreationist, Aurobindo. But not this morning.

Outside A.B.'s 1LDK: his home corridor, part of a well-planned, spacious, senses-delighting labyrinth featuring several public spaces, constituting the 150th floor of his urbmon.

His urbmon, affectionately dubbed "The Big Stink": one of over a hundred colossal, densely situated high-rise habitats that amalgamated into New Perthpatna.

New Perthpatna: one of over a hundred such Reboot Cities sited across the habitable zone of Earth, about twenty-five per cent of the planet's landmass, collectively home to nine billion souls.

A.B. immediately ran into one of those half-million souls of The Big Stink: Zulqamain Safranski.

Zulqamain Safranski was the last person A.B. wanted to see.

Six months ago, A.B. had logged an ASBO against the man.

Safranski was a parkour. A harmless hobby – if conducted in the approved sports areas of the urbmon. But Safranski blithely parkour'd his ass all over the common spaces, often bumping into or startling people as he ricocheted from ledge to bench. After a bruising encounter with the aggressive urban bounder, A.B. had filed his protest, attaching AD tags to already filed but overlooked video footage of the offenses. Not altogether improbably, A.B.'s complaint had been the one to tip the scales against Safranski, sending him via police trundlebug to the nearest Sin Bin, for a punitively educational stay.

But now, all too undeniably, Safranski was back in New Perthpatna, and instantly in A.B.'s chance-met (?) face.

The buff, choleric but laughably diminutive fellow glared at A.B., then said, spraying spittle upward, "You just better watch your ass night and day, Bang-a-gong, or you might find yourself doing a *lâché* from the roof without really meaning to."

A.B. tapped his ear and, implicitly, his implanted vib audio pickup. "Threats go from your lips to the ears of the wrathful Ekh Dagina – and to the ASBO Squad as well."

Safranski glared with wild-eyed malice at A.B., then stalked off, his planar butt muscles, outlined beneath the tight fabric of his mango-colored plugsuit, somehow conveying further ire by their natural contortions.

A.B. smiled. Amazing how often people still forgot the panopticon nature of life nowadays, even after a century of increasing immersion in and extension of null-privacy. Familiarity bred forget-fulness. But it was best always to recall, at least subliminally, that everyone heard and saw everything equally these days. Just part of the Reboot Charter, allowing a society to function in which people could feel universally violated, universally empowered.

At the elevator banks closest to home, A.B. rode up to the 201st floor, home to the assigned space for the urbmon's Power Administration Corps. Past the big active mural depicting drowned Perth, fishes swimming round the BHP Tower. Tags in the air led him to the workpod that Jeetu Kissoon had chosen for the time being.

Kissoon looked good for ninety-seven years old: he could have passed for A.B.'s slightly older brother, but not his father. Coffee-bean skin, snowy temples, laugh lines cut deep, only slightly coun-terbalanced by somber eyes.

When Kissoon had been born, all the old cities still existed, and many, many animals other than goats and chickens flourished. Kissoon had seen the cities abandoned, and the Big Biota Crash, as well as the whole Reboot. Hard for young A.B. to conceive. The man was a walking history lesson. A.B. tried to honor that.

But Kissoon's next actions soon evoked a yawp of disrespectful protest from the younger man.

"Here are the two other Jocks I've assigned to accompany you."

Interactive dossiers hung before A.B.'s gaze. He two-fingered through them swiftly, growing more stunned by the second. Finally he burst out: "You're giving me a furry and a keek as helpers?"

"Tigerishka and Gershon Thales. They're the best available. Live with them, and fix this glitch."

Kissoon stabbed A.B. with a piercing stare, and A.B. realized this meatspace proximity had been demanded precisely to convey the intensity of Kissoon's next words.

"Without power, we're doomed."

2

45th Parallel Blues

Jet-assisted flight was globally interdicted. Not enough resources left to support regular commercial or recreational aviation. No military anywhere with a need to muster its own air force. Jet engines were too harmful to a stressed atmosphere.

And besides, why travel? Everywhere was the same. Vib served fine for most needs.

The habitable zone of Earth consisted of those lands – both historically familiar and newly disclosed from beneath vanished icepack – above the 45th parallel north, and below the 45th parallel south. The rest of the Earth's landmass had been desertified or drowned: sand or surf.

The immemorial ecosystems of the remaining climactically tolerable territories had been devastated by Greenhouse change, then, ultimately and purposefully, wiped clean. Die-offs, migratory invaders, a fast-forward churn culminating in an engineered ecosphere. The new conditions supported no animals larger than mice and only a monoculture of GM plants.

Giant aggressive hissing cockroaches, of course, still thrived.

A portion of humanity's reduced domain hosted forests specially designed for maximum carbon uptake and sequestration. These fast-growing, long-lived hybrid trees blended the genomes of eucalyptus, loblolly pine and poplar, and had been dubbed "eulollypops".

The bulk of the rest of the land was devoted to the crops necessary and sufficient to feed nine billion people: mainly quinoa, kale and soy, fertilized by human wastes. Sugarbeet plantations provided feedstock for bio-polymer production.

And then, on their compact footprints, the hundred-plus Reboot Cities, ringed by small but efficient goat and chicken farms.

Not a world conducive to sightseeing Grand Tours.

On each continent, a simple network of maglev trains, deliberately held to a sparse schedule, linked the Reboot Cities (except for the Sin Bins, which were sanitarily excluded from easy access to the network). Slow but luxurious aerostats serviced officials and businessmen. Travel between continents occurred on SkySail-equipped water ships. All travel was predicated on state-certified need.

And when anyone had to deviate from standard routes – such as a trio of Power Jockeys following the superconducting transmission lines south to France – they employed a trundlebug.

Peugeot had designed the first trundlebugs over a century ago, the Ozones. Picture a large rolling drum fashioned of electrochromic biopoly, featuring slight catenaries in the lines of its body from end to end. A barrel-shaped compartment suspended between two enormous wheels large as the cabin itself. Solid-state battery packs channeled power to separate electric motors. A curving door spanned the entire width of the vehicle, sliding upward.

Inside, three seats in a row, the center one commanding the failsafe manual controls. Storage behind the seats.

And in those seats: Aurobindo Bandjalang working the joystick with primitive recreationist glee and vigor, rather than vibbing the trundlebug; Tigerishka on his right and Gershon Thales on his left.

A tense silence reigned.

Tigerishka exuded a bored professionalism only slightly belied by a gently twitching tailtip and alertly cocked tufted ears. Her tigrine pelt poked out from the edges of her plugsuit, pretty furred face and graceful neck the largest bare expanse.

A.B. thought she smelled like a sexy stuffed toy. Disturbing.

She turned her slit-pupiled eyes away from the monotonous racing landscape for a while to gnaw delicately with sharp teeth at a wayward cuticle around one claw.

Furries chose to express non-inheritable parts of the genome of various extinct species within their own bodies, as a simultaneous expiation of guilt and celebration of lost diversity. Although the Vaults at Reboot City Twenty-nine (formerly Svalbard, Norway) safely held samples of all the vanished species that had been foolish enough to compete with humanity during this Anthropocene Age, their non-human genomes awaiting some far-off day of re-instantiation, that sterile custody did not sit well with some. The furries wanted other species to walk the earth again, if only by partial proxy.

In contrast to Tigerishka's stolid boredom, Gershon Thales manifested a frenetic desire to maximize demands on his attention. Judging by the swallow-flight motions of his hands, he had half a dozen virtual windows open, upon what landscapes of information A.B. could only conjecture. (He had tried vibbing into Gershon's eyes but had encountered a pirate privacy wall. Hard to build team camaraderie with that barrier in place but A.B. had chosen not to call out the man on the matter just yet.)

No doubt Gershon was hanging out on keek fora. The keeks loved to indulge in endless talk.

Originally calling themselves the "punctuated equilibriumists", the cult had swiftly shortened their awkward name to the "punk eeks" and then to the "keeks".

The keeks believed that after a long period of stasis, the human species had reached one of those pivotal Darwinian climacterics that would launch the race along exciting if unpredictable new vectors. What everyone else viewed as a grand tragedy – implacable and deadly climate change leading to the Big Biota Crash – they interpreted as a useful kick in humanity's collective pants. They discussed a thousand, thousand schemes intended to further this leap, most of them just so much mad vaporware.

A.B. clucked his tongue softly as he drove. Such were the assistants he had been handed, to solve a crisis of unknown magnitude.

Tigerishka suddenly spoke, her voice a velvet growl. "Can't you push this bug any faster? The cabin's starting to stink like simians already."

New Perthpatna occupied the site that had once hosted the Russian city of Arkhangelsk, torn down during the Reboot. The closest malfunctioning solar collectors in what had once been France loomed 2,800 kilometers distant. Mission transit time: an estimated thirty-six hours, including overnight rest.

"No, I can't. As it is, we're going to have to camp at least eight hours for the batteries to recharge. The faster I push us, the more power we expend, and the longer we'll have to sit idle. It's a calculated tradeoff. Look at the math."

A.B. vibbed Tigerishka a presentation. She studied it, then growled in frustration.

"I need to run! I can't sit cooped up in a smelly can like this for hours at a stretch! At home, I hit the track every hour."

A.B. wanted to say, *I'm not the one who stuck those big-cat codons in you, so don't yell at me!* But instead he notched up the cabin's HVAC and chose a polite response. "Right now, all I can do is save your nose some grief. We'll stop for lunch, and you can get some exercise then. Can't you vib out like old Gershon there?"

Gerson Thales stopped his air haptics to glare at A.B. His lugubrious voice resembled wet cement plopping from a trough. "What's that comment supposed to imply? That I'm wasting my time? Well, I'm not. I'm engaged in posthuman dialectics at Saltation Central.

Very stimulating. You two should try to expand your minds in a similar fashion."

Tigerishka hissed. A.B. ran an app that counted to ten for him using gently breaking waves to time the calming sequence.

"As mission leader, I don't really care how anyone passes the travel time. Just so long as you all perform when it matters. Now how about letting me enjoy the drive."

The "road" actually required little of A.B.'s attention. A wide border of rammed earth, kept free of weeds by cousins to A.B. beard removers, the road paralleled the surprisingly dainty superconducting transmission line that powered a whole city. It ran straight as modern justice toward the solar collectors that fed it. Shade from the rows of eulollypops planted alongside cut down any glare and added coolness to their passage.

Coolness was a desideratum. The further south they traveled, the hotter things would get. Until, finally, temperatures would approach fifty degrees at many points of the Solar Girdle. Only their plugsuits would allow the Power Jockeys to function outside under those conditions.

A.B. tried to enjoy the sensations of driving, a recreationist pastime he seldom got to indulge. Most of his workday consisted of indoor maintenance and monitoring, optimization of supply and demand, the occasional high-level debugging. Humans possessed a fluidity of response and insight no kybes could yet match. A field expedition marked a welcome change of pace from this indoor work. Or would have, with comrades more congenial.

A.B. sighed, and kicked up their speed just a notch.

After traveling for nearly five hours, they stopped for lunch, just a bit north of where Moscow had once loomed. No Reboot City had ever been erected in its place, more northerly locations being preferred.

As soon as the wide door slid upward, Tigerishka bolted from the cabin. She raced laterally off into the endless eulollypop forest, faster than a baseline human. Thirty seconds later, a rich, resonant, hair-raising caterwaul of triumph made both A.B. and Gershon Thales jump.

Thales said drily, "Caught a mouse, I suppose."

A.B. laughed. Maybe Thales wasn't such a stiff.

A.B. jacked the trundlebug into one of the convenient stepdown charging nodes in the transmission cable designed for just such a purpose. Even an hour's topping up would help. Then he broke out sandwiches of curried goat salad. He and Thales ate companionably. Tigerishka returned with a dab of overlooked murine blood at the corner of her lips, and declined any human food.

Back in the moving vehicle, Thales and Tigerishka reclined their seats and settled down to a nap after lunch, and their drowsiness soon infected A.B. He put the trundlebug on autopilot, reclined his own seat and soon was fast asleep as well.

Awaking several hours later, A.B. discovered their location to be nearly atop the 54th parallel, in the vicinity of pre-Crash Minsk.

The temperature outside their cosy cab registered a sizzling thirty-five, despite the declining sun.

"We'll push on toward Old Warsaw, then call it a day. That'll leave just a little over 1,100 klicks to cover tomorrow."

Thales objected. "We'll get to the farms late in the day tomorrow – too late for any useful investigation. Why not run all nite on autopilot?"

"I want us to get a good night's rest without jouncing around. And besides, all it would take is a tree freshly down across the road, or a new sinkhole to ruin us. The autopilot's not infallible."

Tigerishka's sultry purr sent tingles through A.B.'s scrotum. "I need to work out some kinks myself."

Night halted the trundlebug. When the door slid up, furnace air blasted the trio, automatically activating their plugsuits. Sad old fevered planet. They pulled up their cowls and felt relief.

Three personal homestatic pods were decanted and popped open upon vibbed command beneath the allée. They crawled inside separately to eat and drop off quickly to sleep.

Stimulating caresses awakened A.B. Hazily uncertain what hour this was that witnessed Tigerishka's trespass upon his homeopod, or whether she had visited Thales first, he could decisively report in the morning, had such a report been required by Jeetu Kissoon and the Power Administration Corps, that she retained enough energy to wear him out.

3

The Sands of Paris

The vast, forbidding, globe-encircling desert south of the 45th parallel depressed everyone in the trundlebug. A.B. ran his tongue around lips that felt impossibly cracked and parched, no matter how much water he sucked from his plugsuit's kamelbak.

All greenery gone, the uniform trackless and silent wastes baking under the implacable sun brought to mind some alien world that had never known human tread. No signs of the mighty cities that had once reared their proud towers remained, nor any traces of the sprawling suburbs, the surging highways. What had not been disassembled for re-use elsewhere had been buried.

On and on the trundlebug rolled, following the superconductor line, its enormous wheels operating as well on loose sand as on rammed earth.

A.B. felt anew the grievous historical impact of humanity's folly upon the planet and he did not relish the emotions. He generally devoted little thought to that sad topic.

An utterly modern product of his age, a hardcore Rebooter through and through, Aurobindo Bandjalang was generally happy with his civilization. Its contorted features, its limitations and constraints, its precariousness and its default settings he accepted implicitly, just as a child of trolls believes its troll mother to be utterly beautiful.

He knew pride in how the human race had managed to build a hundred new cities from scratch and shift billions of people north and south in only half a century, outracing the spreading blight and killer weather. He enjoyed the hybrid multicultural melange that had replaced old divisions and rivalries, the new blended mankind. The nostalgic stories told by Jeetu Kissoon and others of his generation were entertaining fairytales, not the chronicle of any lost Golden Age. He could not lament what he had never known. He was too busy keeping the delicate structures of the present day up and running and happy to be so occupied.

Trying to express these sentiments and lift the spirits of his comrades, A.B. found that his evaluation of Reboot civilization was not universal.

"Every human of this fallen Anthropocene age is shadowed by the myriad ghosts of all the other creatures they drove extinct," said Tigerishka, in a surprisingly poetic and somber manner, given her usual blunt and unsentimental earthiness. "Whales and dolphins, cats and dogs, cows and horses – they all peer into and out of our sinful souls. Our only shot at redemption is that some day, when the planet is restored, our coevolved partners might be re-embodied."

Thales uttered a scoffing grunt. "Good riddance to all that nonsapient genetic trash! *Homo sapiens* is the only desirable endpoint of all evolutionary lines. But right now, the dictatorial Reboot has our species locked down in a dead end. We can't make the final leap to our next level until we get rid of the chaff."

Tigerishka spat, and made a taunting feint toward her co-worker across A.B.'s chest, causing A.B. to swerve the car and Thales to recoil. When the keek realized he hadn't actually been hurt, he grinned with a sickly superciliousness.

"Hold on one minute," said A.B. "Do you mean that you and the other keeks want to see another Crash?"

"It's more complex than that. You see—"

But A.B.'s attention was diverted that moment from Thales's explanation. His vib interrupted with a Demand Four call from his apartment.

Vib nodes dotted the power transmission network, keeping people online just like at home. Plenty of dead zones existed elsewhere but not here, adjacent to the line.

A.B. had just enough time to place the trundlebug on autopilot before his vision was overlaid with a feed from home.

The security system on his apartment had registered an unauthorized entry.

Inside his 1LDK, an optical distortion the size of a small human moved around, spraying something similar to used cooking oil on A.B.'s furniture. The hands holding the sprayer disappeared inside the whorl of distortion.

A.B. vibbed his avatar into his home system. "Hey, you! What the fuck are you doing!"

The person wearing the invisibility cape laughed, and A.B. recognized the distinctive crude chortle of Zulqamain Safranski.

"Safranski! Your ass is grass! The ASBO's are on their way!"

Unable to stand the sight of his lovely apartment being dese-crated, frustrated by his inability to take direct action himself, A.B. vibbed off.

Tigerishka and Thales had shared the feed and commiserated with their fellow Power Jock. But the experience soured the rest of the trip for A.B., and he stewed silently until they reached the first of the extensive constructions upon which the Reboot Cities relied for their very existence.

The Solar Girdle featured a tripartite setup, for the sake of security of supply.

First came the extensive farms of solar updraft towers: giant chimneys that fostered wind flow from base to top, thus powering their turbines.

Then came parabolic mirrored troughs that followed the sun and pumped heat into special sinks, lakes of molten salts, which in turn ran different turbines after sunset.

Finally, serried ranks of photovoltaic panels generated electricity directly. These structures, in principle the simplest and least likely to fail, were the ones experiencing difficulties from some kind of dust accretion.

Vibbing GPS coordinates for the troublespot, A.B. brought the trundlebug up to the infected photovoltaics. Paradoxically, the steady omnipresent whine of the car's motors registered on his attention only when he had powered them down.

Outside the vehicle's polarized plastic shell, the sinking sun glared like the malign orb of a Cyclops bent on mankind's destruction.

When the bug-wide door slid up, dragon's breath assailed the Power Jocks. Their plugsuits strained to shield them from the hostile environment.

Surprisingly, a subdued and pensive Tigerishka volunteered for camp duty. As dusk descended, she attended to erecting their intel-ligent shelters and getting a meal ready: chicken croquettes with roasted edamame.

A.B. and Thales sluffed through the sand for a dozen yards to the nearest infected solarcell platform. The keek held his pocket lab in gloved hand.

A little maintenance kybe, scuffed and scorched, perched on the high trellis, valiantly but fruitlessly chipping with its multitool at a hard siliceous shell irregularly encrusting the photovoltaic surface.

Thales caught a few flakes of the unknown substance as they fell, and inserted them into the analysis chamber of the pocket lab.

"We should have a complete readout of the composition of this stuff by morning."

"No sooner?"

"Well, actually, by midnight. But I don't intend to stay up. I've done nothing except sit on my ass for two days, yet I'm still exhausted. It's this oppressive place—"

"Okay," A.B. replied. The first stars had begun to prinkle the sky. "Let's call it a day."

They ate in the bug, in a silent atmosphere of forced companionability, then retired to their separate shelters.

A.B. hoped with mild lust for another nocturnal visit from a prowling Tigerishka but was not greatly disappointed when she never showed to interrupt his intermittent drowsing. Truly, the desert sands of Paris sapped all his usual joie de vivre.

Finally falling fast asleep, he dreamed of the ghostly waters of the vanished Seine, impossibly flowing deep beneath his tent. Somehow, Zulqamain Safranski was diverting them to flood A.B.'s apartment ...

4

The Red Queen's Triathalon

In the morning, after breakfast, A.B. approached Gershon Thales, who stood apart near the trundlebug. Already the sun thundered down its oppressive cargo of photons, so necessary for the survival of the Reboot Cities, yet, conversely, just one more burden for the overstressed Greenhouse ecosphere. Feeling irritable and impatient, anxious to be back home, A.B. dispensed with pleasantries.

"I've tried vibbing your pocket lab for the results but you've got it offline, behind that pirate software you're running. Open up, now."

The keek stared at A.B. with mournful stolidity. "One minute, I need something from my pod."

Thales ducked into his tent. A.B. turned to Tigerishka. "What do you make—"

Blinding light shattered A.B.'s vision for a millisecond in a painful nova, before his MEMS contacts could react protectively by going opaque. Tigerishka vented a stifled yelp of surprise and shock, showing she had gotten the same actinic eyekick.

A.B. immediately thought of vib malfunction, some misdirected feed from a solar observatory, say. But then, as his lenses de-opaqued, he realized the stimulus had to have been external.

When he could see again, he confronted Gershon Thales holding a pain gun whose wide bell muzzle covered both of the keek's fellow Power Jocks. At the feet of the keek rested an exploded spaser grenade.

A.B. tried to vib but got nowhere.

"Yes," Thales said, "we're in a dead zone now. I fried all the optical circuits of the vib nodes with the grenade."

A large enough burst of surface plasmons could do that? Who knew? "But why?"

With his free hand, keeping the pain gun unwavering, Thales reached into a plugsuit pocket and took out his lab. "These results. They're only the divine sign we've been waiting for. Reboot civilization is on the way out now. I couldn't let anyone in the PAC find out. The longer they stay in the dark, the more irreversible the changes will be."

"You're claiming this creeping crud is that dangerous?"

"Did you ever hear of ADRECS?"

A.B. instinctively tried to vib for the info and hit the blank frustrating walls of the newly created dead zone. Trapped in the twentieth century! Recreationist passions only went so far. Where was the panopticon when you needed it?

"Aerially Delivered Re-forestation and Erosion Control System," continued Thales. "A package of geoengineering schemes meant to stabilize the spread of deserts. Abandoned decades ago. But apparently, one scheme's come alive again on its own. Mutant instruction drift is my best guess. Or Darwin's invisible hand."

"What's come alive then?"

"Nanosand. Meant to catalyze the formation of macroscale walls that would block the flow of normal sands."

"And that's the stuff afflicting the solarcells?"

"Absolutely. Has an affinity for bonding with the surface of the cells and can't be removed with destroying them. Self-replicating. Best estimates are that the nanosand will take out thirty per cent of production in just a month, if left unchecked. Might start to affect the turbines too."

Tigerishka asked, in an intellectually curious tone of voice that A.B. found disconcerting, "But what good does going offline do? When PAC can't vib us, they'll just send another crew."

"I'll wait here and put them out of commission too. I only have to hang in for a month."

"What about food?" said Tigerishka. "We don't have enough provisions for a month, even for one person."

"I'll raid the fish farms on the coast. Desalinate my drinking water. It's just a short round trip by bug."

A.B. could hardly contain his disgust. "You're fucking crazy, Thales. Dropping the power supply by thirty per cent won't kill the cities."

"Oh, but we keeks think it will. You see, Reboot civilization is a wobbly three-legged stool, hammered together in a mad rush. We're not in the Red Queen's Race, but the Red Queen's Triathalon. Power, food and social networks. Take out any one leg, and it all goes down. And we're sawing at the other two legs as well. Look at that guy who vandalized your apartment. Behavior like that is on the rise. The urbmons are driving people crazy. Humans weren't meant to live in hives."

Tigerishka stepped forward and Thales swung the gun more towards her unprotected face. A blast of high-intensity microwaves would leave her screaming, writhing and puking on the sands.

"I want in," she said and A.B.'s heart sank through his boots. "The only way other species will ever get to share this planet is when most of mankind is gone."

Regarding the furry speculatively and clinically, Thales said, "I could use your help. But you'll have to prove yourself. First, tie up Bandjalang."

Tigerishka grinned vilely at A.B. "Sorry, apeboy."

Using biopoly cords from the bug, she soon had A.B. trussed with circulation-deadening bonds and stashed in his homeopod.

What were they doing out there? A.B. squirmed futilely. He banged around so much, he began to fear he was damaging the life-preserving tent so he stopped. Wiped out after hours of struggle, he fell into a stupor made more enervating by the suddenly less-than-ideal heat inside the homeopod, whose compromised systems strained to deal with the desert conditions. He began to hallucinate about the subterranean Seine again and realized he was very, very thirsty. His kamelbak was dry when he sipped at its straw.

At some point, Tigerishka appeared and gave him some water. Or did she? Maybe it was all just another dream.

Outside the smart tent, night came down. A.B. heard wolves howling, just like they did on archived documentaries. Wolves? No wolves existed. But someone was howling.

Tigerishka having sex. Sex with Thales. Bastard. Bad guy not only won the battle but got the girl as well ...

A.B. awoke to the pins and needles of returning circulation: discomfort of a magnitude unfelt by anyone before or after the Lilliputians tethered Gulliver.

Tigerishka was bending over him, freeing him.

"Sorry again, apeboy, that took longer than I thought. He even kept his hand on the gun right up until he climaxed."

Something warm was dripping on A.B.'s face. Was his rescuer crying? Her voice belied any such emotion. A.B. raised a hand that felt like a block of wood to his own face and clumsily smeared the liquid around, until some entered his mouth.

He imagined that this forbidden taste was equally as satisfying to Tigerishka as mouse fluids.

Heading north, the trundlebug seemed much more spacious with just two passengers. The corpse of Gershon Thales had been left behind, for eventual recovery by experts. Dessication and cooking would make it a fine mummy.

Once out of the dead zone, A.B. vibbed everything back to Jeetu Kissoon and got a shared commendation that made Tigerishka purr. Then he turned his attention to his personal queue of messages.

The ASBO Squad had bagged Safranski. But they apologised for some delay in his sentencing hearing. Their caseload was enormous these days.

Way down at the bottom of his queue was an agricultural newsfeed. An unprecedented kind of black rot fungus had made inroads into the kale crop on the farms supplying Reboot City Twelve.

Calories would be tight in New Perthpatna, but only for a while. Or so they hoped.

This story is indebted to Gaia Vince and her article in *New Scientist*, "Surviving in a Warmer World"

TERRAFORMING TERRA

Jack Williamson

Jack Williamson (1908–2006) almost made it to 100 years old, and he kept on writing to the end. He had the longest career of any SF writer, almost eighty years. His earliest story appeared in the very first science-fiction magazine, Amazing Stories, *in 1928, showing the influence of Abraham Merritt. He became one of the major writers of the 1930s writing such bizarre "thought variant" stories for* Astounding Stories *as "Born of the Sun" (1934), where it turns out that the planets are eggs and Earth is about to hatch. He produced his fair share of early space opera, notably his* Legion of Space *series, but also penned* The Legion of Time *(1938), where he highlighted the significance of those small moments, which he called the Jonbar hinge, upon which life-changing events can depend, His* Seetee *stories, written in the 1940s, gave rise to the concept of contra-terrene matter. At this time he produced another significant work,* The Humanoids *(1948), which considered the problem of an overly helpful artificial intelligence. Williamson's fiction was often at the cutting edge of scientific advance. He considered genetic engineering in* Dragon's Island *(1951), a theme he revisited in* Manseed *(1982). He continued to win Awards right to the end. The following novelette formed the first part of his novel* Terraforming Earth *(2001), which won the Campbell Memorial Award in 2002. This also takes us through the apocalypse and way beyond.*

1

WE ARE CLONES, the last survivors of the great impact. The bodies of our parents have lain a hundred years in the cemetery on the rubble slope below the crater rim. I remember the day my robot-father brought the five of us up to see the Earth, a hazy red-spattered ball in the black Moon sky.

"It looks – looks sick." Looking sick herself, Dian raised her face to his. "Is it bleeding?"

"Bleeding red-hot lava all over the land," he told her. "The rivers all bleeding iron-red rain into the seas."

"Dead." Arne made a face. "It looks dead."

"The impact killed it." His plastic head nodded. "You were born to bring it back to life."

"Just us kids?"

"You'll grow up."

"Not me," Arne muttered. "Do I have to grow up?"

"So what do you want?" Tanya grinned at him. "To stay a snot-nosed kid forever?"

"Please." My robot-father shrugged in the stiff way robots have, and his lenses swept all five of us, standing around him in the dome. "Your mission is to replant life on Earth. The job may take a lot of time, but you'll be born and born again till you get it done."

We knew our natural parents from their letters to us and their images in the holo tanks and the robots they had programmed to bring us up. My father had been Duncan Yare, a lean man with kind grey eyes and a neat black beard when I saw him in the holo tanks. He had a voice I loved, even when he was the robot.

The dome was new to us, big and strange, full of strange machines, wonderfully exciting. The clear quartz wall let us see the stark earth-lit moonscape all around us. We had clone pets. Mine was Spaceman. He growled and bristled at a black-shadowed monster rock outside and crouched against my leg. Tanya's cat had followed us.

"Okay, Cleo," she called when it mewed. "Let's look outside."

Cleo came flying into her arms. Jumping was easy, here in the Moon's light gravity. My robot-father had pointed a thin blue plastic arm at the cragged mountain wall that curved away on both sides of the dome.

"The station is dug into the rim of Tycho—"

"The crater," Arne interrupted him. "We know it from the globe."

"It's so big!" Tanya's voice was hushed. She was a spindly little girl with straight black hair that her mother made her keep cut short, and bangs that came down to her eyebrows. Cleo sagged in her arms, almost forgotten. "It – it's homongoolius!"

She stared out across the enormous black pit at the jagged peak towering into the blaze of Earth at the center. Dian had turned to look the other way, at the bright white rays that fanned out from the boulder slopes far below, spreading to the pads and gantries and hangars where the spacecraft had landed, and reaching on beyond, across the waste of black-pocked, grey-green rocks and dust to the black and starless sky.

"Homongoolius?" Dian mocked her. "I'd say fractabulous!"

"Homon-fractabu-what?" Pepe made fun of them both. He was short and quick, as skinny as Tanya was, and just as dark. He liked to play games, and never combed his hair. "Can't you speak English?"

"Better than you." Dian was a tall pale girl who never wanted a pet. The robots had made dark-rimmed glasses for her because she loved to read the old paper books in the library. "And I'm learning Latin."

"What good is Latin?" Cloned together, we were all the same age, but Arne was the biggest. He had pale blue eyes and pale blond hair, and he liked to ask questions. "It's dead as Earth."

"It's something we must save." Dian was quiet and shy and always serious. "The new people may need it."

"What new people?" He waved his arm at the Earth. "If everybody's dead—"

"We have the frozen cells," Tanya said. "We can grow new people."

Nobody heard her. We were all looking out at the dead moonscape. The dome stood high between the rock-spattered desert and the ink-black shadow that filled the crater pit. Looking down, I felt giddy for an instant, and Arne backed away.

"Fraidy cat!" Tanya jeered him. "You're grey as a ghost."

Retreating farther, he flushed red and looked up at the Earth. It hung high and huge, capped white at the poles and swirled with great white storms. Beneath the clouds, the seas were streaked brown and yellow and red where rivers ran off the dark continents.

"It was so beautiful," Dian whispered. "All blue and white and green in the old pictures."

"Before the impact," my father said. "Your job is to make it beautiful again."

Arne squinted at it and shook his head. "I don't see how—"

"Just listen," Tanya said.

"Please." My robot-father's face was not designed to smile, but his voice could reflect a tolerant amusement. "Let me tell you what you are."

"I know," Arne said. "Clones—"

"Shut up," Tanya told him.

"Clones," my robot-father nodded. "Genetic copies of the humans who got here alive after the impact."

"I know all that," Arne said. "I saw it on my monitor. We were born down in the maternity lab, from the frozen cells our real parents left. And I know how the asteroid killed the Earth. I saw the simulation on my monitor."

"I didn't," Tanya said. "I want to know."

"Let's begin with Calvin DeFalco." Our robot-parents were all shaped just alike, but each with a breastplate of a different color. Mine was bright blue. He had cared for me as long as I remembered, and I loved him as much as my beagle. "Cal was the man who built the station and got us here. He died for your chance to go back—"

Stubbornly, Arne pushed out his fat lower lip. "I like it better here."

"You're a dummy," Tanya told him. "Dummies don't talk."

He stuck his tongue out at her, but we all stood close around my robot-father, listening.

"Calvin DeFalco was born in an old city called Chicago. He was as young as you are when his aunt took him to a museum where he saw the skeletons of the great dinosaurs that used to rule the Earth. The bones were so big that they frightened him. He asked her if they could ever come back.

"She tried to tell him he was safe. They were truly dead, she said, killed by a giant asteroid that struck the coast of Mexico. That frightened him more. She told him not to worry. Big impacts came millions of years apart. But he did worry about how anybody could survive another impact.

"His first idea was a colony on Mars. He trained to be an astronaut and led the only expedition that ever got there. It turned out to be unfriendly, unfit for any self-sustaining colony. Most of the crew was lost, but Cal returned so famous he was able to persuade the world governments to set up Tycho Station.

"Live men and women worked here to build it, but they went home when the humanform robots were perfected. They left the robots to run the observatory and relay observations. If they ever saw trouble coming they were to call a warning to Earth—"

"But the killer did hit!" Arne broke in. "Why didn't they stop it?"

"Shhh!" Tanya scolded him. "Just listen."

He rolled his eyes at her.

"Everything went dreadfully wrong." My robot-father's voice fell with my real father's sadness. "The asteroid was mostly iron and bigger than the one that killed the dinosaurs. It came fast, on an orbit close around the Sun that hid it from the telescopes. Nobody saw it till there was no time to steer it away. But still they had a little luck."

"Luck?" Arne made a snarly face. "When the whole world was killed?"

"Luck for you," my robot-father told him. "Your father wasn't on what Cal called his survival squad. That was the little handful of people picked for essential skills and chosen to form a sturdy gene pool. He was Arne Linder, a geologist who had written a book about terraforming Mars – changing it to make it fit for people. Cal had wanted him on the Mars expedition, but he didn't like risk. Without the odd stroke of luck that got him to the Moon, you wouldn't exist."

Arne gulped and blinked.

"Cal had been flying a supply plane out to the station every three months. The impact caught it on the ground in New Mexico, partly loaded for the next flight, but it was not yet fueled. The survival team was scattered everywhere. Linder was in Iceland, thousands of miles away. And your mother—"

His lenses turned and his voice warmed for Tanya. "She was Tanya Wu, the team biologist. Her job was installing the maternity lab. The warning caught her in Massachusetts, far across the continent, gathering frozen cells and embryos for the cryonics vault. She got here just in time to save herself and her cat. Your Cleopatra is its second clone."

Cleo was purring in Tanya's arms, her yellow eyes blinking sleepily at the blazing Earth.

"And you, Pepe—" The lenses swung to him. "Your father was Pepe Navarro, an airplane pilot. On that last day, he was in Iceland with Linder on a seismic survey. They just barely got back to White Sands." The lenses gleamed at Arne. "That's why you're here."

"Me!" Dian begged him. "What about me?"

"You?" My robot-father's face showed no feelings, but his voice laughed at her eagerness in a kind but teasing way. "Your clone mother was Diana Lazard. She was the curator of the hall of humanities in a big museum till Cal picked her to help him select what they must plan to save. Our museum level is filled with her books and artefacts. Sealed now, but you'll all study there when you are older."

"It's Dunk's turn." Tanya grinned at me.

"Okay." His voice smiled at her and Cleo before he turned more seriously to me. "I was a science news reporter. Cal had hired me to do publicity for the station. It cost a lot of money, and we had to sell it to the sceptics. I happened to be at White Sands when the asteroid fell waiting to do a story on the new maternity lab. My own good luck."

"And Spaceman?" I asked. "He was your dog?"

"Actually, no." He almost laughed. "I never had time for a pet, but Cal liked dogs. Spaceman's clone dad was a stray that happened to run across the field just before we took off. Cal called him. He jumped aboard, and here he is. A really lucky dog."

"Lucky?" Arne stood scowling out across the blazing moonscape, where nothing had ever lived. "When he's dead? Like our folks are dead, and all the Earth?" He looked at me and Spaceman, with something like a sneer. "Do you call us lucky to be clones?"

My father had no answer ready.

"We're alive," Tanya said. "Don't you like to be alive?"

"Here?" I saw something like a shiver. "I don't know."

"I do." Pepe caught my father's plastic hand. "I want to know all about the impact and what we can do about it."

"I hoped you would." My father hugged him and spoke to all of us. "The asteroid was a chunk of heavy rock, potato-shaped and ten miles long, probably a fragment from some larger collision. Cal had worked hard to have the station ready, but nobody could have been ready for anything so big.

"The warning got to White Sands about midnight on Christmas Eve. We might have had more time, but the duty man had come late from a party and gone to sleep at his post. We all might have died, but for a janitor who happened to see a red light flashing and called Cal. By then, we had only six hours.

"On holiday, people were away from home, impossible to reach. Although the supply plane was standing on the pad, we had a million things to do and no time for anything. Cal tried to keep the news off the air for fear of total chaos. A smart precaution, maybe, he couldn't explain our haste to get off the pad. Fuel had been ordered but not delivered. We had to wait for Dr Linder and Dr Wu and more supplies. A hellish time."

My robot-father's voice had gone quick and trembly.

"But also a time of magnificent heroism. Cal finally had to tell our people there on the field – tell them they had only hours to live. You can imagine how desperately they must have wanted to be with their families, but most of them stayed at the job, working like demons.

"In spite of us, the news got out. Dozens of reporters and camera crews swarmed to the field. Cal had to confirm the story, but he begged them not to kill whatever chance we had. 'Kiss your wives goodbye,' I heard him tell them, 'kneel in prayer, or just get drunk.' I don't know what they reported, but all the TV and radio stations soon went silent.

"We were still on the ground when the asteroid came down in the Bay of Bengal, south of Asia. We had too little time to get into the air before the shockwaves got through the Earth to us at White Sands. The P waves first, just a few minutes ahead of the more destructive surface waves.

"Navarro and Linder got in from Iceland. Dr Wu landed in a chartered jet. The work crews loaded what they could. We made it,

but barely. We were hardly a thousand feet off the pad when
buildings around the field began to crumble and yellow dust came
up to hide everything.

"Earth died behind us."

2

"But you got away!" Pepe was round-eyed with wonder. "You
were heroes!"

"We didn't feel heroic." My robot-father's voice was solemnly
slow and low, almost a whisper. "Think of all we'd lost. We felt
very lonely."

His naked plastic body quivered with something like a shudder
and his eye lenses slowly swept us all.

"Christmas Day." He went silent, remembering. "It should have
been a happy time. My married sister lived in Las Cruces, a city near
the base. She had two kids, just five years old. I'd bought trikes for
them. She was making dinner, baked turkey and dressing, yams,
cranberry sauce—"

His voice caught and he stopped for a second.

"Foods you've never had, but we liked them for Christmas. My
father and mother were coming from Ohio. He had just retired. She
was in a wheelchair from a car accident, but they were going on
around the world. A trip they had planned all their lives. They never
knew they were about to die. My sister called, but I couldn't tell—"
He stopped again, and his voice seemed strange. "Couldn't even say
goodbye."

"What's a trike?" Arne wanted to know.

My father just stood there, looking up at the iron-stained Earth,
till Pepe nudged his plastic arm. "Tell us how you got away."

"I hadn't been on the survival team. Cal brought me in place of
an anthropologist who was on a dig in Mexico. I guess we should
have been glad to get away. But there on the plane, looking back at
the terrible cloud already hiding half the Earth, none of us felt good
about anything."

He looked at Dian.

"Your mother opened her laptop and lay crying over it till Dr Wu
gave her something that put her to sleep."

"She lost her nerve." Arne made a face at Tanya. "My father was braver."

"Maybe." My father made something like a laugh. "Pepe's father was our pilot, and cool enough. He took us all the way out to orbit before he gave the controls to Cal. He'd brought a liter of Mexican tequila. He drank most of it and sang sad Spanish songs and finally slept till we got to the Moon."

"It's dreadful to see." Dian stood gazing up at the Earth, speaking almost to herself. "The rivers all running red, like blood pouring into the oceans."

"Red mud," my robot-father said. "Silt colored red by all the iron that came from the asteroid. Rain washes it off the land because there's no grass or anything to hold it."

"Sad." When she looked at him I saw tears in her eyes. "You had a sad time."

"Tell us," Tanya said. "Tell us how it really was."

"Bad enough." He nodded. "Climbing east from New Mexico, we met the surface wave coming around the Earth from the impact point. The solid planet was rippling like a liquid ocean. Buildings and fields and mountains were rising toward the sky and dissolving into dust.

"The impact blew an enormous cloud of steam and shattered rock and white-hot vapour up through the stratosphere. Night had already fallen on Asia. We passed far north, but we saw the cloud, already facing and flattening, but still glowing dull red inside.

"Clouds had covered all the Earth by the time we came around again. A rusty brown at first, but the color faded as the dust settled out. Higher clouds condensed till the whole planet was bright and white as Venus. It was beautiful." His voice fell. "Beautiful and terrible."

"Everybody?" Whispering, Dian wiped at her tear. "Was everybody killed?"

"Except us." His plastic head nodded very slowly. "The robots here at the station recorded the last broadcasts. The impact made a burst of radiation that burned communications out for thousands of miles. The surface wave spread silence all around the world.

"A few pilots in high-flying aircraft tried to report what they saw, but I don't know who was left to hear. Radio and TV stations went off the air, but a few hardy souls kept on sending to the end. A cruise liner in the Indian Ocean had time to call for help. We picked up a reporter's video of the shattering Taj Mahal, the way he saw it by moonlight.

"An American astronomer guessed the truth. We caught a White House spokesman trying to deny it. Just a sudden solar flare, he said, with no verified reports. His voice was cut off before he finished. Watching from a thousand miles up, we saw the great wave rolling up out of the Atlantic. It washed all the old cities off the coast. The last words we heard came from White Sands. A drunk signal technician wishing us a Merry Christmas."

"You got here." Pepe grinned cheerfully. "But what happened to Mr Defalco?"

"There's a robot for him," Tanya said. "I saw his frozen cells in the vault."

"A tragedy." My robot-father's stiff face had no expression, but his voice was bleak. "Cal got with us to the Moon, but he died before he had the computer programmed to teach his clones, but he was the real hero. Earth had been hit so hard that our mission looked impossible, but he never gave up.

"He tried to keep us too busy to fret about anything. We unloaded the plane and stored the seed and embryos and frozen life cells in the cryonic vault. We had to get used to lunar gravity, which meant a lot of sweating in the centrifuge to keep our bodies fit. We had to clean the hydroponic gardens and get them growing again.

"Still hoping somebody or something had survived, Cal spent most of the nights up here at the telescopes. Earth was then a huge white pearl, dazzling with sunlight but mottled with volcanic explosions. He never saw the surface.

"The second year, he decided to go back—"

"Back to that?" Arne was startled. "Was he crazy?"

"That's what we told him. We'd seen no sign of life – nothing at all through those glaring clouds – but he kept imagining isolated survivors somehow hanging on. If anybody was there, he wanted to help.

"Three of us went down. Pepe at the controls. Cal with his search gear. I kept a video narrative. Flying low enough to look, all we saw was death. The impact had burned cities and forests and grasslands.

The polar ice had thawed. Lowlands were flooded, coastlines changed. We found the land like you see it now, black and barren pouring red mud into the oceans. No spark of green anywhere.

"Hoping for anything alive in the oceans, Cal had Pepe bring us down on the shore of a new sea that ran far into the Amazon valley. I got a whiff of the air when we opened the lock. It had a burnt-sulfur stink and set us all to coughing. In spite of it, Cal was determined to get samples of mud and water to test for microscopic life.

"We had no proper gear but he tried to improvise, with a plastic bag around his head and an oxygen bottle with a tube to his mouth. We watched from the plane. A dismal view. Jagged slopes of dead black lava from a cone north of us. No sun anywhere. A towering storm rising in the west, alive with lightning.

"Cal had a radio. I tried to copy what he said, but the plastic made him hard to hear. He tramped down to the water, stooping to pick up rocks and drop them in his sample bucket. 'Nothing green,' I heard him say. 'Nothing moving.' He looked at the smoking volcano behind him and the blood-colored sea ahead. 'Nothing anywhere.'

"Pepe was begging him to come back, but he muttered something I couldn't make out and stumbled on over the frozen lava, down to a muddy little stream. Squatting there at the edge of it, he scraped up something for his bucket. We saw him double up with a coughing fit, but he got back to his feet and waded on down the beach, into a surf that was foaming pink.

"Pepe called again, warning him to come back. He waved a sample bottle. 'Our best chance.' His voice was a strangled croak, but I got a few words. 'If anything survived in the sea. I hope—'

"*Hope*. Choking on that last word, he tried to get his breath and failed. He lost the radio and his bucket and stumbled a few yards toward us before he tripped and fell. The oxygen bottle floated away. We saw him grabbing for it, but the next wave took it out of his reach."

"You left him there?" Dian's voice rose sharply. "Left him to die?"

"We left him dead. Pepe wanted to help him, but he'd gone too far. His oxygen gone, the air had killed him."

"Air?"

"Bad air." My robot-father's helpless shrug was almost human. "Mixed in the volcanic gases in the whiff I caught, there was cyanide."

"Cyanide?" Pepe frowned. "Who put it there?"

"It came from cometary cyanogen from the asteroid."

"Poisoned air!" Arne turned pale. "And you want us to go back?"

"To help nature clean it." His lenses swept the five of us. "If no green plants are left to restore the oxygen, you must replant them. Cal died with his work undone. It's yours to finish."

3

The mission left to us, to us alone, we died and let the robots sleep while an ice age passed on Earth. The maternity lab delivered us again, and once more our dead parents brought us up.

My robot-father was always with me. He taught me to spell, taught me science and geometry, counted time when I was working out on the treadmill in the centrifuge.

"Keep yourself fit," he used to tell me. "I can last forever, but you're only human."

He made me work till I was panting and dripping sweat.

"You have your clone father's genes," he reminded me again. "You'll never be him, but I want you to promise you'll never give up our noble mission."

My hand on my heart, I promised.

Pepe's robot-father taught him the multiplication tables and rocket engineering and trained him to box. The boxing was to make him quick with his wits and quick on his feet.

"You'll need all that," he said, "when you get to Earth."

Pepe liked to compete. He was always wanting to work out with Arne and me. He beat me till I'd had enough. Arne was big enough to knock him across the centrifuge, but he kept coming back for more.

Tanya's robot-mother taught her how to care for a baby-sized doll, taught her biology and the genetics she might need for terraforming Earth. Working in the maternity lab, she learned to clone frogs and dissect them, but she refused to dissect any kind of cat.

Arne's robot-father helped him to learn to walk, taught him the geology terraforming science. His first experimental project was a colony of cloned ants in a glass-walled farm.

"We can't exist alone," his clone father told him. "We evolved as part of a biocosm. In the cryonic vault, we have seed and spores and cells and embryos to help you rebuild it."

In the nursery and the playroom while we were small, later in the classroom and the gym, we learned to love the robots. They loved us as well as robots could. They were immortal. Sometimes I envied them.

I felt sad for our parents and their Earth, dead a hundred thousand or perhaps a million years. The robots couldn't say how long. They had been awakened only when the computer found Earth once more warm enough for life.

We saw them only in their images, speaking to us from the holo tanks. My own holo father, when he was my teacher, appeared as a tall slim man in a dark suit, wearing a narrow black mustache. Counting pushups when I worked out in the centrifuge, he looked younger and wore a red sweatsuit and no mustache. More relaxed at times when he talked of his wife and their home and their work together, he was in a purple dressing gown. Lecturing from the tank, he sometimes waved an empty pipe.

He tried to teach me the art of history.

"I was doing books and scripts about the project before the impact," he said. "You're to carry on the story I began. That will be important to whoever follows us."

Except for the gold plate on her flat chest, Tanya's robot-mother looked like all the other robots, but her holo mother was tall and beautiful, not flat-chested at all. She had bright grey-green eyes and thick black hair that fell to her waist when she left it free.

In the classroom tank, teaching us biology, she wore a white lab jacket. In the gym tank, teaching us to dance, she was lovely in a long black gown. Down at the pool on the bottom level, she appeared in a red swimsuit she used to wear into my dreams. There was no real piano, but she sometimes played a grand piano in the tank, singing songs she had written from her memories of life and love on Earth.

Tanya grew up as tall as she was, with the same bright greenish eyes and sleek black hair. She learned to sing the same songs in the same rich voice. We all loved her, or all of us but Dian, who never seemed to care if anybody loved her.

Dian's holo mother, Dr Diana Lazard, was smaller than Tanya's, with a chest as flat as the grey name-plate on her robot. She wore dark glasses that made her eyes hard to see. Her hair was a red-gold color that might have been beautiful if she'd let it grow longer, but she kept it short and commonly hid it under a tight black tam. She taught Dian French and Russian and the histories of literature and art, and showed the rest of us nearly all we ever knew about the old Earth.

"Knowledge. Art. Culture." Her everyday voice was dry and flat, but it could ring when she spoke of those treasures and her fear they would be forever lost. "They matter more than anything."

In her classroom, we put on VR headsets that let her guide us over the world that had been. In a virtual airplane, we flew over the white-spired Himalayas and dived down to the river that had carved out the Grand Canyon and crossed Antarctica to the ice desert at the pole. We saw the pyramids and the Acropolis and the newer Sky Needle. She guided us through the Hermitage and the Louvre and the Prado. She wanted all of us to love them, and all lost Earth.

Dian did. Growing up in her mother's image, she cut her hair just as short and kept it under the same black tam and wore the same dark glasses.

If she cared for anybody, it was Arne.

His clone father, Dr Linder, had been a muscular giant whose athletic scholarships had paid his way to degrees in physics and geology. Just as big and just as smart, Arne ran every day on the treadmill in the centrifuge. He learned everything our parents taught and wore the VR gear to tour the lost world with Dian and played chess with her. Perhaps they made love; I never knew.

We had no children. As much as most of us might have wanted them, they were not in DeFalco's plan. The maternity lab, as Tanya's mother explained, was only for clones. The robots gave us contraceptives when we needed them.

Tanya did. Our biologist, she understood sex and enjoyed it. So did Pepe. From their teens, they were always together, never hiding their affection. In spite of Pepe, however, Tanya was generous to me.

Once, dancing with her in the gym, I was so overcome with her scent and her voice and the feel of her lithe body in my arms that I whispered a confession. With Pepe glaring after us, she led me out of the room and up to the dome.

The Earth was new, a long curve of red fire slashed across the black and soundless night, lighting the dead moonscape to a ghostly pink. In the dimness of the dome, she stripped to reveal her enchantment, stripped me while I stood trembling with a dazed elation.

In the Moon's mild gravity, we needed no bed. She laughed at my ignorance and proceeded to teach me. Expert at it, she seemed to relish the lesson as keenly as I did. We were a long time there, the dance over and only the robots awake when we went back down. Kissing me a long goodnight that I shall never forget, she whispered that with practice I might be better than Pepe. Sadly for me, however, it never happened again.

She must have given Pepe some consolation, because he held me no grudge. Afterward, in fact, he seemed more amiable than ever, perhaps because of our shared devotion. He got on less well with Arne, who played his endless chess with Dian and roamed the old Earth in his VR cap to study DeFalco's plan for restoring the planet. He wanted to be our leader. That leader, of course, should have been DeFalco's clone, but the robot with his name on the white plate stood dead in its corner of the stock room, grey beneath millennia of Moon dust.

The year we were twenty-five, our robot parents gathered us into the gym. We found our gene parents already there in the big holo tank, all in their most formal images and looking very serious.

"The time has come for your own flight to Earth." My father spoke for them. "Your training is complete. Remote sensors show the ice age is over. The robots have fueled the two-place Moon jumper and loaded it with seed pellets. Two of you can go, taking off when you are ready."

"I am." Glancing at Tanya, Pepe lifted his voice. "Today, if we can."

"You will be the pilot." My father smiled and turned to Arne. "Linder, you're the trained terraformer. You will go to disperse the seed."

Flushing pink, Arne shook his head.

4

Arne stood shaking his head, scowling at our parents in the holo tank. Dian stepped to his side and slid her arm around him.

"Damn DeFalco!" His lip jutted defiantly. "Damn his crazy plan! It doesn't fit the facts. The asteroid was bigger than he ever imagined. It sterilized the planet and shattered a lot of the crust. It's still recovering, the ice caps receding, but there's still alarming seismic instability. I think we ought to let it wait for another generation."

"Arne!" Tanya shook her head in pained reproof. "Its albedo says it's warm enough. Ready for us now."

"If you believe albedos."

Our holo parents stood frozen in the tank, their eyes fixed on Arne as if the master computer had never been programmed for such a rebellion, but Tanya made a face at him.

"Arny Barny!" Mocking him, her voice turned shrill as it was when she was three. "Under all the bluff, you've always been a fraidy cat. Or are you just a coward?"

"Please, Tammy." Pepe touched her arm. "We're all grown up." He turned very soberly to Arne. "And we can't forget why Dr DeFalco put us here."

"DeFalco's dead."

"Given time, we'll all be dead. And dead again." Pepe shrugged. "But really we don't have to care. We can always be replaced."

"Three cheers for Cal DeFalco!" Arne had flushed with emotion, but he shook his head at Tanya with a sort of forced deliberation. "You call me a coward. I'd say prudent. I know geology and the science of terraforming. I've spent thousands of hours surveying the Earth with telescopes and spectroscopes and radar, studying oceans and floodplains and lowlands.

"And I've found nowhere fit for life. The seas are still contaminated with heavy metals from the asteroid, the rivers still leaching more lethal stuff off the continents. We'd find the atmosphere unbreathable. Oxygen depleted. Carbon dioxide enough to kill you. Sulfur dioxide from constant new eruptions. Climates too severe to let life take root anywhere. If we've got to make some crazy effort in spite of all the odds, at least let's wait for another ten or twenty years—"

"Wait for what?" Tanya cut in more sharply. "If an ice age wasn't long enough to cleanse the planet, what kind of miracle do you expect in ten or twenty years?"

"We can gather data." Arne dropped his voice, appealing to reason. "We can update the plan to fit the Earth as we expect it to be in ten or 20,000 years. We can train for our own mission, if we must finally undertake it."

"We've trained." Pepe waited for Tanya to nod. "We've studied. We're as ready as we'll ever be. We're going. I say now."

"Not me." Arne hugged Dian to him, and she smiled into his face. "Not us."

"We'll miss you." Pepe shrugged and turned to me. "How about it, Dunk?"

I gulped and caught my breath to say okay, but Tanya had already clutched his arm. "I'm the biologist. I understand the problems. I've found oxygen masks ready for us in the stock room. Just take me down. I know how to sow the seed."

They took off together, Pepe flying the space plane, Tanya filing radio reports as they surveyed the Earth from low orbit. She described the shrunken ice caps, the high sea levels, the shifted shorelines that made familiar features hard to recognize.

"We need soil where seed can grow," she said. "Hard to pinpoint from space if it does exist at all. Rocks do crumble into silt, but the rains are scouring most of that into the sea for lack of roots to hold it. We'll try to seed from orbit, but I want to land for a closer look."

Dian asked them to look for any relics of human civilization.

"Relics?" Tanya was sarcastic. "Ice and time have erased the great pyramids. The big dams. The Great Wall of China. Everything large enough to look for."

"No surprise," Arne muttered. "The impact has remade the Earth, but not for us."

"Our job." Pepe's voice. "To make it fit."

"A brand-new world!" Tanya's irony was gone. "Waiting for the spark of life."

On the mike, Arne had technical questions about spectrometer readings of solar radiation reflected from the surface and refracted through the atmosphere, questions about polar ice, about air and ocean circulation. Data, he said, that we ought to record for the next generation.

"We're here to replant the planet." Tanya grew impatient. "And too low over the equator to see atmosphere or ocean circulation patterns. Heavy clouds hide most of the surface. We'll need the radar to search for a landing site."

Arne never said he wished he had gone down with them, but he kept on with his questions till I thought he felt guilty.

Dropping into an orbit that grazed the atmosphere, they sowed the planet with life-bombs, heat-shielded cylinders loaded with seed pellets. Clearing weather over east Africa revealed a narrow sea in the Great Rift Valley, which had deepened and opened wider. Tanya wanted to land there.

"The most likely spot we've seen. It should be warm and wet enough. The water looks blue, probably fresh, with no great pollution. Besides, it happens to be near where *Homo sapiens* evolved. A symbolic spot for a second creation, though Pepe says I'm crazy to think about it.

"He says our job is already done. We've scattered seed over every continent and dropped algae bombs into all the major oceans. He says nature can take care of the rest, but I'm the biologist. I want soil and air and water samples to save for the next generation.

"Arne ought to be here." She was serious, with no sarcasm. "He's the terraformer, more expert than we are. He's missing the thrill of his life."

Elation bubbled in her voice.

"We feel like gods. Descending to the dead world with the fire of life. Pepe says we ought to head back to the Moon while we can, but I won't – I can't – give up the actual landing."

Beginning the final descent on the other side of Earth, they were out of contact while I bit my nails for an hour.

"Down safe!" She was exuberant when we heard her again. "Pepe set us down on the west shore of this Kenyan sea. A splendid day with a high sun and a great view across a neck of the water to a wall of dark cliffs and the slopes of a new volcanic mountain almost as tall as Kilimanjaro. A tower of smoke is climbing out of the cone. The sky above us is blue as the sea, though maybe not for long. I see a storm cloud rising in the west."

She was silent for a moment.

"Another thing – a very odd thing. Landing on its tail, the plane stands tall. From the cockpit we can see far out across the sea. Most of it calm, there's an odd little patch of whitecaps. Odd because they're moving toward us, with no sign of wind anywhere else.

"I can make out—"

Her voice broke off. I heard the quick catch of her breath and Pepe's muffled exclamation.

"Those whitecaps!" Her voice came back, lifted sharply. "Not whitecaps at all. They're something – something alive!"

She must have moved away from the microphone. Her voice faded, though I made out a few words of Pepe's.

"...impossible...nothing green, no photosynthesis, no energy for our kind of life...we've got to know..."

I caught no more till at last Tanya was back at the mike.

"Something swimming!" Her voice was quick and breathless. "Swimming at the surface. We can't see much except the splashing, but it must have descended from something that survived the impact. Pepe doubts that any large creature could live with so little oxygen, but anaerobic life did evolve on the old ocean floors. The black plumes, the giant tube worms, the bacteria that fed them—"

I heard Pepe's muted voice. The mike clicked, went dead, stayed dead while Dian and Arne came up to listen with me.

"Something has cut them off!" Dian shudderend. "An attack by those swimming things?"

"No way to know, but I did try to warn them." Arne must have repeated that a dozen times as the hours went by. "The planet simply isn't ready for us. It may never be."

In the hangars we had a dozen spare space planes that had ferried freight or workmen to the Moon. I suggested that we should think of a rescue flight.

"We'd be fools to go." Arne shook his head. "If they need help, they need it now, not next week. Our duty is to stay here, gather the data we can, record it for a generation that may have a better chance."

"I'm afraid," Dian whispered. "I wish—"

"Wish for what?" Arne snapped. "There's nothing we can do. Nothing but wait."

We waited forever, till the mike clicked at last and we heard Pepe.

"Navarro here, on board alone. Tanya's been off the plane for hours. In her breathing mask, collecting whatever she can. I've begged her to come back before her air runs out, but she's fascinated with those swimmers. We watched one crawling up out of the water. Something like a red octopus, though she says it looks no kin to any octopus that ever existed before the impact. A mass of thick, blood-red coils. It splayed itself on the beach and lay still in the sun.

"She wondered if it might have some kind of photosynthetic symbiote in its blood. Something red instead of green, that feeds it on solar energy. I don't see any way for her to tell, but she's still out there with her binoculars and her video and her sample bucket.

"I've begged her to get back with what she has, but she always needs a few more minutes. She keeps working towards the beach. The red things are amphibians, she says. A dozen of them out there now. An unexpected life form that she thinks could be a problem later. Leave that for later, I told her, but she keeps slogging on. The beach is mud, silt washed down off the hills in the west. She says the things are digging in it, maybe for something they eat. She wants to see. "But now—"

His voice lifted and stopped while he must have been watching. I heard no more till it came back, still begging her. She had gone too far. The mud was deeper than it looked. Her air had run low. She could watch the creatures from the cockpit till she knew them better. Faintly, I caught her answer.

"Just one more minute."

For a long-seeming time I heard nothing at all.

"'One more minute.' He echoed her words.

"It's close to night. That storm's rolling down on us. The wind's getting up. A few raindrops already – Stop, Tanny! Stop!" His voice went high. "Mind the mud."

"Give me just another minute." Her radio voice, so faint I hardly heard it. "These creatures – they're a new evolution. We've got to know what they are. Never mind the risk."

"I mind it," he called again to her. "Tanny, please—"

He stopped to hear something from her that I failed to catch. For a time he was silent again, except for the rush of his rapid breath.

"Navarro again." His voice was back, bitterly resigned. "She can't resist those red monsters. At first they sprawled flat, soaking up the sun, but now they're moving. One jumped at another. The other dodged and sprang to meet it. Now—"

He stopped to watch and shout another warning.

"The things are really quite a show. They look legless, maybe boneless, but amazingly active and quick. A riddle, if they need no oxygen. But I wish—"

He yelled again, and waited.

"They're a crazy tangle of long red tentacles roiling the mud. Fighting? Mating? She has to know. Binoculars now, then the camera. She's too close. Getting data, but I don't like this mud. Maybe bottomless, with no plant life to hold it. Her feet are sinking in it. She's stumbling, struggling—

"My God!" He was screaming into the microphone. "Hold still! I'm coming."

"Don't!" Her voice came thinly, desperate yet oddly calm. "Arne, please! Get back to the Moon. Report what you can. Don't mind me. There'll be another clone."

I heard the whir and clang of the lock, and then nothing at all.

5

The three of us left at Tycho lived out our natural lives with no more news from Earth. The robots slept again, a million years perhaps; we had no clocks that ran so long. The computers woke them when the sensors found the Earth grown green enough. We grew up again, listening to the robots and the holos, struggling once more to learn the roles we must play.

"Meat robots!" Arne was always the critic. "Created and programmed to play God for old DeFalco."

"Hardly gods." Tanya was bright and beautiful and sure of nearly everything. "But at least alive."

"Meat copies." Arne mocked her. "Copies of the holo ghosts in the tank."

"More than copies, too," Tanya said. "Genes aren't everything. We're ourselves."

"Maybe," Arne muttered. "But still slaves of old DeFalco and his idiot plan."

"So what?" Tanya wore a thick sheaf of sleek black hair, and she tossed it scornfully back. "It's the reason we're here. I expect to do my bit."

"Maybe you, but I've heard my father talk."

We all knew his father's image in the tanks. A bronze-bearded giant, Dr Arne Linder had been a distinguished geologist back before the impact. We'd read his books in Dian's library.

Born in old Norway, he had married Sigrid Knutson, a tall blonde beauty he had known when they were children. We learned more about his life from Pepe Navarro's journal. The warning caught them in Iceland. Flying back to the Moon base, he begged Navarro to drop him off in Washington, where his wife was a translator in the Norwegian Embassy.

He had left her pregnant, their first child due. He felt frantic to be with her, but Navarro said they had no time to stop anywhere. They fought in the cockpit. Navarro knocked him out and got them to the base in time to save their lives.

"Dreadful for him," Dian said. "He never got over grieving for Sigrid, or feeling he had failed her."

Our new Arne must have caught something of that bitterness. While the greener Earth had always beckoned the rest of us back to finish our mission, he had never learned to like it. Even as a child, he used to haunt the dome, scowling through the big telescope.

"Those black spots." He used to mutter and shake his head. "I don't know what they are. I don't want to know."

They were dark grey patches scattered here and there across all the continents. The instruments showed only naked rock and soil, bare of life.

"Only old lava flow, most likely," Tanya said.

"Cancers." He muttered and shook his head. "Cancers in the green."

"A silly notion," she scolded him. "We'll find the truth when we land."

"Land there?" He looked sick. "Not if I can help it!"

Our holo parents had been too long in the computers for such matters to concern them, but they were real enough to us. My father had been a journalist, reporting from all over the world. His videos of the monuments and history and culture of Russia and China and the old America held an eerie fascination, yet they always filled me with a black regret for all we could never recover.

He never spoke much about himself, but I found more about him from a long narrative, an odd mix of fact and fiction, that he had dictated to the computer. He called it *The Last Day*. Writing for a future he hoped might want to know about the past, he spoke about his family and everybody he had known, telling what they had meant to him. That much was the fact. The fiction was the way he imagined their last moments.

One chapter was about Linder's wife. Best man at their wedding and dancing with her at the reception, he felt haunted by her tragedy. The baby had come, he imagined, while Linder was in Iceland. She was already at home from the hospital, trying to reach him with her news, when DeFalco called on that last morning.

Although he told her nothing about the falling asteroid, his haste and his tone of voice alarmed her. She tried and tried again to reach Linder at his hotel in Reykjavik. He was never there. Frantic, she tried to call friends at the White Sands Moon Base. The phone lines were jammed.

Listening to the radio, watching holo stations, she learned of the communications blackout spreading over Asia. The baby sensed her terror and began to cry. She nursed it and crooned to it and prayed for Arne to call or come home. When the holo phone rang, it was a friend in flight operations at White Sands, who thought she would be relieved to know her husband was safe. She had just seen him rushing aboard the escape plane.

She must have felt relief, my father thought, but also dreadful despair. She knew she and the baby were about to die. Trying not to feel that he had betrayed her, she prayed for him. With the wailing baby in her arms, she sang to it and prayed for its soul till the surface shock brought the building down upon them.

Hearing the emotion in my father's voice, I shared something of his sorrow, a grief that always left me whenever we climbed into the dome to see the reborn Earth and talked of how to restore it. Our instruments revealed nothing of those anomalous creatures Wu and Navarro had seen crawling out into the Sun. The depleted oxygen had been replenished. Spinning its swift days and nights high in our black sky, Earth waxed and waned through our long months, inviting us home with green life splashed over the land.

Identical genes never made us entirely identical. We all had to struggle for some compromise between ourselves, our genes, and the demands of our mission. I was never my clone brother, whose dried and frozen body had lain in the Moon dust below the crater wall almost forever.

Reading his letters to me about his frustrated devotion to Tanya, I felt it hard to understand. Grown up again, she loved the mission the way her mother had. Avoiding any risk of discord, she favored all three of us equally, Pepe, Arne and I. If Dian felt hurt, she gave no sign.

"Arrogance!" Arne's clone brother had written in his diary. "Anthropocentric arrogance. We've found a new biocosm already blooming. We have no right to harm it. A crime worse than genocide."

The new Arne shrugged when I asked what he thought of the passage.

"Another man writing, too long ago. I get his point about the mission, but I'll do what I must. Frankly, I don't get what he said about Dian, if they really were in love. All she cares about now is her dusty books and her frozen art and chess with her computer."

DeFalco's clone should have been our leader, but he had died without a clone. When the time had come for our return, Arne gathered us in the library reading room to plan it.

"First of all," he asked, "why should we go back?"

"Of course we must." Tanya spoke sharply, irked at him. "That's the reason we exist."

"An overblown dream." His nose tilted up. "Old DeFalco's impact was not the first. It won't be the last. Maybe not the worst. But a new evolution has always replaced the old with something probably better. Nature working as it should. Why should we meddle?"

"Because we're human," Tanya said.

"Is that so great?" He sniffed at her. "When you look at the old Earth, at all the wanton savagery and genocide, our record's not so bright. Navarro and Wu found a new evolution already in progress. It could flower into something better than we are."

"Those red monsters on the beach?" She shuddered. "I'll go with our own kind."

Arne looked around the table and saw us all against him.

"If we're going back," he said, "I'm the leader. I understand terraforming."

"Maybe." Tanya frowned. "But that's not enough. We'll have to get down into low orbit and make a new survey to select the landing site. Pepe is the space pilot." She smiled at him. "If we make a safe landing, we'll have things to build. Pepe is the engineer."

We voted. Dian raised her hand for Arne, Tanya and Pepe. When that left me to break the tie, I nominated Tanya. Arne sat scowling till he surrendered to her smile. Voting on the landing site, again we chose the coast of that same inland sea. Pepe picked the day. When it came, we gathered in space gear at the spaceport elevator. Only three of us at first, anxiously eager, impatiently waiting for Arne and Dian.

"She's gone!" Arne came running down the passage. "I've looked everywhere. Her rooms, the museum, the gym and the shops, the common rooms. I can't find her."

6

The robots found her in her spacesuit a thousand feet down the crater's inner wall. She had struck jagged ledges, bounced and rolled and struck again. Blood had sprayed the faceplate, and she was stiff as iron before they got her back inside. Arne found a note in her computer.

"Farewell and good fortune, if any of you miss me. I've chosen not to go because I see no useful place for me at the Earth outpost, even if you get one set up. I lack the hardihood for pioneering. Even at the best, the colonists will have no time or need for me before another group of clones can grow."

"Hardly true." Gravely, Pepe shook his head. "The mission will take us all."

The robots dug a new grave in the plot of rocks and dusk outside the crater where our parents and our older siblings had lain so long; beside them the sad little row of smaller mounds that covered my beagles. We buried her there, still rigid in her space gear. Arne spoke briefly, his voice hollow and somber in his helmet.

"I do miss her. It's a terrible time for me, because I think I killed her. I've read the diaries of ourselves in love. I think she loved me again, though she never told me, or said much to anybody. Perhaps I should have guessed, but I'm not my brother."

"We'll have another chance." Tanya tried to comfort him. "But we can't help what we are."

We watched the robots fill the grave and delayed the launch again while he made a marker to set at the head of it, a metal plate that should stand forever here on the airless Moon, bearing only this legend:

DIAN LAZARD
NUMBER THREE

"Three." His voice in the helmet was a bitter rumble. "Numbers. That's all we are."

"More than that," Tanya protested. "We're human. More than human, if you remember why we're here."

"Not by choice," he grumbled. "I wish old DeFalco had left my father back on Earth."

Muttering and swallowing whatever else he wanted to say, he knelt at the foot of the grave. The rest of us waited silently, isolated from one another in our clumsy armor. Shut up in her own tiny world, Dian had seemed content with the precious artefacts she cared for. I felt sad that I had never really got to know her.

Arne rose from his knees and Tanya led us from the cemetery to the loaded plane. Our five individual robots had to be left on the station, but the sixth, the one DeFalco had not lived to program, came with us. We called it Calvin.

From orbit, we studied those dark blots again and found them changed.

"They've moved since we were children," Arne said. "Moved and grown. I don't like them. I don't think the planet's ready for us."

"Ready or not," Tanya grinned and leaned cheerfully to slap his back, "here we go."

"I can't imagine—" Muttering, he scowled at the ulcered Earth. What could they be?"

"Bare lavas, maybe, where the rains have left no soil where anything could grow?"

"Maybe burns?" She waited for her turn to study the data. "The spectrometers show oxygen levels high. More oxygen could mean hotter forest fires."

"No smoke." He shook his head. "Fires don't burn for years."

"Let's go on down."

She had Pepe drop us into a landing orbit above the equator. Low over Africa, we found the Great Rift grown still wider. That inland sea had risen, flooding the ancient shore, yet she decided to land near it.

"Why?" Arne demanded. "Have you forgotten those monsters on the beach?"

"I want to see if they've evolved."

"I don't like that." He nodded at the monitor. "That black area just west of the rift. I've watched it creeping across central Africa, erasing what I think was dense rain forest. Something ugly!"

"If it's a challenge, I want to cope with it now."

She had Pepe set us down on the bank of a new river, just a few miles from that narrow, cliff-walled sea.

We rolled dice to be first off the plane. Winning with a six, I opened the air lock and stood a long time there, staring west across the grassy valley floor to a wall of dark forest till Tanya nudged me to make room for her.

Pepe stayed on the plane, but the rest of us climbed down. Tanya picked blades from the grass at our feet and found them the same Kentucky Blue she and Pepe had sowed so long ago. When we looked through binoculars, however, the forest was nothing they had planted. Massive palm-like trees lifted feathery green plumes and enormous trumpet-shaped purple blooms out of a dense tangle of thick crimson vines.

"A jungle of riddles," Tanya whispered. "The trees could be descended from some cactus species. But the undergrowth?" She stared a long time and whispered again, "A jungle of snakes! Slick red snakes!"

I saw them at last, when she passed the binoculars to me. Heavy red coils, rooted in the ground, they wrapped the black stalks of things that looked like gigantic toadstools. Writhing like actual snakes, they kept striking as if at invisible insects.

"A new evolution!" Tanya took the glasses back. "Maybe from the swimmers we saw on that beach? Maybe red from mutant photosynthetic symbiotes? I want a closer look."

"Don't forget," Arne muttered. "Closer looks have killed you."

We saw nothing else moving till Pepe's radio voice came from the cockpit, high above us. "Look north! Along the edge of the jungle. Things hopping like kangaroos. Or maybe grasshoppers."

We found a creature venturing warily over a ridge, standing tall to look at us, sinking out of sight, hopping on toward us to stand and stare again, rumbling with something like the purr of a gigantic cat. A biped, it had a thick tail that balanced its forequarters and made a third leg when it stood. Others came slowly on behind it, jumping high but pausing as if to graze.

"Our retrojets must have scared everything away," Pepe called again. "But now! Farther up the slope. A couple of monsters that would dwarf the old elephants. Half a dozen smaller, maybe younger."

"A danger to us?" Arne called uneasily.

"Who knows? The big ones have stopped to look. And listen, too. They've spread ears as wide as they are. They do look able to smash us if they like."

"Shouldn't we take off?"

"Not yet."

Arne had reached for the binoculars, but Tanya kept them, sweeping the forest edge and the riverbank and the herd of hopping grazers.

"A wonderland!" She was elated. "And a puzzle box. We must have slept longer than I thought, for all this evolutionary change."

Arne climbed back into the plane and came down with a heavy rifle he mounted on a tripod. He squinted through the telescopic sight, waiting for the monsters.

"Don't shoot," Tanya said, "unless I tell you to."

"Okay, if you tell me in time."

He held the rifle on them till they stopped a few hundred yards from us. Armored with slick purple-black plates that shimmered under the tropic sun, they looked a little like elephants, more like military tanks. The tallest came ahead, spread its wing-like ears again, opened enormous bright-fanged jaws, bellowed like a foghorn.

Arne crouched behind his gun.

"Don't," Tanya warned him. "You couldn't stop them."

"I've got to try. No time to take off."

He kept the gun level. We watched those great jaws yawning wider. A thunderous bellow scattered the hoppers. She caught his shoulder and pulled him away from his weapon. The monster stood there a long time, watching us through huge, black-slitted eyes as if waiting for an answer to its challenge, till finally it turned to lead its family on around us and down to the river. They splashed in and disappeared.

"Nothing I expected." Tanya stood frowning after them. "No large land animal could have survived. Perhaps a few sea creatures did. The whales were prehistoric land dwellers that migrated into the sea. Maybe they've returned as amphibians."

The alarmed hoppers settled down. Tanya had us stand still in the shadow of the plane as they grazed in toward us, till Pepe shouted again.

"If you want a killer, here it comes!"

The hopper leader stood tall again, with a kind of purring scream. The grazers reared and scattered in panic. Something swift and tiger-striped pounced out of the grass and darted to overtake a baby before it could leap again. Arne's rifle crashed, and the two tumbled down together.

"I told you," Tanya scolded him. "Don't do that."

"Specimens." He shrugged. "You ought to take a look."

He stayed on guard with the gun while I went on with her to study his kills. No larger than a dog, the infant hopper was hairless, covered with fine grey scales, its belly torn open and entrails exposed. Tanya spread the mangled body on the grass for my camera.

"It's well shaped for its apparent ecological niche, but that's about all I can say." She shook her head in frustration. "We must have had a hundred million years of change."

The killer was a compact mass of powerful muscle, clad in sleek black fur. She opened its bloody jaws to show the fangs to my camera, had me move the body to show the teats and claws.

"A mammal." She spoke for the microphone. "Descended perhaps from rats or mice that somehow got through alive."

Still aglow with the elation of discovery, she forgave Arne for his kill.

"A new world for a new race!" she exulted.

"Maybe," Arne muttered. "But ours? More likely a brand new biology, where we'll never belong."

"We'll see." She shrugged and looked around again at the sea where the great amphibians lived and the jungle that had bred the killer. "We're here to see."

She set the robot to scraping soil from the top of a rocky knob to level a site for our lab and living quarters. We unloaded supplies and set up the first geodesic dome. The robot began cutting stone for a defensive wall. She took me on short expeditions along the shore and up the ridge to record the flora and fauna we found. She was soon asking Pepe about fuel for the plane.

"The reserve still aboard might get us back to the Moon, with half a drop left in the tanks."

"With only one aboard?"

"Safe enough."

Then I want you to go back for what we need to replant our own biocosm. Seed, frozen eggs and embryos, equipment for the lab."

"To replant ourselves?" Arne scowled at her. "With that black biocosm just over the ridge?"

She shrugged. "We face risks. We must cope when we can. Leave our records when we can't." She turned to me. "You'll go back with Pepe. Holograph the data we can send you. Hold the fort."

"And leave us marooned?" Arne went pale. "Just the two of us?"

"Pepe will be back," she told him. "You have enough to do here. Testing soils. Prospecting for oil and ores we'll need."

Pepe and I went back to the Moon. My beagle was happy to have me home. The robots loaded and refueled the plane. Pepe took off and left me alone and very lonely. The robots were poor companions and the holos had nothing new to say, but Spaceman was a comfort until I got news from Earth.

Pepe had inflated another geodome for a hydroponic garden. Arne surveyed land for a farm. When the rainy season ended, the robotic Calvin built a diversion dam to draw irrigation water from the river.

"Arne enjoys shooting a yearling jumper when we need meat," Tanya reported. "A tasty change from the irradiated stuff we brought from the Moon. The hippo-whales come and go between the river and the grass. They stopped twice to stare and bellow, but they ignore us now. I think our tiny human island really is secure, though Arne still frets about the black spot. He's gone now to climb the western cliffs for a look beyond the rim."

Her next transmission came only hours later.

"Arne's back." Her voice was tight and quick. "Exhausted and in panic. Something chased him. A storm, he calls it, but nothing we can understand. A cloud so dark it hides the sun. A roar that isn't wind. Something falling that isn't rain. He says our days on Earth are done."

7

The monitor went blank. All I heard was static. Outside the dome Earth hung full in the lunar night. I watched Africa slide out of sight, watched the black-patched Americas crawl through an endless day, watched Africa return, heard Tanya's voice.

"We're desperate."

Her face was drawn haggard and streaked with something black. In the window beyond her head, I saw a dead black slope reaching up to the dark laval flows that edged the rift valley.

"The bugs have overwhelmed us." Her voice was hoarse and hurried. "Bugs! They're what made those blighted areas that always worried Arne. You must preserve the few facts we've learned.

"These marauding insects have evolved, I imagine, from mutations that enabled some locust or cicada to survive the impact. Evidently they now enter migratory phases like the old locusts. A strange life cycle, as I understand it. I believe they're periodic, like the seventeen-year cicada.

"They must spend decades or even centuries underground, feeding on plant roots or juices. Emergence may be triggered when they've killed too many of their hosts. Emerging, they're voracious, consuming everything organic they reach and then migrating to fresh territory to leave their eggs and begin another cycle.

"Their onslaught on us was dreadful. They blackened the sky. Their roar became deafening. Falling like hail, they ate anything that had ever been alive. Trees, brush, grass, live wood and dead wood, live animals and dead. They coupled in their excrement, buried their eggs in it, died. Their bodies made a carpet of dark rot. The odor was unendurable.

"We're safe in the plane, at least for now, but total desolation surrounds us. The bugs ate our plastic geodomes. They ate the forest and the grass. They killed and ate the hoppers, bones and all. They shed and ate their wings. They died and ate the dead. They're all gone now. Nothing alive but their eggs in the dust, waiting for wind and water to bring new seed from anywhere to let the land revive, while they hatch and multiply and wait to kill again.

"Dark dust rises when the wind blows now, bitter with the stink of death. The hippos came out, wandered forlornly in search of anything to graze, and dived back in the river. Nothing alive is left in sight. Nothing but ourselves, in a stillness as terrible as their roar.

"How long we can last, I don't know. Arne wanted to give up and get back to the Moon, but there's no fuel for that. We aren't equipped for any long trek across this devastation, but Pepe has ripped metal off the plane and welded it into a makeshift boat. If the bugs didn't get across the sea, perhaps we can make a new start beyond it.

"The plane must be abandoned, with our radio gear. This will be our last transmission. Keep your eye on the Earth and record what you can.

"And Dunk—" With a catch in her voice, she stopped to wipe at a tear. "I couldn't wish you were with us, but I want you to know I miss you. Next time, whenever that comes, I hope to know you better. As Pepe likes to say, *Hasta la vista!*"

One thousand years after, we've been reborn to try again. Much of Earth is still darkly scarred, but those dark spots are gone from Africa and Europe. We're going down to Earth, all five of us, with a cryostat filled with seed and cells to replant the planet if we must. Dian is bringing a few of her precious artefacts and the narrow chance we find anybody apt to care.

We're landing on the delta of the Nile. It drains into the Red Sea now, but its valley is still a vivid green slash across red-brown desert. Pepe has picked a landing spot a little north of where the pyramids stood. We're overloaded. Pepe thinks we'll have to spend so much fuel on survey and landing that we can't come back, but we're prepared to stay. I'll record more detail as we drop out of low orbit.

"Technology!" Pepe's shout of triumph rang from the cockpit on our first pass above the Nile. "They've got technology. I heard radio squeals and whistles, and then a burst or weird music. I think our job is done."

"If it is—" Dian was at the telescope, but I heard the awed words she murmured almost to herself. "A new world ready to welcome us!"

"Maybe." Waiting uneasily for a turn at the telescope, Arne shook his head. "We haven't met them yet."

"Maybe?" Pepe mocked him. "We came to meet them, and I think they'll have enough to show us. I see bright lines across the ancient delta. Some run all the way to the river. Canals, I imagine. And—"

His voice caught.

"A grid! There on the western edge. A pattern of closer lines. Could be the streets of a city." He was silent as Earth rolled under us. "Buildings!" His voice lifted suddenly. "It *is* a city. With the sun shifting, I can make out a tower at the center. A new Alexandria!"

"Try for contact," Tanya told him. "Ask for permission for us to set down."

"Down to what?" Arne drowned. "They didn't ask us here."

"What's the risk?" Dian asked him. "What have we got to lose?"

Pepe tried when we came around again.

"Squeals." Frowning in the headphones, he made a face of wry frustration. "Whistles. Scraps of eerie music. Finally voices, but nothing I could understand."

"There!" Tanya was at the telescope. "Out in the edge of the desert, west of the city. A pattern like a wheel."

He studied it.

"I wonder—" His voice paused and quickened. "An airport! The wheel spokes are runways. And there's a wide white streak that could be a road into the city. If we knew how to ask—"

"No matter," she told him. "We've no fuel to search much farther. Put us down, but out where we won't make a problem."

On the next pass, we glided down. The city roofs raced beneath us. Red tile, yellow tile and blue, aligned along stately avenues. The airport rushed beneath us. We were low above the tall control tower when I felt the heavy thrust of the retrorockets.

We tipped down for a vertical landing. The thundering cushion of fire and steam hid everything till I felt the jolt of landing. The rocket thrust gone, we could breathe again. Tanya opened the cabin door to let us look out.

The steam was gone, though I caught its hot scent. I rubbed the sun dazzle out of my eyes and found clumps of spiny yellow-green desert brush around us. The terminal building towered far off in the east. We stayed aboard, uneasily waiting. At the radio, Pepe got hums and squawks and shouting voices.

"Probably yelling at us." He twirled his knobs, listened, tried to echo the voices he heard, shook his head again. "Could be English," he mustered. "Angry English, from the sound of it, but I can't make anything out."

We sat there under the desert blaze till the plane got too hot for comfort.

"Will they know?" Arne shrunk back from the door. "Know we brought their forefathers here?"

"If they don't," Tanya said, "we'll find a way to tell them."

"How?" Sweating from more than the heat, he asked Pepe if we could take off again.

"Not for the Moon," Pepe said. "Not till we must."

Tanya and I climbed down to the ground. Spaceman came with us, running out to sniff and growl at something in the brush and slinking back to tremble against my knee. Arne followed a few minutes later, standing in the shade of the plane and staring across the brush at the distant tower. A bright red light began flashing there.

"Flashing to warn us off," he muttered.

I had brought my videocam, Tanya had me shoot clumps of the thorny brush and then a rock matted over with something like red moss.

"Data on the crimson symbiote reported by the last expedition." She spoke crisply into my mike. "Apparently surviving now in a mutant Bryophyte—"

"Hear that?" Arne cupped his hand to his ear. "Something hooting."

What I heard was a pulsing mechanical scream. Spaceman growled and cowered closer to my leg till we saw an ungainly vehicle lurching over a hill and rolling toward us on tall wheels, flashing colored lights.

"Now's our chance," Tanya said, "to give them the gifts we've brought. Show them we mean no harm."

Clumsy under the heavy gravity we climbed back into the plane and came down with our offerings. Dian carried one of her precious books, the *Poems of Emily Dickinson*, wrapped in brittle ancient plastic. Arne brought a loudhailer, perhaps the same one DeFalco had used to warn the mob away from the escape craft. Pepe stayed in the cockpit.

"We come from the Moon." Arne pushed ahead of us to meet the vehicle, bawling through his hailer. "We come in peace. We come with gifts."

The vehicle had no windows, no operator we could see. Spaceman ran barking to meet it. Arne dropped the bullhorn and stood in front of it, waving his arms. Hooting louder, it almost ran over us before it swerved and rolled on around us to butt against the plane. Heavy metal arms reached out to grab and tip it. Pepe scrambled out as it was lifted off the ground. The hooting stopped, and the machine hauled it away, while Spaceman whimpered and huddled against my feet.

"Robotic, I guess." Pepe stared after it, scratching his head. "Sent out to salvage the wreck."

Baffled and anxious, we stood there sweating. Flying insects buzzed around us. Some of them stung. Tanya had me get a closeup of one on my arm. A hot wind blew out of the desert west, sharp with a scent like burned toast. We started walking toward the tower.

"We're idiots," Arne muttered at Tanya. "We should have stayed in orbit."

She made no answer.

We plodded on, battling the gravity and swatting at insects, till we came over a rocky rise and saw the wide white runways spread out ahead, the tower at the hub was still miles away. Parked aircraft scattered the broad triangles between the flight strips. A few stood upright for vertical landing and ascent, like our own craft, but most had wings and landing gear like those I knew from pictures of the past.

We dropped flat when a huge machine with silver wings came roaring overhead, stopped again when a silent vehicle came racing to meet us. Arne lifted his bullhorn and lowered it when Tanya frowned. Brave again, Spaceman growled and bristled till it stopped. Three men in white got out, speaking together and staring at him. He stood barking at them till one of them pointed something like an ancient flashlight at him. He whined and crumpled down. They gathered him up and took him away in the van.

"Why the dog?" Arne scowled in bafflement. "With no attention to us?"

"Dogs are extinct," Tanya said.

"Hey!" A startled cry from Pepe. "We're moving!"

The parked aircraft beside the strip were gliding away from us. Flowing without ripples, without a sound, with no mechanism visible, the slick white pavement was carrying us toward the terminal building. Pepe bent to feel it with his fingers, dropped to put his ear against it.

"A thousand years of progress since we came to fight the bugs!" He stood up and shrugged at Tanya. "Old DeFalco would be happy."

Scores of people were leaving the parked aircraft to ride the crawling pavement. Men in pants and skirt-like kilts. Women in shorts and trailing gowns. Children in rainbow colors as if on holiday. Although I saw nothing much like our orange-yellow jump-suits, nobody seemed to notice. People streamed out of the terminal ahead. Most of them, I saw, wore bright little silver balls on bracelets or necklaces.

"Sir?" Arne called to a man near us. "Can you tell us—"

With a hiss as if for silence, the man frowned and turned away. They all stood very quietly, alone or in couples or little family groups, gazing solemnly ahead.

Pepe jogged my arm as we came around the building and into a magnificent avenue that led toward the heart of the city. I caught my breath and stood gawking at a row of immense statues spaced down the middle of the parkway.

"Look at that!" Arne raised his arm to point ahead. "I think they do remember us."

A woman in a long white gown gestured sternly to hush him, and the pavement bore us on toward a tall needle that stabbed into the sky at the end of the avenue. A thin crescent at its point shone like a bright new Moon. Statues, needle, crescent, they were all bright silver. A bell began to boom somewhere ahead, slow deep-toned notes like far thunder. The murmur of voices ceased. All eyes lifted toward the crescent. I saw Pepe cross himself.

"A ceremonial," he whispered. "I think they worship the Moon."

I heard him counting under his breath as the bell pealed. "Twenty-nine," he murmured. "The lunar month."

The soundless pavement took us on till he started and jogged my arm again, pointing at the towering figure just ahead. More than magnificent, a blinding silver dazzle in the slanting morning sun, it must have been a hundred feet tall. Shading my eyes, I blinked and looked and blinked again.

It was my father. In the same jacket and necktie his holo image had worn when it spoke from the tank, flourishing the same tobacco pipe he had waved to punctuate his lectures. The pipe, I thought, could be only a magic symbol now; DeFalco had saved no tobacco seed.

Those nearest the statue dropped to their knees, kissing their lunar pendants. Eyes lifted, they breathed their prayers and rose again as we moved on toward the next monumental figure, even taller than my father's. It was Pepe himself, in the flight jacket and cap his clone father had worn to the Moon, one gigantic arm lifted as if to beckon us on toward the needle and the crescent. People pressed toward it, kneeling to kiss heir pendants and pray.

"He never dreamed." His own eyes lifted, Pepe shook his head in awe. "Never dreamed that he might become a god."

Tanya came next, taller still, splendid in the sunlit shimmer of her lab jacket, raising an enormous test tube toward the tower. Arne next, waving his rock-hunter's hammer. Finally Dian, the tallest, holding a silver book. I heard our actual Dian gasp when she read the title cut into the metal.

The Poems of Emily Dickinson.

Below the needle and the crescent, the pavement carried us into a vast open circle ringed with great silver columns. Slowing it crowded us together. At a single thunderous peal, people stood still, gazing up at a balcony high on the face of the spire.

A tiny-seeming man robed in bright silver appeared there, arms raised high. The bell pealed again, echoes rolling from the columns. His voice thundered, louder than the bell. The worshipers sang an answer, a slow and solemn chant. He spoke again, and Pepe gripped my arm.

"English!" he whispered. "A queer accent, but it's got to be English!"

The speaker stopped, arms still lifted toward the sky. The bell pealed, its deep reverberations dying slowly into silence. People around us fell to their knees, faces raised to the crescent. We knelt with them, all of us but Arne. He stalked on forward, bullhorn high.

"Hear this!" he bawled. "Now hear this!"

People around him hissed in protest, but he strode on toward the tower.

"We are your gods!" He paused to let his voice roll back from the columns. "We live on the Moon. We have returned—"

A tall woman in a silver robe came off her knees to shout at him, waving a silver baton. He stopped to gesture at Dian and the rest of us.

"Look!" he shouted. "You must know us—"

She waved the baton at him. His voice choked off. Gasping for breath, he dropped the bullhorn and crumpled to the pavement. The woman swung the baton toward us. Dian rose, waving her book and declaiming Dickinson:

This is my letter to the world
That never wrote to me—

Dimly, I recall the desperate quaver in her voice, the hushed outrage on the woman's face. The baton swept us. A puff of mist chilled and stung my cheek. The pavement seemed to tilt, and I must have fallen.

8

For a long time I thought I was back at Tycho Station, confined to the bed in our tiny clinic. A robot stood over me, as patiently motionless as any robot. A fan hummed softly. The air was warm, with an odd fresh scent. I felt a sense of groggy comfort till a numb stiffness on my cheek brought recollection back: that avenue of gigantic silver figures, the stern-faced woman in her silver robe, the icy mist from her silver baton.

Shocked wide awake, I tried to get off the bed and found no strength. The robot tipped its lenses, bent to catch my wrist and take my pulse. I saw the difference then; its slick plastic body was the pale blue of the walls, though it had the half-human shape of our robots on the Moon.

Earth gravity turned me giddy. The robot eased me back to the bed and seemed to listen when I spoke, though its answer was nothing I could understand. When I stirred again, it helped me to a chair and left the room to bring a human physician, a lean dark man who wore a silver crescent on a neat white jacket. Briskly efficient, he listened at my heart, felt my belly, shook his head at what I tried to say, and turned to leave the room.

"My friends?" I shouted at him. "Where are they?"

He shrugged and walked out. The robot stood watching till I felt able to stand and then took my arm to guide me outside, into a circular garden ringed with a circular building. Its lenses followed intently while I walked gravel paths through strange plants that edged the air with scents new to me. The other doors, I thought, might be hiding my companions, but it caught my arm when I tried to knock. When I persisted, it drew a little silver baton clipped to its waist and beckoned me silently back into the room.

Under its guard, I was treated well enough. Although my words seemed to mean nothing, it nodded when I rubbed my lips and my belly, and brought a tray of food: fruits that we have never grown on the Moon, a plate of crisp brown nut-flavored cakes, a glass of very good wine. I ate with a sudden appetite.

Silent most of the time, now and then it burst into speech. Clearly, it had questions. So did I, desperate questions about these remote children of ours and what they might do with us. It listened blankly when I spoke and locked the door when it left the room, with no hint of any answers.

Haunted by our images along that monumental avenue, I slept badly that night, dreaming that they were lumbering in hot pursuit while we fled across a lifeless landscape pitted with deep craters those black insects had eaten into the planet.

Terror chilled me. Did these people want to sacrifice us in that sacred circle? Drown us in the Nile? Feed us to the insects? Freeze us into silver metal and stand us on guard against the next invasion of heretic clones? I woke up shivering, afraid to know.

Next morning the robot brought an odd-looking machine, and admitted a slim, quick little woman who looked a little like Dian, though she was wrinkled and dark from a sun that never shone below our Tycho dome. Perhaps a sort of nun, she wore a tall silver turban and fingered a silver Moon pendant. She set up the machine to project words on the wall.

The moon is distant from the sea,
And yet with amber hands
She leads him, docile as a boy,
Along appointed sands.

Familiar words. I'd heard Dian recite them in a tone of adoration, though I was never sure exactly what they meant. They became stranger now, as the woman chanted them like a prayer. She repeated them two or three times in the same solemn tones and then read them more slowly, watching through dark-rimmed glasses to see my response, until at last I could nod to a spark of recognition. Vowel sounds had simply shifted. *Moon* was *mahan*, *see* was *say*.

She came back again and again, using her machine to teach me like a child. Even when the sounds became familiar, everything else was baffling: plants and animals, clothing and tools, maps of the world and the symbols of math. Yet at last I was able to ask about my companions.

"Uhl-weese." She frowned and shook her head.

Unwise. Why, she didn't say. When I tried to tell her we were visitors from the Moon, she scolded and seemed to pity me. Caressing her sacred pendant, she spoke of the paradise the Almighty Five had made of the Moon, where the blessed were allowed to dwell in an everlasting joy.

Paradise, unfortunately, was not meant for the likes of me. Pretenders who unwisely tried to steal sacred things or powers were to be consumed forever by the black demons in their hell beneath the earth.

In olden days, she told me darkly, divine fire might have descended to redeem my errant soul. In these more enlightened times, luckily for me, those who attempted to misuse the Holy Book were regarded as either psychotics in need of treatment or shysters deserving eternal torment.

She tried to save me with instruction in the lunar truth, drawn from a massive volume in silver boards that had theological footnotes to explicate almost every holy word. Dickinson's oriole had become the trickster god, Pepe, who cheated as he enchanted. Dian was not only the Moon Mother but also the soul who selected her own society of those who lived to earn their place with her in paradise. The book itself was her letter to the world that never wrote to her.

I was unconverted until one day when I was walking with the robot in the garden and stepped of the path to pick a purple flower. The robot said "Noot, noot," and took the flower from me, but it had failed to see me palm a little ball of crumpled paper. When I was able to spread it out in the privacy of my bathroom, it was a note from Tanya, written on a blank page torn from her notebook.

They want to think we're crazy, though they have trouble explaining how we got here in a sort of craft they never saw before. My witch doctor has a theory. He's trying to convince me that we came from South America, which has not yet been colonized. He talks of a lost party that set out a couple of centuries ago to fight the black insects there. The expedition seems to have ended with a crash into the Amazon rain forest in an area the insects were just invading. Rescue efforts failed, but he believes we must be descendants of survivors. He thinks we somehow salvaged or repaired the wrecked craft that brought us back. If we want to get out of here, I think we'd better go along.

I rolled the paper up and dropped it next day where I had found it. In the end we all went along, though Arne held out until Dian was allowed to persuade him. He grumbled bitterly till he found work on a Nile dredge, improving the channel and turning a swamp into new land for docks and warehouses. He says he is happier now than he ever was twiddling his thumbs on the Moon.

Although the ages seem to have erased every relic of our own times, these people are eagerly searching their own past for evidence of the Holy Clones. They have given Dian a museum position, where she can make good use of her skills at restoring and preserving antiquities and perhaps finally establish herself as an inspired interpreter of holy writ.

Pepe qualified for a pilot's license while Tanya studied methods for the control of the predatory insects. They are gone now with a new expedition to reclaim the Americas.

Although all the history I know is heresy, sternly outlawed here, I've found a university job as a janitor. It gives me access to radio equipment that can reach the lunar station. We can't help hoping that our own silver colossi will endure to watch this new Egypt grow into a finer civilization than our own ever was. Yet Tycho must be kept alive, lest disaster strikes again.

WORLD WITHOUT END

F. Gwynplaine MacIntyre

This final trilogy of stories takes us right to the far ends of existence on Earth.

Fergus Gwynplaine MacIntyre is a Scottish-born writer, playwright and journalist, long resident in the United States. His work, often humorous and noted for its detailed research and rigorous plotting, has appeared in many magazines and anthologies. His books include the novel The Woman Between the Worlds *(1994) and a collection of humorous imaginings* MacIntyre's Improbable Bestiary *(2005).*

H E STOLE MY death. After all these long years I forget his face. I remember his hands, the long tapering fingers holding the hypodermic shaft and pressing its needle into my skinny-skank arm as I beg him to give me a drug I never tried before. Ooh, yeah. Too right, that's good.

When I met him, back in 2023, I was a street bint: selling my snatch to kerb-crawlers and other pervs, just to get enough dosh to buy my next high. When the ecstasy wore off and I came down again, I'd go back on the game again. Another night, another street.

Now I've got every street in the world to myself.

I've exhausted all the pencils in the world. I've used up all the pens, markers, biros, highlighters. Once, when I was still living in London, I broke into a museum and twocked a rusty old typewriter I found there but it only lasted me a couple of years while I banged out these notes to myself. (Whoever else is going to read them?) I've outlived hard drives, soft drives, flash drives, tweets, flippits, thinxes and all the other fiddly-fancy ways to store text. I've gone back to the beginning, I have.

I write with charcoal on walls. There's no shortage of walls hereabouts, and when I run out of charcoal I just burn something.

The sun gets bigger every day. I used to think it only seems to get bigger cus it's coming closer, and that. No. It's really growing bigger, I'm sure. And redder.

The nights are fewer and shorter now, and when night comes I don't recognize the stars. I was never good at their names: I only know Charles's Wain and Orion. A few thousand years after I lost my death, the stars in Orion scarpered off in different directions. Now the stars are all strange, except for the sun overhead. Too right I know *that* one.

I remember my father. When I think of him all I see is a mouth shouting at me and two hard square fists. I remember his voice telling me I was just a whore and a slapper and yelling at me that I'd never amount to nowt. He got that last bit wrong though: only I'm the most important person in the world, now.

Cus I'm the only one left.

I can't remember my mam. I've forgotten the faces and the voices of everyone I ever loved. The only people I can still recall are the bastards I'll hate till the day I die. Which likely means I'll hate them forever. Most of all, I hate my dad and the filthy perv who stole my death.

I was out in the street when I turned fifteen, and I was on the game and sixteen when I met him. One of those clever lads from the Uni, he was, reading science. While I was pulling him off in the alley, he kept nattering to me about something he was working on. *Nanotech*, that was the word. And summat called the Hayflick limit, which meant bugger-all to me at the time, only I sussed it out later. Said he hadn't kept track of his own experiment, and wasn't sure he could ever repeat the results. I wanted him to stop jawing so I could just concentrate on getting him off and then get on to my next punter, but he kept blagging about little tiny robots and such. I was wearing a skimpy miniskirt and a halter. He saw the tracks all in the veins in my arms and my legs and he knew I was on the stuff. Then he jabbed a needle into my arm, injected something. It felt like fire in my blood, ooh I wanted it I wanted it.

I'd already got his money, so he just did up his flies and he left. I pulled a few more punters, then I went back to the bedsit I was sharing with two other girls on the game. I was on the blob that night, so I pulled the used tampon out of my fadge and chucked it away, but I couldn't find a clean one to put in. I found my last clean pair of knickers, and put those on. I felt like all my blood was on fire, and for a while I couldn't sleep. Then I passed out, like.

When I woke up, there was a hole in my new knickers ... just there, across the fadge. There was also a hole in the mattress, underneath.

I wasn't hungry, but that's normal when you're doing ecstasy. Thing is, I wasn't hungry for a high, either. For the first time in all I could remember, I wasn't hungry or thirsty for owt. I put on a skirt, then I looked for my make-up. When you're on the game, you age fast, and you want a bit of slap to cover the wrinkles and that.

Then I noticed that the tracks in my arms had gone. And the ones in my legs were fading.

I got my make-up and went to the mirror. While I was putting on my slap and my lippy, I saw that the lines in my face were gone. All this time, I'd been sixteen going on forty. Now I looked more a proper age sixteen again.

I remembered that fellow from Uni, and I figured whatever was in that drug he'd needled me with, I wanted more of it. But I had no notion of where to find that punter again.

Till then, I'd been going days at a trot without a proper meal, spending all my dosh on ecstasy and other drugs. After I met that perv from the Uni, it took me a couple of days to twig that I wasn't hungry any more, nor I didn't want the drugs neither. But every day, I kept finding holes in my knickers, so I always felt a breeze round my fadge. After a week without any meals, and not wanting any, I started to feel like maybe I was

(gap)

and wondering if I was going to stay sixteen years old for the rest of my life. Whenever I cut myself, or got beaten up by a punter, the hurt would heal right away. Except my teeth, and that. Before I'd met that perv, I'd had a few teeth knocked out that never grew back, and some chipped teeth that only got worse. Strange that everything else heals now, but never my teeth.

I stopped going on the blob. I'd figured out that, whenever I sat down, or when my fanny ever touched against owt, that's how those tiny nano-robots inside me would get energy to keep working: whenever I pulled away, a few bits and bobs of whatever my fadge had touched would be missing, as if it had melted off, like. Didn't matter what: cloth, wood, metal, plastic. My lady-bits had become some kind of dispose-all, eating anything. Glass, too. So I'm a human bottle bank.

There was only so long I could stay in one neighbourhood without someone noticing I never get any older. I tried to avoid the dole office, the labour exchange, the Nash ... the National Health System, I mean. Anyplace where government folk would see me. When they made everyone get ID microchips under their skin, I knew the game was up. After I'd been microchipped a few weeks, my skin pushed the microchip out again. The people at Central Entry knew straight away.

Central Entry's security team came to nick me. They took me to a govvy lab down at Centry. They did no end of tests on me, and somebody twigged that the microbots in my bloodstream are regenerating my body – except my teeth – so that everything heals and I never get older. Some government wonk with big words explained to me about how my telomeres stay the same, and the Hayflick limit, and that. Another govvy told me the nanobots in my blood are (I heard this word often enough to remember it) *self-replicating*.

Then they locked me up, so they could study me. Special Act of Parliament or summat, so they could keep me locked up in a lab.

The doctors were especially interested in how I never need to eat nor drink, because the nanobots inside me get energy and materials from whatever touches my fadge. I still need to sleep, though.

They gave me a private room but it was just a cell, cus I was never allowed to leave except when they took me out for tests. They stuck needles in me, and took all the blood out of my body twice over, trying to take out the tiny robots. They did tests on my fadge, and that, and several times my lady-bits melted the tips of their scientific thingies. Then they put me back the room again. With the door locked.

Once, they turned off the vents in my cell, and I could hear all the air pumping out. I couldn't talk, with no air and that. I couldn't breathe, neither. About three hours later, the air came back and I started breathing again, then some doctors came to see me. Said it was an accident. *Liars!*

There's a water tap in here, but I only drink water once in a while when I'm dead bored. That's dead bored, not dead. Once I went without water for two months, no probs. One of the doctors said summat about the nanobots rehydrating my cells. He also said as how the nano-wotsis had adapted to my personal DNA and that, so injecting some of my blood into somebody else won't work the trick.

I never get hungry or thirsty. At least I still need to sleep.

After seven or eight years of getting poked and jabbed, I tried to
(gap)
and they tried as long as they could to keep the lab safe from the snot-rot (what I heard a nurse call it), or the Global Pandemic (what a doctor called it), but finally it showed up in the lab and they all started dying. The stuff eats flesh and bones and all, and that. I heard rumours from the lab staff about people just melting into huge puddles of snot, or at least it looks like snot, with nowt left but their clothes and shoes and maybe bits and bobs of their teeth.

One morning I woke up and nobody answered the signal to come to my cell, no matter how many times I pushed the button. I tried to force the door open, or a window, but the security thingies kept stopping me same as ever. The automatic voice kept warning me not to try again.

After a long time, the lights went out and the air cycle stopped. I kept trying the door but just getting the warning. I screamed for somebody, anybody. Finally, the automatic voice stopped. After another long time, I tried the door and it opened.

It took me a while and more aggro to get out of the lab, but I did.

Everybody was dead. I could see the big piles of snot and clothes where some people had been lately, and inside the buildings some little piles of dust where the snot had dried up.

Most of the animals were dead too. Plenty of trees and plants, though. And insects. There were birds for a few weeks, then they all started dying.

I found a car that worked without the security link to its owner's ID chip. I'd never twigged how to drive properly, but when you're the only driver on the road it's easy-peasy. I got out of London and I headed for the

(gap)

in the motorboat I'd found to get to France. I went along the coast till the boat needed a recharge and I couldn't keep it going. Then I found another car I could start, and for a couple of years I just

(gap)

and wouldn't you bloody well know it that whatever killed everything else won't kill the insects, and there's more of them all the time! Ugh! Flies and beetles and nasties, and there seem to be more every day. And I'm seeing new sorts of insects now: flies all glittery like red metal, and beetles with big yellow eyes, and I'm sure there weren't any of those before the snot-rot killed off all the people. At least the rats mostly

(gap)

Once in a long while I find an old stash of food in plasti-clings so it never went off nor got mouldy, and sometimes I'll eat something just to remember what food tastes like. Sometimes the wrap is broken and the food's gone off, but I'll eat it anyway. Not as if it will kill me ha ha. Once I ate some cheese that had gone all mouldy, just for the new experien

(gap)

and I came running up shouting at them to take me along, take me with them back to wherever they bloody came from. I know they saw me. I'm sure they heard me. Two of them looked at me with I guess those were eyes. But the bug-men just went back into their big metal ball. It made a humming noise and then it glowed and then it just wasn't there anymore. It didn't go up to the sky or like that. It just *went*.

I waited a while for the bug-men to come back, or anyone else to show up, but finally I knew they would never

(gap)

About every ten or twelve years I'd try to kill myself again, but of course it never worked and I stopped hurting myself. That bastard who stole my death, you'd think he'd of fixed it so I could never feel pain, neither. Every time I tried to kill myself the cut would bleed and hurt like flipping hell but it always healed back.

The first few years weren't so bad cus I found a stash of 3-Vs and a viewer and some power packs, so at least I could still watch holovids and that. I watched all the discs with stories on them, over and over, till I knew them all off by heart. Then I finally got so bored I started watching the educational discs too, and I learnt some physics stuff and that. Things got worse when I couldn't find more batteries that worked and I couldn't recharge the dead ones.

It's so bloody not fair. Batteries get to die but I don't.

I was never much for reading, but when I couldn't watch any more 3-Vs, I found a library that had thousands of textdisks. I tried to read one, but the viewers wouldn't go. Then in the cellar I found hundreds of those old books and mags people had before the disks. I was off my nut with boredom so I started reading.

Then I thought I'd have a go at writing and that's how I started this diary. Not that anyone will ever read it, unless the bug-men come back. I couldn't thumbtext like how people used to write, but I found some old pens and that.

I decided if I was to write things down then I should do the job properly and learn all the right spelling and commas and apostro-things and that, and maybe learn some big words if I could find them in books. So I tried to keep a proper diary of all my

(gap)

I stopped counting the years a long time back. It was easier when there were different seasons. After I went immortal, winter never bothered me except for being harder to travel and all. After all the plants died, I could still keep track of seasons because of winter coming and going. The best part about winter is there are fewer insects.

For a long time, the mosquitos wouldn't leave off me. Nor the flies. But they all seem to be dead now. Except these beetles. Everywhere I go, millions of beetles. I wish they would die.

I wish *I* could die.

By now I know I'm at least three thousand years old, except I'm still only sixteen.

I still remember my father. I still remember him shouting at me, and beating me. I hate him I hate him. Besides me, the only thing that never dies is the hate.

(gap)

The sun gets bigger every day, and redder. There aren't seasons anymore, unless you count it's always summer.

Getting hotter. I sweat a lot but that means the nano-bastards inside me just work harder to replace it and my fadge melts more of whatever I sit down on to get more energy and mass and that. I forget most of what those doctors told me but I remember that part.

I remember the moon. Before all the grass went away, I used to like going to sleep in a field under the stars, looking up at the friendly moon while I drifted to sleep.

The moon went away a long time ago. I don't know where it went.

Once in a long while I try to

(gap)

Somehow the nano-things changed. A while back I noticed that I don't need to sleep any more. I've tried sleeping but it never comes. I'm tired all the time but I can't sleep.

It's just so bloody not fair. All this long time, the only thing left about me that was still normal is that I could sleep. Now the bastard who stole my death has stolen my sleep too. At least make it so I stop getting tired!

When I twigged that the nanobots had changed inside me, I started hoping I could die soon. Some hope! I'm still here.

After the seasons stopped, for a while I started counting days and nights. All the wood and most of the metal are just dust rust now: only plastic and porcelain are left from when people were alive. And stone. I found an old piece of light plastic I could make scratches on, and I added a scratch every morning when the sun came up. Little scratches, rows of ten. I took the plastic with me whenever I went somewhere else, to keep track. By now everywhere I go looks a lot the same as everywhere else.

After I made 1,347 scratches on the plastic, I ran out of room to make more. After a long time, I found another piece of plastic I could scratch. I scratched 1,347 at the top, then kept adding one scratch every day in rows of ten. I did that for a long time.

I've been alone for at least 12,000 years now.

I've decided to forgive my father.

(gap)

I'm going blind in one eye. The left one. I can't remember the last time anything excited me, but I got excited and all when I noticed it.

If something's going wrong with me and now it doesn't heal, maybe those stinking nano-things are finally breaking down inside me.

My teeth wore down to stumps a long long time ago. I remember one of those lab doctors telling me this would happen and offering to yank all my teeth while I still had them. Now I wish they'd done it. I had one toothache that lasted about three centuries, but it finally stopped.

I think the years are getting shorter now, as if it's taking shorter whiles for the Earth to go around the sun. It's so bright all the time, I have trouble telling when it's night now, and all the

(gap)

I WANT TO DIE I WANT TO DIE I BLOODY DAMN WANT TO DIE

(gap)

Even though I stopped needing to breathe a long time ago, I just always kept up breathing by reflex, and that. Sometimes when I got bored enough I'd hold my breath for six or seven hours, but when I stopped it I'd always start breathing again. Without trying. I remember a very long time ago, when I could still sleep, one night I put my head in a plasti-cling and I tied it tight round my neck so there was no air. When I woke up the next day I'd stopped breathing for several hours but it didn't make a difference, so I took the thing off and my breathing started same as always.

That was long long long ago. It's been getting harder to breathe for a long time now. It's not me that's changing, it's the air. It feels thicker than it used to be, and hotter, and stickier. I think there's something poison in it too, but not poison enough to kill me. For a long time it hurt to take a breath, and I got excited again cus I hoped I was dying. But it just got harder and harder to breathe, and it hurt more and more.

One day I noticed I wasn't breathing any more. I hoped my body was shutting down at last at last at last but no apparently it just decided from now on breathing was too much work so it just slacked off.

A long time ago, every once in a while I'd find a river that was mostly nasty stuff instead of water but I'd take a quick drink just to remember water. I can't remember the last time I saw a river. Nor lakes.

The cities mostly went to dust a long time ago. I went back to the seashore, where it used to be I mean, so I could see the changes in the ocean. I'm sure all the fish died thousands of years back. For a while some of that algy-stuff was still alive in the ocean but now I don't think so.

The ocean's getting smaller. Every time I walk down the beach the sand and stones are longer and the ocean is shorter.

For a while, there were some kind of nasty wiggle-things alive I never saw before. I'm sure they weren't around until after all the people died, so there's no science-y name for them. Ugh! Just wiggle-things with too many legs and all slime. And long feely bits instead of eyes. They came up in the mud near the ocean, when there was still mud. For a while I was actually glad to see them because at least something new was alive. They're gone now.

Sometimes I scream but no one hears me.

I used to be able to cry. Now the tears never come no matter how much I want them. It's just so bloody not fair. I can't eat I can't drink I can't sleep I can't breathe and now I can't even cry. I've lost everything that ever made me human except I can't die.

(gap)

ought to be some way to turn off the sun it's so bright all the time and when

(gap)

It's happening faster. Used to be if I hurt myself the cut or the hurt would heal at the normal speed for healing. Yesterday I found a jagged piece of plastic with a sharp edge, so I took it in one hand and I deliberately slit open my other arm all the way from my wrist to my shoulder. I started bleeding and I hoped the nano-things would all leak out. While I watched it the whole bloody cut healed in about nineteen seconds. I heal faster now.

It's just so bloody not fair.

(gap)

Those bug-men and their big metal round thing never came back but after a long time some green shiny people showed up. Not shaped like humans but green and shiny. I think they were all female, no men. They started building a city and planting new sorts of plants and changing the air so it got easier to breathe. Too right I came running to meet them. Their words are just a lot of squeaking noises but they tried to teach me anyway and I tried to learn but it was just too hard. The sky is so bright all the time now, I could just barely see a few stars in the little bit of night, but one of the green ladies pointed up at the sky and I think she was showing me what star they came from, I mean what star their planet is from.

For a long time I lived in their city as a kind of pet and they were mostly nice to me except when they didn't understand what I wanted. They did all kinds of things to me that I guess were medical tests but I let them do it partly because I wanted the green ladies to like me and partly because I hoped they'd find out how to cure me so I can die. After they stopped testing me they were mostly nice to me.

The beautiful shiny green ladies had all sorts of lovely art and precious things they made, not like the statues and paintings and like all back when other humans were alive. The green ladies make this beautiful art out of glowing hot gas that just hangs in the air for a while, then melts. One of the green ladies showed me this sculpture of red gas she'd made, then she pointed up at the sun overhead, and I sussed that they make their lovely sculptures from the same stuff as the sun. I know it's called *plasma gas* cus I learnt it off one of those holovids. After a long while, the lovely green ladies even managed to show me how to work one of their thingies so I could make words and pictures in the air out of burning hot plasma gas.

Then something happened suddenly and all the green ladies left in a hurry. I never knew why. They left behind for me their city and some machines but I couldn't suss how to make those machines work. It was nice they were here while it lasted though.

I wish the green ladies had taken me with them.

(gap)

The sun is right over me all the time now. Big red hot bloody hot.

Every once in a while I travel back to someplace where I was before and I find something I wrote a long time ago. I'm having trouble remembering what I wrote so long ago, so any time I find my own writing it's a surprise like reading summat for the first time.

My right eye is going blind like my left one did. I never sleep but I have nightmares awake thinking what it will be like for me when I can't eat drink sleep breathe and also CAN'T SEE and I will go through blind Eternity feeling my way forever. It's so bloody not fair.

It won't be long now before the Earth melts or drops into the sun. I don't much care which. What I want to know is will it finally kill me? If it does, peace at last.

What bloody scares me is the thought that I'll fall into the sun and die ... but then inside the sun I'll heal again, and die again, and so on forever. Too right it will hurt.

The sun has to die some day. I mean it won't be day anymore when it happens but you know what I mean. Just my stinking luck if Earth falls into the sun and I keep living anyway, and I have to feel the sun killing me all the time while the nano-things keep me alive for millions millions bloody billions more years till the sun finally burns out. I wonder if I can write words in burning plasma inside the sun like those green ladies from somewhere else taught me once. I wish the green ladies would come back. I hope maybe the

(gap)

Everywhere hot lava. Melting melting everything and I burn all over and it hurts it bloody hurts but as fast as I heal I get burnt again stop it stop it stop.

I can still see a bit with one eye. I'm writing this last part with a black flaky stone against a hard white stone but the stone's going soft. The sun's coming closer. After all these millions of years I suddenly remember an old happy song it goes here comes the sun it's all right, but no it's NOT all right. Everything is so hot and all melted. I'm sure it will come any

(gap)

At last at last at last billions of years falling into the sun hurry up will I die now or will it get worse now I'll know if

(gap)

oh damn its not fair

THE CHILDREN OF TIME

Stephen Baxter

Stephen Baxter began his career in 1987 with "The Xeelee Flower", a story that introduced his future history series, which includes the novels Raft *(1991),* Flux *(1993) and* Ring *(1994). He attracted a wider readership with* The Time Ships *(1995), his sequel to H.G. Wells' The Time Machine, and went on to establish himself as one of Britain's most innovative and entertaining science fiction writers. His more recent books include the apocalyptic* Flood *(2008) and its sequel* Ark *(2009).*

I

JAAL HAD ALWAYS been fascinated by the ice on the horizon. Even now, beyond the smoke of the evening hearth, he could see that line of pure bone white, sharper than a stone blade's cut, drawn across the edge of the world.

It was the end of the day and a huge sunset was staining the sky. Alone, restless, he walked a few paces away from the rich smoky pall, away from the smell of broiling racoon meat and bubbling goat fat, the languid talk of the adults, the eager play of the children.

The ice was always there on the northern horizon, always out of reach no matter how hard you walked across the scrubby grassland. He knew why. The ice cap was retreating, dumping its pure whiteness into the meltwater streams, exposing land crushed and gouged and strewn with vast boulders. So while you walked towards it, the ice was marching away from you.

And now the gathering sunset was turning the distant ice pink. The clean geometric simplicity of the landscape drew his soul; he stared, entranced.

Jaal was eleven years old, a compact bundle of muscle. He was dressed in layers of clothing, sinew-sewn from scraped goat skin and topped by a heavy coat of rabbit fur. On his head was a hat made by his father from the skin of a whole raccoon, and on his feet he wore the skin of pigeons, turned inside-out and the feathers coated with grease. Around his neck was a string of pierced cat teeth.

Jaal looked back at his family. There were a dozen of them, parents and children, aunts and uncles, nephews and nieces, and one grandmother, worn down aged forty-two. Except for the very smallest children everybody moved slowly, obviously weary. They had walked a long way today.

He knew he should go back to the fire and help out, do his duty, find firewood or skin a rat. But every day was like this. Jaal had ancient, unpleasant memories from when he was very small, of huts burning, people screaming and fleeing. Jaal and his family had been walking north ever since, looking for a new home. They hadn't found it yet.

Jaal spotted Sura, good-humouredly struggling to get a filthy skin coat off the squirming body of her little sister. Sura, Jaal's second cousin, was two years older than him. She had a limpid, liquid ease of movement in everything she did.

She saw Jaal looking at her and arched an eyebrow. He blushed, hot, and turned away to the north. The ice was a much less complicated companion than Sura.

He saw something new.

As the angle of the sun continued to change, the light picked out something on the ground. It was a straight line, glowing red in the light of the sun, like an echo of the vast edge of the ice itself. But this line was close, only a short walk from here, cutting through hummocks and scattered boulders. He had to investigate.

With a guilty glance back at his family, he ran away, off to the north, his pigeon-skin boots carrying him silently over the hard ground. The straight-edge feature was further away than it looked, and as he became frustrated he ran faster. But then he came on it. He stumbled to a halt, panting.

It was a ridge as high as his knees – a ridge of stone, but nothing like the ice-carved boulders and shattered gravel that littered the rest of the landscape. Though its top was worn and broken, its sides were *flat*, smoother than any stone he had touched before, and the sunlight filled its creamy surface with colour.

Gingerly he climbed on the wall to see better. The ridge of stone ran off to left and right, to east and west – and then it turned sharp corners, to run north, before turning back on itself again. There was a pattern here, he saw. This stone ridge traced a straight-edged frame on the ground.

And there were more ridges; the shadows cast by the low sun picked out the stone tracings clearly. The land to the north of here was covered by a tremendous rectangular scribble that went on as far as he could see. All this was made by people. He knew this immediately, without question.

In fact this had been a suburb of Chicago. Most of the city had been scraped clean by the advancing ice but the foundations of this suburb, fortuitously, had been flooded and frozen in before the glaciers came. These ruins were already 100,000 years old.

"Jaal. Jaal! ..." His mother's voice carried to him like the cry of a bird.

He couldn't bear to leave what he had found. He stood on the eroded wall and let his mother come to him.

She was weary, grimy, stressed. "Why must you do this? Don't you *know* the cats hunt in twilight?"

He flinched from the disappointment in her eyes, but he couldn't contain his excitement. "Look what I found, mother!"

She stared around. Her face showed incomprehension, disinterest. "What is it?"

His imagination leapt, fuelled by wonder, and he tried to make her see what he saw. "Maybe once these rock walls were tall, tall as the ice itself. Maybe people lived here in great heaps, and the smoke of their fires rose up to the sky. Mother, will we come to live here again?"

"Perhaps one day," his mother said at random, to hush him.

The people would never return. By the time the returning ice had shattered their monocultural, over-extended technological civilization, people had exhausted the Earth of its accessible deposits of iron ore and coal and oil and other resources. People would survive: smart, adaptable, they didn't need cities for that. But with nothing but their most ancient technologies of stone and fire, they could never again conjure up the towers of Chicago. Soon even Jaal, distracted by the fiery eyes of Sura, would forget this place existed.

But for now he longed to explore. "Let me go on. Just a little further!"

'No," his mother said gently. "The adventure's over. It's time to go. Come now." And she put her arm around his shoulders, and led him home.

II

Urlu crawled towards the river. The baked ground was hard under her knees and hands, and stumps of burned-out trees and shrubs scraped her flesh. There was no green here, nothing grew, and nothing moved save a few flecks of ash disturbed by the low breeze. She was naked, sweating, her skin streaked by charcoal. Her hair was a mat, heavy with dust and grease. In one hand she carried a sharpened stone. She was eleven years old. She wore a string of pierced teeth around her neck. The necklace was a gift from her grandfather, Pala, who said the teeth were from an animal called a rabbit. Urlu had never seen a rabbit. The last of them had died in the Burning, before she was born, along with the rats and the raccoons, all the small mammals that had long ago survived the ice with mankind. So there would be no more rabbit teeth. The necklace was precious.

The light brightened. Suddenly there was a shadow beneath her, her own form cast upon the darkened ground. She threw herself flat in the dirt. She wasn't used to shadows. Cautiously she glanced over her shoulder, up at the sky.

All her life a thick lid of ash-laden cloud had masked the sky. But for the last few days it had been breaking up, and today the cloud had disintegrated further. And now, through high drifting cloud, she saw a disc, pale and gaunt.

It was the sun. She had been told its name, but had never quite believed in it. Now it was revealed, and Urlu helplessly stared up at its geometric purity.

She heard a soft voice call warningly. "Urlu!" It was her mother.

It was no good to be daydreaming about the sky. She had a duty to fulfil, down here in the dirt. She turned and crawled on.

She reached the bank. The river, thick with blackened dirt and heavy with debris, rolled sluggishly. It was so wide that in the dim light of noon she could barely see the far side. In fact this was the Seine, and the charred ground covered traces of what had once been Paris. It made no difference where she was. The whole Earth was like this, all the same.

To Urlu's right, downstream, she saw hunters, pink faces smeared with dirt peering from the ruined vegetation. The weight of their expectation pressed heavily on her.

She took her bit of chipped stone, and pressed its sharpest edge against the skin of her palm. It had to be her. The people believed that the creatures of the water were attracted by the blood of a virgin. She was afraid of the pain to come, but she had no choice; if she didn't go through with the cut one of the men would come and do it for her, and that would hurt far more.

But she heard a wail, a cry of loss and sorrow, rising like smoke into the dismal air. It was coming from the camp. The faces along the bank turned, distracted. Then, one by one, the hunters slid back into the ruined undergrowth.

Urlu, hugely relieved, turned away from the debris-choked river, her stone tucked safely in her hand.

The camp was just a clearing in the scorched ground-cover, with a charcoal fire burning listlessly in the hearth. Beside the fire an old man lay on a rough pallet of earth and scorched brush, gaunt, as naked and filthy as the rest. His eyes were wide, rheumy, and he stared at the sky. Pala, forty-five years old, was Urlu's grandfather. He was dying, eaten from within by something inside his belly.

He was tended by a woman who knelt in the dirt beside him. She was his oldest daughter, Urlu's aunt. The grime on her face was streaked by tears. "He's frightened," said the aunt. "It's finishing him off."

Urlu's mother asked, "Frightened of what?"

The aunt pointed into the sky.

The old man had reason to be frightened of strange lights in the sky. He had been just four years old when a greater light had come to Earth.

After Jaal's time, the ice had returned a dozen times more before retreating for good. After that, people rapidly cleared the land of the legacy of the ice: descendants of cats and rodents and birds, grown large and confident in the temporary absence of humanity. Then people hunted and farmed, built up elaborate networks of trade and culture, and developed exquisite technologies of wood and stone and bone. There was much evolutionary churning in the depths of the sea, out of reach of mankind. But people were barely touched by time, for there was no need for them to change.

This equable afternoon endured for thirty million years. The infant Pala's parents had sung him songs unimaginably old.

But then had come the comet's rude incursion. Nearly a hundred million years after the impactor that had terminated the summer of the dinosaurs, Earth had been due another mighty collision.

Pala and his parents, fortuitously close to a cave-ridden mountain, had endured the fires, the rain of molten rock, the long dust-shrouded winter. People survived, as they had lived through lesser cataclysms since the ice. And with their ingenuity and adaptability and generalist ability to eat almost anything, they had already begun to spread once more over the ruined lands.

Once it had been thought that human survival would depend on planting colonies on other worlds, for Earth would always be prone to such disasters. But people had never ventured far from Earth: there was nothing out there; the stars had always remained resolutely silent. And though since the ice their numbers had never been more than a few million, people were too numerous and too wide-spread to be eliminated even by a comet's deadly kiss. It was easy to kill a lot of people. It was very hard to kill them all.

As it happened old Pala was the last human alive to remember the world before the Burning. With him died memories thirty million years deep. In the morning they staked out his body on a patch of high ground.

The hunting party returned to the river, to finish the job they had started. This time there was no last-minute reprieve for Urlu. She slit open her palm, and let her blood run into the murky river water. Its crimson was the brightest colour in the whole of this grey-black world.

Urlu's virginal state made no difference to the silent creature who slid through the water, but she was drawn by the scent of blood.

Another of the planet's great survivors, she had ridden out the Burning buried in deep mud, and fed without distaste on the scorched remains washed into her river. Now she swam up towards the murky light.

All her life Urlu had eaten nothing but snakes, cockroaches, scorpions, spiders, maggots, termites. That night she feasted on crocodile meat.

By the morning she was no longer a virgin. She didn't enjoy it much, but at least it was her choice. And at least she wouldn't have to go through any more blood-letting.

III

The catamaran glided towards the beach, driven by the gentle current of the shallow sea and the muscles of its crew. When it ran aground the people splashed into water that came up to their knees, and began to unload weapons and food. The sun hung bright and hot in a cloudless blue dome of a sky, and the people, small and lithe, were surrounded by shining clouds of droplets as they worked. Some of them had their favourite snakes wrapped around their necks.

Cale, sitting on the catamaran, clung to its seaweed trunks. Looking out to sea, he could see the fine dark line that was the floating community where he had been born. This was an age of warmth, of high seas which had flooded the edges of the continents, and most people on Earth made their living from the rich produce of coral reefs and other sun-drenched shallow-water ecosystems. Cale longed to go back to the rafts, but soon he must walk on dry land, for the first time in his life. He was eleven years old.

Cale's mother, Lia, splashed through the water to him. Her teeth shone white in her dark face. "You will never be a man if you are so timid as this." And she grabbed him, threw him over her shoulder, ran through the shallow water to the beach, and dumped him in the sand. "There!" she cried. "You are the first to set foot here, the first of all!"

Everybody laughed, and Cale, winded, resentful, blushed helplessly.

For some time Cale's drifting family had been aware of the line on the horizon. They had prepared their gifts of sea fruit and carved coral, and rehearsed the songs they would sing, and carved their weapons, and here they were. They thought this was an island full of people. They were wrong. This was no island, but a continent.

Since the recovery of the world from Urlu's great Burning, there had been time enough for the continents' slow tectonic dance to play out. Africa had collided softly with Europe, Australia had kissed Asia, and Antarctica had come spinning up from the south pole. It was these great geographical changes – together with a slow, relentless heating-up of the sun – which had given the world its long summer.

While the rafts had dreamed over fecund seas, seventy million years had worn away. But even over such a tremendous interval people were much the same as they had always been.

And now here they were, on the shore of Antarctica – and Cale was indeed the first of all.

Unsteadily he got to his feet. For a moment the world seemed to tip and rock beneath him. But it was not the world that tipped, he understood, but his own imagination, shaped by a life on the rafts.

The beach stretched around him, sloping up to a line of tall vegetation. He had never seen anything like it. His fear and resentment quickly subsided, to be replaced by curiosity.

The landing party had forgotten him already. They were gathering driftwood for a fire and unloading coils of meat – snake meat, from the fat, stupid, domesticated descendants of one of the few animals to survive the firestorm of Urlu's day. They would have a feast, and they would get drunk, and they would sleep; only tomorrow would they begin to explore.

Cale discovered he didn't want to wait that long. He turned away from the sea, and walked up the shallow slope of the beach.

A line of hard trunks towered above his head, smooth-hulled. These "trees", as his father had called them, were in fact a kind of grass, something like bamboo. Cale came from a world of endless flatness; to him these trees were mighty constructs indeed. And sunlight shone through the trees from an open area beyond.

A few paces away a freshwater stream decanted onto the beach and trickled to the sea. Cale could see that it came from a small gully that cut through the bank of trees. It was a way through, irresistible.

The broken stones of the gully's bed stung his feet, and sharp branches scraped at his skin. The rocks stuck in the gully walls were a strange mix: big boulders set in a greyish clay, down to pebbles small enough to have fit in Cale's hand, all jammed together. Even the bedrock was scratched and grooved, as if some immense, spiky fish had swum this way.

Here in this tropical rainforest, Cale was surrounded by the evidence of ice.

He soon reached the open area behind the trees. It was just a glade a few paces across, opened up by the fall of one mighty tree. Cale stepped forward, making for a patch of green. But iridescent wings beat, and a fat, segmented body soared up from the green, and Cale stumbled to a halt. The insect was huge, its body longer than he was tall. Now more vast dragonflies rose up, startled, huddling for protection. A sleeker form, its body yellow-banded, came buzzing out of the trees. It was a remote descendant of a wasp, a solitary predator. It assaulted the swarming dragonflies, ripping through shimmering wings. All this took place over Cale's head in a cloud of flapping and buzzing. It was too strange to be frightening.

He was distracted by a strange squirming at his feet. The patch of green from which he had disturbed the first dragonfly was itself moving, flowing over the landscape as if liquid. It was actually a crowd of creatures, a mass of wriggling worms. From the tops of tottering piles of small bodies, things like eyes blinked.

Such sights were unique to Antarctica. There was no other place like this, anywhere on Earth.

When its ice melted away, the bare ground of Antarctica became an arena for life. The first colonists had been blown on the wind from over the sea: vegetation, insects, birds. But this was not an age for birds, or indeed mammals. As the world's systems compensated for the slow heating of the sun, carbon dioxide, the main greenhouse gas, was drawn down into the sea and the rocks, and the air became oxygen-rich. The insects used this heady fuel to grow huge, and predatory wasps and cockroaches as bold as rats made short work of Antarctica's flightless birds.

And there had been time for much more dramatic evolutionary shifts, time for whole phyla to be remodelled. The squirming multiple organism that fled from Cale's approach was a descendant of the siphonophores, colonial creatures of the sea like Portuguese men o' war. Endlessly adaptable, hugely ecologically inventive, since colonizing the land these compound creatures had occupied fresh water, the ground, the branches of the grass-trees, even the air.

Cale sensed something of the transient strangeness of what he saw. Antarctica, empty of humans, had been the stage for Earth's final gesture of evolutionary inventiveness. But relentless tectonic drift had at last brought Antarctica within reach of the ocean-going communities who sailed over the flooded remnants of India, and the great experiment was about to end. Cale gazed around, eyes wide, longing to discover more.

A coral-tipped spear shot past his head, and he heard a roar. He staggered back, shocked.

A patch of green ahead of him split and swarmed away, and a huge form emerged. Grey-skinned, supported on two narrow forelegs and a powerful articulated tail, this monster seemed to be all head. A spear stuck out from its neck. The product of another transformed phylum, this was a chondrichthyan, a distant relation of a shark. The beast opened a mouth like a cavern, and blood-soaked breath blasted over Cale.

Lia was at Cale's side. "Come on." She hooked an arm under his shoulders and dragged him away.

Back on the beach, munching on snake meat, Cale soon got over his shock. Everybody made a fuss of him as he told his tales of giant wasps and the huge land-shark. At that moment he could not imagine ever returning to the nightmares of the forest.

But of course he would. And in little more than a thousand years his descendants, having burned their way across Antarctica, accompanied by their hunting snakes and their newly domesticated attack-wasps, would hunt down the very last of the land-sharks, and string its teeth around their necks.

IV

Tura and Bel, sister and brother, grew up in a world of flatness, on a shoreline between an endless ocean and a land like a tabletop. But in the distance there were mountains, pale cones turned purple by the ruddy mist. As long as she could remember Tura had been fascinated by the mountains. She longed to walk to them – even, she fantasized, to climb them.

But how could she ever reach them? Her people lived at the coast, feeding on the soft-fleshed descendants of neotenous crabs. The land was a plain of red sand, littered with gleaming salt flats, where nothing could live. The mountains were forever out of reach.

Then, in Tura's eleventh year, the land turned unexpectedly green.

The ageing world was still capable of volcanic tantrums. One such episode, the eruption of a vast basaltic flood, had pumped carbon dioxide into the air. As flowers in the desert had once waited decades for the rains, so their remote descendants waited for such brief volcanic summers to make them bloom.

Tura and her brother hatched the plan between them. They would never get this chance again; the greening would be gone in a year, perhaps never to return in their lifetimes. No adult would ever have approved. But no adult need know.

And so, very early one morning, they slipped away from the village. Wearing nothing but kilts woven from dried sea grass, their favourite shell necklaces around their necks, they looked very alike. As they ran they laughed, excited by their adventure, and their blue eyes shone against the rusted crimson of the landscape.

Bel and Tura lived on what had once been the western coast of North America – but, just as in Urlu's dark time of global catastrophe, it didn't really matter where you lived. For this was the age of a supercontinent.

The slow convergence of the continents had ultimately produced a unity that mirrored a much earlier mammoth assemblage, broken up before the dinosaurs evolved. While vast unending storms roamed the waters of the world-ocean, New Pangaea's interior collapsed to a desiccated wasteland, and people drifted to the mouths of the great rivers, and to the sea coasts. This grand coalescence was accompanied by the solemn drumbeat of extinction events; each time the world recovered, though each time a little less vigorously than before.

The supercontinent's annealing took two hundred million years. And since then, another two hundred million years had already gone by. But people lived much as they always had.

Tura and Bel, eleven-year-old twins, knew nothing of this. They were young, and so was their world; it was ever thus. And today, especially, was a day of wonder, as all around them plants, gobbling carbon dioxide, fired packets of spores through the air, and insects scrambled in once-in-a-lifetime quests to propagate.

As the sun climbed the children tired, their pace falling, and the arid air sucked the sweat off their bodies. But at last the mountains came looming out of the dusty air. These worn hills were ancient, a relic of the formation of New Pangaea. But to Tura and Bel, standing before their scree-covered lower slopes, they were formidable heights indeed.

Then Tura saw a splash of green and brown, high on a slope. Curiosity sparked. Without thinking about it she began to climb. Bel, always more nervous, would not follow.

Though at first the slope was so gentle it was no more than a walk, Tura was soon higher than she had ever been in her life. On she climbed, until her walk gave way to an instinctive scramble on all fours. Her heart hammering, she kept on. All around her New Pangaea unfolded, a sea of Mars-red dust worn flat by time.

At last she reached the green. It was a clump of trees, shadowed by the mountain from the dust-laden winds and nourished by water from subsurface aquifers. Instinctively Tura rubbed her hand over smooth, sturdy trunks. She had never seen trees before.

As the sun brightened, Earth's systems compensated by drawing down carbon dioxide from the air. But this was a process with a limit: even in Jaal's time the remnant carbon dioxide had been a trace. Already the planet had shed many rich ecosystems – tundra, forests, grasslands, meadows, mangrove swamps. Soon the carbon dioxide concentration would drop below a certain critical level after which only a fraction of plants would be able to photosynthesize. The human population, already only a million strung out around the world's single coastline, would implode to perhaps ten thousand.

People would survive. They always had. But these trees, in whose cool shade Tura stood, were among the last in the world.

She peered up at branches with sparse crowns of spiky leaves, far above her head. There might be fruit up there, or water to be had in the leaves. But it was impossible; she could not climb past the smoothness of the lower trunk.

When she looked down Bel's upturned face was a white dot. The day was advancing; as the sun rode higher the going across the dry dust would be even more difficult. With regret she began her scrambled descent to the ground.

As she lived out her life on the coast of Pangaea, Tura never forgot her brief adventure. And when she thought of the trees her hands and feet itched, her body recalling ape dreams abandoned half a billion years before.

V

Ruul was bored.

All through the echoing caverns the party was in full swing. By the light of their hearths and rush torches people played and danced, talked and laughed, drank and fought, and the much-evolved descendants of snakes and wasps curled affectionately around the ankles of their owners. It was a Thousand-Day festival. In a world forever cut off from the daylight, subterranean humans pale as worms marked time by how they slept and woke, and counted off the days of their lives on their fingers.

Everyone was having fun – everyone but Ruul. When his mother was too busy to notice, he crept away into the dark.

Some time ago, restlessly exploring the edge of the inhabited cave, where tunnels and boreholes stretched on into the dark, he had found a chimney, a crack in the limestone. It looked as if you could climb up quite a way. And when he shielded his eyes, it looked to him as if there was light up there, light of a strange ruddy hue. There might be another group somewhere in the caverns above, he thought. Or it might be something stranger yet, something beyond his imagination.

Now, in the dim light of the torches, he explored the chimney wall. Lodging his fingers and toes in crevices, began to climb.

He was escaping the party. Eleven years old, neither child nor adult, he just didn't fit, and he petulantly wished the festival would go away. But as he ascended into profound silence the climb itself consumed all his attention, and the why of it faded from his mind.

His people, cavern-bound for uncounted generations, were good at rock-climbing. They lived in caverns in deep limestone karsts, laid down in long-vanished shallow seas. Once these hollows had hosted ecosystems full of the much-evolved descendants of lizards, snakes, scorpions, cockroaches, even sharks and crocodiles. The extreme and unchanging conditions of Pangaea had encouraged intricacy and interdependency. The people, retreating underground, had allowed fragments of these extraordinary biotas to survive.

Soon Ruul climbed up out of the limestone into a softer sandstone, poorly cemented. It was easier to find crevices here. The crimson light from above was bright enough to show him details of the rock through which he was passing. There was layer upon layer of it, he saw, and it had a repetitive pattern, streaks of darkness punctuated by lumpy nodules. When he touched one of the nodules, he found a blade surface so sharp he might have cut his fingers. It was a stone axe – made, used, and dropped long ago, and buried somehow in the sediments that had made this sandstone. Growing more curious he explored the dark traces. They crumbled when he dug into them with a fingernail, and he could smell ash, as fresh as if a fire had just burned here. The dark layers were hearths.

He was climbing through strata of hearths and stone tools, thousands of layers all heaped up on top of one another and squashed down into the rock. People must have lived in this place a very long time. He was oppressed by a huge weight of time, and of changelessness.

But he was distracted by a set of teeth he found, small, triangular, razor-edged. They had holes drilled in them. He carefully prised these out of the rock and put them in a pouch; perhaps he would make a necklace of them later.

With aching fingertips and toes, he continued his climb.

Unexpectedly, he reached the top of the chimney. It opened out into a wider space, a cave perhaps, filled with that ruddy light. He hoisted himself up the last short way, swung his legs out onto the floor above, and stood up.

And he was stunned.

He was standing on flat ground, a plain that seemed to go on forever. It was covered in dust, very red, so fine it stuck to the sweat on his legs. He turned slowly around. If this was the floor of a cave – well, it was a cave with no walls. And the roof above must be far away too, so far he could not see it; above him was nothing but a dome of darkness. He had no word for *sky*. And in one direction, facing him, something lifted over the edge of the world. It was a ruddy disc, perfectly circular, just a slice of it protruding over the dead-flat horizon. It was the source of the crimson light, and he could feel its searing heat.

Ruul inhabited a convoluted world of caverns and chimneys; he had never seen anything like the purity of this utterly flat plain, the perfectly circular arc of that bow of light. The clean geometric simplicity of the landscape drew his soul; he stared, entranced.

Three hundred million years after the life and death of Tura and Bel, this was what Earth had become. The sediments on which Ruul stood were the ruins of the last mountains. The magmatic currents of a cooling world had not been able to break up the new supercontinent, as they had the first. Meanwhile the sun's relentless warming continued. By now only microbes inhabited the equatorial regions, while at the poles a few hardy, tough-skinned plants were browsed by sluggish animals heavily armoured against the heat. Earth was already losing its water, and Pangaea's shoreline was rimmed by brilliant-white salt flats.

But the boy standing on the eroded-flat ground was barely changed from his unimaginably remote ancestors, from Tura and Cale and Urlu and even Jaal. It had never been necessary for humans to evolve significantly, for they always adjusted their environment so they didn't have to – and in the process stifled evolutionary innovation.

It was like this everywhere. After the emergence of intelligence, the story of any biosphere tended to get a lot simpler. It was a major reason for the silence of the stars.

But on Earth a long story was ending. In not many generations from now, Ruul's descendants would succumb; quietly baked in their desiccating caves, they would not suffer. Life would go on, as archaic thermophilic microbes spread their gaudy colours across the land. But man would be gone, leaving sandstone strata nearly a billion years deep full of hearths and chipped stones and human bones.

"Ruul! Ruul! Oh, there you are!" His mother, caked by red dust, was clambering stiffly out of the chimney. "Somebody said you came this way. I've been frantic. Oh, Ruul – what are you doing?"

Ruul spread his hands, unable to explain. He didn't want to hurt his mother, but he was excited by his discoveries. "Look what I found, mother!"

"What?"

He babbled excitedly about hearths and tools and bones. "Maybe people lived here in great heaps, and the smoke of their fires rose up to the sky. Mother, will we come to live here again?"

"Perhaps one day," his mother said at random, to hush him.

But that wasn't answer enough for Ruul. Restless, curious, he glanced around once more at the plain, the rising sun. To him, this terminal Earth was a place of wonder. He longed to explore. "Let me go on. Just a little further!"

"No," his mother said gently. "The adventure's over. It's time to go. Come now." And she put her arm around his shoulders, and led him home.

THE STAR CALLED WORMWOOD

Elizabeth Counihan

I could have concluded this anthology with any of several stories, but there is something about the ending of this story that seemed just right, and brings our journey through an apocalyptic future almost full circle.

Elizabeth Counihan is from a writing family. Her father was a BBC journalist and her grandfather a novelist. Elizabeth was a family doctor in the National Health Service for many years but is now concentrating on writing. Her stories have appeared in Asimov's, Realms of Fantasy, Nature Futures *and several other magazines and anthologies. She is the editor of the British fantasy magazine* Scheherazade.

IN THE WEEK that Anya died a comet approached the Earth. At first a bright spark in the east, it enlarged, trailing a cloud of shimmering white – a glowing snowball, flung into the sky above the frozen landscape of Siberia. Anya did not see it. She lay, ninety-nine years old, in the last ice palace, tended by machines older than she was. Their antennae perceived the new celestial body. Their voices reported it, echoing through vaulted chambers and long-abandoned halls where, here and there, a small creature twitched a whisker or pricked a furry ear before returning to the business of living. The voices whispered in Anna's room. She could no longer speak but electronic eyes interpreted the movement of her lips, and recorded that her last word was "Wormwood". Her breath rattled in a last sigh and her eyes closed.

The machines went to the burial place and drew out a core of ice. Anya's body was wrapped in an embroidered sheet and placed feet first in the bore hole. Finally, as they had been taught, the machines reverently capped her grave with powdered ice and played the music appropriate to the death of a lady of the palace. The sound was heard only by the wolves and bears of the wilderness. Her grave, the last in row upon row of similar graves, lay under the bleak gaze of the comet.

The comet hurtled on, over wrinkled mountains, arid plains, sun-drenched ocean. Wild dogs howled at its passing; owls blinked under its bright gaze.

Kuri squatted beside a thorn tree, his shadow black and dwarfish under the equatorial sun. He reached out a dark, bony hand and picked up a fragment of yellow ringlass from the jigsaw of coloured shards at his feet, laying it carefully to one side with pieces he had already chosen. After a few moments' thought, chin in cupped hand, he selected a second piece, green this time and laid it with the others. He removed his wide-brimmed hat and half-filled it with the selected glass then, rising stiffly, walked towards his house beside the lake. His body was wiry and naked, his knobbly feet bare; without his hat, only a tangle of grey and black hair protected his head from the sun.

His way to the domed building lay across a hundred metres of flat desert, fringed at its margin by dark reeds. From there the jade-green lake stretched into the west. A feather of white vapour spiralled from the volcano on Crocodile Island and dispersed in the shimmering air. Kuri stopped halfway to catch his breath, his throat rasped by the harsh taint of the volcano. He gazed with narrowed eyes, half-blinded by the beauty of his ancient home, placed like a jewel of many colours between him and the lake. At this time of day the windows were almost inaudible, a subdued harmony, but to the sight they blazed with the brilliance of the noonday sun.

There was a flicker of movement near the water. Kuri shaded his eyes with his free hand then grinned and whistled loudly through his fingers. The moving shape bounded towards him on all fours but rose onto hind legs when it reached his side. The creature, yellow-brown like the earth, planted a slender fore paw on each side of his chest. Green eyes, adoring as a dog's, gazed up at him from a flat, cat-like face. Her tongue rasped his skin.

He bent and kissed her between the ears, then said, "Drink, Jade."

"Drink? Water? Juice drink?" she answered in her breathy growl. She rubbed her head against his hand and he stroked her under the chin.

"Juice. In the house," he said. She raced back towards the glowing building, her tail waving like a yellow plume. Kuri followed more slowly still clutching his hat. The glass vibrated gently, picking up the resonance of the house. His feet left one more line of prints in the dusty earth. He looked back; today's line went only to the thorn tree and the previous day's reached no further, yet he was very tired. He squinted to see older tracks. There were Jade's paw marks skittering here, there and everywhere and the bigger marks of her cousins, the wild adapts. He saw the slots of jumpbuck and, with a stir of anxiety, the recent pug marks of a fanged leopard. Plodding into the distance and only faintly discernible were the wide prints of his own dromedary. Was it then so long since he had ridden it inland? He realized with some surprise that it was two months at least. He turned slowly, looking in vain for signs of his own tracks extending further than the thorn tree and the pile of ringlass sparkling in the sun. He looked at his hand, black and wrinkled; at his arm thin and sere as a dead thorn-branch. A shade fell across his soul.

Kuri shrugged and trudged on. He was thirsty and there was work to do on the east window. The dark entrance to his home was cool and inviting below the blazing windows. He ducked to avoid the curved roof of the tunnel and plunged below ground like a fox to earth. Breathing heavily again, he sat down in the cool light of the northern window that glowed high above him. Jade skipped up to him on her hind legs, holding a beaker between her front paws. He drank, and his skin rained cold drops of sweat. He turned to Jade but she had anticipated his next wish, and was proffering a square of damp lake-weed. He smiled at the little creature; in the window light her tawny coat was dappled purple and bronze like a child's toy. She pirouetted on two legs as if she knew he found her antics comical.

"Good Jade," he said, wiping his forehead. "You must go out this evening. Play with your friends."

"Kuri play with Jade?" she said.

"I'm too old to play. Old creatures don't play." She dropped to all fours and rubbed against his knee. Using her mouth she took the weed from his hand, growling playfully, shaking her head about; then seeing he wasn't going to join the game, trotted out of the house to return it to the water.

Kuri sighed and stretched his creaking bones. He wanted to sleep but wanted even more to return to his task. He lurched to his feet and fetched another juice drink from the cold store. He went over to the east side of his dwelling and, with a critical eye, gazed up at the sun-shaped east window, brilliant in orange and yellow and yet transmitting no heat to him. He could not remember who had installed the window – his mother? Perhaps even his grandfather. He frowned trying to recall that distant time when three people had lived here – no four: there had been his brother, Omu, who had died from a snakebite.

He bent stiffly and picked up his krar, twanging its three strings in turn. A high keening resonated from the window above him. He shook his head in distaste then played a series of chords. The keening descended in pitch but was still unpleasing to his ear. This must have been the original artist's idea of the rising sun – too harsh, too strident for him.

He emptied his hat of the glass pieces and piled them onto a basketful he had selected on previous days. Then he ambled round the chamber picking up tools here and there, taking them and the glass over to the east side. Finally he uttered a word of command and a wooden platform emerged creakily from the wall and swung towards him, lowering itself to floor level. He piled everything on to it and clambered up, directing the platform until it had risen on a swivelling arm to the roof. Even so close to the blazing sun of the window he was neither dazzled nor overheated, such was the wonder of ringlass.

Once Kuri had decided the effect he wanted he worked quickly, tapping out crescents of citrine and gamboge from the solar orb. As he removed the pieces the true heat of the day blasted through the lattice like a wind from the volcano. He mopped his forehead with the brim of his hat then jammed it on his head. The lattice itself writhed in discomfort and gratefully hugged the replacement sections, softer shades of rose and ochre, that he offered it. As each new piece was inserted he tuned it with his krar, slicing tiny slivers of glass from the sections he was altering until both sight and sound merged with the image in his head.

By the time he lowered the mechanism to the ground the sun was sinking towards the western window which already vibrated gently in anticipation. Kuri slumped to the floor, too exhausted even to fetch himself another drink. He looked around for Jade but she was not sleeping in her usual place, under the cool light of the northwest spiral, the only silent window. In his mind's eye he saw her, among the reeds, skipping and pouncing with her adapt cousins. That would be only right.

He licked dry lips. She must prepare for a future without him – quite soon, he thought. But then he heard her familiar call, the repeated little noise she made when she was bringing him food. She bounded in through the entrance tunnel, a wriggling fish held in her jaws. She dropped it at his feet and ran outside again, mewing joyfully. Kuri smiled, shaking his head. "I'm not hungry," he whispered to himself.

Jade returned with another fish and skipped around while he persuaded his body to stand upright. He killed both fish with practised efficiency, then put them in a net.

"Let's eat outside," Kuri said, knowing that would please her. He collected a knife and his cooking gear and went through the tunnel.

There was an evening wind blowing in from the lake, bringing the soda tang of its water and the sulphur of the volcano. The smell increased his thirst.

"Drink, Jade," he croaked, "water this time." He cleaned the fish and lit the stove while she fetched a pouch of fresh water from the purifier. Dropping the pouch in front of Kuri she ran, snarling, at a couple of vultures that were eyeing the fish. They flapped off, one remaining at a distance, shrouded on the dusky sand, the other swooping in low watchful circles. Kuri drank deeply, then tossed the fish into a pan, where they sizzled. The entrails he threw to Jade, who worried them enthusiastically.

The music of the west window rose to a crescendo. Kuri turned towards the lake. All the brilliance of the windows on the eastern side had been quenched by approaching night and from his point of view the building was in shadow, silhouetted against the western sky. The west window itself was hidden by the dark beehive of his home. Behind it the waters of the lake changed from jade to molten crimson as they received the sun. Lapped in harmony, he grinned for sheer joy. The sound of the west window was perfect; but when he thought of the east – something still lacked. He frowned and turned back to his cooking. "I'm not hungry," he repeated under his breath.

As if they had heard him a flock of tiny birds flew in from the lake, shrilling above the sonorous tones of the window. Most darted straight for their roosts in the thorn bushes and palm trees along the shore, but a canny few landed on the ground beside Kuri and bounced up and down waiting for scraps. Kuri tore off a chunk of fish, put a morsel in his mouth and scattered the remainder well clear of Jade. She was crouched beside him, grooming herself. Now her ears pricked and she stretched, unsheathing her claws.

"Leave them, Jade," Kuri said. "Fish is much nicer." He gave her a piece, and she tossed it into the air to cool it, catching it deftly, then eating it with little growls of pleasure. Kuri swilled the last of his mouthful with the aid of another drink of water. The music trailed away. He turned back once more. The water was now darkest indigo, the only other colour a dusky ember-red gleaming fitfully from the volcano. The birds retreated and were silent. He heard the lapping of the water, the soughing of the wind, Jade's sleepy purring. He smiled down at her, the thing he loved best. Everything was as it should be, as it always had been, throughout his long life. Death would come when it came.

He looked eastwards where the stars were already brilliant.

Something was different, an unfamiliar celestial body, faint, haloed in white.

Were his eyes failing at last? No – everything else was as sharp and bright as usual, the stars, the planets, the orbiters that his ancestors had sent into space thousands of years in the past. But now there was a new thing in the heavens.

Nearby he heard the cough of a fanged leopard. He whistled for Jade and the two retreated indoors.

After three nights Kuri realized that the new star was a comet. Each night it was bigger, at first a hazy patch of bright light, then round like a tiny sun, surrounded by a white corona. On the third night he saw the tail, spreading out, spangled by the stars, then lost among them. He had little knowledge of such things, whether this one had been predicted by astronomers or was a new visitor to the sky. Was it hurtling towards the Earth on a path of destruction or would it pass him by? Were there any wise men left alive to solve this riddle? Or was he the last human stargazer to see and wonder?

The next morning he donned loose trousers and went to saddle up his reluctant dromedary. She had been free for so many weeks that, apart from coming to him for titbits, she had decided to ignore him. She had also elected to forget her name, "Beast" (short for "The Beast Who Spits") because that was what she did best. Each time Kuri approached her she lumbered off to a safe distance, then stopped and stared superciliously. Jade was no use in this situation. When she perceived Kuri's difficulty she tried to help but the dromedary spat with supreme accuracy and, when the adapt approached snarling, lashed out dangerously.

In the end guile and persistence won but not before the cool of the morning had been burned away. By then Kuri was gasping painfully and his sweat-soaked trousers clung to his legs. Determination burned through his pounding headache. The work could not wait. Grumbling, the dromedary knelt and he climbed up. Jade yowled piteously but he told her he would be back for supper; she was to catch some fish and watch out for crocodiles.

Once started, Beast trundled down the familiar road and Kuri rested, even slept a little, huddled under a blanket and with his hat jammed on his head. When he opened his eyes again the lake had disappeared behind the hills. The air shimmered. Even the sound of the dromedary's footsteps was stifled. Her rancid smell enveloped him like a filthy cloak. He flapped his hat at the flies hustled around his eyes. He reached for a water pouch, draining it in a few gulps. They passed a troop of baboons, lolling in the shade of a rock, too idle to pester him for food. The only living things in the sun were two basking mambas, coiled like black ropes.

They reached the city by early afternoon, descending from the barren hills to a sudden oasis, a ring of green foliage and coloured blossoms, its walls. To Kuri it was simply "The City", the only one he had ever seen, although he knew that it was one of many and that once it had had a name. The gateway was in the form of a rearing elephant, one foot raised. But there was no malice in the gate. It recognized the visitor and trumpeted a fanfare of welcome. He and the dromedary passed easily beneath the archway of its legs. Kuri did not so much as glance at the massive stone foot poised above him ready to crush any intruder.

As always the city was full of life. Birds fluted and chirruped from every tree. Jewelled carp flashed in the shaded pools and streams. Butterflies drifted on the air like floating blossoms. On the paving there were black-eyed snakes and amber scorpions. Baboons, jumping from the trees, noisily demanded attention. He glimpsed wandering smallbuck at each turn of the way.

But there were no other humans, ever.

Kuri steered his animal between a towering basalt jackal and a fanged leopard formed from living bone. Wild adapts peered from the windows of both. He smiled and waved to them, pleased that they, rather than the baboons, had found a way inside. The dromedary continued along the familiar way, following the curves of the Great Snake Building and reached a courtyard surrounding a central pool. Here he dismounted, leaving her to drink and graze at will. He lowered himself, gulping clear water from the pool, then pulled himself onto a marble bench in the shade of the palms and oleanders. He lay inert, cooled by a breeze that was free, here, from the taint of the volcano. When his strength had returned a little he made for the largest of the buildings framing the courtyard, a giant crystal made in the shape of a krar; the place where ringlass was still being formed, year after year, century after century.

He knew exactly what he wanted.

It was dusk as he reached the lake. Beast had been wayward again and difficult to catch. He had stopped several times on the way to rest and drink. Now the volcano's fumes were black against the first stars. The comet already blazed in the eastern sky behind him.

There were two shapes in front of his house. The smaller bounded towards him uttering squeals of delight. He clambered down, carrying a basket of the new ringlass, then he dismissed the dromedary with a slap on the rump. She loped off, grunting. Jade was upon him, springing onto her hind legs, trying to lick his face. The second, larger adapt hesitated, as if making to run away, but remained. Kuri heard a faint growl. The creature's tail was held high, bristling and defiant. It called to Jade, a plaintive mew. She looked back and answered, then darted away, stopping and looking back at Kuri.

"It's good, Jade," he said. "It's Brown Boy, isn't it? Go with him." But Jade, after touching noses with the other adapt, ran back to Kuri. Brown Boy trotted off into the shadow of the reed beds, from where he continued to call at intervals.

She had caught more fish for him but, when he had cleaned them, he found himself unable to eat. Jade, as usual, devoured the entrails but she was clearly worried, running up to him, saying, "Kuri eat. Kuri eat." When they went to bed she nuzzled against him, but he said, "I can't make love to you any more, Jade. I'm too old, too tired." He stroked her belly.

He heard the other adapt calling from the reed beds. "Go with Brown Boy. He will give you cubs," he whispered.

But she would not.

Kuri continued his reconstruction of the east window. He removed the centre of the solar shape, now a corona of pale golds and oranges, then fitted the inner circle with tiny beads of plain ringlass, something he had never used before on any of the windows. As he tuned this new work with his krar his absorption deepened. He did not stop to eat – had no desire for food. Instead he drank – water, juice, more water. Even Jade's plaintive cries failed to distract him.

By night the comet grew until its light was bright as moonlight.

Kuri completed his work on the third day. The new ringlass chimed in tune with the krar; the outer rings of coloured glass resonated in harmony. He was satisfied.

At sunset he found himself unable to stand. He crawled through the tunnel, then knelt on the sand facing the lake, waiting for the night. For the last time he watched the sun plunge towards the water and stain it red as blood. He heard the farewell song of the west window. Jade crept up and crouched beside him, whimpering. He patted her head.

Darkness fell.

Then there was a new vibration, faint at first but soon emerging high and clear, like the resonance of a glass harp. A light rose behind Kuri but he did not look back but gazed transfixed at his creation.

The light struck the East Window. He saw the comet, brilliant as a second moon, reflected in the diamond-white centre. He heard a voice reaching towards Earth from the depths of space, growing louder and clearer. The outer circles of the window chimed in marvellous harmony. And then, new and unexpected, the other windows took up the song – the blazing chords of the South, the wayward dissonance of the North, the trumpeted glory of the West. The dark dome vibrated, wavering before his eyes. He knew that startled birds took flight from the reeds, jackals cried in the distance. He could see shadows beside him. He realized that Brown Boy was beside Jade, that a small troop of adapts had formed a semicircle in front of the house.

But this was only a dim halo of awareness at the fringes of sight. With all his being he gazed at the window on to Paradise, heard the music of the spheres.

He slumped forward.

In the morning Brown Boy called to Jade to come with him. She had lain the whole night in vigil beside Kuri's body, crying his name. Brown Boy nuzzled her gently. She looked up at him, questioning, pleading, her eyes reflecting the colour of the lake. She rose and stretched, then paced with drooping tail to the edge of the water. He followed her and like her, scooped a mouthful of pumice pebbles. Following her lead he deposited them on the curled body of the last in the line of his creators. Jade ran back for more pebbles. Brown Boy lifted his head and called. More adapts emerged from the reeds.

Soon Kuri, the last of his kind, lay buried in the very place where his primal ancestors had first lifted their heads from the earth to ask "what?" and "why?".

The adapts spent one more night gazing in wonder at the white blaze of Kuri's window, swaying to the music that stirred their blood. At last Brown Boy looped his tail about Jade's shoulders and drew her away to begin a new life.

The windows of Kuri's house continued to greet each phase of the day but as the newcomer faded the white heart of the East Window became silent until, perhaps, in the years to come the comet should retrace its path, to remind the Earth of the beings that had ruled it for so short a time.

But now the star that had been called Wormwood continued westward across Africa. Its brightness startled flocks of birds into wakefulness, caused great beasts to trumpet and bray, glinted in the eyes of prowling raptors and hopping rodents. It traced a path of wandering silver across the ocean, glinting on metalled dolphins and the gauzy wings of flying-fish.

Somewhere along the coast of Brazil a group of tree-like beings waved their branches in the wind. The branch tips brushed against each other, connections that wound and unwound. As the comet poured its light over them, the light-sensitive tips quested upwards. Others whipped out, clasping their fellows.

"What?" they whispered. "Why?"